The Lady Chosen

&

A Gentleman's Honor

The Lady Chosen

&

A Gentleman's Honor

STEPHANIE
LAURENS

AVON BOOKS
An Imprint of HarperCollins*Publishers*

This is a work of fiction. Names, characters, places and incidents either are the product of the author's imagination or are used fictitiously. Any resemblance to actual events, locales, organizations, or persons, living or dead, is entirely coincidental and beyond the intent of either the author or the publisher.

AVON BOOKS, INC.
An Imprint of HarperCollins*Publishers*
10 East 53rd Street
New York, New York 10022

Published by arrangement with the author
ISBN 0-7394-3703-8

Printed in the U.S.A.

Contents

ॐ

The Lady Chosen

&

A Gentleman's Honor

The Lady Chosen

Prologue

⚮

The Pavilion, Brighton
October 1815

"His Royal Highness's straits must be dire indeed if he needs must summon His Britannic Majesty's best simply to bask in the reflected glory."

The drawled comment contained more than a little cynicism; Tristan Wemyss, fourth Earl of Trentham, glanced across the stuffy music room, packed with guests, sycophants, and all manner of toadies, at its subject.

Prinny stood in the center of a circle of admirers. Decked out in gold braid and crimson, with epaulets high and fully fringed, their Regent was in genial and expansive good humor, retelling heroic tales of derring-do drawn from the dispatches of recent engagements, most notably that of Waterloo.

Both Tristan and the gentleman standing beside him, Christian Allardyce, Marquess of Dearne, knew the real stories; they had been there. Easing free of the throng, they'd retreated to the side of the opulent chamber to avoid hearing the artful lies.

It was Christian who'd spoken.

"Actually," Tristan murmured, "I'd viewed tonight more in the nature of a distraction—a feint, if you will."

Christian raised heavy brows. "Listen to my stories of England's greatness—don't worry that the Exchequer's empty and the people are starving?"

Tristan's lips quirked downward. "Something like that."

Dismissing Prinny and his court, Christian surveyed the others crowding the circular room. It was an all-male company primarily composed of representatives from every major regiment and arm of the services recently active; the chamber was a sea of colorful dress uniforms, of braid, polished leather, fur, and even feathers. "Telling that he chose to stage what amounts to a victory reception in Brighton rather than London, don't you think? I wonder if Dalziel had any say in that?"

"From all I've gathered, our Prince is no favorite in London, but it seems our erstwhile commander has taken no chances with those names he volunteered for the guest list tonight."

"Oh?"

They were talking quietly, out of habit disguising their communication as nothing more than a social exchange between acquaintances. Habit died hard, especially since, until recently, such practices had been vital to staying alive.

Tristan smiled vaguely, indeed *through* a gentleman who glanced their way; the man decided against intruding. "I saw Deverell at the table—he was seated not far from me. He mentioned that Warnefleet and St. Austell were here, too."

"You can add Tregarth and Blake—I saw them as I was arriving—" Christian broke off. "Ah, I see. Dalziel has only allowed those of us who have sold out to appear?"

Tristan caught his eye; the smile that was never far from his mobile lips deepened. "Can you imagine Dalziel allowing even Prinny to identify his most secret of secret operatives?"

Christian hid a smile, raised his glass to his lips, and sipped.

Dalziel—he went by no other name or honorific—was the Foreign Office taskmaster who, from his office buried in the depths of Whitehall, managed His British Majesty's foreign spy network, a network that had been instru-mental in handing victory to England and her allies both in the Peninsula campaign and more recently at Waterloo. Together with a certain Lord Whitley, his opposite number in the Home Office, Dalziel was responsible for all covert operations both within England and beyond its borders.

"I didn't realize Tregarth or Blake were in the same boat as we two, and I know of the others only by repute." Christian glanced at Tristan. "Are you sure the others are leaving?"

"I know Warnefleet and Blake are, for much the same reasons as we. As for the others, it's purely conjecture but I can't see Dalziel compromising an operative of St. Austell's caliber, or Tregarth's or Deverell's for that matter, just to pander to Prinny's latest whim."

"True." Christian again looked out over the sea of heads.

Both he and Tristan were tall, broad-shouldered, and lean, with the honed strength of men used to action, a strength imperfectly concealed by the elegant cut of their evening clothes. Beneath those clothes, both bore the scars of years of active service; although their nails were perfectly manicured, it would be some months yet before the telltale signs of their unusual, often ungentlemanly erstwhile occupation faded from their hands—the calluses, the roughness, the leatherlike palms.

They and their five colleagues known to be present had all served Dalziel and their country for at least a decade, Christian for nearly fifteen years. They'd served in whatever guise had been required, from nobleman to streetsweeper, from clerk to navvy. There had, for them, been only one measure of success—discovering the information they'd been sent behind enemy lines to acquire and surviving long enough to get it back to Dalziel.

Christian sighed, drained his glass. "I'm going to miss it."

Tristan's laugh was short. "Aren't we all?"

"Be that as it may, given that we're no longer on His Majesty's payroll"—Christian set his empty glass down on a nearby sideboard—"I fail to see why we need stand here talking, when we could be much more comfortable doing the same elsewhere . . ." His grey gaze met the eyes of a gentleman clearly considering approaching; the gentleman considered again and turned away. "And without running the risk of having to do the pretty for whichever toady captures us and demands to hear our story."

Glancing at Tristan, Christian raised a brow. "What say you— shall we adjourn to pleasanter surrounds?"

"By all means." Tristan handed his empty glass to a passing footman. "Do you have any particular venue in mind?"

"I've always been partial to the Ship and Anchor. It has a very cosy snug."

Tristan inclined his head. "The Ship and Anchor, then. Dare we leave together, do you think?"

Christian's lips curved. "Heads together, talking earnestly in hushed and urgent tones—if we make for the door unobtrusively but determinedly, I can see no reason we shouldn't walk straight through."

They did. Everyone who saw them assumed one had been sent to summon the other for some secret but highly significant purpose; the footmen rushed to get their coats, and then they strode out, into the crisp night.

Both paused, drew in a deep breath, clearing the stultifying stuffiness of the overheated Pavilion from their lungs, then, exchanging faint smiles, they stepped out.

Leaving the Pavilion's brightly lit entrance, they emerged onto North Street. Turning right, they walked with the relaxed gait of men who knew where they were going toward Brighton Square and the Lanes beyond. Reaching the narrow cobbled ways lined with fishermen's cottages, they dropped into single file, at every crossroads changing place, eyes always watching, searching the shadows . . . if either realized, realized they were now at home, at peace, no longer fugitives, no longer at war, neither commented nor tried to suppress the behavior that had become second nature to them both.

They headed steadily south, toward the sound of the sea, soughing in the darkness beyond the shore. Finally, they turned into Black Lion Street. At the end of the street lay the Channel, the border beyond which they'd lived most of the past decade. Halting beneath the swaying sign of the Ship and Anchor, they both paused, eyes on the darkness framed by the houses at the end of the street. The smell of the sea, the brine on the wind, the familiar tang of seaweed reached them.

Memory held them both for an instant, then, as one, they turned. Christian pushed open the door, and they went inside.

Warmth enveloped them, the sounds of English voices, the hop-infused scent of good English ale. Both relaxed, an indefinable tension falling from them. Christian walked up to the bar. "Two pots of your best."

The landlord nodded a greeting and quickly pulled the pints.

Christian glanced at the half-closed door behind the bar. "We'll sit in your snug."

The landlord glanced at him, then set the frothing tankards on the bar. He shot a quick glance at the snug door. "As to that, sir, you're welcome, I'm sure, but there's a group o' gen'lemen in there already, and they might not welcome strangers, like."

Christian raised his brows. He reached for the flap in the counter and lifted it, stepping past as he picked up one tankard. "We'll risk it."

Tristan hid a grin, tossed coins on the counter for the ale, hoisted the second tankard, and followed on Christian's heels.

He was standing at Christian's shoulder when Christian sent the snug door swinging wide.

The group gathered about two tables pushed together looked around; five pairs of eyes locked on them.

Five grins dawned.

Charles St. Austell sat back in the chair at the far end of the table and magnanimously waved them in. "You are better men than we. We were about to take bets on how long you'd stand it."

* * *

The others stood so the tables and chairs could be rearranged. Tristan shut the door, set down his tankard, then joined in the round of introductions.

Although they'd all served under Dalziel, they'd never met all seven together. Each knew some of the others; none had previously met all.

Christian Allardyce, the eldest and longest-serving, had operated in the east of France, often in Switzerland, Germany, and the other smaller states and principalities; with his fairish coloring and facility for languages, he'd been a natural in that sphere.

Tristan himself had served more generally, often in the heart of things, in Paris and the major industrial cities; his fluency in French as well as German and Italian, his brown hair, brown eyes, and easy charm had served him and his country well.

He'd never crossed paths with Charles St. Austell, the most outwardly flamboyant of the group. With his tumbling black locks and flashing dark blue eyes, Charles was a magnet for ladies young and old. Half-French, he possessed both the tongue and the wit to make the most of his physical attributes; he'd been Dalziel's principal operative in the south of France, in Carcasonne and Toulouse.

Gervase Tregarth, a Cornishman with curling brown hair and sharp hazel eyes, had, so Tristan learned, spent much of the last decade in Britanny and Normandy. He knew St. Austell from the past, but in the field they'd never met.

Tony Blake was another scion of an English house who was also half-French. Black-haired, black-eyed, he was the most elegant of the group, yet there was an underlying sharpness beneath the smooth veneer; he was the operative Dalziel had most often used to intercept and interfere with the French spymasters' networks, a hideously dangerous undertaking centered on the northern French ports. That Tony was alive was a testament to his mettle.

Jack Warnefleet was outwardly a conundrum; he appeared so overtly English, startlingly handsome with fairish brown hair and hazel eyes, that it was hard to imagine he'd been consistently successful in infiltrating all levels of French shipping and many business deals as well. He was a chameleon even more than the rest of them, with a cheery, hail-fellow-well-met geniality few saw beyond.

Deverell was the last man Tristan shook hands with, a personable gentleman with an easy smile, dark brown hair, and greenish eyes. Despite being uncommonly handsome he possessed the knack of blending in with any group. He had served almost exclusively in Paris and had never been detected.

The introductions complete, they sat. The snug was now comfortably full; a fire burned cheerily in one corner as in the flickering light they settled about the table, almost shoulder to shoulder.

They were all large men; they had all at some point been guardsmen in one regiment or another, until Dalziel had found them and lured them into serving through his office.

Not that he'd had to persuade all that hard.

Savoring his first sip of ale, Tristan ran his eye around the table. Outwardly, they were all different, yet they were, very definitely, brothers beneath the skin. Each was a gentleman born of some aristocratic lineage, each possessed similar attributes, abilities, and talents although the relative balance differed. Most importantly, however, each was a man capable of dicing with danger, one who would accept the challenge of a life-and-death engagement without a flicker—more, with an inbred confidence and a certain devil-may-care arrogance.

There was more than a touch of the wild adventurer in each of them. And they were loyal to the bone.

Deverell set down his tankard. "Is it true we've all sold out?" There were nods and glances all around; Deverell grinned. "Is it polite to inquire why?" He looked at Christian. "In your case, I assume Allardyce must now become Dearne?"

Wryly, Christian inclined his head. "Indeed. Once my father died, and I came into the title, any choice evaporated. If it hadn't been for Waterloo, I would already be mired in issues pertaining to sheep and cattle, and no doubt leg-shackled to boot."

His tone, faintly disgusted, brought commiserating smiles to the others' faces.

"That sounds all too familiar." Charles St. Austell looked down the table. "I hadn't expected to inherit, but while I was away, both my elder brothers failed me." He grimaced. "So now I'm the Earl of Lostwithiel and, so my sisters, sisters-in-law, and dear mother constantly remind me, long overdue at the altar."

Jack Warnefleet laughed, not exactly humorously. "Entirely unexpectedly, I've joined the club, too. The title was expected—it was the pater's—but the houses and the blunt came via a great-aunt I barely knew existed, so now, I've been told, I rank high on the list of eligibles and can expect to be hunted until I surrender and take a wife."

"*Moi, aussi.*" Gervase Tregarth nodded to Jack. "In my case it was a cousin who succumbed to consumption and died ridiculously young, so now I'm the Earl of Crowhurst, with a house in London I haven't even seen and a need, so I've been informed, to get myself a wife and heir, given I'm now the last of the line."

Tony Blake made a dismissive sound. "At least you don't have a French mother—believe me, when it comes to hounding one to the altar, they take the cake."

"I'll drink to that." Charles raised his tankard to Tony. "But does that mean you, too, have returned to these shores to discover yourself encumbered?"

Tony wrinkled his nose. "Courtesy of my father, I've become Viscount Torrington—I'd hoped it would be years yet, but . . ." He shrugged. "What I didn't know was that over the past decade the pater had taken an interest in various investments. I'd expected to inherit a decent livelihood—I hadn't expected to succeed to great wealth. And then I discover the entire ton knows it. On my way down here I stopped briefly in town to call on my godmother." He shuddered. "I was nearly mobbed. It was horrendous."

"It's because we lost so many at Waterloo." Deverell gazed into his tankard; they were all silent for a moment, remembering lost comrades, then all lifted their cups and drank.

"I have to confess I'm in much the same straits." Deverell set down his tankard. "I'd no expectations when I left England, only to discover on my return that some distant cousin twice removed had turned up his toes, and I'm now Viscount Paignton, with the houses, the income—and just like you all, the dire need of a wife. I can manage the land and funds, but the houses, let alone the social obligations—they're a web far worse than any French plot."

"And the consequences of failing could drive you to your grave," St. Austell put in.

There were dark murmurs of assent all around. All eyes turned to Tristan.

He smiled. "That's quite a litany, but I fear I can trump all your tales." He looked down, turning his tankard between his hands. "I, too, returned to find myself encumbered—with a title, two houses and a hunting box, and considerable wealth. However, both houses are home to an assortment of females, great-aunts, cousins, and other more distant connections. I inherited from my great-uncle, the recently departed third Earl of Trentham, who loathed his brother—my grandfather—and also my late father, and me.

"His argument was we were wastrel ne'er-do-wells who came and went as we pleased, traveled the world, and so on. In all fairness, I must say that now I've met my great-aunts and their female army, I can see the old boy's point. He must have felt trapped by his position, sentenced to live his life surrounded by a tribe of doting, meddling females."

A *frisson,* a shudder, ran around the table.

Tristan's expression grew grim. "Consequently, when his own son's son died, and then his son as well, and he realized I would inherit from him, he devised a devilish clause to his will. I've inherited title, land, and houses, and wealth for a year—but if I fail to marry within that year, I'll be left with the title, the land, and the houses—all that's entailed—but the bulk of the wealth, the funds needed to run the houses, will be given to various charities."

There was silence, then Jack Warnefleet asked, "What would happen to the horde of old ladies?"

Tristan looked up, eyes narrow. "That's the devilish heart of it—they'd remain my pensioners, in my houses. There's nowhere else for them to go, and I could hardly turf them into the streets."

All the others stared at him, appreciation of his predicament dawning in their faces.

"That's a dastardly thing to do." Gervase paused, then asked, "When's your year up?"

"July."

"So you've got next Season to make your choice." Charles set his tankard down and pushed it away. "We're all in large measure in the same boat. If I don't find a wife by then, my sisters, sisters-in-law, and dear mother will drive me demented."

"It's not going to be plain sailing, I warn you." Tony Blake glanced around the table. "After escaping from my godmother's, I sought refuge in Boodles." He shook his head. "Bad mistake. Within an hour, not one, but *two* gentlemen I'd never before met approached and asked me to dinner!"

"Set on *in your club?*" Jack voiced their communal shock.

Grimly, Tony nodded. "And there was worse. I called in at the house and discovered a pile of invitations, literally a foot high. The butler said they'd started arriving the day after I'd sent word I'd be down—I'd warned my godmother I might drop in."

Silence fell as they all digested that, extrapolated, considered . . .

Christian leaned forward. "Who else has been up to town?"

All the others shook their heads. They'd only recently returned to England and had gone straight to their estates.

"Very well," Christian continued. "Does this mean that when next we each show our faces in town, we'll be hounded like Tony?"

They all imagined it. . . .

"Actually," Deverell said, "it's likely to be much worse. A lot of families are in mourning at the moment—even if they're in town, they won't be going about. The numbers calling should be down."

They all looked at Tony, who shook his head. "Don't know—I didn't wait to find out."

"But as Deverell says, it must be so." Gervase's face hardened. "But such mourning will end in good time for next Season, then the harpies will be out and about, looking for victims, more desperate and even more determined."

"Hell!" Charles spoke for them all. "We're going to be"—he gestured—"precisely the sort of targets we've spent the last decade *not being.*"

Christian nodded, serious, sober. "In a different theater, maybe, but it's still a form of war, the way the ladies of the ton play the game."

Shaking his head, Tristan sat back in his chair. "It's a sad day when, having survived everything the French could throw at us, we, England's heroes, return home—only to face an even greater threat."

"A threat to our futures like none other, and one we haven't, thanks to our devotion to king and country, as much experience in facing as many a younger man," Jack added.

Silence fell.

"You know . . ." Charles St. Austell poked his tankard in circles. "We've faced worse before, and won." He looked up, glanced around. "We're all much of an age—there's what? Five years between us? We're all facing a similar threat, and have a similar goal in mind, for similar reasons. Why not band together—help each other?"

"One for all and all for one?" Gervase asked.

"Why not?" Charles glanced around again. "We're experienced enough in strategy—surely we can, and should, approach this like any other engagement."

Jack sat up. "It's not as if we'd be in competition with each other." He, too, glanced around, meeting everyone's eyes. "We're all alike to some degree, but we're all different, too, all from different families, different counties, and there's not too *few* ladies but too *many* vying for our attentions—that's our problem."

"I think it's an excellent idea." Leaning his forearms on the table, Christian looked at Charles, then at the others. "We all have to wed. I don't know about you, but I'll fight to the last gasp to retain control of my destiny. *I* will choose my wife—I will not have her foisted, by whatever means, upon me. Thanks to Tony's fortuitous reconnoitering, we now know the enemy will be waiting, ready to pounce the instant we appear." He glanced around again. "So how are we going to seize the initiative?"

"The same way we always have," Tristan replied. "Information is key. We share what we learn—dispositions of the enemy, their habits, their preferred strategies."

Deverell nodded. "We share tactics that work, and warn of any perceived pitfalls."

"But what we need first, more than anything," Tony cut in, "is a safe refuge. It's always the first thing we put in place when going into enemy territory."

They all paused, considered.

Charles grimaced. "Before your news, I would have imagined our clubs, but that clearly won't do."

"No, and our houses are not safe for similar reasons." Jack frowned. "Tony's right—we need a refuge where we can be certain we're safe, where we can meet and exchange information." His brows rose. "Who knows? There might be times when it would be to our advantage to conceal our connections with each other, at least socially."

The others nodded, exchanging glances.

Christian put their thoughts into words. "We need a club of our own. Not to live in, although we might want a few bedchambers in case of need, but a club where we can meet, and from which we can plan and conduct our campaigns in safety without having to watch our backs."

"Not a bolt-hole," Charles mused. "More a castle . . ."

"A stronghold in the heart of enemy territory." Deverell nodded decisively. "Without it, we'll be too exposed."

"And we've been away too long," Gervase growled. "The harpies will fall on us and tie us down if we waltz into the ton unprepared. We've forgotten what it's like . . . if we ever truly knew."

It was a tacit acknowledgment that they were indeed sailing into unknown and therefore dangerous waters. Not one of them had spent any meaningful time in society after the age of twenty.

Christian looked around the table. "We have five full months before we need our refuge—if we have it established by the end of February, we'll be able to return to town and slip in past the pickets, disappear whenever we wish . . ."

"My estate's in Surrey." Tristan met the others' gazes. "If we can decide on what we want as our stronghold, I can slip into town and make the arrangements without creating any ripples."

Charles's eyes narrowed; his gaze grew distant. "Someplace close to everywhere, but not too close."

"It needs to be in an area easily reachable, but not obvious." Deverell tapped the table in thought. "The fewer in the neighborhood who recognize us the better."

"A house, perhaps . . ."

They tossed around their requirements, and quickly agreed that a house in one of the quieter areas outside but close to Mayfair yet away from the heart of town would serve them best. A house with reception rooms and space enough for them all to congregate, with a room in which they could meet with ladies if necessary, but the rest of the house to be female-free, with at least three bedchambers in case of need, and kitchens and staff quarters—and a staff who understood their requirements . . .

"That's it." Jack slapped the table. "Here!" He grabbed up his tankard and raised it. "I give you Prinny and his unpopularity—if it weren't for him, we wouldn't be here today and wouldn't have had the opportunity to make all our futures that much safer."

With wide grins, they all drank, then Charles pushed back his chair, rose, and lifted his tankard. "Gentlemen—I give you our club! Our last bastion against the matchmakers of the ton, our secured base from which we'll infiltrate, identify, and isolate the lady we each want, then take the ton by storm and capture her!"

The others cheered, thumped the table, and rose.

Charles inclined his head to Christian. "I give you the bastion which will allow us to take charge of our destinies and rule our own hearths. Gentlemen!" Charles raised his tankard high. "I give you the Bastion Club!"

They all roared their approval and drank.

And the Bastion Club was born.

One

Lust and a virtuous woman—only a fool combined the two.

Tristan Wemyss, fourth Earl of Trentham, reflected that he'd rarely been called a fool, yet here he stood, gazing out of a window at an undoubtedly virtuous lady and indulging in all manner of lustful thoughts.

Understandable, perhaps; the lady was tall, dark-haired, and possessed a willowy, subtly curvaceous figure displayed to advantage as, strolling the back garden of the neighboring house, she paused here and there, bending to examine some foliage or flower in the lush and strangely riotous garden beds.

It was February, the weather as bleak and chill as in that month it was wont to be, yet the garden next door displayed abundant growth, thick leaves in dark greens and bronzes from unusual plants that seemed to thrive despite the frosts. Admittedly, there were trees and shrubs leafless and lifelorn scattered throughout the deep beds, yet the garden exuded an air of winter life quite absent from most London gardens in that season.

Not that he possessed any interest in horticulture; it was the lady who held his interest, with her gliding, graceful walk, with the tilt of her head as she examined a bloom. Her hair, the color of rich mahogany, was coiled in a coronet about her head; he couldn't from this distance divine her expression, yet her face was a pale oval, features delicate and pure.

A wolfhound, shaggy and brindle-coated, snuffled idly at her heels; it usually accompanied her whenever she wandered outside.

His instincts, well honed and reliable, informed him that today the lady's attention was perfunctory, in abeyance, that she was killing time while she waited for something. Or someone.

"M'lord?"

Tristan turned. He was standing in the bay window of the library on the first floor in the rear corner of the terrace house at Number 12 Montrose Place. He and his six coconspirators, the members of the Bastion Club, had bought the house three weeks ago; they were in the process of equipping it to serve as their private stronghold, their last bastion against the matchmakers of the ton. Situated in this quiet area of Belgravia mere blocks from the southeast corner of the park, beyond which lay Mayfair, where they all possessed houses, the house was perfect for their needs.

The library window overlooked the back garden, and also the back garden of the larger house next door, Number 14, in which the lady lived.

Billings, the carpenter in charge of the renovations, stood in the doorway studying a battered list.

"I think as we've about done all the new work, 'cepting for this set of cupboards in the office." Billings looked up. "If you could take a look and see if we've got the idea right, we'll get it done, then we'll start the painting, polishing, and cleaning up, so's your people can settle in."

"Very good." Tristan stirred. "I'll come now." He cast a last glance at the garden next door, and saw a towheaded boy racing across the lawn toward the lady. Saw her turn, see, wait expectantly . . . clearly the news she'd been anticipating.

Quite why he found her fascinating he had no idea; he preferred blonds of more buxom charms and despite his desperate need of a wife, the lady was too old to be still on the marriage mart; she would certainly already be wed.

He drew his gaze from her. "How long do you think it will be before the house is habitable?"

"Few more days, p'raps a week. Belowstairs is close to done."

Waving Billings ahead, Tristan followed him out of the door.

"Miss, miss! The gentl'man's here!"

At last! Leonora Carling drew in a breath. She straightened, spine stiffening in anticipation, then unbent to smile at the bootboy. "Thank you, Toby. Is it the same gentleman as before?"

Toby nodded. "The one as Quiggs said is one of the owners."

Quiggs was a journeyman-carpenter working on the house next door; Toby, always curious, had befriended him. Through that route Leonora had learned enough of the gentlemen-owners' plans for next door to decide she needed to learn more. A lot more.

Toby, tousle-haired, bright color in his cheeks where the wind had nipped, jigged from foot to foot. "You'll need to look sharpish if'n you want to catch 'im though—Quiggs said as Billings was having a last word, and then the gentl'man'd likely leave."

"Thank you." Leonora patted Toby's shoulder, drawing him with her as she walked quickly toward the back door. Henrietta, her wolfhound, loped at their heels. "I'll go around right now. You've been most helpful—let's see if we can persuade Cook that you deserve a jam tart."

"*Cor!*" Toby's eyes grew round; Cook's jam tarts were legendary.

Harriet, Leonora's maid, who'd been with the household for many years, a comfortable but shrewd female with a mass of curling red hair, was waiting in the hall just inside the back door. Leonora sent Toby to request his reward; Harriet waited only until the boy was out of earshot before demanding, "You're not going to do anything rash, are you?"

"Of course not." Leonora glanced down at her gown; she tweaked the bodice. "But I must learn whether the gentlemen next door were those who previously wanted this house."

"And if they are?"

"If they are, then either they were behind the incidents, in which case the incidents will cease, or alternatively they know nothing of our attempted burglaries, or the other happenings, in which case . . ." She frowned, then pushed past Harriet. "I must go. Toby said the man would be leaving soon."

Ignoring Harriet's worried look, Leonora hurried through the kitchen. Waving aside the usual household queries from Cook, Mrs. Wantage, their housekeeper, and Castor, her uncle's ancient butler, promising to return shortly and deal with everything, she pushed through the swinging baize-covered door into the front hall.

Castor followed. "Shall I summon a hackney, miss? Or do you wish for a footman . . . ?"

"No, no." Grabbing her cloak, she swung it about her shoulders and quickly tied the strings. "I'm just stepping into the street for a minute—I'll be back directly."

Snatching her bonnet from the hall stand, she plonked it on her head; looking into the hall mirror, she swiftly tied the ribbons. She spared a glance for her appearance. Not perfect, but it would do. Interrogating unknown gentlemen was not something she often did; regardless, she wasn't about to quail or quake. The situation was all too serious.

She turned to the door.

Castor stood before it, a vague frown creasing his brow. "Where shall I say you've gone if Sir Humphrey or Mr. Jeremy should ask?"

"They won't. If they do, just tell them I've gone to call next door." They'd think she'd gone to visit at Number 16, not Number 12.

Henrietta sat beside the door, bright eyes locked on her, canine jaws parted, tongue lolling, hoping against hope . . .

"Stay here."

With a whine, the hound flopped to the flags and, in patent disgust, laid her huge head on her paws.

Leonora ignored her. She gestured impatiently at the door; as soon as Castor opened it, she hurried out onto the tiled front porch. At the top of the steps, she paused to scan the street; it was, as she'd hoped, deserted. Relieved, she rapidly descended into the fantasy of the front garden.

Normally, the garden would have distracted her, at least made her look and take note. Today, hurrying down the main path, she barely saw the bushes, the bright berries bobbing on the naked branches, the strange lacy leaves growing in profusion. Today, the fantastical creation of her distant cousin Cedric Carling failed to slow her precipitate rush for the front gate.

The new owners of Number 12 were a group of lords—so Toby had heard, but who knew? At the very least they were tonnish gentlemen. Apparently they were refurbishing the house, but none of them planned to live in it—an unquestionably odd, distinctly suspicious circumstance. Combined with all else that had been going on . . . she was determined to discover if there was any connection.

For the past three months, she and her family had been subjected to determined harrassment aimed at persuading them to sell their house. First had come an approach through a local agent. From dogged persuasion, the agent's arguments had degenerated into belligerence and pugnacity. Nevertheless, she'd eventually convinced the man, and presumably his clients, that her uncle would not sell.

Her relief had been short-lived.

Within weeks, there'd been two attempts to break into their house. Both had been foiled, one by the staff, the other by Henrietta. She might have dismissed the occurences as coincidence if it hadn't been for the subsequent attacks on her.

Those had been much more frightening.

She'd told no one bar Harriet of those incidents, not her uncle Humphrey or her brother Jeremy or any other of the staff. There was no point rattling the servants, and as for her uncle and brother, if she managed to make them believe that the incidents had actually happened and weren't a figment of her untrustworthy female imagination, they would only restrict her movements, further compromising her ability to deal with the problem. To identify those responsible and their reasons, and ensure no further incidents occurred.

That was her goal; the gentleman from next door would, she hoped, get her one step further along her road.

Reaching the tall wrought-iron gate set into the high stone wall, she hauled it open and whisked through, turning to her right, toward Number 12—

And crashed into a walking monument.

"Oh!"

She cannoned off a body like stone.

It gave not an inch, but it moved like lightning.

Hard hands gripped her arms above the elbows.

Sparks flared and sizzled, struck by the collision. Sensation flashed from where his fingers grasped.

He held her steady, stopping her from falling.

Also trapping her.

Her lungs seized. Her eyes, widening, clashed, then locked with a hard hazel gaze, one surprisingly sharp. Even as she noticed, he blinked; his heavy lids descended, screening his eyes. The planes of his face, until then chiseled granite, softened into an expression of easy charm.

His lips changed the most—from a rigid, determined line into curving, beguiling mobility.

He smiled.

She hauled her gaze back up to his eyes. Blushed.

"I'm so sorry. Pray excuse me." Flustered, she stepped back, disengaged. His fingers eased; his hands slid from her. Was it her imagination that labeled the move reluctant? Her skin prickled; her nerves skittered. Oddly breathless, she hurried on, "I didn't see you coming . . ."

Her gaze flicked beyond him—to the house at Number 12. She registered the direction from which he'd been walking, and the trees along the boundary wall between Number 12 and Number 14, the only ones that could have hidden him during her earlier survey of the street.

Her fluster abruptly evaporated; she looked at him. "Are you the gentleman from Number 12?"

He didn't blink; not a flicker of surprise at such a strange greeting—almost an accusation given her tone—showed in that charmingly mobile face. He had sable brown hair, worn slightly longer than was fashionable; his features possessed a distinctly autocratic cast. An instant, brief but discernible, passed, then he inclined his head. "Tristan Wemyss. Trentham, for my sins." His gaze moved past her to the open gate. "I take it you live here?"

"Indeed. With my uncle and brother." Lifting her chin, she drew a tight breath, fixed her eyes on his, glinting green and gold beneath his dark lashes. "I'm glad I caught you. I wished to ask if you and your friends were the purchaser who attempted to buy my uncle's house last November, through the agent Stolemore."

His gaze returned to her face, studying it as if he could read far more than she would like therein. He was tall, broad-shouldered; his scrutiny gave her no opportunity to assess further, but the impression she'd gleaned was one of quiet elegance, a fashionable facade behind which unexpected strength lurked. Her senses had registered the contradiction between how he looked and how he felt in the instant she'd run into him.

Neither name nor title meant anything to her yet; she would check in Debrett's later. The only thing that struck her as out of place was the light tan that colored his skin . . . an idea stirred, but, held by his gaze, she couldn't pin down the impression. His hair fell in gentle waves about his head, framing a broad forehead above arched dark brows that now drew into a frown.

"No." He hesitated, then added, "We heard of the proposed sale of Number 12 in mid-January, through an acquaintance. Stolemore handled the sale, true enough, but we dealt directly with the owners."

"Oh." Her certainty dissipated; her belligerence deflated. Nevertheless, she felt forced to ask, "So you weren't behind the earlier offers? Or the other incidents?"

"Earlier offers? I take it someone was keen to buy your uncle's house?"

"Indeed. Very keen." They'd well-nigh driven her demented. "However, if it wasn't you or your friends . . ." She paused. "Are you sure none of your friends . . . ?"

"Quite sure. We were in this together from the first."

"I see." Determined, she drew breath, lifted her chin even higher. He was a full head taller than she; it was difficult to adopt a censorious stance. "In that case, I feel I must ask what you intend to do with Number 12, now you have bought it. I understand neither you nor your friends will be taking up residence."

Her thoughts—her suspicions—were there to be read, clear in her lovely blue eyes. Their shade was arresting, neither violet nor plain blue; they reminded Tristan of periwinkles at twilight. Her sudden appearance, the brief—all too brief—moment of collision when, against all odds, she'd run into his arms . . . in light of his earlier thoughts of her, in light of the obsession that had been building over the past weeks while, from the library of Number 12, he'd watched her walk her garden, the abrupt introduction had left him adrift.

The obvious direction of her thoughts rapidly hauled him back to earth.

He raised a brow, faintly haughty. "My friends and I merely wish for a quiet place in which to meet. I assure you our interests are in no way nefarious, illicit, or . . ." He'd been going to say "socially unacceptable"; the matrons of the ton would probably not agree. Holding her gaze, he glibly substituted, "Such as to cause any raised eyebrows even among the most prudish."

Far from being put in her place, she narrowed her eyes. "I thought that's what gentlemen's clubs were for. There are any number of such establishments only blocks away in Mayfair."

"Indeed. We, however, value our privacy." He wasn't going to explain the reasons for their club. Before she could think of some way to probe further, he seized the initiative. "These people who tried to buy your uncle's house. How insistent were they?"

Remembered aggravation flared in her eyes. "Too insistent. They made themselves—or rather the agent—into a definite pest."

"They never approached your uncle directly?"

She frowned. "No. Stolemore handled all their offers, but that was quite bad enough."

"How so?"

When she hesitated, he offered, "Stolemore was the agent for the sale of Number 12. I'm on my way to speak with him. Was it he who was obnoxious, or . . . ?"

She grimaced. "I really can't say that it was he. Indeed, I suspect it was the party he was acting for—no agent could remain in business if he habitually behaved in such a manner, and at times Stolemore seemed embarrassed."

"I see." He caught her gaze. "And what were the other 'incidents' that occurred?"

She didn't want to tell him, was wishing she'd never mentioned them; that was clear in her eyes, in the way her lips set.

Unperturbed, he simply waited; his gaze locked with hers, he let the silence stretch, his stance unthreatening, but immovable. As many had before, she read his message arright. Somewhat waspishly replied, "There have been two attempts to break into our house."

He frowned. "Both attempts after you'd refused to sell?"

"The first was a week after Stolemore finally accepted defeat and went away."

He hesitated, but it was she who put his thoughts into words.

"Of course, there's nothing to connect the attempted burglaries with the offer to buy the house."

Except that she believed the connection was there.

"I thought," she continued, "that if you and your friends had been the mystery purchasers interested in our house, then that would mean that the attempted burglaries and"—she caught herself, hauled in a breath—"were not connected but to do with something else."

He inclined his head; her logic, as far as it went, was sound, yet it was plain she hadn't told him all. He debated whether to press her, to ask outright if the burglaries were the sum total of the reasons why she'd come barreling out to do battle with him, deliberately disregarding the social niceties. She cast a quick glance toward her uncle's gate. Questioning her could wait; at this juncture, Stolemore might be more forthcoming. When she glanced back at him, he smiled. Charmingly. "I believe you now have the better of me."

When she blinked at him, he went on, "Given we're to be neighbors of sorts, I think it would be acceptable for you to tell me your name."

She eyed him, not warily but assessingly. Then she inclined her head, held out her hand. "Miss Leonora Carling."

His smile broadening, he grasped her fingers briefly, was visited by an urge to hold on to them for longer. She wasn't married after all. "Good afternoon, Miss Carling. And your uncle is?"

"Sir Humphrey Carling."

"And your brother?"

A frown started to grow in her eyes. "Jeremy Carling."

His smile remained, all reassurance. "And have you lived here long? Is it as peaceful a neighborhood as it seems at first glance?"

Her narrowing eyes told him she hadn't been deceived; she answered only his second question. "Entirely peaceful."

Until recently. Leonora held his disturbingly sharp gaze, and added, as repressively as she could, "One hopes it will remain so."

She saw his lips twitch before he glanced down.

"Indeed." With a wave, he invited her to walk with him the few steps back to the gate.

She turned, only then realized her acquiescence was a tacit acknowledgment that she'd come racing out purely to meet him. She glanced up, caught his gaze—knew he'd seen the action for the admission it was. Bad enough. The glint she glimpsed in his hazel eyes, a flash that made her senses seize, her breath catch, was infinitely more disturbing.

But then his lashes veiled his eyes, and he smiled, as charmingly as before. She felt increasingly sure the expression was a mask.

He halted before the gate and held out his hand.

Courtesy forced her to surrender her fingers once more to his grasp.

His hand closed; his sharp, too-farseeing eyes trapped her gaze. "I'll look forward to extending our acquaintance, Miss Carling. Pray convey my greetings to your uncle; I will call to pay my respects shortly."

She inclined her head, consciously clinging to graciousness while she longed to pull her fingers free. It was an effort to keep them from fluttering in his; his touch, cool, firm, a fraction too strong, affected her equilibrium in a most peculiar way. "Good afternoon, Lord Trentham."

He released her and bowed elegantly.

She turned, went through the gate, then swung it shut. Her eyes touched his briefly before she faced the house.

That fleeting connection was enough to steal her breath once again.

Walking up the path, she tried to force her lungs to work, but could feel his gaze still on her. Then she heard the scrape of boots as he turned, the sound of firm footsteps as he headed down the pavement. She finally breathed in, then exhaled in relief. What was it about Trentham that so set her on edge?

And on the edge of what?

The feel of his hard fingers and faintly callused palm about her hand lingered, a sensual memory imprinted on her mind. Recollection niggled, but as before proved elusive. She'd never met him before, of that she was sure, yet something about him was faintly familiar.

Inwardly shaking her head, she climbed the porch steps and determinedly forced her mind to the duties she'd left waiting.

Tristan strolled down Motcomb Street toward the huddle of shops midway along that housed the office of Earnest Stolemore, House and Land Agent. His discussion with Leonora Carling had sharpened his senses, stirring instincts that, until recently, had been a critical element in his daily life. Until recently his life had depended on those instincts, in reading their messages accurately, and reacting correctly.

He wasn't sure what he made of Miss Carling—Leonora as he thought of her, only reasonable given he'd been silently watching her for three weeks. She'd been physically more attractive than he'd deduced from afar, her hair a rich mahogany in which veins of garnet glowed, those unusual blue eyes large and almond-shaped beneath finely drawn dark brows. Her nose was straight, her face finely boned, cheekbones high, her skin pale and flawless. But it was her lips that set the tone of her appearance; full, generously curved, a dusky rose, they tempted a man to take, to taste.

His instantaneous reaction, and hers, had not escaped him. Her response, however, intrigued him; it was almost as if she hadn't recognized that flash of sensual heat for what it was.

Which raised certain fascinating questions he might well be tempted to pursue, later. At present, however, it was the pragmatic facts she'd revealed that exercised his mind.

Her fears about the attempted burglaries might be simply a figment of an overactive feminine imagination aroused by what he assumed had been Stolemore's intimidatory tactics in trying to gain the sale of the house.

She might even have imagined the incidents entirely.

His instincts whispered otherwise.

In his previous occupation, reading people, assessing them, had been crucial; he'd long ago mastered the knack. Leonora Carling was, he would swear, a strong-willed, practical female with a healthy vein of common sense. Definitely not the sort to start at shadows, let alone imagine burglaries.

If her supposition was correct, and the burglaries were connected with Stolemore's client's wish to buy her uncle's house . . .

His eyes narrowed. The full picture of why she'd come out to beard him formed in his mind. He didn't, definitely didn't, approve. Face set, he strolled on.

To the green-painted frontage of Stolemore's enterprise. Tristan's lips curved; no one viewing the gesture would have labeled it a smile. He caught sight of his reflection in the glass of the door as he reached for the handle, as he turned it, substituted a more comforting face. Stolemore, no doubt, would satisfy his curiosity.

The bell over the door jangled.

Tristan entered. The rotund figure of Stolemore was not behind his desk. The small office was empty. A doorway opposite the front door was masked by a curtain; it led into the tiny house of which the office was the front room.

Shutting the door, Tristan waited, but there was no sound of shuffling feet, of the lumbering gait of the heavily built agent.

"Stolemore?" Tristan's voice echoed, far stronger than the tinkling bell. Again he waited. A minute ticked by and still there was no sound. None.

He had an appointment, one Stolemore would not have missed. He had the bank draft for the final payment for the house in his pocket; the way the sale had been arranged, Stolemore's commission came from this last payment.

Hands in his greatcoat pockets, Tristan stood perfectly still, his back to the door, his gaze fixed on the thin curtain before him.

Something was definitely not right.

He drew in his attention, focused it, then walked forward, slowly, absolutely silently, to the curtain. Reaching up, he abruptly drew the folds aside, simultaneously stepping to the side of the doorway.

The jingle of the curtain rings died.

A narrow, dimly lit corridor led on. He entered, keeping his shoulders angled, his back toward the wall. A few steps along he came to a stairway so narrow he wondered how Stolemore got up it; he debated but, hearing no sound from upstairs, sensing no presence, he continued along the corridor.

It ended in a tiny lean-to kitchen built onto the back of the house.

A figure lay slumped on the flags on the other side of the rickety table that took up most of the space.

Otherwise, the room was uninhabited.

The figure was Stolemore; he'd been savagely beaten.

There was no one else in the house; Tristan was certain enough to dispense with caution. From the look of the bruises on Stolemore's face, he'd been attacked some hours ago.

One chair had tipped over. Tristan righted it as he edged around the table, then went down on one knee by the agent's side. The briefest examination confirmed Stolemore was alive, but unconscious. It appeared he'd been staggering to reach the pump handle set in the bench at the end of the small kitchen. Rising, Tristan found a bowl, placed it under the spout, and wielded the handle.

A large handkerchief was protruding from the nattily dressed agent's coat pocket; Tristan took it and used it to bathe Stolemore's face.

The agent stirred, then opened his eyes.

Tension stabbed through the large frame. Panic flared in Stolemore's eyes, then he focused, and recognized Tristan.

"Oh. *Argh* . . ." Stolemore winced, then struggled to rise.

Tristan grabbed his arm and hauled him up. "Don't try to talk yet." He hoisted Stolemore onto the chair. "Do you have any brandy?"

Stolemore pointed to a cupboard. Tristan opened it, found the bottle and a glass, and poured a generous amount. He pushed the glass to

Stolemore, recorked the bottle and placed it on the table before the agent.

Slipping his hands into his greatcoat pockets, he leaned back against the narrow counter. Gave Stolemore a minute to regain his wits.

But only a minute.

"Who did it?"

Stolemore squinted up at him through one half-closed eye. The other remained completely closed. He took another sip of brandy, dropped his gaze to the glass, then murmured, "Fell down the stairs."

"Fell down the stairs, walked into a door, hit your head on the table . . . I see."

Stolemore glanced up at him fleetingly, then lowered his gaze to the glass and kept it there. "Was an accident."

Tristan let a moment slip by, then quietly said, "If you say so."

At the note in his voice, one of menace that chilled the spine, Stolemore looked up, lips parting. His eye now wide, he rushed into speech. "I can't tell you anything—bound by confidentiality, I am. And it don't affect you gentlemen, not at all. I swear."

Tristan read what he could from the agent's face, difficult given the swelling and bruising. "I see." Whoever had punished Stolemore had been an amateur; he or indeed any of his ex-colleagues could have inflicted much greater damage yet left far less evidence.

But there was no point, given Stolemore's present condition, in going further down that road. He would simply lose consciousness again.

Reaching into his pocket, Tristan withdrew the banker's draft. "I've brought the final payment as agreed." Stolemore's eyes fastened on the slip of paper as he drew it back and forth between his fingers. "You have the title deed, I take it?"

Stolemore grunted. "In a safe place." Slowly, he pushed up from the table. "If you'll stay here for a minute, I'll fetch it."

Tristan nodded. He watched Stolemore hobble to the door. "No need to rush."

A small part of his mind tracked the lumbering agent as he moved through the house, identified the location of his "safe place" as under the third stair. For the most part, however, he stayed leaning against the counter, quietly adding two and two.

And not liking the number he came up with.

When Stolemore limped back, a title deed tied with ribbon in one hand, Tristan straightened. He held out a commanding hand; Stolemore gave him the deed. Unraveling the ribbon, he unrolled the deed, swiftly checked it, then rerolled it and slipped it into his pocket.

Stolemore, wheezing, had slumped back into the chair.

Tristan met his eyes. Raised the draft, held between two fingers. "One question, and then I'll leave you."

Stolemore, his gaze all but blank, waited.

"If I was to guess that whoever did this to you was the same person or persons who late last year hired you to negotiate the purchase of Number *14* Montrose Place, would I be wrong?"

The agent didn't need to answer; the truth was there in his bloated face as he followed the carefully spaced words. Only when he had to decide how to reply did he stop to think.

He blinked, painfully, then met Tristan's gaze. His own remained dull. "I'm bound by confidentiality."

Tristan let a half minute slide by, then inclined his head. He flicked his fingers; the bank draft sailed down to the table, sliding toward Stolemore. He put out a large hand and trapped it.

Tristan pushed away from the counter. "I'll leave you to your business."

Half an hour after returning to the house, Leonora escaped the demands of the household and took refuge in the conservatory. The glass-walled and -roofed room was her own special place within the large house, her retreat.

Her heels clicked on the tiled floor as she walked to the wrought-iron table and chairs set in the bow window. Henrietta's claws clicked in soft counterpoint as she followed.

Presently heated against the cold outside, the room was filled with rioting plants—ferns, exotic creepers, and strange-smelling herbs. Combining with the scents, the faint yet pervasive smell of earth and growing things soothed and reassured.

Sinking into one of the cushioned chairs, Leonora looked out over the winter garden. She should report meeting Trentham to her uncle and Jeremy; if he called later and mentioned it, it would appear odd if she hadn't. Both Humphrey and Jeremy would expect some description of Trentham, yet assembling a word picture of the man she'd met on the pavement less than an hour ago was not straightforward. Dark-haired, tall, broad-shouldered, handsome, dressed elegantly, and patently of the first stare—the superficial characteristics were simple to define.

Less certain was the impression she'd gained of a man outwardly charming and inwardly quite different.

That impression had owed more to his features, to the sharpness in his heavy-lidded eyes, not always concealed by his long lashes, the almost grimly determined set of mouth and chin before they'd softened, the harsh lines of his face before they'd eased, adopting a cloak of beguiling charm. It was an impression underscored by other physical attributes—like the fact he'd not even flinched when she'd run full tilt into him. She was taller than the average; most men would at least have taken a step back.

Not Trentham.

There were other anomalies, too. His behavior on meeting a lady he'd never set eyes on before, and could not have known anything of, had been too dictatorial, too definite. He'd actually had the temerity to interrogate her, and he'd done it, even knowing she'd noticed, without a blink.

She was accustomed to running the house, indeed, to running all their lives; she'd performed in that role for the past twelve years. She was decisive, confident, assured, in no way intimidated by the male of the species, yet Trentham . . . what was it about him that had made her, not exactly wary but watchful, careful?

The remembered sensations their physical contact had evoked, not once but multiple times, rose in her mind; she frowned and buried them. Doubtless some disordered reaction on her part; she hadn't expected to collide with him—it was most likely some strange symptom of shock.

Moments passed; she sat staring through the windows, unseeing, then shifted, frowned, and focused her mind on defining where she and her problem now were.

Regardless of Trentham's disconcerting presence, she'd extracted all she'd needed from their meeting. She'd learned the answer to what had been her most pressing question—neither Trentham nor his friends were behind the offers to buy this house. She accepted his word unequivocally; there was that about him that left no room for doubt. Likewise, he and his friends were not responsible for the attempts to break in, nor the more disturbing, infinitely more unnerving attempts to scare her witless.

Which left her facing the question of who was.

The latch clicked; she turned as Castor walked in.

"The Earl of Trentham has called, miss. He's asked to speak with you."

A rush of thoughts tumbled through her mind; a flurry of unfamiliar feelings flitted in her stomach. Inwardly frowning, she quelled them and rose; Henrietta rose, too, and shook herself. "Thank you, Castor. Are my uncle and brother in the library?"

"Indeed, miss." Castor held the door for her, then followed. "I left his lordship in the morning room."

Head high, she glided into the front hall, then stopped. She eyed the closed door of the morning room.

And felt something inside her tighten.

She paused. At her age, she hardly needed to be miss-ish over being alone for a short time in the morning room with a gentleman. She could go in, greet Trentham, learn why he'd asked to speak with her, all in private, yet she couldn't think of anything he might have to tell her that would require privacy.

Caution whispered. The skin above her elbows pricked.

"I'll go and prepare Sir Humphrey and Mr. Jeremy." She glanced at Castor. "Give me a moment, then show Lord Trentham into the library."

"Indeed, miss." Castor bowed.

Some lions were better left untempted; she had a strong suspicion Trentham was one. With a swish of her skirts, she headed for the safety of the library. Henrietta padded behind.

Two

ॐ☙

Extending along one side of the house, the large library possessed windows facing both the front and back gardens. If either her brother or her uncle had been aware of the outside world, they might have noticed the large visitor walking up the front path.

Leonora assumed they'd both been oblivious.

The sight that met her eyes as she opened the door, entered, then quietly shut it, confirmed her supposition.

Her uncle, Sir Humphrey Carling, was seated in an armchair angled before the hearth, a heavy tome open on his knees, an especially strong quizzing glass distorting one pale blue eye as he squinted at the faded hieroglyphics inscribed on the pages. He had once been an imposing figure, but age had stooped his shoulders, thinned his once leonine head of hair, and drained his physical strength. The years, however, had made no discernible impact on his mental faculties; he was still revered in scientific and antiquarian circles as one of the two foremost authorities in translating obscure languages.

His white head, hair thin, straggling, and worn rather long despite Leonora's best efforts, was bowed to his book, his mind clearly in . . . Leonora believed the present tome hailed from Mesopotamia.

Her brother, Jeremy, her junior by two years and the second of the two foremost authorities in translating obscure languages, sat at the desk nearby. The surface of the desk was awash with books, some open, others stacked. Every maid in the house knew she touched anything on that desk at her peril; despite the chaos, Jeremy always instantly knew.

He'd been twelve when, together with Leonora, he'd come to live with Humphrey after the deaths of their parents. They'd lived in Kent then; although Humphrey's wife had already passed on, the wider family had felt that the countryside was a more suitable environment for two still growing and grieving children, especially as everyone accepted that Humphrey was their favorite relative.

It was no great wonder that Jeremy, bookish from birth, had been infected with Humphrey's passion to decipher the words of men and civilizations long dead. At twenty-four, he was already well on the way to carving out a niche for himself in that increasingly competitive sphere; his standing had only grown when, six years ago, the household had moved to Bloomsbury so Leonora could be introduced to society under her aunt Mildred, Lady Warsingham's aegis.

Yet Jeremy was still her little brother; her lips curved as she took in his wide but slight shoulders, the mop of brown hair that regardless of any brushing was perennially tousled—she was sure he ran his fingers through it, yet he swore he didn't, and she'd never caught him at it.

Henrietta headed across the floor for the spot before the hearth. Leonora walked forward, unsurprised when neither man looked up. A maid had once dropped a silver epergne on the tiles outside the library door, and neither had noticed.

"Uncle, Jeremy—we have a visitor."

Both looked up, blinked in identical, blankly distant fashion.

"The Earl of Trentham has called." She continued toward her uncle's chair, patiently waiting for their brains to wander back to the real world. "He's one of our new neighbors at Number 12." Both sets of eyes followed her, both still blank. "I told you the house was bought by a group of gentlemen. Trentham is one of them. I gather he's been overseeing the renovations."

"Ah—I see." Humphrey closed his book, set it aside with his quizzing glass. "Good of him to call."

Positioning herself behind her uncle's chair, Leonora didn't miss the rather more puzzled look in Jeremy's brown eyes. Plain brown, not hazel. Comforting, not razor-sharp.

Like the eyes of the gentleman who walked into the room in Castor's wake.

"The Earl of Trentham."

Pronouncement made, Castor bowed and withdrew, closing the door.

Trentham had paused just before it, his gaze raking the company; as the latch clicked, he smiled. His charming mask very much to the fore, he walked toward the group about the hearth.

Leonora hesitated, suddenly unsure.

Trentham's gaze lingered on her face, waiting . . . then he looked at Humphrey.

Who gripped his chair's arms and, with obvious effort, started to rise. Leonora quickly stepped close to lend a hand.

"I pray you won't disturb yourself, Sir Humphrey." With a graceful gesture, Trentham waved Humphrey back. "I'm grateful for your time in seeing me." He bowed, acknowledging Humphrey's formal nod. "I was passing and hoped you would forgive the informality as we are in effect neighbors."

"Indeed, indeed. Pleased to make your acquaintance. I understand you're making some changes at Number 12 prior to settling in?"

"Purely cosmetic, to make the place more habitable."

Humphrey waved at Jeremy. "Allow me to present my nephew, Jeremy Carling."

Jeremy, who had risen, reached across the desk and shook hands. Initially politely, but as his gaze met Trentham's, his eyes widened; interest flared across his face. "I say! You're a military man, aren't you?"

Leonora looked at Trentham, stared. How had she missed it? His stance alone should have alerted her, but combined with that faint tan and his hardened hands . . .

Self-preservatory instincts flared and had her mentally stepping well back.

"Ex-military." With Jeremy clearly waiting, wanting to know, Trentham added, "I was a major in the Guards."

"You've sold out?" Jeremy had what Leonora considered an unhealthy interest in the recent campaigns.

"After Waterloo, many of us did."

"Are your friends ex-Guards, too?

"They are." Glancing at Humphrey, Trentham went on, "That's why we bought Number 12. A place to meet that's more private and quieter than our clubs. We're not used to the bustle of town life anymore."

"Aye, well, I can understand that." Humphrey, never one for tonnish life, nodded feelingly. "You've come to the right pocket of London for peace and quiet."

Swiveling, Humphrey looked up at Leonora, smiled. "Nearly forgot you there, my dear." He looked back at Trentham. "My niece, Leonora."

She curtsied.

Trentham's gaze held hers as he bowed. "Actually, I encountered Miss Carling earlier in the street."

Encountered? She leapt in before Humphrey or Jeremy could wonder. "Lord Trentham was leaving as I went out. He was good enough to introduce himself."

Their gazes met, directly, briefly. She looked down at Humphrey.

Her uncle was appraising Trentham; he clearly approved of what he saw. He waved to the chaise on the other side of the hearth. "But do sit down."

Trentham looked at her. Gestured to the chaise. "Miss Carling?"

The chaise sat two. There was no other seat; she would have to sit beside him. She met his gaze. "Perhaps I should order tea?"

His smile took on an edge. "Not on my account, I pray."

"Or me," Humphrey said.

Jeremy merely shook his head, moving back to his chair.

Drawing in a breath, her head discouragingly high, she stepped from behind the armchair and crossed to the end of the chaise closer to the fire and Henrietta, sprawled in a shaggy heap before it. Trentham very correctly waited for her to sit, then sat beside her.

He didn't purposely crowd her; he didn't have to. Courtesy of the short chaise, his shoulder brushed hers.

Her lungs seized; warmth slowly spread from the point of contact, sliding beneath her skin.

"I understand," he said, as soon as he'd elegantly disposed his long limbs, "that you've had considerable interest from others in purchasing this house."

Humphrey inclined his head; his gaze shifted to her.

She plastered on an innocent smile, airily waved. "Lord Trentham was on his way to see Stolemore—I mentioned we'd met."

Humphrey snorted. "Indeed! The knuckleheaded bounder. Couldn't get it through his skull that we weren't interested in selling. Luckily, Leonora convinced him."

That last was said with sublime vagueness; Tristan concluded that Sir Humphrey had no real idea how insistent Stolemore had been, or to what lengths his niece had been forced to go to dissuade the agent.

He glanced again at the books piled on the desk, at the similar mounds heaped about Sir Humphrey's chair, at the papers and clutter that spoke eloquently of a scholarly life. And scholarly abstraction.

"So!" Jeremy leaned forward, arms folded across an open book. "Were you at Waterloo?"

"Only on the fringes." The distant fringes. Of the enemy camp. "It was a widespread engagement."

Eyes alight, Jeremy questioned and probed; Tristan had long ago mastered the knack of satisfying the usual questions without stumbling, of giving the impression he'd been a normal regimental officer when in fact he'd been anything but.

"In the end, the allies deserved to win, and the French deserved to lose. Superior strategy and superior commitment won the day."

And lost altogether too many lives in the process. He glanced at Leonora; she was staring into the fire, patently distancing herself from the conversation. He was well aware that prudent mamas warned their daughters away from military men. Given her age, she'd doubtless heard all the stories; he shouldn't have been surprised to find her pokering up, determinedly holding aloof.

Yet . . .

"I understand"—he returned his attention to Sir Humphrey—"that there've been a number of disturbances in the neighborhood." Both men looked at him, unquestionably intelligent but not connecting with his meaning. He was forced to expand, "Attempted burglaries, I believe?"

"Oh." Jeremy smiled dismissively. "Those. Just a would-be thief trying his luck, I should think. The first time, the staff were still about. They heard him and caught a glimpse, but needless to say he didn't stop to give his name."

"The second time"—Sir Humphrey took up the tale—"Henrietta here raised a fuss. Not even certain there was anyone there, heh, old girl?" He rubbed the somnolent hound's head with his shoe. "Just got the wind up—could have been anything, but roused us all, I can tell you."

Tristan shifted his gaze from the placid hound to Leonora's face, read her tight lips, her closed, noncommittal expression. Her hands were clasped in her lap; she made no move to interject.

She was too well-bred to argue with her uncle and brother before him, a stranger. And she may well have resigned the battle of puncturing their detached and absentminded confidence.

"Whatever the case," Jeremy cheerfully concluded, "the burglar's long gone. Quiet as a grave around here at night."

Tristan met his eyes, and decided to agree with Leonora's judgment. He would need more than suspicions to convince Sir Humphrey or Jeremy to heed any warning; he consequently said nothing of Stolemore in the remaining minutes of his visit.

It drew to a natural close and he rose. He made his farewells, then looked at Leonora. Both she and Jeremy had risen, too, but it was she he wished to speak with. Alone.

He kept his gaze on her, let the silence stretch; her stubborn resistance was, to him, obvious, but her capitulation came sufficiently fast for both her uncle and brother to remain transparently unaware of the battle conducted literally before their noses.

"I'll see Lord Trentham out." The glance that went with the clipped words held an arctic chill.

Neither Sir Humphrey nor Jeremy noticed. As, with an elegant nod, he turned from them, he could see in their eyes that they were already drifting back to whatever world they customarily inhabited.

Who stood at the helm of this household was increasingly clear.

Leonora opened the door and led Trentham into the front hall. Henrietta lifted her head, but for once didn't follow; she settled down again before the fire. The desertion struck Leonora as unusual, but she didn't have time to dwell on it; she had a dictatorial earl to dismiss.

Cloaked in chilly calm, she swept to the front door and halted; Castor slipped past and stood ready to open the door. Head high, she met Trentham's hazel eyes. "Thank you for calling. I bid you a good day, my lord."

He smiled, something other than charm in his expression, and held out his hand.

She hesitated; he waited . . . until good manners forced her to surrender her fingers into his clasp.

His untrustworthy smile deepened as his hand closed strongly about hers. "If you could spare me a few minutes of your time?"

Under his heavy lids, his gaze was hard and clear. He had no intention of releasing her until she acceded to his wishes. She tried to slip her fingers free; his grip tightened fractionally, enough to assure her she could not. Would not. Until he permitted it.

Her temper erupted. She let her disbelief—*how dare he?*—show in her eyes.

The ends of his lips quirked. "I have news you'll find interesting."

She debated for two seconds, then, on the principle that one shouldn't cut off one's nose to spite one's face, she turned to Castor. "I'll walk Lord Trentham to the gate. Leave the door on the latch."

Castor bowed and swung the door wide. She allowed Trentham to lead her out. He paused on the porch. The door shut behind them; he glanced back as he released her, then met her gaze and waved at the garden.

"Your gardens are amazing—who planted them, and why?"

Assuming that, for some reason, he wished to ensure they were not overheard, she went down the steps by his side. "Cedric Carling, a distant cousin. He was a renowned herbalist."

"Your uncle and brother—what's their primary interest?"

She explained as they strolled down the winding path to the gate.

Brows rising, he glanced at her. "You spring from a family of authorities on eccentric subjects." His hazel eyes quizzed her. "What's your specialty?"

Head rising, she halted. Met his gaze directly. "I believe you had some news you thought might interest me?"

Her tone was pure ice. He smiled. For once with neither charm nor guile. The gesture, strangely comforting, warmed her. Thawed her . . .

She fought off the effect, kept her eyes on his—watched as all levity faded and seriousness took hold.

"I met with Stolemore. He'd been given a thorough thrashing, very recently. From what he let fall, I believe his punishment stemmed from his failure to secure your uncle's house for his mysterious buyer."

The news rocked her, more than she cared to admit. "Did he give any indication who . . . ?"

Trentham shook his head. "None." His eyes searched hers; his lips tightened. After a moment, he murmured, "I wanted to warn you."

She studied his face, forced herself to ask, "Of what?"

His features once more resembled chiseled granite. "Unlike your uncle and brother, I don't believe your burglar has retired from the field."

He'd done all he could; he hadn't meant to do even that much. He didn't, in fact, have the right. Given the situation within the Carling ménage, he'd be well advised not to get involved.

The next morning, seated at the head of the table in the breakfast room of Trentham House, Tristan idly scanned the news sheets, kept one ear on the twitterings of the three of the six female residents who'd decided to join him for tea and toast, and otherwise kept his head down.

He should, he was well aware, be reconnoitering the social field *à propos* of identifying a suitable wife, yet he couldn't summon any enthusiasm for the task. Of course, all his old dears were watching him like hawks, waiting for any sign that he would welcome assistance.

They'd surprised him by being remarkably sensitive in not pushing their help upon him thus far; he sincerely hoped they'd hold to that line.

"Do pass the marmalade, Millie. Did you hear that Lady Warrington has had her ruby necklace copied?"

"Copied? Great heavens—are you sure?"

"I had it from Cynthia Cunningham. She swore it was true."

Their scandalized accents faded as his mind returned to the events of the day before.

He hadn't intended to return to Montrose Place after seeing Stolemore. He'd left the shop in Motcomb Street deep in thought; when next he'd looked up, he'd been in Montrose Place, outside Number 14. He'd surrendered to instinct and gone in.

All in all, he was glad he had. Leonora Carling's face when he'd told her his suspicions had remained with him long after he'd left.

"Did you see Mrs. Levacombe making eyes at Lord Mott?"

Lifting one of the news sheets, he held it before his face.

He'd shocked himself by his readiness, unquestioning and immediate, to use force to extract information from Stolemore. Admittedly, he'd been trained to be utterly ruthless in pursuit of vital information. What shocked him was that by some warping of his mind information pertaining to threats against Leonora Carling had assumed the status of vital to him. Previous to yesterday, such status had been attained only by king and country.

But he'd now done all he legitimately could. He'd warned her. And maybe her brother was right and they'd seen the last of the burglar.

"My lord, the builder from Montrose Place has sent a boy with a message."

Tristan looked up at his butler, Havers, who had come to stand by his elbow. About the table, the chatter died; he debated, then inwardly shrugged. "What's the message?"

"The builder thinks there's been some tampering, nothing major, but he'd like you to view the damage before he repairs it." Holding Tristan's gaze, Havers wordlessly conveyed the fact that the message had been rather more dramatic. "The boy's waiting in the hall if you wish to send a reply."

Premonition clanging, instincts alert, Tristan tossed his napkin on the table and rose. He inclined his head to Ethelreda, Millicent, and Flora, all elderly cousins many times removed. "If you'll excuse me, ladies, I have business to attend."

He turned, leaving them agog, the room wrapped in pregnant silence.

The twittering broke in a storm as he stepped into the corridor.

In the hall, he shrugged into his greatcoat, picked up his gloves. With a nod to the builder's boy, standing in awe, eyes wide with wonderment as he drank in the rich trappings of the hall, he turned to the front door as a footman swung it wide.

Tristan strode out and down the steps into Green Street; the builder's boy on his heels, he headed for Montrose Place.

"You see what I mean?"

Tristan nodded. He and Billings stood in the rear yard of Number

12. Leaning down, he examined the minute scratches on the lock of the rear window at the back of what would, within days, be the Bastion Club. Part of the "tampering" Billings had summoned him to see. "Your journeyman has sharp eyes."

"Aye. And there were one or two things disturbed like. Tools we always leave just so that had been pushed aside."

"Oh?" Tristan straightened. "Where?"

Billings waved indoors. Together, they entered the kitchen. Billings stumped through a short corridor to a dark side door; he waved to the floor before it. "We leave our things here at night, out of sight of prying eyes."

The builder's gang was working; thumps and a steady *scritch-scratch* drifted down from the floors above. There were few tools left before the door, but the marks in the fine dust where others had lain were clearly visible.

Along with a footprint, close by the wall.

Tristan hunkered down; one close look confirmed that the print had been made by a gentleman's leather-soled boot, not the heavy working boots the builders wore.

He was the only gentleman who'd been about the house recently, certainly within the time the coating of fine sawdust had fallen, and he hadn't been anywhere near this door. And the print was too small; definitely a man's, but not his. Rising, he looked at the door. A heavy key was in the lock. He took it out, turned, and walked back to the kitchen where windows allowed light to stream in.

Telltale flecks of wax were visible, both along the key's shank and its teeth.

Billings peered around his shoulder; suspicion darkened his face. "An impression?"

Tristan grunted. "Looks like it."

"I'll order new locks." Billings was outraged. "Never had such a thing happen before."

Tristan turned the key in his fingers. "Yes, get in new locks. But don't fit them until I give you the word."

Billings glanced at him, then nodded. "Aye, m'lord. I'll do that." He paused, then added, "We're finished with the second floor if you'd like to take a gander?"

Tristan looked up. Nodded. "I'll just put this back."

He did so, carefully aligning the key precisely as it had been, so it wouldn't impede another key being inserted from the outside. Waving Billings ahead, he followed him up the kitchen stairs to the ground floor. There, the workmen were busily preparing what would be a comfortable drawing room and cosy dining room for the finishing touches of paint and polish. The only other rooms at that level were a small parlor beside the front door that the club members had agreed should be set aside for interviewing any females they might be forced to meet, a boothlike office for the club porter and another larger office toward the rear for the club's majordomo.

Climbing the stairs in Billings's wake, Tristan paused on the first floor to glance briefly at the painting and polishing going on in the library and the meeting room before heading up to the second floor where the three bedrooms were located. Billings conducted him through each room, pointing out the finishes and specific touches they'd requested, all in place.

The rooms smelled new. Fresh and clean, yet substantial and solid. Despite the winter chill, there was no hint of damp.

"Excellent." In the largest bedroom, the one above the library, Tristan met Billings's eye. "You and your men are to be commended."

Billings inclined his head, accepting the compliment with a craftsman's pride.

"Now"—Tristan swung to the window; like the library below it commanded an excellent view of the Carling's rear garden—"how long will it be before the staff quarters are habitable? In light of our nighttime visitor, I want to get someone in here as soon as possible."

Billings considered. "There's not much more we need to do in the attic bedrooms. We could finish those up by evening tomorrow. Kitchen and belowstairs will take a day or two more."

His gaze on Leonora strolling the rear garden with her hound at her heels, Tristan nodded. "That will do admirably. I'll send for our majordomo—he'll be here late tomorrow. His name's Gasthorpe."

"Mr. Billings!"

The call floated up the stairs. Billings turned. "If there's nothing else, m'lord, I should tend to that."

"Thank you, no. Everything appears most satisfactory. I'll make my own way out." Tristan nodded a dismissal; with a deferential nod in reply, Billings went.

Minutes ticked by. Hands in his greatcoat pockets, Tristan remained before the window, staring down at the graceful figure drifting about the garden far below. And tried to decide why, what it was that was driving him to act as he was about to. He could rationalize his actions, certainly, but were his logical reasons the whole truth? The real truth?

He watched the hound press close to Leonora's side, saw her look down, lift a hand to stroke the dog's huge head, lifted in canine adoration.

With a snort, he turned away; with a last glance around, he headed downstairs.

"Good morning." He turned his most beguiling smile on the old butler, adding just a hint of masculine commiseration in the face of feminine waywardness. "I wish to speak with Miss Carling. She's walking in the back garden at present—I'll join her there."

Title, bearing, and the excellent cut of his coat—and his bald-faced boldness—won through; after only the slightest hesitation, the butler inclined his head. "Indeed, my lord. If you'll step this way?"

He followed the old man down the hall and into a cosy parlor. A fire crackled in the grate; a piece of embroidery, barely started, lay on a small sidetable.

The butler gestured to a pair of French doors standing ajar. "If you'd like to go through?"

With a nod, Tristan did, emerging onto a small paved terrace that gave onto the lawns. Descending the steps, he strolled around the corner of the house and sighted Leonora examining blooms on the opposite side of the main lawn. She was looking the other way. He headed toward her; as he approached, the hound scented him and turned, alert but waiting to judge his intentions.

Courtesy of the lawn, Leonora didn't hear him. He was still a few yards away when he spoke. "Good morning, Miss Carling."

She whirled. She stared at him, then glanced—almost accusingly—at the house.

He hid a smile. "Your butler showed me through."

"Indeed? And to what do I owe this pleasure?"

Before answering the cool and distinctly prickly greeting, he held out a hand to the hound; she inspected, accepted, nudging her head under his palm, inviting him to pat. He did, then turned to the less tractable female. "Am I right in thinking that your uncle and brother see no continuing threat arising from the attempted burglaries?"

She hesitated. A frown formed in her eyes.

He slid his hands into his greatcoat pockets; she hadn't offered her hand, and he wasn't fool enough to push his luck. He studied her face; when she remained silent, he murmured, "Your loyalty does you credit, but in this instance, might not be your wisest choice. As I see it, there's something—some action—which the two attempts to break in here are part of. They're not finite acts in themselves, but incidents in a continuing whole."

That description hit the mark; he saw the flare of connection in her eyes.

"I suspect there are incidents which already have followed, and there will almost certainly be incidents to come." He hadn't forgotten there was more, something in addition to the burglaries she'd yet to tell him. But that was the closest he dared come to pressing her; she was not the sort he could browbeat or bully. He was accomplished in both roles, but with some, neither worked. And he wanted her cooperation, her trust.

Without both, he might not learn all he needed to know. Might not succeed in lifting the threat he sensed hanging over her.

Leonora held his gaze, and reminded herself she knew better than to trust military men. Even ex-military; they were assuredly the same. One couldn't rely on them, on anything they said let alone anything they promised. Yet why was he here? What had prompted him to return? She tilted her head, watching him closely. "Nothing has happened recently. Maybe whatever"—she gestured— "whole the burglaries were part of is no longer centered here."

He let a moment elapse, then murmured, "That doesn't appear to be the case."

Turning, he faced the house, scanned its bulk. It was the oldest house in the street, built on a grander scale than the terrace houses that in later years had been constructed on either side, walls abutting on both left and right.

"Your house shares walls, presumably basement walls, too, with the houses on either side."

She followed his gaze, glancing at the house, not that she needed to to verify that fact. "Yes." She frowned. Followed his logic.

When he said nothing more, but simply stood by her side, she set her lips and, eyes narrowing, glanced up at him.

He was waiting to catch that glance. Their gazes met, locked. Not quite in a battle of wills, more a recognition of resolutions and strengths.

"What's happened?" She knew something had, or that he'd discovered some new clue. "What have you learned?"

Despite its apparent mobility, his face was difficult to read. A heartbeat passed, then he drew one hand free of his greatcoat pocket.

And reached for hers.

Slid his fingers around her wrist, slid his hand around her much smaller one. Closed it. Took possession of that much.

She didn't stop him; couldn't have. Everything within her stilled at his touch. Then quivered in response. The heat of his hand engulfed hers. Once again, she couldn't breathe.

But she was growing used to the reaction, enough to pretend to ignore it. Lifting her head, she raised a brow in distinctly haughty question.

His lips curved; she knew absolutely that the expression was not a smile.

"Come—walk with me. And I'll tell you."

A challenge; his hazel eyes held hers, then he drew her to him, laid her hand on his sleeve as he stepped closer, beside her.

Dragging in a tight breath, she inclined her head, fell into step beside him. They strolled across the lawn, back toward the parlor, her skirts brushing his boots, his hand over hers on his arm.

She was screamingly aware of his strength, sheer masculine power close, so close, by her side. There was heat there, too, the beckoning presence of flame. The arm beneath her fingers felt like steel, yet warm, alive. Her fingertips itched, her palm burned. By an effort of will, she forced her wits to work. "So?" She slanted him a glance, as chill as she could make it. "What have you discovered?"

His hazel eyes hardened. "There's been a curious incident next door. Someone broke in, but carefully. They tried to leave as little as possible to alert anyone, and nothing was taken." He paused, then added, "Nothing bar an impression of the key to a side door."

She digested that, felt her eyes widen. "They're coming back."

He nodded, his lips a thin line. He looked at Number 12, then glanced at her. "I'll be keeping watch."

She halted. "Tonight?"

"Tonight, tomorrow. I doubt they'll wait long. The house is nearly ready for occupation. Whatever they're after—"

"It would be best to strike now, before you have servants installed." She swung to face him, tried to use the movement to slip her hand free of his.

He lowered his arm, but closed his hand more firmly about hers.

She pretended to be oblivious. "You'll keep me—us—informed of what transpires?"

"Of course." His voice was subtly lower, more resonant, the sound sliding through her. "Who knows? We might even learn the reason behind . . . all that's gone before."

She kept her eyes wide. "Indeed. That would be a blessing."

Something—some hint not of laughter, but of wry acceptance—showed in his face. His eyes remained locked with hers. Then, with blatant deliberation, he shifted his fingers and stroked the fine skin over her inner wrist.

Her lungs seized. Hard. She actually felt giddy.

She would never have believed such a simple touch could so affect her. She had to look down and watch the mesmerizing caress. Realized in that instant that this would never do; she forced herself to swallow, to diguise her reaction, to turn her locked attention to good effect.

Continuing to look at his hand holding hers, she stated, "I realize you have only recently returned to society, but this really is not the done thing."

She'd intended the statement to be coolly distant, calmly censorious; instead, her voice sounded tight, strained, even to her ears.

"I know."

The tenor of those words jerked her eyes back to his face, to his lips. To his eyes. And the intent therein.

Again moving with that deliberation she found shocking, he held her stunned gaze, and raised her hand.

To his lips.

He brushed them across her knuckles, then, still holding her gaze, turned her hand, now boneless, and placed a kiss—warm and hot—in her palm.

Lifting his head, he hesitated. His nostrils flared slightly, as if he was breathing her scent. Then his eyes flicked to hers. Captured them. Held them as he bent his head again, and set his lips to her wrist.

To the spot where her pulse leapt like a startled hind, then raced.

Heat flared from the contact, streaked up her arm, slid through her veins.

If she'd been a weaker woman, she'd have collapsed at his feet.

The look in his eyes kept her upright, sent reaction rushing through her, stiffening her spine. Had her lifting her head. But she didn't dare take her eyes from his.

That predatory look didn't fade, but, eventually, his lashes swept down, hiding his eyes.

His voice when he spoke was deeper, murmurous thunder rolling in, subtly yet definitely menacing. "Tend your garden." Once again he caught her gaze. "Leave the burglars to me."

He released her hand. With a nod, he turned and strode away, over the lawn toward the parlor.

Tend your garden.

He hadn't been speaking of plants. "Tend your hearth" was the more common injunction directing women to focus their energies in the sphere society deemed proper—on their husband and children, their home.

Leonora didn't have a husband or children, and didn't appreciate being reminded of the fact. Especially on the heels of Trentham's practiced caresses and the unprecedented reactions they'd evoked.

Just what had he thought he was doing?

She suspected she knew, which only further fired her ire.

She kept herself busy through the rest of the day, eliminating any chance of dwelling on those moments in the garden. From reacting to the spur she'd felt at Trentham's words. From giving rein to her irritation and letting it drive her.

Not even when Captain Mark Whorton had asked to be released from their engagement when she'd been expecting him to set their wedding day had she permitted herself to lose control. She'd long ago accepted responsibility for her own life; steering a safe path meant keeping the tiller in her hands.

And not allowing any male, no matter how experienced, to provoke her.

After luncheon with Humphrey and Jeremy, she spent the afternoon on social calls, first to her aunts, who were delighted to see her even though she'd purposely called too early to meet any of the fashionable who would later grace her Aunt Mildred's drawing room, and subsequently to a number of elderly connections it was her habit to occasionally look in upon. Who knew when the old dears would need help?

She returned at five to oversee dinner, ensuring her uncle and brother remembered to eat. The meal consumed, they retreated to the library.

She retired to the conservatory.

To evaluate Trentham's revelations and decide how best to act.

Seated in her favorite chair, her elbows on the wrought-iron table, she ignored his edict and turned her mind to burglars.

One point was unarguable. Trentham was an earl. Even though it was February and the ton correspondingly thin on the London streets, he'd no doubt be expected at some dinner or other, invited to some elegant soirée. If not that, then doubtless he'd go to his clubs, to game and enjoy the company of his peers. And if not that, then there were always the haunts of the demimonde; given the aura of predatory sexuality he exuded, she wasn't so innocent as to believe he wasn't acquainted with them.

Leave the burglars to him? She stifled a dismissive snort.

It was eight o'clock and pitch-dark beyond the glass. Next door, Number 12 loomed, a black block in the gloom. With no light gleaming in any window or winking between curtains, it was easy to guess it was uninhabited.

She'd been a good neighbor to old Mr. Morrissey; irascible old scoundrel that he'd been, he'd nevertheless been grateful for her visits. She'd missed him when he'd died. The house had passed to Lord March, a distant connection who, having a perfectly good mansion in Mayfair, had had no use for the Belgravia house. She hadn't been surprised that he'd sold it.

Trentham, or his friends, were apparently acquainted with his lordship. Like his lordship, Trentham was probably, at that moment, preparing for a night on the town.

Leaning back in the chair, she tugged at the stiff little drawer that clung to the underside of the circular table. Wrestling it open, she considered the large, heavy key that rested within, half-buried by old lists and notes.

She reached in and retrieved the key, laid it on the table.

Had Trentham thought to change the locks?

CHAPTER

Three

❦❦❦

He couldn't risk lighting a match to check his watch. Stoically, Tristan settled his shoulders more comfortably against the wall of the porter's alcove off the front hall. And waited.

About him, the shell of the Bastion Club lay silent. Empty. Outside, a bitter wind blew, sending flurries of sleet raking across the windows. He estimated it was past ten o'clock; in such freezing weather, the burglar was unlikely to dally much beyond midnight.

Waiting like this, silent and still in the dark for a contact, a meeting, or to witness some illicit event had been commonplace until recently; he hadn't forgotten how to let time slip past. How to free his mind from his body so he remained a statue, senses alert, attuned to all around him, ready to snap back to the moment at the slightest movement, while his mind roamed, keeping him occupied and awake, but elsewhere.

Unfortunately, tonight, he didn't appreciate the direction in which his mind wanted to go. Leonora Carling was certain distraction; he'd spent most of the day lecturing himself on the unwisdom of pursuing the sensual response he evoked in her—and she, correspondingly and even more strongly, evoked in him.

He was well aware she didn't recognize it for what it was. Didn't see it as a danger despite her susceptibility. Such innocence would normally have dampened his ardor; with her, for some ungodly reason, it only whetted his appetite further.

His attraction to her was a complication he definitely did not need. He had to find a wife, and that quickly; he required a sweet-tempered, biddable, gentle female who would cause him not a moment's angst, who would run his houses, keep his troop of elderly relatives in line, and otherwise devote herself to bearing and raising his children. He did not expect her to spend much time with him; he had for too long been alone—he now preferred it that way.

With the clock ticking on the outrageous terms of his great-uncle's will, he couldn't afford to be distracted by a strong-willed, independent-minded, prickly termagent, one he suspected was a spinster by design, and was, moreover, possessed of a waspish tongue and, when she chose to deploy it, a distinctly chilly hauteur.

There was no purpose in thinking of her.

He couldn't seem to stop.

He shifted, easing his shoulders, then leaned back again. What with taking up the reins of his inheritance, getting accustomed to having a tribe of old dears under his feet on a daily basis, inhabiting his houses and complicating his life, as well as considering how best to secure a wife, he'd let the small matter of a mistress or any other avenue of sexual release slide to the back of his mind.

In hindsight, not a wise decision.

Leonora had cannoned into him and set spark to tinder. Their subsequent exchanges hadn't doused the flame. Her haughty dismissiveness was the equivalent of a blatant challenge, one to which he instinctively reacted.

His morning's ruse of using their sensual connection to distract her from the burglars, while tactically sound, had been personally unwise. He'd known it at the time, yet had cold-bloodedly reached for the one weapon that had promised the greatest chance of success; his overriding aim had been to ensure her mind was fixed on matters other than the putative burglar.

Outside the wind howled. Again he straightened, silently stretched, then settled against the wall once more.

Fortunately for all concerned, he was too old, too wise, and far too experienced to allow lust to dictate his actions. During the day, he'd formulated a plan for dealing with Leonora. Given he'd stumbled onto this mystery and she was, no matter what her uncle and brother thought, threatened by it, then given his training, given his nature, it was understandable, indeed right and proper, for him to resolve the situation and remove the threat. Thereafter, however, he would leave her alone.

The distant scrape of metal on stone reached him. His senses focused, expanded, straining to catch any further evidence that the burglar was near.

A trifle earlier than he'd expected, but whoever it was was most likely an amateur.

He'd returned to the house at eight o'clock, slipping in via the rear alleyway and the shadows of the back garden. Entering through the kitchen, he'd noted that the builders had left only a few tools gathered in a corner. The side door had been as he'd left it, the key in the lock but not turned, the teeth not engaged. The scene set, he'd retreated to the porter's alcove, leaving the door at the top of the kitchen stairs propped open with a brick.

The porter's alcove commanded an uninterrupted view of the ground floor hall, the stairs leading upward, and the door to the kitchen stairs. No one could enter from the ground or the upper floors and get access to the basement level without him seeing them.

Not that he expected anyone to come that way, but he'd wanted to leave the way clear for the burglar belowstairs. He was willing to wager the "burglar" would head for some area of the basement; he wanted to let the man settle to his task before he intervened. He wanted evidence to confirm his suspicions. And then he intended to interrogate the "burglar."

It was difficult to imagine what a real burglar would expect to steal from a vacant house.

His ears caught the soft slap of a leather sole on stone. Abruptly, he turned and faced the front door.

Against all the odds, someone was coming in that way.

A wavering outline appeared on the etched-glass panels of the door. He slipped noiselessly out of the porter's booth and merged with the shadows.

Leonora slid the heavy key into the lock and glanced down at her companion.

She'd retired to her bedchamber supposedly to sleep. The servants had locked up and retired. She'd waited until the clock had struck eleven, reasoning that by then the street would be deserted, then she'd slipped downstairs, avoiding the library where Humphrey and Jeremy were still poring over their tomes. Collecting her cloak, she'd let herself out of the front door.

There was, however, one being she couldn't so easily avoid.

Henrietta blinked up at her, long jaws agape, ready to follow her wherever she went. If she'd tried to leave her in the front hall and go out alone at this hour, Henrietta would have howled.

Leonora narrowed her eyes at her. "Blackmailer." Her whisper was lost in the strafing wind. "Just remember," she continued, more by way of bolstering her own courage than instructing Henrietta, "we're only here to watch what he does. You have to be absolutely quiet."

Henrietta looked at the door, then nudged it with her nose.

Leonora turned the key, pleased when it slid smoothly around. Removing it, she pocketed it, then drew her cloak close. Curling one hand about Henrietta's collar, she grasped the doorknob and turned it.

The bolt slid back. She opened the door just wide enough for her and Henrietta to squeeze through, then swung around to shut it. The wind gusted; she had to release Henrietta and use both hands to force the door closed—silently.

She managed it. Heaving an inward sigh of relief, she turned.

The front hall was shrouded in stygian gloom. She stood still as her eyes began to adjust, as the sense of emptiness—the strangeness of a remembered place stripped of all its furnishings—sank into her.

She heard a faint click.

Beside her, Henrietta abruptly sat, posture erect, a suppressed whimper, not of pain but excitement escaping her.

Leonora stared at her.

The air around her stirred.

The hair on her nape lifted; her nerves leapt. Instinctively, she dragged in a breath—

A hard palm clamped over her lips.

A steely arm locked about her waist.

Hauled her back against a body like sculpted rock.

Strength engulfed her, trapping her, subduing her.

Effortlessly.

A dark head bent close.

A voice in which fury was barely leashed hissed in her ear, *"What the devil are you doing here?"*

Tristan could barely believe his eyes.

Despite the gloom, he could see hers, wide with shock. Could sense the leap and race of her pulse, the panic that gripped her.

Knew absolutely that it was only partially due to surprise. Sensed his own response to that fact.

Ruthlessly reined it in.

Lifting his head, he scanned with his senses but could detect no other movement in the house. But he couldn't talk to her, even in whispers, in the front hall; devoid of furnishings, its surfaces polished and clean, any sound would echo.

Tightening his arm about her waist, he lifted her off her feet and carried her to the small parlor they'd set aside for interrogating females. Spared a moment to wonder at their farsightedness. He had to take his hand from her face to turn the knob, then they were inside, and he shut the door.

He still had her in his arm, feet off the ground, her back locked to him.

She wriggled, hissed, "Put me down!"

He debated, in the end, grim-faced, complied. Speaking face-to-face would be easier; keeping her wriggling her derriere against him was senseless torture.

The instant her feet touched the floor, she spun around.

And collided with his finger, raised to point at her nose. "I didn't tell you about the incident here so you could waltz in and put yourself in the middle of it!"

Startled, she blinked; her eyes rose to his face. Quite stunned; she'd never had any man take such a tone with her. He seized the initiative. "I told you to leave this to *me.*" He spoke in a deep but furious whisper, at a level that wouldn't carry.

Her eyes narrowed. "I recall what you said, but this person, whoever he is, is *my* problem."

"It's *my* house he's going to be breaking into. And anyway—"

"Besides," she continued as if she hadn't heard him, chin lifting but like him keeping her voice low, "you're an *earl.* I naturally assumed you'd be out socializing."

The jab pricked his frustration. He spoke through his teeth. "I'm not an earl by choice, and I avoid socializing as much as I can. *But* that's neither here nor there. *You* are a woman. A female. You have no purpose here. Especially given *I'm* here."

Her mouth fell open as he grabbed her elbow and spun her to face the door.

"I'm not—!"

"Keep your voice down." He marched her forward. "And you most certainly are. I'm going to see you out of the front door, then you're going straight home and staying there come what may!"

She dug in her heels. "But what if he's out there?"

He halted, looked at her. Realized she was staring beyond the hall door toward the dark, tree-shrouded front garden. His thoughts followed hers.

"Damn!" He released her, squelched a more explicit curse.

She looked at him; he looked at her.

He hadn't checked the front door; the would-be intruder could have taken an impression of that key, too. He couldn't check now without lighting a match, and that he couldn't risk. Regardless, it was perfectly possible the "burglar" would check the front of the house before proceeding to the alley behind. Bad enough she'd come in, running the risk of scaring off the burglar or worse, encountering him, but to send her out now would be madness.

The intruder had already proved to be violent.

He drew in a deep breath. Nodded tersely. "You'll have to stay here until it's over."

He sensed she was relieved, in the dimness couldn't be sure.

She inclined her head haughtily. "As I said, this may be your house, but the burglar's my problem."

He couldn't resist growling, "That's debatable." In his lexicon, burglars were not a woman's problem. She had an uncle *and* a brother—

"It's my house—at least, my uncle's—that he's trying to gain access to. You know that as well as I."

That was unarguable.

A faint scratching reached them—from the hall door.

Saying "Damn!" again seemed redundant; with an eloquent glance at her, he opened the door. Shut it behind the shaggy heap that walked in. "Did you have to bring your dog?"

"I didn't have a choice."

The dog turned to look at him, then sat, lifting her great head in an innocent pose, as if intimating that he of all people should understand her presence.

He suppressed a disgusted growl. "Sit down." He waved Leonora to the window seat, the only place to sit in the otherwise empty room; luckily the window was shuttered. As she moved to comply, he continued, "I'm going to leave the door open so we can hear."

He could forsee problems if he left her alone and returned to his post in the hall. The scenario that most exercised his mind was what might happen when the burglar arrived; would she stay put, or rush out? This way, at least, he would know where she would be—at his back.

Opening the door silently, he set it ajar. The wolfhound slumped to the floor at Leonora's feet, one eye on the gap in the door. He moved to stand beside the door, shoulders against the wall, head turned to watch the dark emptiness of the hall.

And returned to his earlier thought, the one she'd interrupted. Every instinct he possessed insisted that women, ladies of Leonora's ilk especially, should not be exposed to danger, should not take part in any dangerous enterprises. While he acknowledged such instincts arose from the days when a man's females embodied the future of his line, to his mind those arguments still applied. He felt seriously irritated that she was there, that she'd come there, not defying so much as negating, stepping around, her uncle and her brother and their rightful roles. . . .

Glancing at her, he felt his jaw set. She probably did it all the time.

He had no right to judge—her, Sir Humphrey, or Jeremy. If he read all three arright, neither Sir Humphrey nor Jeremy possessed any ability to control Leonora. Nor did they attempt to. Whether that was because she'd resisted and browbeaten them into acquiescence, or because they simply did not care enough to insist in the first place, or alternatively, were too sensitive to her willful independence to rein her in, he couldn't tell.

Regardless, to him, the situation was wrong, unbalanced. Not how things ought to be.

Minutes ticked by, stretched to half an hour.

It had to be close to midnight when he heard a metallic scrape—a key turning in the old lock belowstairs.

The wolfhound lifted her head.

Leonora straightened, alerted both by Henrietta's sudden attention and the unfurling tension emanating from Trentham, until then apparently relaxed against the wall. She'd been conscious of his glances, of his irritation, his frowns, but had vowed to ignore them. Learning the burglar's purpose was her aim, and with Trentham present they might even succeed in catching the villain.

Excitement gripped her, escalated as Trentham motioned her to stay where she was and restrain Henrietta, then flitted, wraithlike, through the door.

He moved so silently, if she hadn't been watching, he'd have simply disappeared.

Instantly, she rose and followed, equally silent, grateful the builders had left drop sheets spread everywhere, muting the click of Henrietta's claws as the wolfhound fell in at her heels.

Reaching the hall door, she peered out. Spied Trentham as he merged with the dense shadows at the top of the kitchen stairs. She squinted as she drew her cloak about her; the servants' door seemed to be propped open.

"*Ow!* Ooof!"

A string of curses followed.

"Here! Get *orf!*"

"What the hell are you doing here, you crazy old fool?"

The voices came from below.

Trentham was gone down the kitchen stairs before she could blink. Grabbing up her skirts, she raced after him.

The stairs were a black void. She rushed down without thinking, heels clattering on the stone steps. Behind her, Henrietta woofed, then growled.

Reaching the landing midway down, Leonora gripped the banister and looked down into the kitchen. Saw two men—one tall and cloaked, the other large but squat and much older—wrestling in the middle of the flags where the kitchen table used to sit.

They'd frozen at Henrietta's growl.

The taller man looked up.

In the same instant she did, he saw Trentham closing in.

With a huge effort, the taller man swung the older one around and shoved him at Trentham.

The old man lost his footing and went flying back.

Trentham had a choice; sidestep and let the old man fall to the stone flags, or catch him. Watching from above, Leonora saw the decision made, saw Trentham stand his ground and let the old man fall against him. He steadied him, would have set him on his feet and gone after the tall man, already racing toward a narrow corridor, but the old man grappled, struggling—

"Be still!"

The order was rapped out. The old man stiffened and obeyed.

Leaving him swaying on his feet, Trentham went after the tall man—

Too late.

A door slammed as Trentham disappeared down the corridor. An instant later, she heard him swear.

Hurrying down the stairs, she pushed past the old man and raced to the back of the kitchen, to the windows that looked down the path to the rear gate.

The tall man—he had to be their "burglar"—raced from the side of the house and plunged down the path. For one instant he was lit by a faint wash of moonlight; eyes wide, she drank in all she could, then he disappeared beyond the hedges bordering the kitchen garden. The gate to the alley lay beyond.

With an inward sigh, she drew back, replayed all she'd seen in her mind, committed it to memory.

A door banged, then Trentham appeared on the paving outside. Hands on his hips, he surveyed the garden.

She tapped on the window; when he looked her way, she pointed down the path. He turned, then went down the steps and loped toward the gate, no longer racing.

Their "burglar" had escaped.

Turning to the old man, now sitting at the bottom of the stairs, still wheezing and trying to catch his breath, she frowned. "What are you doing here?"

He talked, but didn't answer, mumbling a great deal of fustian by way of excuses but failing to clarify the vital point. Clad in an ancient frieze coat, with equally ancient and worn boots and frayed mittens on his hands, he gave off an aroma of dirt and leaf mold readily detectable in the freshly painted kitchen.

She folded her arms, tapped her toe as she looked down at him. "Why did you break in?"

He shuffled, mumbled, and muttered some more.

She was at the limit of her patience when Trentham returned, entering via the door down the dark corridor.

He looked disgusted. "He had the foresight to take *both* keys."

The comment wasn't made to anyone in particular; Leonora understood that the fleeing man had locked the side door against Trentham. While he halted, hands in his pockets and studied the old man, she wondered how, keyless, he had managed to get through that locked door.

Henrietta had seated herself a yard from the old man; he eyed her warily.

Then Trentham commenced his interrogation.

With a few well-phrased questions elicited the information that the old man was a beggar who normally slept in the park. The night had turned so raw he'd searched for shelter; he'd known the house was empty, so he'd come there. Trying the back windows, he'd found one with a loose lock.

With Trentham standing like some vengeful deity on one side and Henrietta, spike-toothed jaws gaping, on the other, the old codger clearly felt he had no option but to make a clean breast of it. Leonora suppressed an indignant sniff; apparently she hadn't appeared sufficiently intimidatory.

"I didn't mean no harm, sir. Just wanted to get out of the cold."

Trentham held the old man's gaze, then nodded. "Very well. One more question. Where were you when the other man tripped over you?"

"In through there." The old man pointed across the kitchen. "Farther from the windows is warmer. The bu—blighter hauled me out here. Think he was planning on throwing me out."

He'd pointed to a small pantry.

Leonora glanced at Trentham. "The storerooms beyond share basement walls with Number 14."

He nodded, turned back to the old man. "I've a proposition for you. It's mid-February—the nights will be freezing for some weeks." He glanced around. "There's dust cloths and other coverings around for tonight. You're welcome to find a place to sleep." His gaze returned to the old man. "Gasthorpe, who'll be majordomo here, will be taking up residence tomorrow. He'll bring blankets and start to make this place habitable. However, all the servants' bedrooms are in the attic."

Tristan paused, then continued, "In light of our friend's unwelcome interest in this place, I want someone sleeping down here. If you're willing to act as our downstairs nightwatchman, you can sleep here every night legitimately. I'll give orders you're to be treated as one of the household. You can stay in and be warm. We'll rig up a bell so all you need do if anyone tries to gain entry is ring it, and Gasthorpe and the footmen will deal with any intruder."

The old man blinked as if he couldn't quite take in the suggestion, wasn't sure he wasn't dreaming.

Without allowing any trace of compassion to show, Tristan asked, "Which regiment were you in?"

He watched as the old shoulders straightened, as the old man's head lifted.

"Ninth. I was invalided out after Corunna."

He nodded. "As were many others. Not one of our better engagements—we were lucky to get out at all."

The rheumy old eyes widened. "You were there?"

"I was."

"Aye." The old man nodded. "Then you'll know."

Tristan waited a moment, then asked, "So will you do it?"

"Keep watch for ye every night?" The old man eyed him, then nodded again. "Aye, I'll do it." He looked around. "Be strange after all these years, but . . ." He shrugged, and pushed himself up from the stairs.

He bobbed his head deferentially to Leonora, then moved past her, looking around the kitchen with new eyes.

"What's your name?"

"Biggs, sir. Joshua Biggs."

Tristan reached for Leonora's arm and propelled her onto the stairs. "We'll leave you on duty, Biggs, but I doubt there'll be any further disturbance tonight."

The old man looked up, raised a hand in a salute. "Aye, sir. But I'll be here if there is."

Fascinated by the exchange, Leonora returned her attention to the present as they regained the front hall. "Do you think the man who fled was our burglar?"

"I seriously doubt we have more than one man, or group of men, intent on gaining access to your house."

"Group of men?" She looked at Trentham, cursed the darkness that hid his face. "Do you really think so?"

He didn't immediately answer; despite not being able to see, she was sure he was frowning.

They reached the front door; without releasing her, he opened it, met her gaze as they stepped out onto the front porch, Henrietta padding behind them. Faint moonlight reached them.

"You were watching—what did you see?"

When she hesitated, marshaling her thoughts, he instructed, "Describe him."

Letting go of her elbow, he offered his arm; absentmindedly she laid her hand on his sleeve, and they went down the steps. Frowning in concentration, she walked beside him toward the front gate. "He was tall—you saw that. But I got the impression he was young." She slanted a glance at him. "Younger than you."

He nodded. "Go on."

"He was easily as tall as Jeremy, but not much taller, and leanish rather than stout. He moved with that sort of gangling grace younger men sometimes have—and he ran well."

"Features?"

"Dark hair." Again she glanced at him. "I'd say even darker than yours—possibly black. As to his face . . ." She looked ahead, seeing again in her mind's eye the fleeting glimpse she'd caught. "Good features. Not aristocratic, but not common, either."

She met Trentham's gaze. "I'm perfectly sure he was a gentleman."

He didn't argue, indeed, didn't seem surprised.

Emerging onto the pavement into the teeth of the wind slicing up the street, he drew her close, into the lee of his shoulders; they put their heads down and swiftly walked the few yards to the front gate of Number 14.

She should have made a stand and left him there, but he'd swung the gate open and whisked her in before the potential difficulties of his seeing her all the way to the front door occurred to her.

But the garden, as always, soothed her, convinced her that no problem would arise. Like inverted feather dusters, a profusion of lacy fronds lined the path, here and there an exotic-looking flower head held high on a slender stalk. Bushes shaped the beds; trees accented the graceful design. Even in this season, a few starry white blooms peeked from under the protective hoods of thick, dark green leaves.

Although the night sent chill fingers sneaking along the twisting path, the wind could only batter at the high stone wall, could whip only the topmost branches of the trees.

On the ground, all was still, quiet; as always the garden struck her as a place that was alive, patiently waiting, benign in the dark.

Rounding the last bend in the path, she looked ahead, through the bushes and waving branches saw light shining from the library windows. At the far end of the house, abutting Number 16, the library was distant enough for there to be no danger of Jeremy or Humphrey hearing their footsteps on the gravel and looking out.

They might, however, hear an altercation on the front porch.

Glancing at Trentham, she saw that his eyes, too, had been drawn to the lighted windows. Halting, she drew her hand from his arm and faced him. "I'll leave you here."

He looked down at her, but didn't immediately reply.

As far as Tristan could see, he had three options. He could accept her dismissal, turn his back, and walk away; alternatively, he could take her arm, march her up to the front door, and, with suitable and pointed explanations, hand her into her uncle and brother's keeping.

Both options were cowardly. The first in bowing to her refusal to accept the protection she needed and running away—something he'd never done in his life. The second because he knew neither her uncle nor her brother, no matter how outraged he managed to make them, was capable of controlling her, not for more than a day.

Which left him no option bar the third.

Holding her gaze, he let all he felt harden his tone. "Coming to wait for the burglar tonight was an incredibly foolhardy thing to do."

Up went her head; her eyes flashed. "Be that as it may, if I hadn't, we wouldn't even know what he looks like. You didn't see him—I did."

"And what"—his voice had taken on the icy tone he would have used to dress down a wantonly reckless subaltern—"do you think would have happened had I not been there?"

Reaction, hard and sharp, speared through him; until that moment, he hadn't allowed himself to envisage that event. Eyes narrowing as real fury took hold, he stepped, deliberately intimidating, toward her. "Let me hypothesize—correct me if I'm wrong. On hearing the fight belowstairs you would have rushed down—into the teeth of things. Into the fray. And what then?" He took another step and she gave ground, but only fractionally. Then her spine locked; her head rose even higher. She met his gaze defiantly.

Lowering his head, bringing their faces close, his eyes locked with hers, he growled, "Regardless of what happened to Biggs, and having seen the villain's efforts with Stolemore, it wouldn't have been pretty, what—just *what* do you imagine would have happened to you?"

His voice had not risen but deepened, roughened, gained in power as his words brought the reality of what she had risked home to him.

Her spine stiff, her gaze as chill as the night about them, she opened her lips. "Nothing."

He blinked. "Nothing?"

"I would have set Henrietta on him."

The words stopped him. He glanced down at the wolfhound, who sighed heavily, then sat.

"As I said, these would-be intruders are *my* problem. I'm perfectly capable of dealing with any matters that arise myself."

He shifted his gaze from the hound to her. "You hadn't intended to bring Henrietta with you."

Leonora didn't succumb to the temptation to shift her eyes. "Nevertheless, as it happened, I did. So I wasn't in any danger."

Something changed—behind his face, behind his eyes. "Just because Henrietta is with you, you aren't in any danger?"

His voice had altered again; cold, hard, but flat, as if all the passion that had invested it a moment earlier had been drawn in, compressed.

She replayed his words, hesitated, yet could see no reason not to nod. "Precisely."

"Think again."

She'd forgotten how fast he could move. How totally helpless he could make her feel.

How totally and completely helpless she was, yanked into his arms, crushed against him, and ruthlessly kissed.

The impulse to struggle flared, but was extinguished before it took hold. Drowned beneath a tidal wave of feelings. Hers, and his.

Something between them ignited; not anger, not shock—something closer to avid curiosity.

She closed her hands in his coat, grabbed hold, held on as a rush of sensation swept her up, caught her, held her trapped. Not just by his arms but by myriad strands of fascination. By the shift of his lips, cool and hard on hers, the restless flexing of his fingers on her upper arms as if he longed to reach further, explore and touch, longed to pull her closer yet.

Spiraling thrills cascaded through her; licks of excitement teased her nerves, built her fascination. She'd been kissed before, but never like this. Never had pleasure and greedy need leapt to such a simple caress.

His lips moved on hers, ruthless, relentless, until she surrendered to the unsubtle pressure and parted them.

Her world shook when he pressed them wider yet and his tongue slid in to meet hers.

She tensed. He ignored it and caressed, then probed. Something within her rocked, teetered, then cracked. Sensation spilled down her veins, flowing steadily through her, hot, scalding, bright.

Another flash, another sharp shock of sensation. She would have gasped but he caught her to him, one steely arm sliding about her and tightening—distracting her as he deepened the kiss.

By the time her senses refocused, she was too enthralled, too enmeshed in the novel delights to think about breaking free.

Tristan sensed it, knew it in his bones, tried not to let his hunger take advantage. She'd been kissed before, but he'd stake his considerable reputation that she'd never yielded her mouth to any man.

But it, and she, were now his to enjoy, to savor, at least as far as a kiss would allow.

Madness, of course. He knew that now, but in that heated moment when she'd blithely consigned her protection to a hound—a hound who was sitting patiently by while he ravished her mistress's soft mouth—all he'd seen was red. He hadn't realized how much of that haze had been due to lust.

He knew now.

He'd kissed her to demonstrate her inherent weakness.

In doing so had uncovered his own.

He was hungry—starved; by some blessing of fate so was she. They stood in the silent garden, locked together, and simply enjoyed, took, gave. She was a novice, but that only added a piquancy, a delicate touch of enchantment to know that it was he who was leading her along paths she'd never trod.

Into realms she hadn't before explored.

The warmth of her, the supple strength, the blatantly feminine curves pressed to his chest—the fact he had her locked in his arms sank through his senses, sank evocative talons deep.

Until he knew just what he wanted, knew beyond doubt what Pandora's box he'd opened.

Leonora clung as the kiss went on, as it progressed, expanded, opening up new horizons, educating her senses. Some part of her reeling mind knew without question that she wasn't in any danger, that Trentham's arms were a safe haven for her.

That she could accept the kiss and all it brought if not with impunity, then at least without risk.

That she could grasp the brief glimpse of passion he offered, seize the moment and, starved, ease her hunger at least that much, own to wanting more without fear, knowing that when it ended she would be able—would be allowed—to step back. To remain herself, locked away and safe.

Alone.

So she made no move to end it.

Until Henrietta whined.

Trentham lifted his head instantly, looked down at Henrietta, but he didn't let her go.

Blushing, very glad of the darkness, she pushed back, felt his chest, warm rock, beneath her hands. Still frowning, glancing around at the shadows, he eased his hold on her.

Clearing her throat, she stepped back, out of his arms, putting clear distance between them. "She's cold."

He looked at her, then at Henrietta. "Cold?"

"Her coat's wiry hair, not fur."

He looked at her; she met his gaze, and suddenly felt terribly awkward. How did one part from a gentleman who'd just . . .

She looked down, snapped her fingers at Henrietta. "I'd better take her in. Good night."

He said nothing as she turned and started for the front steps. Then suddenly she sensed him shift.

"Wait."

She turned, raised a brow, as haughty as she could make it.

His face had hardened. "The key." He held out a hand. "To the front door of Number 12."

Heat rushed to her cheeks again. Reaching into her pocket, she drew it out. "I used to visit old Mr. Morrissey. He had terrible trouble doing his household accounts."

He took the key, weighed it in his palm.

She glanced up; he caught her gaze.

After a moment, very quietly he said, "Go inside."

It was too dark to read his eyes, yet caution whispered, told her to obey. Inclining her head, she turned to the front steps. She climbed them, opened the door she'd left on the latch, slipped in, and quietly closed it behind her, conscious all the while of his gaze on her back.

Sliding the key into his pocket, Tristan stood on the path amid the waving fronds and watched until her shadow disappeared into the house. Then he swore, turned, and walked away into the night.

CHAPTER

Four

ॐ◯ॐ

It wasn't the first time in his career that he'd made a tactical blunder. He needed to put it behind him, pretend it hadn't happened, and stick to his strategy of rescuing the damn woman, then moving on, getting on with the fraught business of finding himself a wife.

The next morning, as he strode up the front path to the door of Number 14, Tristan kept repeating that litany, along with a pointed reminder that an argumentative, willful, trenchantly independent lady of mature years was assuredly not the sort of wife he wanted.

Even if she tasted like ambrosia and felt like paradise in his arms.

How old was she anyway?

Nearing the front porch, he thrust the question out of his mind. If this morning went as he planned, he'd be much better placed to adhere to his strategy.

Pausing at the bottom of the steps, he looked up at the front door. He'd tossed and turned all night, not only with the inevitable effects of that unwise kiss, but even more because, stirred by the earlier events of the night, his conscience wouldn't settle. Whatever the truth about the "burglar," the matter was serious. Experience insisted it was so; his instincts were convinced of it. Even though he had no intention of leaving Leonora to deal with it on her own, he didn't feel comfortable in not alerting both Sir Humphrey and Jeremy Carling to the danger.

He'd come determined to make a real attempt to bring home to them the true tenor of the situation. It was their right to protect Leonora; he couldn't in all honor usurp their role while leaving them in ignorance.

Straightening his shoulders, he went up the steps.

The ancient butler answered his knock.

"Good morning." Charm to the fore, he smiled. "I'd like to speak to Sir Humphrey, and also Mr. Carling, if they're available."

The man's starchy demeanor eased; he opened the door wide. "If you'll wait in the morning room, my lord, I'll inquire."

He stood in the middle of the morning room and prayed Leonora didn't hear of his arrival. What he wanted to achieve would be easier accomplished between gentlemen, without the distracting presence of the object central to their discussion.

The butler returned and conducted him to the library. He entered and found Sir Humphrey and Jeremy alone, and heaved a small sigh of relief.

"Trentham! Welcome!" Seated as he had been on Tristan's earlier visit, in the armchair by the fire with—Tristan was almost certain—the same book open on his knee, Humphrey waved him to the chaise. "Sit down, sit down, and tell us what we can do for you."

Jeremy, too, looked up and nodded a greeting. Tristan returned the nod as he sat. Again, he got the impression little had changed on Jeremy's desk except, perhaps, the particular page he was studying.

Catching his glance, Jeremy smiled. "Indeed, I'll be grateful for a respite." He waved at the book before him. "Deciphering this Sumerian script is deuced hard on the eyes."

Humphrey snorted. "Better that than this." He indicated the tome on his knees. "More than a century later, but they weren't any neater. Why they couldn't use decent quills—" He broke off, then grinned engagingly at Tristan. "But you've not come to hear about that. You mustn't let us get started, or we can talk scripts for hours."

Tristan's mind boggled.

"So!" Humphrey closed the tome on his lap. "How can we help you, heh?"

"It's not so much a matter of help." He was feeling his way, unsure of his best approach. "I thought I should let you know that there was an attempted burglary at Number 12 last night."

"Good God!" Humphrey was as taken aback as Tristan could have wished. "Dashed bounders! Getting a great deal too above themselves these days."

"Indeed." Tristan grabbed back the reins before Humphrey could bolt. "But in this case, the builders noticed that some tampering had occurred on the previous night, so we mounted a watch last night. The felon returned and entered the house—we would have caught him but for some unexpected obstacles. As things fell out, he escaped, but it appeared he was . . . let us say not the expected low-class villain. Indeed, he bore all the signs of being a gentleman."

"A gentleman?" Humphrey was astounded. "A *gentleman* breaking into houses?"

"So it seems."

"But what would a gentleman be after?" Frowning, Jeremy met Tristan's gaze. "It seems quite nonsensical to me."

Jeremy's tone was dismissive; Tristan squelched his exasperation. "Indeed. Even more amazing is that a burglar would bother breaking into a completely empty house." He looked at Humphrey, then Jeremy. "There's literally nothing in Number 12, and given the builders' paraphernalia and presence throughout the day, that fact must be patently obvious."

Both Humphrey and Jeremy only looked more puzzled, as if the entire subject was completely beyond them. Tristan knew all about deceptiveness; he was starting to suspect he was watching a practiced performance. His voice hardened. "It occurred to me that the attempt to gain access to Number 12 might be linked to the two attempted burglaries here."

Both faces turned to him remained blank and vague. Too blank and vague. They understood everything, but were steadfastly refusing to react.

He deliberately let the silence grow awkward. Eventually, Jeremy cleared his throat. "How so?"

He nearly gave up; only a trenchant determination fueled by something very like anger that they shouldn't be allowed so easily to abdicate their responsibilities and retreat into their long-dead world, leaving Leonora to cope by herself in this one, had him leaning forward, with his gaze capturing theirs. "What if the burglar *isn't* your usual run of thief, and all evidence suggests that's so, but instead he's after something specific—some item that has value to him. If that item is here, in *this* house, then—"

The door opened.

Leonora swept in. Her eyes found him; she beamed. "My lord! How delightful to see you again."

Rising, Tristan met her eyes. She wasn't delighted—she was in a flat panic. She glided up; inwardly disgusted with how poorly things had gone, he seized the inherent advantage and held out his hand.

She blinked at it, but after only the slightest hesitation surrendered her fingers. He bowed; she curtsied. Her fingers quivered in his.

The courtesies satisfied, he drew her to sit beside him on the chaise. She had no option but to do so. As, tense and on edge, she sank onto the damask, Humphrey said, "Trentham's just told us there was a burglary next door—just last night. Blackguard escaped, unfortunately."

"Indeed?" Eyes wide, she turned to Tristan as he sat again, angling herself so she could watch his face.

He caught her eye. "Just so." His dry tone wasn't wasted on her. "I was just suggesting that the attempt to gain access to Number 12 might be connected to the previous attempts to gain entry here."

She, he knew, had arrived at the same conclusion, and that sometime ago.

"I still don't see any real link." Jeremy leaned on his book and fixed Tristan with a steady but still dismissive gaze. "I mean, burglars try their hand wherever they might, don't they?"

Tristan nodded. "Which is why it seems odd that this 'burglar'— and I think we can safely assume all the attempts have been by the same party—continues to push his luck in Montrose Place despite his failures to date."

"Hmm, yes, well, perhaps he'll take the hint and go away, given he couldn't get into either of our houses?" Humphrey raised his brows hopefully.

Tristan hung on to his temper. "The very fact he's tried three times suggests he won't go away—that whatever he's after he's driven to get."

"Yes, but that's just it, don't you see." Sitting back, Jeremy spread his hands wide. "What on earth could he want here?"

"That," Tristan retorted, "is the question."

Yet every suggestion that the "burglar" might be after something contained in their researches, some information, concealed or otherwise, or some unexpectedly valuable tome, met with denials and incomprehension. Other than speculating that the villain might be after Leonora's pearls, something Tristan found difficult to believe—and from the look on her face, so did Leonora—neither Humphrey nor Jeremy had any ideas to advance.

It was patently clear they had no interest in solving the mystery of the burglar, and were both of the opinion that ignoring the matter entirely was the surest route to getting it to disappear.

At least for them.

Tristan didn't approve, but he recognized their type. They were selfish, absorbed in their own interests to the exclusion of all else. Over the years, they'd learned to leave anything and everything to Leonora to deal with; because she always had, they now viewed her efforts as their right. She haggled with the real world while they remained engrossed in their academic one.

Admiration for Leonora—exceedingly reluctant for it was definitely something he didn't want to feel—along with a deeper understanding and a niggling sense that she deserved better bloomed and slid through him.

He could make no headway with Humphrey or Jeremy; eventually he had to concede defeat. He did, however, exact a promise that they would bend their minds to the question and inform him immediately if they thought of any item that could be the burglar's goal.

Catching Leonora's eye, he rose. Throughout, he'd been conscious of her tension, of her watching him like a hawk ready to jump in and deflect or confuse any comment that might reveal her part in the previous night's activities.

He held her gaze; she read his message and rose, too.

"I'll see Lord Trentham out."

With easy smiles, Humphrey and Jeremy bade him farewell. Following Leonora to the door, he paused on the threshold and looked back.

Both men were already head down, back in the past.

He looked at Leonora. Her expression stated she knew what he'd seen. One brow rose quizzically, as if she was wryly amused that he'd thought he could change things.

He felt his face harden. Waving her on, he followed, closing the door behind them.

She led him to the front hall. Drawing level with the door to the parlor, he touched her arm.

Met her gaze when she looked at him. "Let's walk in the back garden." When she didn't immediately acquiesce, he added, "I want to talk to you."

She hesitated, then inclined her head. She led him through the parlor—he noticed the piece of embroidery still precisely as it had been previously—out through the French doors and down onto the lawn.

Head high, she walked on; he fell in beside her. And said nothing. Waited for her to ask what he wished to talk about, grasping the moment to work on a strategy for convincing her to leave the matter of the mysterious burglar to him.

The lawn was lush and well tended, the beds circling it thick with odd plants he'd never seen before. The late Cedric Carling must have been a collector as well as an authority on herbal horticulture . . . "How long ago did your cousin Cedric die?"

She glanced at him. "Over two years ago." She paused, then continued, "I can't see that there'd be anything valuable in his papers, or we would have heard long ago."

"Most likely." After Humphrey and Jeremy, her open acuity was refreshing.

They'd walked across the width of the lawn; she halted where a sundial was set on a pedestal standing just within the boundary of a deep bed. He stopped beside and a little behind her. Watched as she put out a hand, with her fingertips traced the engraving in the bronze face.

"Thank you for not mentioning my presence in Number 12 last night." Her voice was low but clear; she kept her gaze on the sundial. "Or what happened on the path."

She drew breath, lifted her head.

Before she could say more—tell him the kiss hadn't meant anything, had been a silly mistake, or some similar nonsense he'd feel forced to prove wrong—he raised his hand, set one fingertip to her nape, and traced slowly, deliberately, down her spine, all the way down to below her waist.

Her breath caught, then she swung to face him, periwinkle blue eyes wide.

He trapped her gaze. "What happened last night, especially those moments on the path, is between you and me."

When she continued to stare at him, searching his eyes, he elaborated, "Kissing you and telling anyone is not within my code, and definitely not my style."

He saw the flash of reaction in her eyes, saw her consider asking, waspishly, just what his style was, but caution caught her tongue; she raised her head, haughtily inclined it as she looked away.

The moment was going to turn awkward, and he still hadn't thought of any approach likely to deflect her from the burglaries. Casting about in his mind, he looked past her. And saw the house beyond the garden wall, the house next door, which also, like Number 12, shared a wall with Number 14.

"Who lives there?"

She glanced up, followed his gaze. "Old Miss Timmins."

"She lives alone?"

"With a maid."

He looked down into Leonora's eyes; they were already filled with speculation. "I'd like to call on Miss Timmins. Will you introduce me?"

She was only too happy to do so. To leave the disconcerting moment in the garden—her thudding heart had yet to slow to its normal rhythm—and plunge instead into further investigations. By Trentham's side.

Quite why she found his company so stimulating Leonora didn't know. She wasn't even sure she approved, or that her Aunt Mildred, let alone her Aunt Gertie, would either, if they knew. He was, after all, a military man. Young girls might have their heads turned by broad shoulders and a magnificent uniform, but ladies such as she were supposed to be too wise to fall victim to such gentlemen's wiles. They were invariably second sons, or sons of second sons, looking to make their way in the world through an advantageous marriage . . . except Trentham was now an earl.

Inwardly, she frowned. Presumably that excused him from the general prohibition.

Regardless, as she walked briskly down the street beside him, her gloved hand on his sleeve, the sense of his strength engulfing her, the excitement of the hunt simmering in her veins, there was no question in her mind but that she felt immeasurably more alive when with him.

When she'd heard he'd called, she'd panicked. She'd felt sure he had come to complain of her infraction in going into Number 12 last night. And possibly, even worse, to mention—in whatever manner— their indiscretion on the path. Instead, he'd made not the slightest allusion to her part in the night's activities; even though she was sure he'd sensed her agitation, he'd said and done nothing to tease her.

She'd expected a lot worse from a military man.

Reaching the gate of Number 16, Trentham swung it wide, and they went through, walking up the path and climbing the steps to the small front porch side by side. She pulled the bell, heard it ring deep within the house, smaller than Number 14, a terrace similar in style to Number 12.

Footsteps pattered, approaching, then came the sound of bolts being drawn back. The door opened a little way; a sweet-faced maid peeped out.

Leonora smiled. "Good morning, Daisy. I know it's a trifle early, but if Miss Timmins can spare a few minutes, we have a new neighbor, the Earl of Trentham, who'd like to make her acquaintance."

Daisy's eyes had grown round as she took in Trentham, standing blocking the sunlight at Leonora's side. "Oh, yes, miss. I'm sure she'll see you—she always likes to know what's going on." Opening the door fully, Daisy waved them in. "If you'll wait in the morning room, I'll tell her you're here."

Leonora led the way into the morning room and sat on the chaise.

Trentham didn't sit. He paced. Prowled. Looking at the windows. Examining the locks.

She frowned. "What—"

She broke off as Daisy hurried back in. "She says as she'll be delighted to receive you." She bobbed to Trentham. "If you'll come this way, I'll take you up to her."

They climbed the stairs, following Daisy; Leonora was aware of the glances Trentham directed this way and that. If she didn't know better, she'd think *he* was the burglar looking for the best way in. . . .

"Oh." Halting at the top of the stairs, she swung to face him. Whispered, "Do you think the burglar might try here next?"

He frowned, waved her on. With Daisy sailing ahead, she had to turn and hurry to catch up. Trentham merely lengthened his stride. With him on her heels, she glided into Miss Timmins's drawing room.

"Leonora, my dear." Miss Timmins's voice quavered. "How sweet of you to call."

Miss Timmins was old and frail and rarely ventured outside. Leonora often called; over the past year, she'd noticed the brightness in Miss Timmins's soft blue eyes fading, as if a flame were burning low.

Smiling in return, she pressed Miss Timmins's clawlike hand, then stepped back. "I've brought the Earl of Trentham to call. He and some friends have bought the house beyond ours, Number 12."

Gently vague, her prim grey curls neatly brushed and dressed, her pearls looped about her throat, Miss Timmins shyly gave Trentham her hand. Nervously murmured a greeting.

Trentham bowed. "How do you do, Miss Timmins. I hope you've been keeping well through these cold months?"

Miss Timmins flustered, but still clung to Trentham's hand. "Yes, indeed." She seemed caught by his eyes. After a moment, she ventured, "It's been such a shocking winter."

"More sleet than usual, certainly." Trentham smiled, all charm. "May we sit?"

"Oh! Yes, of course. Please do." Miss Timmins leaned forward. "I heard you're a military man, my lord. Tell me, were you at Waterloo?"

Leonora sank into a chair and watched, amazed, as Trentham—a self-confessed military man—charmed old Miss Timmins, who wasn't, generally, comfortable with men. Yet Trentham seemed to know just what to say, just what an old lady thought appropriate to talk about. Just what snippets of gossip she'd like to hear.

Daisy brought tea; as she sipped, Leonora cynically wondered just what goal Trentham was pursuing.

Her answer came when he set down his cup and assumed a more serious mien. "Actually, I had a purpose in calling beyond the pleasure of meeting you, ma'am." He caught Miss Timmins's gaze. "There have been a number of incidents in the street lately, of burglars trying to gain entry."

"Oh, dear me!" Miss Timmins rattled her cup onto its saucer. "I must tell Daisy to be doubly sure she locks every door."

"As to that, I wonder if you would mind if I look around the ground floor and belowstairs, to make sure there's no easy way inside? I would sleep much more soundly if I knew your house, with only you and Daisy here, was secure."

Miss Timmins blinked, then beamed at him. "Why, of course, dear. So thoughtful of you."

After a few more comments of a more general nature, Trentham rose. Leonora rose, too. They took their leave, with Miss Timmins instructing Daisy that his-lordship-the-earl would be looking around the house to make sure all was safe.

Daisy beamed, too.

In parting, Trentham assured Miss Timmins that should he discover any less than adequate lock, he would take care of its replacement—she wasn't to bother her head.

From the look in Miss Timmins's old eyes as she pressed his hand in farewell, his-lordship-the-earl had made a conquest.

Disturbed, when they reached the stairs and Daisy had gone ahead, Leonora paused and caught Trentham's eye. "I hope you intend making good on that promise."

His gaze was steady and remained so; eventually he replied, "I will." He studied her face, then added, "I meant what I said." Stepping past her, he started down the stairs. "I *will* sleep more soundly knowing this place is secure."

She frowned at the back of his head—the man was a complete conundrum—then followed him down the stairs.

She trailed after him as he systematically checked every single window and door on the ground floor, then descended to the basement and did the same there. He was thorough and, to her eyes, coolly professional, as if securing premises against intruders had been a frequent task in his erstwhile occupation. It was increasingly difficult to dismiss him as "just another military man."

In the end, he nodded to Daisy. "This is better than I expected. Has she always been worried about intruders?"

"Oh, yes, sir, m'lord. Ever since I came here to do for her, and that's going on six years, now."

"Well, if you lock every lock and shoot every bolt, you'll be as safe as you could be."

Leaving a grateful and reassured Daisy, they walked down the garden path. Reaching the gate, Leonora, who'd been pursuing her own thoughts, glanced at Trentham. "Is the house truly secure?"

He looked at her, then held the gate open. "As secure as it can be. There's no way to stop a determined intruder." He fell into step beside her as they paced along the pavement. "If he uses force—breaking a window or forcing a door—he'll get in, but I don't think our man is likely to be so direct. If we're right in thinking it's Number 14 he wants access to, then to get that via Number 16, he'll have to have a few nights undetected to tunnel through the basement walls. He won't get that if he's too obvious about how he gets in."

"So as long as Daisy is vigilant, all should be well."

When he didn't say anything, she looked at him. He sensed her glance, caught her eye. Grimaced. "On our way in, I was wondering how to introduce some man into the household, at least until we've laid this burglar by the heels. But she's frightened of men, isn't she?"

"Yes." She was astonished he'd been so perceptive. "You're one of the few I've ever known her to talk to beyond the barest commonplace."

He nodded, looked down. "She'd be too uncomfortable with a man under her roof, so it's lucky those locks are so sound. We'll have to put our faith in them."

"And do everything we can to catch this burglar soon."

Her determination rang in her voice.

They'd reached the gate of Number 14. Tristan halted, met her gaze. "I suppose there's no point insisting you leave the matter of the burglar in my hands?"

Her periwinkle blue eyes hardened. "None."

He exhaled, looked away down the street. He wasn't above lying for a good cause. Wasn't above using distractions, either, despite their inherent danger.

Before she could shift away, he caught her hand. Turned his head and trapped her gaze. Held it while with his fingers he sought, then flicked the opening in her glove wide, then raised her wrist, the inner face now exposed, to his lips.

Felt the quiver that raced through her, watched her head lift, her eyes darken.

He smiled, slowly, intently. Softly decreed, "What's between you and me remains between you and me, but it hasn't gone away."

Her lips set; she tugged, but he didn't release her, instead, with his thumb, languidly caressed the spot he'd kissed.

She caught her breath, then hissed, "I'm not interested in any dalliance."

Eyes on hers, he raised a brow. "No more am I." He was interested in distracting her. They'd both be better off with her concentrating on him rather than on the burglar. "In the interests of our acquaintance"— in the interests of his sanity—"I'm willing to make a deal."

Suspicion glowed in her eyes. "What deal?"

He chose his words carefully. "If you promise to do no more than keep your eyes and ears open, to do no more than watch and listen and report all to me when next I call, I'll agree to share with you all I discover."

Her expression turned haughtily dismissive. "And what if you don't discover anything?"

His lips remained curved, but he let his mask slide, let his true self show briefly. "Oh, I will." His voice was soft, faintly menacing; its tone held her.

Again, slowly, deliberately, he raised her wrist to his lips.

Holding her gaze, kissed.

"Do we have a deal?"

She blinked, refocused on his eyes, then her breasts swelled as she drew in a deep breath. And nodded. "Very well."

He released her wrist; she all but snatched it back.

"But on one condition."

He raised his brows, now as haughty as she. "What?"

"I'll watch and listen and do no more if you promise to call and tell me what you've discovered *as soon* as you discover it."

His gaze locked with hers, he considered, then let his lips ease. He inclined his head. "As soon as practicable, I'll share any discovery."

She was mollified, and surprised to be so. He hid a grin and bowed. "Good day, Miss Carling."

She held his gaze for a moment longer, then inclined her head. "Good day, my lord."

Days passed.

Leonora watched and listened, but nothing of any moment occurred. She was content with their bargain; there was in truth little else she could do beyond watch and listen, and the knowledge that if anything did occur, Trentham expected to be involved in dealing with it was unexpectedly heartening. She'd grown used to acting alone, indeed eschewed the help of others who in general were more likely to get in her way, yet Trentham was undeniably able—with him involved, she felt confident of resolving the issue of the burglaries.

Staff started to appear at Number 12; Trentham occasionally called in there, as duly reported by Toby, but did not venture to knock on the Carlings' front door.

The only factor that disturbed her equanimity was her recollections of that kiss in the night. She'd tried to forget it, simply put it from her mind, an aberration on both their parts, yet forgetting the way her pulse leapt whenever he came near was much harder. And she had absolutely no idea how to interpret his comment that what lay between them hadn't gone away.

Did he mean he intended to pursue it?

But then he'd declared he wasn't interested in dalliance any more than she was. Despite his past occupation, she was learning to take his words at face value.

Indeed, his tactful dealings with the old soldier Biggs, his discretion in not speaking of her nighttime adventures, and his unprecedented charming of Miss Timmins, going out of his way to reassure and see to the old lady's safety, had in large part ameliorated her prejudice.

Perhaps Trentham was one of those whose existence proved the rule—a trustworthy military man, one who could be relied on, at least in certain matters.

Despite that, she wasn't entirely certain she could rely on him to tell her all and anything he discovered. Nevertheless, she would have allowed him a few more days' grace if it hadn't been for the watcher.

At first, it was simply a sensation, a prickling of her nerves, an eerie feeling of being observed. Not just in the street, but in the back garden, too; that last unnerved her. The first of the earlier attacks on her had occurred just inside the front gate; she no longer walked in the front garden.

She began taking Henrietta with her wherever she went, and if that wasn't possible, a footman.

With time, her nerves would doubtless have calmed, steadied.

But then, strolling in the back garden late one afternoon as the abbreviated February twilight closed in, she glimpsed a man standing almost at the rear of the garden, beyond the hedge that bisected the long plot. Framed by the central arch in the hedge, a lean, dark figure swathed in a dark cloak, he stood among the vegetable beds—and watched her.

Leonora froze. He wasn't the same man who had accosted her in January, the first time by the front gate, the second time in the street. That man had been smaller, slighter; she'd been able to fight back, to break free.

The man who now watched her looked infinitely more menacing. He stood silent, still, yet it was the stillness of a predator waiting for his moment. There was only a stretch of lawn between them. She had to fight the urge to raise a hand to her throat, had to battle an instinct to turn and flee—battle the conviction that if she did he'd be on her.

Henrietta ambled up, saw the man, and growled low in her throat. The rumbling warning continued, subtly escalating. Hackles rising, the hound placed herself between Leonora and the man.

He remained still for an instant longer, then whisked around. His cloak flapped; he disappeared from Leonora's sight.

Heart thudding uncomfortably, she looked down at Henrietta. The wolfhound remained alert, senses focused. Then a distant thud reached Leonora's ears; an instant later, Henrietta wuffed and relaxed from her stance, turning to calmly continue their progress back to the parlor doors.

A chill swept Leonora's spine; eyes wide, scanning the shadows, she hurried back to the house.

The next morning at eleven o'clock—the earliest hour at which it was acceptable to call—she rang the doorbell of the elegant house in Green Street that the urchin sweeping at the corner had told her belonged to the Earl of Trentham.

An imposing but kindly-looking butler opened the door. "Yes, ma'am?"

She drew herself up. "Good morning. I am Miss Carling, from Montrose Place. I wish to speak with Lord Trentham, if you please."

The butler looked genuinely regretful. "Unfortunately, his lordship is not presently in."

"Oh." She'd assumed he would be, that like most fashionable men he was unlikely to set foot beyond his door before noon. After a frozen moment in which nothing—no other avenue of action—occurred to her, she lifted her gaze to the butler's face. "Is he expected to return soon?"

"I daresay his lordship will be back within the hour, miss." Her determination must have shown; the butler opened the door wider. "If you would care to wait?"

"Thank you." Leonora let a hint of approval color the words. The butler had the most sympathetic face. She stepped across the threshold and was instantly struck by the airiness and light in the hall, underscored by the elegant furnishings. As the butler closed the door, she turned to him.

He smiled encouragingly. "If you'll come this way, miss?"

Insensibly reassured, Leonora inclined her head and followed him down the corridor.

Tristan returned to Green Street at a little after noon, no further forward and increasingly concerned. Climbing his front steps, he fished out his latch key and let himself in; he had still not grown accustomed to waiting for Havers to open the door, relieve him of his cane and coat, all things he was perfectly capable of doing himself.

Setting his cane in the hall stand, tossing his coat across a chair, he headed, soft-footed, for his study. Hoping to slip past the arches of the morning room without being spotted by any of the old dears. An exceedingly faint hope; regardless of their occupations, they always seemed to sense his flitting presence and glance up just in time to smile and waylay him.

Unfortunately, there was no other way to reach the study; his great-uncle who'd remodeled the house had, he'd long ago concluded, been a glutton for punishment.

The morning room was a light-filled chamber built out from the main house. A few steps below the level of the corridor, it was separated from it by three large arches. Two hosted huge flower arrangements in urns, which gave him some cover, but the middle arch was the doorway, open country.

As silent as a thief, he neared the first arch and, just out of sight, paused to listen. A babble of female voices reached him; the group was at the far end of the room, where a bow window allowed morning light to stream over two chaises and various chairs. It took a moment to attune his ear to pick out the individual voices. Ethelreda was there, Millie, Flora, Constance, Helen, and yes, Edith, too. All six of them. Chattering on about knots—French knots?—what were they?—and gross-something and leaf-stitch . . .

They were discussing embroidery.

He frowned. They all embroidered like martyrs, but it was the one arena in which real competition flourished between them; he'd never heard them discussing their shared interest before, let alone with such gusto.

Then he heard another voice, and his surprise was complete.

"I'm afraid I've never been able to get the threads to lie just so."

Leonora.

"Ah, well, dear, what you need to do—"

He didn't take in the rest of Ethelreda's advice; he was too busy speculating on what had brought Leonora there.

The discussion in the morning room continued, Leonora inviting advice, his old dears taking great delight in supplying it.

Vivid in his mind was that piece of embroidery lying discarded in the parlor in Montrose Place. Leonora might have no talent for embroidery, but he'd have sworn she had no real interest in it, either.

Curiosity pricked. The nearest flower arrangement was tall enough to conceal him. Two swift steps and he was behind it. Peering between the lilies and chrysanthemums, he saw Leonora seated in the middle of one of the chaises surrounded on all sides by his collection of old dears.

Winter sunlight poured through the window at her back, a glimmering wash spilling over her, striking garnet glints from her coronet of dark hair yet leaving her face and its delicate features in faint and mysterious shadow. In her dark red walking dress, she looked like a medieval madonna, an embodiment of feminine virtue and passion, of feminine strength and fragility.

Head bowed, she was examining an embroidered antimacassar laid across her knees.

He watched her encourage her elderly audience to tell her more, to participate. Also saw her step in, swiftly tamping down a sudden spurt of rivalry, soothing both parties with tactful observations.

She had them captivated.

And not only them.

He heard the words in his mind.

Inwardly humphed.

Yet he didn't turn away. Silent, he simply stood, watching her through the screen of flowers.

"Ah—my lord!"

With incomparable reflexes, he stepped forward and turned, his back to the morning room. They'd be able to see him, but the movement would make it seem he'd just walked by.

He viewed his butler with a resigned eye. "Yes, Havers?"

"A lady has called, my lord. A Miss Carling."

"Ah! Trentham!"

He turned as Ethelreda called.

Millie stood and beckoned. "We have Miss Carling here."

All six beamed at him. With a nod of dismissal to Havers, he stepped down and crossed toward the group, not quite certain of the impression he was receiving—almost as if they believed they'd been keeping Leonora there, trapped, cornered, some special delight just for him.

She rose, a light blush in her cheeks. "Your cousins have been very kind in keeping me company." She met his gaze. "I came because there have been developments in Montrose Place that I believe you should know."

"Yes, of course. Thank you for coming. Let's repair to the library, and you can tell me your news." He held out his hand; inclining her head, she surrendered hers.

He drew her from the midst of his elderly champions, nodded to them. "Thank you for entertaining Miss Carling for me."

He had no doubt of the thoughts behind their brilliant smiles.

"Oh, we enjoyed it."

"So delightful . . ."

"Do call again, dear."

They beamed and bobbed; Leonora smiled her thanks, then let him place her hand on his sleeve and lead her away.

Side by side they climbed the steps to the corridor; he didn't need to glance back to know six pairs of eyes were still avidly watching.

As they passed into the front hall, Leonora glanced at him. "I didn't realize you had such a large family."

"I haven't." He opened the library door and ushered her in. "That's the problem. There's just me, and them. And the rest."

Drawing her hand from his sleeve, she turned to look at him. "Rest?"

He waved her to the chairs angled to the blaze roaring in the hearth. "There's eight more at Mallingham Manor, my house in Surrey."

Her lips twitched; she turned and sat.

His smile faded. He dropped into the opposite chair. "Now cut line. Why are you here?"

Leonora lifted her gaze to his face, saw within it all she'd come to find—reassurance, strength, ability. Drawing breath, she leaned back in the chair, and told him.

He didn't interrupt; when she'd finished he asked questions, clarifying where and when it was she'd felt under observation. At no point did he seek to dismiss her intuitive certainty; he treated all she reported as fact, not fancy.

"And you're sure it was the same man?"

"Positive. I caught only a glimpse as he moved, but he had that same loose-limbed motion." She held his gaze. "I'm sure it was he."

He nodded. His gaze drifted from her as he considered all she'd said. Eventually, he glanced at her. "I don't suppose you told your uncle or brother about any of this?"

She raised her brows, mock-haughtily. "I did, as it happens."

When she said nothing more, he prompted, "And?"

Her smile wasn't as lighthearted as she would have liked. "When I mentioned the feeling of being watched, they smiled and told me I was overreacting to the recent troubling events. Humphrey patted my shoulder and told me I shouldn't worry my head about such things, that there really was no need—it would all blow over soon enough.

"As for the man at the bottom of the garden, they were sure I was mistaken. A trick of the light, the shifting shadows. An overactive imagination. I really shouldn't read so many of Mrs. Radcliffe's novels. Besides, as Jeremy pointed out—in the manner of one stating an absolute proof—the back gate is always kept locked."

"Is it?"

"Yes." She met Trentham's hazel eyes. "But the wall is covered on both sides with ancient ivy. Any reasonably agile man would have no difficulty climbing over."

"Which would account for the thud you heard."

"Precisely."

He sat back. Elbow on one chair arm, chin propped on that fist, one long finger idly tapping his lips, he looked past her. His eyes glinted, hard, almost crystalline sharp beneath his heavy lids. He knew she was there, wasn't ignoring her, but was, at present, absorbed.

She hadn't before had such a chance to study him, to take in the reality of the strength in his large body, appreciate the width of his shoulders disguised though they were by the superbly tailored coat—Shultz, of course—or the long, lean legs, muscles delineated by tightly fitted buckskins that disappeared into glossy Hessians. He had very large feet.

He was always elegantly dressed, yet it was a quiet elegance; he did not need or wish to draw attention to himself—indeed, eschewed all opportunity to do so. Even his hands—she might dub them his best feature—were adorned only by a plain gold signet ring.

He'd spoken of his style; she felt confident in defining it as quiet, elegant strength. Like an aura it hung about him, not something derived from clothes or manner, but something inherent, innate, that showed through.

She found such quiet strength unexpectedly attractive. Comforting, too.

Her lips had eased into a gentle smile when his gaze shifted back to her. He raised a brow, but she shook her head, remained silent. Their gazes held; relaxed in the chairs in the quiet of his library, they studied each other.

And something changed.

Excitement, an insidious thrill, slid slowly through her, a subtle flick, a temptation to illicit delight. Heat blossomed; her lungs slowly seized.

Their eyes remained locked. Neither moved.

It was she who broke the spell. Shifted her gaze to the flames in the hearth. Breathed in. Reminded herself not to be ridiculous; they were in his house, in his library—he would hardly seduce her under his own roof with his servants and elderly cousins standing by.

He stirred and sat up. "How did you get here?"

"I walked through the park." She glanced at him. "It seemed the safest way."

He nodded, rose. "I'll drive you home. I need to look in at Number 12."

She watched while he tugged the bellpull, gave orders to his butler when that worthy arrived. When he turned back to her, she asked, "Have you learned anything?"

Tristan shook his head. "I've been investigating various avenues. Searching for any whispers of men seeking something from Montrose Place."

"And did you hear anything?"

"No." He met her gaze. "I didn't expect to—that would be too easy."

She grimaced, then rose as Havers returned to say his curricle was being brought around.

While she donned her pelisse and he shrugged into his greatcoat and dispatched a footman to fetch his driving gloves, Tristan racked his brains for any avenue he'd left unexplored, any door open to him he hadn't been through. He'd tapped any number of ex-servicemen, and some who were still serving in various capacities, for information; he was now certain that what they were dealing with was something peculiar to Montrose Place. There had been no whispers of gangs or individuals behaving in like manner anywhere else in the capital.

Which only added weight to their supposition that there was something in Number 14 the mystery burglar wanted.

As they bowled around the park in his curricle, he explained his deductions.

Leonora frowned. "I've asked the servants." Lifting her head, she tucked back a strand of hair whipping in the breeze. "No one has any idea of anything that might be particularly valuable." She glanced at him. "Beyond the obvious answer of something in the library."

He caught her glance, then looked to his horses. After a moment, asked, "Is it possible your uncle and brother would hide something important—for instance if they made a discovery and wanted to keep it secret for a time?"

She shook her head. "I often act as hostess for their learned dinners. There's a great deal of competition and rivalry in their field, but far from being secretive about any discoveries, the usual approach is to shout any new finding, no matter how minor, from the rooftops, and that as soon as possible. By way of claiming rights, if you take my meaning."

He nodded. "So that's unlikely."

"Yes, but . . . if you were to suggest that Humphrey or Jeremy might have stumbled across something quite valuable, and simply not seen it for what it was—or rather they would recognize it but not attribute an accurate value to it"—she looked at him—"I'd have to agree."

"Very well." They'd reached Montrose Place; he drew rein outside Number 12. "We'll have to assume something of the sort is at the heart of this."

Tossing the reins to his tiger who'd jumped from the back and come running, he climbed down to the pavement, then handed her down.

Linking their arms, he walked her to the gate of Number 14.

At the gate, she drew back and faced him. "What do you think we should do?"

He met her gaze directly, without any hint of his usual mask. An instant passed, then he said, softly, "I don't know."

His hard gaze held hers; his hand found hers, his fingers twined with hers.

Her pulse leapt at his touch.

He raised her hand, brushed his lips across her fingers.

Held her gaze over them.

Then, lingeringly, touched his lips to her skin again, blatantly savoring.

Dizziness threatened.

His eyes searched hers, then he murmured, deep and low, "Let me think things through. I'll call on you tomorrow, and we can discuss how best to go on."

Her skin burned where his lips had brushed. She managed a nod, stepped back. He let her fingers slide from his. Pushing the iron gate, she stepped through, shut it. Looked at him through it. "Until tomorrow, then. Good-bye."

Her pulse thrumming through her veins, throbbing in her fingertips, she turned and walked up the path.

Five

"Is this the place?"

Tristan nodded to Charles St. Austell and reached for the door-knob of Stolemore's establishment. By the time he'd dropped by one of his smaller clubs, the Guards, the previous evening, he'd already decided to call on Stolemore and be rather more persuasive. Encountering Charles, up from the country on business, also taking refuge at the club, had been too good a stroke of fortune to overlook.

Either of them could be menacing enough to persuade almost anyone to talk; together, there was no doubt Stolemore would tell them all Tristan wished to know.

He'd only had to mention the matter to Charles, and he'd agreed. Indeed, he'd leapt at the chance to help, to once again exercise his peculiar talents.

The door swung inward; Tristan led the way in. This time, Stolemore was behind the desk. He looked up as the bell tinkled, his gaze sharpening as he recognized Tristan.

Tristan strolled forward, his gaze trained on the hapless agent. Stolemore's eyes widened. His gaze deflected to Charles. The agent paled, then tensed.

Behind him, Tristan heard Charles move; he didn't look around. His senses informed him Charles had turned the wooden sign on the door to CLOSED, then came the rattle of rings on wood; the light faded as Charles drew the curtains across the front windows.

Stolemore's expression, eyes filled with apprehension, said he understood their threat very well. He grasped the edge of his desk and eased his chair back.

From the corner of his eye, Tristan watched Charles cross soft-footed to lounge, arms folded, against the edge of the curtained doorway leading deeper into the house. His grin would have done credit to a demon.

The message was clear. To escape the small office Stolemore would have to go through one or other of them. Although the agent was a heavy man, heavier than either Tristan or Charles, there was no doubt in any of their minds that he would never make it.

Tristan smiled, not humorously yet gently enough. "All we want is information."

Stolemore licked his lips, his gaze flicking from him to Charles. "On what?"

His voice was rough, underlying fear grating.

Tristan paused as if savoring the sound, then softly replied, "I want the name and all the details you have on the party who wished to purchase Number 14 Montrose Place."

Stolemore swallowed; again he edged back, his gaze shifting between them. "I don't go talking about my clients. Worth my reputation to give out information like that."

Again Tristan waited, his eyes never leaving Stolemore's face. When the silence had stretched taut, along with Stolemore's nerves, he softly inquired, "And what do you imagine it's going to cost you not to oblige us?"

Stolemore paled even more; the lingering bruises from the beating administered by the very people he was protecting were clearly visible beneath his pasty skin. He turned to Charles, as if gauging his chances; an instant later, he looked back at Tristan. Puzzlement flowed behind his eyes. "Who are you?"

Tristan replied, his tone even, uninflected, "We're gentlemen who do not like seeing innocents taken advantage of. Suffice to say the recent activities of your client do not sit well with us."

"Indeed," Charles put in, his voice a dark purr, "you could say he's rattling our cages."

The last words were laden with menace.

Stolemore glanced at Charles, then quickly looked back at Tristan. "All right. I'll tell you—but on condition you don't tell him it was me gave you his name."

"I can assure you that when we catch up with him, we won't be wasting time discussing how we found him." Tristan raised his brows. "Indeed, I can guarantee he'll have much more pressing claims on his attention."

Stolemore smothered a nervous snort. He reached for a drawer in the desk.

Tristan and Charles moved, silent, deadly; Stolemore froze, then glanced nervously at them, now positioned so he was directly between them. "It's just a book," he croaked. "I swear!"

A heartbeat passed, then Tristan nodded. "Take it out."

Barely breathing, Stolemore very slowly withdrew a ledger from the drawer.

The tension eased a fraction; the agent placed the book on the desk and opened it. He fumbled, hurriedly shuffling pages, then he ran his finger down one, and stopped.

"Write it down," Tristan said.

Stolemore obliged.

Tristan had already read the entry, committed it to memory. When Stolemore finished and pushed the slip of paper with the address across the desk, he smiled—charmingly, this time—and picked it up.

"This way"—he held Stolemore's gaze as he tucked the paper into his inner coat pocket—"if anyone should ask, you can swear with a clear conscience that you told no one his name or address. Now—what did he look like? There was just one man, I take it?"

Stolemore nodded in the direction in which the slip of paper had disappeared. "Just him. Nasty piece of work. Looks gentlemanly enough—black hair, pale skin, brown eyes. Well dressed but not Mayfair quality. I took him for a nob from the country; he behaved arrogantly enough. Youngish, but he's got a mean streak and a hasty temper." Stolemore raised a hand to the bruises about one eye. "If I never see him again, it'll be too soon."

Tristan inclined his head. "We'll see what we can do to arrange it."

Turning, he walked to the door. Charles followed on his heels.

Outside on the pavement, they paused.

Charles grimaced. "Much as I would love to come and cast an eye over our stronghold"—his devilish grin dawned—"and over our delectable neighbor, I have to hie back to Cornwall."

"My thanks." Tristan held out his hand.

Charles grasped it. "Anytime." A hint of self-deprecation tinged his smile. "Truth to tell, I enjoyed it, minor though it was. I feel like I'm literally rusting in the country."

"The adjustment was never going to be easy, even less so for us than for others."

"At least you've got something to keep you occupied. All I have is sheep and cows and sisters."

Tristan laughed at Charles's patent disgust. He clapped him on the shoulder, and they parted, Charles heading back to Mayfair while Tristan headed in the opposite direction.

To Montrose Place. It was not quite ten o'clock. He would check with Gasthorpe, the ex–sergeant major they'd hired as the Bastion Club's majordomo who was overseeing the final stages of preparing the club for its patrons, then he'd call on Leonora as he'd promised.

As he'd promised, discuss how to go on.

At eleven o'clock, he knocked on the door of Number 14. The butler showed him to the parlor; Leonora rose from the chaise as he entered.

"Good morning." She bobbed a curtsy as he bowed over her hand.

The sun had managed to struggle free of the clouds; the beams of sunshine playing over the foliage in the back garden drew Tristan's gaze.

"Walk with me in the garden." He retained possession of her hand. "I'd like to see this back wall of yours."

She hesitated, then inclined her head; she would have led the way, but he didn't free her fingers. Instead, he curved his hand more definitely about hers. She threw him a brief glance as side by side they walked to the French doors. Opening them, they passed through; as they went down the steps, he drew her hand through his arm.

Aware of the skittering of her pulse, the way it quivered beneath his fingers.

She lifted her head. "We need to go through that arch in the hedges." She pointed. "The wall is at the back of the kitchen gardens."

Which gardens were extensive. With Henrietta ambling behind, they strolled down the central path, past rows of cabbages followed by endless rows lying fallow, long mounds covered with leaves and other debris waiting, slumbering, until spring returned.

He halted. "Where was he standing when you saw him?"

Leonora glanced around, then pointed to a spot just a little way ahead, about twenty feet inside the back wall. "It must have been about there."

He released her, turning to look back up the path, through the archway to the lawn. "You said he whisked out of your sight. In which direction did he go? Did he turn and walk back toward the wall?"

"No—he went sideways. If he'd turned and run back down the path, I would have been able to see him for longer."

He nodded, surveying the ground in the direction she'd indicated. "That was two evenings ago." It hadn't rained since. "Has your gardener been working here?"

"Not in the last few days. There's not much to do here in winter."

He put a hand on her arm, pressed briefly. "Stay here." He continued down the path, treading carefully along the edge. "Tell me when I get to where he was standing."

She watched, then said, "About there."

He circled the area, eyes on the ground, then moved between the beds away from the path in the direction the man had gone.

He found what he was looking for a foot from the base of the wall, where the man had stepped heavily before jumping onto the thick creeper. He crouched down; Leonora came bustling up. The footprint was clearly delineated.

"Hmm . . . yes."

He glanced up to find her bending near, studying the impression. She caught his eye. "That looks about right."

He rose; she straightened. "It's the same size and shape as the print I found in the dust by the side door of Number 12."

"The door the burglar came in through?"

He nodded and turned to the creeper-covered wall. He scanned it carefully, but it was Leonora who found the evidence.

"Here." She lifted a broken twig, then let it fall.

"And here." He pointed higher, where the creeper had been dislodged from the wall. He glanced at the heavy gate. "I don't suppose you have the key?"

The look she threw him was coolly superior. She drew an old key from her pocket.

He swiped it from her fingers. Pretended not to see the flare of irritation in her eyes. Moving past her, he fitted the key to the huge old lock and turned it. The gate groaned protestingly as he hauled it open.

There were two clear prints in the alley running behind the houses, in the accumulated dirt covering the rough flags. A brief glance was enough to confirm they were from the same boot, made as the man jumped down from the wall. Thereafter, however, there were no clear traces.

"That's conclusive enough." He took Leonora's arm, urged her back to the gate.

They reentered the garden, Leonora shooing Henrietta before them. Tristan closed and relocked the gate. Leonora was the only one who walked in the garden; he'd been watching long enough to be certain of that. That the burglar had singled her out worried him. Reminded him of his earlier conviction that she hadn't told him all.

Turning from the gate, he held out the key. She took it, looked down to slip it into her pocket.

He glanced around. The gate lay to one side of the path, not in line with the archway in the hedge; they were out of sight of the lawn and the house. Courtesy of the fruit trees lining the side walls, they were also screened from any neighbors.

He looked down as Leonora raised her head.

He smiled. Infused all the art of which he was capable into the gesture.

She blinked, but, somewhat to his chagrin, seemed less addled than he'd hoped.

"Those earlier attempts to break in here—the burglar didn't see you, did he?"

She shook her head. "The first time, only the servants were about. The second time, when Henrietta raised the alarm, we all came tumbling down, but he was long gone by then."

She offered nothing more. Her periwinkle blue eyes remained clear, unclouded. She hadn't stepped back; they were close, her face turned up so she could look into his.

Attraction flared, raced over his skin.

He let it. Let it flow and build, didn't try to suppress it. Let it show in his face, in his eyes.

Hers, locked on his, widened. She cleared her throat. "We were going to discuss how best to go on."

The words were breathless, uncharacteristically weak.

He paused for a heartbeat, then leaned closer. "I've decided we should play it by ear."

"By ear?" Her lashes fluttered down as he leaned closer yet.

"Hmm. Just follow our noses."

He did precisely that, lowered his head and set his lips to hers.

She stilled. She'd been watching, skittish, but had not anticipated such a direct attack.

He was too experienced to signal his intentions. Not on any battlefield.

So he didn't immediately take her in his arms, instead simply kissed her, his lips on hers, subtly tempting.

Until she parted hers and let him in. Until he cradled her face, sank deep and drank, savored, took.

Only then did he reach for her, and draw her to him, unsurprised, as his tongue tangled with hers, that she stepped toward him without thought. Without hesitation.

She was caught in the kiss.

As was he.

Such a simple thing—it was just a kiss. Yet as Leonora felt her breasts meet his chest, felt his arms close around her, there seemed to be so much more. So much she'd never before felt, never before even realized existed. Like the warmth that raced through them—not just through her but through him, too. The sudden tension, not of rejection, not of reining back, but of wanting.

Her hands had risen to rest against his shoulders. Through the contact, she sensed his reaction, both his ease in this sphere, his expertise, and beneath that a deeper yearning.

His hand on her back, strong fingers splayed over her spine, urged her closer; she acquiesced, and his lips turned demanding. Commanding. She met them, gave her mouth and felt the first lick of glory in his hunger. Against her, his body felt like oak, strong and unbending, yet the mobile lips that held hers, that played, teased and made her want, were so alive, so assured.

So addictive.

She was about to sink against him, about to willingly slide deeper under his spell, when she sensed him ease back, felt his hands slide to her waist and grip lightly.

He broke off the kiss and lifted his head.

Looked into her eyes.

For a moment, she could only blink at him, wondering why he'd stopped. Regret flashed through his eyes, superceded by resolve, a hard glint in the hazel. As if he hadn't wanted to stop but felt he must.

A fleeting madness gripped her—a strong urge to reach her hand to his nape and draw him, and those fascinating lips, back to her.

She blinked again.

He set her back on her feet, steadying her.

"I should go."

Her wits snapped back into place, back into the real world. "How have you decided to proceed?"

He looked at her; she could have sworn a frown crossed behind his eyes. His lips thinned. She waited, her gaze steady.

Eventually, he replied, "I called on Stolemore this morning." He grasped her hand, wound her arm in his, and steered them back along the path.

"And?"

"He consented to tell me the name of the purchaser so intent on buying this house. One Montgomery Mountford. Do you know him?"

She looked ahead, mentally running through all her and her family's acquaintances. "No. He's not one of Humphrey's or Jeremy's colleagues, either—I help with their correspondence, and that name hasn't arisen."

When he said nothing more, she glanced at him. "Did you get an address?"

He nodded. "I'll go there and see what I can learn."

They'd reached the archway. She halted. "Where is it?"

He met her gaze; again she got the impression he was irritated. "Bloomsbury."

"Bloomsbury?" She stared. "That's where we used to live."

He frowned. "Before here?"

"Yes. I told you we moved here two years ago, when Humphrey inherited this house. For the four years before that, we lived in Bloomsbury. In Keppell Street." She caught his sleeve. "Perhaps it's someone from there, who for some reason . . ." She gestured. "Who knows why, but there must be a connection."

"Perhaps."

"Come on!" She set off for the parlor doors. "I'll come with you. There's plenty of time before lunch."

Tristan swallowed a curse and set off after her. "There's no need—"

"Of course there is!" She flicked him an impatient glance. "How will you know if this Mr. Mountford is in some odd way connected with our past?"

There was no good answer to that. He'd kissed her with the connected aims of further arousing her sensual curiosity and thus distracting her enough to allow him to pursue the burglar on his own, and had apparently failed on both counts. Swallowing his irritation, he followed her up the steps.

And through the French doors.

Exasperated, he halted. He wasn't used to following another's lead, let alone tripping on a lady's heels. "Miss Carling!"

She halted before the door. Head rising, spine stiffening, she faced him. Her eyes met his. "Yes?"

He struggled to mask his glare. Intransigence glowed in her fine eyes, invested her stance. He debated for an instant, then, like all experienced commanders when faced with the unexpected, adjusted his tactics.

"Very well." Disgusted, he waved her on. Giving way on a relatively minor point might well strengthen his hand later.

She sent him a beaming smile, then opened the door and led the way into the hall.

Lips compressed, he followed. It was only Bloomsbury, after all.

Indeed, being Bloomsbury, her presence on his arm proved a bonus. He'd forgotten that in the middle-class neighborhood into which Mountford's address took them, a couple attracted less attention than a single, well-dressed gentleman.

The house in Taviton Street was tall and narrow. It proved to be a lodging house. The landlady opened the door; neat and severe in dull black, she narrowed her eyes when he asked for Mountford.

"He's gone. Left last week."

After the foiled attempt at Number 12. Tristan affected mild surprise. "Did he say where he was going?"

"No. Just handed me my shillings on the way out." She sniffed. "I wouldn't have got them if I hadn't been right here."

Leonora edged in front of him. "We're trying to find a man who might know something of an incident in Belgravia. We're not even sure Mr. Mountford's the right man. Was he tall?"

The landlady considered her, then thawed. "Aye. Medium-tall." Her eyes flicked to Tristan. "Not as tall as your husband here, but tallish."

A faint blush tinged Leonora's fine skin; she hurried on. "Lightly built rather than heavy?"

The landlady nodded. "Black-haired, a bit too pale to be healthy. Brown eyes but a cold fish, if you ask me. Youngish in looks but in his middle twenties, I'd say. Thought a lot of himself, he did, and kept to himself, too."

Leonora glanced up, over her shoulder. "That sounds like the man we're searching for."

Tristan met her gaze, then looked at the landlady. "Did he have any visitors?"

"No, and that was strange. Usually, young gentlemen like that, I have to have a strong word about visitors, if you take my meaning."

Leonora smiled weakly. He drew her back. "Thank you for your help, ma'am."

"Aye, well, I hope you catch up with him and he can help you."

They stepped back off the tiny front porch; the landlady started to close the door, then stopped.

"Wait a minute—I just remembered." She nodded at Tristan. "He did have a visitor, once, but he didn't come in. Stood on the pavement just like you're doing and waited until Mr. Mountford came out to join him."

"What did this visitor look like? Did you get a name?"

"He didn't give one, but I remember thinking as I went up to fetch Mr. Mountford that I wouldn't need one. I just told him the gentleman was foreign, and sure enough, he knew who it was."

"Foreign?"

"Aye. He had an accent you couldn't miss. One of those that sounds like they're growling at you."

Tristan stilled. "What did he look like?"

She frowned, shrugged. "Just like any spic-and-span gentleman. Very neat he was—I do remember that."

"How did he stand?"

The landlady's face eased. "Now that's something I can tell you—he stood like he had a poker strapped to him. He was that stiff, I thought as how he'd break if he bowed."

Tristan smiled charmingly. "Thank you. You've been a great help."

The landlady turned a soft shade of pink. She bobbed a curtsy. "Thank you, sir." After an instant, she shifted her gaze to Leonora. "I wish you good luck, ma'am."

Leonora inclined her head graciously and allowed Trentham to steer her away. She half wished she'd asked the landlady what she was wishing her good luck with—finding Mountford, or keeping Trentham to his supposed wedding vows?

The man was a menace with that lethal smile.

She glanced up at him, then tucked the thought away along with the rest the day had brought. Better not to dwell on them while he was beside her.

He was pacing along, his expression impassive.

"What do you make of Mountford's visitor?"

Tristan glanced at her. "Make?"

Her eyes narrowed, her lips thinned; the look she bent on him told him she was more than seven. "What nationality do you think he is? You clearly have some idea."

The woman was annoyingly acute. Still, there was no harm in telling her. "German, Austrian, or Prussian. That peculiarly stiff stance plus the diction suggests one of the three."

She frowned, but said no more. He hailed a hackney and helped her in. They were bowling back to Belgravia when she asked, "Do you think the foreign gentleman could be behind the burglaries?" When he didn't immediately answer, she went on, "What possible thing could attract a German, Austrian, or Prussian to Number 14 Montrose Place?"

"That," he admitted, his voice low, "is something I'd dearly like to know."

She glanced sharply at him, but when he volunteered nothing more, she surprised him by looking ahead and keeping her counsel.

He handed her down outside Number 14; she waited while he paid the jarvey, then linked her arm in his as they turned to the gate. She kept her gaze down as he swung it open, and they passed through.

"We're giving a small dinner party tonight—just a few of Humphrey's and Jeremy's friends." She glanced briefly up at him, faint color in her cheeks. "I wondered if you would care to join us? It would give you a chance to form an opinion of the sort of secrets Humphrey or Jeremy might have stumbled upon."

He hid a cynical smile. Raised his brows in innocent consideration. "That's not a bad idea."

"If you're free . . . ?"

They'd reached the porch steps. Taking her hand, he bowed. "I
would be delighted." He met her gaze. "At eight?"

She inclined her head. "Eight." As she turned away, her eyes
touched his. "I'll look forward to seeing you then."

Tristan watched her climb the steps, waited until, without looking
back, she disappeared through the door, then he turned and let his lips
curve.

She was as transparent as glass. She wanted to question him over
his suspicions regarding the foreign gentleman. . . .

His smile faded; his face resumed its customary impassive mien.

German, Austrian, or Prussian. He knew enough for those options
to set warning bells clanging, but he didn't have enough information
yet to do anything decisive—other than delve deeper.

Who knew? Mountford's acquaintance with the foreigner might
be pure coincidence.

As he reached the front gate and swung it wide, a familiar sensation spread across the back of his shoulders.

He knew better than to believe in coincidence.

Leonora spent the remainder of the day in restless anticipation. Once
she'd given her orders for dinner and airily informed Humphrey and
Jeremy of their extra guest, she took refuge in the conservatory.

To calm her mind and decide on her best tack.

To revisit all she'd learned that morning.

Such as that Trentham was not averse to kissing her. And she was
not averse to responding. That was certainly a change, for she'd never
before found anything particularly compelling in the act. Yet with
Trentham . . .

Sinking back against the cushions of the wrought-iron chair, she
had to admit she would have happily followed wherever he led, at least
within reason. Kissing him had proved quite pleasurable.

Just as well he'd stopped.

Eyes narrowing on a white orchid bobbing gently in the draft, she
replayed all that had happened, all she'd felt. All she'd sensed.

He'd stopped not because he'd wished to, but because he'd
planned to. His appetite had wanted more, but his will had decreed he
should end the kiss. She'd seen that brief clash in his eyes, caught the
hard hazel gleam as his will had triumphed.

But why? She shifted again, very conscious of the way the brief interlude had remained, a nagging abrasion in her mind. Perhaps the answer lay there—the curtailing of the kiss had left her . . . dissatisfied. On some level she hadn't previously been aware of, unfulfilled.

Wanting more.

She frowned, absentmindedly tapped a finger on the table. With his kisses, Trentham had opened her eyes and engaged her senses. Teased them with a promise of what might be—and then left it at that.

Deliberately.

After telling her they should follow their noses.

She was a lady; he was a gentleman. Theoretically, it wouldn't be proper for him to press her further, not unless she invited his attentions.

Her lips curved cynically; she suppressed a soft snort. She might be inexperienced; she wasn't foolish. He hadn't curtailed their kiss because of any obedience to social mores. He'd stopped deliberately to entice, to build her awareness, to provoke her curiosity.

To make her want.

So that when next he wanted, and wanted more, wanted to take the next step along the path, she would be eager to accede.

Seduction. The word slipped into her mind, trailing the promise of illicit excitement and fascination.

Was Trentham seducing her?

She'd always known she was handsome enough; catching men's eyes had never been difficult. Yet she'd never before been interested enough to pay attention, to play any of the accepted games. Hadn't seen anything to enthuse her.

So now she was twenty-six, the despair of her aunt Mildred, definitely past her last prayers.

Trentham had come along and teased her senses awake, then left them alert and hungry for more. Anticipation of a sort she'd never before known had gripped her, but she wasn't yet sure what she wanted—what *she* wished their interaction to be.

Drawing a breath, she slowly exhaled. She didn't have to make any decisions yet. She could afford to wait, watch, and learn—to follow her nose and then make up her mind whether she approved of where that took her; she hadn't discouraged him, nor led him to believe she wasn't interested.

Because she was. Very interested.

She'd thought that aspect of life had passed her by, that circumstances had left those thrills beyond her reach.

For her, marriage was no longer an option—perhaps fate had sent Trentham as consolation.

* * *

When she turned and saw him crossing the drawing room toward her, her words echoed in her mind.

If this was consolation, what was the prize?

His broad shoulders were clothed in evening black, the coat a masterpiece of understated elegance. His grey silk waistcoat shone softly in the candlelight; a diamond pin winked from his cravat. As she was learning to expect, he'd avoided any intricacy; the cravat was tied in a simple style. Dark hair neatly brushed and sheening, framing his strong features, every element of his appearance—clothes, assurance, and manners—all proclaimed him a gentleman of the haut ton, accustomed to rule, accustomed to obedience.

Accustomed to his own way.

She curtsied and gave him her hand. He took it and bowed, lifted a brow at her as he straightened and raised her.

Challenge gleamed in his eyes.

She smiled, content to meet it, knowing she looked well in her apricot silk gown. "Permit me to introduce you, my lord."

He inclined his head, and anchored her hand on his sleeve, leaving his hand over hers.

Possessively.

Serene, with no hint of awareness showing, she led him to where Humphrey and his friends, Mr. Morecote and Mr. Cunningham, were already deep in discussion. They broke off to acknowledge Trentham, to exchange a few words, then she led him on, introducing him to Jeremy, Mr. Filmore, and Horace Wright.

She'd intended to pause there, to let Horace, the liveliest of their scholarly acquaintances, entertain them while she played the part of demure lady, but Trentham had other ideas. With his usual assumption of command, he eased her out of the conversation and guided her back to their initial position by the hearth.

None of the others, engrossed in their arguments, noticed.

Prompted by caution, she drew her hand from his sleeve and turned to face him. He caught her eye. His lips curved in a smile that showed white teeth, along with appreciation. Of her intention, but also of her—of her shoulders rising from the wide neckline of her gown, of her hair dressed in curls that tumbled about her ears and nape.

Watching his eyes drift over her, she felt her lungs tighten, fought to suppress a shiver—not of cold. Heat rose in her cheeks; she hoped he'd imagine it was due to the fire.

Lazily his gaze ambled upward and returned to hers.

The expression in his hard hazel eyes jolted her, made her breath seize. Then his lids swept down, thick lashes screening that disturbing gaze.

"Have you kept house for Sir Humphrey for long?"

His tone was the usual social drawl, languid and apparently bored. Managing to drag in a breath, she inclined her head and answered.

She used the opening to deflect their conversation into a description of the area in Kent in which they'd previously lived; paeans on the joys of the countryside seemed much safer than courting the fell intent in his eyes.

He responded with mention of his estate in Surrey, yet his eyes told her he was playing with her.

Like a very large cat with a particularly succulent mouse.

She kept her chin high, refused to acknowledge her awareness by the slightest sign. She breathed a sigh of relief when Castor appeared and announced the meal—only to realize that as the only lady present, Trentham would naturally lead her in.

Meeting his gaze directly, she placed her hand on his proffered sleeve and allowed him to steer her through the doors into the dining room.

He seated her at the end of the table, then took the chair on her right. Under cover of the jocular exchanges as the other gentlemen sat, he met her gaze, arched a brow.

"I'm impressed."

"Indeed?" She glanced around, as if to check that everything was in order, as if it was the table that had motivated his comment.

His lips curved dangerously. He leaned closer. Murmured, "I expected you to break before now."

She met his gaze. "Break?"

His eyes widened. "I felt certain you'd be determined to wring from me just what our next step should be."

His expression remained innocent; his eyes were anything but. Every utterance had two meanings, and she couldn't tell which he meant.

After a moment, she murmured, "I'd thought to restrain myself until later."

Looking down, she shook out her napkin as Castor placed her soup plate before her. Picking up her spoon, she coolly—much more coolly than she felt—met Trentham's eyes.

He held her gaze as the footman served him, then his lips curved. "That would no doubt be wise."

"My dear Miss Carling, I had meant to ask—"

Horace, on her other side, claimed her attention. Trentham turned to Jeremy with some inquiry. As usually occurred at such gatherings, the conversation rapidly turned to ancient writings. Leonora ate, sipped, and watched, surprised to see Trentham joining in, until she realized he was subtly probing for any suggestion of a secret find among the group.

She pricked up her ears; when the opportunity presented, she threw in a question, opening up yet another avenue of possibility among the ruins of ancient Persia. But no matter in which direction she or Trentham steered them, the six scholars were patently unaware of any potentially precious find.

Finally, the covers were removed and she rose. The gentlemen did, too. As was their habit, her uncle and Jeremy intended taking their friends to the library to consume port and brandy while poring over their latest research; normally, she retired at this point.

Naturally, Humphrey invited Trentham to join the male congregation.

Trentham's eyes met hers; she held his gaze, willing him to decline and allow her to conduct him to the door . . .

His lips curved; he turned to Humphrey. "Actually, I noticed you have a large conservatory. I've been thinking of adding one to my town house and wondered if I might prevail upon you to allow me to inspect yours."

"The conservatory?" Humphrey beamed genially and looked to her. "Leonora knows most about that—I'm sure she'll be pleased to show you around."

"Yes, of course. I'll be happy to . . ."

The tenor of Trentham's smile was pure seduction; he moved toward her. "Thank you, my dear." He looked back at Humphrey. "I will need to leave soon, however, so in case I don't see you again, I do thank you for your hospitality."

"It was entirely our pleasure, my lord." Humphrey shook hands.

Jeremy and the others exchanged farewells.

Then Trentham turned to her. Raised a brow and waved to the door. "Shall we?"

Her heart was beating faster, but she inclined her head calmly. And led him out.

Six

෪෬ඏ෬ඏ

The conservatory was her domain. Other than the gardener, no one else came there. It was her sanctuary, her refuge, her place of safety. As she led the way down the central aisle and heard the door click behind her, for the first time within the glass walls, she felt a *frisson* of danger.

Her slippers slapped softly on the tiles; her silk skirts swished. Lower yet came Trentham's soft tread as he followed her down the path.

Excitement and something sharper gripped her. "Through the winter, the room's heated by steam piped from the kitchen." Reaching the end of the path, halting in the deepest curve of the bow windows, she dragged in a breath. Her heart was thudding so loudly she could hear it, feel the pulse in her fingers. She reached out, touched one fingertip to the glass pane. "There are two layers of glass to help keep the heat in."

The night outside was black; she focused on the pane, and saw Trentham approaching, his image reflected in the glass. Two lamps burned low, one on either side of the room; they threw enough light to see one's way, to gain some idea of the plants.

Trentham closed the distance between them, his stride slow, a large, infinitely predatory figure; not for an instant did she doubt he was watching her. His face remained in shadow, until, halting close behind her, he lifted his gaze and met hers in the glass.

His eyes locked with hers.

His hands slid around her waist, closed, held her.

Her mouth was dry. "Are you really interested in conservatories?"

His gaze drifted down. "I'm interested in what this conservatory contains."

"The plants?" Her voice was a thread.

"No. You."

He turned her, and she was in his arms. He bent his head and covered her lips, as if he had the right. As if in some strange way she belonged to him.

Her hand came to rest on his shoulder. Gripped as he parted her lips and surged in. He held her anchored before him as he savored her mouth, unhurriedly, as if he had all the time in the world.

And intended taking it.

The engagement made her head spin. Pleasurably. Warmth spread beneath her skin; the taste of him—hard, male, dominant—sank into her.

For long moments, they both simply took, gave, explored. While something within them both tightened.

He broke the kiss, lifted his head, but only enough to draw her closer yet. His hand, spread across her back, burned through the fine silk of her gown. He looked into her eyes from beneath heavy, almost slumbrous lids.

"What was it you wanted to talk to me about?"

She blinked, valiantly struggled to reassemble her wits. Watched him watch her attempt it. Requesting enlightenment on what his next step would be would assuredly be tempting fate; he was waiting for the question.

"Never mind." Boldly, she reached up and drew his lips back to hers.

They were curved as they met hers, but he obliged; together they sank back into the exchange, let it draw them deeper. He drew back again.

"How old are you?"

The question feathered across her senses, into her mind. Her lips throbbed, hungry still; she brushed them across his.

"Does it matter?"

His lids lifted; their gazes touched. A moment passed. "Not materially."

She licked her lips, looked at his. "Twenty-six."

Those wicked lips curved. Once again, danger tickled her spine.

"Old enough."

He drew her to him, against him; once again he bent his head.

Once again she met him.

Tristan sensed her eagerness, her enthusiasm. That much, at least, he'd won. She'd handed him the situation on a platter; it had been too good to pass up—another chance to build her awareness, to expand her horizons. Enough at least so that next time he sought to distract her sensually he'd have some chance of success.

She'd snapped out of his hold too easily that afternoon, evaded his snare, shaken free of any lingering fascination far too readily for his liking.

His nature had always been dictatorial. Tyrannical. Predatory.

He came from a long line of hedonistic males who had, with few exceptions, always taken what they'd wanted.

He definitely wanted her but in a way that was somehow different, to a depth that was unfamilar. Something within him had changed, or perhaps more correctly emerged. Some part of him he'd never before had reason to wrestle with; never before had any woman called it forth.

She did. Effortlessly. But she had no idea of what she did, far less of what she tempted.

Her mouth was a delight, a cavern of honeyed sweetness, warm, beguiling, infinitely alluring. Her fingers tangled in his hair; her tongue dueled with his, quick to learn, eager to experience.

He gave her what she wanted, yet reined his demons back. She pressed closer, all but inviting him to deepen the kiss. An invitation he saw no reason to decline.

Slender, supple, subtly curvaceous, her softer limbs and softer flesh were a potent feminine prod to his totally masculine need. The feel of her in his arms fed his desire, stoked the sensual fires that had sprung up between them.

Play it by ear. Follow their noses. The simplest way forward.

She was so unlike the wife he'd imagined—the wife some part of him, was still stubbornly insisting was the sort he should be searching for—he wasn't yet ready to resign that position completely, at least not openly.

He sank deeper into her mouth, drew her closer still, savoring her warmth and its age-old promise.

Time enough to examine where they were once they'd got there; letting matters develop as they would while he dealt with the mysterious burglar was only wise. Regardless of whatever was growing between them, his priorities at this point were unwaveringly clear. Removing the threat hanging over her was his primary and overriding concern; nothing, but nothing, would deflect him from that goal—he was too experienced to permit any interference.

Time enough once he'd accomplished that mission and she was safe, secure, to turn his mind to dealing with the desire that some benighted fate had sown between them.

He could feel it welling, growing in strength, in intent, more ravenous with every minute she spent in his arms. It was time to call a halt; he had no compunction in shutting his demons in, in gradually drawing back from the exchange.

He lifted his head. She blinked dazedly up at him, then drew in a sharp breath and glanced around. He eased his hold and she stepped back, her gaze returning to his face.

Her tongue came out, traced her upper lip.

He was suddenly conscious of a definite ache. He straightened, drew breath.

"What—" She cleared her throat. "What are your plans in relation to the burglar?"

He looked at her. Wondered what it would take to totally strip her wits away. "The new Registry they're compiling at Somerset House. I want to learn who Montgomery Mountford is."

She thought for only a moment, then nodded. "I'll come with you. Two people looking will be faster than one."

He paused as if considering, then inclined his head. "Very well. I'll call for you at eleven."

She stared at him; he couldn't read her eyes but knew she was surprised.

He smiled. Charmingly.

Her expression turned suspicious.

His smile deepened into a genuine gesture, cynical and amused. Capturing her hand, he raised it to his lips. "Until tomorrow."

She met his eyes. Her brows rose haughtily. "Shouldn't you take some notes on the conservatory?"

He held her gaze, turned her hand, and placed a lingering kiss in her palm. "I lied. I already have one." Releasing her hand, he stepped back. "Remind me to show it to you sometime."

With a nod and a final challenging glance, he left her.

She was still suspicious when he arrived to take her up in his curricle the next morning.

He met her gaze, then handed her up; she stuck her nose in the air and pretended not to notice. He climbed up, took the reins, and set his greys pacing.

She looked well, striking in a deep blue pelisse buttoned over a walking gown of sky-blue. Her bonnet framed her face, her fine features touched with delicate color as if some artist had taken his brush to the finest porcelain. As he guided his skittish pair through the crowded streets, he found it hard to understand why she'd never married.

All the tonnish males in London couldn't be that blind. Had she hidden herself away for some reason? Or had her managing disposition, her trenchant self-reliance, her propensity to take the lead, proved too much of a challenge?

He was perfectly aware of her less-than-admirable traits, yet for some unfathomable reason, that part of him that she and only she had tempted forth insisted on seeing them as, not even anything so mild as a challenge—more a declaration of war. As if she was an opponent blatantly defying him. All nonsense, he knew, yet the conviction ran deep.

It had, in part, dictated his latest tack. He had agreed to her request to accompany him to Somerset House; he would have suggested it if she hadn't—there would be no danger there.

While with him, she was safe; if out of his sight, left to her own devices, she would undoubtedly try to come at the problem—*her* problem as she'd so trenchantly declared—from some other angle. Ordering her to cease investigating on her own, forcing her to do so, was beyond his present powers. Keeping her with him as much as possible was unquestionably the safest course.

Tacking down the Strand, he mentally winced. His rational arguments sounded so logical. The compulsion behind them—the compulsion he used such arguments to excuse—was novel and distinctly unsettling. Disconcerting. The sudden realization that the well-being of a lady of mature years and independent mind was now critical to his equanimity was just a tad shocking.

They arrived at Somerset House; leaving the curricle in the care of his tiger, they entered the building, footsteps echoing on the cold stone. An assistant peered at them from behind a counter; Tristan made his request and they were directed down a corridor to a cavernous hall. Regimented rows of wooden cabinets filled the space; each cabinet possessed multiple drawers.

Another assistant, advised of their search, pointed to a particular set of cabinets. The letters "MOU" were inscribed in gold on the polished wooden fronts. "I would suggest you start there."

Leonora walked briskly to the cabinets; he followed rather more slowly, thinking of what the drawers must contain, estimating how many certificates might be found in each drawer . . .

His conjecture was borne out when Leonora pulled open the first drawer. "Good Lord!" She stared at the mass of paper crammed into the space. "This could take days!"

He pulled open the drawer beside her. "Just as well you invited yourself along."

She made a sound suspiciously like a suppressed snort and started checking the names. It wasn't as bad as they'd feared; in short order they located the first Mountford, but the number of people born in England with that surname was depressingly large. They persevered, and ultimately discovered that yes, indeed, there was a Montgomery Mountford.

"But"—Leonora stared at the birth certificate— "this means he's seventy-three!"

She frowned, then pushed the certificate back, looked at the next, and the next. And the next.

"Six of them," she muttered, her exasperated tone confirming what he'd expected. "And not one of them could possibly be him. The first five are too old, and this one is thirteen."

He put a hand briefly on her shoulder. "Check carefully on either side in case a certificate's been misfiled. I'll check with the assistant."

Leaving her frowning, flicking through the certificates, he walked to the supervisor's desk. A quiet word and the supervisor sent one of his assistants scurrying. Three minutes later a dapper individual in the sober garb of a government functionary arrived.

Tristan explained what he was looking for.

Mr. Crosby bowed. "Indeed, my lord. However, I do not believe that name is one of those protected. If you'll allow me to verify?"

Tristan waved, and Crosby walked down the room.

Dispirited, Leonora shut the drawers. She returned to his side, and they waited until Crosby reappeared.

He bowed to Leonora, then looked at Tristan. "It is as you suspected, my lord. Unless there's a certificate missing—which I very much doubt—then there is no Montgomery Mountford of the age you're searching for."

Tristan thanked him and steered Leonora outside. They paused on the steps and she turned to him.

Met his gaze. "Why would someone use an assumed name?"

"Because," he pulled on his driving gloves, felt his jaw set, "he's up to no good." Retaking her elbow, he urged her down the steps. "Come—let's go for a drive."

He took her into Surrey, to Mallingham Manor, now his home. He did so impulsively, he supposed to distract her, something he felt was increasingly necessary. A felon using an assumed name boded no good at all.

From the Strand, he headed across the river, immediately alerting her to the change in direction. But when he explained he needed to attend to business at his estate so he could return to town free to pursue the question of Montgomery Mountford, phantom burglar, she accepted the arrangement readily.

The road was direct and in excellent condition; the greys were fresh and eager to stretch their legs. He turned the curricle in between the elegant wrought-iron gates in good time for luncheon. Setting the pair pacing up the drive, he noted Leonora's attention was fixed on the huge house ahead, standing amid manicured lawns and formal parterres. The gravel drive swept up to a circular forecourt before the imposing front doors.

He followed her gaze; he suspected he saw the house as she did, for he'd yet to grow used to the idea that this was now his, his home. A manor house had stood on the spot for centuries, but his great-uncle had renovated and refurbished with zeal. What now faced them was a Palladian mansion built of creamy sandstone with pediments over every long window and mock battlements above the long line of the facade.

The greys swept into the forecourt. Leonora exhaled. "It's beautiful. So elegant."

He nodded, allowing himself to acknowledge it, permitting himself to admit that his great-uncle had got something right.

A stable lad came running as he stepped to the ground. Leaving the curricle and pair to his tiger's care, he helped Leonora down, then led her up the steps.

Clitheroe, his great-uncle's butler, now his, opened the doors before they reached them, beaming in his usual genial way. "Welcome home, my lord." Clitheroe included Leonora in his smile.

"Clitheroe, this is Miss Carling. We'll be here for luncheon, then I'll tend to business before we return to town."

"Indeed, my lord. Shall I inform the ladies?"

Shrugging out of his greatcoat, Tristan suppressed a grimace. "No. I'll take Miss Carling to meet them. I assume they're in the morning room?"

"Yes, my lord."

He lifted Leonora's pelisse from her shoulders and gave it to Clitheroe. Placing her hand on his sleeve, with his other hand he gestured down the hall. "I believe I mentioned that I had various females—family and connections—resident here?"

She glanced at him. "You did. Are they cousins like the others?"

"Some, but the two most notable are my great-aunts Hermione and Hortense. At this time of day, the group are invariably to be found in the morning room." He met her eyes. "Gossiping."

He paused and threw open a door. As if to prove his point, the flurry of feminine chatter within immediately ceased.

As he conducted her into the long room filled with light courtesy of a succession of windows along one wall, all looking out over a pastoral scene of gentle lawns leading down to a distant lake, Leonora found herself subjected to wide-eyed, unblinking stares. His ladies—she counted eight—were positively agog.

They were not, however, disapproving.

That was instantly apparent as Trentham, with his usual polished grace, introduced her to his eldest great-aunt, Lady Hermione Wemyss. Lady Hermione beamed and bade her a sincere welcome; Leonora curtsied and responded.

And so it went around the circle of lined faces, all exhibiting various degrees of joy. Just as the six old ladies in his London house had been sincerely thrilled to meet her, so, too, were these women. Her first thought, that perhaps, for whatever reason, they did not venture into society and so were starved for visitors, and therefore would have been delighted with whoever had come to call, died a quick death; as she sank onto the chair Trentham placed for her, Lady Hortense launched into an account of their latest round of visits and the excitement surrounding the local church fete.

"Always something happening around here, you know," Hortense confided. "Not dull at all."

The others nodded and eagerly chimed in, telling her of the local sights and the amenities of the estate and village before inviting her to tell them something of herself.

Completely assured in such company, she responded easily, telling them of Humphrey and Jeremy and their endeavors, and Cedric's gardens—all the sorts of things older ladies liked to know.

Trentham had remained standing by her chair, one hand on its back; now he stepped back. "If you'll excuse me, ladies, I'll rejoin you for luncheon."

They all beamed and nodded; Leonora glanced up and met his gaze. He inclined his head, then his attention was claimed by Lady Hermione; he bent to listen to her. Leonora couldn't hear what was said. With a nod, Trentham straightened, then walked from the room; she watched his elegant back disappear through the door.

"My dear Miss Carling, do tell us—"

Leonora turned back to Hortense.

She might have felt deserted, but that proved impossible in the present company. The old ladies quite plainly set themselves to entertain her; she couldn't help but respond. Indeed, she found herself intrigued by the myriad snippets they let fall of Trentham and his predecessor, his great-uncle Mortimer. She put together enough to understand the route by which Trentham had inherited, heard from Hermione of her brother's sour disposition and disaffection with Trentham's side of the family.

"Always insisted they were wastrels." Hermione snorted. "Nonsense, of course. He was just jealous they could jaunter all over while he had to stay at home and mind the family acres."

Hortense nodded sagely. "And Tristan's behavior these past months has proved how wrong Mortimer was." She caught Leonora's eye. "Very sound man, Tristan. Not one to shirk his duties, whatever they might be."

This pronouncement was greeted with wise nods all around. Leonora suspected it had some significance beyond the obvious, but before she could think of any way to inquire tactfully, a colorful description of the vicar and the rectory household distracted her.

Some part of her liked, even reveled in the simple gossip of country life. When the butler arrived to announce that luncheon awaited them, she rose with an inward start, realizing how much she'd enjoyed the unexpected interlude.

Although the ladies had been pleasant and gentle companions, it was the subject matter that had held her, the talk of Trentham and the general round of country events.

She had, she realized, missed it.

Trentham was waiting in the dining room; he pulled out a chair and seated her by his side.

The meal was excellent; the conversation never flagged, yet neither was it strained. Despite its unusual composition, the household seemed relaxed and content.

At the end of the meal, Tristan caught Leonora's eye, then pushed back his chair and glanced around the table. "If you'll excuse us, there are a few last matters I need to attend to, and then we must return to town."

"Oh, indeed."

"Of course—so nice to meet you, Miss Carling."

"Do get Trentham to bring you down again, my dear."

He rose, taking Leonora's hand, helping her to her feet. Conscious of impatience, he waited while she exchanged farewells with his tribe of old dears, then led her out of the room and into his private wing.

By mutual agreement, the resident ladies did not intrude into his private domain; conducting Leonora through the archway and into the long corridor in some irrational way soothed him.

He'd left her with the group knowing they'd keep her amused, reasoning he'd be able to concentrate on his business affairs and deal with them more expeditiously if spared her physical presence. He hadn't reckoned with his irrational compulsion—the one that needed to know not just where she was, but how she was faring.

Throwing open a door, he ushered her into his study. "If you'll take a seat for a few minutes, I have a few matters to deal with, then we can be on our way."

She inclined her head and walked to the armchair angled before the hearth. He watched her settle comfortably, eyes on the blaze. His gaze rested on her for a moment, then he turned and crossed to his desk.

With her in the room—safe, content, and quiet—he found it easier to concentrate; he quickly approved various expenditures, then settled to check a number of reports. Even when she rose and walked to the window to stand looking out on the vista of lawns and trees, he barely glanced up, just enough to register what she was doing, then returned to his work.

Fifteen minutes later, he'd cleared his desk sufficiently to be able to remain in London for the next several weeks, and single-mindedly devote his attention to her phantom burglar. And, subsequently, if matters continued to head in that direction, to her.

Pushing back his chair, he looked up—and found her leaning against the window frame, watching him.

Her periwinkle blue gaze was steady. "You don't appear the least like one of society's lions."

He held her gaze, equally direct. "I'm not."

"I thought all earls—especially unmarried ones—were by definition."

He lifted a brow as he rose. "This earl never expected the title." He crossed toward her. "I never imagined having it."

She raised a brow back, eyes quizzing as he reached her. "And the unmarried?"

He looked down at her, after a moment said, "As you've just noted, that adjective only gains status when attached to the title."

She studied his face, then looked away.

He followed her gaze out of the window to the peaceful scene beyond. He glanced down at her. "We have time for a stroll before starting back."

She glanced at him, then looked back at the gently rolling landscape. "I was just thinking how much I've missed country pleasures. I would like a stroll."

He led her into an adjoining parlor and out through French doors onto a secluded terrace. Steps led down to the lawn, still green despite winter's harshness. They started to amble; his gaze on her, he asked, "Would you like your pelisse?"

She looked at him, smiled, shook her head. "It's not that cold in the sunshine, weak though it is."

The bulk of the house protected them from the breeze. He glanced back at it, then faced forward. And found her watching him.

"It must have been a shock to discover you'd inherited all that"— her wave indicated more than the roof and walls—"given you hadn't expected it."

"It was."

"You seem to have managed quite well. The ladies seem thoroughly content."

A smile touched his lips. "Oh, they are." His bringing her here had ensured that.

He looked ahead to the lake. She followed his gaze. They walked to the shore, then idled along the bank. Leonora spotted a family of ducks. She stopped, shading her eyes with her hand to better see them.

Pausing a few steps away, he studied her, let his gaze dwell on the picture she made standing by his lake in the dappled sunshine, and felt a content he hadn't before experienced warm him. It seemed senseless to pretend that the impulse to bring her here hadn't been driven by a primitive instinct to have her safe behind walls that were his.

Seeing her here, being with her here, was like discovering another piece of a still scattered jigsaw.

She fitted.

How well left him uneasy.

He was normally impatient of inaction, yet was content to walk by her side, doing essentially nothing. As if being with her made it permissible for him to simply be, as if she was sufficient reason for his existence, at least in that moment. No other woman had had that effect on him. The realization only escalated his need to nullify the threat to her.

As if sensing his suddenly hardening mood, she glanced at him, wide eyes searching his face. He slipped on his mask and smiled easily.

She frowned.

Before she could ask, he took her arm. "Let's go this way."

The rose garden even in hibernation distracted her. He led her on into the extensive formal shrubbery, slowly circling back toward the house. A small marble temple, austerely classical, stood at the center of the shrubbery.

Leonora had forgotten just how pleasant walking in a large, well-designed and well-tended garden could be. In London, Cedric's fantastical creation lacked the soothing vistas, the magnificent sweeps that could only be achieved in the country, and the parks were too limited in view and too crowded. Certainly not soothing. Here, walking with Trentham, peace slid like a drug through her veins, as if a well that had been almost dry was refilling.

Placed at the junction of the shrubbery paths, the temple was simply perfect. Lifting her skirts, she climbed the steps. Inside, the floor was a delicate mosaic in black, grey, and white. The Ionic columns that supported the domed roof were white veined with grey.

Turning, she looked back at the house, framed by the high hedges. The perspective was superb. "It's magnificent." She smiled at Trentham as he halted beside her. "No matter any difficulties, you can't be sorry that this is yours."

She extended her arms, her hands, including the gardens, the lake, and the surrounding countryside in the statement.

He met her gaze. Held it for a long moment, then quietly said, "No. I'm not sorry."

She caught his tone, the existence of some deeper meaning in his words. She let her frown show.

His lips, until then straight, as serious as his expression, curved, she thought a touch wryly. Reaching out, he shackled her wrist, then slid his hand down to close about hers.

He lifted it, raised her wrist to his lips. Eyes holding hers, he kissed, let his lips linger as her pulse leapt, then throbbed.

As if that had been a signal he'd been waiting for, he reached for her, drew her closer. She permitted it, went into his arms, more than curious, openly eager.

He bent his head and her lashes fluttered down; she lifted her lips and he took them. Smoothly slid between, took possession of her mouth, and her senses.

She yielded them readily, totally unafraid; she was more than confident in her reading of him—he would never harm her. But where he was heading with his intoxicating kisses—what came next, and when—she still didn't know; she had no experience on which to draw.

She'd never been seduced before.

That that was his ultimate aim she accepted; she could see no other reason for his actions. He'd asked her age, stated she was old enough. At twenty-five, she'd been deemed on the shelf; now twenty-six, she was—clearly to his mind as well as hers—her own woman. A spinster whose life was no one's business but her own; her actions would impinge on no one else, her decisions were her own to make.

Not that she was necessarily going to accede to his wishes. She would make up her mind if and when the time came.

It wouldn't come today, not in an open temple visible from his house. Free of any prospect of having to think, she sank into his arms and kissed him back.

Dueled with him, let herself flow into the exchange, felt heat rise between them, along with that fascinating tension—a tenseness that sent excitement rippling along her nerves, sent anticipation coursing beneath her skin.

Her body tightened; heat welled and pooled.

Emboldened, she pushed her hands up, over his shoulders, slid them to his nape. Splaying her fingers, she speared them slowly through his dark locks. Thick and heavy, they slid through and over her fingers, even as his tongue slid deeper.

He angled his head and drew her nearer, until her breasts were crushed to his chest, her thighs brushing his, her skirts tangling around his boots. His arms locked around her, lifting her against him; his strength captured her. The kiss deepened into a melding of mouths, a far more intimate exchange. She half expected to be shocked—felt she should be—yet instead all she knew was that burgeoning heat, a certain assuredness both in him and her, and a dizzying hunger.

That escalating hunger was theirs—not hers, not his, but something growing between them.

It beckoned.

Enticed.

Fed Tristan's need.

But it was her need that he played to, that he watched and gauged, that ultimately had him easing his hold on her, gathering her in one arm while he raised a hand to her face. To trace her cheek, frame her jaw, hold her still while he methodically plundered. Yet at no stage did he seek to overwhelm her; that, he knew, was not the route to ensnare her.

To seduce her was an instinct he no longer sought to fight. He eased his fingers from the delicate curve of her jaw and sent them lower, flirting with her senses until her lips turned demanding, then caressing lightly, enough to educate her imagination, enough to feed her hunger, not enough to sate it.

Her breasts swelled beneath his tracing touch; he ached to take more, to claim more, but held back. Strategy and tactics were his strong suit; in this as in all things, he was playing to win.

When her fingers clenched on his skull, he consented to palm her breast, to fondle, still lightly, still inciting rather than satisfying. He felt her senses leap, sensed her nerves tightening. Felt her nipple pebble against his palm.

Had to drag a breath deep and hold it, then, gradually, step by step, he eased back from the kiss. Gradually unclenched the muscles locking her to him. Gradually let her surface from the kiss.

But he didn't take his hand from her breast.

When he released her lips and lifted his head, he was still lightly tracing, back and forth across the swell, teasingly circling her nipple. Her lashes fluttered, then she opened her eyes, looked into his.

Her lips were lightly swollen, her eyes wide.

He looked down.

She followed his gaze.

Her lungs locked.

He counted the seconds before she remembered to breathe, knew she had to be dizzy. But she didn't step back.

It was he who shifted his caressing hand to her upper arm, grasped gently, then slid his hand down to hers. He lifted it to his lips, met her eyes as, faint color in her cheeks, she looked up at him.

He smiled, but hid the true tenor of the gesture. "Come." Setting her hand on his sleeve, he turned her to the house. "We need to start back to town."

The journey was a godsend. Leonora took full advantage of the hour during which Trentham was engrossed with his cattle, smoothly tacking through the traffic that grew heavier as they entered the capital, to calm her mind. To try to restore—reclaim—her customary assurance.

She glanced at him often, wondering what he was thinking, but other than an occasional enigmatic glance—leaving her certain he was partly amused but still quite intent—he said nothing. Aside from all else, his tiger was up behind them, too close to allow any private words.

Indeed, she wasn't sure she wanted any. Any explanation. Not that he'd shown any sign of giving her one, but that seemed to be part of the game.

Part of the building exhilaration, the excitement. The craving.

That last she hadn't expected, but she certainly felt it—could now understand what she never had before—what caused women, even ladies of eminent sense, to cater to a gentleman's physical demands.

Not that Trentham had made any real demands. Yet. That was her point.

If she could know when he would, and what those demands might be, she'd be better placed to plan her response.

As matters were . . . she was left to speculate.

She was sunk in that endeavor when the curricle slowed. She blinked and looked around, and discovered they were home. Trentham drew the curricle up before Number 12. Handing the reins to the tiger, he climbed down, then lifted her to the pavement.

Hands about her waist he looked down at her.

She looked back, and made no attempt to move away.

His lips curved. He opened them—

Footsteps crunched on gravel nearby. They both turned to look.

Gasthorpe, the majordomo, a thickset man with crisp salt-and-pepper hair, came hurrying down the path from Number 12. Reaching them, he bowed. "Miss Carling."

She'd made a point of meeting Gasthorpe the day after he'd taken up residence. She smiled and inclined her head.

He turned to Trentham. "My lord, forgive the interruption, but I wanted to make sure you called in. The carters have delivered the furniture for the first floor. I would be grateful if you would cast your eye over the items, and advise me if you approve."

"Yes, of course. I'll be in in a moment—"

"Actually"—Leonora gripped Trentham's arm, drawing his gaze to her face—"I would love to see what you've done to Mr. Morrissey's house. May I come in while you check the furniture?" She smiled. "I would be happy to help—a lady's eye is often quite different in such matters."

Trentham looked at her, then glanced at Gasthorpe. "It's rather late. Your uncle and brother—"

"Won't have noticed I left the house." Her curiosity was rampant; she kept her eyes wide, fixed on Trentham's face.

His lips twisted, then set; again he glanced at Gasthorpe. "If you insist." She took his arm and he turned toward the path. "But only the first floor has been furnished as yet."

She wondered why he was being so uncharacteristically diffident, then put it down to being a gentleman more or less in charge of fitting out a house. Something he no doubt felt ill equipped to do.

Ignoring his reticence, she swept up the path beside him. Gasthorpe had gone ahead and stood holding the door. She stepped over the threshold and paused to look around. She'd last glimpsed the hall in the shadows of night, when the painters' cloths had been down, the room stripped and bare.

The transformation was now complete. The hall was surprisingly light and airy, not dark and gloomy—an impression she associated with gentlemen's clubs. However, there was not a single item of delicacy to soften the austere, starkly elegant lines; no sprigged wallpaper, not even any scrollwork. It was rather cold, almost bleak in its eschewing of all things feminine, yet she could see men—men like Trentham—gathering there.

They wouldn't notice the softness that was missing.

Trentham didn't offer to show her the downstairs rooms; with a gesture, he directed her to the stairs. She climbed them, noting the high gloss on the banister, the thickness of the stair carpet. Clearly expense had not been a consideration.

On the first floor, Trentham moved past her and led the way to the room at the front of the house. A large mahogany table stood in the middle of the floor, eight matching chairs upholstered in ocher velvet surrounding it. A sideboard stood against one wall, a long bureau against another.

Tristan glanced around, swiftly surveying their meeting room. All was as they'd envisaged it; catching Gasthorpe's eye, he nodded, then with a wave, directed Leonora back across the landing.

The small office with its desk, bank of drawers, and two chairs, need no more than a cursory glance. They moved on to the room at the back of the house—the library.

The merchant from whom they'd purchased the furniture, Mr. Meecham, was overseeing the siting of a tall bookcase. He glanced briefly their way, but immediately returned his attention to directing his two assistants, waving first one way, then that, until they had the heavy bookcase positioned to his satisfaction. They set it down with audible grunts.

Meecham turned to Tristan with a wide smile. "Well, my lord." He bowed, then looked around with patent satisfaction. "I flatter myself you and your friends will be excellently comfortable here."

Tristan saw no reason to argue; the room looked inviting, clean, and uncluttered yet with plenty of deep armchairs dotted about and numerous side tables waiting to support a glass of fine brandy. There were two bookcases, presently empty. Although the room was the library, it was unlikely they would retire here to read novels. News sheets assuredly, periodicals and reports, and sporting magazines; the library's primary function would be as a place of quiet relaxation where if any words were spoken, they would be in a deep murmur.

Glancing around, he could see them all here, private, quiet, but companionable in their silence. Returning his gaze to Meecham, he nodded. "You've done well."

"Indeed, indeed." Gratified, Meecham waved his two workers from the room. "We'll leave you to enjoy what we've thus far wrought. I'll have the rest of the items delivered within the week."

He bowed low; Tristan nodded a dismissal.

Gasthorpe caught his eye. "I'll see Mr. Meecham out, my lord."

"Thank you, Gasthorpe—I won't need you again. We'll see ourselves out."

With a nod and a speaking look, Gasthorpe left.

Tristan inwardly winced, but what could he do? Explaining to Leonora that females were not supposed to be inside the club, not beyond the small front parlor, would inevitably lead to questions he— and his fellow club members—would much rather were never asked. Answering would be too risky, akin to tempting fate.

Much better to give ground when it didn't really matter and couldn't really hurt than explain what was behind the formation of the Bastion Club.

Leonora had drifted from his side. After trailing her fingers along the back of one armchair, noting the amenities, he thought with approval, she'd wandered to the window and now stood looking out.

At her own back garden.

He waited, but she didn't return. Heaving an inward, somewhat resigned sigh, he crossed the room, the rich Turkish carpet muffling his steps. He stopped by the side of the window, leaned against the frame.

She turned her head and met his gaze.

"You used to stand here and watch me, didn't you?"

He considered every option before replying, "At times."

Her eyes remained steady on his, then she looked back at the garden. "That's how you knew who I was when I ran into you that first day."

To that he said nothing, then was left wondering what track her mind was taking.

After a long moment, her gaze fixed beyond the glass, she murmured, "I'm not very good at this business." She gestured briefly, her hand waving between them. "I haven't had any real experience."

He inwardly blinked. "So I'd assumed."

She turned her head, met his gaze. "You'll have to teach me."

As she faced him, he straightened. She closed the distance between them. He frowned, his hands instinctively circling her waist. "I'm not certain—"

"I'm perfectly willing to learn." Her gaze dropped to his lips; hers curved, innocently sensual. "Even eager."

Lifting her gaze to his eyes, she stretched upward, palms to his chest, lifted her lips to his. Softly murmured, "But you know that."

And kissed him.

The invitation was so blatant it captured him utterly. Temporarily suspended his wits, left him at his senses' mercy.

And his senses were merciless. They wanted more.

More of her, of the soft, luscious haven of her mouth, of her pliant, innocently beguiling lips. Of her body, tentatively yet determinedly pressing against his much harder frame.

That last shook him, shook enough of his wits into place for him to take control. What she was thinking he didn't know, but with her lips on his, her mouth all his, her tongue dueling increasingly hotly with his, he couldn't spare enough of his mind to follow the contortions of hers.

Later.

Now . . . all he could do—all he could force his body and senses to do—was follow her lead.

And teach her more.

He let her press close, gathered her fully into his arms. Let her feel his body hardening against hers, let her sense what she invoked, the response her body, supple, curvaceous and blatantly tempting, all female softness and feminine heat, provoked.

During their wanderings through the house, she'd opened her pelisse. Sliding a hand beneath the heavy wool, he set his palm to her breast. Not lightly tracing as he had before, but claiming possessively. Giving her now what their earlier interlude had teasingly promised, tauntingly foretold.

She gasped, clung, but not once did she waver; her lips cleaved to his, innocently demanding. Unfrightened, unshocked. Determined. Enthralled. She was caught, totally fascinated. He deepened the kiss, touched, caressed.

Felt the flames start to smolder. Felt desire slowly rise, stretch languidly, then reach out in hunger.

Leonora felt it, too, although she couldn't name it, that wash of heated emptiness deep within. It infused her, and him, intrigued and beckoned. Ensnared. She had to get closer, somehow deeper into the exchange; sliding her hands up, she twined them about his neck, sighed when the movement pressed her breast firmly into his hard palm.

His hand closed and her senses rocked. His fingers shifted, seeking, finding, and her wits, her very being, stilled.

Then fractured, shattered, as those knowing fingers tightened, tightened . . . until she gasped through their kiss.

His fingers eased and heat flooded her, a rushing tide she'd never felt before. Her breasts swelled; the bodice of her walking dress was suddenly too tight. The thin film of her chemise chafed.

He seemed to know; he dealt with her bodice's tiny buttons with practiced ease, and she could breathe again. Only to catch her breath on a rush of pleasure, on a spike of anticipation when he boldly slid his hand beneath the gaping gown to caress, to fondle. His touch screened by fine silk, to build her yearning once again, so that she ached for more definite contact. Burned to feel his skin against hers, desperate to feel still more.

Her lips were hungry, her demands clear. Tristan couldn't resist. Didn't try.

Two quick tugs and her chemise was loose; hooking one finger between her full breasts he drew the fine fabric down.

Then set his hand to her bounty.

Felt the deep shudder that racked her in his soul.

He closed his hand, hungrily possessive, and her heart leapt.

His followed.

Into a furnace of greedy, eager giving, of sensual taking, of appreciation, and a dawning recognition of mutual need.

Hands and lips fed the hunger, eager, inciting. Enthralled.

There was a change in their interaction. He sensed it, surprised to find himself, although still in control, no longer dictating their play. Her developing assurance, her interest and understanding, invested her lips, directed the way she met him, the slow sensuous stroking of her tongue against his, the seductive caress of her fingers in his hair, the openly confident, determinedly fascinated way she sank against him, all supple limbs and soft heat, bathing in the flames of a mutual conflagration he'd never imagined sharing with an innocent woman.

Lust and a virtuous woman.

The thought echoed in his brain even while she filled his senses. She was more than he'd expected even while he was something other than she'd thought. Something beyond her experience, yet she was something beyond his.

The flames between them were definite, real, scorching, firing thoughts of passion, of greater intimacy, of the satiation of that mutual need.

It hadn't occurred to him that they might travel this far so soon. He in no way regretted it, yet . . .

Deeply entrenched instincts had him drawing back, easing her back. Slowing their caresses, lightening them. Letting the flames gradually subside to a simmer.

He lifted his head, looked at her eyes. Watched her lashes rise, then met her clear, startlingly blue gaze.

Read in it not shock, not the slightest hint of retreat or fluster, but instead an awakened interest. A question.

What next?

He knew, but this was not, yet, the time to explore that avenue. He recalled where they were, what his mission was. He felt his face harden. "It's getting dark. I'll see you home."

Leonora inwardly frowned, but then her gaze slipped past his shoulder to the window; night had indeed fallen. She blinked, stepped back as he released her. "I hadn't realized it was so late."

Naturally not; her wits had been in a whirl. A pleasurable whirl, one that had opened her eyes considerably more. Ignoring her chemise, doggedly refusing to let her mind dwell on what had just occurred—later, when he wasn't around to see her blushes—she adjusted and refastened her bodice, then buttoned her pelisse.

His gaze, sharp as ever, hadn't left her. She lifted her head and met it directly. He searched her eyes, then raised a brow. "I take it"—his gaze shifted from her to sweep the room—"you approve of the decor?"

She raised a haughty brow back. "I daresay it's eminently suitable for your purpose." *Whatever that might be.*

Head high, she swung toward the door. She felt his gaze on her back as she crossed the room, then he stirred and followed.

She had very little experience of men. Especially not men like Trentham. That, Leonora felt, was her greatest weakness, one that left her at an unfair disadvantage whenever she was with him.

Stifling a humph, she dragged her silky quilt about her and climbed into the old armchair before the fire blazing in her room. It was icy outside, too cold even to sit in the conservatory and think. Besides, a quilt and an armchair before the fire seemed much more suitable given the issues she was determined to think about.

Trentham had escorted her home and requested an interview with her uncle and Jeremy. She'd taken him to the library, listened while he questioned them as to whether they'd stumbled onto any possibility that might be the burglar's aim. She could have told him that neither of them would have spared a thought for the burglar let alone his objective since he, Trentham, had last mentioned the matter—and so it had proved. Neither had any ideas or suggestions; the puzzled look in their eyes clearly stated they were surprised he was still intersted in the affair at all.

He saw it as well as she; his jaw set, but he thanked them and politely enough took his leave.

Only she had sensed his disapproval; her uncle and brother had remained, as ever, determinedly oblivious.

With Henrietta padding beside her, canine appreciation for Trentham transparent, she'd walked with him to the front hall. She'd dismissed Castor earlier; they'd been alone in the soft lamplight, in a place in which she'd always felt secure.

Then Trentham had looked at her, and she hadn't felt safe at all.

She'd felt hot. Warmth had spread beneath her skin; a light flush rose to her cheeks. All in response to the look in his eyes, to the thoughts she could see behind them.

They'd been standing close. He'd lifted a hand, traced her cheek, then slid one finger beneath her chin and tipped up her face. Set his lips to hers in a swift, unfulfilling kiss.

Raising his head, he'd caught her gaze. Held it for a moment, then murmured, "Take care."

He'd released her just as Castor came hurrying from the nether regions. He'd departed without a backward glance, leaving her to wonder, to speculate. To plan.

If she dared.

That, she decided, snuggling into the quilt's warmth, was the crucial question. Did she dare satisfy her curiosity? It was, in truth, more than curiosity; she had a burning desire to know, to experience all that could lie between a man and a woman physically and emotionally.

She'd always *expected* to learn those facts at some point in her life. Instead, fate and society had conspired to keep her ignorant, the commonly accepted decree holding that only married ladies could participate, experience, and thus know.

All well and good if one was a young girl. At twenty-six, she no longer fitted that description; to her mind, the proscription no longer applied.

No one had ever advanced any explanation of the moral logic behind society's acceptance that married ladies, once they'd presented their husbands with an heir, could indulge in affairs as long as they remained discreet.

She intended to be the very soul of discretion, and she had no vows to break.

If she wished to avail herself of Trentham's offer to introduce her to the pleasures she'd thus far been denied, there were, in her view, no social conventions she need consider. As for the somewhat indefinite quibble of her falling with child, there had to be some way around such things or London would be awash with by-blows and half the ton's matrons perpetually pregnant; she was sure Trentham would know how to manage.

Indeed, it was in part his experience, that air of competence and expertise, that attracted her, that had made it possible that afternoon for her to grasp the invitation he'd offered.

Clearly, she'd read that invitation correctly; the subtle, step-by-step advancement of their engagement, from touch, to kiss, to sensual caress confirmed it. Now she'd taken the first step into his arms, he'd shown her enough for her to have some inkling of what she'd missed, of what lay ahead.

He'd introduced her to a degree of intimacy that was clearly the prelude to all she wished to know. He was willing to be her partner in adventure, her mentor in that sphere. To guide her, teach her, show her. In return, of course . . . but she understood that and, after all, who was she saving herself for?

Marriage and its attendant dependency was a yoke that simply didn't fit her. Having accepted that years ago, her only real regret, a silent and somewhat suppressed regret, had been that she would never experience physical intimacy or that particular brand of sensual pleasure.

Now Trentham had appeared, dangling temptation before her.

Eyes on the flames glowing hotly in the hearth, she considered reaching for it.

If she didn't act now and grab the chance fate had finally consented to allow her, who knew for how long his interest, and therefore his offer, would stand? Military gentlemen were not renowned for their constancy; she had firsthand experience of that.

Her mind slid away, assessing the possibilities, distracted by them. The fire slowly died to red-hot embers.

When the chill in the air finally penetrated her absorption, she realized she'd made her decision. Her mind had been engrossed, had been for some time, with two questions.

How was she to convey that decision to Trentham?

And how could she manage their interaction so that the reins remained in her hands?

Tristan received the letter by the first post the next morning.

After the customary salutations, Leonora had written:

With respect to the item the burglar seeks, I have decided it would be wise to search my late cousin Cedric's workshop. The room is quite extensive, but has been closed up for some years, indeed, since before we took possession of the house. It may be that a determined search will turn up some item of real but esoteric value. I will commence my search immediately after luncheon; should I discover anything of note, I will of course inform you.

Yours, etc.
Leonora Carling

He read the letter three times. His well-honed instincts assured him there was more to it than the superficial meaning of the words, yet her hidden agenda eluded him. Deciding he'd been a covert operative for too long and was now seeing plots where there patently were none, he set the letter aside and put his mind determinedly to business.

His, and hers.

He dealt with hers first, listing the various avenues available for identifying the man masquerading as Montgomery Mountford. After considering the list, he wrote a summons and sent a footman to deliver it, then settled to write a series of letters the recipients would prefer not to receive. Nevertheless, debts were debts, and he was calling them in in a good cause.

An hour later, Havers conducted a nondescript, rather shabby individual into the study. Tristan sat back and waved him to a chair. "Good morning, Colby. Thank you for coming."

The man was wary, but not servile. He ducked his head and sat in the chair, glancing quickly around as Havers closed the door, then looking back at Tristan. "Mornin', sir—beggin' your pardon, it's m'lord, ain't it?"

Tristan merely smiled.

Colby's nervousness increased. "What can I help you with, then?"

Tristan told him. Despite his appearance, Colby was the recognized underworld baron of the patch of London that included Montrose Place. Tristan had made his acquaintance, or rather made sure Colby knew of him, when they'd settled on Number 12 for the club.

On hearing of the strange goings-on in Montrose Place, Colby sucked his teeth and looked severe. Tristan had never believed that the attempted burglaries were the handiwork of the local louts; Colby's reaction and subsequent assurance confirmed that.

His eyes narrowed, Colby now looked more like the potentially dangerous specimen he was. "I'd like to meet this fine gentleman of yours."

"He's mine." Tristan made the statement blandly.

Colby glanced at him, assessing, then nodded. "I'll put the word around you're wanting a word with 'im. If any of the boys hear of 'im, I'll be sure to let you know."

Tristan inclined his head. "Once I lay hands on him, you won't see him again."

Colby nodded, once, bargain accepted. Information in exchange for removal of a competitor. Tristan rang for Havers, who saw Colby out.

Tristan finished the last of his requests for information, then gave them to Havers with strict instructions for delivery. "No livery. Use the heaviest footmen."

"Indeed, my lord. I apprehend we wish to make a show of strength. Collison would be best in that regard."

Tristan nodded, fighting a smile as Havers withdrew. The man was a godsend, dealing with the myriad demands of the old dears, yet with equal aplomb accommodating the rougher side of Tristan's affairs.

Having accomplished all he could regarding Montgomery Mountford, Tristan gave his attention to the day-to-day business of keeping his head above water with the details and demands of the earldom. While the clock ticked and time passed without his making any real headway in the matter of making said earldom secure.

For one of his temperament, that last irked.

He had Havers bring him luncheon on a tray and continued to whittle down the stack of business letters. Scrawling a note to his steward on the last, he sighed and pushed the completed pile aside.

And turned his mind determinedly to marriage.

To his wife-to-be.

Telling that he didn't think of her as a bride, but as his wife. Their association was not based on social superficialties, but on practical, ungilded day-to-day interactions. He could easily picture her by his side, as his countess dealing with the demands of their future life.

He should, he supposed, have considered a range of candidates. If he asked, his resident gossipmongers would be thrilled to provide him with a list. He'd toyed with the notion, or at least had told himself he was, yet appealing to others for assistance in such a personal and vitally crucial decision was simply not his style.

It was also redundant, a waste of time.

To the right of the blotter lay Leonora's letter. His gaze locking on it, on the delicate script reminiscent of the writer, he sat and brooded, turning his pen end over end between his fingers.

The clock struck three. He looked up, then threw the pen down, pushed back his chair, stood and headed for the hall.

Havers met him there, helped him into his greatcoat, handed him his cane, then swung the door wide.

Tristan walked out, went quickly down the steps, and headed for Montrose Place.

He found Leonora in the workshop, a large chamber tucked into the basement of Number 14. The walls were solid stone, thick and cold. A row of windows high along one wall looked out at ground level toward the front of the house. They would have admitted reasonable light once, but were now fogged and cracked.

They were, Tristan instantly noted, too small for even a child to crawl through.

Leonora hadn't heard him walk in; she had her nose buried in some musty tome. He scraped a sole on the flags. She looked up—and smiled in delighted welcome.

He smiled back, let the simple gesture warm him; he strolled in, looking about. "I thought you said this place had been closed up for years?"

There were no cobwebs, and all surfaces—tables, floors, and shelves—were clean.

"I sent in the maids this morning." She met his gaze as he turned to her. "I'm not particularly partial to spiders."

He noticed a pile of dusty letters stacked on the bench beside her; his levity faded. "Have you found anything?"

"Nothing specific." She closed the book; a cloud of dust puffed out from the pages. She gestured to the wooden rack, a cross between bookshelves and pigeonholes covering the wall behind the bench. "He was neat, but not methodical. He seems to have kept everything, stretching back over the years. I've been sorting bills and accounts from letters, shopping lists from drafts of learned papers."

He picked up the old parchment topping the pile. It was a letter inscribed in faded ink. He initially thought the script a woman's, but the contents were clearly scientific. He glanced at the signature. "Who's A. J.?"

Leonora leaned closer to check the letter; her breast brushed his arm. "A. J. Carruthers."

She moved away, lifting the old tome back to the shelf. He squelched a flaring urge to draw her back, to reestablish the sensual contact.

"Carruthers and Cedric corresponded frequently—it seems they were working on some papers before Cedric died."

With the tome safely stored, Leonora turned. He continued flicking through the letters. Her gaze on the pile of parchments, she moved closer. Misjudged and moved too far—she brushed, shoulder to thigh, against him.

Desire ignited, flamed between them.

Tristan tried to breathe in. Couldn't. The letters slipped from his fingers. He told himself to step back.

His feet wouldn't move. His body craved the contact too much to deny it.

She glanced fleetingly up at him through her lashes, then, as if embarrassed, eased fractionally back, creating a gap of less than an inch between them.

Too much, yet not enough. His arms were rising to haul her back, when he realized and lowered them.

She reached quickly for the letters and spread them out.

"I was"—her voice was husky; she paused to clear her throat—"going to sort through these. There might be something in them that will point to a discovery."

It took longer than he liked for him to refocus on the letters; he'd clearly been celibate for too long. He breathed in, exhaled. His mind cleared. "Indeed—they might allow us to decide if it's something Cedric discovered that Mountford's after. We shouldn't forget he wanted to buy the house—it's something he expected would be left behind."

"Or something he could gain access to by virtue of being the purchaser, before we moved out."

"True." He fanned the letters over the bench top, then looked up at the large pigeonholes. Stepping away from temptation, he turned down the room, following the bench, scanning the shelves above it, searching for more letters. He pulled out all he saw, leaving them on the bench top. "I want you to go through every letter you can find, and collect all those written in the year preceding Cedric's death."

Following him, Leonora frowned at his back, then tried to peer around at his face. "There'll be hundreds."

"However many, you'll need to study them all. Then make a list of the correspondents, and write and ask each one if they know of anything Cedric was working on that could have commercial or military significance."

She blinked. "Commercial or military significance?"

"They'll know. Scientists may be as absorbed in their work as your uncle and brother, but they usually recognize the possibilities in what they're working on."

"Hmm." Gaze fixed between his shoulder blades, she continued following at his heels. "So I'm to write to each contact he made in his last year."

"Every last one. If there was anything of significance, someone will know."

He reached the end of the room and swung around. She looked down—and walked into him. He caught her; she looked up, feigning surprise.

Didn't have to fabricate her leaping pulse, her suddenly thudding heart.

He'd focused on her lips; her gaze fell to his.

Then he glanced at the door.

"All the staff are busy." She'd made sure of that.

His gaze returned to her face. She met it but briefly; when he didn't immediately move, she wriggled her hands free and reached up, sliding one to his nape, curling the fingers of the other into his lapel.

"Stop being so stuffy and kiss me."

Tristan blinked. Then she shifted in his arms, unintentionally teasing that part of his anatomy most susceptible to her nearness.

Without another thought, he bent his head.

He escaped nearly an hour later, feeling distinctly bemused. It had been years—decades—since he'd indulged in any such mildly illicit behavior, yet far from boring him, his senses were smugly content, luxuriating in the stolen pleasures.

Striding down the front path, he raked his hand through his hair and hoped it would pass muster. Leonora had developed a penchant for thoroughly mussing his normally elegant cut. Not that he was complaining. While she'd been mussing, he'd been savoring.

Her mouth, her curves.

Lowering his arm, he noticed a smear of dust on his sleeve. He brushed it off. The maids had dusted all surfaces; they hadn't dusted the letters. When they'd finally separated, he'd had to brush telltale streaks off both himself and Leonora. In her case, not just from her clothes.

The image of how she'd appeared at that point swam across his mind. Her eyes had been bright but darkened, her lids heavy, her lips swollen from his kisses. Drawing his attention even more to her mouth—a mouth that increasingly evoked mental images not generally associated with virtuous gentlewomen.

Closing the front gate behind him, he suppressed a wholly masculine smirk—and ignored the effect such thoughts inevitably had. The afternoon's discoveries had improved his mood significantly. Reviewing the day, he felt he'd gained on a number of fronts.

He'd come to view Cedric's workshop determined to move the investigation into the burglaries forward. Impatience was sharpening its spurs; it was his duty to marry, thus protecting his tribe of old dears from destitution, but before he could marry Leonora, he had to nullify the threat to her. Eliminating that threat was his top priority; it was too immediate, too definite to give second place. Until he successfully completed his mission, he'd remain focused first and always on that.

So having escalated his own investigations through the various layers of the underworld, he'd come to assess what avenues for advancement Cedric's workshop might suggest.

Cedric's letters would indeed be useful. First in eliminating his works as a potential target for the burglar, second in keeping Leonora amused.

Well, perhaps not amused, but certainly busy. Too busy to have time to embark on any other avenue of attack.

He'd accomplished a great deal for one day. Satisfied, he strode on, and turned his mind to the morrow.

Devising her own seduction, or at least actively encouraging it, was proving more difficult than Leonora had thought. She'd expected to get rather further in Cedric's workshop, but Trentham had failed to close the door when he'd entered. Crossing the room and closing it herself would have been too blatant.

Not that matters hadn't progressed; they just hadn't progressed as far as she'd wished.

And now he'd lumbered her with the task of going through Cedric's correspondence. At least he'd restricted their search to the last year of Cedric's life.

She'd spent the rest of the day reading and sorting, squinting at faded writing, deciphering illegible dates. This morning, she'd brought all the relevant letters up to the parlor and spread them on the occasional tables. The parlor was the room in which she conducted all household business; sitting at her escritoire, she dutifully inscribed all the names and addresses onto a list.

A long list.

She then composed a letter of inquiry, advising the recipient of Cedric's death and requesting they contact her if they had any information regarding anything of value, discoveries, inventions, or possessions, that might reside in her late cousin's effects. Instead of mentioning the burglar's interest, she stated that, due to space constraints, it was intended that all nonvaluable papers, substances, and equipment would be burned.

If she knew anything of experts, should they know of anything the least valuable, the idea of it being burned would have them reaching for their pen.

After luncheon, she commenced the arduous task of copying her letter, addressing each copy to one of the names on her list.

When the clock chimed and she saw it was three-thirty, she set down her pen and stretched her aching back.

Enough for today. Not even Trentham would expect her to get through the inquiries all in one day.

She rang for tea; when Castor brought the tray, she poured and sipped.

And thought of seduction.

Hers.

A distinctly titillating subject, especially for a twenty-six-year-old reluctant-but-resigned virgin. That was a reasonable description of what she'd been, but she was resigned no more. Opportunity had beckoned, and she was determined to play.

She glanced at the clock. Too late to call at Trentham House for afternoon tea. Besides, she didn't want to find herself surrounded by his old ladies; that would not advance her cause.

But losing a whole day in inaction wasn't her style, either. There had to be some way, some excuse she could use to call on Trentham—and get him to herself in appropriate surrounds.

"Would you like me to show you around, miss?"

"No, no." Leonora crossed the threshold of the Trentham House conservatory and cast a reassuring smile at Trentham's butler. "I'll just amble about and await his lordship. If you're sure he'll return soon?"

"I'm certain he'll arrive home before dark."

"In that case . . ." She smiled and gestured about her, moving deeper into the room.

"Should you require anything, the bellpull is to the left." Serene and unperturbed, the butler bowed and left her.

Leonora looked around. Trentham's conservatory was much larger than theirs; indeed, it was monstrous. Recalling his supposed need of information on such rooms, she humphed. His was not just larger, it was better, the temperature much more even, the floor beautifully tiled in blue-and-green mosaics. A small fountain tinkled somewhere—she couldn't see through the artfully arranged, lush and verdant growth.

A path led on; she strolled down it.

It was four o'clock; outside the glass-paned walls the light was fading fast. Trentham clearly wouldn't be long, but why he would feel impelled by falling night to return to his house she couldn't fathom. The butler, however, had been quite definite on the point.

She reached the end of the path and stepped into a clearing ringed by high banks of shrubs and flowering bushes. It contained a circular pond set into the floor; the small fountain at its center was responsible for the tinkling. Beyond the pond, a wide window seat, heavily cushioned, followed the curve of the windowed wall; sitting on it, one could either view the garden outside, or look inward, contemplating the pond and the well-stocked conservatory.

Crossing to the window seat, she sank onto the cushions. They were deep, comfortable—perfect for her needs. She considered, then stood and walked on, along another path following the curved outer wall. Better she meet Trentham standing; he towered over her as it was. She could lead him back to the window seat—

A flash of movement in the garden caught her eye. She stopped, looked; she couldn't see anything unusual. The shadows had deepened while she'd been ambling; gloom now gathered beneath the trees.

Then, out of one such pocket of darkness, a man emerged. Tall, dark, lean, he wore a tattered coat and stained corduroy breeches, a battered cap pulled low on his head. He glanced furtively around as he strode rapidly for the house.

Leonora sucked in a breath. Wild thoughts of yet another burglar flooded her mind; recollection of the man who twice had attacked her stole her breath. This man was much larger; if he got his hands on her, she wouldn't be able to break free.

And his long legs were carrying him straight to the conservatory.

Sheer panic held her motionless in the shadow of the massed plants. The door would be locked, she told herself. Trentham's butler was excellent—

The man reached the door, reached for the handle, turned it.

The door swung inward. He stepped through.

Faint light from the distant hallway reached him as he closed the door, turned, straightened.

"Good God!"

The exclamation exploded from Leonora's tight chest. She stared, unable to believe her eyes.

Trentham's head had snapped around at her first squeak.

He stared back at her, then his lips thinned and he frowned—and recognition was complete.

"Sssh!" He motioned her to silence, glanced toward the corridor, then, soft-footed, approached. "At the risk of repeating myself, what the damn hell are you doing here?"

She simply stared at him—at the grime worked into his face, at the dark stubble shading his jaw. A smudge of soot ran upward from one brow and disappeared beneath his hair, now hanging lank and listless under that cap—a worn tartan monstrosity that looked even worse at close range.

Her gaze drifted down to take in his coat, tattered and none too clean, to his breeches and knitted stockings, and the rough work boots he had on his feet. Reaching them, she paused, then ran her gaze all the way back up to his eyes. Met his irritated gaze.

"Answer my question and I'll answer yours—what in all Hades are you supposed to be?"

His lips thinned. "What do I look like?"

"Like a navvy from the most dangerous slum in town." A definite aroma reached her; she sniffed. "Perhaps down by the docks."

"Very perceptive," Tristan growled. "Now what brought you here? Have you discovered something?"

She shook her head. "I wanted to see your conservatory. You said you'd show it to me."

The tension—the apprehension—that had flashed through him on seeing her there leached away. He looked down at himself, and grimaced. "You've called at a bad time."

She frowned, her gaze once more on his disreputable attire. "But what *have* you been doing? Where have you been, dressed like that?"

"As you so perceptively guessed, the docks." Searching for any clue, any hint, any whisper of one Montgomery Mountford.

"You're a trifle old to be indulging in larks." She looked up and caught his gaze. "Do you frequently do such things?"

"No." Not anymore. He had never expected to don these clothes again, but on doing so that morning, had felt peculiarly justified in his refusal to throw them out. "I've been visiting the sort of dens that would-be burglars haunt."

"Oh. I see." She looked up at him with now openly eager interest. "Did you learn anything?"

"Not directly, but I've passed the word—"

"Oh, is she in here, then, Havers?"

Ethelreda. Tristan swore beneath his breath.

"We'll just keep her company until dear Tristan arrives."

"No need for her to mope about all alone."

"Miss Carling? Are you there?"

He swore again. They were all there—coming this way. "For God's sake!" he muttered. He went to grab Leonora, then remembered his hands were filthy. He kept his palms away from her. "You'll have to distract them."

It was an outright plea; he met her eyes, infused every ounce of beseeching candor of which he was capable into his expression.

She looked at him. "They don't know you go out masquerading as a lout, do they?"

"No. And they'll have fits if they see me like this."

Fits would be the least of it; Ethelreda had a horrible tendency to swoon.

They were casting about along the paths, drawing inexorably nearer.

He held out his hands, begging. *"Please."*

She smiled. Slowly. "All right. I'll save you." She turned and started toward the source of feminine twittering, then glanced back over her shoulder. Caught his eye. "But you owe me a favor."

"Anything." He sighed with relief. "Just get them out of here. Take them to the drawing room."

Her smile deepening, Leonora turned and went on. Anything, he'd said. An excellent outcome from an otherwise useless exercise.

CHAPTER
Eight

ᕙᕗᕙᕗ

Arranging to be seduced, Leonora was perfectly sure, wasn't supposed to be this difficult. The next day, while sitting in the parlor copying her letter, copy after copy, doggedly working through Cedric's correspondents, she reevaluated her position and considered all avenues for advance.

The previous afternoon she'd dutifully deflected Trentham's cousins to the drawing room; he'd joined them fifteen minutes later, clean, spotless, his usual debonair self. Having used her interest in conservatories to explain her visit to the ladies, she'd duly asked him various questions to which he'd denied all knowledge, instead suggesting he have his gardener call on her.

Asking him to conduct her on a tour would have been fruitless; his cousins would have accompanied them.

Regretfully, she'd crossed his conservatory off her mental list of suitable venues for seduction; an appropriate time could be managed, and the window seat provided an excellent location, but their privacy could never be assured.

Trentham had summoned his carriage, helped her into it, and sent her home. Unfulfilled. Even hungrier than when she'd left.

Even more determined.

Still, the excursion had not been without gain; she now had one trump card in hand. She intended to use it wisely. That meant clearing the time, location, and privacy hurdles simultaneously. She had no idea how rakes managed it. Perhaps they simply waited for opportunity to arise, then pounced.

After waiting patiently all these years, and having finally made up her mind, she wasn't inclined to sit back and wait any longer. The right opportunity was what was required; if necessary, she'd have to create it.

All well and good, but she couldn't think how.

She racked her brain throughout the day. And the next. She even considered taking up her Aunt Mildred's permanent offer to take her about within the ton. Despite her disinterest in society's balls and parties, she was aware such events provided venues in which gentlemen and ladies could meet privately. However, from snippets Trentham's cousins had let fall, as well as his own caustic comments, she'd gathered he had little enthusiasm for the social round. No point making such an effort herself if he wasn't likely to be present to be met, privately or otherwise.

When the clock struck four, she tossed down her pen and stretched her arms over her head. She was almost at the end of her letter-writing exercise, but when it came to venues in which to be seduced, her mind remained stubbornly blank.

"There has to be somewhere!" She pushed up from her chair, irritated and impatient. Frustrated. Her gaze went to the window. The day had been fine, but breezy. Now the wind had eased; evening was closing in, benign if cool.

She headed for the front hall, grabbed her cloak, didn't bother with her bonnet; she wouldn't be out long. She glanced around, expecting Henrietta, then realized the hound was out for her constitutional in the nearby park, led on a lead by one of the footmen.

"Damn!" She wished she'd been in time to join them.

The gardens, both front and back, were protected; she wanted— *needed*—to walk in the open air. She needed to breathe, to let the coolness refresh her, to blow away her frustration and reinvigorate her brain.

She hadn't walked outside alone for weeks, yet the burglar could hardly be watching all the time.

With a swish of her skirts, she turned, opened the front door, and walked outside.

She left the door on the latch and went down the steps, then followed the path to the gate. Reaching it, she peered out. The light was still good; in both directions the street, always a quiet one, lay empty. Safe enough. Pulling open the gate, she walked through, tugged it closed behind her, then set off walking briskly along the pavement.

Passing Number 12, she glanced in, but saw no sign of movement. She'd heard via Toby that Gasthorpe had now hired a full staff, but most were not yet in residence. Biggs, however, returned there every night, and Gasthorpe himself rarely left the house; there had been no further felonious activity there.

Indeed, since she'd last seen the man at the bottom of their garden, and he'd run off, there'd been no further incidents of any kind. The sense of being watched had receded; although occasionally she still felt under observation, the feeling was more distant, less threatening.

She walked on, pondering that, considering what it might mean in terms of Montgomery Mountford and whatever it was he was so intent on removing from her uncle's house. While arranging to be seduced was certainly a distraction, she hadn't forgotten Mr. Mountford.

Whoever he was.

The thought evoked others; she recalled Trentham's recent searches. Direct and to the point, decisive, active, yet try as she might, she couldn't imagine any other gentleman masquerading as he had done.

He'd appeared very comfortable in his disguise.

He'd looked even more dangerous than he usually did.

The image teased; she remembered hearing of ladies who indulged in passionate affairs with men of distinctly rougher background than their own. Could she—would she later—be susceptible to such longings?

She honestly had no idea, which only confirmed how much she'd yet to learn, not just of passion, but of herself, too.

With every day that passed, she became more aware of that last.

She reached the end of the street and stopped on the corner. The breeze was stronger there; her cloak billowed. Holding it down, she looked toward the park, but saw no gangling hound returning with footman in tow. She considered waiting, but the breeze was too chilly and strong enough to unravel her hair. Turning, she retraced her steps, feeling considerably restored.

Her gaze on the pavement, she determinedly turned her mind to passion, specifically how to sample it.

The shadows were lengthening; dusk was approaching.

She'd reached the boundary of Number 12 when she heard footsteps striding quickly up behind her.

Panic flared; she whirled, backing against the high stone wall even while her intellect calmly pointed out the unlikelihood of any attack.

One look at the face of the man rushing toward her, and she knew intellect lied.

She opened her mouth and screamed.

Mountford snarled and grabbed her. Hands locking cruelly about both arms, he dragged her to the middle of the wide pavement and shook her.

"Hey!"

The shout came from the end of the street; Mountford paused. A heavyset man was running their way.

Mountford swore. His fingers bit viciously into her arms as he swung to look the other way.

He swore again, a vulgar expletive, a hint of fear showing. His lips curled in a snarl.

Leonora looked, and saw Trentham closing fast. Some way behind him came another man, but it was the look on Trentham's face that shocked her—and momentarily transfixed Mountford.

He shook free of that killing look, glanced at her, then hauled her to him—and flung her forcefully back. Into the wall.

She screamed. The sound cut off when her head hit the stone. She was only vaguely aware of sliding slowly down, crumpling in a mass of skirts on the pavement.

Through a white fog, she saw Mountford racing across the street, avoiding the men running in from either end. Trentham didn't give chase, but came straight for her.

She heard him swear, distantly noted he was swearing at her, not Mountford, then she was wrapped in his strength and hoisted to her feet. He held her against him, supporting her; she was standing, yet he was taking most of her weight.

She blinked; her vision cleared. Leaving her staring into a face in which some primitive emotion akin to fury warred with concern.

To her relief, concern won.

"Are you all right?"

She nodded, swallowed. "Just a trifle dazed." She put up a hand to the back of her head, gingerly felt, then smiled, albeit tremulously. "Only a small bump. No serious damage."

His lips thinned, his eyes narrowed on hers, then he glanced in the direction Mountford had fled.

She frowned and tried to ease from his hold. "You should have followed him."

He didn't let her go. "The others are after him."

Others? Two and two . . . "Have you had people watching the street?"

He glanced at her briefly. "Of course."

No wonder she hadn't felt threatened by the continuing observation. "You might have told me."

"Why? So you could stage some witless act like this?"

She ignored that and stared across the street. Mountford had raced into the garden of the house opposite; the two other men, both heavier and slower, had followed.

No one reappeared.

Trentham's lips were a grim line. "Is there an alley behind those houses?"

"Yes."

He bit back a sound; she suspected it was another curse. He looked at her assessingly, then consented to ease the arm he'd locked about her. "I'd credited you with more sense—"

She raised a hand, stopped his words. "I had absolutely no reason to think Mountford would be out here. Come to that, if you had men watching from both ends of the street, why did they let him past them?"

He glanced again in the direction his men had gone. "He must have spotted them. Presumably he reached you in the same way he left, via an alley and someone's garden."

His gaze returned to her face, searched it. "How are you feeling?"

"Reasonable." Better than she'd expected; Mountford's rough handling had shaken her more than the collision with the wall. She drew breath, let it out. "Just a bit shaky."

He nodded curtly. "Shock."

She focused on him. "What are you doing here?"

Accepting that his men weren't about to return, Mountford between them, Tristan released her and took her arm. "The furniture for the third floor was delivered yesterday. I'd promised Gasthorpe I'd check and approve it. Today is his day off—he's gone to Surrey to visit his mother and won't be back until tomorrow. I'd thought to kill two birds by checking the house as well as the furniture."

He studied her face, still too pale, then turned her along the pavement. Pacing slowly, he led her along the wall of Number 12 toward Number 14 beyond. "I left it later than I'd intended. Biggs should be inside by now, so all will no doubt be well until Gasthorpe returns."

She nodded, walking by his side, leaning on his arm. They drew level with the gate of Number 12, and she stopped.

She drew in a deep breath, then met his eyes. "If you don't mind, perhaps I could come in and help you check the furniture." She smiled, definitely tremulously, then looked away. Somewhat breathlessly added, "I'd prefer to stay with you for a little while longer, to catch my breath before going in to face the household."

She ran her uncle's household; there'd no doubt be people waiting to speak to her as soon as she went in.

He hesitated, but Gasthorpe wasn't around to disapprove. And on the list of activities likely to lift a woman's spirits, viewing new furniture probably ranked high. "If you wish." He steered her through the gate and up the path to the door. While she was viewing, he'd use the time to think of how better to protect her. He couldn't, unfortunately, expect her to remain a prisoner within doors.

Taking the key from his pocket, he unlocked the front door. Frowned as he handed her over the threshold. "Where's your hound?"

"She's being taken for a walk in the park." She glanced back at him as he closed the door. "The footmen take her—she's too strong for me."

He nodded, noting that once again she'd followed his thought— that if she walked at all, then she should walk with Henrietta. But if the dog was too strong, then beyond the garden that wasn't a viable option.

She led the way to the stairs; he followed. They'd reached the first steps when a cough drew their attention to the door to the kitchens.

Biggs stood in the opening. He saluted. "On watch here, m'lud."

Tristan smiled his charming smile. "Thank you, Biggs. Miss Carling and I are just taking stock of the new furniture. We'll let ourselves out later. Carry on."

Biggs bobbed to Leonora, snapped off another salute, then turned and descended into the kitchens. The faint aroma of a pie drifted to their nostrils.

Leonora met his gaze, a smile in her eyes, then she turned, grasped the banister, and went on.

He watched, but she didn't falter. However, when they reached the second-floor landing, she glanced at him and drew in a tight breath.

Frowning anew, he took her arm. "Here." He urged her into the largest bedroom, the one over the library. "Sit down." A large armchair sat angled to the window; he led her to it.

She subsided into the chair with a little sigh. Smiled weakly up at him. "I don't faint."

He narrowed his eyes at her; she was no longer pale, but there was an odd tenseness about her. "Just sit there and study the furniture you can see. I'll check the other rooms, then you can give me your verdict."

Leonora nodded, closed her eyes, and let her head rest against the chair's back. "I'll wait here."

He hesitated, looking down at her, then he turned and left her.

When he was gone, she opened her eyes and studied the room. The large bow window looked over the back garden; during the day it would let in ample light, but now, with night encroaching, the room was gathering shadows. A fireplace stood in the center of the wall opposite her chair; a fire was set but not lit.

A chaise was positioned at an angle to the fireplace; beyond it, in the far corner of the room, stood a massive armoire in dark polished wood.

The same polished wood adorned the even more massive four-poster bed. Staring at the expanse of ruby silk coverlet, she thought of Trentham; presumably his friends were similarly large. Dark red brocade curtains were looped back about the carved posts at the head of the bed. The last light lingered on the curves and twists in the ornately carved headboard, repeated on the turned posts at the bed's foot. With its thick mattress, the bed was a substantial piece, solid, stable.

The central feature of the room; the focus of her senses.

It was, she decided, the perfect venue for her seduction.

Far better than his conservatory.

And there was no one to interrupt, to interfere. Gasthorpe was in Surrey and Biggs in the kitchens, too far away to hear anything—provided they closed the door.

She turned to look at the solid oak door.

The encounter with Mountford had only deepened her determination to press ahead. She wasn't so much shaky as tense; she needed to feel Trentham's arms around her to convince herself she was safe.

She wanted to be in his arms, wanted to be close to him. Wanted the physical contact, the shared sensual pleasure. Needed the experience, now more than ever.

Two minutes later, Trentham strolled back in.

She waved to the door. "Close that so I can see the tallboy."

He turned and did as she asked.

She dutifully studied the tall chest of drawers thus revealed.

"So"—ambling up, he halted beside the chair and looked down at her—"do the amenities meet with your approval?"

She looked up at him, slowly smiled. "Indeed, they appear quite perfect."

Rakes undoubtedly had it right; when opportunity presented, one had to pounce.

She held up her hand.

Tristan grasped it and smoothly drew her to her feet. He'd expected her to step away; instead, she'd shifted her feet—she straightened directly in front of him, so close her breasts brushed his coat.

She looked into his face, then moved closer still. Reached up and drew his head down to hers. Pressed her lips to his in a blatant, open-mouthed kiss, one he only just stopped himself from falling headfirst into.

His control uncharacteristically quaked. He gripped her waist—hard—to stop himself from devouring her.

She ended the caress and drew back, but only a fraction; she lifted her lids and met his gaze. Her eyes glinted vibrantly blue beneath her lashes. Holding his gaze, she reached for the ties of her cloak, tugged, then let the garment fall to the floor. "I wanted to thank you."

Her voice was husky, low; its timbre slid through him. His body clenched, recognizing her meaning; he was pulling her closer, tight, body to body, lowering his head, before the echo had died.

She stopped him with one finger, sliding the tip across his lower lip. Her gaze followed the motion; instead of moving away, she moved closer yet—let herself sink against him. "You were there when I needed you."

Unthinking, he gathered her to him; her lids lifted, and she met his eyes. Slid her hand up to his nape again. Her lids drifted down, and she stretched upward against him. "Thank you."

He took her mouth as she offered it. Sank deep and drank, felt not just pleasure but reassurance slide through his veins. It seemed only right that she thanked him like this; he saw no reason to refuse the moment, to do anything other than sate his senses with the tribute she surrendered.

Her arms slid up, twined about his neck; she pressed close, her body a promise of bliss.

Between them, the embers they'd left smoldering flared, then flames leapt beneath their skins. He felt the fire ignite; confident he had her measure, he let it burn.

Let his fingers find their way to her breasts; when the sweet mounds were tight and straining, he reached for her laces. Dealt with them and the ribbons of her chemise with practiced ease.

Her breasts spilled into his hands; she gasped through the kiss. Possessively kneading, he held her, drew her on, urged the flames higher.

He broke from the kiss, nudged her head up, set his lips to the taut tendon in her throat. Traced it down to where her pulse beat frantically, then licked, laved. Sucked.

She gasped; the sound echoed in the silence, drove him on. Steering her around, he sank onto the chair's arm, drawing her with him, pressing her gown and chemise to her waist.

So he could feast.

She'd offered her bounty; he accepted. With lips and tongue, took and claimed. Traced the full curves. Pressed hot kisses to the tightly ruched peaks. Listened to her fractured breathing. Felt her fingers tightening on his skull as he teased.

Then he took one pebbled nipple into his mouth, rasped it lightly, and she tensed. He sucked gently, then soothed the taut nubbin with his tongue. Waited until she'd relaxed before drawing it deep and suckling.

She cried out, her body bowing in his arms.

He showed no mercy, suckling voraciously first at one breast, then the other.

Her fingers spasmed, holding him to her. He slid his hands down from her waist, back and over her hips, and captured her bottom; spreading his thighs, he drew her hips to him. Wedged her close so her stomach rode against him, both easing and teasing the fiery ache.

Closing his hands, he kneaded, and felt more than heard her gasp. He didn't stop but explored more intimately, holding her at his mercy, his lips taunting and teasing her swollen breasts while he evocatively shifted her lower body, molding hips, stomach, and thighs to him as he wished.

Then she dragged in a breath and bent her head. He released her breasts, looked up, and she captured his mouth. Slid in, caressed and heated him, stole his breath, gave it back.

He felt her fingers at his throat, then she flicked his cravat loose. Their mouths melded; they took and gave while her fingers slid down his chest.

Opening his shirt.

Tugging it free of his waistband. Trailing her fingertips over his chest, taunting, feather-light. Maddening.

"Take off your coat."

The words whispered through his brain. His skin was burning; it seemed a good idea.

He released her for a second, stood, shrugged.

Cravat, coat, and shirt fell back across the chair.

Bad move.

The instant her naked breasts touched his bare chest, he knew that was so.

Didn't care.

The sensation was so erotic, so blissfully attuned to some deeper need that he shrugged aside the warning as easily as he had the shirt. He gathered her to him, sank into her welcoming mouth, aware to his bones of the light touch of her hands on his skin, innocent, tentatively exploring.

Aware of the rush of pleasure her touch evoked, of the answering heat flaring within her.

He didn't press but let her feel and learn as she wished, his ego pleased beyond belief by her eager desire. He held her close; hands splayed over her naked back, he traced the fine muscles bracketing her spine.

Delicate, supple yet with their own feminine strength, an echo of all she was.

He'd never been with a woman he wanted more, one who promised so completely to sate him. Not just sexually, but at some deeper level, one he didn't, in his present state, recognize or understand. Whatever it was, the compulsive need she evoked was strong.

Stronger than any lust, any mere desire.

His control had never had to cope with such a feeling.

It cracked, shattered, and he didn't even know.

Didn't even have the sense to pull back when her questing fingers wandered lower. When she traced, tantalizingly, in open wonderment, he only groaned.

Startled, she drew her hand away; he grabbed it. His hand locked around hers he guided it back, urged her to learn him as he intended to learn her. Drew back from the kiss and watched her face as she did.

Gloried in her innocence, and even more in her awakening.

His lungs constricted until he was giddy. He continued to watch her, kept his senses focused on her, away from the conflagration she was causing, from the urgent need pulsing through him.

Only when she glanced up beneath her lashes, lips parted, rosy from his kisses, did he move to draw her to him again, to again take her mouth and sweep her deeper into the magic.

Deeper under his spell.

When he finally released her lips, Leonora could barely think. Her skin was on fire; so was his. Everywhere they touched, flames leapt, singed. Her breasts ached, brushed to excruciating sensitivity by the coarse dark hair across his chest.

That chest was a sculpted wonder of hard muscle over heavy bone. Her spread fingers found scars, nicks here and there; the light tan of his face and neck extended over his chest, as if he occasionally worked outside without a shirt. Inside without a shirt he was a wonder, appearing to her senses like a god come to life. She'd only seen male bodies like his in books of ancient sculptures, yet his was alive, real, utterly male. The feel of his skin, the resilience of his muscles, the sheer strength he possessed overwhelmed her.

His lips, his tongue, teased hers, then he lifted his head and brushed a kiss to her temple.

Whispered in the heated dark, "I want to see you. Touch you."

He drew back just enough to catch her eyes. His were dark pools, compellingly intent.

His strength surrounded her, caged her; his hands stroked her bare skin. She felt them slide to her sides, then tense to press her gown and chemise lower.

"Let me."

Command and question both. She breathed slowly out, infinitesimally nodded.

He pushed her gown down. Once past the swell of her hips, both gown and chemise fell of their own accord.

The soft silken swoosh was audible in the room.

Darkness had closed in, yet enough light still lingered. Enough for her to study his face as he looked down, as, still holding her within the circle of one arm, with his other hand he traced from her breast to her waist, to her hip, flaring outward, then inward across her upper thigh.

"You are so beautiful."

The words fell from his lips; he didn't even seem to notice, as if he hadn't consciously said them. His features were set, the harsh planes austere, his lips a hard line. There was no softness in his face, no hint of his charm.

All lingering reservations of the rightness of her actions were cindered in that moment. Turned to ashes by the stark emotion in his face.

She didn't know enough to name it, but whatever that emotion was it was what she wanted, what she needed. She'd lived her life longing to be looked at by a man in just such a way, as if she were more precious, more desirable than his soul.

As if he'd willingly trade his soul for what she knew would happen next.

She reached for him as he reached for her.

Their lips met, and the flames roared.

She would have been frightened if he hadn't been there, solid and real for her to hold on to, her anchor in the maelstrom that swirled through them, around them.

His hands slid down and around, closed over her bare bottom; he kneaded, and heat raced across her skin. Fever followed, a hot urgent ache that swelled and grew as he evocatively plundered her mouth, as he held her close, lifted her hips against him, and suggestively molded her softness to the rigid line of his erection.

She moaned, hot, hungry and wanting.

Wanton. Eager. Determined.

He hoisted her higher; instinctively she wrapped her arms about his shoulders, her long legs about his hips.

Their kiss turned incendiary.

He broke from it only to demand, "Come. Lie with me."

She answered with a scorching kiss.

Tristan carried her to the side of the bed, and tumbled them both onto it. They bounced, and he angled over her, pressing her down, wedging one leg between hers.

Their lips locked, melded. He sank into the kiss, letting his wandering senses luxuriate in the heavenly delight of having her under him, naked and wanting. Some primitive, wholly male part of his soul rejoiced.

Wanted more.

He let his hands roam, shaping her breasts, then sliding lower, caressing her hips, then pressing beneath to cup her bottom and squeeze. He nudged her thighs wider, freed one hand, and placed it on her stomach.

Felt the feminine muscles beneath his palm jump, contract.

He slid his fingers lower, tangling in the dark curls at the apex of her thighs. Reaching through them, he stroked the soft, sweet flesh they concealed. Felt her shudder.

Easing her thighs wider he cupped her. Sensed the quick intake of her breath. He opened her mouth and kissed her more deeply, then eased back from the kiss, leaving their lips brushing, touching, letting her senses surface sufficiently for her to know and feel.

Their breaths mingled, heated and urgent; from beneath heavy lids, their eyes met, held.

Locked as he shifted his hand and touched her. Stroked, caressed, intimately traced. Her breasts rose and fell; her teeth closed on her lower lip as he opened her. As he teased, glorying in the slick heat of her body, then slowly, deliberately, slid one long finger into her.

Her breathing fractured; her eyes closed. Her body rose beneath his.

"Stay with me." He stroked slowly, in, out, letting her grow accustomed to his touch, to the sensation.

Her breathing ragged, she forced open her eyes; gradually, her body unclenched.

Slowly, gradually, flowered for him.

He watched it happen, watched the sensual delight rise and sweep her away, watched her eyes darken, felt her fingers tense, nails sinking into his muscles.

Then her breathing broke. Spine bowing, head pressing back, she closed her eyes. "Kiss me." A desperate plea. "Please—kiss me." Her voice broke on a gasp as sensation built, coiled, tightened.

"No." Eyes locked on her face, he pushed her on. "I want to watch you."

She was fighting for breath, clinging to sanity.

"Lie back and let it happen. Let go."

He caught a glimpse of brilliant blue from beneath her lashes. He slipped another finger in with the first, thrust deeper, faster.

And she fractured.

He watched her climax take her, listened to the soft cry that fell from her swollen lips, felt her sheath contract, powerful and tight, then relax, aftershocks rippling through the velvet heat.

His fingers still inside her, he leaned down, and kissed her.

Long, deep, giving her all he could, letting her taste his desire, see his wanting, then, step by step, drawing back.

When he withdrew his fingers, stroked them through her wet curls, then lifted his head, her fingers, tangled in the hair at his nape, closed, clutched. She opened her eyes, studied his, his face, read his decision.

He tried to ease back, to let her breathe; to his surprise, she tightened her grip, held him to her.

Held his gaze, then licked her lips. "You owe me a favor." Her voice was a hoarse whisper; it strengthened with her next words. "Anything, you said. So promise you won't stop."

He blinked. "Leonora—"

"No. I want you with me. Don't stop. Don't pull away."

He gritted his teeth. She'd blindsided him. Naked, spread beneath him, her body pliant in aftermath . . . and she was begging him to take her. "It's not that I don't want you—"

She shifted one sleek thigh.

He sucked in a breath.

Groaned. Shut his eyes. Couldn't shut off his senses. Grimly resolved, he placed his palms on the bed and pushed up, away from her heat.

Opened his eyes.

And stopped.

Hers were swimming.

Tears?

She blinked hard, but didn't shift her gaze from his. "*Please.* Don't leave me."

Her voice broke on the words.

Something inside him did, too.

His resolve, his certainty, shattered.

He wanted her so much he could barely think, yet the last thing he should do was sink into her soft heat, take her, claim her, like this, now. But he wasn't proof against the need in her eyes, a need he couldn't place, but knew he had to fill.

About them, the house was silent, still. Outside the window, night had fallen. They were alone, draped in shadows, naked on a wide bed.

And she wanted him inside her.

He drew a deep breath, bowed his head, then abruptly pulled back and sat up.

"All right."

One part of his mind was bellowing: *"Don't do it!"* The thunder in his blood, and even more a wave of emotional conviction drowned it out.

He unfastened his trousers, then stood to strip them off. Glanced back at her as he straightened, met her eyes. "Just remember this was your idea."

She smiled a soft madonna's smile, but her eyes remained wide, watchful. Waiting.

He looked at her, then looked around, stalked to where her clothes had fallen and swiped up her gown. Shaking it out, turning the skirts inside out, he returned to the bed. Dropping beside her, he scooped her hips up in one arm and spread the skirts beneath her.

Glanced at her face in time to see one delicate brow arch upward, but she made no comment, simply settled back again.

Met his eyes. Still waiting.

Read his thoughts as she often did. "I'm not going to change my mind."

He felt his face harden. Felt desire rip through him. "So be it."

She had cooled; he hadn't. He seriously doubted she had any idea of what she did to him, to what level she called to him, especially with them naked in the dappled dark, alone in an essentially empty house.

It was impossible to shake the aura of illicit danger; it was so much a part of him, he didn't even try. She wanted this, knowingly. As he stretched beside her, propped on one elbow and reached for her, he didn't try to hide anything, any part of him, from her.

Least of all the dark, primitive desire she evoked.

Their eyes had adjusted long ago; they could see each other's faces and expressions, even, given they were so close, the emotions in each other's eyes. He sensed the trepidation that quivered through her as he drew her to him. At the same time read the determination in her face, and didn't pause.

He kissed her, not as he had before but as a lover who had been given free rein. He entered like a conqueror, laid claim as he wished, laid waste to her senses.

Initially passive, waiting to see, Leonora instinctively rose to his challenge. Her body stirred, came alive once more; she lifted one hand, and speared her fingers once more into his hair.

And clung tight as, once again, the flames erupted between them. This time, he made no effort to hold them, contain them; instead, he let them rage. Deliberately sent them raging with each possessive sweep of his hard palms as he shaped her body beneath his, as he claimed every inch of her softness, explored at will, even more intimately.

She shuddered, and let him. Let him sweep her into the fiery sea, the conflagration of desire, passion and simple, unavoidable need.

He touched her in ways she had never imagined, until she clung and sobbed. Until she was awash with heat and longing, with desire burning so fiercely she felt literally on fire. He shifted over her, spread her thighs, and settled between. In the deepening darkness, he was literally a god, powerful and intent as, braced above her, he looked down on her. Then he bent his head and took her mouth again, and his sheer vitality—the fact he was all hard muscle and bone, and hot, heated blood—captured her.

The crinkly roughness of his haired skin chafed, abraded, reminded her how soft her own skin was, how sensitive. Reminded her how vulnerable and defenseless she was against his strength.

He shifted, reached down, caught one of her knees, and lifted her leg to his hip. Set it there, then traced back with his palm, around, until he found her slick and swollen, hot and ready.

And then he was pressing into her, hard, hot, and much larger than she'd realized. Her lungs seized. She felt her body stretching. He pressed inexorably in.

She gasped, tried to pull away from the kiss.

He didn't let her.

Instead, he held her down, held her trapped, and slowly, slowly filled her.

Her body arched as he did, bowed, tightened, tensed against his invasion. She felt the restriction, felt the pressure build, but he didn't stop; he pressed deeper, deeper, until the barrier simply gave, and he surged through. And on.

Until she was so full of him she could barely breathe, until she felt him throbbing high and deep inside her. She felt her body give, surrender, then accept.

Only then did he stop, hold still, the solid reality of him buried deep within her.

He drew back from the kiss, opened his eyes, looked down into hers from two inches away. Their breaths, ragged and broken, hot and heated, mingled.

"Are you all right?"

The words reached her, deep and gravelly; she considered how she felt with the hot weight of him holding her down, his muscled hardness trapping her spread and so vulnerable beneath him. With his erection buried intimately within her.

She nodded. Her lips were hungry for his; she touched them to his, tasted him, then sent her tongue exploring, savoring the unique flavor. She felt more than heard him groan, then he moved within her.

At first just a little, rocking his hips against her.

But soon that wasn't enough, not for either of them.

What followed was a journey of discovery. She hadn't imagined intimacy would be this consuming, this demanding, this fulfilling. This hot, this sweaty, this involving. He didn't speak again, didn't ask what she thought, asked for no permission as he took her. As he filled her, sank into her body, sheathed himself in her heat.

Yet throughout, again and again his eyes touched hers, checking, reassuring, encouraging. They communicated without words, and she followed him eagerly. Wantonly.

Into a landscape of passion.

It rolled on, unfolding, scene upon scene, and she realized just how much the simple act of joining could be.

How enthralling. How fascinating.

How demanding. How addictive.

How, at the very end as they tumbled through space and she felt him with her, fulfilling.

Given his expertise, she'd expected him to withdraw from her before he spilled his seed. She didn't want that; instinct drove her to sink her nails into his flexing buttocks and hold him to her.

He looked at her; almost blindly, their eyes met. Then he closed his eyes on a groan, and let it happen, let the last powerful surge take him even deeper into her, locking them together as he spent himself within her.

She felt his warmth flood her.

Her lips curved in a satisfied smile, and she finally let go, and let oblivion take her.

Slumped across the bed, Tristan tried to make sense of what had happened.

Leonora lay across him, still intimately entwined. He felt no urge to disengage. She was half-asleep; he hoped she'd remain so until he found his mental feet.

He'd collapsed on top of her, sated literally out of his mind. A novel occurrence. Later, he'd roused enough to roll to the side, taking her with him. He'd pulled the coverlet over them to protect her cooling limbs from the chill invading the room.

It was full dark, but not that late. No one would be unduly worried by her absence, not yet. Experience suggested that despite what had seemed a journey to the stars, it would not even be six o'clock; he had time to consider where they were now, and how best to go forward.

He was too experienced not to understand that going forward usually meant understanding where one had been.

That was his problem. He was not at all sure he understood all that had just taken place.

She'd been attacked; he'd arrived in time to rescue her, and they'd come in here. All seemed straightforward to that point.

Then she'd wanted to thank him. He'd seen no reason not to let her.

It was after that that matters had become complicated.

He vaguely recalled thinking that indulging her was a perfectly sensible way of taking her mind off the attack. True enough, but her thanks, rendered in the manner she'd chosen, had both soothed and invoked a darker need of his own, a reaction to the incident, a compulsion to put his mark on her, to make her irrevocably his.

Put like that, it seemed a primitive, somewhat uncivilized response, yet he couldn't deny that was what had driven him to strip her, to touch her, to know her intimately. He hadn't understood enough to fight it, hadn't seen the danger.

He glanced down at Leonora's dark head, at her hair, tumbled and jumbled, warm against his shoulder.

He hadn't intended this.

This, he now realized, increasingly so as his brain caught up with the ramifications, with the full extent of what all *this* now meant to him—*this* was a major complication in a plan that hadn't been running all that smoothly to begin with.

He felt his face harden. His lips thinned. If he hadn't been wary of waking her, he would have sworn.

It didn't take much thinking to know that now there was only one way forward. No matter what options his strategist's mind devised, his instinctive, deeply entrenched reaction never wavered.

She was his. Absolutely. In incontrovertible fact.

She was in danger, under threat.

There was only one option left.

Please . . . don't leave me.

He hadn't been able to resist that plea, knew he wouldn't, even now, were she to make it again. There'd been some need so deep, so vulnerable in her eyes, it had been impossible for him to deny. Despite the upheaval it was going to cause, he couldn't, didn't, regret anything.

In reality, nothing had changed, only the relative timing.

What was required was a restructuring of his plan. On a significant scale, admittedly, but he was too much a tactician to waste time grumbling.

* * *

Reality seeped slowly into Leonora's mind. She stirred, sighed, luxuriating in the warmth that surrounded her, enveloped her, engulfed her. Filled her.

Lashes fluttering, she opened her eyes, blinked. Realized what the source of all that comforting warmth was.

A blush—she prayed it was a blush—suffused her. She shifted enough to look up.

Trentham glanced down at her. A frown, rather vague, filled his eyes. "Just lie still."

Beneath the covers, one large palm closed about her bottom and he shifted her, settled her more comfortably on him. About him.

"You'll be sore. Just relax and let me think."

She stared at him, then looked down—at her hand spread on his naked chest. Relax, he said. They were naked, limbs tangled, and he was still inside her. No longer filling her as he had, but still definitely there . . .

She knew men were generally unaffected by their own nakedness, yet this seemed—

Dragging in a breath, she stopped thinking about it. If she did, if she started letting herself dwell on all she'd learned, all she'd experienced, stunned amazement and wonder would keep her here for hours.

And her aunts were coming to dinner.

She'd dwell on the magic later.

Lifting her head, she looked at Trentham. He was still vaguely frowning. "What are you thinking about?"

He glanced at her. "Do you know any bishops?"

"Bishops?"

"Hmm—we need a special license. I could apply to—"

She braced her hands on his chest, pushed up, and got his immediate attention. Eyes wide, she stared down at him. "Why do we need a special license?"

"Why . . ." He stared, bemusedly, back at her. Eventually said, "That's the very last thing I expected you to say."

She frowned at him. Clambered up and off him, twisting to sit in the coverlet. "Stop teasing." She looked around. "Where are my clothes?"

Silence reigned for a heartbeat, then he said, "I'm not teasing."

His tone had her looking, very quickly, back at him. Their eyes locked; what she saw in his set her heart thumping. "That's not . . . funny."

"I didn't think any of this was 'funny.' "

She sat and looked at him; her spurt of panic receded. Her brain started to function again. "I don't expect you to marry me."

His brows rose; she dragged in a breath. "I'm twenty-six. Past marriageable age. You don't have to feel that because of this"—her wave encompassed the coverlet cocoon and all it contained—"you have to make any honorable sacrifice. You don't need to feel you seduced me and so must make amends."

"As I recall, you seduced me."

She blushed. "Indeed. So there's no reason you need to find a bishop."

It was definitely time to get dressed. She spied her chemise on the floor and turned to crawl out of the cocoon.

Steely fingers closed like a manacle about her wrist.

He didn't tug or restrain her; he didn't have to. She knew she couldn't break free until he consented to let her go.

She sank back into the coverlet. He was staring up at the ceiling; she couldn't see his eyes.

"Let's just see if I've got this straight."

His voice was even, but there was an edge to it that left her wary.

"You're a twenty-six-year-old virgin—I beg your pardon, ex-virgin. You have no other entanglements, romantic or otherwise. Correct?"

She would have loved to tell him this was pointless, but from experience she knew humoring difficult males was the fastest way to deal with their megrims. "Yes."

"Am I also correct in stating that you set out deliberately to seduce me?"

She pressed her lips together, then conceded, "Not immediately."

"But today. That"—his thumb had started to draw distracting little circles on the inside of her wrist—"was intended. Deliberate. You were set on having me . . . what? Initiate you?"

He turned his head and looked at her. She blushed, but forced herself to nod. "Yes. Just that."

"Hmm." He went back to staring at the ceiling. "And now, having accomplished your goal, you expect to say: 'Thank you, Tristan, that was very nice,' and carry on as if it never happened."

She hadn't thought that far. She frowned. "I assumed, eventually, we'd go our separate ways." She studied his profile. "There's no consequences to this, no reason we need do anything because of it."

The corner of his lips lifted; she couldn't tell which of the possible moods the gesture reflected.

"Except," he stated, his voice still even, but with the accents increasingly clipped, "you've miscalculated."

She really didn't want to ask, especially given his tone, but he simply waited, so she had to. "How?"

"*You* may not expect me to marry you. However, as the one who was seduced, *I* expect *you* to marry *me.*"

He turned his head, met her gaze—let her read in the blazing hazel of his eyes that he was absolutely serious.

She stared—read the message twice. Her jaw actually slackened, then she snapped her lips shut. "*That* is nonsensical! You don't want to marry me—you *know* you don't. You're simply being difficult." With a twist and a tug, she wrenched her wrist free, aware she managed only because he let her. She scrambled from the bed. Anger, fear, irritation, and trepidation were a heady mix. She made for her chemise.

Tristan sat up as she left the bed, his gaze locking on the bruises circling her upper arms. Then he remembered the attack, and breathed again. Mountford had marked her, not him.

Then she bent and swiped up her chemise, and he saw the smudges on her hips, the faint bluish marks his fingers had left on the alabaster skin of her bottom. She turned, struggling into the chemise, and he saw similar marks on her breasts.

Softly swore.

"What?" She yanked her chemise down and glared at him.

Lips compressed, he shook his head. "Nothing." He stood, and reached for his trousers.

Something dark, something powerful and dangerous was churning inside him. Burgeoning, struggling to break free.

He couldn't think.

He grabbed her dress from the bed and shook it out; there was only the slightest stain, and a small red spot. The sight rattled his control. He blocked it out, and carried the gown to her.

She took it, conveying her thanks with a haughty inclination of her head. He nearly laughed. She thought he was letting her walk free.

He shrugged into his shirt, quickly buttoned it, tucked it into his waistband, then quickly and expertly knotted his cravat. All the while he watched her. She was used to having a maid; she couldn't do up her gown on her own.

When he was fully dressed, he picked up her cloak. "Here. Let me." He handed her the cloak; she glanced at him, then took it. And turned, presenting him with her back.

He quickly laced up her gown. As he tied off the laces, his fingers slowed. He hooked one finger beneath the laces, anchoring her before him. Leaning down, he spoke softly in her ear. "I haven't changed my mind. I intend to marry you."

She stood poker straight, looking ahead, then she turned her head and met his eyes. "I haven't changed my mind either. I don't want to get married." She held his gaze, then added, "I never truly did."

He hadn't been able to shift her.

The argument had raged all the way down the stairs, reduced to hissed whispers as they crossed the ground floor because of Biggs, only to escalate again when they reached the relative safety of the garden.

Nothing he'd said had swayed her.

When, driven to complete and total exasperation by the notion that a lady of twenty-six whom he'd just very pleasurably initiated into the delights of intimacy should refuse to wed him, title, wealth, houses, and all, he'd threatened to march straight up her garden path and demand her hand from her uncle and her brother, revealing all if she made that necessary, she'd gasped, halted, turned to him—and nearly slain him with a look of horrified vulnerability.

"You said what was between us would remain between us."

There'd been real fear in her eyes.

He'd backed down.

In real disgust had heard himself gruffly assuring her that of course he wouldn't do any such thing.

Hoisted with his own petard.

Worse, hoisted with his honor.

Late that night, slumped before the fire in his library, Tristan tried to find a way through the morass that had, without warning, appeared around his feet.

Slowly sipping French brandy, he replayed all their exchanges, tried to read the thoughts, the emotions, behind her words. Some he couldn't be certain of, some he couldn't define, but of one thing he felt reasonably sure. She honestly didn't think she—a twenty-six-year-old ape-leader—her words—was capable of attracting and holding the honest and honorable attentions of a man like him.

Raising his glass, eyes on the flames, he let the fine liquor slide down his throat.

Admitted, quietly, to himself, that he didn't truly care what she thought.

He had to have her—in his house, within his walls, in his bed. Safe. Had to; he no longer had any choice. The dark, dangerous emotion she'd stirred to life and now unleashed would not permit any other outcome.

He hadn't known he had it in him, that degree of feeling. Yet that evening, when he'd been forced to stand on the garden path and watch her—let her—walk away from him, he'd finally realized what that roiling emotion was.

Possessiveness.

He'd come very close to giving it free rein.

He'd always been a protective man, witness his erstwhile occupation, and now his tribe of old dears. He'd always understood that much of himself, but with Leonora his feelings went far beyond any protective instinct.

Given that, he didn't have much time. There was a very definite limit to his patience; there always had been.

Rapidly he mentally scanned all the arrangements he'd put in place in pursuit of Mountford, including those he'd initiated that evening after returning from Montrose Place.

For the moment, that line would hold. He could turn his attention to the other front on which he was engaged.

He had to convince Leonora to marry him; he had to change her mind.

How?

Ten minutes later he rose and went to seek his old dears. Information, he'd always maintained, was the key to any successful campaign.

The dinner with her aunts, a not-infrequent event in the weeks leading up to the Season when her aunt Mildred, Lady Warsingham, would come to try and convince Leonora to cast her hat into the matrimonial ring, was a near disaster.

A fact directly attributable to Trentham, even in his absence.

The next morning, Leonora was still having trouble subduing her blushes, still battling to keep her mind from dwelling on those moments when, panting and heated, she'd lain beneath him and watched him above her, moving in that deep, compulsive rhythm, her body accepting the surges of his, the rolling, relentless physical fusion.

She'd watched his face, seen passion strip away all his charm and leave the harsh angles and planes etched with something far more primitive.

Fascinating. Enthralling.

And utterly distracting.

She threw herself into sorting and rearranging every scrap of paper in her escritoire.

At twelve, the doorbell pealed. She heard Castor cross the hall and open the door. The next instant Mildred's voice rang out. "In the parlor, is she? Don't worry—I'll see myself in."

Leonora pushed her piles of papers into the escritoire, closed it, and rose. Wondering what had brought her aunt back to Montrose Place so soon, she faced the door and patiently waited to find out.

Mildred swept in, stylishly turned out in black and white. "Well, my dear!" She advanced on Leonora. "Here you sit, all by yourself. I wish you would consent to come with me on my visits, but I know you won't, so I won't bother bemoaning that."

Leonora dutifully kissed Mildred's scented cheek, and murmured her gratitude.

"Dreadful child." Mildred subsided onto the chaise and settled her skirts. "Now, I had to come because I have simply *wonderful* news! I have tickets for Mr. Kean's new play for this very evening. The theater is already sold out for weeks ahead—it's going to be the play of the Season. But by a fabulous stroke of magnanimous fate, a dear friend gave me tickets, and I have a spare. Gertie will come, of course. And you will come, too, won't you?" Mildred looked at her beseechingly. "You know Gertie will mutter all through the performance otherwise—she always behaves when you're there."

Gertie was her other aunt, Mildred's older, unmarried sister. Gertie had strong views about gentlemen, and while she refrained from voicing these in Leonora's presence, deeming her niece still too young and impressionable to hear such caustic truths, she had never spared her sister from her blistering observations, blessedly delivered *sotto voce.*

Sinking into the armchair opposite Mildred, Leonora hesitated. Visiting the theater with her aunt generally meant meeting at least two gentlemen Mildred had decided were eligible partis for her hand. But such a visit also meant watching a play, during which no one would dare talk. She would be free to lose herself in the performance. With luck, it might succeed in distracting her from Trentham and *his* performance.

And a chance to see the inimitable Edmund Kean was not to be lightly refused.

"Very well." She refocused on Mildred in time to see triumph fleetingly light her aunt's eyes. She narrowed her own. "But I refuse to be paraded like a well-bred mare during the interval."

Mildred dismissed the quibble with a wave. "If you wish, you may remain in your seat throughout the break. Now, you will wear your midnight blue silk, won't you? I know you care nothing for your appearance, so you may do it to please me."

The hopeful look in Mildred's eyes was impossible to deny; Leonora felt her lips curve. "As such a sought-after opportunity comes through you, I can hardly refuse." The midnight blue gown was one of her favorites, so appeasing her aunt cost her nothing. "But I warn you—I won't put up with any Bond Street beau whispering sweet nothings in my ear during the performance."

Mildred sighed. She shook her head as she rose. "When we were girls, having eligible gentlemen whisper in our ears was the highlight of the night." She glanced at Leonora. "I'm due at Lady Henry's, then Mrs. Arbuthnot's, so I must away. I'll call for you in the carriage around eight."

Leonora nodded her agreement, then saw her aunt to the door.

She returned to the parlor more pensive. Perhaps going out into the ton, at least for the few weeks before the Season proper commenced, might be wise.

Might distract her from the lingering effects of her seduction.

Might help her recover from the shock of Trentham offering to marry her. And the even greater shock of him insisting that she should.

She didn't understand his reasoning, but he'd seemed very set on it. A few weeks in society being exposed to other men would no doubt remind her why she'd never wed.

She suspected nothing. Not until the carriage drew up before the theater steps and a harried groom opened the door did the faintest glimmer of a suspicion cross her mind.

And by then it was too late.

Trentham stepped forward and calmly held out his hand to assist her from the carriage.

Jaw slack, she stared at him.

Mildred's elbow dug into her ribs; she started, then threw a swift, fulminating glance at her aunt before haughtily reaching out and placing her fingers in Trentham's palm.

She had no choice. Carriages were banking up; the steps of the theater hosting the most talked-about play was not the place to create a scene—to tell a gentleman what one thought of him and his machinations. To inform her aunt that this time she'd gone too far.

Cloaked in chilly hauteur, she allowed him to help her down, then stood, feigning icy indifference, idly surveying the fashionable hordes streaming up the theater steps and through the open doors while he greeted her aunts and assisted them to the pavement.

Mildred, resplendent in her favorite black and white, forcefully linked her arm in Gertie's and forged her way up the steps.

Coolly, Trentham turned to her and offered his arm.

She met his gaze, to her surprise saw no triumph in his hazel eyes, but rather a careful watchfulness. The sight mollified her somewhat;

she consented to lay the tips of her fingers on his sleeve and allow him to guide her in her aunts' wake.

Tristan considered the angle of Leonora's chin and preserved his silence. They joined her aunts in the foyer, where the crush had brought them to a standstill. He took the lead and with no great difficulty cleared a path to the stairs upward, drawing Leonora with him; her aunts followed close behind. Once on the stairs the press of bodies eased; covering Leonora's hand on his sleeve, he led his party up to the semicircular corridor leading to the boxes.

He glanced at Leonora as they neared the door of the box he'd hired. "I've heard that Mr. Kean is the best actor of the day, and tonight's play a worthy showcase for his talents. I thought you might enjoy it."

She met his eyes briefly, then inclined her head, still haughtily aloof. Reaching the box, he held aside the heavy curtain screening the doorway; she swept in, her head high. He waited for her aunts to pass him, then followed, allowing the curtain to fall closed behind him.

Lady Warsingham and her sister bustled to the front of the box and disposed themselves in two of the three seats along the front. Leonora had paused in the shadows by the wall; her narrowed gaze was fixed on Lady Warsingham, who was busy noting all the notables in the other boxes, exchanging nods, determinedly not looking Leonora's way.

He hesitated, then approached.

Her attention swung to him; her eyes flared. "How did you manage this?" She spoke in a hissed whisper. "I never told you she was my aunt."

He raised a brow. "I have my sources."

"And the tickets." She glanced out at the boxes, quickly filling with those lucky enough to have secured a place. "Your cousins told me you never go out in society."

"As you can see, that's not strictly true."

She glanced back at him, expecting more.

He met her gaze. "I've little use for society in general, but I'm not here to spend my evening with the ton."

She frowned, somewhat warily asked, "Why are you here then?"

He held her gaze for a heartbeat, then murmured, "To spend my evening with you."

A bell clanged in the corridor. He reached for her arm and guided her to the remaining chair at the front of the box. She threw him a skeptical glance, then sat. He drew the fourth chair around, set it to her left, angled toward her, and settled to watch the performance.

It was worth every penny of the small fortune he'd paid. His eyes rarely strayed to the stage; his gaze remained on Leonora's face, watching the emotions flitting across her features, delicate, pure; and, in this setting, unguarded. Although initially aware of him, Edmund Kean's magic quickly drew her in; he sat and watched, content, perceptive, intrigued.

He had no idea why she'd refused him—why, according to her, she had no interest in marriage at all. Her aunts, subjected to his most subtle interrogation, had been unable to shed any light on the matter, which meant he was going into this battle blind.

Not that that materially affected his strategy. As far as he'd ever heard, there was only one way to win a reluctant lady.

When the curtain came down at the end of the first act, Leonora sighed, then remembered where she was, and with whom. She glanced at Trentham, was unsurprised to find his gaze steady on her face.

She smiled. Coolly. "I'd very much like some refreshment."

His eyes held hers for a moment, then his lips curved and he inclined his head, accepting the commission. His gaze went past her and he rose.

Leonora swiveled and saw Gertie and Mildred on their feet, gathering their reticules and shawls.

Mildred beamed at her and Trentham; her gaze settled on his face. "We're off to parade in the corridor and meet everyone. Leonora hates to be subjected to the crush, but I'm sure we can rely on you to entertain her."

For the second time that evening, Leonora's jaw fell slack. Stunned, she watched her aunts bustle out, watched Trentham hold the heavy curtain aside for them to escape. Given her earlier insistence on avoiding the ritual parade, she could hardly complain, and there was nothing the least improper in her and Trentham remaining in the box alone; they were in public, under the gaze of any number of the ton's matrons.

He let the curtain fall and turned back to her.

She cleared her throat. "I really am quite parched . . ." Refreshments were available by the stairs; reaching the booth and returning would keep him occupied for a good portion of the interval.

His gaze rested on her face; his lips were lightly curved. A tap sounded by the doorway; Trentham turned and held the curtain aside. An attendant ducked past, carrying a tray with four glasses and a bottle of chilled champagne. He placed the tray on the small table against the back wall.

"I'll pour."

The attendant bowed to her, then Trentham, and disappeared through the curtain.

Leonora watched as Trentham eased the cork from the bottle, then poured the delicately fizzy liquid into two of the long flutes. She was suddenly very glad she'd worn her midnight blue gown—suitable armor for this type of situation.

Picking up both glasses, he crossed to where she still sat, swiveled on her chair so she sat sideways to the pit.

He handed her one glass. She reached for it, somewhat surprised that he made no move to use the moment, to touch her fingers with his. He released the glass, caught her gaze as she glanced up.

"Relax. I won't bite."

She arched a brow at him, sipped, then asked, "Are you sure?"

His lips quirked; he glanced out at the patrons milling in the other boxes. "These surrounds are hardly conducive."

He looked back at her, then reached for Gertie's chair, turned it so its back was to the throng, and sat, stretching his long legs out before him, elegantly at ease.

He sipped, his gaze on her face, then asked, "So tell me. Is Mr. Kean really as good as they say?"

She realized he would have no notion; he'd been away with the army for the last several years. "He's an artist without peer, at least at the moment." Deeming the topic a safe one, she related the highlights of Mr. Kean's career.

He put a question here and there. When the subject had run its course, he let a moment pass, then quietly said, "Speaking of performances . . ."

She met his eyes, and nearly choked on her champagne. Felt a slow blush rise to her cheeks. She ignored it, lifted her chin. Met his gaze directly. She was, she reminded herself, an experienced lady now. "Yes?"

He paused, as if considering not what to say but how to say it. "I wondered . . ." He raised his glass, sipped, his lashes screening his eyes. "How much of an actress are you?"

She blinked, let her frown show in her eyes, let her expression convey her incomprehension.

His lips quirked self-deprecatingly. His eyes returned to hers. "If I were to say you'd enjoyed our . . . last interlude, would I be wrong?"

Her blush intensified but she refused to look away. "No." Remembered pleasure flooded her, gave her strength to waspishly state, "You know perfectly well I enjoyed . . . all of it."

"So that didn't contribute to your aversion to marrying me?"

It suddenly occurred to her what he was asking. "Of course not." The idea he might think such a thing . . . she frowned. "I told you—my decision was reached long ago. My stance has nothing to do with you."

Could a man like him really need reassurance on such a point? She could tell nothing from his eyes, his expression.

Then he smiled, gently, yet the gesture was more predatory than charming. "I just wanted to be sure."

He hadn't resigned the battle to get her to accept him—*that* message she read with ease. Determinedly ignoring the effect of all that lounging masculinity mere feet away, she fixed him with a polite look and asked after his cousins. He replied, allowing the change of subject.

The audience started returning to their seats; Mildred and Gertie rejoined them. Leonora was aware of the sharp glances both her aunts cast her; she kept her expression calm and serene, and gave her attention to the stage. The curtain went up; the play recommenced.

To his credit, Trentham made no move to distract her. She was once again aware his gaze remained primarily on her, but refused to acknowledge the attention in any way. He couldn't force her to marry him; if she held to her refusal, he'd eventually go away.

Just as she'd imagined he would.

The notion of being proved right for once brought her no joy. Inwardly frowning at such a hint of susceptibility, she forced herself to concentrate on Edmund Kean.

When the curtain came down, tumultuous applause filled the theater; after Mr. Kean had taken countless bows, the audience, finally satisfied, turned to leave. Swept away by the drama, Leonora smiled easily and gave Trentham her hand, paused beside him as he lifted the curtain to allow Mildred and Gertie to pass out, then let him guide her in their wake.

The corridor was too crowded to allow any private conversation; the jostling crowd, however, gave plenty of scope for any gentleman wishing to tease a lady's senses. To her surprise, Trentham made no move to do so. She was highly conscious of him, large, solid, and strong beside her, protecting her from the pressure of shifting bodies. From his occasional glances, she knew he was aware of her, yet his attention remained focused on steering them efficiently through the throng and out into the street.

Their carriage drew up as they gained the pavement.

He handed Gertie and Mildred up, then turned to her.

Met her gaze. Lifted her hand from his sleeve.

Holding her gaze, he raised her fingers to his lips, kissed—the warmth of the lingering caress spread through her.

"I hope you enjoyed the evening."

She couldn't lie. "Thank you. I did."

He nodded and handed her up. His fingers slid from hers with only the faintest hint of reluctance.

She sat; he stepped back and closed the door. He signaled to the coachman. The carriage lurched, then rumbled off.

The impulse to sit forward and peer back out of the window to see if he stood watching nearly overcame her. Hands clasped in her lap, she stayed where she was and stared across the carriage.

He might have refrained from any illicit caress, any attempt to ruffle her senses, but she'd seen—experienced—enough to appreciate the reality behind his mask. He hadn't given up yet.

She told herself he would. Eventually.

Seated opposite, Mildred stirred. "Such polished manners—so masterful. You have to admit there are few gentlemen about these days who are so . . ." Lost for words, she gestured.

"Manly," Gertie supplied.

Both Leonora and Mildred looked at her in surprise. Mildred recovered first. "Indeed!" She nodded. "You're quite right. He behaved just as he ought."

Shaking free of the shock of hearing Gertie, the gentleman-hater, approve of any male—then again, this was Trentham, the charmer—she should have expected it—Leonora asked, "How did you meet him?"

Mildred shifted, settling her skirts. "He called this morning. Given you were already acquainted, accepting his invitation seemed perfectly sensible."

From Mildred's point of view. Leonora refrained from reminding her aunt that she'd said an old friend had given her the tickets; she'd long known what lengths Mildred would go to to get her into the presence of an eligible gentleman. And there was no doubt Trentham was eligible.

The thought brought him once more to mind—not as he'd been in the theater, but as he'd been in the golden moments they'd shared in the upstairs bedroom. Each moment, each touch, were imprinted on her memory; just the thought was enough to evoke again, not just the sensations but all the rest—all she'd felt.

She'd tried hard to keep the memories from her, not to think or dwell on the emotion that had filled her when she'd realized he intended drawing back from consummation—the emotion that had driven her to utter her plea.

Please . . . don't leave me.

The words haunted her, the memory alone enough to make her feel acutely vulnerable. Exposed.

Yet his response . . . despite all, regardless of what else she knew of him, how she judged his character, his machinations, she owed him for that.

For giving her all she'd wanted.

For being hers to command in that moment, for giving himself to her as she'd wished.

She let the memory slide from her; it was still too evocative to wrap herself in. Instead, she turned to the evening, considered all that had and hadn't been. Including the way she'd reacted to him, to his nearness. That had changed. No longer did her nerves leap and jump. Now, when he was close, when they touched, her nerves glowed. It was the only word she could find for the sensation, for the warm comfort it brought. Perhaps an echo of remembered pleasure. Regardless, far from being on edge, she'd felt comfortable. As if rolling naked together on a bed indulging in the act of intimacy had fundamentally changed her responses to him.

For the better, as she saw it. She no longer felt at such a disadvantage, no longer felt physically tense, keyed up in his presence. Curious, but true. Their time alone in the box had been comfortable, pleasant.

If she was honest, totally enjoyable despite his probing.

She sighed, and leaned back against the squabs. She could hardly upbraid Mildred with any sincerity. She'd enjoyed the evening far more, and in quite a different way, than she'd expected.

Ten

⊰⊚⌣⊚⊱

When he called to take her driving in the park the next morning, she was stunned. When she tried to refuse, he simply looked at her.

"You've already admitted you don't have any engagements."

Only because she'd thought he wanted to tell her about his investigations.

His hazel eyes remained fixed on hers. "You should tell me about the letters you sent to Cedric's acquaintances. You can tell me just as well in the park as here." His gaze sharpened. "Besides, you must be longing to get out in the fresh air. Today is not the sort of day to let slip by."

She narrowed her eyes at him; he was seriously dangerous. He was right, of course; the day was glorious, and she'd been toying with the idea of a brisk walk, but after her last excursion hesitated to go out alone.

He was too wise to press further, but simply waited . . . waited for capitulation as he was wont to do.

She pulled a face at him. "Very well. Wait while I get my pelisse."

He was waiting in the hall when she came down the stairs. As she walked by his side to the gate, she told herself she really should not allow this ease she felt with him to develop much further. Being with him was altogether too comfortable. Too pleasant.

The drive did nothing to break the spell. The breeze was fresh, tangy with the promise of spring; the sky was blue with wispy clouds that merely flirted with the sun. The warmth was a welcome relief from the chill winds that had blown until recently; the first swelling buds were visible on the branches beneath which Trentham steered his greys.

On such a day, the ladies of the ton were out and about, but the hour was still early, the Avenue not overly crowded. She nodded here and there to those of her aunts' acquaintances who recognized her, but largely gave her attention to the man beside her.

He drove with a light touch she knew enough to admire, and an unthinking confidence that told her more. She tried to keep her eyes off his hands, long fingers expertly managing the ribbons, and failed.

A moment later, she felt heat rise in her cheeks and forced her gaze away. "I sent the last letters off this morning. With luck someone will reply within a week."

Tristan nodded. "The more I think of it, the more likely it seems that whatever Mountford is after, it's something to do with your cousin Cedric's work."

Leonora glanced at him; wisps of her hair had come loose and flirted about her face. "How so?"

He looked to his horses—away from her mouth, her soft luscious lips. "It had to be something a purchaser would get with the house. If your uncle had been willing to sell, would you have cleared out Cedric's workshop?" He glanced at her. "I got the impression it had been forgotten, dismissed from everyone's minds. I hardly think that applies to anything in the library."

"True." She nodded, trying to tame her wayward locks. "I wouldn't have bothered going into the workshop if it hadn't been for Mountford's efforts. However, I think you're overlooking one point. If *I* was after something and had a reasonable idea where it might be, I might arrange to buy the house, not intending to complete the sale, you understand, and then ask to visit to measure up rooms for furnishings or remodeling." She shrugged. "Easy enough to get time to look around and perhaps remove things."

He considered, imagined, then reluctantly grimaced. "You're right. That leaves us with the possibility that it, whatever it is, could be just about anything secreted anywhere in the house." He glanced at her. "A house full of eccentrics."

She met his gaze, raised her brows, then tipped her nose in the air and looked away.

He called the next day and swept aside her reservations with invitations to a special preview of the latest exhibition at the Royal Academy.

She cast him a severe glance as he ushered her through the gallery doors. "Do all earls get such special privileges?"

He met her gaze. "Only special earls."

Her lips curved before she looked away.

He hadn't expected to gain all that much from the excursion, to his mind a minor exercise in his wider strategy. Instead, he found himself engrossed in a spirited discussion on the merits of landscapes over portraiture.

"People are so alive! They're what life's about."

"But the scenes are the essence of the country, of England—the people are a function of the place."

"Nonsense! Just look at this costermonger." She pointed to an excellent line drawing of a man with a barrow. "One glance and you'd know exactly where he came from—even what borough of London. The people personify the place—they're a representation of it, too."

They were in one of the smaller rooms in the labyrinthine gallery; from the corner of his eye, he saw the other group in the chamber move on through the door, leaving them alone.

Leaning on his arm, studying a busy river scene populated with half a regiment of dockworkers, Leonora hadn't noticed. Obedient to his tug, she strolled on to the next work—a plain and simple landscape.

She humphed, glanced back at the river scene, then up at him. "You can't expect me to believe you'd rather have an empty landscape than a picture of people."

He looked into her face. She stood close; her lips, her warmth, beckoned. Her hand lay trustingly on his arm.

Desire and more unexpectedly surfaced.

He didn't try to mask it, to screen it from his face or his eyes.

"People in general don't interest me." He met her gaze, let his voice deepen. "But there's one picture of you I'd like to see again, to experience again."

She held his gaze. A soft blush slowly rose in her cheeks, but she didn't look away. She knew exactly what image he was thinking of—of her naked and wanting beneath him. She drew a brief breath. "You shouldn't say that."

"Why not? It's the truth."

He felt her quiver.

"It's not going to happen—you won't see that picture again."

He studied her, felt both humble and amazed that she didn't see him for what he was—that she believed, not naively but with simple conviction, that if she stood firm, he wouldn't step beyond the bounds of honor and seize her.

She was wrong, but he valued her trust, treasured it too much to unnecessarily shake it.

So he raised a brow, smiled. "On that I fear we're unlikely to agree."

As he'd anticipated, she sniffed, put her nose in the air, and turned to the next work of art.

He let one day go by—a day he spent checking with his various contacts, all those whom he'd set the task of locating Montgomery Mountford—before returning to Montrose Place and inveigling Leonora to accompany him on a drive to Richmond. He'd done his forward planning; the Star and Garter was apparently the place to see and be seen.

It was the "be seen" aspect he required.

Leonora felt curiously lighthearted as she walked beneath the trees, her hand locked in Trentham's. Not precisely *de rigueur,* but when she'd pointed that out, he'd merely raised a brow and continued holding her hand.

Her mood was due to him; she couldn't imagine feeling this way with any other gentleman she'd known. She knew it was dangerous, that she would miss the unexpected closeness, the totally unanticipated sharing—the subtle thrill of walking beside a wolf—when he finally gave in and bade her adieu.

She didn't care. When the time came, she'd mope, but for now she was determined to grasp the moment, a fleeting interlude as spring bloomed. Not in her wildest dreams had she imagined such a state of ease could arise from intimacy, from one simple act of physical sharing.

There wouldn't be any repetition. Despite what she'd thought, he hadn't intended it to happen in the first place, and no matter what he said, he wouldn't precipitate another encounter against her wishes. Now that she knew he felt honor-bound to marry her, she knew better than to lie with him again. She wasn't such a fool as to tempt fate further.

No matter how she felt when with him.

No matter how much fate tempted her.

She slanted him a glance.

He caught it, raised a brow. "A penny for your thoughts."

She laughed, shook her head. "My thoughts are much too precious." *Much* too dangerous.

"What are they worth?"

"More than you can possibly pay."

When he didn't immediately reply, she glanced at him.

He met her gaze. "Are you sure?"

She was about to dismiss the question with a laugh, then she read his true meaning in his eyes. Realized on a rush of understanding that, as so often seemed to occur, his thoughts and hers were very much in tune. That he knew what she'd been thinking—and quite literally meant he'd pay anything she asked . . .

It was all there in his eyes, engraved in crystalline hazel, sharp and clear. He rarely adopted his mask with her now, not when they were private.

Their steps had slowed; they halted. She dragged in a tight breath. "Yes." Regardless of the price he was prepared to pay, she couldn't—wouldn't—accept.

They stood facing each other while a long moment passed. It should have turned awkward, but, as in the gallery, a deeper under-standing—an acceptance each of the other—prevented it.

Eventually, he simply said, "We'll see."

She smiled, easily, companionably, and they resumed their walk.

After inspecting the deer and ambling under the oaks and beeches, they returned to his curricle and repaired to the Star and Garter.

"I haven't been here for years," she admitted as she took her seat at a table by the window. "Not since the year I came out."

She waited while he ordered tea and crumpets, then said, "I have to admit I have difficulty seeing you as a young man on the town."

"Probably because I never was one." He settled back, held her gaze. "I went into the Guards at twenty, more or less straight from Oxford." He shrugged. "It was the accepted route in my branch of the family—we were the military arm."

"So where were you stationed? You must have attended balls in the nearest town?"

He kept her entertained with tales of his exploits, and that of his peers, then turned the table and drew out her memories of her first Sea-son. She had enough she could say to make a decent showing; if he realized her accounts were edited, he gave no sign.

They'd moved on to her observations of the ton and its present inhabitants when a party at a nearby table, all standing to leave, tipped over a chair. She glanced around—and realized, from the fixed stares of the three girls and their mother that the reason for the commotion was that all attention had been locked on them.

The mother, an overdressed matron, cast a supercilious, purse-lipped glance their way, then moved to gather her chicks. "Come, girls!"

Two moved to obey; the third stared for a moment longer, then turned and hissed, her whisper clearly audible, "Did Lady Mott say when the wedding would be?"

Leonora continued to stare at the retreating backs. Her wits were tumbling, shooting off in all directions; as scene after scene replayed in her mind, she felt chilled, then overheated. Temper—an eruption more powerful than any she'd known—overtook her. Slowly, she turned her head, and met Trentham's gaze.

Read in the hard hazel not an ounce of contrition, not even a hint of exculpation, but simple, clear, and unequivocal confirmation.

"You *fiend.*" She breathed the word. Her fingers tightened on the handle of her teacup.

His eyes didn't so much as flicker. "I wouldn't advise it."

He hadn't shifted from his lounging pose, but she knew how fast he could move.

She suddenly felt dizzy, giddy; she couldn't breathe. She pushed up out of her chair. "Let me out of here."

Her voice wavered but he acted; she was dimly aware that he was watching her closely. He got her outside, swept aside all hurdles; she was too overwrought to stand on pride and not take advantage of the escape he arranged.

But the instant her half boots touched the grass in the park, she jerked her hand from his arm and strode out. Away from him. Away from the temptation of hitting him—trying to hit him; she knew he wouldn't let her.

Gall burned her throat; she'd thought him out of his depth in the ton, but it was she who had had her eyes closed. Lulled into doe-eyed trust by a wolf—who hadn't even bothered to wear wool!

She gritted her teeth against a scream, one directed against herself. She'd known what he was like from the first—a remarkably ruthless man.

Abruptly, she came to a halt. Panic would get her nowhere, especially with a man like him. She had to think, had to act—in the right way.

So what had he done? What had he actually accomplished? And how could she negate or reverse it?

She stood still as her wits slowly realigned. A measure of calm descended; it wasn't—couldn't be—as bad as she'd thought.

She spun around and wasn't the least surprised to discover him two feet away, watching her.

Carefully.

She locked her eyes on his. "Have you said anything to anyone about us?"

His gaze didn't waver. "No."

"So that girl was simply . . ." She gestured with both hands.

"Extrapolating."

She narrowed her eyes. "As you knew everyone would."

He didn't reply.

She continued to look daggers at him as the realization that all was not lost—that he hadn't created a social snare she couldn't simply step out of—seeped through her. Her temper subsided; her annoyance did not. "This is not a game."

A moment went by before he said, "All life is a game."

"And you play to win?" She infused the words with something close to contempt.

He stirred, then reached out, took her hand.

To her utter surprise, he jerked her to him.

She gasped as she landed against his chest.

Felt his arm lock her to him.

Felt smoldering embers burst into flame.

He looked down at her, then carried the hand he'd trapped to his lips. Slowly brushed his lips to her fingers, then across her palm, lastly pressed them to her wrist. Holding her gaze, holding her captive all the while.

His eyes burned, reflecting all she could sense flaring between them.

"What's between you and me remains between you and me, but it hasn't gone away." He held her gaze. "And it won't."

He lowered his head. She dragged in a breath. "But I don't want it."

From under his lashes, his eyes met hers, then he murmured, "Too late."

And kissed her.

She'd called him a fiend, and she'd been right.

By noon the next day, Leonora knew what it felt like to be under siege.

When Trentham—damn his arrogant hide—had finally consented to release her, she'd been left in no doubt whatsoever that they were locked in combat.

"I am not going to marry you." She'd made the declaration with as much strength as she'd been able to muster, in the circumstances not as much as she'd have liked.

He'd looked at her, growled—actually growled—then grabbed her hand and marched off to his curricle.

On the way home, she'd preserved a frigid silence, not because various pithy phrases hadn't been burning her tongue, but because of his tiger, perched behind them. She'd had to wait until Trentham handed her to the pavement before Number 14 to fix him with a narrow-eyed glare, and demand, "Why? Why me? Give me one sane reason why you want to marry me."

Hazel eyes glinting, he'd looked down at her, then bent closer and murmured, "Do you remember that picture we spoke of?"

She'd quelled a sudden urge to step back. Searched his eyes briefly before asking, "What of it?"

"The prospect of seeing it every morning and every night constitutes an eminently sane reason to me."

She'd blinked; a blush had risen to her cheeks. For an instant, she'd stared at him, her stomach clenching tight, then she'd stepped back. "You're crazed."

She'd spun on her heel, pushed open the front gate, and stalked up the garden path.

The invitations had started arriving with the first post that morning.

One or two she could have ignored; fifteen by lunchtime, and all from the most powerful hostesses, were simply impossible to dismiss. How he had managed it she didn't know, but his message was clear—she could not avoid him. Either she met him on neutral ground, meaning within the social round of the ton, or . . .

That implied "or" was seriously worrisome.

He was not a man she could easily predict; her failure to foresee his objectives to date was what had got her into this mess in the first place.

"Or . . ." sounded far too dangerous, and when it came down to it, no matter what he did, as long as she adhered to the simple word "No" she would be perfectly safe, perfectly secure.

Mildred, with Gertie in tow, arrived at four o'clock.

"My dear!" Mildred sailed into the parlor like a black-and-white galleon. "Lady Holland called and insisted I bring you to her soirée this evening." Subsiding with a silken swish onto the chaise, Mildred turned eyes filled with zeal upon her. "I had no idea Trentham had such connections."

Leonora suppressed a growl of her own. "Nor had I." Lady Holland, for heaven's sake! "The man's a fiend!"

Mildred blinked. "Fiend?"

She resumed her activity—pacing before the hearth. "He's doing this to"—she gestured wildly—"flush me out!"

"Flush you . . ." Mildred looked concerned. "My dear, are you feeling quite the thing?"

Turning, she looked at Mildred, then switched her gaze to Gertie, who had paused before an armchair.

Gertie met her eyes, then nodded. "Very likely." She lowered herself into the chair. "Ruthless. Dictatorial. Not one to let anything stand in his way."

"Exactly!" The relief of having found someone who understood was great.

"Still," Gertie continued, "you do have a choice."

"Choice?" Mildred looked from one to the other. "I do hope you're not going to encourage her to fly in the face of this unlooked-for development?"

"As to that," Gertie responded, entirely unmoved, "she'll do as she pleases—she always has. But the real question here is, is she going to let him dictate to her, or is she going to make a stand?"

"Stand?" Leonora frowned. "You mean ignore all these invitations?" Even she found the thought a trifle extreme.

Gertie snorted. "Of course not! Do that, and you'll dig your own grave. But there's no reason to let him get away with thinking he can force you into anything. As I see it, the most telling response would be to accept the most sought-after invitations with delight, and attend with the clear aim of enjoying yourself. Go and meet him in the ballrooms and if he dares press you there, you can give him his congé with half the ton looking on."

She thumped her cane. "Mark my words, you need to teach him he's not omnipotent, that he won't get his way by such machinations." Gertie's old eyes gleamed. "Best way to do that is to give him what he thinks he wants, then show him that it isn't what he really wants at all."

The look on Gertie's face was unashamedly wicked; the thought it evoked in Leonora's mind was definitely attractive.

"I take your point . . ." She stared into the distance, her mind juggling possibilities. "Give him what he's angled for, but . . ." Refocusing on Gertie, she beamed. "Of course!"

The number of invitations had grown to nineteen; she felt almost giddy with defiance.

She swung to Mildred; she'd been watching Gertie, a rather bemused expression on her face. "Before Lady Holland's, perhaps we should attend the Carstairs's rout?"

They did; Leonora used the event as a refresher to dust off and buff up her social skills. By the time she walked into Lady Holland's elegant rooms, her confidence was riding high. She knew she looked well in her deep topaz silk, her hair piled high, topaz drops in her ears, pearls looped about her throat.

Following in Mildred's and Gertie's wake, she curtsied before

Lady Holland, who shook her hand and uttered the usual pleasantries, all the while observing her through shrewd and intelligent eyes.

"I understand you've made a conquest," her ladyship remarked.

Leonora raised her brows lightly, let her lips curve. "Entirely unintentionally, I assure you."

Lady Holland's eyes widened; she looked intrigued.

Leonora let her smile deepen; head high, she glided on.

From where he'd retreated to lounge against the drawing-room wall, Tristan watched the exchange, saw Lady Holland's surprise, caught the amused glance she shot him as Leonora moved into the crowd.

He ignored it, fixed his gaze on his quarry, and pushed away from the wall.

He'd arrived unfashionably early, uncaring that her ladyship, who had always taken an interest in his career, would correctly guess his reasons. The past two hours had been ones of inaction, of unutterable boredom, reminding him why he'd never felt he'd missed anything in joining the army at twenty. Now Leonora had consented to arrive, he could get on with things.

The invitations he'd arranged through his own offices and those of his town-bound old dears would ensure that for the next week he'd be able to come up with her every night, somewhere in the ton.

Somewhere conducive to furthering his goal.

Beyond that, even if the damn woman still held firm, society being what it was, the invitations would continue of their own accord, creating opportunities for him to exploit until she surrendered.

He had her in his sights; she wouldn't escape.

Closing the distance between them, he came up alongside her as her aunts sank onto a chaise by one side of the room. His appearance preempted a number of other gentlemen who had noticed Leonora and thought to test the waters.

He'd discovered that Lady Warsingham was by no means unknown within the ton; nor was her niece. The prevailing view of Leonora was that she was a willful lady stubbornly and intractably opposed to marriage. Although her age placed her beyond the ranks of the marriageable misses, her beauty, assurance, and behavior cast her in the light of a challenge, at least in the eyes of men who viewed challenging ladies with interest.

Such gentlemen would no doubt take note of *his* interest and look elsewhere. If they were wise.

He bowed to the older ladies, both of whom beamed at him.

He turned to Leonora and encountered an arch and distinctly chilly glance. "Miss Carling.

She gave him her hand and curtsied. He bowed, raised her, and set her hand on his sleeve.

Only to have her lift it off and turn to greet a couple who'd strolled up.

"Leonora! I declare we haven't seen you for an age!"

"Good evening, Daphne. Mr. Merryweather." Leonora touched cheeks with the brown-haired Daphne, a lady of bounteous charms, then shook hands with the gentleman whose coloring and features proclaimed him Daphne's brother.

She shot Tristan a glance, then smoothly included him, introducing him as the Earl of Trentham.

"I say!" Merryweather's eyes lit. "I heard you were in the Guards at Waterloo."

"Indeed." He uttered the word as repressively as he could, but Merryweather failed to take the hint. He babbled on with the usual questions; inwardly sighing, Tristan gave his practiced answers.

Leonora, more attuned to his tones, shot him a curious glance, but then Daphne claimed her attention.

His hearing acute, Tristan quickly realized the tenor of Daphne's inquiries. She assumed Leonora had no interest in him; although married, it was clear Daphne did.

From the corner of his eye, he saw Leonora cast him an assessing glance, then she leaned closer to Daphne, lowered her voice . . .

He suddenly saw the danger.

Reaching out, he very deliberately closed his fingers about Leonora's wrist. Smiling charmingly at Merryweather, he shifted, including Daphne in the gesture as, entirely unsubtly, he drew Leonora to him—away from Daphne—and linked her arm with his. "I do hope you'll excuse us—I've just sighted my erstwhile commander. I really should pay my respects."

Both Merryweather and Daphne smiled and murmured easy farewells; before Leonora could gather her wits, he inclined his head and drew her away, into the crowd.

Her feet moved; her gaze was locked on his face. Then she looked ahead. "That was rude. You're not a serving officer—there's no reason you need make your bow to your ex-commander."

"Indeed. Especially as he's not present."

She shot him a narrowed-eyed look. "Not just a fiend but a lying fiend."

"Speaking of fiendish, I think we should set some rules for this engagement. For however long we spend fencing within the ton—a length of time entirely in your control, I might add—you will refrain from setting any harpies such as the lovely Daphne on me."

"But why are you here if not to sample and select among the fruits of the ton?" She gestured about them. "It's what all tonnish gentleman do."

"God knows why—I don't. I, as you very well know, am here for only one purpose—in pursuit of you."

He paused to lift two glasses of champagne from a footman's tray. Handing one to Leonora, he guided her to a less congested area before a long window. Positioning himself so he could keep the room in view, he sipped, then continued, "You may play the game between us in any way you like, but if you possess any self-preservatory instincts at all, you will keep the game between us and not involve any others." He lowered his gaze, met her eyes. "Female, or male."

She considered him; her brows lightly rose. "Is that a threat?" She calmly sipped, apparently unperturbed.

He studied her eyes, serene and untroubled. Confident.

"No." Raising his glass, he clinked the edge to hers. "That's a promise."

He drank and watched her eyes flare.

But she had her temper firmly in hand. She forced herself to sip, to appear to be surveying the crowd, then lowered her glass. "You can't simply come along and take me over."

"I don't want to take you over. I want you in my bed."

That earned him a faintly scandalized glance, but no one else was near enough to hear.

Her blush subsiding, she held his gaze. "That is something you can't have."

He let the moment stretch, then raised a brow at her. "We'll see."

She studied his face, then raised her glass. Her gaze went past him.

"Miss Carling! By Jove! A delight to see you—why it must be years."

Leonora smiled, and held out her hand. "Lord Montacute. A pleasure—and yes, it has been years. Can I make you known to Lord Trentham?"

"Indeed! Indeed!" His lordship, ever genial, shook hands. "Knew your father—and your great-uncle, too, come to that. Irascible old blighter."

"As you say."

Remembering her aim, Leonora brightly asked, "Is Lady Montacute here tonight?"

His lordship waved vaguely. "Somewhere about."

She kept the conversation rolling, foiling all Trentham's attempts to dampen it—dampening Lord Montacute was beyond even Trentham's abilities. Simultaneously, she scanned the crowd for further opportunities.

It was pleasing to discover she hadn't lost the knack of summoning a gentleman with just a smile. In short order, she'd collected a select group, all of whom could hold their own conversationally. Lady Holland's gatherings were renowned for their wit and repartee; with a gentle prod here, a verbal poke there, she started the ball rolling—after that, their discourses took on a life of their own.

She had to suppress a too-revealing smile when Trentham, despite himself, was drawn in, becoming engaged with Mr. Hunt in a discussion of suppression orders as pertaining to the popular press. She stood by his side and presided over the group, ensuring the talk never flagged. Lady Holland drifted up, paused beside her, then nodded and met her eye.

"You have quite a talent, my dear." She patted Leonora's arm, her gaze sliding briefly to Trentham, then archly back to Leonora before she moved on.

A talent for what? Leonora wondered. Keeping a wolf at bay?

Guests had started leaving before the discussions waned. The group broke up reluctantly, the gentlemen drifting off to find their wives.

When she and Trentham once more stood alone, he looked at her. His lips slowly set, his eyes hardened, glinted.

She arched a brow, then turned toward where Mildred and Gertie stood waiting. "Don't be a hypocrite—you enjoyed it."

She wasn't sure, but she thought he growled. She didn't need to look to know he prowled at her heels as she crossed the room to her aunts.

He behaved, if not with joyous charm, then at least with perfect civility, escorting them down the stairs and out to their waiting carriage.

Tristan handed her aunts up, then turned to her. Deliberately stepping between her and the carriage, he took her hand, met her eyes.

"Don't think to repeat that exercise tomorrow."

He shifted and handed her to the carriage door.

One foot on the step, she met his gaze, and arched a brow. Even in the dimness, he recognized the challenge.

"You chose the field—I get to choose the weapons."

She inclined her head serenely, then ducked and entered the carriage.

He closed the door with care—and a certain deliberation.

Eleven

Over breakfast the next morning, Leonora considered her social calendar; the evenings were now much fuller than they had been three days ago.

"You choose," Mildred had told her as she'd descended from the carriage last night.

Munching her toast, Leonora weighed the possibilities. Although the Season proper was some weeks distant, there were two balls that evening to which they'd been invited. The major event was the ball at Colchester House in Mayfair, the more minor and assuredly less formal, a ball at the Masseys' house in Chelsea.

Trentham would expect her to attend the Colchester affair; he'd wait for her to appear there, as he had last night at Lady Holland's.

Pushing away from the table, Leonora rose and headed for the parlor to dash off a note to Mildred and Gertie that she fancied visiting the Masseys that evening.

Sitting at her escritoire, she wrote the brief note, inscribed her aunts' names, then rang for a footman. It was her hope that, in this instance, absence would make the heart grow *less* fond; quite aside from the fact her nonappearance at Colchester House would annoy Trentham, there was also the definite possibility that, if left alone in such an arena, he might find his eye drawn to some other lady, perhaps even become distracted with one of Daphne's ilk . . .

Inwardly frowning, she looked up as the footman entered, and handed over the note for delivery.

That done, she sat back and determinedly turned her mind to more serious matters. Given her stubborn refusal of his suit, she was perhaps naive in thinking Trentham would continue to aid her in the matter of

Montgomery Mountford, yet when she tried to imagine him losing interest, removing the men he had watching the house, she couldn't. Regardless of their personal interactions, she knew he wouldn't leave her to deal with Mountford alone.

Indeed, in light of what she'd learned of his character, the notion seemed laughable.

They would remain in undeclared partnership until the riddle of Mountford was solved; it therefore behooved her to push as hard as she could on that front. Keeping clear of Trentham's snares while dealing with him on a daily basis would not be easy; prolonging the danger was senseless.

She couldn't expect any answers to her letters for at least a few days more. So what else could she do?

Trentham's suggestion that Cedric's work was most likely Mountford's target had struck a chord. Besides Cedric's letters, the workshop had contained more than twenty ledgers and journals. She'd brought them up to the parlor and stacked them in a corner. Eyeing them, she recalled her late cousin's fine, faded, cramped writing.

Rising, she went upstairs and inspected Cedric's bedroom. It was inches deep in dust and strewn with cobwebs. She set the maids the task of cleaning the room; she'd search it tomorrow. For today . . . she descended to the parlor and settled to work through the journals.

By the time evening arrived, she'd uncovered nothing more exciting than the recipe for a concoction to remove stains from porcelain; it was difficult to believe Mountford and his mysterious foreigner were interested in that. Setting aside the ledgers, she went upstairs to change.

The Masseys' house was centuries old, a rambling villa built on the riverbank. The ceilings were lower than now fashionable; there was a wealth of dark wood in beams and paneling, but the shadows were dispersed by lamps, candelabra, and sconces liberally scattered through the rooms. The large interconnecting chambers were perfect for less formal entertaining. A small orchestra scraped away at the river end of the dining room, for the occasion converted into an area for dancing.

After greeting their hostess in the hall, Leonora entered the drawing room, telling herself she'd enjoy herself. That the boredom caused by lack of purpose that customarily afflicted her would not affect her tonight because she did indeed have a purpose.

Unfortunately, enjoying herself with other gentlemen if Trentham was not there to see . . . it was difficult to convince herself there was all that much to be gained from the evening. Nevertheless, she was there, gowned in silk of a deep turbulent blue no young unmarried lady could ever wear. As she didn't particularly want to chat, she might as well dance.

Leaving Mildred and Gertie with a group of their cronies, she made her way down the room, stopping to exchange greetings here and there, but always moving on. A dance had just ended when she stepped through the doors into the dining room; quickly scanning those present, she considered which of the gentlemen—

Hard fingers, a hard palm, closed about her hand; her senses reacted, informing her who stood at her shoulder even before she turned and met his gaze.

"Good evening." His eyes on hers, Trentham raised her hand to his lips. Searched her eyes. Raised a brow. "Would you care to dance?"

The look in his eyes, the tenor of his voice—just like that, he made her come alive. Made her nerves tighten, her senses sing. Sent a rush of pleasurable anticipation sliding through her. She drew breath, her imagination eagerly supplying what dancing with him would feel like. "I . . ." She looked away, across the sea of dancers waiting for the next measure to begin.

He said nothing, simply waited. When she glanced back at him, he met her gaze. "Yes?"

His hazel eyes were sharp, watchful; behind them lurked faint amusement.

She felt her lips set, lifted her chin. "Indeed—why not?"

He smiled, not his charming smile but in predatory appreciation of her meeting his challenge. He led her forward as the opening strains of a waltz began.

It would have to be a waltz. The instant he drew her into his arms, she knew she was in trouble. Valiantly battling to dampen her response to having him so near, to feeling his strength engulf her again, his hand spread over the silk at her back, she cast about for distraction.

Let a frown form in her eyes. "I thought you would attend the Colchesters' affair."

The ends of his lips lifted. "I knew you'd be here." His eyes quizzed her—wicked, dangerous. "Believe me, I'm perfectly content with your choice."

If she'd harbored any doubt as to what he was alluding, the turn at the end of the room explained all. If they'd been at the Colchesters, waltzing in their huge ballroom, he wouldn't have been able to hold her so close, to curl his fingers so possessively about her hand, to draw her so tight through the turn their hips brushed. Here, the dance floor was crowded with other couples all absorbed with each other, immersed in the moment. There were no matrons lining the walls, watching, waiting to disapprove.

His thigh parted hers, all restrained power as he swung her through the turn; she couldn't suppress a reactive shiver—couldn't stop her nerves, her whole body responding.

Tristan watched her face, wondered if she had any idea of just how responsive she was, of what seeing her eyes flare, then darken, seeing her lashes sweep down, her lips part, did to him.

He knew she didn't know.

That only made it worse, only heightened the effect, and left him in even greater pain.

The insistent ache had been escalating over the past days, a nagging aggravation he'd never before had to contend with. Before, the itch had been a simple one to scratch. This time . . .

His every sense was focused on her, on the sway of her supple body in his arms, on the promise of her warmth, the elusive, teasing torment of the passion she seemed intent on denying.

That last was something he wouldn't permit. Shouldn't permit.

The music ended, and he was forced to halt, forced to release her, something he did reluctantly, a fact her wide eyes said she realized.

She cleared her throat, smoothed her gown. "Thank you." She looked around. "Now—"

"Before you waste time planning anything else—like attracting another gentleman to dance with you—while I'm with you, you'll dance with no one else."

Leonora turned to face him. "I beg your pardon?"

She honestly couldn't believe her ears.

His eyes remained hard. He raised a brow. "Do you want me to repeat it?"

"No! I want to forget I ever heard such an outrageous piece of impertinence."

He seemed totally unaffected by her increasing ire. "That would be unwise."

She felt her temper rise; they'd kept their voices low, but there was no doubt which way the discussion was heading. Drawing herself up, drawing every ounce of haughtiness she possessed about her, she inclined her head. "If you'll excuse me—"

"No." Steely fingers closed about her elbow; he nodded across the room. "See that door over there? We're going to go through it."

She drew in a huge breath, held it. Carefully enunciated, "I realize your experience of the *ton*—"

"The *ton* bores me to death." He glanced down at her, started unobtrusively but effectively steering her toward the closed door. "I'm therefore unlikely to pay much attention to its strictures."

Her heart was thumping. Looking into his eyes—hard, faceted hazel—she realized she wasn't playing with just a wolf, but a *wild* wolf. One who didn't acknowledge any rules beyond his own. "You *cannot* simply . . ."

Abduct me. Ravish me.

The intent in his eyes left her breathless.

His gaze remained on her face, gauging, judging, as he expertly herded her across the crowded room. "I suggest we repair to a place where we can discuss our relationship in private."

She'd been private with him any number of times; there was no need for her senses to leap at the word. No need for her imagination to run riot. Irritated that it had, she made a firm bid to take charge again. Lifting her head, she nodded. "Very well. I agree. Clearly we need to address our differing views and set matters straight."

She wasn't going to marry him; that was the point he needed to accept. If she emphasized that fact, clung to it, she'd be safe.

They reached the door and he opened it; she stepped through into a corridor running alongside the reception rooms. The passage was wide enough for two to walk abreast; one side was lined with carved paneling in which doors were set, the other was a wall of windows looking out over the private gardens.

In late spring and summer the windows would be opened and the corridor would become a delightful venue in which guests could stroll. Tonight, with a raw wind blowing and the promise of frost in the air, all the doors and windows were closed, the passage deserted.

Moonlight streamed in providing light enough to see. The walls were stone, the doors solid oak. Once Trentham shut the door behind them they stood in a silvered, private world.

He released her arm, offered his; she pretended not to notice. Head high, she paced slowly along. "The pertinent point we need to address—"

She broke off when his hand closed about hers. Possessively. She halted, looked down at her fingers swallowed in his palm.

"That," she said, her gaze fixed on the sight, "is a perfect example of the issue we need to discuss. You cannot go around grabbing my hand, seizing me as if I in some way belonged to you—"

"You do."

She looked up. Blinked. "I beg your pardon?"

Tristan looked into her eyes; he wasn't averse to explaining. "You. Belong. To me." It felt good to state it, reinforcing the reality.

Her eyes widened; he continued, "Regardless of what you imagined you were doing, you gave yourself to me. *Offered* yourself to me. I accepted. Now you're mine."

Her lips thinned; her eyes flashed. "That is not what happened. You're deliberately—God alone knows why—misconstruing the incident."

She said nothing more but glared up at him belligerently.

"You're going to have to work a lot harder to convince me that having you naked beneath me on the bed in Montrose Place was a figment of my imagination."

Her jaw firmed. "*Misconstruing*—not imagining."

"Ah—so you admit that you did, indeed—"

"What *happened,*" she snapped, "as you very well know, is that we enjoyed"—she gestured—"a pleasant interlude."

"As I recall, you begged me to . . . 'initiate you' was, I believe, the term we agreed on."

Even in the poor light, he could see her blush. But she nodded. "Just so."

Turning, she walked along the corridor; he kept pace beside her, her hand still locked in his.

She didn't immediately speak, then she drew in a deep breath. He realized he was going to get at least part of an explanation.

"You have to understand—and accept—that I don't wish to marry. Not you, not anyone. I have no interest in the state. What happened between us . . ." She lifted her head, looked down the long corridor. "That was purely because I wanted to know. To experience . . ." She looked down, walked on. "And I thought you were a sensible choice to be my teacher."

He waited, then prompted, his tone even, nonaggressive, "Why did you think that?"

She waved between them, slipping her hand from his to do so. "The attraction. It was obvious. It was simply there—you know it was."

"Yes." He was starting to see . . . he halted.

She stopped, too, and faced him. Met his gaze, searched his face. "So you do understand, don't you? It was just so I would know . . . that's all. Just once."

Very carefully, he asked, "Done. Finished. Over?"

She lifted her head. Nodded. "Yes."

He held her gaze for a long moment, then murmured, "I did warn you, on the bed at Montrose Place, that you'd miscalculated."

Her head rose another notch, but she evenly stated, "That was when you felt you had to marry me."

"I *know* I have to marry you, but that isn't my point."

Exasperation flared in her eyes. "What is your point?"

He could feel a grim, definitely cynical, totally self-deprecatory smile fighting for expression; he kept it from his face, kept his features impassive. "That attraction you mentioned. Has it died?"

She frowned. "No. But it will—you know it will. . . ." She stopped because he was shaking his head.

"I know no such thing."

Wary irritation crept into her face. "I accept that it hasn't faded *yet,* but you know perfectly well gentlemen do not remain attracted to women for long. In a few weeks, once we've identified Mountford and you'll no longer be meeting me on a daily basis, you'll forget me."

He let the moment stretch while assessing his options. Eventually asked, "And if I don't?"

Her eyes narrowed. She opened her lips to reiterate that he would.

He cut her off by stepping nearer, closer, crowding her against the windows.

Immediately, heat bloomed between them, beckoning, enticing. Her eyes flared, her breathing caught, then continued more rapidly. Her hands rose, fluttered to rest lightly against his chest; her lashes lowered as he leaned closer.

"Our *mutual* attraction hasn't faded in the least—it's grown stronger." He breathed the words along her cheek. He wasn't touching her, holding her, other than with his nearness. "You say it'll fade—I say it won't. I'm sure I'm right—you're sure you are. You want to address the matter—I'm willing to be party to an agreement."

Leonora felt giddy. His words were dark, forceful, black magic in her mind. His lips touched, butterfly light, to her temple; his breath fanned her cheek. She dragged in a tight breath. "What agreement?"

"If the attraction fades, I'll agree to release you. Until it does, you're mine."

A shiver slithered down her spine. "Yours. What do you mean by that?"

She felt his lips curve against her cheek.

"Exactly what you're thinking. We've been lovers—are lovers." His lips drifted lower to caress her jaw. "We remain so while the attraction lasts. If it continues, as I'm sure it will, beyond a month, we marry."

"A month?" His nearness was sapping her wits, leaving her dizzy.

"I'm willing to indulge you for a month, no more."

She struggled to concentrate. "And if the attraction fades—even if it doesn't completely die but *fades* within a month, you'll agree that a marriage between us is not justified?"

He nodded. "Just so."

His lips cruised over hers; her unruly senses leapt.

"Do you agree?"

She hesitated. She'd come out here to address what lay between them; what he was suggesting seemed a reasonable way forward . . . she nodded. "Yes."

And his lips came down on hers.

She mentally sighed with pleasure, felt her senses unfurl like petals under the sun, wallowing, glorying, absorbing the delight. Savoring the urge—their mutual attraction.

It would fade—she knew it, absolutely beyond doubt. It might be waxing stronger at the moment simply because, at least for her, it was so new, yet ultimately, inevitably, its power would wane.

Until then . . . she could learn more, understand more. Explore further. At least a little bit further. Sliding her hands up, she wound her arms about his neck and kissed him back, parted her lips for him, surrendered her mouth, felt the addictive warmth blossom between them when he accepted the invitation.

He shifted closer, pinning her against the window; one hard hand closed about her waist, holding her steady while their mouths melded, while their tongues dueled and tangled, caressed, explored, claimed anew.

Hunger flared.

She felt it in him—a telltale hardening of his muscles, self-restraint imposed, desire harnessed—and felt her own response, a rising tide of heated longing that welled and washed through her. That had her pressing closer, sliding a hand to trace his jaw, tempting him to deepen the kiss.

He did, and for a moment the world fell away.

Flames flared, roared.

Abruptly he drew back. Broke the kiss enough to murmur against her lips, "We need to find a bedchamber."

She was giddy, wits whirling. She tried, but couldn't concentrate. "Why?"

His lips returned to hers, taking, needing, giving. He drew away, his breathing not quite steady. "Because I want to fill you—and you want me to. It's too dangerous here."

The gravelly words shocked her, thrilled her. Shook a few of her wits into place. Enough so she could think beyond the heat coursing her veins, the pounding in her blood.

Enough to realize.

It was too dangerous anywhere!

Not because he was wrong, but because he was absolutely right.

Just hearing him say the words had escalated her need, deepened that heated longing, the emptiness she knew he could and would fill. She wanted, desperately, to know again the pleasure of having him join with her.

She pulled out of his arms. "No—we can't."

He looked at her. Blinked dazedly. "Yes, we can." The words were uttered with simple conviction, as if he was assuring her they could walk in the park.

She stared at him. Realized she had no hope of arguing convincingly against it; she'd never been a good liar.

Before he could seize her wrist—as he usually did—and haul her off to a bed, she whirled and fled.

Down the corridor. She sensed him behind her; swerved and flung open one of the many doors. Rushed through.

Her mouth fell open in a silent O. She stopped, teetering on her toes just inside a large linen press. They were alongside the dining room; tablecloths and napkins were neatly stacked on shelves on either side. At the end of the tiny chamber, filling the gap between the shelves, was a bench for folding.

Before she could turn, she felt Trentham behind her. Filling the doorway, blocking her escape.

"Excellent choice." His voice purred, deep and dark. His hand curved around her bottom; he pushed her forward, stepping in behind her.

Shutting the door.

She swung around.

Tristan swept her into his arms, brought his lips down on hers, and let his reins loose. Kissed her witless, let desire rule, let the pent-up passions of the last week pour through him.

She sank against him, caught up in the maelstrom. He drank in her response. Felt her fingers tense, then her nails sank into his shoulders as she met him, appeased him, then tormented him.

Urged him on.

Why she'd taken against a bed he had no idea; perhaps she wanted to expand her horizons. He was only too willing to accommodate her, to demonstrate all that could be accomplished even in such surroundings.

A narrow fanlight above the door let in a shaft of moonlight, enough for him to see. Her gown reminded him of a storm-wracked sea from which her breasts rose, heated and swollen, aching for his touch.

He closed his hands about them and heard her moan. Heard the entreaty, the urgency in the sound.

She was as heated, as needy, as he. With his thumbs, he circled her nipples, hard pebbles beneath the silk, tight and hot and wanting.

Sinking deeper into her mouth, plundering evocatively, deliberately presaging what was to come, he released her breasts and swiftly dealt with her laces, let the dark gown collapse about her waist while he found and unfastened the tiny buttons down the front of her chemise.

He pushed the straps from her shoulders, bared her to the waist; without breaking the kiss, he fastened his hands about her waist and lifted her, sat her on the bench, cupped her breasts one in each hand, broke from the kiss, and bent his head to pay homage.

She gasped, fingers tightening on his skull, spine bowing as he feasted. Her breathing was fractured, desperate; he pushed her ruthlessly on, laving, then suckling, until she sobbed.

Until his title fell from her lips on a pleading gasp.

"Tristan." He licked a tortured nipple, then raised his head. Took her lips again in a searing kiss.

Lifted her skirts, frothed the soft petticoats up about her waist, spreading her knees as he did, stepping between.

He clamped one hand about her naked hip.

Trailed the fingers of the other up the silky inner face of one thigh, and cupped her.

The shudder that wracked her nearly brought him to his knees. Forced him to break from the kiss, drag in a huge breath, and reach desperately for some small measure of control.

Enough to hold back from ravishing her.

He stepped nearer, pressing her knees wider, opening her to his touch. Her lids fluttered; her eyes glinted through the screen of her lashes.

Her lips were swollen, parted, her breathing ragged, her breasts alabaster mounds rising and falling, her skin pearly in the silvery light.

He caught her gaze, trapped it, held her with him as he eased a finger into her tight sheath. Her breath hitched, then rushed out as he reached deeper. Her fingers sank into his upper arms. She was slick, wet, so hot she scalded him. He wanted nothing more than to sink his aching erection into that beckoning heat.

Their gazes locked, he readied her, pressing deep, working his hand so she was fully prepared, releasing her hip to unbutton his trousers, then guiding himself to her entrance. Gripping her hip, he held her, and nudged in.

Watched her face, watched her watching him watch her as he pressed deeper. Releasing her hip, he spread his hand over her bottom, and eased her forward. With his other hand lifted her leg.

"Wrap your legs about my hips."

She dragged in a breath and did. Cradling her bottom in both hands, he drew her to the edge of the bench, and pressed in, inch by inch deeper, feeling her body give, accept and take him in.

Her eyes remained locked on his as their bodies came together; when he finally thrust the last inch, embedding himself inside her, she caught her breath. Her lashes swept down, her eyes closed, her face passion blank as she savored the moment.

He was with her, watching, knowing, feeling.

Only when her lashes fluttered up, and she again met his gaze did he move.

Slowly.

His heart was thundering, his demons raging, desire pounding in his veins, but he kept a tight rein—the moment was too precious to lose.

The startling intimacy as he drew slowly back, then filled her again, and watched her eyes darken even more. He repeated the movement, attuned to her heartbeat, to her need, to the urgency in her—not a hard, driving need like his but a softer, more feminine hunger.

One he needed to sate even more than his own.

So he kept the pace slow, and watched her rise, watched her eyes glaze, heard her breath strangle—watched her come apart in his arms. Listened to her cries until he had to kiss her to mute the telltale sounds, the sweetest symphony he'd ever heard.

He held her, sunk deep in her body, deep in her mouth, when she shuddered, fractured, and climaxed about him. Knew only a fleeting surprise when she took him with her.

Into bliss.

The slow, hot, deeply fulfilling dance slowed, halted. Left them locked together, breathing hard, foreheads touching. The thudding of their hearts filled their ears. Their lashes lifted, gazes touched.

Lips brushed, breaths mingled.

Their warmth held them.

He was sheathed to the hilt in her clinging heat and had no desire to move, to break the spell. Her arms locked about his neck, her legs locked about his hips, she made no effort to shift, to edge away—to leave him.

She seemed even more dazed, more vulnerable, than he.

"Are you all right?"

He whispered the words, watched her eyes focus.

"Yes." The reply came on a soft exhalation. She licked her lips, looked briefly at his. Cleared her throat. "That was . . ."

Leonora couldn't find any word that sufficed.

His lips kicked up at the end. "Stupendous."

She met his gaze, knew better than to nod. Could only wonder at the madness that had gripped her.

And the hunger, the raw need that had gripped him.

His eyes were dark, but softer, not sharp as they usually were. He seemed to sense her wonder; his lips curved. He touched them to hers.

"I want you." His lips brushed hers again. "In every possible way."

She heard the truth, recognized its ring. Had to wonder. "Why?"

He nudged her head back, set his lips cruising her jaw. "Because of this. Because I'll never have enough of you."

She could sense the power of his hunger rising again. Felt the sensation of him within her grow more definite.

"Again?" She heard the stunned amazement in her voice.

He answered with a low growl that might have been a very male chuckle. "Again."

She never should have agreed—acquiesced—to that heated second mating among the tablecloths.

Sipping her tea at the breakfast table the next morning, Leonora made a firm resolution not to be so weak in future—during the rest of the month that was left to them. Trentham—Tristan as he'd insisted she call him—had finally escorted her back to the reception rooms with a smug, wholly male, proprietory air she'd found irritating in the extreme. Especially given she suspected his smugness derived from his entrenched belief that she would find his lovemaking so addictive she'd blindly agree to marry him.

Time would teach him his error. In the meantime, it behooved her to exercise some degree of caution.

She hadn't, after all, intended to acquiesce to even a first mating, let alone the second.

Nevertheless . . . she had learned more, had definitely added to her store of experience. Given the terms of their agreement, she had nothing to fear—the impulse, the physical need that brought them together *would* gradually wane; an occasional indulgence was no great matter.

Except for the possibility of a child.

The notion floated into her mind. Reaching for another slice of toast, she considered it. Considered, surprised, her initial impulsive reaction to it.

Not what she'd expected.

A frown growing in her eyes, she waited for common sense to reassert itself.

Eventually acknowledged that her interaction with Trentham was teaching her, revealing to her, things about herself she'd never known.

Never even suspected.

Through the following days, she kept herself busy, studying Cedric's journals and dealing with Humphrey and Jeremy and the customary round of daily life in Montrose Place.

In the evenings, however . . .

She started to feel like the perennial Cinderella, going to ball after ball and night after night inevitably ending in the arms of her prince. An exceedingly handsome, masterful prince who never failed, despite her firm resolve, to sweep her off her feet . . . and into some private place where they could indulge their senses, and that flaring need to be together, to share their bodies and be one.

His success was startling; she had no idea how he managed it. Even when she avoided the obvious choice of entertainment, guessing which event he would expect her to attend and attending some other, he never failed to materialize at her side the instant she walked into the room.

As for his knowledge of their hostesses' houses, that was beginning to border on the bizarre. She had spent far more time than he in the ton, and that more recently, yet with unerring accuracy he would lead her to a small parlor, or a secluded library or study, or a garden room.

By the end of the week she was starting to feel seriously hunted.

Starting to realize she might have underestimated the feeling between them.

Or, even more frightening, had totally misjudged its nature.

Twelve

There was very little Tristan didn't know about establishing a network of informers.

Lady Warsingham's coachman saw no difficulty in providing the local streetsweeper with news of whither he'd been instructed he would be heading each evening; one of Tristan's footmen would go strolling at noon to meet with the streetsweeper and return with the news.

His own household staff were proving exemplary sources, intrigued and eager to supply him with details of the houses Leonora chose to grace with her presence. And Gasthorpe had exercised his own initiative and handed Tristan a vital contact.

Toby, the Carlings's bootboy, inhabited the kitchen of Number 14 and therefore was privy to his masters' and mistress's intended directions. The lad was always eager to hear the ex–sergeant major's tales; in return, he innocently provided Tristan with intelligence on Leonora's daytime activities.

That evening, she'd elected to attend the Marchioness of Huntly's gala. Tristan sauntered in a few minutes before he estimated the Warsingham party would arrive.

Lady Huntly greeted him with a twinkle in her eye. "I understand," she said, "that you have a particular interest in Miss Carling?"

He met her gaze, wondering . . . "Most particular."

"In that case, I should warn you that a number of my nephews are expected to attend tonight." Lady Huntly patted his arm. "Just a word to the wise."

He inclined his head and moved into the crowd, wracking his brains for the relevant connection. Her nephews? He was about to go and look for Ethelreda or Millicent, both of whom were somewhere in the room, to request clarification, when he recalled Lady Huntly had been born a Cynster.

Muttering a curse, he executed an immediate about-face and took up a position close by the main doors.

Leonora entered a few minutes later; he claimed her hand the instant she was free of the receiving line.

She raised her brows at him; he could see a comment regarding overt possessiveness forming in her mind. Placing his hand over hers, he squeezed her fingers. "Let's get your aunts settled, then we can dance."

She met his eyes. "Just a dance."

A warning, one he had no intention of heeding. Together, they escorted her aunts to a group of chaises where many of the older ladies had gathered.

"Good evening, Mildred." A bedezined old dame nodded regally.

Lady Warsingham nodded back. "Lady Osbaldestone. I believe you'll remember my niece, Miss Carling?"

The old dame, still handsome in her way but with terrifyingly sharp black eyes, surveyed Leonora, who curtsied. The old harridan snorted. "Indeed I remember you, miss—but you've no business being a miss still." Her gaze moved on to Tristan. "Who's this?"

Lady Warsingham performed the introductions; Tristan bowed.

Lady Osbaldestone humphed. "Well, one can hope you'll succeed in changing Miss Carling's mind. The dancing's through there."

With her cane, she waved toward an archway beyond which couples were whirling. Tristan seized the implied dismissal. "If you'll excuse us?"

Without waiting for further permission, he whisked Leonora away.

Pausing beneath the archway, he asked, "Lady Osbaldestone— who's she?"

"A *bona fide* terror of the ton. Pay her no heed." Leonora surveyed the dancers. "And I warn you, tonight we are *only* going to dance."

He made no reply; taking her hand, he led her onto the floor and whirled her into a waltz. A waltz he used to maximum effect, unfortunately, given the limitations of a half-empty dance floor, not as great an effect as he would have liked.

The next dance was a cotillion, an exercise he had little use for; it provided too few opportunities to tweak his partner's senses. It was too early yet to inveigle her away to the tiny salon overlooking the gardens; when she admitted to being parched, he left her by the side of the room and went to fetch two glasses of champagne.

The refreshment room gave off the ballroom; he was only absent for a moment, yet when he returned he discovered Leonora in conversation with a tall, dark-haired man he recognized as Devil Cynster.

His internal curses were vitriolic, but when he approached, neither Leonora nor Cynster, who was not thrilled at the interruption, would have detected anything beyond urbanity in his expression.

"Good evening." Handing Leonora her glass, he nodded to Cynster, who returned the nod, his pale gaze sharpening.

One aspect that was instantly apparent was that they were very much alike, not just in height, in the width of their shoulders, in their elegance, but also in their characters, their natures—their temperaments.

An instant passed while both assimilated that fact, then Cynster held out his hand. "St. Ives. My aunt mentioned you were at Waterloo."

Tristan nodded, shook hands. "Trentham, although I wasn't that then."

He mentally scrambled for the best way to answer the inevitable questions; he'd heard enough of the Cynsters' involvement in the recent campaigns to guess that St. Ives would know enough to detect his usual sliding around the truth.

St. Ives was watching him closely, assessingly. "What regiment were you in?"

"The Guards." Tristan met the pale green gaze, deliberately omitting any further definition. St. Ives's gaze narrowed; he held it, murmured, "You were in the heavy cavalry, as I recall. Together with some of your cousins, you relieved Cullen's troop on the right flank."

St. Ives stilled, blinked, then a wry, quite genuine smile curved his lips. His gaze returned to Tristan's; he inclined his head. "As you say."

Only someone with a very high level of military clearance would know of that little excursion; Tristan could almost see the connections being made behind St. Ives's clear green eyes.

He noted St. Ives's quick, reassessing glance before, with an almost indiscernible movement they both saw and understood, he drew back.

Leonora had been looking from one to the other, sensing a communication she could not follow, irritated by it. She opened her lips—

St. Ives turned to her and smiled with devastating, purely predatory force. "I was intending to sweep you off your feet, but I believe I'll leave you to Trentham's tender mercies. Not the done thing to cross a fellow officer, and there seems little doubt he deserves a clear shot."

Leonora's chin came up; her eyes narrowed. "I am not some enemy to be captured and conquered."

"That's a matter of opinion." Tristan's dry comment brought her gaze swinging his way.

St. Ives's smile grew, unrepentant; he sketched a bow and withdrew, saluting Tristan from behind Leonora's back.

Tristan saw that last with relief; with luck, St. Ives would warn off his cousins, and any others of their ilk.

Leonora cast a frowning glance at St. Ives's retreating back. "What did he mean by you 'deserving a clear shot'?"

"Presumably because I sighted you first."

She swung back, her frown deepening. "I am not some form of"— she gestured, glass and all—"*prey.*"

"As I said, that's a matter of opinion."

"Nonsense." She paused, eyes on his, then continued, "I sincerely hope you're not thinking in such terms, for I warn you I have no intention of being captured, conquered, let alone tied up."

Her diction had grown more definite with every word; her last phrase had nearby gentlemen turning to view her.

"This"—Tristan caught her hand and wound her arm in his—"is not the place to discuss my intentions."

"Your *intentions?*" She lowered her voice. "As far as I'm concerned, you have none *vis à vis* me. None that have any likelihood of coming to fruition."

"I'm desolate to have to contradict you, of course. However . . ." He kept talking, fencing with her as he steered her to a side door. But as he reached to open it, she realized. And dug in her heels.

"No." She narrowed her eyes at him even more. "Just dancing tonight. There's no reason we need be private."

He raised a brow at her. "Retreating in disarray?"

Her lips thinned; her eyes were mere slits. "Nothing of the sort, but you won't catch me with such an obvious lure."

He heaved an exaggerated sigh. In point of fact, it was too early— the rooms insufficiently crowded—for them to risk slipping away. "Very well." He turned her back into the room. "That sounds like a waltz starting up."

Lifting her glass from her fingers, he handed both glasses to a passing footman, then swept her onto the dance floor.

Leonora relaxed into the dance, let her senses free; at least here, in the presence of others, it was safe to do so. In private, she trusted neither him nor herself. Experience had taught her that once in his arms, she couldn't rely on her intellect to guide her. Rational logical arguments never seemed to win when pitted against that warm rush of needy yearning.

Desire. She knew enough now to name it, the passion that drove them, that fired their attraction. She'd acknowledged it as such to herself, but knew better than to allow her understanding to show.

However, as she whirled through the dance in Trentham's arms, relaxed but with her senses exhilaratingly alive, it was a different aspect of their interaction that concerned her.

An aspect Devil Cynster's words and their ensuing discussion had brought into sharper focus.

She held her tongue until the dance ended, but then they were joined by two other couples, and conversation became general. When the musicians struck up the opening bars to a cotillion, she met Trentham's gaze in fleeting warning, then accepted Lord Hardcastle's hand.

Trentham—Tristan—let her go with no reaction beyond a hardening of his gaze. Heartened, she returned to his side once the dance ended, but when the next measure proved to be a country dance, she again accepted an offer from another—young Lord Belvoir, a gentleman who might one day be of Tristan's and St. Ives's ilk, but was now merely an entertaining companion much of her own age.

Again, Tristan—she'd started to think of him by his given name—he'd teased it from her often enough under circumstances sufficiently unique and memorable that she was unlikely to forget it—bore her defection with outwardly stoic calm. Only she was near enough to see the hardness, the possessiveness, and, more than anything else, the watchfulness in his eyes.

It was that last that underscored her thoughts of how he viewed her, and finally had her throwing caution to the wind in an attempt to reason with her wolf. Her wild wolf; she didn't forget, but sometimes it was necessary to take risks.

She bided her time until the small group they were a part of dispersed. Before others could join them, she placed her hand on Tristan's arm and nudged him toward the door he'd previously headed for.

He glanced at her, raised his brows. "Have you had second thoughts?"

"No. I've had other thoughts." She met his eyes fleetingly, and continued toward the door. "I want to talk—just *talk*—to you, and I suppose it had better be in private."

Reaching the door, she paused and met his gaze. "I presume you do know of somewhere in this mansion we can be assured of being alone?"

His lips curved in a wholly male grin; opening the door, he handed her through. "Far be it from me to disappoint you."

He didn't; the room he led her to was small, furnished as a sitting room in which a lady of the house could sit in comfortable privacy and look out over the manicured gardens. Reached through a maze of intersecting corridors, it was some distance from the reception rooms, a perfect venue for private conversation, verbal or otherwise.

Inwardly shaking her head—how did he do it?—she went straight to the windows, to stand and look out on the fog-shrouded garden. There was no moon, no distraction outside. She heard the door click shut, then felt Tristan approaching. Dragging in a breath, she swung to face him, put a palm to his chest to hold him back. "I want to discuss how you see me."

He didn't outwardly blink, but she'd obviously taken a tack he hadn't expected. "What—"

She stopped him with an upraised hand. "It's becoming increasingly clear that you view me as some sort of challenge. And men like you are constitutionally incapable of letting a challenge lie." She eyed him severely. "Am I right in thinking you view getting my agreement to marry you in such a light?"

Tristan returned her regard. Increasingly wary. It was difficult to think how else he would view it. "Yes."

"Ah-ha! That, you see, is our problem."

"Which problem is that?"

"The problem of you not being able to take my 'no' for an answer."

Propping his shoulder against the window frame, he looked down at her face, at her eyes glowing with zeal at her supposed discovery. "I don't follow."

She made a dismissive sound. "Of course you do, you just don't want to think about it because it doesn't fit your stated *intentions*."

"Bear with my muddled male mind and explain."

She threw him a long-suffering look. "You can hardly deny that any number of ladies have been—and more will be once the Season proper starts—throwing themselves at your head."

"No." It was one of the reasons he clung to her side, one of the reasons he wanted to gain her agreement to their wedding as soon as possible. "What have they to do with us?"

"Not us so much as *you*. You, like most men, have little appreciation for what you can have without a fight. You equate fighting for something with its value—the harder and more difficult the struggle, the more valuable the object attained. As with wars, so with women. The more a lady resists, the more desirable she becomes."

She fixed him with her clear, periwinkle blue gaze. "Am I right?"

He thought before nodding. "It's a reasonable hypothesis."

"Indeed, but you see where that leaves us?"

"No."

She gave an exasperated hiss. "You want to marry me because I won't marry you—not for any other reason. That"—she waved both hands—"primitive instinct of yours is what's driving you—and it's getting in the way of our attraction fading. It would be fading but—"

He reached out, caught one of her waving hands, and yanked her to him. She landed against his chest, gasped as his arms closed around her. He felt her body react as it always had, always did, to his. "Our mutual attraction hasn't faded."

She hauled in a tight breath. "That's because you're confusing it. . . ." Her words faded as he lowered his head. "I said we'd only talk!"

"That's illogical." He brushed her lips with his, pleased when hers clung. He shifted, settling her more comfortably in his arms. Setting her hips to his, the soft curve of her stomach cradling his erection. He looked down into her eyes, wide, darkening. His lips curved, but not in a smile. "You're right—it is a primitive instinct that's driving me. But you picked the wrong one."

"What—"

Her mouth was open—he filled it. Took possession in a long, slow, thorough kiss. She tried to resist, hold back, but then surrendered.

When, eventually, he lifted his head, she sighed, murmured, "What's illogical about talking?"

"It's not consistent with your conclusion."

"My conclusion?" She blinked at him. "I hadn't even got to my conclusion."

He brushed her lips again so she wouldn't see his wolfish grin. "Let me state it for you. If, as you hypothesize, the only reason I want to marry you—the only true reason driving our mutual attraction—is because you're resisting, why not try *not* resisting and see what happens?"

She stared dazedly up at him. "Not resisting?"

He shrugged lightly, his gaze falling to her lips. "If you're right, you'll prove your point." He took her lips, her mouth again, before she could consider what would happen if she was wrong.

His tongue stroked hers; she shivered delicately, then kissed him back. Stopped resisting, as she generally did when they'd reached this point; he wasn't fool enough to believe that meant anything more than that she'd inwardly shrugged and decided to take what she might, still firmly convinced the desire between them would wane.

He knew it wouldn't, at least on his part. What he felt for her was quite different from anything he'd felt before—not for any other woman, not for anyone at all. Protective, deeply to-his-bones possessive, and unquestionably right. It was that conviction of rightness that drove him to have her again and again, even in the teeth of her determined denials, to demonstrate the breadth and depth, the increasing power of all that was growing between them.

A stunning revelation in any circumstances, but he set himself to paint the sensual reality between them in bold and striking colors the better to impress her with its power, its potency, its undisguised truth.

She felt it, broke from the kiss, from beneath heavy lids met his eyes. Sighed. "I really did intend that tonight we would only dance."

There was no resistance, no reluctance, only acceptance.

He closed his hands about her bottom and shifted suggestively against her. Bent his head to brush her lips. "We are going to dance— it just won't be to a waltz."

Her lips curved. Her hand tightened on his nape and she drew him to her. "To our own music, then."

He took her mouth, caught their reins, and deliberately set them aside.

The daybed angled to the windows was the obvious place to lay her, to lie alongside her and feast on her breasts. Until her soft gasps were urgent and needy, until she arched and her fingers clung to his skull.

Suppressing a triumphant smile, he slid farther down the daybed, raising her skirts, pressing them high about her waist to expose her hips, and her long slender legs. Tracing her curves, fingers first trailing, then gripping to part her thighs, opening her to him.

Then he bent his head and set his lips to her softness.

She cried out, tried to catch his shoulders, but they were beyond her reach. Her fingers tangled in his hair, clenched as he laved, licked, then lightly suckled.

"*Tristan!* No . . ."

"Yes." He held her down and pressed deeper, savoring the tart taste of her, step by step knowingly winding her tight . . .

She was quivering on the crest of climax when he shifted, freed his erection from the confines of his trousers, and rose over her. She gripped his forearms, nails sinking deep, her knees rising to grip his flanks. Sensual entreaty etched every line of her face; urgency drove her restless body, shifting wantonly, beckoning beneath his.

Her spine bowed as he entered her; he drove home and she climaxed, a glorious rippling release. He caught her up, drove her on. She clung, sobbed, and matched him, as committed as he as they swept up the mountain, with each forceful thrust climbed the jagged peaks, then tension splintered, fractured, fell away, and they soared into the void, into the sublime heat of their sharing.

Into that moment when all barriers fell away, and there was just him and her, joined in naked honesty, wrapped in that powerful reality.

Chests heaving, hearts thundering, heat coursing beneath their skins, they stilled, waited, locked intimately together, for the glory to wane. Their gazes touched, held—neither made any move to shift, to part.

She raised a hand, traced his cheek. Her eyes searched his, wondering . . .

He turned his head, pressed an openmouthed kiss to her palm.

Knew when she drew a deep breath that although her body and her senses were still sunk in the bliss, her mind had snapped free; she'd already resumed thinking.

Resigned, he looked into her eyes. Raised one brow.

"You said I'd picked the wrong primitive instinct—that it wasn't the response to a challenge that was driving you." She held his gaze. "If not that, then what? Why"—with one hand, she waved weakly— "are we here?"

He knew the answer, couldn't manage a smile. "We're here because I want you."

She made a derisive sound. "So it's just lust—"

"No." He pressed into her and gained her complete attention. "Not lust—not anything like it. But you're not hearing what I'm saying. I. Want. *You.* Not any other woman; no other will do. Only you."

She frowned.

His lips curved, not in a smile. "That's why we're here. That's why I'll pursue you no matter what comes until you agree to be mine."

Only you.

Sipping tea at the breakfast table the next morning, Leonora examined those words.

She wasn't at all sure she understood the implications, understood what Tristan had meant to convey. Men, at least those of his ilk, were a species unknown to her; she felt uneasy in attributing too much meaning—or the meaning she would have intended—to his phrase.

There were further complications.

The ease with which he'd subverted her determined intentions at Huntly House—just as he had on the evenings before that—made thinking she could stand against him and his practiced seduction a frankly ludicrous hope.

No more pretending on that front; if she seriously wanted to deny him, she'd have to unearth a chastity belt. And even then . . . he could almost certainly pick locks.

And there was more yet to consider.

While it was perfectly obvious that testing her hypothesis by not resisting would play into his hands, if she was right in her estimation of the reason behind his passion, then not resisting the notion of marrying him would indeed see his interest wane.

But what if it didn't?

She'd spent half the night wondering, imagining . . .

A gentle cough from Castor jerked her back to reality; she had no idea how long her mind had been wandering, caught by an unexpected vista, entranced by a prospect she'd long ago thought she'd turned her back on. Frowning, she pushed aside her uneaten toast and rose.

"When the footman takes Henrietta for her walk, please ask him to summon me—I'll accompany them today."

"Indeed, miss." Castor bowed as she left the room.

That evening, together with Mildred and Gertie, Leonora swept into Lady Catterthwaite's ballroom. They were neither early nor late. After greeting their hostess, they joined the fray. With every passing day, more of the fashionable returned to town and the balls grew commensurately more crowded.

Lady Catterthwaite's ballroom was small and cramped. Accompanying her aunts to where a grouping of chairs and chaises gave the older female guests a place to sit and watch their charges, and exchange all the latest news, Leonora was surprised to find no Trentham waiting for her—waiting to step out of the crowd and waylay her. Claim her.

She helped Gertie settle in an armchair, inwardly frowning at how accustomed to his attentions she'd grown. Straightening, she nodded to her aunts. "I'm going to mingle."

Mildred was already speaking with an acquaintance; Gertie nodded, then turned to join the circle.

Leonora glided into the already considerable crowd. Attracting a gentleman, joining a group of acquaintances would be easy enough, yet she had no desire to do either. She was . . . not precisely concerned, but certainly wondering over Tristan's nonappearance. Last night, after he'd so deliberately uttered the words "only you," she'd sensed a change in him, a sudden wariness, a watchfulness she'd been unable to interpret.

He hadn't cut himself off from her, hadn't precisely withdrawn, but she'd sensed a self-protective recoil on his part, as if he'd gone too far, said more than was safe . . . or, perhaps, true.

The possibility nagged; she was already having trouble enough trying to fathom his motives—coping with the fact that his motives had, entirely beyond her wishes or her will, become important to her— that the idea he might not be open with her, honest with her . . . that way lay a morass of uncertainty in which she had no intention of becoming mired.

It was precisely the sort of situation that most strongly supported her inflexible stance against marriage.

She continued drifting aimlessly, stopping here and there to exchange greetings, then, entirely unexpectedly, directly ahead of her in the crowd, she saw a pair of shoulders she recognized instantly.

They were clad in scarlet, as they had been years ago. As if sensing her regard, the gentleman glanced around and saw her. And smiled.

Delighted, he turned and held out his hands. "Leonora! How lovely to see you."

She returned his smile and gave him her hands. "Mark. I see you haven't sold out."

"No, no. A career soldier, that's me." Brown-haired, fair-skinned, he turned to include the lady standing by his side. "Allow me to present my wife, Heather."

Leonora's smile slipped a fraction, but Heather Whorton smiled sweetly and shook hands. If she recalled that Leonora was the lady her husband had been engaged to before he'd offered for her hand, she gave no sign. Relaxing, somewhat to her surprise Leonora found herself regaled with an account of the Whortons' life over the past seven or so years, from the birth of their first child to the arrival of their fourth, to the rigors of following the drum or alternatively the long separations imposed on military families.

Both Mark and Heather contributed; it was impossible to miss how dependent on Mark his wife was. She hung on his arm, but even more, seemed totally immersed in him and their children—indeed, she seemed to have no identity beyond that.

That was not the norm in Leonora's circle.

As she listened and smiled politely, commenting as appropriate, the truth of how badly she and Mark would have suited sank in. From his responses to Heather, it was patently clear that he rejoiced in her need of him—a need Leonora would never have had, would never have allowed herself to develop.

She'd long ago realized she hadn't loved Mark; at the time of their engagement she'd been a young and distinctly naive seventeen—she'd thought she wanted what all other young ladies wanted—lusted after—a handsome husband. Listening to him now, and remembering, she could admit that she hadn't been in love with him but with the idea of being in love, of getting married and having her own household. Of gaining what for girls of that age had been the Holy Grail.

She listened, observed, and sent up a heartfelt prayer; she truly had had a lucky escape.

Tristan strolled nonchalantly down the stairs of Lady Catterthwaite's ballroom. He was later than usual; a message received earlier in the day from one of his contacts had necessitated another visit to the docks—night had fallen before he'd returned to Trentham House.

Pausing two steps from the bottom, he scanned the room, but failed to find Leonora. He did, however, locate her aunts. A niggle of concern pricking his nape, he stepped down to the floor and headed their way.

Impelled by a need to find Leonora, an impulse whose strength unnerved him.

Their interlude the previous evening, the explanation he'd given her, that she and she alone could fulfill his need, had only served to underscore, to exacerbate, his growing sense of vulnerability. He felt as if he were going into battle missing part of his armor, that he was exposing himself, his emotions, in a reckless, foolish, wantonly idiotic fashion.

His intincts were to immediately and comprehensively guard against any such weakness, to cover it up, shore it up with all speed.

He couldn't help being the type of man he was, had long ago accepted his nature. Knew there was no sense fighting his escalating need to secure Leonora, to make her unequivocally his.

To have her agree to marry him with all speed.

Reaching the gaggle of older ladies, he bowed before Mildred and shook hands with both her and Gertie. He then had to endure a round of introductions to the circle of eager, interested, matronly faces.

Mildred saved him by waving toward the crowd. "Leonora is here, somewhere in the melee."

"About time you got here!" Grumbling under her breath, Gertie, sitting to one side of the group, drew his attention. "She's over there." She pointed with her cane; Tristan turned, looked, and saw Leonora chatting with an officer from some infantry regiment.

Gertie snorted. "That blackguard Whorton's toadying up to her—can't imagine she's enjoying it. You'd best go and rescue her."

He'd never been one to rush in without understanding the game.

Although the trio of which Leonora was one was at some distance, they were, from this angle, clearly visible. Although he could see only Leonora's profile, her stance and her occasional gesture assured him she was neither upset nor worried. She also showed no sign of wanting to slip away.

He looked back at Gertie. "Whorton—I assume he's the captain she's talking with?" Gertie nodded. "Why do you call him a black-guard?"

Gertie narrowed her old eyes at him. Her lips compressed in a tight line, she considered him closely; from the first, she'd been the less encouraging of Leonora's aunts, yet she hadn't attempted to thrust a spoke in his wheel. Indeed, as the days had passed, he thought she'd come to look on him more favorably.

He apparently passed muster, for she suddenly nodded and looked again at Whorton. Her dislike was evident in her face.

"He jilted her, that's why. They were engaged when she was seventeen, before he went away to Spain. He came back the next year, and came straightaway to see her—we were all expecting to learn when the wedding bells would ring. But then Leonora showed him out, and returned to tell us he'd asked her to release him. Seemed he'd found his colonel's daughter more to his liking."

Gertie's snort was eloquent. "That's why I call him a blackguard. Broke her heart, he did."

A complex swirl of emotions swept through Tristan. He heard himself ask, "She released him?"

"Of course she did! What lady wouldn't, in such circumstances? The bounder didn't want to marry her—he'd found a better billet."

Gertie's fondness for Leonora rang in her voice, colored her distress. Impulsively, he patted her shoulder. "Don't worry—I'll go and rescue her."

But he wasn't going to make Whorton into a martyr in the process. Aside from all else, he was damned glad the bounder hadn't married Leonora.

Eyes on the trio, he tacked through the crowd. He'd just been handed a vital piece of the jigsaw of Leonora and her attitude to marriage, but he couldn't yet spare the time to stop, consider, jiggle, and see exactly how it fitted, nor what it would tell him.

He came up beside Leonora; she glanced up at him, smiled.

"Ah—there you are."

Taking her hand, he raised it briefly to his lips, then placed it on his sleeve as was his habit. Her brows lifted faintly, in resignation, then she turned to the others. "Allow me to introduce you."

She did; he heard with a jolt that the other lady was Whorton's wife. His polite mask in place, he returned the greetings.

Mrs. Whorton smiled sweetly at him. "As I was saying, it's proved quite an effort to organize our sons' schooling . . ."

To his definite surprise, he found himself listening to a discussion of where to send the Whorton brats for their education. Leonora gave her opinion from her experience with Jeremy; Whorton quite clearly intended giving her advice due consideration.

Contrary to Gertie's supposition, Whorton made no attempt to attach Leonora, nor to evoke any long-ago sympathies.

Tristan watched Leonora closely, but could detect nothing beyond her customary serene confidence, her usual effortless social grace.

She wasn't a particularly good actress; her temper was too definite. Whatever her feelings over Whorton had been, they were no longer strong enough to raise her pulse. It beat steadily beneath his fingers; she was truly unperturbed.

Even discussing children who, had things been different, might have been hers.

He suddenly wondered how she felt about children, realized he'd been taking her views *vis à vis* his heir for granted.

Wondered if she was already carrying his child.

His gut clenched; a wave of possessiveness flowed over him. He didn't so much as flutter an eyelash, yet Leonora glanced at him, a faint frown—one of questioning concern—in her eyes.

The sight saved him. He smiled easily; she blinked, searched his eyes, then turned back to Mrs. Whorton's chatter.

Finally, the musicians tuned up. He seized the moment to part from the Whortons; he led Leonora directly to the floor.

Drew her into his arms, whirled her into the waltz.

Only then focused on her face, on the long-suffering look in her eyes.

He blinked, raised a brow.

"I realize you military men are accustomed to acting with dispatch, but within the ton's ballrooms, it's customary to *ask* a lady if she wishes to dance."

He met her gaze. After a moment, said, "My apologies."

She waited, then raised her brows high. "Aren't you going to ask me?"

"No. We're already waltzing—asking you is redundant. And you might refuse."

She blinked at him, then smiled, clearly amused. "I must try that sometime."

"Don't."

"Why not?"

"Because you won't like what happens."

She held his gaze, then sighed exaggeratedly. "You're going to have to work on your social skills. This dog-in-the-manger attitude won't do."

"I know. Believe me, I'm working on a solution. Your help would be appreciated."

She narrowed her eyes, then tipped up her nose and looked away. Feigning temper because he'd had the last word.

He swung her into a sweeping turn, and thought of the other little matter, a pertinent and possibly urgent matter, he now had to address.

Military men. Her memories of Whorton, no matter how ancient and buried, could not have been happy ones—and she almost certainly classed him and the captain as men of the same stamp.

Thirteen

〜

"Excellent!" Leonora looked up as Tristan walked in. Quickly tidying her escritoire, she shut it and rose. "We can walk in the park with Henrietta, and I can tell you my news."

Tristan raised a brow at her, but obediently held the door and followed her back out into the hall. She'd told him last night that she'd received quite a few replies from Cedric's acquaintances; she'd asked him to call to discuss them—she'd made no mention of walking her hound.

He helped her into her pelisse, then shrugged on his greatcoat; the wind was chilly, whipping through the streets. Clouds hid the sun, but the day was dry enough. A footman arrived with Henrietta straining on a leash. Tristan fixed the hound with a warning glance, then took the leash.

Leonora led the way out. "The park is only a few streets away."

"I trust," Tristan said, following her down the garden path, "that you've been exercising with your dog?"

She shot him a glance. "If by that you mean to ask have I been strolling the streets without her, no. But it's definitely restricting. The sooner we lay Mountford by the heels, the better."

Bustling forward, she swung open the gate, held it while he and Henrietta passed through, then swung it shut.

He caught her hand, trapped her gaze as he wound her arm in his. "So cut line." Holding her beside him, he let Henrietta tow them in the direction of the park. "What have you learned?"

She drew breath, settled her arm in his, looked ahead. "I'd had great hopes of A. J. Carruthers—Cedric had communicated most frequently with Carruthers in the last few years. However, I didn't receive any reply from Yorkshire, where Carruthers lived, until yesterday. *Before* that, however, over the previous days, I received three replies from other herbalists, all scattered about the country. All three wrote that they believed Cedric *had* been working on some special formula, but none of them knew any details. Each of them, however, suggested I contact A. J. Carruthers, as they understood Cedric had been working most closely with Carruthers."

"Three independent replies, all believing Carruthers would know more?"

Leonora nodded. "Precisely. Unfortunately, however, A. J. Carruthers is dead."

"Dead?" Tristan halted on the pavement and met her gaze. The green expanse of the park lay across the street. "Dead how?"

She didn't misunderstand, but grimaced. "I don't know—all I do know is that he's dead."

Henrietta tugged; Tristan checked, then led both females across the street. Henrietta's huge and shaggy form, her gaping jaws filled with sharp teeth, gave him a perfect excuse to avoid the fashionable area thronging with matrons and their daughters; he turned the questing hound toward the more leafy and overgrown region beyond the western end of Rotten Row.

That area was all but deserted.

Leonora didn't wait for his next question. "The letter I received yesterday was from the solicitor in Harrogate who acted for Carruthers and oversaw his estate. He informed me of Carruthers's demise, but said he couldn't otherwise help with my query. He suggested that Carruthers's nephew, who inherited all Carruthers's journals and so on, might be able to shed some light on the matter—the solicitor was aware that Carruthers and Cedric had corresponded a great deal in the months prior to Cedric's death."

"Did this solicitor mention exactly when Carruthers died?"

"Not exactly. All he said was that Carruthers died some months after Cedric, but that he'd been ill for some time before." Leonora paused, then added, "There's no mention in the letters Carruthers sent to Cedric of any illness, but they might not have been that close."

"Indeed. This nephew—do we have his name and direction?"

"No." Her grimace was frustration incarnate. "The solicitor advised that he'd forwarded my letter to the nephew in York, but that was all he said."

"Hmm." Looking down, Tristan walked on, assessing, extrapolating.

Leonora glanced at him. "It's the most interesting piece of information we've found yet—the most likely, indeed, the *only* possible link to something that might be what Mountford seeks. There's nothing specific in Carruthers's letters to Cedric, other than oblique references to something they were working on—no details at all. But we need to pursue it, don't you think?"

He looked up, met her eyes, nodded. "I'll get someone on it tomorrow."

She frowned. "Where? In Harrogate?"

"And York. Once we have the name and direction, there's no reason to wait to pay this nephew a visit."

His only regret was that he couldn't do so personally. Traveling to Yorkshire would mean leaving Leonora beyond his reach; he could surround her with guards, yet no amount of organized protection would be sufficient to reassure him of her safety, not until Mountford, whoever he was, was caught.

They'd been strolling, neither slowly nor briskly, towed along in Henrietta's wake. He realized Leonora was studying him, a rather odd look on her face.

"What?"

She pressed her lips together, her eyes on his, then she shook her head, looked away. "You."

He waited, then prompted, "What about me?"

"You knew enough to realize someone had taken an impression of a key. You waited for a burglar and closed with him without turning a hair. You can pick locks. Assessing premises for their ability to withstand intruders is something you've done before. You got access to special records from the Registry, records others wouldn't even know existed. With a wave of your hand"—she demonstrated—"you can have men watching my street. You dress like a navvy and frequent the docks, then change into an earl—one who somehow always knows where I'll be, one with exemplary knowledge of our hostesses' houses.

"And now, just like that, you'll arrange for people to go hunting for information in Harrogate and York." She pinned him with an intent but intrigued look. "You're the oddest ex-soldier-cum-earl I've ever met."

He held her gaze for a long moment, then murmured, "I wasn't your average soldier."

She nodded, looking ahead once more. "So I gathered. You were a major in the Guards—a soldier of Devil Cynster's type—"

"No." He waited until she met his gaze. "I—"

He broke off. The moment had come sooner than he'd anticipated. A rush of thoughts jostled through his mind, the most prominent being how a woman who'd been jilted by one soldier would feel about being lied to by another. Perhaps not quite lied to, but would she see the difference? His instincts were all for keeping her in the dark, for keeping his dangerous past and his equally dangerous propensities from her. For keeping her in sublime ignorance of that side of his life, and all it said of his character.

Her eyes on his face, she continued slowly strolling, head tilting as she studied him. And waited.

He drew breath, softly said, "I wasn't like Devil Cynster, either."

Leonora looked into his eyes; what she saw there she couldn't interpret. "What sort of soldier were you, then?"

The answer, she knew, held a vital key to understanding who the man beside her truly was.

His lips twisted wryly. "If you could get access to my record, it would say I joined the army at twenty and rose to the rank of major in the Guards. It would give you a regiment, but if you checked with soldiers in that regiment, you'd discover few knew me, that I hadn't been sighted since shortly after I first joined."

"So what sort of regiment were you in? Not the cavalry."

"No. Not the infantry, either, nor the artillery."

"You said you'd been at Waterloo."

"I was." He held her gaze. "I was on the battlefield, but not with our troops." He watched her eyes widen, then quietly added, "I was behind enemy lines."

She blinked, then stared at him, thoroughly intrigued. "You were a *spy?*"

He grimaced lightly, looked ahead. "An agent working in an unofficial capacity for His Majesty's government."

A host of impressions swamped her—observations that suddenly made sense, other things that were no longer so mysterious—yet she was far more interested in what the revelation meant, what it said of him. "It must have been terribly lonely, as well as being horrendously dangerous."

Tristan glanced at her; that wasn't what he'd expected her to say, to think of. His mind ranged back, over the years . . . he nodded. "Often."

He waited for more, for all the predictable questions. None came. They'd slowed; impatient, Henrietta woofed and tugged. He and Leonora exchanged a glance, then she smiled, tightened her hold on his arm and they stepped out more briskly, circling back toward the streets of Belgravia.

She had a pensive expression on her face, faraway and distant, yet not troubled, not irritated, not concerned. When she felt his gaze, she glanced at him, met his eyes, then smiled and looked ahead.

They crossed the thoroughfare and paced down the street, then turned into Montrose Place. Reaching her gate, he swung it wide, ushered her through, then followed her in. She was waiting to link her arm in his; she was still deep in thought.

He stopped before the steps. "I'll leave you here."

She glanced up at him, then inclined her head and reached for Henrietta's lead. She met his gaze; her eyes were a startling blue. "Thank you."

Those periwinkle blue eyes said she was speaking of much more than his help with Henrietta.

He nodded, thrust his hands into his pockets. "I'll have someone on their way to York tonight. I believe you'll be attending Lady Manivers' rout?"

Her lips lifted. "Indeed."

"I'll see you there."

Her eyes held his for a moment, then she inclined her head. "Until then."

She turned away. He watched her go inside, waited until the door shut, then turned and walked away.

Dealing with Tristan, Leonora decided, had become unbelievably complicated.

It was the following morning; she lolled in her bed and stared at the sunbeams making patterns on the ceiling. And tried to sort out what, exactly, was going on between them. Between Tristan Wemyss, ex-spy, ex–unofficial agent of His Majesty's government, and her.

She'd thought she'd known, but day by day, night by night, he kept . . . not so much changing as revealing greater and ever more intriguing depths. Facets of his character that she'd never imagined he might possess, aspects she found deeply appealing.

Last night . . . all had progressed as it usually did. She'd tried, not too hard, admittedly—she'd been distracted by all she'd learned that afternoon—but she nevertheless had made an effort to hold to a celibate line. He'd seemed even more determined, more ruthless than usual in storming her position—and taking her.

He'd whisked her off to a secluded room, one draped in shadows. There, on a daybed, he'd taught her to ride him—even now, just thinking of those moments made her blush. Remembered sensation sent warmth washing through her. The muscles in her thighs now ached, yet in that position she'd been better able to appreciate how much pleasure she gave him. How much sensual delight he took in her body. For the first time in all their interactions, she'd taken the lead, experimented, and gloried in her ability to pleasure him.

Addictive. Enthralling. Deeply satisfying.

That, however, had been the least of the revelations the evening had brought.

When, finally slumped in his arms, heated and replete, she'd nipped his shoulder and told him she liked the sort of soldier he was, he'd sent one hard palm stroking slowly, pensively, down her spine, then said, "I'm not like Whorton, I promise you."

She'd blinked, then struggled up onto her elbows to frown down into his face. "You're not anything like Mark." Her mind had been groggy; the rock-hard, tanned, scarred body beneath her was nothing like what she'd ever imagined Mark's might be, and as for the man within it . . .

Tristan's eyes had been dark pools, impossible to read. His hand had continued slowly, reassuringly stroking. He must have read her confusion in her face. "I want to marry you—I won't change my mind. You don't need to worry I'll hurt you like he did."

Realization had dawned. She'd pushed up, stared down at him. "Mark didn't hurt me."

He'd frowned. "He jilted you."

"Well, yes. But . . . I was actually quite happy to be jilted."

Of course, she'd had to explain. She'd done so with greater candor than she'd previously brought to the subject; stating the reality aloud had more clearly established the truth in her mind as well as his.

"So you see," she'd concluded, "it wasn't any deep and lasting slight—not in any way. I don't have any"—she'd waved—"adverse feelings toward soldiers because of it."

He'd considered her, searched her face. "So you don't hold my former career against me?"

"Because of what happened with Whorton? No."

His frown had only deepened. "If it wasn't Whorton jilting you that gave you a distaste for men and marriage, what did?" His gaze had sharpened; even in the shadows she'd been able to feel its edge. "Why haven't you married?"

She hadn't been ready to answer that.

She'd brushed it aside, clung to a more immediate point. "Is that why you told me about your career—to distinguish yourself from Whorton?"

He'd looked disgruntled. "If you hadn't asked, I wouldn't have told you."

"But I did ask. Is that why you answered?"

He'd hesitated, his reluctance clear, then admitted, "Partially. I would have had to tell you sometime . . ."

"But you told me this afternoon because you wanted me to see you as different from Whorton, different from how you imagined I saw him—"

He'd hauled her down and kissed her. Distracted her.

Effectively.

She hadn't known what to make of his reasoning—his motives, his reactions—last night. She still didn't. Yet . . . he'd obviously felt threatened enough by her experience with Whorton, and how he believed that affected her view of military men, to tell her the truth. To break with what she suspected was habit and neither hide nor conceal his past.

A past she felt sure none of his family knew. That few others of any sort knew.

He was a man with shadows behind him, yet circumstances had dictated he step into the light, and he needed someone—someone who understood, who could understand him, someone he could trust—beside him.

She could see that, acknowledge that much.

Slowly stretching under the covers, she sighed deeply. Because of his earlier suggestion, she'd allowed herself to imagine what being married to him would be like; her response to the vision had been completely different to what she'd expected. To what her response to all such thoughts of marriage had been in the past.

Now . . . now that she was imagining being *his* wife, the prospect enticed. With age and experience—maturity, perhaps—she'd come to value things—things like the gentle round of country life—far more than she had previously; she'd gradually come to realize such elements were important to her. They provided an outlet for her natural abilities—her organizational and managerial talents; without such outlets she'd feel stifled . . .

Just as, indeed, she felt increasingly stifled in her uncle's house.

The realization was not so much a shock as an earthquake, one that literally rocked the concepts she'd thought for so long were the foundations of her life. That realization was not a small thing to assimilate, to absorb.

The sunbeams danced on the ceiling; the household was awake—the day called to her. Yet she remained in the cocoon of her bed and instead opened her mind. Let her thoughts free.

Followed where they led.

The girlish dreams she'd buried long ago had revived, subtly re-created, altered so that this time they were attractive to the woman she now was—this time, they fitted her.

She could see, imagine—start to desire if she let herself—a future as Tristan's wife. His countess. His helpmate.

Swirling through those dreams, lending them greater fascination and power, was the enticement of being the one—the only one according to him—who could give him all he wanted. That, very possibly, he needed. When they were together, she could sense the power of what had grown between them, that welling emotion deeper than passion, stronger than desire. The emotion that in those quiet, intense and private moments wrapped them about.

The emotion they shared.

It was something ephemeral between them, something most easy to see in those heated moments when both their guards were completely down, yet it was also there, peeking through, like something caught from the corner of an eye in their more public exchanges.

He'd asked why she'd never married; the truth was, she'd never truly studied the reason. The instinctive, deeply held belief—the one that had made letting Whorton go so easy—was something so buried in her mind, so much a part of her, she'd never taken it out and examined it, never truly concerned herself with it before. It had simply been there, a certainty.

Until Tristan had appeared, and laid all he was before her.

He did, now, have the right to question, to ask for her reasons, to demand they were sound.

It was time to look deeper, into her heart, into her soul, and discover whether her old instincts were still relevant, whether they remained relevant to the new world on whose threshold she and Tristan now stood.

He'd seized her hand, dragged her to that threshold, forced her to open her eyes and truly see . . . and he wasn't going to go away. To simply draw back and leave her.

He'd been right; the attraction between them wouldn't fade.

It hadn't. It had grown.

Lips setting, she flung back the covers, got out of bed, and determinedly crossed to the bellpull.

Reexamining and possibly restructuring the basic tenets of one's life was not an undertaking that could be accomplished in a few rushed minutes.

Unfortunately, throughout that day and those following, rushed minutes were all Leonora could find. Yet as the events of each passing day strengthened and deepened the connection between her and Tristan, the need to revisit the reason underlying her aversion to marriage grew.

Their slow progress on the matter of Mountford, either locating the man masquerading by that name or identifying whatever it was he was after, only added pressure by way of Tristan's increasing protectiveness, which spilled over into a more primitive possessiveness.

Even though he battled to hide it, she saw. And understood.

Tried not to let it prod her temper; he couldn't, it seemed, help it.

February had finally given way to March; the first hint of spring blew in to soften winter's bleakness. The ton started to return to the capital in earnest, to prepare for the upcoming Season. While earlier the entertainments had been small, largely informal, the social calendar was growing ever more crowded, the events equally so.

Lady Hammond's ball bade fair to be the first acknowledged crush of the year. Arriving with Mildred and Gertie, Leonora stood patiently on the stairs leading up to the ballroom together with half a hundred others all waiting to greet their hostess. Looking around, she noted familiar faces, nodded, exchanged smiles. There were weeks yet before the Season proper; in years past, she was sure town hadn't been so crowded so early in the year. Even in the park . . .

"My dear, of *course* we're here early."

The lady behind Leonora had just met an old friend.

"Everyone will be, mark my words. Or at least, every family with a daughter to bring out. It's quite criminal the number of gentlemen who were lost in all those wars . . ."

The lady continued; Leonora stopped listening—she'd seen the light. Pity the eligible gentlemen as yet unmarried.

Eventually, she, Mildred, and Gertie gained the ballroom door; after making her curtsy to Lady Hammond, an old acquaintance of her aunts', she followed Mildred and Gertie to one of the alcoves set with chairs and chaises to accommodate chaperones and the older generation.

Her aunts found seats among their cronies; after turning aside a number of arch queries, Leonora retreated.

Into the crowd. Tristan would have some difficulty locating her; he hadn't joined the queue to the ballroom by the time she'd gained the top of the stairs, which meant it would be some time before he could join her.

Tonight, the crowd was too dense to amble through with only nods and smiles; she had to stop and chat, to exchange greetings and opinions and social conversation. She'd never found that difficult, some-times boring perhaps, but tonight so many were newly come to town that there was plenty to catch up with, to hear, to laugh at and be amused. Nevertheless, aware she was attracting a certain degree of attention from gentlemen too recently returned to the ballrooms to have registered Tristan's interest, she did not remain for too long within one group, but kept drifting.

Dealing with one wolf at a time seemed wise.

"Leonora!"

She turned, and smiled at Crissy Wainwright, a plump and these days somewhat buxom blond who had been presented in the same year she had. Crissy had quickly snared a lord and married; successive con-finements had kept her away from London for some years. Crissy all but elbowed her way through the crowd. "Phew!" Reaching Leonora, she snapped open her fan. "It's a madhouse. And here I thought I was wise coming up to town early."

"Many had the same idea, it seems." Leonora took Crissy's hand; they pressed fingers, touched cheeks.

"Mama is going to be miffed." Eyes dancing, Crissy glanced at Leonora. "She was all for stealing a march on all others with daughters to establish this Season—she's got my youngest sister to puff off, and she's set her sights on this earl who has to marry."

Leonora blinked. "An earl who has to marry?"

Crissy leaned closer and lowered her voice. "It seems this poor soul has only recently inherited and has to marry before July or lose his wealth. But he'll retain his houses and his dependents, neither of which would be easy to maintain on a pauper's budget."

A chill touched Leonora's spine. "I hadn't heard. Which earl?"

Crissy waved. "Doubtless no one thought to mention it—you're not interested in a husband, after all." She grimaced. "I always thought you were quite touched, being so set against marriage, but now . . . I have to admit there are times I think you had it right." Her expression clouded briefly, but then brightened. "Indeed, I'm here determined to enjoy myself and not think about being married at all. If this poor earl is as hunted as it sounds he'll be, maybe I'll offer him a safe harbor? I've heard he's astonishingly handsome—so rare when combined with wealth and title—"

"What title?" Leonora broke in without compunction; Crissy could ramble for hours.

"Oh—didn't I say? It's Trillingwell, Trellham—something like that."

"Trentham?"

"Yes! That's it." Crissy swung to face her. "You have heard."

"I assure you I hadn't, but I do thank you for telling me."

Crissy blinked, then studied her face. "Why, you sly thing—you know him."

Leonora narrowed her eyes to slits—not at Crissy but at a dark head she could see tacking toward her through the crowd. "I do indeed know him." In the biblical sense, what was more. "If you'll excuse me . . . I daresay we'll meet again if you're to remain in town."

Crissy grabbed her hand as she stepped out.

"Just tell me—is he as handsome as they say?"

Leonora raised her brows. "He's too handsome for his own good." Twisting free of Crissy's slackening grip, she stalked into the crowd, on a direct collision course with the earl who had to marry.

Tristan knew something was wrong the instant Leonora appeared abruptly before him. The daggers stabbing from her eyes were difficult to miss; the fingertip she jabbed into his chest was even more pointed.

"I want to talk to you. Now!"

The words were hissed, her temper clearly seething.

He consulted his conscience; it remained clear. "What's happened?"

"I'll be delighted to tell you, but I suspect you'd prefer to hear me out in private." Her eyes bored into his. "What little nook have you found for us tonight?"

He held her gaze and considered the tiny servants' pantry, which, he'd been assured, was the only possible venue for totally private engagements in Hammond House. Unlit, it would be dark and closed in—perfect for what he'd had in mind . . . "There is no place in this house suitable for any private conversation."

Especially not if she lost her temper, the leash of which looked to be already fraying.

Her eyes snapped. "Now is the time to live up to your reputation. Find one."

His talents swung into action; he took her hand, set it on his sleeve, somewhat relieved that she permitted it. "Where are your aunts?"

She waved to the side of the room. "In the chairs over there."

He headed that way, his attention on her, avoiding all the glances cast his way. Bending close, he spoke softly. "You've developed a headache—a *migraine.* Tell your aunts you feel quite ill and must leave immediately. I'll offer to drive you home in my carriage—" He broke off, halted, beckoned a footman; when the footman arrived, he issued a terse order—the footman hurried off.

They resumed their progress. "I've already sent for my carriage." He glanced at her. "If you could soften your spine, wilt a little, we might have some chance of pulling this off. We have to ensure your aunts stay here."

That last wasn't easy, but whatever the particular bee Leonora had got stuck in her bonnet, she was bound and determined to have her moment with him; it wasn't so much her acting abilities that won the day as the impression she radiated that if people did not fall in with her stated wishes, she was liable to become violent.

Mildred cast him an anxious glance. "If you're sure . . . ?"

He nodded. "My carriage is waiting—you have my word I'll take her straight home."

Leonora glanced at him, eyes narrow; he kept his expression impassive.

With the air of females bowing to a stronger—and somewhat incomprehensible—will, Mildred and Gertie remained where they were and allowed him to escort Leonora from the room, and thence from the house.

As instructed, his carriage was waiting; he handed Leonora in, then followed. The footman shut the door; a whip cracked, and the carriage lurched forward.

In the dark, he caught her hand, squeezed it. "Not yet." He spoke softly. "My coachman doesn't need to hear, and Green Street is only around the corner."

Leonora glanced at him. "Green Street?"

"I promised to take you home. My home. Where else are we to find a private room with adequate lighting for a discussion?"

She had no argument with that; indeed, she was glad he recognized the need for lighting—she wanted to be able to see his face. Inwardly seething, she grudgingly waited in silence.

His hand remained closed about hers. As they rattled through the night, his thumb stroked, almost absentmindedly. She glanced at him; he was gazing out of the window—she couldn't tell if he even realized what he was doing, much less if he intended it to soothe her temper.

The touch was soothing, but it didn't dampen her ire.

If anything, it stoked it.

How dare he be so insufferably complacent, so confident and assured, when she'd just discovered his ulterior motive, which he must have guessed she'd learn?

The carriage turned, not into Green Street, but into a narrow lane, the mews serving a row of large houses. It rocked to a halt. Tristan stirred, opened the door, and descended.

She heard him speak to his coachman, then he turned to her, beckoned. She gave him her hand and alighted; he whisked her through a garden gate before she had a chance to get her bearings.

"Where are we?"

Tristan had followed her through the gate; he shut it behind them. On the other side of the high stone wall, she heard the carriage rumble off.

"My gardens." He nodded to the house on the other side of an expanse of lawn visible through a screen of bushes. "Arriving via the front door would necessitate explanations."

"What about your coachman?"

"What about him?"

She humphed. His hand touched her back and she started along the path through the bushes. As they stepped free of the concealing shadows, he took her hand and came up beside her. The narrow path followed the garden beds bordering that wing of the house; he led her past the conservatory, past what looked like a study, and on to the long room she recognized as the morning room where his old ladies had entertained her weeks earlier.

He halted before a pair of French doors. "You didn't see this." He placed his hand, palm flat, on the frame of the doors where they met, just where the lock linked them. He gave one sharp push, and the lock clicked; the doors swung inward.

"Good gracious!"

"Sssh!" He swept her in, then closed the doors. The morning room lay in darkness. At such a late hour, this wing of the house was deserted. Taking her hand, he drew her across the room to the steps leading up to the corridor. Pausing in the shadows on the steps, he looked to the left, to where the front hall was bathed in golden light.

Peeking past him, she could see no evidence of footmen or butler.

He turned and urged her to the right, along a short, unlighted corridor. Reaching past her, he opened the door at the end and pushed it wide.

She entered; he followed and quietly shut the door.

"Wait," he breathed, then moved past her.

Faint moonlight gleamed on a heavy desk, illuminated the large chair behind it and four other chairs placed around the room. A number of cabinets and chests of drawers lined the walls. Then Tristan drew the curtains and all light vanished.

An instant later came the scrape of tinder; flame flared, lighting his face, limning the austere planes as he adjusted the lamp's wick, then reset the glass.

The warm glow spread and filled the room.

He looked at her, then waved her to the two armchairs set before the hearth. When she reached them, he came up beside her and lifted her cloak from her shoulders. He laid it aside, then bent to the embers still glowing in the hearth; sinking into one of the armchairs, she watched as he efficiently restoked the fire until it was again an acceptable blaze.

Straightening, he looked down at her. "I'm going to have some brandy. Do you want anything?"

She watched him cross to a tantalus against the wall. She doubted he would have sherry in his study. "I'll have a glass of brandy, too."

He glanced at her again, brows rising, but he poured brandy into two balloons, then returned and handed her one. She had to use both hands to hold it.

"Now." He sank into the other armchair, stretched his legs out before him, crossed his ankles, then sipped, and fixed his hazel gaze on her. "What is this all about?"

The brandy was a distraction; she set the balloon carefully on the small table beside the chair.

"This," she said, uncaring of how waspish she sounded, "is about you *needing* to marry."

He met her accusing gaze directly; he sipped again—the brandy balloon seemed a part of his large hand. "What of it?"

"*What of it?* You *have* to marry because of something to do with your inheritance. You'll lose it if you don't marry by July—is that right?"

"I'll lose the bulk of the funds but retain the title and everything entailed."

She dragged in a breath past the constriction suddenly gripping her lungs. "So—you have to marry. You don't actually *want* to marry, me or anyone else, but you have to, and so you thought I would suit. You need a wife, and I will do. Have I finally got that correct?"

He stilled. In a heartbeat changed from an elegant gentleman relaxed in the chair to a predator poised to react. All that truly changed was a sudden flaring tension, but the effect was profound.

Her lungs had locked tight; she could barely breathe.

She didn't dare take her eyes from his.

"No." When he spoke his voice had deepened, darkened. The brandy balloon looked fragile in his grip; as if realizing, he eased his fingers. "That's not how it was—how it is."

She swallowed. And tipped up her chin. She was pleased when her voice remained steady—still haughty, disbelieving. Defiant. "How is it, then?"

His gaze didn't leave her. After a moment, he spoke, and there was that in his voice that warned her not even to entertain the notion that he wasn't speaking the absolute truth. "I have to marry, that much you have right. Not because I've any personal need for my great-uncle's funds, but because, without them, keeping my fourteen dependents in the manner to which they're accustomed would be impossible."

He paused, let the words and their meaning sink in. "So yes, I have to front the altar by the end of June. However, regardless, I had and have absolutely no intention of allowing my great-uncle, or the ton's matrons, to interfere in my life—to dictate whom I will take as my bride. It's obvious that, if I so wished, a wedding to some suitable lady could be arranged, signed, sealed, and consummated in less than a week."

He paused, sipped, his gaze locked with hers. He spoke slowly, distinctly. "June is still some months away. I saw no reason to rush. Consequently, I made no effort to consider any suitable ladies"—his voice deepened, strengthened—"and then I saw you, and all such considerations became redundant."

They were sitting feet apart, yet what had grown between them, what now existed between them sprang to life at his words—a palpable force, filling the space, all but shimmering in the air.

It touched her, held her, a web of emotion so immensely strong she knew she could never break free. And, very likely, nor could he.

His gaze had remained hard, openly possessive, unwavering. "I have to marry—I would at some point have been forced to seek a wife. But then I found you, and all searching became irrelevant. *You* are the wife I want. You are the wife I will have."

She didn't—couldn't—doubt what he was telling her; the proof was there, between them.

The tension grew, became unbearable. They both had to move; he did first, coming out of the chair in a fluid, graceful motion. He held out his hand; after a moment, she took it. He drew her to her feet.

Looked down at her, his face graven, hard. "Do you understand now?"

Tipping up her face, she studied his—his eyes, the harsh, austere planes that communicated so little. Drew breath, felt forced to ask, "Why? I still don't understand why you want to marry me. Why you want me, and me alone."

He held her gaze for a long moment; she thought he wasn't going to answer, then he did.

"Guess."

It was her turn to think long and hard, then she licked her lips and murmured, "I can't." After an instant, she added, with brutal honesty, "I don't dare."

Fourteen

He'd insisted on escorting her home. Only their hands had touched; she'd been intensely grateful. He'd been watching her; she'd sensed his need, so flagrantly possessive, had appreciated the fact he'd reined it in—that he seemed to understand that she needed time to think, to absorb all he'd said, all she'd learned.

Not just of him, but of herself.

Love. If that was what he'd meant, it changed everything. He hadn't said the word, yet standing close to him, she could feel it, whatever it was—not desire, not lust, but something much stronger. Something much finer.

If it was love that had grown between them, then walking away from him, from his proposal, was, perhaps, no longer an option. Walking away would be the coward's way out.

The decision was hers. Not just her happiness but his, too, hinged on it.

With the house silent and still about her, the clock on the landing ticking through the small hours, she lay in her bed and forced herself to face the reason that had kept her from marriage.

It wasn't an aversion—nothing so definite and absolute. An aversion she could have identified and assessed, convinced herself to set aside, or overcome.

Her problem lay deeper, it was much more intangible, yet all through the years time and again it had had her shying away from marriage.

And not just marriage.

Lying in her bed, staring up at the moon-washed ceiling, she listened to the telltale clicking on the polished boards outside her bedroom door as Henrietta stretched, then padded off downstairs to wander. The sound faded. No more distraction remained.

She drew breath, and forced herself to do what she had to. To take a long look at her life, to examine all the close friendships and relationships she'd not allowed to develop.

The only reason she'd ever considered marrying Mark Whorton was because she'd recognized from the first that she would never be close, emotionally close, to him. She would never have become to him what Heather, his wife, had—a woman dependent and happily so. He'd needed that, a dependent wife. Leonora had never been a candidate for supplying that need; she had simply not been capable of it.

Thanks be to all the gods he'd had the sense to, if not see the truth, then at least act on what he'd perceived to be a dissonance between them.

The same dissonance did not exist between her and Tristan. Something else did. Possibly love.

She had to face it—to face the fact that this time, with Tristan, she fitted the bill of his wife. Precisely, exactly, in every respect. He'd recognized it instinctively; he was the type of man accustomed to acting on his instincts—and he had.

He wouldn't—didn't—expect her to be dependent, to indeed change in any way. He wanted her for what she was—the woman she was and could be—not to fulfill some ideal, some erroneous vision, but because he knew she was right for him. He was in absolutely no danger of setting her on any pedestal; conversely, through all their interactions, she'd realized he was not just capable of but disposed to worshiping her absolutely.

Her—the real her—not some figment of his imagination.

The thought—the reality—was so deeply, gut-wrenchingly attractive . . . she wanted it, could not let it go. But to grasp it, she would have to accept the emotional closeness that, with Tristan, would be— already was—a foregone conclusion, a vital part of what bound them.

She had to face what had kept her from allowing such a closeness with anyone else.

It wasn't easy going back through the years, forcing herself to strip away all the veils, all the facades she'd erected to hide and excuse the hurts. She hadn't always been as she now was—strong, capable, not needing others. Back then, she hadn't been self-sufficient, self-reliant, hadn't emotionally been able to cope, not with everything, not by herself. She'd been just like any other young girl, needing a shoulder to cry on, needing warm arms to hold her, to reassure her.

Her mother had been her touchstone, always there, always understanding. But then, one summer day, her mother and father both had died.

She still remembered the coldness, the icy loss that had settled about her, locking her in its prison. She hadn't been able to cry, had had no idea how to mourn, how to grieve. And there'd been no one to help her, no one who understood.

Her uncles and aunts—all the rest of the family—were older than her parents had been, and none had any children of their own. They'd patted her, praised her for being so brave; not one had glimpsed, had had any inkling of the anguish she'd hidden inside.

She'd kept hiding it; that was what had seemed expected of her. But every now and then, the burden had become too great, and she'd tried—*tried*—to find someone to understand, to help her find her way past it.

Humphrey had never understood; the staff at the house in Kent had no idea what was wrong with her.

No one had helped.

She'd learned to hide her need away. Step by step, incident by incident through the years of her girlhood, she'd learned *not* to ask help of anyone, not to open herself emotionally to anyone, not to trust any other person enough to ask for help—not to rely on them; if she didn't, they couldn't refuse her.

Couldn't turn her away.

The connections slowly clarified in her mind.

Tristan, she knew, wouldn't turn her away. Wouldn't refuse her.

With him, she'd be safe.

All she had to do was find the courage to accept the emotional risk she'd spent the last fifteen years teaching herself never to take.

He called at noon the next day. She was arranging flowers in the garden hall; he found her there.

She nodded in greeting, conscious of his sharp gaze, of how closely he studied her before leaning his shoulder against the doorframe, only two feet away.

"Are you all right?"

"Yes." She glanced at him, then looked back at her flowers. "You?"

After a moment, he said, "I've just come from next door. You'll see more of us coming and going in future."

She frowned. "How many of you are there?"

"Seven."

"And you're all ex- . . . Guards?"

He hesitated, then replied. "Yes."

The idea intrigued. Before she could think of her next question, he stirred, shifted closer.

She was instantly aware of his nearness, of the flaring response that rushed through her. She turned her head and looked at him.

Met his gaze—fell into it.

Couldn't look away. Could only stand there, her heart thudding, her pulse throbbing in her lips as he leaned slowly closer, then brushed an achingly incomplete kiss over her mouth.

"Have you made up your mind yet?"

He breathed the words over her hungry lips.

"No. I'm still thinking."

He drew back enough to catch her eyes. "How much thinking does it take?"

The question broke the spell; she narrowed her eyes at him, then turned back to her flowers. "More than you know."

He resettled against the doorframe, his gaze on her face. After a moment, he said, "So tell me."

She pressed her lips tight, went to shake her head—then remembered all she'd thought of in the long watches of the night. She drew a deep breath, slowly let it out. Kept her eyes on the flowers. "It's not a simple thing."

He said nothing, just waited.

She had to draw another breath. "It's been a long time since I . . . trusted anyone, anyone at all to . . . do things for me. To help me." That had been one outcome, possibly the most outwardly obvious, of her shrinking from others.

"You came to me—asked for my help—when you saw the burglar at the bottom of your garden."

Lips tight, she shook her head. "No. I came to you because you were my only way forward."

"You saw me as a source of information?"

She nodded. "You did help, but I never asked you—you never offered, you simply gave. That"—she paused as it came clear in her mind, then went on—"that's what's been happening between us all along. I never asked for help—you simply gave it, and you're strong enough that refusing was never a real option, and there seemed no reason to fight you given we were seeking the same end . . ."

Her voice quavered and she stopped.

He moved closer, took her hand.

His touch threatened to shatter her control, but then his thumb stroked; an indefinable warmth flooded her, soothed, reassured.

She lifted her head, dragged in a shaky breath.

He stepped closer yet, slid his arms around her, drew her back against him.

"Stop fighting it." The words were dark, a sorceror's command in her mind. "Stop fighting me."

She sighed, long, deep; her body relaxed against the warm solid rock of his. "I'm trying. I will." She pressed her head back, looked up over her shoulder. Met his hazel eyes. "But it won't happen today."

He gave her time. Reluctantly.

She spent her days trying to decipher Cedric's journals, searching for any mention of secret formulae, or of work done in association with Carruthers. She'd discovered that the entries weren't in any chronological order; on any given topic they were almost random— first in one book, then in another—linked, it seemed, by some unwritten code.

Her nights she spent in the ton, at balls and parties, always with Tristan by her side. His attention, fixed and unwavering, was noted by all; the few brave ladies who had attempted to distract him were given short shrift. Extremely short indeed. Thereafter, the ton settled to speculate on their wedding date.

That evening, as they strolled about Lady Court's ballroom, she explained about Cedric's journals.

Tristan frowned. "What Mountford's after *must* be something to do with Cedric's work. There seems nothing else in Number 14 that might account for this much interest."

"How much interest?" She glanced at him. "What have you learned?"

"Mountford—I still don't have a better name—is still about London. He's been sighted, but keeps moving; I haven't been able to catch up with him yet."

She didn't envy Mountford when he did. "Have you heard anything from Yorkshire."

"Yes and no. From the solicitor's files, we traced Carruthers's principal heir—one Jonathon Martinbury. He's a solicitor's clerk in York. He recently completed his articles, and was known to have been planning to travel to London, presumably to celebrate." He glanced at her, met her gaze. "It seems he received your letter, sent on from the solicitor in Harrogate, and brought his plans forward. He left on the mail coach two days later, but I've yet to locate him in town."

She frowned. "How odd. I would have thought, if he'd altered his plans in response to my letter, he would have called."

"Indeed, but one should never try to predict the priorities of young men. We don't know why he'd decided to visit London in the first place."

She grimaced. "True."

No more was said that night. Ever since their talk in his study, and their subsequent exchange in the garden hall, Tristan had refrained from arranging to indulge their senses beyond what could be achieved in the ballrooms. Even there, they were both intensely aware of each other, not just on the physical plane; each touch, each sliding caress, each shared glance, only added to the hunger.

She could feel it crawling her nerves; she didn't need to meet his often darkened eyes to know it rode him even harder.

But she had wanted time, and he gave her that.

One thing asked for—one thing received.

As she climbed the stairs to her bedroom that night, she acknowledged that, accepted it.

Once she was sunk in her bed, cozy and warm, returned to it.

She couldn't hesitate for forever. Not even for another day. It wasn't fair—not to him, not to her. She was toying with, tormenting, both of them. For no reason, not one that had relevance or power anymore.

Outside her door, Henrietta growled, then her nails scrabbled, clicked; the sound faded as the hound headed for the stairs. Leonora registered the fact, but distantly; she remained focused, undistracted.

Accept Tristan, or live without him.

Not a choice. Not for her. Not now.

She was going to take the chance—accept the risk and go forward.

The decision firmed in her mind; she waited, expecting some pulling back, some instinctive recoil, but if it was there, it was swamped beneath an upwelling tide of certainty. Of sureness.

Almost of joy.

It suddenly occurred to her that deciding to accept that inherent vulnerability was at least half the battle. Certainly for her.

She suddenly felt lighthearted, immediately started plotting how to tell Tristan of her decision—how to most appropriately break the news . . .

She had no idea how much time had passed when the realization that Henrietta had not returned to her position before her door slid into her mind.

That distracted her.

Henrietta often wandered the house at night, but never for long. She always returned to her favorite spot on the corridor rug outside Leonora's door.

She wasn't there now.

Leonora knew it even before, tugging her wrapper around her, she eased open her door and looked.

At empty space.

Faint light from the stairhead reached down the corridor; she hesitated, then, pulling her wrapper firmly about her, headed for the stairs.

She remembered Henrietta's low growl before the hound had gone off. It might have been in response to a cat crossing the back garden. Then again . . .

What if Mountford was trying to break in again?

What if he harmed Henrietta?

Her heart leapt. She'd had the hound since she was a tiny scrap of fur; Henrietta was in truth her closest confidante, the silent recipient of hundreds of secrets.

Gliding wraithlike down the stairs, she told herself not to be silly. It would be a cat. There were lots of cats in Montrose Place. Maybe two cats, and that was why Henrietta hadn't yet come back upstairs.

She reached the bottom of the main stairs and debated whether to light a candle. Belowstairs would be black; she might even stumble over Henrietta, who would expect her to see her.

Stopping by the side table at the back of the front hall, she used the tinderbox left there to strike a match and light one of the candles left waiting. Picking up the simple candlestick, she pushed through the green baize door.

Holding the candle high, she walked down the corridor. The walls leapt out at her as the candlelight touched them, but all seemed familiar, normal. Her slippers slapping on the cold tile, she passed the butler's pantry and the housekeeper's room, then came to the short flight of stairs leading down to the kitchens.

She paused and looked down. All below was inky black, except for patches of faint moonlight slanting in through the kitchen windows and through the small fanlight above the back door. In the diffuse light from the latter, she could just make out the shaggy outline of Henrietta; the hound was curled up against the corridor wall, her head on her paws.

"Henrietta?" Straining her eyes, Leonora peered down.

Henrietta didn't move, didn't twitch.

Something was wrong. Henrietta wasn't that young. Greatly fearing the hound had suffered a seizure, Leonora grabbed up her trailing night rail and rushed down the stairs.

"Henriet—*oh!*"

She stopped on the last stair, mouth agape, face-to-face with the man who had stepped from the black shadows to meet her.

Candlelight flickered over his black-avised face; his lips curled in a snarl.

Pain exploded in the back of her skull. She dropped the candle, pitched forward as all light extinguished and everything went black.

For an instant, she thought it was simply the candle going out, then from a great distance she heard Henrietta start to howl. To bay. The most horrible, bloodcurdling sound in the world.

She tried to open her eyes and couldn't.

Pain knifed through her head. The black intensified and dragged her down.

Returning to consciousness wasn't pleasant. For some considerable time, she hung back, hovered in that land that was neither here nor there, while voices washed over her, concerned, some sharp with anger, others with fear.

Henrietta was there, at her side. The hound whined and licked her fingers. The rough caress drew her inexorably back, through the mists, into the real world.

She tried to open her eyes. Her lids were inordinately heavy; her lashes fluttered. Weakly, she raised a hand, and realized there was a wide bandage circling her head.

All talk abruptly ceased.

"She's awake!"

That came from Harriet. Her maid rushed to her side, took her hand, patted it. "Don't you fret. The doctor's been, and he says you'll be good as new in no time."

Leaving her hand limp in Harriet's clasp, she digested that.

"Are you all right, sis?"

Jeremy sounded strangely shaken; he seemed to be hovering close by. She was lying stretched out, her feet elevated higher than her head, on a chaise . . . she must be in the parlor.

A heavy hand awkwardly patted her knee. "Just rest, my dear," Humphrey advised. "Heaven knows what the world is coming to, but . . ." His voice quavered and trailed away.

An instant later came a rough growl, "She'll do better if you don't crowd her."

Tristan.

She opened her eyes, looked straight at him, standing beyond the end of the chaise.

His face was more rigidly set than she'd ever seen it; the cast of his patrician features screamed a warning to any who knew him.

His blazing eyes were warning enough to anyone at all.

She blinked. Didn't shift her gaze. "What happened?"

"You were hit on the head."

"That much I'd gathered." She glanced at Henrietta; the hound pushed closer. "I went down to look for Henrietta. She'd gone downstairs but hadn't come back. She usually does."

"So you went after her."

She looked back at Tristan. "I thought something might have happened. And it had." She looked back at Henrietta, frowned. "She was by the back door, but she didn't move . . ."

"She was drugged. Laudanum in port, trickled under the back door."

She reached for Henrietta, palmed the shaggy face, looked into the bright brown eyes.

Tristan shifted. "She's fully recovered—lucky for you, whoever it was didn't use enough to do more than make her snooze."

She dragged in a breath, winced when her head ached sharply. Looked again at Tristan. "It was Mountford. I came face-to-face with him at the bottom of the stairs."

For one instant, she thought he would actually snarl; the violence she glimpsed in him, that flowed across his features was frightening. Even more so because part of that aggression was directed, quite definitely, at her.

Her revelation had shocked the others; they were all looking at her, not Tristan.

"Who's Mountford?" Jeremy demanded. He looked from Leonora to Tristan. "What is this about?"

Leonora sighed. "It's about the burglar—he's the man I saw at the bottom of our garden."

That piece of information had Jeremy's and Humphrey's jaws dropping. They were horrified—doubly so because not even they could any longer close their eyes, pretend the man was a figment of her imagination. Imagination hadn't drugged Henrietta nor cracked Leonora's skull. Forced to acknowledge reality, they exclaimed, they declared.

The noise was all too much. She closed her eyes and slipped gratefully away.

Tristan felt like a violin string stretched to snapping point, but when he saw Leonora's eyes close, saw her brow and features smooth into the blankness of unconsciousness, he dragged in a breath, swallowed his demons, and got the others out of the room without roaring at them.

They went, but reluctantly. Yet after all he'd heard, all he'd learned, to his mind they'd forfeited any right they might have had to watch over her. Even her maid, devoted though she seemed.

He sent her to prepare a tisane, then returned to stand looking down at Leonora. She was still pale, but her skin was no longer deathly white as it had been when he'd first reached her side.

Jeremy, no doubt prodded by incipient guilt, had had the sense to send a footman next door; Gasthorpe had taken charge, sending one footman flying to Green Street, and another for the doctor he'd been instructed was the one always to summon. Jonas Pringle was a veteran of the Peninsula campaigns; he could treat knife and gunshot wounds without turning a hair. A knock on the head was a minor affair, but his assurance, backed by experience, had been what Tristan had needed.

Only that had kept him marginally civilized.

Realizing Leonora might not wake for some time, he raised his head and looked through the windows. Dawn was just starting to streak the sky. The urgency that had propelled him through the last hours started to ebb.

Pulling one of the armchairs around to face the chaise, he dropped into it, stretched out his legs, fixed his gaze on Leonora's face, and settled to wait.

She resurfaced an hour later, lids fluttering, then opening as she drew in a sharp, pain-filled breath.

Her gaze fell on him, and widened. She blinked, glanced around as well as she could without moving her head.

He lifted his jaw from his fist. "We're alone."

Her gaze returned to him; she studied his face. Frowned. "What's wrong?"

He'd spent the last hour rehearsing how to tell her; now the time had come, he was too tired to play any games. Not with her. "Your maid. She was hysterical when I got here."

She blinked; when her lids lifted, he saw in her eyes that she'd already jumped ahead, seen what must have happened, but when she met his gaze, he couldn't interpret her expression. Surely she couldn't have forgotten the earlier attacks. Equally, he couldn't imagine why she'd be surprised at his reaction.

His voice was rougher than he intended when he said, "She told me about two early attacks on you. Specifically on you. One in the street, one in your front garden."

Her eyes on his, she nodded, winced. "But it wasn't Mountford."

That was news. News that sent his temper soaring. He shot to his feet, unable any longer to pretend to a calmness that was far beyond him.

He swore, paced. Then swung to face her. *"Why didn't you tell me?"*

She met his gaze, didn't cower in the least, then quietly said, "I didn't think it was important."

"Not . . . important." Fists clenched, he managed to keep his tone reasonably even. "You were threatened, and you didn't think that was important." He locked his eyes on hers. "You didn't think *I* would think that important?"

"It wasn't—"

"No!" He cut off her words with a slicing motion. Felt compelled to pace again, glancing briefly at her, struggling to get his thoughts in order, in sufficient order to communicate to her.

Words burned his tongue, too heated, too violent to let loose.

Words he knew he would regret the instant he uttered them.

He had to focus; he brought all his considerable training to bear, forcing himself to cut to the heart of the matter. Ruthlessly to strip away every last veil and face the cold hard truth—the central solid reality that was the only thing that truly mattered.

Abruptly, he halted, drew in a tense breath. Swung to face her, locked his eyes on hers. "I've come to care for you." He had to force the words out; low and gravelly, they grated. "Not just a little, but deeply. More deeply, more completely, than I've cared for anything or anyone in my life."

He drew a tight breath, kept his gaze on her eyes. "Caring for someone means, however reluctantly, giving some part of yourself into their keeping. They—the one cared for—becomes the repository of that part of you"—his eyes held hers—"of that something you've given that's so profoundly precious. That's so profoundly important. They, therefore, become *important*—deeply, profoundly important."

He paused, then more quietly stated, "As you are to me."

The clock ticked; their gazes remained locked. Neither moved.

Then he stirred. "I've done all I can to explain, to make you understand."

His expression closed; he turned to the door.

Leonora tried to rise. Couldn't. "Where are you going?"

Hand on the knob, he looked back at her. "I'm leaving. I'll send your maid to you." His words were clipped, but emotion, suppressed, seethed beneath them. "When you can cope with being important to someone, you know where to find me."

"Tristan . . ." With an effort, she swiveled, lifted her hand—

The door shut. Clicked with a finality that echoed through the room.

She stared at the door for a long moment, then sighed and sank back on the chaise. Closed her eyes. She comprehended perfectly what she'd done. Knew she would have to undo it.

But not now. Not today.

She was too weak even to think, and she would need to think, to plan, to work out exactly what to say to soothe her wounded wolf.

The next three days turned into a parade of apologies.

Forgiving Harriet was easy enough. The poor soul had been so overset on seeing Leonora lying senseless on the kitchen flags, she'd babbled hysterically about men attacking her; one minor comment had been enough to attract Tristan's attention. He'd ruthlessly extracted all the details from Harriet, and left her in an even more emotionally wrought state.

When Leonora retired to her bed after consuming a bowl of soup for luncheon—all she could imagine keeping down—Harriet helped her up the stairs and into her room without a word, without once looking up or meeting her eye.

Inwardly sighing, Leonora sat on her bed, then encouraged Harriet to pour out her guilt, her worries and concerns, then made peace with her.

That proved the easiest fence to mend.

Drained, still physically shaken, she remained in her room for the rest of the day. Her aunts called, but after one look at her face, kept their visit brief. At her insistence, they agreed to avoid all mention of the attack; to all who asked after her, she would be simply indisposed.

The next morning, Harriet had just removed her breakfast tray and left her sitting in an armchair before the fire, when a tap sounded on her door. She called, "Come in."

The door opened; Jeremy looked around it.

He spotted her. "Are you well enough to talk?"

"Yes, of course." She waved him in.

He came slowly, carefully shutting the door behind him, then walking quietly across to stand by the mantelpiece and look down at her. His gaze fastened on the bandage still circling her head. A spasm contorted his features. "It's my fault you got hurt. I should have listened—paid more attention. I knew it wasn't your imagination, what you said about the burglars, but it was so much easier to simply ignore it all—"

He was twenty-four, but suddenly he was, once again, her little brother. She let him talk, let him say what he needed to. Let him, too, make his peace, not just with her but himself. The man he knew he should have been.

A draining twenty minutes later, he was sitting on the floor beside her chair, his head leaning against her knee.

She stroked his hair, so soft yet as ever ruffled and unruly.

Suddenly, he shivered. "If Trentham hadn't come . . ."

"If he hadn't, you would have coped."

After a moment, he sighed, then rubbed his cheek against her knee. "I suppose."

She remained in bed for the rest of that day, too. By the next morning, she was feeling considerably better. The doctor called again, tested her vision and her balance, probed the tender spot on her skull, then pronounced himself satisfied.

"But I would advise you to avoid any activity that might exhaust you, at least for the next few days."

She was considering that—considering the apology *she* had to make and how exhausting, mentally and physically, that was likely to be—as she slowly, carefully, went down the stairs.

Humphrey was sitting on a bench in the hall; using his cane, he slowly rose as she descended. He smiled, a little lopsidedly. "There you are, my dear. Feeling better?"

"Indeed. A great deal better, thank you." She was tempted to launch into questions about the household, anything to avoid what she foresaw was to come. She put the urge from her as unworthy; Humphrey, like Harriet and Jeremy, needed to speak. Smiling easily, she accepted his arm when he offered it and steered him into the parlor.

The interview was worse—more emotionally involved—than she'd expected. They sat side by side on the chaise in the parlor, looking out over the gardens but seeing nothing of them. To her surprise, Humphrey's guilt stretched back many more years than she'd realized.

He broached his recent shortcomings head-on, apologizing gruffly, but then he looked back, and she'd discovered he'd spent the last days thinking much more deeply than she'd guessed.

"I should have made Mildred come down to Kent more often—I knew it at the time." Staring through the window, he absentmindedly patted Leonora's hand. "You see, when your aunt Patricia died, I shut myself away—I swore I'd never care for anyone like that again, never leave myself open to so much hurt. I liked having you and Jeremy about the house—you were my distractions, my anchors to the daily round; with you two about, it was easy to forget my hurt and lead a normal enough life.

"But I was absolutely determined never to let any person get close, and become important to me. Not again. So I always kept myself distanced from you—from Jeremy, too, in many ways." His old eyes weary, half-filled with tears, he turned to her. Smiled weakly, wryly. "And so I failed you, my dear, failed to take care of you as I ought, and I'm immensely ashamed of that. But I failed myself, too, in more ways than one. I cut myself off from what might have been between us, you and me, and with Jeremy, too. I shortchanged us all in that regard. But I still didn't achieve what I wanted—I was too arrogant to see that caring about others is not wholly a conscious decision."

His fingers tightened about hers. "When we found you lying on the flags that night . . ."

His voice quavered, died.

"Oh, Uncle." Leonora raised her arms and hugged him. "It doesn't matter. Not anymore." She rested her head on his shoulder "It's past."

He hugged her back, but brusquely replied, "It *does* matter, but we won't argue, because you're right—it's in the past. From now on, we go forward as we should have been." He ducked his head to look into her face. "Eh?"

She smiled, a trifle teary herself. "Yes. Of course."

"Good!" Humphrey released her and hauled in a breath. "Now—you must tell me all you and Trentham have discovered. I gather there's some question about Cedric's work?"

She explained. When Humphrey demanded to see Cedric's journals she fetched a few from the stack in the corner.

"Hmm . . . humph!" Humphrey read down one page, then eyed the stack of journals. "How far have you got with these?"

"I'm only onto the fourth, but . . ." She explained that the journals were not filled in chronological order.

"He'll have had some other order—a journal for each idea, for instance." Humphrey shut the book on his lap. "No reason Jeremy and I can't put our other work aside and give you a hand with these. Not your forte, but it is ours, after all."

She managed not to gape. "But what about the Mesapotamians—and the Sumerians?"

The work they were both engaged in was a commission from the British Museum.

Humphrey snorted, waved the protest aside as he levered to his feet. "The museum can wait—this patently can't. Not if some nefarious and dangerous bounder is after something here. Besides"—on his feet, he straightened and grinned at Leonora—"who else is the museum going to get to do such translations?"

An unarguable point. She rose and crossed to the bellpull. When Castor entered, she instructed him to move the stack of journals to the library. The journal he'd been looking at tucked under his arm, Humphrey shuffled out in that direction, Leonora assisting him; a footman carrying the journals passed them in the hall—they followed him into the library.

Jeremy looked up; as always open books covered his desk.

Humphrey waved his stick. "Clear a space. New task. Urgent matter."

"Oh?"

To Leonora's surprise, Jeremy obeyed, shutting books and moving them so the footman could set the towering stack of journals down.

Jeremy immediately took the top one and opened it. "What are they?"

Humphrey explained; Leonora added that they were assuming there was some valuable formula buried somewhere in the journals.

Already absorbed in the volume in his hands, Jeremy humphed.

Humphrey returned to his seat, and returned to the volume he'd carried from the parlor. Leonora considered, then left to check with the servants, and review all household matters.

An hour later, she reentered the library. Both Jeremy and Humphrey had their heads down; a frown was fixed on Jeremy's face. He looked up when she lifted the top volume off the pile of journals.

"Oh." He blinked somewhat myopically at her.

She sensed his instinctive wish to take the book back. "I thought I'd help."

Jeremy colored, glanced at Humphrey. "Actually, it's not going to be easy to do that, not unless you can stay here most of the day."

She frowned. "Why?"

"It's the cross-referencing. We've only just made a start, but it's going to be a nightmare until we discover the connection between the journals, and their correct sequence, too. We'll have to do it verbally— it's simply too big a job, and we need the answer too urgently, to attempt to write down connections." He looked at her. "We're used to it. If there are other avenues that need to be investigated, you might be better employed—we might get this mystery solved sooner if you gave your attention to them."

Neither wanted to exclude her; it was there in their eyes, in their earnest expressions. But Jeremy spoke the truth; they were the experts in this field—and she really did not fancy spending the rest of the day and the evening, too, squinting at Cedric's wavering script.

And there were numerous other matters on her plate.

She smiled benignly. "There are other avenues it would be worthwhile exploring, if you can cope without me?"

"Oh, yes."

"We'll manage."

Her smile widened. "Good, then I'll leave you to it."

Turning, she went to the door. Glancing back as she turned the knob, she saw both heads down again. Still smiling, she left.

And determinedly turned her mind to her most urgent task: tending to her wounded wolf.

Fifteen

Accomplishing that goal—making her peace with Tristan—arranging to do so, required a degree of ingenuity and bold-faced recklessness she'd never before had to employ. But she had no choice. She summoned Gasthorpe, boldly gave him orders, arranged to hire a carriage and be conveyed to the mews behind Green Street, the coachman to wait for her return.

All, of course, with the firm insistence that under no circumstances was his-lordship-the-earl to be informed. She'd discovered a ready intelligence in Gasthorpe; although she hadn't liked subverting him from his loyalty to Tristan, when all was said and done, it was for Tristan's own good.

When, in the darkness of late evening, she stood in the bushes at the end of Tristan's garden and saw light shining from the windows of his study, she felt vindicated in every respect.

He hadn't gone out to any ball or dinner. Given her absence from the *ton*, the fact that he, too, wasn't attending the usual events would be generating intense speculation. Following the path through the bushes and farther to where it skirted the house, she wondered how immediate he would wish their wedding to be. For herself, having made her decision, she didn't truly care . . . or, if she did, she would rather it was sooner than later.

Less time to anticipate how things would work out—much better to take the plunge and get straight on with it.

Her lips lifted. She suspected he would share that opinion, if not for quite the same reasons.

Pausing outside the study, she stood on tiptoe and peeked in; the floor was considerably higher than the ground. Tristan was seated at his desk, his back to her, his head bent as he worked. A pile of papers sat on his right; on his left, a ledger lay open.

She could see enough to be sure he was alone.

Indeed, as he turned to check an entry in the ledger and she glimpsed his face, he *looked* very much alone. A lone wolf who'd had to change his solitary ways and live among the ton, with title, houses, and dependents, and all the associated demands.

He'd given up his freedom, his exciting, dangerous, and lonely life, and picked up the reins that had been left to his care without complaint.

In return, he'd asked for little, either in excuse, or as reward.

The one thing he had asked of this new life was to have her as his wife. He'd offered her all she could hope for, given her all she could and would accept.

In return, she'd given him her body, but not what he'd wanted most. She hadn't given him her trust. Or her heart.

Or rather, she had, but she'd never admitted it. Never told him.

She was there to rectify that omission.

Turning away, taking care to tread silently, she continued toward the morning room. She'd guessed he would stay in and work at estate matters, all the matters he'd no doubt been neglecting while concentrating on catching Mountford. The study was where she'd hoped he'd be; she'd seen both library and study, and it was the study that held the most definite impression of him, of being the room to which he would retreat. His lair.

She was glad to have been proved right; the library was in the other wing, across the front hall.

Reaching the French doors through which they'd entered on her previous visit, she placed herself squarely before them, braced her hands on the frame as he had—using both hands rather than just one—and pushed sharply.

The doors rattled, but remained closed.

"Damn!" She frowned at them, then stepped close and put her shoulder to the spot. She counted to three, then flung her weight against the doors.

They popped open; she only just saved herself from sprawling on the floor.

Regaining her balance, she whirled and closed the doors, then, catching her cloak about her, slunk silently into the room. She waited, breath bated, to see if anyone had been alerted; she didn't think she'd made much noise.

No footsteps sounded; no one came. Her heartbeat gradually slowed.

Cautiously, she went forward. The last thing she wished was to be discovered breaking into this house in order to meet illicitly with its master; if she were caught, once they wed, she'd have to dismiss, or bribe, the entire staff. She didn't want to have to face the choice.

She checked the front hall. As before, at this time of night there were no footmen hovering; Havers, the butler, would be belowstairs. Her way was clear; she slipped into the shadows of the corridor leading to the study with a prayer on her lips.

In thanks for what she'd thus far received, and with hope that her luck would hold.

Halting outside the study door, she faced the panels, and tried to imagine, in a last-minute rehearsal, how their conversation would go . . . but her mind stubbornly remained blank.

She had to get on with it, with her apology and her declaration. Drawing in a deep breath, she grasped the doorknob.

It jerked out of her grip; the door was flung wide.

She blinked, and found Tristan beside her. Towering over her.

He looked past her, down the corridor, then seized her hand and pulled her into the room. Lowering the pistol he held in his other hand, he released her and closed the door.

She stared at the pistol. "Good heavens!" She lifted stunned eyes to his face. "Would you have shot me?"

His eyes narrowed. "Not you. I didn't know who . . ." His lips thinned. He turned away. "Creeping up on me is never wise."

She opened her eyes wide. "I'll remember that in future."

He prowled to a sideboard and laid the pistol in the display case atop it. His gaze was dark as he glanced back at her, then returned to stand by the desk.

She remained where she'd halted, more or less in the middle of the room. It wasn't a big room, and he was in it.

His gaze rose to her face. Hardened. "What are you doing here? No—wait!" He held up a hand. "First tell me how you got here."

She'd expected that tack. Clasping her hands, she nodded. "You didn't call—not that I'd expected it"—she had, but had realized her error—"so I had to call here. As we've previously discovered, me calling during the customary visiting hours is unlikely to provide us with much chance of private conversation, so . . . ." She dragged in a huge breath and rushed on, "I summoned Gasthorpe, and hired a coach through him—I insisted he keep the matter strictly private, so you mustn't hold that against him. The coach—"

She told him all, stressing that the coach with coachman and footman was waiting in the mews to take her home. When she came to the end of her recitation, he let a moment pass, then faintly raised his brows—the first change in his expression since she'd entered the room.

He shifted and leaned back against the edge of the desk. His gaze remained on her face. "Jeremy—where does he think you are?"

"He and Humphrey are quite sure I'm asleep. They've thrown themselves into making sense of Cedric's journals; they're engrossed."

A subtle change rippled across his features, sharpening, hardening; she quickly added, "Despite that, Jeremy did make sure the locks were all changed, as you suggested."

He held her gaze; a long moment passed, then he inclined his head fractionally, acknowledging she'd read his thoughts accurately. Dampening an urge to smile, she went on, "Regardless, I've been keeping Henrietta in my room at night, so she won't wander . . ." And disturb her, worry her. She blinked, and continued, "So I had to take her with me when I left this evening—she's with Biggs in the kitchen at Number 12."

Tristan considered. Inwardly humphed. She'd covered all the necessary details; he could rest easy on that score. She was there, safe; she'd even arranged her safe return. He settled against the desk, crossed his arms. Let his gaze, fixed on her face, grow even more intent. "So why are you here?"

She met his gaze directly, steadily, perfectly calm. "I've come to apologize."

He raised his brows; she went on, "I should have remembered about those first attacks, and told you of them, but what with all that's happened more recently, they'd drifted to the back of my mind." She studied his eyes, considering rather than searching; he realized she was assembling her words as she went—this was no rehearsed speech.

"Nevertheless, at the time the attacks occurred, we hadn't met, and there was no other who considered me important in that vein, such that I would feel obliged to inform them. Warn them."

She lifted her chin, still held his eyes. "I accept and concede that the situation has now changed, that I'm important to you, and that you therefore need to know. . . ." She hesitated, frowned at him, then reluctantly amended, "Perhaps even have a right to know, of anything that constitutes a threat to me."

Again she paused, as if reviewing her words, then straightened and nodded, her eyes refocusing on his. "So I apologize unequivocally for not telling you of those incidents, for not recognizing that I should."

He blinked, slowly; he hadn't expected an apology in such thorough and crystal-clear terms. His nerves started tingling; a nervous eagerness gripped him. He recognized his typical reaction to being on the brink of success. To having victory—complete and absolute—within his grasp.

Of being only one step away from seizing it.

"You agree that I have a right to know of any threat to you?"

She met his gaze, nodded decisively. "Yes."

He considered for only a heartbeat, then asked, "Do I take it you agree to marry me?"

She didn't hesitate. "Yes."

A tight knot of tension he'd carried for so long he'd become unaware of it unraveled and fell from him. The relief was immense. He drew in a huge breath, felt as if it was the first truly free breath he'd had in weeks.

But he wasn't finished with her—hadn't finished extracting promises from her—yet.

Straightening from the desk, he trapped her gaze. "You agree to be my wife, to act in all ways as my wife, and obey me in all things?"

This time she hesitated, frowned. "That's three questions. Yes, yes, and in all things reasonable."

He raised one brow. " 'In all things reasonable.' It seems we need some definitions." He closed the distance between them, halted directly before her. Looked into her eyes. "Do you agree that wherever you go, whatever you do, should any activity involve the smallest degree of danger to you, then you will inform me of it first, before you undertake it?"

Her lips compressed; her eyes were locked on his. "If possible, yes."

He narrowed his eyes. "You're quibbling."

"You're being unreasonable."

"It's unreasonable for a man to want to know his wife is safe at all times?"

"No. But it's unreasonable to wrap her in some protective cocoon to achieve that."

"That's a matter of opinion."

He growled the words *sotto voce,* but Leonora heard them. He shifted intimidatingly closer; her temper started to rise. She determinedly reined it in. She hadn't come to war with him. He was far too used to conflict; she was determined to have none of it between them. She held his hard gaze, as definite as he. "I'm perfectly willing to do everything possible—everything within reason—to accommodate your protective tendencies."

She invested the words with every ounce of her determination, her commitment. He heard it ring; she saw understanding—and acceptance—flow behind his eyes.

They sharpened until his gaze was crystalline hazel, intent on her. "If that's the best offer you're prepared to make . . . ?"

"It is."

"Then I accept." His gaze dropped to her lips. "Now . . . I want to know to what lengths you're prepared to go to accommodate my other tendencies."

It was as if he'd lowered a shield, abruptly dropped a barrier between them. A wave of sexual heat washed over her; she suddenly remembered he was a wounded wolf—a wild wounded wolf—and she'd yet to appease him. At least on that level. Logically, rationally—in words—she'd made amends, and he'd accepted. But that wasn't the only plane on which they interacted.

Her breath slowly strangled. "What other tendencies?" She got the words out before her voice grew too weak—anything to gain a few more seconds . . .

His gaze drifted lower; her breasts swelled, ached. Then he raised his lids, looked into her face. "Those tendencies you've been running from, trying to avoid, but nevertheless enjoying for the past several weeks."

He shifted closer; his coat brushed her bodice, his thigh touched hers.

Her heart thudded in her throat; desire spread like wildfire beneath her skin. She looked into his face, at his thin, mobile lips, felt her own throb. Then she lifted her gaze to his mesmeric hazel eyes—and the truth broke over her. In all that had passed between them, all they'd shared to date, he hadn't yet shown her, revealed to her, all.

Revealed, let her see, the depths, the true breadth of his possessiveness. Of his passion, his desire to possess her.

He reached for the ties of her cloak, with one tug had them free; the garment slid to the floor, pooling behind her. She'd worn a simple, deep blue evening gown; she watched his gaze roam her shoulders, frankly possessive, frankly hungry, then once more he met her gaze. Raised one brow. "So . . . what will you give me? How much will you yield?"

His eyes were locked with hers; she knew what he wanted.

All.

No reservations, no restrictions.

Knew in her heart, knew by the leaping of her senses that in that they were matched, that regardless of any ideas to the contrary, she was and would always be incapable of denying him exactly what he wanted.

Because she wanted it, too.

Despite his aggressiveness, despite the dark desire that smoldered in his eyes, there was nothing here for her to fear.

Only enjoy.

While she finished paying his price.

She moistened her lips, glanced at his. "What do you want me to say?" Her voice was low, her tone unashamedly sultry. Meeting his eyes, she arched a haughty brow. "Take me, I'm yours?"

A spark to tinder; the flames flared in his eyes. Crackled between them.

"That"—he reached for her; hands spanning her waist, he drew her uncompromisingly flush against him—"will do nicely."

Bending his head, he set his lips to hers, and whirled them straight into the fire.

She parted her lips to him, welcomed him in, gloried in the heat he sent pouring through her veins.

Gloried in his possession of her mouth, slow, thorough, powerful, a warning of all that was to come.

Lifting her arms, she wound them about his neck, and abandoned herself to her fate.

He seemed to know, to sense her total and complete surrender—to him, to this, to the heated moment.

To the passion and desire that spilled through them.

He raised his hands and framed her face, anchored her as he deepened the kiss. Melding their mouths until they breathed as one, until the same pounding rhythm had laid siege in their veins.

With a low murmur, she pressed to him, wantonly inciting. His hands left her face, drifted down, curving about her shoulders, then boldly tracing her breasts. He closed his fingers, and the flames leapt. She shuddered, and urged him on. Kissed him as hungrily, as demanding as he was. He obliged, his fingers finding the tight peaks of her nipples and squeezing slowly, excruciatingly, tight.

She broke from the kiss on a gasp. His hands didn't stop; they were everywhere, kneading, stroking, caressing. Possessing.

Heating her. Setting fires beneath her skin, making her pulse rage.

"This time, I want you naked."

She could barely make out the words.

"With not a stitch to hide behind."

She couldn't imagine what he thought she might hide. Didn't care.

When he turned her and set his fingers to her laces, she waited only until she felt the bodice loosen to slip the gown from her shoulders. She went to slide her arms from the tiny sleeves—

"No. Wait."

A command she was in no position to disobey; her wits were whirling, her senses in eager tumult, anticipation building with every breath, with every possessive touch. But he wasn't touching her now. Lifting her head, she drew in a shaky, broken breath.

"Turn around."

She did, just as the level of light in the small room increased. Two heavy lamps sat on either end of the huge desk. He'd turned the wicks high; as she faced him he settled, sitting propped against the front edge of the desk midway between the lamps.

He met her gaze, then his lowered. To her breasts, still concealed behind the gauzy shimmer of her silk chemise.

He raised a hand, beckoned. "Come here."

She did, through the tumbling cascade of her thoughts recalled that despite the fact they'd been intimate on numerous occasions, he'd never seen her naked in any degree of light.

One glance at his face confirmed that he intended to see all tonight.

His hand slid about her hip; he drew her to stand before him, between his legs. Took her hands, one in each of his, and laid them, palms flat, on his thighs. "Don't move them until I tell you."

Her mouth was dry; she didn't answer. Just watched his face as he slid the sleeves of her bodice farther down her arms, then reached—not for the ties of her chemise as she'd expected—but for the silk-screened mounds of her breasts.

What followed was a delicious torment. He traced, fondled, weighed, kneaded—all the time watching her, gauging her reactions. Under his practiced ministrations, her breasts swelled, grew heavy and tight. Until they ached. The fine film of silk was just enough to taunt, to tease, to have her gasping with need—the need to have his hands on her.

Skin to burning skin.

"Please . . ." The plea fell from her lips as she looked up at the ceiling, trying to cling to sanity.

His hands left her; she waited, then felt his fingers close about her wrists. He lifted her hands as she lowered her head and looked at him.

His eyes were dark pools lit by golden flames. "Show me."

He guided her hands to the ribbon ties.

Her gaze merged with his, she gripped the ends of the ribbons, and tugged, then, totally enthralled by what she could see in his face, the naked passion, the driving need, she slowly peeled the fine fabric down, exposing her breasts to the light.

And to him. His gaze felt like flame, licking, heating. Without looking up, he caught her hands and drew them back to his thighs. "Leave them there."

Releasing her hands, he raised his to her breasts.

The real torture began. He seemed to know just how much she could take, then he bent his head, soothed an aching nipple with his tongue, then took it into his mouth.

Feasted.

Until she cried out. Until her fingertips clung to the iron muscles of his thighs. He suckled, and her knees quaked. He locked one arm beneath her hips and supported her, held her steady while he did as he wished, imprinted himself on her skin, on her nerves, on her senses.

She cracked open her lids; panting, glanced down. Watched and felt his dark head move against her as he pandered to his desires—and hers.

With each touch of his lips, each swirl of his tongue, each dragging nerve-tingling suction, he ruthlessly, relentlessly stoked the fire within her.

Until she burned. Until, incandescent and empty, she felt like a glowing void, one she yearned for, ached for, desperately needed him to fill. To complete.

She lifted her hands, with a wriggle slid her arms free of her sleeves, then reached for him, traced his jaw with her palms, felt them work as he suckled. She slid her fingers back into his hair; reluctantly, he eased back, released her soft flesh.

Looked into her face, met her eyes, then he set her on her feet. His large palms stroked up, tracing the heated swollen curves, then stroked down, over her waist, possessively following her contours, pushing her gown and chemise down, over the swell of her hips, until with a soft whoosh they fell, puddling about her feet.

His gaze had followed the fabric to her knees. He studied them, then slowly, deliberately, lifted his gaze, past her thighs, lingering on the dark curls at their apex before moving slowly on, upward, over the gentle swell of her stomach, over her navel, her waist, to her breasts, eventually to her face, her lips, her eyes. A long comprehensive survey, one that left her in no doubt that he considered all he saw, all she was, to be his.

She shivered, not with cold but with burgeoning need. She reached for his cravat.

He caught her hands. "No. Not tonight."

Despite the grip of desire, she managed a faint frown. "I want to see you, too."

"You'll see enough of me over the years." He stood; still holding her hands, he stepped to the side. "Tonight . . . I want you. Naked. Mine." He trapped her gaze. "On this desk."

The desk? She looked at it.

He released her hands, locked his about her waist and lifted her, placed her sitting on the front of the desk where he'd been leaning.

The sensation of polished mahogany beneath her bare bottom temporarily distracted her.

Tristan gripped her knees, spread them wide and stepped between. Caught her face in his hands as she looked up, surprised— and kissed her.

Let his reins slide, simply let go, let desire rage and pour through him, and her. Their mouths melded, tongues tangled. Her hands framed his jaw as his drifted lower, needing to find her soft flesh again, needing to feel her urgency, her flaring response to his touch—all the evidence that she truly was his.

Her body was liquid silk under his hands, passion hot and urgent. He gripped her hips and leaned into her, gradually eased her back, at the last pressing her down to lie across his great-uncle's desk.

He drew back from the kiss, half straightened, seized the moment to look down on her, lying naked, heated, and panting, across the gleaming mahogany. The wood was no richer than her hair, still anchored in a knot atop her head.

He thought of that as he set a hand to one bare knee and slowly slid it upward, tracing the firm muscle of her thigh as he leaned down to her and took her mouth again.

Filled it, claimed like a conqueror, then set up a rhythm of thrust and retreat she and her body knew well. She was with him in thought and deed, in desire and urgency. She shifted beneath his hands; locking one about her hip, anchoring her, he trailed the fingers of the other from the spot between her breasts down over her waist, over her stomach to tantalizingly caress the damp curls covering her mons.

She gasped through their kiss. He broke from it, drew back enough to catch her eyes, gleaming an intense violet blue beneath her lashes. "Let down your hair."

Leonora blinked, acutely conscious of his fingertips idly stroking through her curls. Not quite touching her aching flesh. It throbbed; all of her pulsed with longing. With a sensual need impossible to deny.

She lifted her arms, eyes locked with his, and slowly reached for the pins holding her long locks. As she grasped the first, he touched her, set one blunt fingertip to her.

Her body tensed, lightly bowed; she closed her eyes, gripped the pin, and pulled it loose. Sensed his satisfaction in his touch, in his slow, teasing caress. Cracking open her lids, she watched him watching her; fingers searching, she found another pin.

Had to close her eyes again as she pulled it free—and he made free with her body. Touched, stroked.

Then delicately probed.

Just a gentle pressure at the entrance to her body.

Enough to tantalize, not enough to slake.

Eyes closed, she pulled another pin; one large finger glided in a fraction farther.

She was swollen, throbbing, wet. Dragging in a breath, with both hands she searched, pulled, let the pins fall in a rain on the desk.

By the time her hair tumbled loose, he'd buried his fingers in her sheath, penetrating, stroking, stoking. She was gasping for breath, her nerves alive, her body writhing against his hold. Her long hair spread about her shoulders, across the desk. She looked up at him, and saw his gaze drifting over her, taking in her abandonment; stark possession stamped his features.

He caught her gaze, studied her, then leaned down, and kissed her. Took her mouth, captured her senses in a drugging kiss. Then his lips left hers; he nudged her jaw higher, dipped his head to trail hot, openmouthed kisses down the taut line of her throat, down over the swell of her breasts. He lingered there, licking, laving, suckling, but lightly, then his hair brushed the soft undersides as he followed the line of her body lower. She was struggling for breath, far past wanton abandon; feelings, sensations, poured irresistibly through her, filling her, sweeping her on.

Her hands had come to rest on his shoulders; he was still clad in his coat. The tactile reminder emphasized her vulnerability; he had her completely naked, writhing before him, displayed on his desk like a houri . . . she gasped as his lips cruised over her stomach.

He didn't stop.

"Tristan . . . *Tristan!*"

He paid no heed; she had to swallow her screams as he pressed her thighs wider and sank between. Settled to feast as he had once before, but that time she hadn't been naked, exposed. So vulnerable.

She closed her eyes. Tight. Tried to hold back the welling tide . . .

It rose inexorably, lick by lick, subtle flick by flick, until it caught her. Gripped her.

She fractured.

Her body arched.

Her senses shattered. The world disappeared into shards of bright light, into a pulsing radiance that surrounded her, sank into her, through her. Left her bones melted, her muscles limp, left a deep well of heat within her, still empty.

Incomplete.

She was giddy, all but incapable, but she forced her lids up. Glanced at him as he straightened.

His large frame thrummed with restrained aggression, with a finely tuned, powerful tension. His hands gripping her naked thighs, he stood looking down at her, hazel eyes burning as they roamed her body.

What she saw in his face made her lungs seize, her heart hitch, then beat more strongly.

Naked desire etched his features, harshly delineated every line of his face.

Yet there was an aloneness there, too, a vulnerability, a hope.

She saw it, understood it.

Then his eyes met hers. For an instant, time stood still, then she lifted her arms, weak though they were, and beckoned him to her.

He stirred. His eyes locked on hers, he shrugged out of his coat, stripped off his cravat, opened his shirt, baring the muscled contours of his chest, lightly dusted with dark hair. Recollected sensation, of feeling that hair rasp against her sensitized skin as he moved within her, had her breasts swelling to aching fullness, her nipples puckering tight. He saw. Reached for his waistband. Flicked the buttons undone, freed his erection.

He glanced down only briefly, fitting himself to her, then he nudged in, just a fraction.

And looked up. Caught her gaze again, then leaned down, bracing his hands on the table on either side of her head, flicking his fingers through her hair. He leaned closer, brushed her lips.

Eyes locking on hers once more, he pressed into her.

She rose beneath him. Their breaths mingled as she arched, adjusted, took him in. At the last, he thrust deep and filled her. Her breath fell from her lips; she closed her eyes, luxuriating in the feel of him buried inside her. Then she lifted one hand, speared her fingers into his hair, drew his head to hers, and set her lips to his. Opened her mouth to him, invited him in.

Flagrantly invited him to plunder.

And he did.

Each powerful stroke lifted her, shifted her.

They broke from the kiss. Without waiting for instructions, she raised her legs and wrapped them about his hips. Heard him groan, saw blankness sweep his face as he took advantage and sank deeper, thrust harder, farther. Sheathed himself in her.

He closed one hand about her hip, anchoring her against his repetitive invasions. As the tempo mounted, he leaned down to her again, let his lips brush hers, then plunged into her mouth as his body plunged wildly into hers.

As all restraint broke and he gave himself to her.

As she had already given herself, body and soul, mind and heart, to him.

She let go, truly let herself free, let him take her with him as he wished.

Even locked in the throes of an impossibly powerful passion, Tristan sensed her decision, her total surrender to the moment—her surrender to him. She was with him, not just locked together physically but in some other place, in some other way, on some other plane.

He'd never reached that mystical place with any other woman; he'd never dreamed such a soul-searing experience would ever be his. Yet she took him in, rode his every thrust, wrapped him in the heat of her body—and joyously, with true abandonment, gave him all he could wish for, all he had yearned for.

Unconditional surrender.

She had said she would be his. Now she was. Forever.

He needed no further reassurance, no evidence beyond the tight clasp of her body, the supple writhing of her naked curves beneath him.

But he'd always wanted more, and she'd given without him asking.

Not just her body, but this—an unfettered commitment to him, to her, to what lay between them.

It rose up in a tide, impossible to control. It rolled over them both, crashed, swirled, made them gasp, cling. Fight for air. Fight for their hold on life, then lose it as brilliance swamped them, as their bodies clutched, clung, shuddered.

He spilled his seed deep within her, held tight, immobile, as ecstasy drenched them.

Filled them, sank deep, then slowly ebbed and faded.

He let go, felt his muscles relax, let her hold him, cradle him, his forehead bowed to hers.

Wrapped together, lips brushing, together they surrendered to their fate.

* * *

She stayed for hours. Few words were spoken. There was no need between them to explain; neither needed nor wanted inadequate words to intrude.

He'd restoked the fire. Slumped in an armchair before it with her curled in his lap, still naked, with her cloak thrown over her to keep her warm, his arms beneath it, his hands on her bare skin, her hair like wild silk clinging to them both . . . he would have happily remained so forever.

He glanced down at her. The firelight gilded her face. It had earlier gilded her body when she'd stood unabashed before the flames and let him examine each curve, each line. This time, he'd left her largely unmarked; only the imprints of his fingers at her hip where he'd anchored her were visible.

Leonora looked up, caught his eye, smiled, then laid her head back on his shoulder. Under her palm, spread across his bare chest, his heart beat steadily. The beat echoed in her blood. Throughout her body.

Closeness wrapped them about, linked them in a way she couldn't define, certainly hadn't expected.

He hadn't either, yet they'd both accepted it.

Once accepted, it couldn't be denied.

It had to be love, but who was she to say? All she knew was that for her it was immutable. Unchanging, fixed, and forever.

Whatever the future held—marriage, family, dependents, and all—she would have that, that strength, to call on.

It felt right. More right than she'd imagined anything could feel.

She was where she belonged. In his arms. With love between them.

Sixteen

ॐ

The next morning, Leonora breezed down to the breakfast parlor somewhat later than usual; she was normally the first of the family up and about, but this morning she'd slept in. With a definite spring in her step and a smile on her lips, she swept over the threshold—and came to an abrupt halt.

Tristan sat beside Humphrey, listening intently while calmly demolishing a plate of ham and sausages.

Jeremy sat opposite; all three men looked up, then Tristan and Jeremy rose.

Humphrey beamed at her. "Well, my dear! Congratulations! Tristan has told us your news. I have to say I'm utterly delighted!"

"Indeed, sis. Congratulations." Leaning over the table, Jeremy caught her hand and drew her across to plant a kiss on her cheek. "Excellent choice," he murmured.

Her smile became a trifle fixed. "Thank you."

She looked at Tristan, expecting to see some degree of apology. Instead, he met her gaze with a steady, assured—confident—expression. She took due note of that last, inclined her head. "Good morning."

The "my lord" stuck in her throat. She would not soon forget his notion of an appropriate finale to their reconciliation the previous evening. Later, he'd dressed her, then carried her out to the carriage, overridden her by then thoroughly weak protest, and accompanied her to Montrose Place, leaving her in the tiny parlor of Number 12 while he collected Henrietta, then escorting them both to her front door.

Suavely, he took her hand, raised it briefly to his lips, then held her chair for her. "I trust you slept well?"

She glanced at him as he resumed his seat beside her. "Like one dead."

His lips twitched, but he merely inclined his head.

"We've been telling Tristan here that Cedric's journals do not, at first glance, fall into any of the customary patterns." Humphrey paused to eat a mouthful of egg.

Jeremy took up the tale. "They're not organized by subject, which is most usual with such things, and as you'd found"—he dipped his head to Leonora—"the entries are not in any type of chronological order."

"Hmm." Humphrey chewed, then swallowed. "There has to be some key, but it's perfectly possible Cedric kept it in his head."

Tristan frowned. "Does that mean you won't be able to make sense of the journals?"

"No," Jeremy answered. "It just means it'll take us rather longer." He glanced at Leonora. "I vaguely recall you mentioned letters?"

She nodded. "There are lots. I've only looked at the ones in the past year."

"You'd better give them to us," Humphrey said. "All of them. In fact, any scrap of paper of Cedric's you can find."

"Scientists," Jeremy put in, "especially herbalists, are renowned for writing vital information on scraps of whatever comes to hand."

Leonora grimaced. "I'll have the maids gather up everything from the workshop. I've been meaning to search Cedric's bedchamber—I'll do that today."

Tristan glanced at her. "I'll help you."

She turned her head to check his expression to see what he really intended—

"Aaaah! Aieee-ah!"

The hysterical wails came from a distance. They all heard them. The cries continued clearly for an instant, then were muted—by the green baize door, they all realized, when a footman, startled and pale, skidded to a halt in the parlor doorway. "Mr. Castor! You got to come quick!"

Castor, a serving dish in his ancient hands, goggled at him.

Humphrey stared. "What the devil's the matter, man?"

The footman, completely shaken out of his habitual aplomb, bowed and bobbed to those around the table. "It's Daisy, sir. M'lord. From next door." He fixed on Tristan, who was rising to his feet. "She's just rushed in wailing and carrying on. Seems Miss Timmins has fallen down the stairs and . . . well, Daisy says as she's dead, m'lord."

Tristan tossed his napkin on the table and stepped around his chair.

Leonora rose at his shoulder. "Where is Daisy, Smithers? In the kitchen?"

"Yes, miss. She's taking on something terrible."

"I'll come and see her." Leonora swept out into the hall, conscious of Tristan following at her heels. She glanced back at him, took in his grim expression, met his eyes. "Will you go next door?"

"In a minute." His hand touched her back, a curiously comforting gesture. "I want to hear what Daisy has to say first. She's no fool—if she says Miss Timmins is dead, then she probably is. She won't be going anywhere."

Leonora inwardly grimaced and pushed through the door into the corridor leading to the kitchen. Tristan, she reminded herself, was much more accustomed to dealing with death than she was. Not a nice thought, but in the circumstances it held a certain comfort.

"Oh, miss! Oh, *miss!*" Daisy appealed to her the instant she saw her. "I don't know what to do. I couldn't do nothing!" She sniffed, wiped her eyes with the dishcloth Cook pressed into her hand.

"Now, Daisy." Leonora reached for one of the kitchen chairs; Tristan anticipated her, lifting it and setting it for her to sit facing Daisy. Leonora sat, felt Tristan lean his hands on the chair's back. "What you must do now, Daisy—what would be most help to Miss Timmins now—is to compose yourself—just take deep breaths, there's a good girl—and tell us—his-lordship-the-earl and me—what happened."

Daisy nodded, dutifully gulped in air, then blurted out, "Everything started out normal this morning. I came down from my room by the back stairs, riddled the grate and got the kitchen fire going, then got Miss Timmins's tray ready. Then I went to take it up to her . . ." Daisy's huge eyes clouded with tears. "Swept through the door I did, as usual, and plonked the tray on the hall table to tidy my hair and straighten up before I went up—and there she was."

Daisy's voice quavered and broke. Tears gushed, she mopped them furiously. "She was lying there—at the bottom of the stairs—like a little broken bird. I rush over, o'course, and checked, but there was no point. She was gone."

For a moment, no one said anything; they'd all known Miss Timmins.

"Did you touch her?" Tristan asked, his tone quiet, almost soothing.

Daisy nodded. "Aye—I patted her hand, and her cheek."

"Her cheek—was it cold? Do you remember?"

Daisy looked up at him, frowning as she thought. Then she nodded. "Aye, you're right. Her cheek was cold. Didn't think anything of her hands—they always were cold. But her cheek . . . yeah, it was cold." She blinked at Tristan. "Does that mean she'd been dead for a while?"

Tristan straightened. "It means it's likely she died some hours ago. Sometime in the night." He hesitated, then asked, "Did she ever wander at night? Do you know?"

Daisy shook her head. She'd stopped crying. "Not that I ever knew. She never mentioned such a thing."

Tristan nodded, stepped back. "We'll take care of Miss Timmins."

His gaze included Leonora. She stood, too, but glanced back at Daisy. "You'd best stay here. Not just for today, but tonight, too." She saw Neeps, her uncle's valet, hovering, concerned. "Neeps, you can help Daisy get her things after luncheon."

The man bowed. "Indeed, miss."

Tristan waved Leonora before him; she led him out of the kitchen. In the front hall they found Jeremy waiting.

He looked distinctly pale. "Is it true?"

"It must be, I'm afraid." Leonora went to the hall stand and lifted down her cloak. Tristan had followed her; he took it from her hands.

He held it, and looked down at her. "I don't suppose I can convince you to wait with your uncle in the library?"

She met his gaze. "No."

He sighed. "I thought not." He draped the cloak about her shoulders, then reached around her to open the front door.

"I'm coming, too." Jeremy followed them out onto the porch, then down the winding path.

They reached the front door of Number 16; Daisy had left it on the latch. Pushing the door wide, they entered.

The scene was exactly as Leonora had imagined it from Daisy's words. Unlike their house with its wide front hall with the stairs at the rear facing the front door, here, the hall was narrow and the head of the stairs was above the door; the foot of the stairs was at the rear of the hall.

That was where Miss Timmins lay, crumpled like a rag doll. Just as Daisy had said, there seemed little doubt life had left her, but Leonora went forward. Tristan had halted ahead of her, blocking the hall; she put her hands on his back and gently pushed; after an instant's hesitation, he moved aside and let her through.

Leonora crouched by Miss Timmins. She was wearing a thick cotton nightgown with a lacy wrapper clutched around her shoulders. Her limbs were twisted awkwardly, but decently covered; a pair of pink slippers were on her narrow feet.

Her lids were closed, the fading blue eyes shut away. Leonora brushed back the thin white curls, noted the extreme fragility of the papery skin. Taking one tiny clawlike hand in hers, she looked up at Tristan as he paused beside her. "Can we move her? There seems no reason to leave her like this."

He studied the body for a moment; she got the impression he was fixing its position in his memory. He glanced up the stairs, all the way to the top. Then he nodded. "I'll lift her. The front parlor?"

Leonora nodded, released the bony hand, rose and went to open the parlor door. "Oh!"

Jeremy, who'd gone past the body, past the hall table with the breakfast tray and onto the kitchen stairs, came back through the swinging door. "What is it?"

Speechless, Leonora simply stared.

With Miss Timmins in his arms, Tristan came up behind her, looked over her head, then nudged her forward.

She came to with a start, then hurried to straighten the cushions on the chaise. "Put her here." She glanced around at the wreck of the once fastidiously neat room. Drawers were pulled out, emptied on the rugs. The rugs themselves had been pulled up, slung aside. Some of the ornaments had been smashed in the grate. The pictures on the walls, those still on their hooks, hung crazily. "It must have been thieves. She must have heard them."

Tristan straightened from laying Miss Timmins gently down. With her limbs extended and her head on a cushion, she looked to be simply fast asleep. He turned to Jeremy, standing in the open doorway, looking around in amazement. "Go to Number 12 and tell Gasthorpe that we need Pringle again. Immediately."

Jeremy lifted his gaze to his face, then nodded and left.

Leonora, fussing with Miss Timmins's nightgown, rearranging her wrapper as she knew she would have liked, glanced up at him. "Why Pringle?"

Tristan met her gaze, hesitated, then said, "Because I want to know if she fell, or was pushed."

"Fell." Pringle carefully repacked his black bag. "There's not a mark on her that can't be accounted for by the fall, and none that looks like bruises from a man's grip. At her age, there would be bruises."

He glanced over his shoulder at the tiny body laid out on the chaise. "She was fragile and old, not long for this world in any case, but even so. While a man could easily have grabbed her and flung her down the stairs, he couldn't have done it without leaving some trace."

His gaze on Leonora, tidying a vase on a table beside the chaise, Tristan nodded. "That's some small relief."

Pringle snapped his bag closed, glanced at him as he straightened. "Possibly. But there's still the question of why she was out of bed at that hour—somewhere in the small hours, say between one o'clock and three—and what so frightened her, and it was almost certainly fright, enough to make her faint."

Tristan focused on Pringle. "You think she fainted?"

"I can't prove it, but if I had to guess what happened . . ." Pringle waved at the chaos of the room. "She heard sounds from this, and came to see. She stood at the top of the stairs and peered down. And saw a man. Suddenly. Shock, faint, fall. And here we are."

Tristan, gazing at the chaise and Leonora beyond it, said nothing for a moment, then he nodded, looked at Pringle, and offered his hand. "As you say—here we are. Thank you for coming."

Pringle shook his hand, a grim smile flirting about his lips. "I thought leaving the army would mean a humdrum practice—with you and your friends about, at least I won't be bored."

With an exchange of smiles, they parted. Pringle left, closing the front door behind him.

Tristan walked around the back of the chaise to where Leonora stood, looking down at Miss Timmins. He put an arm around Leonora, lightly hugged.

She permitted it. Leaned into him for a moment. Her hands were tightly clasped. "She looks so peaceful."

A moment passed, then she straightened and heaved a huge sigh. Brushed down her skirts and looked around. "So—a thief broke in and searched this room. Miss Timmins heard him and got out of bed to investigate. When the thief returned to the hall, she saw him, fainted, and fell . . . and died."

When he said nothing, she turned to him. Searched his eyes. Frowned. "What's wrong with that as deduction? It's perfectly logical."

"Indeed." He took her hand, turned to the door. "I suspect that's precisely what we're supposed to think."

"Supposed to think?"

"You missed a few pertinent facts. One, there's not a single window lock or door lock forced or unexpectedly left open. Both Jeremy and I checked. Two"—stepping into the hall, ushering her ahead of him, he glanced back into the parlor—"no self-respecting thief would leave a room like that. There's no point, and especially at night, why risk the noise?"

Leonora frowned. "Is there a three?"

"No other room has been searched, nothing else in the house appears disturbed. *Except*"—holding the front door, he waved her ahead of him; she went out onto the porch, waited impatiently for him to lock the door and pocket the key.

"Well?" she demanded, linking her arm with his. "Except *what?*"

They started down the steps. His tone had grown much harder, much colder, much more distant when he replied, "Except for a few, very new, scrapes and cracks in the basement wall."

Her eyes grew huge. "The wall shared with Number 14?"

He nodded.

Leonora glanced back toward the parlor windows. "So this was Mountford's work?"

"I believe so. And he doesn't want us to know."

"What are we looking for?"

Leonora followed Tristan into the bedchamber Miss Timmins had used. They'd returned to Number 14 and broken the news to Humphrey, then gone to the kitchen to confirm for Daisy that her employer was indeed dead. Tristan had asked after relatives; Daisy hadn't known of any. None had called in the six years she'd worked in Montrose Place.

Jeremy had taken on the task of making the necessary arrangements; together with Tristan, Leonora had returned to Number 16 to try to identify any relative.

"Letters, a will, notes from a solicitor—anything that might lead to a connection." He pulled open the small drawer of the table by the bed. "It would be most unusual if she has absolutely no kin."

"She never mentioned any."

"Be that as it may."

They settled to search. She noticed he did things—looked in places—she'd never have thought of. Like the backs and undersides of drawers, the upper surface above a top drawer. Behind paintings.

After a while, she sat on a chair before the escritoire and applied herself to all the notes and letters therein. There was no sign of any recent or promising correspondence. When he glanced at her, she waved him on. "You're much better at that than I."

But it was she who found the connection, in an old, very faded and much creased letter lying at the back of the tiniest drawer.

"The Reverend Mr. Henry Timmins, of Shacklegate Lane, Strawberry Hills." Triumphant, she read the address to Tristan, who had paused in the doorway.

He frowned. "Where's that?"

"I think it's out past Twickenham."

He crossed the room, lifted the letter from her hand, scanned it. Humphed. "Eight years old. Well, we can but try." He glanced at the window, then pulled out his watch and checked it. "If we take my curricle . . ."

She rose, smiled, linked her arm in his. Very definitely approved of that "we." "I'll have to fetch my pelisse. Let's go."

The Reverend Henry Timmins was a relatively young man, with a wife and four daughters and a busy parish.

"Oh, dear!" He abruptly sat down in a chair in the small parlor to which he'd conducted them. Then he realized and started up.

Tristan waved him back, handed Leonora to the chaise, and sat beside her. "So you were acquainted with Miss Timmins?"

"Oh, yes—she was my great-aunt." Pale, he glanced from one to the other. "We weren't at all close—indeed, she always seemed most nervous when I called. I did write a few times, but she never replied . . ." He blushed. "And then I got my preferment . . . and married . . . that sounds so unfeeling, yet she wasn't at all encouraging, you know."

Tristan squeezed Leonora's hand, warning her to silence; he inclined his head impassively. "Miss Timmins passed away last night, but not, I fear, easily. She fell down the stairs sometime very early in the morning. While we have no evidence she was directly attacked, we believe that she came upon a thief in her house—her front parlor was ransacked—and because of the shock, fainted and fell."

Reverend Timmins's face was a study in horror. "Good gracious me! How dreadful!"

"Indeed. We have reason to believe that the burglar responsible is the same man intent on gaining entry into Number 14." Tristan glanced at Leonora. "The Carlings live there, and Miss Carling herself has been subject to several attacks, we presume intended to frighten the household into leaving. There have also been a number of attempts to break into Number 14, and also into Number 12, the house of which I am part owner."

Reverend Timmins blinked. Tristan calmly continued, explaining their reasoning that the burglar they knew as Mountford was attempting to gain access to something hidden in Number 14, and that his forays into Number 12 and last night into Number 16 were by way of seeking entry via the basement walls.

"I see." Frowning, Henry Timmins nodded. "I've lived in terraces like that—you're quite right. The basement walls are often a series of arches filled in. Quite easy to break through the archways."

"Indeed." Tristan paused, then continued, in the same, authoritative tone, "Which is why we've been so set on finding you, why we've been speaking to you so frankly." He leaned forward; clasping his hands between his knees, he captured Henry Timmins's pale blue gaze. "Your great-aunt's death was deeply regrettable, and if Mountford is responsible, he deserves to be caught and brought to book. In the circumstances, I feel it would be poetic justice to use the situation as it now stands—the situation that has arisen because of Miss Timmins's demise—to set a trap for him."

"Trap?"

Leonora didn't need to hear the word to know that Henry Timmins was caught, hooked. So was she. She edged forward so she could watch Tristan's face.

"There's no reason for anyone beyond those who already know to imagine Miss Timmins died other than by natural causes. She'll be mourned by those who knew her, then . . . if I may suggest, you, as heir, should put Number 16 Montrose Place up for rent." With a gesture, Tristan indicated the house about them. "You're clearly not in any need of a house in town at present. On the other hand, being a prudent man, you will not wish to sell precipitously. Renting the property is the sensible course, and no one will wonder at it."

Henry was nodding. "True, true."

"If you're agreeable, I'll arrange for a friend to pose as a house agent and handle the rental for you. Of course, we won't be renting to just anyone."

"You think Mountford will come forward and rent the house?"

"Not Mountford himself—Miss Carling and I have seen him. He'll use an intermediary, but it will be he who wants access to the house. Once he has it, and enters . . ." Tristan sat back; a smile that was no smile curved his lips. "Suffice to say that I have the right connections to ensure he won't escape."

Henry Timmins, eyes rather wide, continued to nod.

Leonora was less susceptible. "Do you really believe that after all this, Mountford will dare show his face?"

Tristan turned to her; his eyes were cold, hard. "Given the lengths to which he's already gone, I'm prepared to wager he won't be able to resist."

They returned to Montrose Place that evening with Henry Timmins's blessings, and, more importantly, a letter to the family solicitor from Henry instructing said solicitor to act on Tristan's directions regarding Miss Timmins's house.

There were lights burning in the rooms on the first floor of the Bastion Club; handing Leonora to the pavement, Tristan saw them, wondered . . .

Leonora shook out her skirts, then slipped her hand in his arm.

He looked down at her, refrained from mentioning how much he liked the little gesture of feminine acceptance. He was learning that she often did small revealing things instinctively, without noticing; he saw no reason to bring such transparency to her attention.

They headed up the path of Number 14.

"Who will you get to play the part of house agent?" Leonora glanced at him. "You can't—he knows what you look like." She ran her gaze over his features. "Even with one of your disguises . . . there's no way of being sure he wouldn't see through it."

"Indeed." Tristan glanced across at the Bastion Club as they climbed the porch steps. "I'll see you in, speak with Humphrey and Jeremy, then I'm going next door." He met her gaze as the front door opened. "It's possible some of my associates are in town. If so . . ."

She arched a brow at him. "Your ex-colleagues?"

He nodded, following her into the hall. "I can't think of any gentlemen more suited to aid us in this."

Charles, predictably, was delighted.

"Excellent! I always knew this notion of a club was a brilliant idea."

It was nearly ten o'clock; having consumed a superb dinner in the elegant dining room downstairs, they—Tristan, Charles, and Deverell—were now seated, sprawled and comfortable, in the library, each cradling a balloon liberally supplied with fine brandy.

"Indeed." Despite his more reserved manner, Deverell looked equally interested. He eyed Charles. "I think I should be the house agent—you've already played one part in this drama."

Charles looked aggrieved. "But I could always play another."

"I think Deverell's right." Tristan firmly took charge. "He can be the house agent—this is only his second visit to Montrose Place, so chances are Mountford and his cronies won't have spotted him. Even if they have, there's no reason he can't play totally vague and say he's handling the matter for a friend." Tristan glanced at Charles. "Meanwhile, there's something else I think you and I should take care of."

Charles instantly looked hopeful. "What?"

"I told you of this solicitor's clerk who inherited from Carruthers." He'd told them the entire story, all the pertinent facts, over dinner.

"The one who came to London and disappeared into the teeming throng?"

"Indeed. I believe I mentioned he'd originally planned to come to town? While searching for information in York, my operative learned that this Martinbury had earlier arranged to meet with a friend, another clerk from his office, here, in town; before he left unexpectedly, he confirmed the meeting."

Charles raised his brows high. "When, and where?"

"Noon tomorrow, at the Red Lion in Gracechurch Street."

Charles nodded. "So we nab him after the meeting—I assume you have descriptions?"

"Yes, but the friend has agreed to introduce me, so all we need do is be there, and then we'll see what we can learn from Mr. Martinbury."

"He couldn't be Mountford, could he?" Deverell asked.

Tristan shook his head. "Martinbury was in York for much of the time Mountford's been active down here."

"Hmm." Deverell sat back, rolled the brandy in his balloon. "If it won't be Mountford who approaches me—and I agree that's unlikely—then who do you think will try to rent the house?"

"My guess," Tristan said, "would be a scrawny, weasel-faced specimen, short to medium height. Leonora—Miss Carling—has seen him twice. He seems certain to be an associate of Mountford's."

Charles opened his eyes wide. "Leonora, is it?" Swiveling in his chair, he fixed Tristan with his dark gaze. "So tell us—how sits the wind in that quarter, hmm?"

Impassive, Tristan studied Charles's devilish face, and wondered what fiendish devilment Charles might concoct if he didn't tell them . . . "As it happens, the notice of our engagement will appear in the *Gazette* tomorrow morning."

"Oh-ho!"

"I see!"

"Well, that was quick work!" Rising, Charles grabbed the decanter and replenished their glasses. "We have to toast this. Let's see." He struck a pose before the fireplace, his glass held high. "Here's to you and your lady, the delightful Miss Carling. Let's drink in acknowledgment of your success in determining your own fate—to your victory over the meddlers—and to the inspiration and encouragement this victory will provide to your fellow Bastion Club members!"

"Hear! Hear!"

Charles and Deverell both drank. Tristan saluted them with his glass, then drank, too.

"So when's the wedding?" Deverell asked.

Tristan studied the amber liquid swirling in his glass. "As soon as we lay Mountford by the heels."

Charles pursed his lips. "And if that takes longer than expected?"

Tristan raised his eyes, met Charles's dark gaze. Smiled. "Trust me. It won't."

Early the next morning, Tristan visited Number 14 Montrose Place; he left before Leonora or any of the family came downstairs, confident he'd solved the riddle of how Mountford had got into Number 16.

As Jeremy had, at his direction, already had the locks on Number 16 changed, Mountford must have suffered another disappointment. All the better for driving him into their snare. He now had no option other than to rent the house.

Leaving Number 14 by the front gate, Tristan saw a workman busy setting up a sign atop the low front wall of Number 16. The sign announced that the house was for rent and gave details for contacting the agent. Deverell had wasted no time.

He returned to Green Street for breakfast, manfully waited until all six of the resident old dears were present before making his announcement. They were more than delighted.

"She's just the sort of wife we wished for you," Millicent told him.

"Indeed," Ethelreda confirmed. "She's such a sensible young woman—we were awfully afraid you might land us with some flibbertigibbet. One of those empty-headed gels who giggle all the time. The good Lord only knows how we would have coped then."

In fervent agreement, he excused himself and took refuge in the study. Ruthlessly blocking out the obvious distraction, he spent an hour dealing with the more urgent matters awaiting his attention, remembering to pen a brief letter to his great-aunts informing them of his impending nuptials. When the clock chimed eleven, he put down his pen, rose, and quietly left the house.

He met Charles at the corner of Grosvenor Square. They hailed a hackney; at ten minutes before noon, they pushed through the door of the Red Lion. It was a popular public house catering to a mixture of trades—merchants, agents, shippers, and clerks of every description. The main room was crowded, yet after one glance, most moved out of Tristan's and Charles's way. They went to the bar, were served immediately, then, ale mugs in hand, turned and surveyed the room.

After a moment, Tristan took a sip of his ale. "He's over there, one table from the corner. The one that keeps looking around like an eager pup."

"That's the friend?"

"Fits the description to a tee. The cap's hard to miss." A tweed cap was sitting on the table at which the young man in question waited.

Tristan considered, then said, "He won't recognize us. Why don't we just take the table next to him, and wait for the right moment to introduce ourselves?"

"Good idea."

Once again the crowd parted like the Red Sea; they installed themselves at the small table in the corner without attracting more than a quick glance and a polite smile from the young man.

He seemed terribly young to Tristan.

The young man continued to wait. So did they. They discussed various points—difficulties they'd both faced on taking up the reins of large estates. There was more than enough there to provide believable cover had the young man been listening. He wasn't; like a spaniel, he kept his eyes on the door, ready to leap up and wave when his friend entered.

Gradually, as the minutes ticked by, his eagerness ebbed. He nursed his pint; they nursed theirs. But when the clang from a nearby belltower sounded the half hour, it seemed certain that he for whom they all waited was not going to appear.

They waited some more, in growing concern.

Eventually, Tristan exchanged a glance with Charles, then turned to the young man. "Mr. Carter?"

The young man blinked, focused properly on Tristan for the first time. "Y-yes?"

"We've not met." Tristan reached for a card, handed it to Carter. "But I believe an associate of mine told you we were concerned to meet with Mr. Martinbury over a matter of mutual benefit."

Carter read the card; his youthful face cleared. "Oh, yes—of course!" Then he looked at Tristan and grimaced. "But as you can see, Jonathon hasn't come." He glanced around, as if to make sure Martinbury hadn't materialized in the last minute. Carter frowned. "I really can't understand it." He looked back at Tristan. "Jonathon's very punctual, and we're very good friends."

Worry clouded his face.

"Have you heard from him since he's been in town?"

Charles asked the question; when Carter blinked at him, Tristan smoothly added, "Another associate."

Carter shook his head. "No. No one at home—York, that is—has had any word from him. His landlady was surprised; she made me promise to tell him to write when I met him. It's odd—he's really a very reliable person, and he is fond of her. She's like a mother to him."

Tristan exchanged a glance with Charles. "I think it's time we searched more actively for Mr. Martinbury." Turning to Carter, he nodded at his card, which the young man still held in his hand. "If you do hear from Martinbury, any contact at all, I'd be obliged if you would send word immediately to that address. Likewise, if you furnish me with your direction, I'll make sure you're informed if we locate your friend."

"Oh, yes. Thank you." Carter dragged a tablet from his pocket, found a pencil, and quickly wrote down the address of his lodging house. He handed the sheet to Tristan. He read it, then nodded and put the note in his pocket.

Carter was frowning. "I wonder if he even reached London."

Tristan rose. "He did." He drained his tankard, set it on the table. "He left the coach when it reached town, not before. Unfortunately, tracing a single man on the streets of London is not at all easy."

He said the last with a reassuring smile. With a nod to Carter, he and Charles left.

They paused on the pavement outside.

"Tracing a single man walking the streets of London may not be easy." Charles glanced at Tristan. "Tracing a dead one is not quite so hard."

"No, indeed." Tristan's expression had hardened. "I'll take the watchhouses."

"And I'll take the hospitals. Meet at the club later tonight?"

Tristan nodded. Then grimaced. "I just remembered . . ."

Charles glanced at him, then hooted. "Just remembered you'd announced your engagement—of course! No longer a life of ease for you—not until you're wed."

"Which only makes me even more determined to find Martinbury with all speed. I'll send word to Gasthorpe if I find anything."

"I'll do the same." With a nod, Charles headed down the street.

Tristan watched him go, then swore, swung on his heel, and strode off in the opposite direction.

Seventeen

The day was fleeing, whipped away by grey squalls, as Tristan climbed the steps of Number 14 and asked to see Leonora. Castor directed him to the parlor; dismissing the butler, he opened the parlor door and went in.

Leonora didn't hear him. She was seated on the chaise, facing the windows, looking out at the garden, at the shrubs bowing before the blustering wind. Beside her, a fire burned brightly in the hearth, crackling and spitting cheerily. Henrietta lay stretched before the flames, luxuriating in their heat.

The scene was comfortable, cozy—warming in a way that had nothing to do with temperature, a subtle comfort to the heart.

He took a step, let his heel fall heavily.

She heard, turned . . . then she saw him and her face lit. Not just with expectation, not just with eagerness to hear what he had learned, but with an open welcome as if a part of her had returned.

He neared and she rose, held out her hands. He took them, raised first one, then the other to his lips, then drew her nearer and bent his head. Took her mouth in a kiss he struggled to keep within bounds, let his senses savor, then reined them in.

When he lifted his head, she smiled at him; their gazes touched, held for a moment, then she sank onto the chaise.

He crouched to pat Henrietta.

Leonora watched him, then said, "Now before you tell me anything else, explain how Mountford got into Number 16 last night. You said there were no forced locks, and Castor told me some tale about you asking after a drainage inspector. What has he to do with anything—or was he Mountford?"

Tristan glanced at her, then nodded. "Daisy's description tallies. It seems he posed as an inspector and talked her into letting him inspect the kitchen, scullery, and laundry drains."

"And when she wasn't looking, he took an impression of a key?"

"That seems most likely. No inspector called here or at Number 12." She frowned. "He's a very . . . calculating man."

"He's clever." After a moment of studying her face, Tristan said, "Added to that, he must be getting desperate. I'd like you to bear that in mind."

She met his gaze, then smiled reassuringly. "Of course."

The look he cast her as he rose to his feet looked more resigned than reassured.

"I saw the sign outside Number 16. That was quick." She let her approval show in her face.

"Indeed. I've handed that aspect over to a gentleman by the name of Deverell. He's Viscount Paignton."

She opened her eyes wide. "Do you have any other . . . associates helping you?"

Sinking his hands into his pockets, the fire warm on his back, Tristan looked down into her face, into eyes that reflected an intelligence he knew better than to underestimate. "I have a small army working for me, as you know. Most of them, you'll never meet, but there is one other who's actively helping me—another part-owner of Number 12."

"As is Deverell?" she asked.

He nodded. "The other gentleman is Charles St. Austell, Earl of Lostwithiel."

"Lostwithiel?" She frowned. "I heard something about the last two earls dying in tragic circumstances . . ."

"They were his brothers. He was the third son and is now the earl."

"Ah. And what is he helping you with?"

He explained about the meeting they'd hoped to have with Martinbury, and their disappointment. She heard him out in silence, watching his face. When he paused after explaining the agreement they'd made with Martinbury's friend, she said, "You think he's met with foul play."

Not a question. His eyes on hers, he nodded. "Everything that was reported to me from York, everything his friend Carter said of him, painted Martinbury as a conscientious, reliable, honest man—not one to miss an appointment he'd taken care to confirm." Again he hesitated, wondering how much he should tell her, then pushed aside his reluctance. "I've started checking the watchhouses for reported deaths, and Charles is checking the hospitals in case he was brought in alive, but then died."

"He could still be alive, perhaps gravely injured, but without friends or connections in London . . ."

He considered the timing, then grimaced. "True—I'll put some others onto checking that. However, given how long it's been without any word from him, we need to check the dead. Unfortunately, that's not the sort of search anyone but Charles and I, or one like us, can undertake." He met her gaze. "Members of the nobility, especially ones with our background, can get answers, demand to see reports and records, that others simply can't."

"So I've noticed." She sat back, considering him. "So you'll be busy during the days. I spent today with the maids, searching every nook and cranny in Cedric's workshop. We found various scraps and jottings which are now with Humphrey and Jeremy in the library. They're still poring over the journals. Humphrey's increasingly certain there ought to be more. He thinks there are sections—pieces of records—missing. Not torn out but written down somewhere else."

"Hmm." Tristan stroked Henrietta's head with his boot, then glanced at Leonora. "What about Cedric's bedchamber? Have you searched there yet?"

"Tomorrow. The maids will help—there'll be five of us. If there's anything there, I assure you we'll find it."

He nodded, mentally running down his list of matters he'd wanted to discuss with her. "Ah, yes." He refocused on her face, caught her gaze. "I put the customary notice in the *Gazette* announcing our betrothal. It was in this morning's edition."

A subtle change came over her face; an expression he couldn't quite place—resigned amusement?—invested her blue eyes.

"I was wondering when you were going to mention that."

Suddenly, he wasn't sure of the ground beneath his feet. He shrugged, his eyes still on hers. "It was just the usual thing. The expected thing."

"Indeed, but you might have thought to warn me—that way, when my aunts descended in a swirl of congratulations a bare ten minutes before the first of a good two dozen callers, all wanting to congratulate me, I wouldn't have been caught like a deer in a hunter's sights."

He held her gaze; for a moment, silence reigned. Then he winced. "My apologies. With Miss Timmins's death and all the rest, it escaped my mind."

She considered him, then inclined her head. Her lips weren't quite straight. "Apology accepted. However, you do realize that, now the news is out, we'll need to make the obligatory appearances?"

He stared down at her. "What appearances?"

"The necessary appearances every engaged couple are expected to make. For instance, tonight, everyone will expect us to attend Lady Hartington's soirée."

"Why?"

"Because it's the major event tonight, and so they can congratulate us, watch us, analyze and dissect, assure themselves it will be a good match, and so on."

"And this is obligatory?"

She nodded.

"Why?"

She didn't misunderstand. "Because if we don't give them that chance, it will fix unwarranted—and quite staggeringly intrusive— attention on us. We won't have a moment's peace. They'll call constantly, and not just within the accepted hours; if they're in the neighborhood, they'll drive down the street and peer out of their carriages. You'll find a couple of giggling girls on the pavement every time you step out of your house, or your club next door. And you won't dare appear in the park, or on Bond Street."

She fixed him with a direct look. "Is that what you want?"

He read her eyes, confirmed she was serious. Shuddered. "Good Lord!" He sighed; his lips thinned. "All right. Lady Hartington's. Should I meet you there, or call for you in my carriage?"

"It would be most appropriate for you to escort my aunts and me. Mildred and Gertie will be here by eight. If you arrive a little after, you can accompany us there, in Mildred's carriage."

He humphed, but nodded curtly. He didn't take orders well, but in this sphere . . . that was one reason he needed her. He cared very little for society, knew both enough and too little of its tortuous ways to feel totally comfortable in its glare. While he had every intention of spending as little time in it as possible, given his title, his position, if a quiet life was his aim, it would never do to thumb his nose openly at the ladies' sacred rites.

Such as passing judgment on newly affianced couples.

He refocused on Leonora's face. "How long do we have to pander to prurient interest?"

Her lips twitched. "For at least a week."

He scowled, literally growled.

"Unless some scandal intervenes, or unless . . ." She held his gaze. He thought, then, still at sea, prompted, "Unless what?"

"Unless we have some serious excuse—like being actively involved in catching a burglar."

He left Number 14 half an hour later, resigned to attending the soirée. Given Mountford's increasingly risky actions, he doubted they'd have long to wait before he made his next move, and stepped into their snare. And then . . .

With any luck, he wouldn't have to attend all that many more of society's events, at least not as an unmarried man.

The thought filled him with grim determination.

He strode along purposefully, mentally planning his morrow and how he'd extend the search for Martinbury. He'd turned into Green Street, was nearly at his front door when he heard himself hailed.

Halting, turning, he saw Deverell descending from a hackney. He waited while Deverell paid off the jarvey, then joined him.

"Can I offer you a drink?"

"Thank you."

They waited until they were comfortable in the library, and Havers had withdrawn, before getting down to business.

"I've had a nibble," Deverell replied in response to Tristan's raised brow. "And I'd swear it's the weasel you warned me of—he slunk up just as I was about to leave. He'd been keeping watch for about two hours. I'm using a small office that's part of a property I own in Sloane Street. It was empty and available, and the right sort of place."

"What did he say?"

"He wanted details of the house at Number 16 for his master. I ran through the usual, the amenities and so on, and the price." Deverell grinned. "He led me to hope his master would be interested."

"And?"

"I explained how the property came to be for rent, and that, in the circumstances, I had to warn his master that the house may only be available for a few months, as the owner might decide to sell."

"And he wasn't put off?"

"Not in the least. He assured me his master was only interested in a short let, and didn't want to know what had happened to the last owner."

Tristan smiled, grim, wolfish. "It sounds like our quarry."

"Indeed. But I don't think Mountford's going to show himself to me. The weasel asked for a copy of the lease agreement and took it away with him. Said his master would want to study it. If Mountford signs it and sends it back with the first month's rent—well, what house agent would quibble?"

Tristan nodded; his eyes narrowed. "We'll let the game play out, but that certainly sounds promising."

Deverell drained his glass. "With luck, we'll have him within a few days."

Tristan's evening started badly and grew progressively worse.

He arrived in Montrose Place early; he was standing in the hall when Leonora came down the stairs. He turned, saw, froze; the vision she presented in a watered-silk gown of deep blue, her shoulders and throat rising like fine porcelain from the wide neckline, her hair glossy, garnet-shot, piled on her head, ripped his breath away. A gauzy shawl concealed and revealed her arms and shoulders, shifting and sliding over the svelte curves; his palms tingled.

Then she saw him, met his eyes, and smiled.

Blood drained from his head; he felt dizzy.

She crossed the hall toward him, the periwinkle blue hue of her eyes lit by that welcoming expression she seemed to save just for him. She gave him her hands. "Mildred and Gertie should be here any minute."

A commotion at the door proved to be her aunts; their advent saved him from having to formulate any intelligent response. Her aunts were full of congratulations and myriad social instructions; he nodded, trying to take them all in, trying to orient himself in this battlefield, all the while conscious of Leonora and that, very soon, she would be all his.

The prize was definitely worth the battle.

He escorted them out to the carriage. Lady Hartington's house wasn't far. Her ladyship, of course, was beyond thrilled to receive them. She exclaimed, twittered, gushed, and archly asked after their wedding plans; impassive, he stood beside Leonora, and listened while she calmly deflected all her ladyship's queries without answering any of them. From her ladyship's expression, Leonora's responses were perfectly acceptable; it was all a mystery to him.

Then Gertie stepped in and ended the inquisition. At a nudge from Leonora, he led her away. As usual, he made for a chaise by the wall.

Her fingertips sank into his arm. "No. No point. Tonight we'd be better served by taking center stage."

With a nod, she directed him to a position almost in the center of the large drawing room. Inwardly frowning, he hesitated, then complied; his instincts were twitching—the spot was so open, they would be easily flanked, even surrounded. . . .

He had to trust her judgment; in this theater, his own was severely underdeveloped. But even in this, being guided by another did not come easily.

Predictably, they were quickly surrounded by ladies young and old wanting to press their congratulations and hear their news. Some were sweet, pleasant, innocent of guile, ladies for whom he deployed his charm. Others set his back up; after one such encounter, brought to a close by Mildred cutting in and all but physically towing the old battle-ax away, Leonora glanced up at him, with her elbow surreptitiously jabbed him in the ribs.

He looked down at her, frowned with his eyes. She smiled serenely back. "Stop looking so grim."

He realized his mask had slipped, quickly reinstalled his charming facade. Meanwhile, *sotto voce,* informed her, "That harridan made me feel murderous, so grim was a mild response." He met her eyes. "I don't know how you can stand such as she—they're so patently insincere, and don't even try to hide it."

Her smile was both understanding and teasing; briefly she leaned more heavily on his arm. "You get used to it. When they become difficult, just let it wash over you, and remember that what they're after is a reaction—deny them that, and you've won the exchange."

He could see what she meant, tried to follow that line, but the situation itself abraded his temper. For the last decade, he'd eschewed any situation that focused attention on him; to stand there, in a ton drawing room, the cynosure of all eyes and at least half the conversations, ran directly counter to what had become ingrained habit.

The evening wore on, for him far too slowly; the number of ladies and gentlemen waiting to speak with them did not appreciably decrease. He continued to feel off-balance, exposed. And out of his depth in dealing with some of the more dangerous specimens.

Leonora took care of them with a sure touch he had to admire. Just the right amount of haughtiness, the right amount of confidence. Thank God he'd found her.

Then Ethelreda and Edith came up; they greeted Leonora as if she was already a member of the family, and she responded in kind. Mildred and Gertie touched fingers; he saw a brief question put by Edith, to which Gertie replied with a short word and a snort. Then glances were exchanged between the older ladies, succeeded by conspiratorial smiles.

Passing before them, Ethelreda tapped his arm. "Bear up, dear boy. We're here, now."

She and Edith moved on, but only as far as Leonora's side. Over the next fifteen minutes, his other cousins—Millicent, Flora, Constance, and Helen—arrived, too. Like Ethelreda and Edith, they greeted Leonora, exchanged pleasantries with Mildred and Gertie, then joined Ethelreda and Edith in a loose gathering alongside Leonora.

And things changed.

The crowd in the drawing room had grown to uncomfortable proportions; there were even more people hovering, waiting to speak with them. It was a crush, and he'd never liked being hemmed in, yet Leonora continued to greet those who pressed forward, introducing him, deftly managing the interactions, but if any lady showed a tendency to spite or coldness, or simply a wish to monopolize, either Mildred and Gertie or one of his cousins would step in and, with a rush of seemingly inconsequential observations, draw such persons away.

In short order, his view of his old dears was shattered and reformed; even the retiring Flora displayed remarkable determination in distracting and removing one persistent lady. Gertie, too, left no doubt as to which mast her flag was pinned.

The reversal of roles kept him off-balance; in this arena, they were the protectors, sure and effective, he the one needing their protection.

Part of that protection was to prevent him from reacting to those who saw his and Leonora's engagement as a loss to themselves, who viewed her as having in some way snared him, when the truth was the exact opposite. It hadn't occurred to him just how real, how strong and powerful, the feminine competition in the marriage mart was, or that Leonora's apparent success in capturing him would make her the focus of envy.

His eyes were now open.

Lady Hartington had chosen to enliven her soirée with a short spell of dancing. As the musicians set up, Gertie turned to him. "Grab the opportunity while you may." She poked his arm. "You've got another hour or more to endure before we can leave."

He didn't wait; he reached for Leonora's hand, smiled charmingly, and excused them to the two ladies with whom they'd been conversing. Constance and Millicent stepped in, smoothly covering his and Leonora's retreat.

Leonora sighed and went into his arms with real relief. "How exhausting. I had no idea it would be this bad, not so early in the year."

Whirling her down the room, he met her gaze. "You mean it could be worse?"

She looked into his eyes, and smiled. "Not everyone's in town yet."

She said no more; he studied her face as they twirled, turned, and precessed back up the room. She seemed to have given herself, her senses, over to the waltz; he followed her lead.

And found a degree of comfort. Of soothing reassurance in the feel of her in his arms, in the reality of her under his hands, in the brush of their thighs as they went through the turns, the flowing harmony with which their bodies moved, in tune, attuned. Together.

When the music finally ended, they were at the other end of the room. Without asking, he set her hand on his sleeve and guided her back to where their supporters waited, a small island of relative safety.

She slanted him a glance, a smile on her lips, understanding in her eyes. "How are you faring?"

He glanced at her. "I feel like a general surrounded by a bevy of personal guards well equipped with initiative and experience." He drew breath, looked ahead to where their group of sweet old ladies were waiting. "The fact they're female is a trifle unsettling, but I have to admit I'm humbly grateful."

A chortle, smothered, answered him. "Indeed, you should be."

"Believe me," he murmured as they neared the others, "I know my limitations. This is a female theater dominated by female strategies too convoluted for any male to fathom."

She threw him a laughing glance, one wholly personal, then they resumed their public personas and went forward to deal with the small horde still waiting to congratulate them.

The night, predictably but to his mind regrettably, ended without affording him and Leonora any opportunity to slake the physical need that had burgeoned, fed by close contact, by the promise of the waltz, by his inevitable reaction to the evening's less civilized moments.

Mine.

That word still rang in his head, prodded his instincts whenever she was close, most especially whenever others seemed not to comprehend that fact.

Not a civilized response but a primitive one. He knew it, and didn't care.

The next morning, he left Green Street restless and unfulfilled, and threw himself into the search for Martinbury. They were all increasingly convinced the object of Mountford's search was something buried in Cedric's papers; A. J. Carruthers had been Cedric's closest confidant, Martinbury was by all accounts the heir to whom Carruthers had entrusted his secrets—and Martinbury had unexpectedly disappeared.

Locating Martinbury, or discovering what they could of his fate, seemed the likeliest route to learning Mountford's aim and dealing with his threat.

The fastest way to end the business so he and Leonora could wed.

But entering watchhouses, gaining men's trust, accessing records in search of the recently deceased, took time. He'd started with those watchhouses closest to the coaching inn where Martinbury had alighted. As, in a hackney, he rumbled home in the late afternoon, no further forward, he wondered if that wasn't a false assumption. Martinbury could have been in London for some days before disappearing.

He entered his house to discover Charles waiting in his library to report.

"Nothing," Charles said the instant he'd shut the door. In one of the armchairs before the hearth, he swiveled to look up at him. "What about you?"

Tristan grimaced. "Same story." He picked up the decanter from the sideboard, filled a glass, then crossed to top up Charles's glass before sinking into the other armchair. He frowned at the fire. "Which hospitals have you checked?"

Charles told him—the hospitals and hospices closest to the inn where the mail coaches from York terminated.

Tristan nodded. "We need to move faster and widen our search." He explained his reasoning.

Charles inclined his head in agreement. "The question is, even with Deverell helping, how do we widen our search and simultaneously go faster?"

Tristan sipped, then lowered his glass. "We take a calculated risk and narrow the field. Leonora mentioned that Martinbury may still be alive, but if he's injured, with no friends or relatives in town, he may simply be lying in a hospital bed somewhere."

Charles grimaced. "Poor bugger."

"Indeed. In reality, that scenario is the only one that's going to advance our cause quickly. If Martinbury's dead, then it's unlikely whoever did the deed will have left any useful papers behind, ones that will point us in the right direction."

"True."

Tristan sipped again, then said, "I'm swinging my people on to searching the hospitals for any gentleman matching Martinbury's description who's still alive. They don't need our authority to do that."

Charles nodded. "I'll do the same—I'm sure Deverell will, too. . . ."

The sound of a male voice in the hall outside reached them. They both looked at the door.

"Speak of the devil," Charles said.

The door opened. Deverell walked in.

Tristan rose and poured him a brandy. Deverell took it and sprawled elegantly on the chaise. In contrast to their sober expressions, his green eyes were alight. He saluted them with his glass. "I bring tidings."

"Positive tidings?" Charles asked.

"The only sort a wise man brings." Deverell paused to sip his brandy; lowering the glass, he smiled. "Mountford took the bait."

"He rented the house?"

"The weasel brought the lease back this morning along with the first month's rent. A Mr. Caterham has signed the lease and intends moving in immediately." Deverell paused, frowning slightly. "I handed over the keys and offered to show them around the property, but the weasel—he goes by the name of Cummings—declined. He said his master was a recluse and insisted on total privacy."

Deverell's frown grew. "I did think of following the weasel back to his hole, but decided the risk of scaring them off was too high." He glanced at Tristan. "Given Mountford, or whoever he is, seems set on going into the house forthwith, letting him pursue that aim and walk into our trap with all speed seemed the wisest course."

Both Tristan and Charles were nodding.

"Excellent!" Tristan stared at the fire, his gaze distant. "So we have him, we know where he is. We'll continue trying to solve the riddle of what he's after, but even if we don't succeed, we'll be waiting for his next move. Waiting for him to reveal all himself."

"To success!" Charles said.

The others echoed the words, then they drained their glasses.

After seeing Charles and Deverell out, Tristan headed for his study. Passing the arches of the morning room, he heard the usual babel of elderly feminine voices and glanced in.

He halted in midstride. He could barely believe his eyes.

His great-aunts had arrived, along with—he counted heads—his other six resident pensioners from Mallingham Manor. All fourteen of his dependent old dears were now gathered under his Green Street roof, scattered about the morning room, heads together . . . plotting.

Uneasiness filled him.

Hortense glanced up and saw him. "There you are, m'boy! *Wonderful* news about you and Miss Carling." She thumped the arm of her chair. "*Just* as we'd all hoped."

He went down the steps. Hermione flapped her hand at him. "Indeed, my dear. We are *excellently* pleased!"

Bowing over her hand, he accepted those and the others' murmured expressions of delight with a mild, "Thank you."

"Now!" Hermione turned to look up at him. "I hope you won't think we've taken too much on ourselves, but we've organized a family dinner for tonight. Ethelreda has spoken with Miss Carling's family—Lady Warsingham and her husband, the elder Miss Carling, and Sir Humphrey and Jeremy Carling—and they are all in agreement, as is Miss Carling, of course. Given there are so many of us, and some of us are getting on in years, and as the proper course would be for us to meet Miss Carling and her family formally at such a dinner, we hoped you, too, would agree to holding it tonight."

Hortense snorted. "Aside from all else, we're too fagged from driving up this afternoon to weather an outing to some other entertainment."

"And, dear," Millicent put in, "we should remember that Miss Carling and Sir Humphrey and young Mr. Carling had a funeral to attend this morning. A neighbor, I understand?"

"Indeed." A vision danced through Tristan's mind, of a comfortable if large dinner party, rather less formal than might be imagined—he knew his great-aunts and their companions quite well . . . He looked around, met their bright, transparently hopeful gazes. "Do I take it you're suggesting this dinner would be in lieu of any appearance in the ton tonight?"

Hortense pulled a face. "Well, if you really wish to attend some ball or other—"

"No, no." The relief that flooded him was very real; he smiled, struggling to keep his delight within bounds. "I see no reason at all your dinner can't go ahead, precisely as you've planned it. Indeed"—his mask slipped; he let his gratitude shine through—"I'll be grateful for any excuse to avoid the ton tonight." He bowed to his aunts, with a glance extended the gesture to the others, deploying his charm to maximum effect. "Thank you."

The words were heartfelt.

They all smiled, bobbed, delighted to have been of use.

"Didn't think you'd be all that enamored of the gadding throng," Hortense opined. She grinned up at him. "If it comes to it, neither are we."

He could have kissed them. Knowing how flustered that would make most of them, he contented himself with dressing with extra care, then being in the drawing room to greet them as they entered, bowing over their hands, commenting on their gowns and coiffures, on their jewels—deploying for them that irresistible charm he knew well how to use but rarely did without some goal in mind.

Tonight, his goal was simply to repay them for their kindness, their thoughtfulness.

He'd never been so thankful to hear of a family dinner in his life.

While they waited in the drawing room for their guests to arrive, he thought of how incongruous their gathering would appear—he standing before the mantelpiece, the sole male surrounded by fourteen elderly females. But they were his family; he did, in truth, feel more comfortable surrounded by them and their amiable chatter than he did in the more glittering, more exciting, but also more malicious world of the ton. They and he shared something—an intangible connection of place and people spread over time.

And into this, Leonora would now come—and she would fit.

Havers entered to announce Lord and Lady Warsingham and Miss Carling—Gertie. On their heels, Sir Humphrey, Leonora, and Jeremy arrived.

Any thought that he would have to act as a formal host evaporated in minutes. Sir Humphrey was engaged by Ethelreda and Constance, Jeremy by a group of the others, while Lord and Lady Warsingham were treated to the Wemyss charm as dispensed by Hermione and Hortense. Gertie and Millicent, who had met the previous evening, had their heads together.

After exchanging a few words with the other old dears, Leonora joined him. She gave him her hand, her special smile—the one she reserved just for him—curving her lips. "I have to say I was extremely glad of your great-aunts' suggestion. After attending Miss Timmins's funeral this morning, attending Lady Willoughby's ball tonight and dealing with the—as you described it—prurient interest, would have severely tried my temper." She glanced up, met his eyes. "And yours."

He inclined his head. "Even though I didn't attend the funeral. How was it?"

"Quiet, but sincere. I think Miss Timmins would have been pleased. Henry Timmins shared the service with the local vicar, and Mrs. Timmins was there, too—a nice woman."

After an instant, she turned to him and lowered her voice. "We found some papers in Cedric's room, hidden in the bottom of his woodbasket. They weren't letters, but sheets of entries similar to those in the journals but most importantly, they weren't in Cedric's hand— they were written by Carruthers. Humphrey and Jeremy are concentrating on those now. Humphrey says they're descriptions of experiments, similar to those in Cedric's journal, but there's still no way to make any sense of them, to know if they mean anything at all. It seems all we've discovered so far contains only part of whatever they were working on."

"Which suggests even more strongly that there is some discovery, one Cedric and Carruthers thought it worthwhile to deal with carefully."

"Indeed." Leonora searched his face. "In case you're wondering, the staff at Number 14 are very much on alert, and Castor will send to Gasthorpe should anything untoward occur."

"Good."

"Have you learned anything?"

He felt his jaw start to set; he pulled his charming mask back into place. "Nothing about Martinbury, but we're trying a new tack that might get us further faster. However, the big news is that Mountford—or whoever he is—has taken the bait. He, acting via the weasel, rented Number 16 late this afternoon."

Her eyes widened; she kept them fixed on his. "So things are starting to happen."

"Indeed."

He turned, smiling, as Constance joined them. Leonora stood by his side and chatted with the ladies as they came up. They told her of the church fete, and of the little routine day-to-day changes, the alterations the seasons brought to the manor. They told her of this and that, remembered snippets of Tristan's early life, of his father and grandfather.

She occasionally glanced at him, saw him extend that ready charm—also saw beneath it. Having met Lady Hermione and Lady Hortense, she could see from where he'd got it; she wondered what his father had been like.

Yet in this sphere Tristan's manners were more genuine; the real man showed through, not just with his strengths but with his weaknesses, too. He was comfortable, relaxing; she suspected that previously, he might well have gone for years without lowering his guard. Even now, the drawbridge chains were rusty.

She moved around the room, chatting here, chatting there, always conscious of Tristan, that he watched her as she watched him. Then Havers announced dinner, and they all went in, she on Tristan's arm.

He sat her beside him at one end of the table; Lady Hermione was at the other end. She made a neat speech expressing her pleasure at the prospect of shortly yielding her chair to Leonora, and led a toast to the affianced couple, then the first course was served. The gentle hum of conversation rose and engulfed the table.

The evening passed pleasantly, truly enjoyably. The ladies repaired to the drawing room, leaving the gentlemen to their port; it wasn't long before they rejoined them.

Her uncle Winston, Lord Warsingham, Mildred's husband, stopped by her side. "An excellent choice, my dear." His eyes twinkled; he'd been concerned by her lack of interest in marriage, but had never sought to interfere. "Might have taken you an unconscionable time to make up your mind, but the result's the thing, heh?"

She smiled, inclined her head. Tristan joined them, and she directed the conversation to the latest play.

And continued, at some level she wasn't sure she understood, to watch Tristan. She didn't always keep her eyes on him, yet she was wholly aware—an emotional watching if such a thing could be, a focusing of the senses.

She'd noticed, again and again, his momentary hesitations when, discussing something with her, he would check, pause, consider, then go on. She'd started to identify the patterns that told her what he was thinking, when and in what vein he was thinking of her. The decisions he was making.

The fact he'd made no move to exclude her from their active investigations heartened her. He could have been much more difficult; indeed, she'd expected it. Instead, he was feeling his way, accommodating her as he could; that bolstered her hope that in the future—the future they'd both committed themselves to—they would rub along well together.

That they would be able to accommodate each other's natures and needs.

His, both nature and needs, were more complex than most; she'd realized that sometime ago—it was part of the attraction he held for her, that he was different from others, that he needed and wanted on a somewhat different scale, on a different plane.

Given his dangerous past, he was less disposed to excluding women, infinitely more disposed to using them. She'd sensed that from the first, that he was less inclined than his less adventurous brethren to coddle females; she now knew him well enough to guess that in pursuit of his duty he would have been coldly ruthless. It was that side of his nature that had allowed her to become as involved as she was in their investigations with only relatively minor resistance.

However, with her, that more pragmatic side had come into direct conflict with something much deeper. With more primitive impulses, all-but-primal instincts, the imperative to keep her forever shielded, tucked away from all harm.

Again and again, that conflict darkened his eyes. His jaw would set, he would glance at her briefly, hesitate, then leave matters as they were.

Adjustment. Him to her, her to him.

They were meshing together, step by step learning the ways in which their lives would interlock. Yet that fundamental clash remained; she suspected it always would.

She would have to bear with it, adjust to it. Accept but not react to his repressed but still present instincts and suspicions. She didn't believe he'd put the latter into words, not even to himself, yet they remained, beneath all his strengths, the weaknesses she'd brought forth. She'd told him, admitted why she didn't easily accept help, could not easily trust him or anyone with things that mattered to her.

Logically, consciously, he believed in her decision to trust him, to accept him into the innermost sphere of her life. At a deeper, instinctive level, he kept watching for signs she would forget.

For any sign she was excluding him.

She'd hurt him once in precisely that way. She wouldn't do so again, but only time would teach him that.

His gift to her had been, from the first, to accept her as she was. Her gift in return would be to accept all he was and give him the time to lose his suspicions.

To learn to trust her as she did him.

Jeremy joined them; her uncle seized the moment to talk estates with Tristan.

"Well, sis." Jeremy glanced around at the company. "I can see you here, with all these ladies, organizing them, keeping the whole household ticking smoothly along." He grinned at her, then sobered. "Their gain. We'll miss you."

She smiled, put her hand on his arm, squeezed. "I haven't left you yet."

Jeremy lifted his gaze to Tristan, beyond her. Half smiled as he looked back at her. "I think you'll find you have."

Eighteen

For all his relative naïveté, Jeremy was correct in one respect—Tristan clearly considered their union already accepted, established, acknowledged.

The Warsinghams were the first to leave, Gertie with them. When Humphrey and Jeremy prepared to follow them, Tristan trapped her hand on his sleeve and declared that he and she had matters pertaining to their future that they needed to discuss in private. He would see her home in his carriage in half an hour or so.

He stated it so glibly, with such complete assurance, everyone meekly nodded and fell into line. Humphrey and Jeremy departed; his great-aunts and cousins bade them good night and retired.

Leaving him to usher her into the library, alone at last.

He paused to give Havers instructions for the carriage. Leonora went to stand before the fire, a goodly blaze throwing heat into the room. Outside, a chill wind blew and heavy clouds blocked the moon; not a pleasant evening.

Holding out her hands to the flames, she heard the door click softly shut, sensed Tristan draw near.

She turned; his hands slid about her waist as she did. Her palms came to rest on his chest. She locked her eyes on his. "I'm glad you arranged this—there are a number of matters we should talk about."

He blinked. He didn't let her go, yet he didn't draw her closer. Their hips and thighs were lightly, teasingly, brushing; her breasts were just touching his chest. His hands spanned her waist; she was neither in his arms nor out of them, yet wholly within his control. He looked down into her eyes. "What matters are those?"

"Matters such as where we'll live—how you imagine our life should run."

He hesitated, then asked, "Do you want to live here, in London, among the ton?"

"Not especially. I've never felt any great attraction to the ton. I'm comfortable enough in it, but I don't crave its dubious excitements."

His lips twitched. He lowered his head. "Thank heaven for that."

She laid a finger across his lips before they could capture hers. Felt his hands release her waist, his palms slide over her silk-clad back. From beneath her lashes, she met his eyes, drew a quick breath. "So we'll live at Mallingham Manor?"

Against her finger, his lips curved distractingly. "If you can bear to live buried in the country."

"Surrey is hardly the depths of buccolic rusticity." She lowered her hand.

His lips came nearer, hovered an inch from hers. "I meant the old dears. Can you cope with them?"

He waited; she struggled to think. "Yes." She understood the old ladies, recognized their ways, foresaw no difficulty dealing with them. "They're well-disposed—I understand them, and they understand us."

He made a derisive sound; it feathered over her lips, made them throb. "You may understand them—they frequently leave me at a total loss. There was something a few months ago about the vicarage curtains that completely passed me by."

She was finding it hard not to laugh; his lips were so close, it seemed terribly dangerous, like letting her guard down with a wolf about to pounce.

"So you truly will be mine?"

She was about to laughingly offer her mouth and herself in proof when something in his tone struck her; she met his eyes—realized he was deadly serious. "I'm already yours. You know it."

His lips, still distractingly near, twisted; he shifted, easing her closer—his restlessness reached her, washed over her in a wave of tangible, shifting uncertainty. With the fuller touch of their bodies heat flared; he bent his head and set his lips to the corner of hers.

"I'm not your average gentleman."

The words whispered over her cheek.

"I know." She turned her head and their lips met.

After a brief exchange, he drew away, sent his lips tracing upward, over her cheekbone to her temple, then down until his breath warmed the hollow beneath her ear.

"I've lived dangerously, beyond all laws, for a decade. I'm not as civilized as I ought to be. You know that, don't you?"

She did, indeed, know that; the knowledge was crawling her nerves, anticipation sliding like heated silk down her veins. More to the immediate point, amazing though it seemed, she realized he was still unsure of her. And that whatever the matter he'd wanted to discuss, it was still on his mind, and she'd yet to hear of it.

Pushing up her hands, she caught and framed his face, and boldy kissed him. Trapped him, caught him, drew him in. Moved into him. Felt his response, felt his hands spread over her back, firm, then mold her to him.

When she finally consented to let him free, he raised his head and looked down at her; his eyes were dark, turbulent.

"Tell me." Her voice was husky, but commanding. Demanding. "What is it you wanted to say?"

A long moment passed; she was conscious of their breaths, of their pulses throbbing. She thought he wasn't going to answer, then he drew a short breath. His eyes had never left hers.

"*Don't.* Go. Into. Danger."

He didn't have to say more, it was there in his eyes. There for her to see. A vulnerability so deeply enmeshed in him, in who he was, that he could never not have it, and still have her.

A dilemma, one he could never resolve, but could only accept. As, in taking her as his wife, he'd chosen to do.

She leaned into him; her hands were still bracketing his face. "I will never willingly place myself in danger. I've decided to be yours— I intend to continue in that role, to remain important to you." She held his gaze. "Believe that."

His features hardened; he ignored her hands and lowered his head. Took her lips, her mouth in a searing kiss that bordered on the wild.

Drew back to whisper against her lips. "I'll try to, if you'll remember this. If you fail, we both will pay the price."

She traced his lean cheek. Waited until he met her eyes. "I won't fail. And neither will you."

Their hearts were thudding; familiar flames licked hungrily over their skins. She searched his eyes. "*This*"—she shifted sinuously against him, felt his breath hitch—"was meant to be. We didn't decree it, you or I, it was there, waiting to snare us. Now the challenge is to make all the rest work—it's not an endeavor we can escape or decline, not if we want this."

"I definitely want this, and more. I'm not letting you go. Not for any reason. Not ever."

"So we're committed, you and I." She held his darkened gaze. "We'll make it work."

Two heartbeats passed, then he bent his head; his hands firmed, lifting her against him.

She dropped her hands to his shoulders, pressed back. *"But . . ."*

He paused, met her eyes. "But what?"

"But we've run out of time tonight."

They had. Tristan tightened his arms, kissed her witless, then shackled his demons, clamoring for her, and, grim-faced, set her on her feet.

She looked as chagrined as he felt—a minor consolation.

Later.

Once they had Mountford by the heels, nothing was going to get in their way.

His carriage was waiting; he escorted Leonora out to it, helped her in, and followed. As the carriage rattled off over the now wet cobbles, he returned to something she'd mentioned earlier. "Why does Humphrey think pieces of Cedric's puzzle are missing? How can he know?"

Leonora settled back beside him. "The journals are details of experiments—what was done and the results, nothing more. What's missing is the rationale that makes sense of them—the hypotheses, the conclusions. Carruthers's letters refer to some of Cedric's experiments, and others which Humphrey and Jeremy reason must be Carruthers's own, and the sheets of descriptions from Carruthers we found in Cedric's room—Humphrey thinks at least some of those match some of the experiments referred to in Carruthers's letters."

"So Cedric and Carruthers appear to have been exchanging details of experiments?"

"Yes. But as yet Humphrey can't be certain whether they were working on the same project together, or whether they were simply exchanging news. Most pertinently, he hasn't found anything to define what their mutual project, assuming there was one, was."

He juggled the information, debating whether it made Martinbury, Carruthers's heir, more or less important. The carriage slowed, then halted. He glanced out, then climbed out before Number 14 Montrose Place and handed Leonora down.

Overhead, the clouds were scudding, the dark pall breaking up before the wind. She tucked her hand into his arm; he glanced at her as he swung the gate wide. They walked up the winding path, both distracted by the eccentric world of Cedric's creation gleaming in the fitful moonlight, the odd-shaped leaves and bushes embroidered with droplets of rain.

Light beamed from the front hall. As they climbed the porch steps the door swung open.

Jeremy looked out, his face tense. He saw them and his features eased. "About time! The blackguard's already started tunneling."

In absolute silence, they faced the wall beside the laundry trough in the basement of Number 14 and listened to the stealthy *scritch-scritch* of someone scraping away mortar.

Tristan motioned Leonora and Jeremy to stillness, then put out a hand, and laid it on the bricks from behind which the noise was emanating.

After a moment, he removed his hand and signaled them to retreat. At the entrance to the laundry, a footman stood waiting. Leonora and Jeremy went silently past him; Tristan paused. "Good work." His voice was just loud enough to reach the footman. "I doubt they'll get through tonight, but we'll organize a watch. Close the door and make sure no one makes any unusual sound in this area."

The footman nodded. Tristan left him and followed the others into the kitchen at the end of the corridor. From their faces, both Leonora and Jeremy were bursting with questions; he waved them to silence and addressed Castor and the other footmen, all gathered and waiting with the rest of the staff.

In short order he organized a rotating watch for the night, and reassured the housekeeper, cook, and maids that there was no likelihood of the villains breaking in undetected while they slept.

"At the rate they're going—and they'll have to go slowly—they can't risk a hammer and chisel—they'll take at least a few nights to loosen enough bricks to let a man through." He glanced around the company gathered about the kitchen table. "Who noticed the scratching?"

A tweeny colored and bobbed. "Me, sir—m'lord. I went in to get the second hot iron and heard it. Thought it was a mouse at first, then I remembered what Mr. Castor had said about odd noises and such, so I came straightaway and told him."

Tristan smiled. "Good girl." His gaze rested on the baskets piled high with folded sheets and linens set between the maids and the stove. "Was it washing day today?"

"Aye." The housekeeper nodded. "We always do our main wash on a Wednesday, then a small wash on Mondays."

Tristan looked at her for a moment, then said, "I have one last question. Have any of you, at any time in the last several months, going back to November or so, seen or been spoken to by either of these two gentlemen?" He proceeded to give quick word sketches of Mountford and his weasely accomplice.

"How did you guess?" Leonora asked when they were back in the library.

The two older maids and two of the footmen had been approached independently at various times in November, the maids by Mountford himself, the footmen by his accomplice. The maids had thought they'd found a new admirer, the footmen a new and unexpectedly well-heeled acquaintance always ready to buy the next pint.

Tristan dropped onto the chaise beside Leonora and stretched out his legs. "I always wondered why Mountford tried first to buy the house. How did he know Cedric's workshop had been locked up and left essentially undisturbed? He couldn't see in—the windows are so old, so fogged and crazed, it's impossible to see anything through them."

"He knew because he'd cozened the maids." Jeremy sat in his usual place behind his desk. Humphrey was in his chair before the hearth.

"Indeed. And that's how he's known other things"—Tristan glanced at Leonora—"like your propensity to walk alone in the garden. At what times you go out. He's been focused on this household for months, and he's done a decent job of reconnoitering."

Leonora frowned. "That begs the question of how he knew there's something here to be found." She looked at Humphrey, one of Cedric's journals open on his lap, a magnifying glass in his hand. "*We* still don't know there's anything valuable here—we're only surmising because of Mountford's interest."

Tristan squeezed her hand. "Trust me. Men like Mountford never are interested unless there's something to gain."

And the notice of foreign gentlemen was even less easy to attract. Tristan kept that observation to himself. He looked at Humphrey. "Any advance?"

Humphrey spoke at length; the answer was no.

At the end of his explanation, Tristan stirred. They were all keyed up; sleep would be difficult knowing that in the basement, Mountford was quietly excavating through the wall.

"What do you expect to happen now?" Leonora asked.

He glanced at her. "Nothing tonight. You can rest easy on that score. It'll take at least three nights of steady working to open a hole big enough for a man without alerting anyone on this side."

"I'm more worried about someone on this side alerting him."

He smiled his predator's smile. "I have men all around—they'll be there night and day. Now Mountford's in there, he won't get away."

Leonora looked into his eyes; her lips formed a silent O.

Jeremy humphed. He picked up a sheaf of the papers they'd found in Cedric's room. "We'd better get on with these. Somewhere here, there has to be a clue. Although why our dear departed relative couldn't use some simple, understandable cross-referencing system I don't know."

Humphrey's snort was eloquent. "He was a scientist, that's why. Never show any consideration for whoever might have to make sense of their works once they're gone. Never come across one who has in all my days."

Tristan stood, stretched. Exchanged a glance with Leonora. "I need to think through our plans. I'll call tomorrow morning and we'll make some decisions." He looked at Humphrey, included Jeremy when he said, "I'll probably bring some associates with me in the morning—can I ask you to give us a report on what you've discovered up to then?"

"Of course." Humphrey waved. "We'll see you at breakfast."

Jeremy barely glanced up.

Leonora saw him to the front door. They stole a quick, unsatisfying kiss before Castor, summoned by some butlerish instinct, appeared to open the door.

Tristan looked down into Leonora's shadowed eyes. "Sleep well. Believe me, you're at no risk."

She met his eyes, then smiled. "I know. I have proof."

Puzzled, he raised a brow.

Her smile deepened. "You're leaving me here."

He searched her face, saw understanding in her eyes. He saluted her, and left.

By the time he reached Green Street, his plan was clear in his mind. It was late; his house was quiet. He went straight to his study, sat at his desk, and reached for his pen.

The next morning, he, Charles, and Deverell met at the Bastion Club shortly after dawn. It was March; dawn wasn't that early, but they needed sufficient light to see by as they circled Number 16 Montrose

Place. They checked every possible escape route, tested the guards Tristan already had in place, and arranged for reinforcements where needed.

At half past seven, they retreated to the club's meeting room to reassess and report all that each individually had done, had set in train since the previous evening. At eight o'clock, they repaired to Number 14, where Humphrey and Jeremy, weary after working most of the night, and an eager Leonora were waiting.

Along with a substantial breakfast. Leonora had clearly given orders that they were to be fed well.

Seated at one end of the table, Leonora sipped her tea; over the rim of her cup, she regarded the trio of dangerous men who had invaded her home.

It was the first time she'd met St. Austell and Deverell; one glance was enough for her to see the similarities between them and Tristan. Likewise, they both evoked the same wariness she'd initially felt with Tristan; she wouldn't trust them, not entirely, not as a woman trusts a man, not unless she came to know them much better.

She looked at Tristan, beside her. "You said you would discuss a plan."

He nodded. "A plan of how best to react to the situation as we currently know it." He glanced at Humphrey. "Perhaps, if I outline the situation, you would correct me if you have more recent information."

Humphrey inclined his head.

Tristan looked down at the table, clearly gathering his thoughts. "We know that Mountford is searching for something he believes hidden in this house. He's been intent, persistent, unswervingly fixed on his goal for months. He seems increasingly desperate, and clearly will not cease until he finds what he's after. We have a connection between Mountford and a foreigner, which may or may not be pertinent. Mountford is now on the scene, trying to gain access to the basement here. He has one known accomplice, a weasel-faced man." Tristan paused to sip his coffee. "That's the opposition as we know it.

"Now, to the something they're after. Our best guess is that it's something the late Cedric Carling, the previous owner of this house and a renowned herbalist, discovered, possibly working with another herbalist, A. J. Carruthers, unfortunately now also deceased. Cedric's journals, and Carruthers's letters and notes, all we've found so far, suggest a collaboration, but the project itself remains unclear." Tristan looked at Humphrey.

Humphrey glanced at Jeremy. Waved him on.

Jeremy met the others' eyes. "We have three sources of information—Cedric's journals, letters to Cedric from Carruthers, and a set of notes from Carruthers, which we believe were enclosures sent with the letters. I've been concentrating on the letters and notes. Some of the notes detail individual experiments discussed and referred to in the letters. From what we've been able to link together so far, it seems certain Cedric and Carruthers were working together on some specific concoction. They discuss the properties of some fluid they were trying to influence with this concoction." Jeremy paused, grimaced. "We have nothing where they state what the fluid is, but from various references, I believe it to be blood."

The effect of that pronouncement on Tristan, St. Austell, and Deverell was marked. Leonora watched them exchange significant glances.

"So," St. Austell murmured, his gaze locked with Tristan's, "we have two renowned herbalists working on something to affect blood, and a possible foreign connection."

Tristan's expression had hardened. He nodded to Jeremy. "That clarifies the one uncertainty I had regarding our way forward. Clearly, Carruthers's heir, Jonathon Martinbury, an upright and honest young man who has mysteriously disappeared after reaching London, apparently coming down in response to a letter regarding Carruthers's and Cedric's collaboration, is a potentially critical pawn in this game."

"Indeed." Deverell looked at Tristan. "I'll swing my people on to that line, too."

Leonora glanced from one to the other. "What line?"

"It's now imperative we locate Martinbury. If he's dead, that will take some time—probably more time than we have with Mountford working downstairs. But if Martinbury's alive, there's a chance we can scour the hospitals and hospices sufficiently well to locate him."

"Convents." When Tristan glanced at her, Leonora elaborated. "You didn't mention them, but there are quite a lot in the city, and most take in the sick and injured as they're able."

"She's right." St. Austell looked at Deverell.

Who nodded. "I'll direct my people that way."

"What people?" Jeremy frowned at the trio. "You talk as if you have troops at your disposal."

St. Austell raised his brows, amused. Tristan straightened his lips and replied, "In a way, we do. In our previous calling, we had need of . . . connections at all levels of society. And there are a lot of ex-soldiers we can call on for assistance. We each know people who are used to going out and looking for things for us."

Leonora frowned Jeremy down when he would have asked more.

"So you've combined your troops and sent them out to search for Martinbury. What does that leave us to do? What's your plan?"

Tristan met her eyes, then glanced at Humphrey and Jeremy. "We still don't know what Mountford's after—we could simply sit back and wait for him to break in, then see what he goes for. That, however, is the more dangerous course. Letting him into this house, letting him at any stage get his hands on what he's after, should be our last resort."

"The alternative?" Jeremy asked.

"Is to go forward following the lines of inquiry we already have. One, seek Martinbury—he may have more specific information from Carruthers. Two, continue to piece together what we can from the three sources we have—the journals, letters, and notes. It's likely those are at least part of what Mountford is after. If he has access to the pieces we're missing, that would make sense.

"Three." Tristan glanced at Leonora. "We've assumed that the something—let's call it a formula—was hidden in Cedric's workshop. That may still be the case. We've only removed all the obvious written materials—if there's something specifically concealed in the workshop, it may still be there. Lastly, the formula may be completed, written down and hidden elsewhere in this house." He paused, then continued, "The risk of letting something like that fall into Mountford's hands is too great to take. We need to search this house."

Recalling how he'd searched Miss Timmins's rooms, Leonora nodded. "I agree." She glanced around the table. "So Humphrey and Jeremy should continue with the journals, letters, and notes in the library. Your people are scouring London for Martinbury. That leaves you three, I take it?"

Tristan smiled at her, one of his charming smiles. "And you. If you could warn your staff and clear the way for us, we three will search. We may need to search from attics to basement, and this is a large house." His smile took on an edge. "But we're very good at searching."

They were.

Leonora watched from the doorway of the workshop as, silent as mice, the three noblemen pried, poked, and prodded into every last nook and cranny, climbed about the heavy shelving, squinting down the backs of cupboards, whisked hidden crevices with canes, and lay on the floor to inspect the undersides of desks and drawers. They missed nothing.

And found nothing but dust.

From there, they worked steadily outward and upward, going through kitchen and pantries, even the now silent laundry, through every room on the lower floor, then they climbed the stairs and, quietly determined, set about applying their unexpected skills to the rooms on the ground floor.

Within two hours, they'd reached the bedchambers; an hour later, they broached the attics.

The luncheon gong was clanging when Leonora, seated on the stairs leading up to the attics—into which she'd flatly refused to venture—felt the reverberations of their descent.

She stood and swung around. Their footfalls, heavy, slow, told her they'd found nothing at all. They came into view, brushing cobwebs from their hair and coats—Shultz would not have approved.

Tristan met her eyes, somewhat grimly concluded, "If any precious formula is secreted in this house, it's in the library."

In Cedric's journals, Carruthers's letters and notes.

"At least we're now sure of that much." Turning, she led them back to the main stairs and down to the dining room.

Jeremy and Humphrey joined them there.

Jeremy shook his head as he sat. "Nothing more, I'm afraid."

"Except"—Humphrey frowned as he shook out his napkin—"that I'm increasingly certain Cedric did not keep any record of his own as to the rationale and conclusions he drew from his experiments." He grimaced. "Some scientists are like that—keep it all in their head."

"Secretive?" Deverall asked, starting on his soup.

Humphrey shook his head. "Not usually. More a case of they don't want to waste time writing down what they already know."

They all started eating, then Humphrey, still frowning, continued, "If Cedric didn't leave any record—and most of the books in the library are ours—there were only a handful of ancient texts in there when we moved in."

Jeremy nodded. "And I went through all of those. There were no records stuck in them, or written in them."

Humphrey continued, "If that's so, then we're going to have to pray Carruthers left some more detailed account. The letters and notes give one hope—and I'm not saying we won't ever get the answer if that's all there is for us to work with—but a properly kept journal with a *consecutive* listing of experiments . . . if we had that, we could sort out which recipes for this concoction were the later ones. Especially which was the final version."

"There are any number of versions, you see." Jeremy took up the explanation. "But there's no way to tell from Cedric's journal which came after which, let alone why. Cedric must have known, and from comments in the letters, Carruthers knew, too, but . . . so far, we've only been able to match a handful of Carruthers's experimental notes with his letters, which are the only things that are dated."

Humphrey chewed, nodded morosely. "Enough to make you tear out your hair."

In the distance, the front doorbell pealed. Castor left them, reappearing a minute later with a folded note on a salver.

He walked to Deverell's side. "A footman from next door brought this for you, my lord."

Deverell glanced at Tristan and Charles as he set down his fork and reached for the note. It was a scrap of plain paper, the writing an ill-formed scrawl in pencil. Deverell scanned it, then looked at Tristan and Charles across the table.

They both sat up.

"What?"

Everyone looked at Deverell. A slow smile curved his lips.

"The good sisters of the Little Sisters of Mercy off the Whitechapel Road have been caring for a young man who answers to the name of Jonathon Martinbury." Deverell glanced at the note; his face hardened. "He was brought to them two weeks ago, the victim of a vicious beating left to die in a gutter."

Arranging to fetch Martinbury—they all agreed he had to be fetched—was an exercise in logistics. In the end, it was agreed that Leonora and Tristan would go; neither St. Austell nor Deverell wanted to risk being seen leaving or returning to Number 14. Even Leonora and Tristan had to be cautious. They left the house via the front door, with Henrietta on her lead.

Once on the street, the line of trees along the boundary of Number 12 screened them from anyone watching from Number 16. They turned in at the gate of the club and, much to Henrietta's disgruntlement, left her in the kitchens there.

Tristan hurried Leonora down the back path of the club, then out into the alleyway behind. From there it was easy to reach the next street, where they hired a hackney and headed with all speed for the Whitechapel Road.

In the infirmary at the convent, they found Jonathon Martinbury. He looked to be a stalwart young man, squarish of both build and countenance, with brown hair visible through the breaks in the bandages wrapping his head. Much of him seemed bandaged; one arm rested in a sling. His face was badly bruised and cut, with a massive contusion above one eye.

He was lucid, if weak. When Leonora explained their presence by saying they'd been searching for him in relation to Cedric Carling's work with A. J. Carruthers, his eyes lit.

"Thank God!" Briefly, he closed his eyes, then opened them. His voice was rough, still hoarse. "I got your letter. I came down to town early, intending to call on you—" He broke off, his face clouding. "Everything since has been a nightmare."

Tristan talked to the sisters. Although concerned, they agreed that Martinbury was well enough to be moved, given he was now with friends.

Between them, Tristan and the convent's gardener supported Jonathon out to the waiting hackney. Leonora and the sisters fussed. Climbing into the carriage severely tried the young man's composure; he was tight-lipped and pale when they had him finally settled on the seat, wrapped in a blanket and cushioned by old pillows. Tristan had given Jonathon his greatcoat; Jonathon's coat had been ripped beyond redemption.

Together with Leonora, Tristan repeated Jonathon's thanks to the sisters and promised a much-needed donation as soon as he could arrange it. Leonora gave him an approving look. He handed her up into the carriage, and was about to follow when a motherly sister came hurrying up.

"Wait! Wait!" Lugging a large leather bag, she huffed out of the convent gate.

Tristan stepped forward and took the bag from her. She beamed in at Jonathon. "A pity after all you've been through to lose that one little piece of good luck!"

As Tristan hoisted the bag onto the carriage floor, Jonathon leaned down, reaching to touch it as if to reassure himself. "Indeed," he gasped, nodding as well as he could. "Many thanks, Sister."

The sisters waved and called blessings; Leonora waved back. Tristan climbed up and closed the door, settling beside Leonora as the carriage rumbled off.

He looked at the large leather traveling bag sitting on the floor between the seats. He glanced at Jonathon. "What's in it?"

Jonathon laid his head back against the squabs. "I think it's what the people who did this to me were after."

Both Leonora and Tristan looked at the bag.

Jonathon drew a painful breath. "You see—"

"No." Tristan held up a hand. "Wait. This journey's going to be bad enough. Just rest. Once we've got you settled and comfortable again, then you can tell us all your story."

"All?" Through half-closed lids Jonathon regarded him. "How many of you are there?"

"Quite a few. Better if you have to tell your tale only once."

A fever of impatience gripped Leonora, centered on Jonathon's black leather bag. A perfectly ordinary traveling bag, but she could imagine what it might contain; she was almost beside herself with frustrated curiosity by the time the carriage finally rolled to a halt in the alleyway alongside the back gate of Number 14 Montrose Place.

Tristan had first halted the carriage in a street closer to the park; he'd left them there, saying he needed to get things in place.

He'd returned more than half an hour later. Jonathon had been sleeping; he was still groggy when they stopped for the last time, and Deverell opened the carriage door.

"Go." Tristan gave her a little push.

She gave Deverell her hand and he helped her down; behind him, the garden gate stood open, with Charles St. Austell beyond—he beckoned her through.

Their largest footman, Clyde, was standing behind Charles with what Leonora realized was a makeshift stretcher in his hands.

Charles saw her looking. "We're going to carry him in. Too slow and painful otherwise."

She glanced at him. "Slow?"

With his head, he indicated the house next door. "We're trying to minimize the chance of Mountford seeing anything."

They'd assumed Mountford or more likely his accomplice would be watching the comings and goings at Number 14.

"I thought we'd have taken him to Number 12." Leonora glanced toward their club.

"Too difficult to disguise getting all of us over there to hear his story." Gently, Charles eased her aside as Tristan and Deverell helped Jonathon through the gate. "Here we are."

Between the four of them, they got Jonathon settled in the stretcher, constructed from folded sheets and two long broom poles. Deverell went ahead, leading the way. Clyde and Charles followed, carrying the stretcher. Carrying Jonathon's bag in one hand, Tristan brought up the rear, Leonora before him.

"What about the hackney?" Leonora whispered.

"Taken care of. I've paid him to rest there for another ten minutes before rumbling off, just in case the sound as he passes behind next door alerts them."

He'd thought of everything—even cutting a new, narrow arch in the hedge dividing the well-screened kitchen garden from the more open lawn. Instead of going up the central path and on through the central archway and then having to cross a wide expanse of lawn, they headed up a narrow side path following the boundary wall with Number 12, then through the newly hacked breach in the hedge, emerging hard by the garden wall, largely concealed in its shadow.

They only had a short distance to cover until the jut of the kitchen wing hid them from Number 16. Then they were free to climb the steps to the terrace and go in through the parlor doors.

When Tristan closed the French doors behind her, she caught his eye. "Very neat."

"All part of the service." His gaze went past her. She turned to see Jonathon being helped out of the stretcher and onto a daybed, already made up.

Pringle was hovering. Tristan caught his eye. "We'll leave you to your patient. We'll be in the library—join us when you're finished."

Pringle nodded, and turned to Jonathon.

They all filed out. Clyde took the stretcher and headed for the kitchens; the rest of them trooped into the library.

Leonora's eagerness to see what Jonathon had in his bag was nothing to Humphrey's and Jeremy's. If Tristan and the others had not been there, she doubted she would have been able to prevent them having the bag fetched and "just checking" what it contained.

The comfortable old library had rarely seemed so full, and even more rarely so alive. It wasn't just Tristan, Charles, and Deverell, all pacing, waiting, hard-faced and intent; their repressed energy seemed to infect Jeremy and even Humphrey. This, she thought, sitting feigning patience on the chaise and with Henrietta, sprawled at her feet, watching them all, must be what the atmosphere in a tent full of knights had felt like just before the call to battle.

Finally, the door opened and Pringle entered. Tristan splashed brandy into a glass and handed it to him; Pringle took it with a nod, sipped, then sighed appreciatively. "He's well enough, certainly well enough to talk. Indeed, he's eager to do so, and I'd suggest you hear him out with all speed."

"His injuries?" Tristan asked.

"I'd say those who attacked him were coldly intent on killing him."

"Professionals?" Deverell asked.

Pringle hesitated. "If I had to guess, I'd say they were professionals, but more used to knives or pistols, yet in this case they were trying to make the attack look like the work of local thugs. However, they failed to take Mr. Martinbury's rather heavy bones into account; he's very bruised and battered, but the sisters have done well, and with time he'll be as good as new. Mind you, if some kind soul hadn't taken him to the convent, I wouldn't have given much for his chances."

Tristan nodded. "Thank you once again."

"Think nothing of it." Pringle handed back his empty glass. "Every time I hear from Gasthorpe, I at least know it'll be something more interesting than boils or carbuncles."

With nods all around, he left them.

They all exchanged glances; the excitement leapt a notch.

Leonora rose. Glasses were quickly drained and set down. She shook out her skirts, then swept to the door, and led them all back to the parlor.

Nineteen

❧✦❧

"It's all still a mystery to me. I can't make head or tail of it—if you can shed any light on the affair I'd be grateful." Jonathon settled his head against the back of the chaise.

"Start at the beginning," Tristan advised. They were all gathered around—in chairs, propped against the mantelpiece—all keenly focused. "When did you first hear of anything to do with Cedric Carling?"

Jonathon's gaze fixed, grew distant. "From A. J.—on her deathbed."

Tristan, and everyone else, blinked. "*Her* deathbed?"

Jonathon looked around at them. "I thought you knew. A. J. Carruthers was my aunt."

"*She* was the herbalist? A. J. Carruthers?" Humphrey's disbelief rang in his tone.

Jonathon, somewhat grim-faced, nodded. "Yes, she was. And that was why she liked living hidden away in north Yorkshire. She had her cottage, grew her herbs and conducted her experiments and no one bothered her. She collaborated and corresponded with a large number of other well-respected herbalists, but they all knew her only as A. J. Carruthers."

Humphrey frowned. "I see."

"One thing," Leonora put in. "Did Cedric Carling, our cousin, know she was a woman?"

"I honestly don't know," Jonathon replied. "But knowing A. J., I doubt it."

"So when did you first hear of Carling or anything to do with this business?"

"I'd heard Carling's name from A.J. over the years, but only as another herbalist. The first I knew of this business was just a few days before she died. She'd been failing for months—her death was no surprise. But the story she told me then—well, she was starting to drift away, and I wasn't sure how much to credit."

Jonathon drew breath. "She told me she and Cedric Carling had gone into partnership over a particular ointment they'd both been convinced would be eminently useful—she was a great one for working on *useful* things. They'd been working on this ointment for over two years, quite doggedly, and from the first they'd made a solemn and binding agreement to share in any profits from the discovery. They'd enacted a legal document—she told me I'd find it in her papers, and I did, later. However, the thing she was most urgent to tell me then was that they'd succeeded in their quest. Their ointment, whatever it was, was effective. They'd reached that point some two months or so before, and then she'd heard no more from Carling. She'd waited, then written to other herbalists she knew in the capital, asking after Carling, and she'd only just heard back that he'd died."

Jonathon paused to look at their faces, then continued, "She was too old and frail to do anything about it then, and she assumed that with Cedric's death, it would take his heirs some time to work through his effects and contact her, or her heirs, about the matter. She told me so I'd be prepared, and know what it was about when the time came."

He dragged in a breath. "She died shortly after, and left me all her journals and papers. I kept them, of course. But what with one thing and another, my work for my articles, and not hearing anything from anyone about the discovery, I more or less forgot about it, until last October."

"What happened then?" Tristan asked.

"I had all her journals in my rooms, and one day I picked one up, and started to read. And that's when I realized she might have been right—that what she and Cedric Carling had discovered might, indeed, be very useful." Jonathon shifted awkwardly. "I'm no herbalist, but it seemed like the ointment they'd created would help to clot blood, especially in wounds." He glanced at Tristan. "I could imagine that that might have quite definite uses."

Tristan stared at him, knew Charles and Deverell were doing the same, and they were all reliving the same day, reliving the carnage on the battlefield at Waterloo. "An ointment to clot blood." Tristan felt his face set. "Very useful indeed."

"We should have kept Pringle," Charles said.

"We can ask his advice fast enough," Tristan answered. "But first let's hear the rest. There's a lot we don't yet know—like who Mountford is."

"Mountford?" Jonathon looked blank.

Tristan waved. "We'll get to him—whoever he is—in time. What happened next?"

"Well, I wanted to come down to London and follow things up, but I was right in the middle of my final examinations—I couldn't leave York. The discovery had sat around doing nothing for two years—I reasoned it could wait until I was finished with my articles and could devote proper time to it. So that's what I did. I discussed it with my employer, Mr. Mountgate, and also with A. J.'s old solicitor, Mr. Aldford."

"Mountford," Deverell put in.

They all looked at him.

He grimaced. "Mountgate plus Aldford equals Mountford."

"Good heavens!" Leonora looked at Jonathon. "Who else did you tell?"

"No one." He blinked, then amended, "Well, not initially."

"What does that mean?" Tristan asked.

"The only other person who was told was Duke—Marmaduke Martinbury. He's my cousin and A. J.'s other heir—her other nephew. She left me all her journals and papers and herbalist things—Duke never had a moment for her interest in herbs—but her estate was otherwise divided between the two of us. And, of course, the discovery as such was part of her estate. Aldford felt duty-bound to tell Duke, so he wrote to him."

"Did Duke reply?"

"Not by letter." Jonathon's lips thinned. "He came to visit me to ask about the matter." After a moment, he went on, "Duke is the black sheep of the family, always has been. As far as I know, he has no real fixed abode, but is usually to be found at whatever racecourse is holding a carnival.

"Somehow—probably because he was strapped for cash and so at home at his other aunt's house in Derby—Aldford's letter found him. Duke came around wanting to know when he could expect his share of the cash. I felt honor-bound to explain the whole to him—after all, A. J's share of the discovery was half his." Jonathon paused, then went on, "Although he was his usual obnoxious self, he didn't, once he understood what the legacy was, seem all that interested."

"Describe Duke."

Jonathon glanced at Tristan, noting his tone. "Leaner than me, a few inches taller. Dark hair—black, actually. Dark eyes, pale skin."

Leonora stared at Jonathon's face, did a little mental rearranging, then nodded decisively. "That's him."

Tristan glanced at her. "You're sure?"

She looked at him. "How many lean, tallish, black-haired young men with"—she pointed at Jonathon—"a nose like that do you expect to stumble over in this affair?"

His lips twitched, but thinned immediately. He inclined his head. "So Duke is Mountford. Which explains a few things."

"Not to me," Jonathon said.

"All will be made clear in time," Tristan promised. "But carry on with your tale. What happened next?"

"Nothing immediately. I finished my exams and arranged to come down to London, then I received that letter from Miss Carling, via Mr. Aldford. It seemed clear that Mr. Carling's heirs knew less than I did, so I brought forward my visit . . ." Jonathon stopped, puzzled, looked at Tristan. "The sisters said you'd sent people asking after me. How did you know I was in London, let alone hurt?"

Tristan explained, succinctly, from the beginning of the odd happenings in Montrose Place to their realization that A. J. Carruthers's work with Cedric held the key to the mysterious Mountford's desperate interest, to how they had tracked and finally found Jonathon himself.

He stared at Tristan, dazed. "Duke?" He frowned. "He is the black sheep, but although he's nasty, mean-tempered, even something of a brute, it's a bully's facade—I'd have said he was something of a coward beneath his bluster. I can imagine he might have done *most* of what you say, but I honestly can't see him arranging to have me beaten to death."

Charles smiled that deadly smile he, Tristan, and Deverell all seemed to have in their repertoires. "Duke might not have—but the people he's very likely now dealing with would have no scruples in disposing of you if you threatened to butt in."

"If what you say is true," Deverell put in, "they're probably having trouble keeping Duke up to scratch. That would certainly fit."

"The weasel," Jonathon said. "Duke has a . . . well, a valet I suppose. A manservant. Cummings."

"That's the name he gave me." Deverell raised his brows. "About as clever as his master."

"So," Charles said, straightening away from the mantelpiece, "what now?"

He looked at Tristan; they all looked at Tristan. Who smiled, not nicely, and rose. "We've learned all we need to this point." Settling his sleeves, he glanced at Charles and Deverell. "I rather think it's time we invited Duke to join us. Let's hear what he has to say."

Charles's grin was diabolical. "Lead the way."

"Indeed." Deverell was already at Tristan's heels as he turned for the door.

"Wait!" Leonora looked at the black bag, sitting beside the chaise, then raised her gaze to Jonathon's face. "Please tell me you have all of A. J.'s journals and her letters from Cedric in there."

Jonathon grinned, a trifle lopsidedly. He nodded. "The purest luck, but yes, I have them."

Tristan turned back. "That's one point we haven't covered. How did they catch you, and why didn't they take the letters and journals?"

Jonathon looked up at him. "Because it was so cold, there were hardly any passengers on the mail coach—it got in early." He glanced at Leonora. "I don't know how they knew I was on it—"

"They'd have had someone watching you in York," Deverell said. "I take it you didn't change your schedule immediately after you got Leonora's letter and rush off?"

"No. It took two days to organize bringing my time away forward." Jonathon sank back on the chaise. "When I got off the coach, there was a message waiting for me, telling me to meet a Mr. Simmons at the corner of Green Dragon Yard and Old Montague Street at six o'clock to discuss a matter of mutual interest. It was a nicely worded letter, well written, good quality paper—I thought it was from you, the Carlings, about the discovery. I didn't really think—you couldn't have known I was on the mail coach, but at the time it all seemed to fit.

"That corner is a few minutes from the coaching inn. If the mail had got in on schedule, I wouldn't have had time to organize a room before going to the meeting. Instead, I had an hour to look about, to find a clean room, and leave my bag there, before going to the rendezvous."

Tristan's unnerving smile remained. "They assumed you hadn't brought any papers with you. They would have searched."

Jonathon nodded. "My coat was ripped apart."

"So, finding nothing, they put you out of the picture and left you for dead. But they didn't check what time the coach pulled in—tsk, tsk. Very slapdash." Charles strolled toward the door. "Are we going?"

"Indeed." Tristan swung on his heel and headed for the door. "Let's fetch Mountford."

Leonora watched the door close behind them.

Humphrey cleared his throat, caught Jonathon's eye, then pointed to the black bag. "May we?"

Jonathon waved. "By all means."

Leonora was torn.

Jonathon was obviously drooping, exhaustion and his injuries catching up with him; she urged him to lie back and recoup. At her suggestion, Humphrey and Jeremy took themselves and the black bag off to the library.

Closing the parlor door behind her, she hesitated. Part of her wanted to hurry after her brother and uncle, to help with and share in the academic excitement of making sense of Cedric and A. J.'s discovery.

More of her was drawn to the real, more physical excitement of the hunt.

She debated for all of ten seconds, then headed for the front door. Opening it, she left it on the latch. Night had fallen, the darkness of evening closing in. On the porch, she hesitated. Wondered if she should take Henrietta. But the hound was still in the kitchens of the Club; she didn't have time to fetch her. She peered across at Number 16, but its front door was closer to the street; she couldn't see anything.

Don't. Go. Into. Danger.

There were three of them ahead of her; what danger could there be?

She hurried down the front steps and ran quickly down the front path.

They were, she assumed, going to pluck Mountford from his hole—she was curious, after all this time, to see what he was really like, what sort of man he was. Jonathon's description was ambivalent; yes, Mountford—Duke—was a violent bully, but not a murderous one.

He'd been violent enough where she was concerned. . . .

She approached the front door of Number 16 with appropriate caution.

It stood half-open. She strained her ears but heard nothing.

She peered past the door.

Faint moonlight threw her shadow deep into the hall. Caused the man framed in the doorway to the kitchen stairs to pause and turn around.

It was Deverell. He motioned her to silence, and to stay back, then he turned and melted into the shadows.

Leonora hesitated for a second; she'd stay back, just not this far back.

Her slippers silent on the tiles, she glided into the hall and followed in Deverell's wake.

The stairs leading down to the kitchens and the basement level were just beyond the hall door. From her earlier visit following Tristan around, Leonora knew that the double flight of stairs ended in a long corridor. The doors to the kitchens and scullery gave off it to the left; on the right lay the butler's pantry, followed by a long cellar.

Mountford was tunneling through from the cellar.

Pausing at the stairhead, she leaned over the banister and peered down; she could make out the three men moving below, large shadows in the gloom. Faint light shone from somewhere ahead of them. As they moved out of her sight, she crept down the stairs.

She paused on the landing. From there she could see the length of the corridor before and below her. There were two doors into the cellar. The nearer stood ajar; the faint light came from beyond it.

Even more faintly, like a *frisson* across her nerves, came a steady, *scritch-scratch*.

Tristan, Charles, and Deverell came together before the door; although she saw them move, assumed they were talking, she heard nothing, not the slightest sound.

Then Tristan turned to the cellar door, thrust it open and walked in.

Charles and Deverell followed.

The silence lasted for a heartbeat.

"Hey!"

"What . . . ?"

Thuds. Bangs. Stifled shouts and oaths. It was more than just a scuffle.

How many men had been in there? She'd assumed only two, Mountford and the weasel, but it sounded like more . . .

A horrendous *crash* shook the walls.

She gasped, stared down. The light had gone out.

In the gloom, a figure burst out of the second cellar door, the one at the end of the corridor. He turned, slammed the door, fiddled. She heard the grating sound of an old iron lock falling into place.

The man ran from the door, raced, hair and coat wildly flapping, up the corridor toward the stairs.

Startled, paralyzed by recognition—the man was Mountford—Leonora hauled in a breath. She forced her hands to her skirts, grasped them to turn and flee, but Mountford hadn't seen her—he skidded to a halt by the nearer cellar door, now wide-open.

He reached in, grabbed the door, and swung it shut, too. Grabbed the knob, desperately worked.

Into a sudden silence came a telltale grating, then the clunk as the heavy lock fell home.

Chest heaving, Mountford stepped back. The blade of a knife held in one fist gleamed dully.

A thud fell on the door, then the handle rattled.

A muffled oath filtered through the thick panels.

"Hah! Got you!" Face alight, Mountford turned.

And saw her.

Leonora whirled and fled.

She was nowhere near fast enough.

He caught her at the top of the stairs. Fingers biting into her arm, he swung her hard back against the wall.

"Bitch!"

The word was vicious, snarled.

Looking into the starkly pale face thrust close to hers, Leonora had a second to make up her mind.

Strangely, that was all it took—just a second for her emotions to guide her, for her wits to catch up. All she had to do was delay Mountford, and Tristan would save her.

She blinked. Wilted a fraction, lost a little of her starch. Infused her best imitation of Miss Timmins's vagueness into her manner. "Oh, dear—you must be Mr. Martinbury?"

He blinked, then his eyes blazed. He shook her. "How do you know that?"

"Well . . ." She let her voice quaver, kept her eyes wide. "You are the Mr. Martinbury who is related to A. J. Carruthers, aren't you?"

For all his reconnoitering, Mountford—Duke—would not have learned what sort of woman she was; she was perfectly certain he wouldn't have thought to ask.

"Yes. That's me." Gripping her arm, he pushed her ahead of him into the front hall. "I'm here to get something of my aunt's that now belongs to me."

He didn't put away the knife, a dagger of sorts. A frenetic tension thrummed through him, about him; his manner was strained, nervous.

She let her lips part, striving to look suitably witless. "Oh! Do you mean the formula?"

She had to get him away from Number 16, preferably into Number 14. Along the way, she had to convince him she was so helpless and unthreatening that he didn't need to keep hold of her. If Tristan and the others came up the stairs now . . . Mountford had her and a dagger, not to her mind a helpful arrangement.

He was studying her through slitted eyes. "What do you know about the formula? Have they found it?"

"Oh, I believe so. At least, I think that's what they said. My uncle, you know, and my brother. They've been working on our late cousin

Cedric Carling's journals, and I *think* they were saying only just a few hours ago that they believe they have the thing clear at last!"

Throughout her artless speech, she'd been drifting toward the front door; he'd been drifting with her.

She cleared her throat. "I realize there must have been some misunderstanding." With an airy wave, she dismissed whatever had occurred downstairs. "But I'm sure if you talk to my uncle and brother, they'd be happy to share the formula with you, given you are A. J. Carruthers's heir."

Emerging into the moonlight on the front porch, he stared at her.

She kept her expression as vacant as she could, tried not to react to his menace. The hand holding the knife was trembling; he seemed uncertain, off-balance, struggling to think.

He looked across at Number 14. "Yes," he breathed. "Your uncle and brother are very fond of you, aren't they?"

"Oh, yes." She gathered her skirts and with absolutely no hurry, descended the steps; he still did not let go of her arm but descended alongside her. "Why, I've kept house for them for more than a decade, you know. Indeed, they'd be lost without me—"

She continued in airy, totally vacuous vein as they went down the path, turned into the street, walked the short distance to the gate of Number 14, and went in. He walked beside her, still holding her arm, not saying anything; he was so tense, nervously starting, twitching, if he'd been a woman she'd have diagnosed incipient hysteria.

When they reached the front steps, he pulled her roughly closer. Held the dagger up for her to see. "We don't need any interference from your servants."

She blinked at the dagger, then, forcing her eyes wide, stared blankly up at him. "The door's on the latch—we won't need to disturb them."

His tension eased a notch. "Good." He propelled her up the steps. He seemed to be trying to look in every direction at once.

Leonora reached for the door; she glanced at Duke's white face, tight, taut, wondered for one instant if she was wise to trust in Tristan . . .

Hauling in a breath, she lifted her head and opened the door. Prayed Castor wouldn't appear.

Duke stepped inside with her, keeping close beside her. His grip on her arm eased as he scanned the empty hall.

Quietly closing the door, she said, her tone easy and light, inconsequential, "My uncle and brother will be in the library. It's this way."

He kept his hand on her arm, still looked this way and that, but went with her quickly and quietly through the hall and into the corridor leading to the library.

Leonora thought furiously, tried to plan what she should say. Duke's nerves were strung tight, any tighter and they'd snap. God only knew what he might do then. She hadn't dared look to see if Tristan and the others were following, but the old locks on the cellar doors might take longer to pick than less heavy modern locks.

She still didn't feel that she'd made the wrong decision—Tristan *would* rescue her, and Jeremy and Humphrey, soon. Until then, it was up to her to keep them all—Jeremy, Humphrey, and herself—safe.

Her ploy had worked so far; she couldn't think of anything better than to continue in that vein.

Opening the library door, she sailed in. "Uncle, Jeremy—we have a guest."

Duke kept pace with her, kicking the door shut behind them.

Inwardly muttering—*when* would he let her go?—she kept a silly, innocuous expression plastered on her face. "I found Mr. Martinbury next door—it seems he's been looking for that formula of Cousin Cedric's. He seems to think it belongs to him—I told him you wouldn't mind sharing it with him . . . ?"

She infused every ounce of quavering helplessness into her voice, every last iota of intent into her eyes. If anyone could confuse and obstruct someone with words written on a page, it was her brother and uncle.

Both were in their usual places; both had glanced up, then remained frozen.

Jeremy met her gaze, read the message in her eyes. His desk was awash with papers; he started to rise from his chair behind it.

Mountford panicked. "Wait!" His fingers tightened on Leonora's arm; he hauled her to him, jerking her off-balance so she fell against him. He brandished his dagger before her face.

"Don't do anything rash!" Wildly, he looked from Jeremy to Humphrey. "I just want the formula—just give it to me, and she won't get hurt."

She felt his chest heave as he dragged in a breath.

"I don't want to hurt anyone, but I *will*. I want that formula."

The sight of the knife had shocked Jeremy and Humphrey; Duke's rising tones were scaring her.

"I say, see here!" Humphrey struggled up out of his chair, uncaring of the journal that slid to the floor. "You can't just come in here and—"

"Shut *up!*" Mountford was dancing with impatience. His eyes kept flicking to Jeremy's desk.

Leonora couldn't help but focus on the blade, waltzing before her eyes.

"Listen, you can have the formula." Jeremy started to come around his desk. "It's here." He waved at the desk. "If you'll—"

"Stop right there! Not one more step, or I'll slice her cheek!"

Jeremy paled. Halted.

Leonora tried not to think about the knife slicing into her cheek. She closed her eyes briefly. She had to think. Had to find a way . . . a way to take control . . . to waste time, to keep Jeremy and Humphrey safe . . .

She opened her eyes and focused on her brother. "Don't come any closer!" Her voice was weak and wavery, totally unlike her. "He might lock you up somewhere, and then I'll be alone with him!"

Mountford shifted, dragging her so he could keep both Humphrey and Jeremy in view but was no longer standing directly before the door. "Perfect," he hissed. "If I lock you two up, just like I locked the others up, then I can take the formula and be on my way."

Jeremy stared at her. "Don't be stupid." He meant every word. Then he glanced at Mountford. "Anyway, there's nowhere he could lock us up—this is the only room on this floor with a lock."

"Indeed!" Humphrey puffed. "A nonsensical suggestion."

"Oh, no," she warbled, and prayed Mountford would believe her act. "Why, he could lock you in the broom closet across the hall. You'd both fit."

The look Jeremy sent her was furious. "You *fool!*"

His reaction played into her hands. Mountford, so nervous he was jigging, jumped on the idea. "Both of you—now!" He waved with the knife. "You"—he pointed at Jeremy—"get the old man and help him to the door. You don't want your sister's lovely face scarred, do you?"

With a final glare at her, Jeremy went and took Humphrey's arm. He helped Humphrey to the door.

"Stop." Mountford pulled her around so they were directly behind the other two, facing the door. "Right—no noise, no nonsense. Open the door, walk to the broom closet, open its door and walk in. Close the door quietly behind you. Remember—I'm watching every move, and my dagger is at your sister's throat."

She saw Jeremy haul in a breath, then he and Humphrey did exactly as Mountford had ordered. Mountford edged forward as they went into the broom closet directly across the wide corridor; he glanced down the corridor toward the front hall, but no one came from that direction.

The instant the broom closet door shut, Mountford pushed her forward. The key was in the lock. Without releasing her, he turned it.

"Excellent!" He turned to her, eyes feverishly bright. "Now you can get me the formula, and I'll be on my way."

He pushed her back into the library. He closed the door and hurried her to the desk. "Where is it?"

Leonora spread her hands and shuffled papers, confusing what little order there had been. "He said it was here . . ."

"Well find it, damn you!" Mountford released her, ran his fingers through his hair.

Frowning as if concentrating, disguising her sudden spurt of relief, Leonora drifted around the large desk, spreading and sorting papers. "If my brother said it was here, I can assure you it will be . . ." She continued rambling, just like any of the dithery old dears she'd helped over the years. And steadily, paper by paper, worked her way around the desk.

"Is this it?" Finally opposite Mountford, she picked up one sheet, squinted at the receipe, then shook her head. "No. But it must be here . . . perhaps it's this one?"

She felt Mountford quiver, made the mistake of glancing up—he caught her eye. Saw . . .

His face blanked, then rage poured into his expression. "Why *you*—!"

He lunged for her.

She weaved back.

"This was a trick, wasn't it? I'll teach you—"

He would have to catch her first. Leonora wasted no time arguing; she put her mind to dodging him, darting this way, then that. The desk was big enough that he couldn't reach her over it.

"Ah!" He launched himself over the desk at her.

With a shriek, she whisked out of his reach. She glanced at the door but he was already scrambling to his feet, his face a mask of fury.

He raced at her. She ran.

Around and around.

The door opened.

She rounded the desk and fled straight for the tall figure who walked in.

Flung herself at him and clutched.

Tristan caught her, then caught her hands, pushed her behind him. "Out."

One word, but the tone was not one to disobey. Tristan didn't look at her. Out of breath, she followed his gaze to Mountford, leaning, panting, on the opposite side of the desk. He was still holding the dagger in one fist.

"Now."

A warning. She backed a few steps, then whirled. He didn't need her there to distract him.

She rushed out into the corridor, intending to summon help, only to realize Charles and Deverell were there, standing in the shadows.

Charles reached past her, caught the door, and pulled it shut. Then he leaned nonchalantly against the frame and grinned somewhat resignedly at her.

Deverell, his lips curved in the same, almost reminiscent wolfish smile, leaned back against the corridor wall.

She stared at them. Pointed to the library. "Mountford's got a dagger!"

Deverell raised his brows. "Only one?"

"Well, yes . . ." A thud reverberated from behind the door. She started, swung around and stared at it—as much of it as she could see past Charles's shoulders. She glared at him. "Why aren't you helping him?"

"Who? Mountford?"

"*No!* Tristan!"

Charles screwed up his face. "I doubt he needs help." He glanced at Deverell.

Who grimaced. "Unfortunately." The word "pity" danced in the air.

Thuds and grunts issued from the library, then a body hit the floor. Hard.

Leonora winced.

Silence reigned for a moment, then Charles's expression changed and he straightened away from the door.

It opened. Tristan stood framed in the doorway.

His gaze locked on Leonora, then flicked to Charles and Deverell. "He's all yours." Reaching out, he took Leonora's arm, pushing her down the corridor. "If you'll excuse us for a moment?"

A rhetorical question; Charles and Deverell were already slipping past him into the library.

Leonora felt her heart thudding; it still hadn't slowed. Swiftly she scanned Tristan, all of him she could see as he drew her down the corridor. His face was set and definitely grim. "Did he hurt you?"

She could barely keep the panic from her voice. Daggers could be deadly.

He flicked her a narrow-eyed glance; if anything his jaw set harder. "Of course not."

He sounded insulted. She frowned at him. "Are you all right?"

His eyes flared. "No!"

They'd reached the front hall; Tristan threw open the morning room door and propelled her in. He followed on her heels, all but slamming the door. "Now! Just refresh my memory—what was it I warned you—only yesterday, I seem to recall—never, *ever* to do?"

She blinked, met his barely restrained fury with her usual steady gaze. "You told me never to go into danger."

"Don't. Go. Into. Danger." He stepped closer, deliberately intimidating. "Precisely. *So*"—his chest swelled as he dragged in a desperate breath, felt the reins of his temper slither free regardless—*"what the devil did you think you were doing by following us next door?"*

He didn't raise his voice, rather, he lowered it. Infused every last ounce of power into his diction so the words cracked like a whip. Stung like one, too.

"I—"

"If that's an example of how you intend obeying me in future, of how you intend going on, despite my clear warning, I take leave to tell you that it *won't do!*" He ran a hand through his hair.

"If—"

"*God!* I aged a decade and more when Deverell told me he'd seen you out there. And *then* we had to subdue Mountford's cronies before we could get at the locks, and *they* were ancient and stiff! I can't remember feeling so damned desperate in my life!"

"I under—"

"No, you *don't!*" He pinned her with a glare. "And don't think this means we're not going to get married, because we are—that's final!"

He emphasized how final with a swift motion of his hand. "But as you can't be trusted to pay attention, to behave with a modicum of common sense—to exercise those wits God definitely gave you and spare me this torment—be damned if I don't have a bloody tower built at Mallingham and *lock you in it!*"

He stopped to drag in a breath, noticed her eyes were glittering strangely. Warningly.

"If you're quite finished?" Her tone was considerably more glacial than his.

When he didn't immediately respond, she went on, "For your information, you have what happened here this evening entirely wrong." She lifted her chin, met his gaze defiantly. "I didn't go into danger—*not at all!*" Her eyes snapped; she held up a finger to stop him from erupting—interrupting.

"What happened was this. I followed you and Charles and Deverell—three gentlemen of not inconsiderable experience and abilities—into a house we all believed held only two far less able men." Her eyes bored into his, defying him to contradict her. "We *all* believed there was no great danger. As it happened, fate took a hand, and the situation became *unexpectedly* dangerous.

"However!" She fixed him with a look as furious as any of his had been. "What you are doggedly failing to see in all this is what to me is the most crucial point!" She flung her hands outward. *"I trusted you!"*

She turned, paced, then with an angry swish faced him and drilled a finger into his chest. "I *trusted* you to get yourself free and come after me and rescue me—*and you did.* I *trusted* you to save me, and yes, you turned up and dealt with Mountford. In typical blinkered male fashion, you're refusing to see this!"

He caught her finger. She locked her eyes on his. Her chin set. "I trusted in you, and you *didn't* fail me. I got it—*we* got it—right."

She held his gaze; a faint sheen invested her blue eyes. "I have a warning for you," she said, her voice low. *"Don't. Spoil. It."*

If he'd learned anything in his long career, it was that, in certain circumstances, retreat was the wisest option.

"Oh." He searched her eyes, then nodded and released her hand. "I see. I didn't realize."

"Humph!" She lowered her hand. "Just as long as you do now . . ."

"Yes." A sense of euphoria was welling inside him, threatening to spill over and sweep him away. "I do see . . ."

She watched him, waited, unconvinced by his tone.

He hesitated, then asked, "You really did *mean* to trust me with your life?"

Her eyes were definitely glittery now, but not with anger. She smiled. "Yes, I definitely did. If I hadn't had you to trust in, I don't know what I would have done."

She moved into his arms; he closed them around her. She tipped up her face to look into his. "With you in my life, the decision was easy." Raising her arms, she draped them over his shoulders. Looked into his eyes. "So now all is well."

He studied her face, then nodded. "Indeed." He was lowering his head to kiss her when his strategist's brain, routinely checking that all was indeed well in their world, snagged on one point.

He hesitated, lifted his lids, waited until she did the same. He frowned. "I assume Jonathon Martinbury's still in the parlor, but what happened to Humphrey and Jeremy?"

Her eyes widened; her expression dissolved into one of mild horror. "Oh, great heavens!"

Twenty

&ᵒ⌇ᵒ&

"I'm so sorry!" Leonora helped Humphrey out of the closet. "Things . . . just happened."

Jeremy followed Humphrey out, kicking aside a mop. He glowered at her. "That was the most hopeless piece of acting I've ever witnessed—and that dagger was *sharp,* for heaven's sake!"

Leonora looked into his eyes, then quickly hugged him. "Never mind—it worked. That's the important thing."

Jeremy humphed and looked at the closed library door. "Just as well. We didn't want to knock and draw attention to ourselves—didn't know if it would distract someone at the wrong moment." He looked at Tristan. "I take it you caught him?"

"Indeed." Tristan waved to the library door. "Let's go in—I'm sure St. Austell and Deverell will have explained his position to him by now."

The scene that met their eyes as they filed into the library suggested that was the case; Mountford—Duke—sat slumped, head and shoulders drooping, in a straight-backed chair in the middle of the library. His hands, hanging limp between his knees, were bound with curtain cord. One booted ankle was lashed to a chair leg.

Charles and Deverell were propped side by side against the front edge of the desk, arms folded, eyeing their prisoner as if imagining what they might do to him next.

Leonora checked, but could see only a graze on one of Duke's cheekbones; nevertheless, despite the lack of outward damage, he didn't look at all well.

Deverell looked up as they headed toward their usual places. Leonora helped Humphrey into his chair. Deverell caught Tristan's eye. "Might be an idea to get Martinbury in to hear this." He glanced around at the limited seating. "We could carry his chaise in."

Tristan nodded. "Jeremy?"

The three of them went out, leaving Charles on watch.

A minute later, a deep woof sounded from the front of the house, followed by the click of Henrietta's claws as she loped toward them.

Surprised, Leonora glanced at Charles.

He didn't shift his gaze from Mountford. "We thought she might prove helpful in persuading Duke to see the error of his ways."

Henrietta was already growling when she appeared in the doorway. Her hackles had risen; she fixed glowing amber eyes on Duke. Rigid, frozen, lashed to the chair, he stared, horrified, back.

Henrietta's growl dropped an octave. Her head lowered. She took two menacing steps forward.

Duke looked ready to faint.

Leonora clicked her fingers. "Here, girl. Come here."

"Come on, old girl." Humphrey tapped his thigh.

Henrietta looked again at Mountford, then snuffled and ambled over to Leonora and Humphrey. After greeting them, she circled, then collapsed in a shaggy heap between them. Resting her huge head on her paws, she fixed an implacably hostile gaze on Duke.

Leonora glanced at Charles. He looked well pleased.

Jeremy reappeared and held the library door wide; Tristan and Deverell carried the chaise from the parlor with Jonathon Martinbury reclining on it into the room.

Duke gasped. He stared at Jonathon; the last vestige of color drained from his face. "Good Lord! What happened to you?"

No actor could have given such a performance; he was transparently shocked by his cousin's state.

Tristan and Deverell set the chaise down; Jonathon met Duke's eyes steadily. "I gather I met some friends of yours."

Duke looked ill. His face waxen, he stared, then slowly shook his head. "But how did they know? *I* didn't know you were in town."

"Your *friends* are determined, and they have very long arms." Tristan sank onto the chaise beside Leonora.

Jeremy closed the door. Deverell had returned to his position beside Charles. Crossing the room, Jeremy pulled out his chair from behind the desk and sat.

"Right." Tristan exchanged glances with Charles and Deverell, then looked at Duke. "You're in a serious and dire position. If you have any wits at all, you'll answer the questions we put to you quickly, straightforwardly, and honestly. And, most importantly, accurately."

He paused, then went on, "We're not interested in hearing your excuses—justifications would be wasted breath. But for understanding's sake, what started you off on this tack?"

Duke's dark eyes rested on Tristan's face; from her position beside Tristan, Leonora could read their expression. All Duke's violent bravado had deserted him; the only emotion now investing his eyes was fear.

He swallowed. "Newmarket. It was last year's Autumn Carnival. I hadn't before dealt with the London centper-cents, but there was this nag . . . I was certain . . ." He grimaced. "Anyway, I got in deep—deeper than I've ever been. And those sharks—they have thugs who act as collectors. I went up north, but they followed. And then I got the letter about A. J.'s discovery."

"So you came to see me," Jonathon put in.

Duke glanced at him, nodded. "When the collectors caught up with me a few days later, I told them about it—they made me write it all down and took it back to the cent-per-cent. I thought the promise would hold him for a while . . ." He glanced at Tristan. "That's when things went from bad to hellish."

He drew breath; his gaze fixed on Henrietta. "The cent-per-cent sold my vowels on, on the strength of the discovery."

"To a foreign gentleman?" Tristan asked.

Duke nodded. "At first it seemed all right. He—the foreigner—encouraged me to get hold of the discovery. He told me how there was clearly no need to include the others"—Duke flushed—"Jonathon and the Carlings, as they hadn't bothered about the discovery for all this time—"

"So you attempted by various means to get into Cedric Carling's workshop, which by asking the servants you'd learned had been closed up since his death."

Again Duke nodded.

"You didn't think to check your aunt's journals?"

Duke blinked. "No. I mean . . . well, she was a woman. She could only have been helping Carling. The final formula had to be in Carling's books."

Tristan glanced at Jeremy, who returned a wry look. "Very well," Tristan continued. "So your new foreign backer encouraged you to find this formula."

"Yes." Duke shifted on the chair. "At first, it seemed quite a lark. A challenge to see if I could get the thing. He was even willing to underwrite buying the house." His face clouded. "But things kept going wrong."

"We can dispense with a list—we know most of it. I take it your foreign friend became more and more insistent?"

Duke shivered. His eyes, when they met Tristan's, looked haunted. "I offered to find the money, buy back my debt, but he wouldn't have it. He wanted the formula—he was willing to give me as much money as it took to get it, but it was get the damned thing for him—or die. He *meant* it!"

Tristan's smile was cold. "Foreigners of his ilk generally do." He paused, then asked, "What's his name?"

What little color had returned to Duke's face fled. A moment passed, then he moistened his lips. "He told me if I told anyone at all about him, he'd kill me."

Tristan inclined his head, gently said, "And what do you imagine will happen to you if you don't tell us about him?"

Duke stared, then glanced at Charles.

Who met his gaze. "Don't you know the punishment for treason?"

A moment passed, then Deverell quietly added, "That's assuming, of course, that you make it to the scaffold." He shrugged. "What with all the ex-soldiers in the prisons these days . . ."

Eyes huge, Duke dragged in a breath and looked at Tristan. "I didn't know it was *treason!*"

"I'm afraid what you've been doing definitely qualifies."

Duke hauled in another breath, then blurted out, "But I don't *know* his name."

Tristan nodded, accepting. "How do you contact him?"

"I don't! He set it up at the beginning—I have to meet him in St. James's Park every third day and report what's happened."

The next meeting was to occur the following day.

Tristan, Charles, and Deverell grilled Duke for a further half hour, but learned little more. Duke was patently cooperating; recalling how keyed up—how panic-stricken, she now realized—he'd been earlier, Leonora suspected he'd realized that they were his only hope, that if he helped, he might escape a situation that had transformed into a nightmare.

Jonathon's assessment had been accurate; Duke was a black sheep with few morals, a cowardly and violent bully, untrustworthy and worse, but he wasn't a killer, and he'd never meant to be a traitor.

His reaction to Tristan's questions about Miss Timmins was revealing. His face a ghastly hue, Duke falteringly recounted how he'd gone up to check on the ground-floor walls, heard a choking sound in the dimness, and looked up, to see the fragile old woman come tumbling down the stairs to land, dead, at his feet. His horror was unfeigned; it was he who had closed the old lady's eyes.

Watching him, Leonora grimly concluded justice of a sort had been served; Duke would never forget what he'd seen, what he'd inadvertently caused.

Eventually, Charles and Deverell hauled Duke off to the club, there to be held in the basement under the watchful eyes of Biggs and Gasthorpe, together with the weasel and the four thugs Duke had hired to help with the excavations.

Tristan glanced at Jeremy. "Have you identified the final formula?"

Jeremy grinned. He picked up a sheet of paper. "I'd just copied it out. It was in A. J.'s journals, all neatly noted. Anyone could have found it." He handed the sheet to Tristan. "It was definitely half Cedric's work, but without A. J. and her records, it would have been the devil to piece together."

"Yes, but will it work?" Jonathon asked. He'd remained silent throughout the interrogation, quietly taking things in. Tristan handed the paper to him; he scanned it.

"I'm no herbalist," Jeremy said. "But if the results as laid out in your aunt's journals are correct, then yes, their concoction will definitely aid clotting when applied to wounds."

"And it was lying there in York for the past two years." Tristan thought of the battlefield at Waterloo, then banished the vision. Turned to Leonora.

She met his eyes, squeezed his hand. "At least we have it now."

"One thing I don't understand," Humphrey put in. "If this foreigner was so set on finding the formula, and he was able to order Jonathon here killed, why didn't he come after the formula himself?" Humphrey raised his shaggy brows. "Mind you, I'm deuced glad he didn't. Mountford was bad enough, but at least we survived him."

"The answer's one of those diplomatic niceties." Tristan rose and resettled his coat. "If a foreigner from one of the embassies was implicated in an attack on, even the death of, an unknown young man or even two from the north, the government would frown, but largely ignore it. However, if the same foreigner was implicated in burglarly and violence in a house in a wealthy part of London, the house of distinguished men of letters, the government would assuredly be most displeased and not at all inclined to ignore anything."

He glanced at them all, his smile coolly cynical. "An attack on property close to the government's heart would create a diplomatic incident, so Duke was a necessary pawn."

"So what now?" Leonora asked.

He hesitated, looking down into her eyes, then smiled faintly, just for her. "Now we—Charles, Deverell, and I—need to take this information to the proper quarters, and see what they want done."

She stared at him. "Your erstwhile employer?"

He nodded. Straightened. "We'll meet again here for breakfast if you're agreeable and make whatever plans we need to make."

"Yes, of course." Leonora reached out and touched his hand in farewell.

Humphrey nodded magnanimously. "Until tomorrow."

"Unfortunately, your meeting with your government contact will have to wait until morning." Jeremy nodded at the clock on the mantelpiece. "It's past ten."

Tristan, heading for the door, turned, smiling, as he reached it. "Actually, no. The State never sleeps."

The State for them meant Dalziel.

They sent word ahead; nevertheless, the three of them had to cool their heels in the spymaster's anteroom for twenty minutes before the door opened, and Dalziel waved them in.

As they sank onto the three chairs set facing the desk, they glanced around, then met each other's eyes. Nothing had changed.

Including Dalziel. He rounded the desk. He was dark-haired, dark-eyed and always dressed austerely. His age was unusually difficult to gauge; when he'd first started working through this office, Tristan had assumed Dalziel to be considerably his senior. Now . . . he was starting to wonder if there were all that many years between them. He had visibly aged; Dalziel had not.

As cool as ever, Dalziel sat behind the desk, facing them. "Now. Explain, if you please. From the beginning."

Tristan did, severely editing his account as he went, leaving out much of Leonora's involvement; Dalziel was known to disapprove of ladies dabbling in the game.

Even so, how much missed that steady dark gaze was a matter for conjecture.

At the end of the tale, Dalziel nodded, then looked at Charles and Deverell. "And how is it you two are involved?"

Charles grinned wolfishly. "We share a mutual interest."

Dalziel held his gaze for an instant. "Ah, yes. Your club in Montrose Place. Of course."

He looked down; Tristan was sure it was so they could blink in comfort. The man was a menace. They weren't even part of his network anymore.

"So"—looking up from the notes he'd scrawled while listening, Dalziel leaned back and steepled his fingers; he fixed them all with his gaze—"we have an unknown European intent—seriously intent—on stealing a potentially valuable formula for aiding wound healing. We don't know who this gentleman might be, but we have the formula, and we have his local pawn. Is that correct?"

They all nodded.

"Very well. I want to know who this European is, but I don't want him to know I know. I'm sure you follow me. What I want you to do is this. First, tamper with the formula. Find someone who can make it look believable—we have no idea what training this foreigner might have. Second, convince the pawn to keep his next meeting and hand over the formula—make sure he understands his position, and that his future hangs on his performance. Third, I want you to follow the gentleman back to his lair and identify him for me."

They all nodded. Then Charles grimaced. "Why are we still doing this—taking orders from you?"

Dalziel looked at him, then softly said, "For the same reason I'm giving those orders with every expectation of being obeyed. Because we are who we are." He raised one dark brow. "Aren't we?"

There was nothing else to say; they understood one another all too well.

They rose.

"One thing." Tristan caught Dalziel's questioning look. "Duke Martinbury. Once he has the formula, this foreigner is liable to want to tie up loose ends."

Dalziel nodded. "That would be expected. What do you suggest?"

"We can make sure Martinbury walks away from the meeting, but after that? In addition, he's due some punishment for his part in this affair. All things considered, impression into the army for three years would fit the bill on both counts. Given he's from Yorkshire, I thought of the regiment near Harrogate. Its ranks must be a little thin these days."

"Indeed." Dalziel made a note. "Muffleton's colonel there. I'll tell him to expect Martinbury—Marmaduke, wasn't it?—as soon as he's finished being useful here."

With a nod, Tristan turned; with the others, he left.

"A fake formula?" His gaze on the sheet containing Cedric's formula, Jeremy grimaced. "I wouldn't know where to start."

"Here! Let me see." Seated at the end of the breakfast table, Leonora held out her hand.

Tristan paused in consuming a mound of ham and eggs to pass the sheet to her.

She sipped her tea and studied it while the rest of them applied themselves to their breakfasts. "Which are the critical ingredients, do you know?"

Humphrey glanced down the table at her. "From what I gathered from the experiments, shepherd's purse, moneywort, and comfrey were all crucial. As to the other substances, it was more a matter of enhancement of action."

Leonora nodded, and set down her cup. "Give me a few minutes to consult with Cook and Mrs. Wantage. I'm sure we can concoct something believable."

She returned fifteen minutes later; they were sitting back, replete, enjoying their coffee. She laid a neatly written formula in front of Tristan and retook her seat.

He picked it up, read it, nodded. "Looks believable to me." He passed it to Jeremy. Looked at Humphrey. "Can you recopy that for us?"

Leonora stared at him. "What's wrong with my copy?"

Tristan looked at her. "It wasn't written by a man."

"Oh." Mollified, she poured herself another cup of tea. "So what's your plan? What do we have to do?"

Tristan caught the inquiring gaze she directed at him over the rim of her cup, inwardly sighed, and explained.

As he'd anticipated, no amount of argument had swayed Leonora from joining him on the hunt.

Charles and Deverell had thought it a great joke, until Humphrey and Jeremy also insisted on playing a part.

Short of tying them up and leaving them in the club under Gasthorpe's eye—something Tristan actually considered—there was no way to prevent them appearing in St. James's Park; in the end, the three of them decided to make the best of it.

Leonora proved surprisingly easy to disguise. She was the same height as her maid Harriet, so could borrow her clothes; with the judicious application of some soot and dust, she made a passable flowerseller.

They decked Humphrey out in some of Cedric's ancient clothes; by disregarding every edict of elegance, he was transformed into a thoroughly disreputable specimen, his thinning white hair artfully straggling, apparently unkempt. Deverell, who'd returned to his house in Mayfair to assume his own disguise, returned, approved, then took Humphrey in charge. They set out in a hackney to take up their positions.

Jeremy was the hardest to easily disguise; his slender length and clear-cut, well-defined features screamed "well-bred." In the end, Tristan took him with him back to Green Street. They returned half an hour later as two rough-looking navvies; Leonora had to look twice before she recognized her brother.

He grinned. "This is almost worth being locked in the closet."

Tristan frowned at him. "*This* is no joke."

"No. Of course not." Jeremy tried to look suitably chastened, and failed miserably.

They bade Jonathon, unhappy but resigned to missing out on all the fun, farewell, promising to tell him all when they returned, then went to the club to check on Charles and Duke.

Duke was exceedingly nervous, but Charles had him in hand. They each had defined roles to play; Duke knew his—had had it explained to him in painstaking detail—but even more important, he'd been told very clearly what Charles's role was. They were all sure that come what may, knowing what Charles would do if he didn't behave as instructed would be enough to ensure Duke's continued cooperation.

Charles and Duke would be the last to leave for St. James's Park. The meeting was scheduled for three o'clock, close by Queen Anne's Gate. It was just after two when Tristan handed Leonora into a hackney, waved Jeremy in, then followed.

They left the hackney at the nearer end of the park. As they strolled onto the lawns, they separated, Tristan going ahead, striding easily, stopping now and then as if looking for a friend. Leonora followed a few yards behind, an empty trug hung over her arm—a flowerseller heading home at the end of a good day. Behind her, Jeremy slouched along, apparently sulking to himself and paying little attention to anyone.

Eventually Tristan reached the entrance known as Queen Anne's Gate. He slouched against the bole of a nearby tree and settled somewhat grumpily to wait. As per his instructions, Leonora angled deeper into the park. A wrought-iron bench sat beside the path wending in from Queen Anne's Gate; she sank onto it, stretched her legs out before her, balancing the empty trug against them, and fixed her gaze on the vista before her, of the treed lawns leading down to the lake.

On the next wrought-iron bench along the path sat an old, white-haired man weighed down by a veritable mountain of mismatched coats and scarves. Humphrey. Closer to the lake, but in line with the gate, Leonora could just see the old plaid cap Deverell had pulled low over his face; he was slumped down against the trunk of a tree, apparently asleep.

Without seeming to notice anyone, Jeremy slouched past; he made his way out of the gate, crossed the road, then stopped to peer into the window of a tailor's shop.

Leonora swung her legs and her trug slightly, and wondered how long they would have to wait.

It was a fine day, not sunny, but pleasant enough for there to be many others loitering, enjoying the lawns and the lake. Enough, at least, for their little band to be entirely unremarkable.

Duke had been able to describe his foreigner in only the most cursory terms; as Tristan had somewhat acidly commented, the majority of foreign gentlemen of Germanic extraction presently in London would fit his bill. Nevertheless, Leonora kept her eyes wide, scanning the strollers who passed before her, as an idle flowerseller with no more work for the day might do.

She saw a gentleman coming along the path from the direction of the lake. He was fastidiously turned out in a grey suit; he wore a grey hat and carried a cane, held rigidly in one hand. There was something about him that caught her eye, tweaked her memory, something odd about the way he moved . . . then she recalled Duke's landlady's description of his foreign visitor. *A poker strapped to his spine.*

This had to be their man.

He passed by her, then stepped to the verge, just short of where Tristan lounged, his gaze fixed on the gate, one hand tapping his thigh impatiently. The man pulled out his watch, checked it.

Leonora stared at Tristan; she was sure he hadn't seen the man. Angling her head as if she'd just noticed him, she paused as if debating with herself, then rose and sauntered, hips swinging in time with her trug, to his side.

He glanced at her, straightened as she came up beside him.

His gaze flicked beyond her, noted the man, then returned to her face.

She smiled, nudged him with her shoulder, angling closer, doing her best to mimic the encounters she'd occasionally witnessed in the park. "Pretend I'm suggesting a little dalliance to enliven the day."

He grinned at her, slowly, showing his teeth, but his eyes remained cold. "What do you think you're doing?"

"That's the man over there, and any minute Duke and Charles will arrive. I'm giving us a perfectly reasonable reason for following the man when he leaves, together."

His lips remained curved; he slid one arm about her waist and pulled her closer, bending his head to whisper in her ear, "You are not coming with me."

She smiled into his eyes, patted his chest. "Unless the man goes into the stews, and that hardly seems likely, I am."

He narrowed his eyes at her; she smiled more brightly, but met his gaze directly. "I've been a part of this drama from the beginning. I think I should be a part of its end."

The words gave Tristan pause. And then fate stepped in and took the decision from him.

The bell towers of London's churches tolled the hour—three clangs, echoed and repeated in multiple keys—and Duke came striding swiftly along the pavement and turned in at Queen Anne's Gate.

Charles, in the guise of a tavern brawler, came sauntering along a little way behind, timing his approach.

Duke halted, saw his man, and marched toward him. He looked neither right nor left; Tristan suspected Charles had drilled him until he was so focused on what he had to do, so desperate to get it right, that paying attention to anything else was presently beyond him.

The wind was in the right quarter; it wafted Duke's words to them. "Do you have my vowels?"

The demand took the foreigner aback, but he recovered swiftly. "I might have. Have you got the formula?"

"I know where it is, and can get it for you in less than a minute, if you have my vowels to give me in return."

Through narrowing eyes, the foreign gentleman searched Duke's pale face, then he shrugged, and reached into his coat pocket.

Tristan tensed, saw Charles lengthen his stride; they both relaxed a fraction when the man drew out a small packet of papers.

He held them up for Duke to see. "Now," he said, his voice cold and crisply accented, "the formula, if you please."

Charles, until then apparently about to stroll past, changed direction and with one step joined the pair. "I have it here."

The foreigner started. Charles grinned, wholly evil. "Don't mind me—I'm just here to make sure my friend Mr. Martinbury comes to no harm. So"—he nodded at the papers, glanced at Duke—"they all there then?"

Duke reached for the vowels.

The foreigner drew them back. "The formula?"

With a sigh, Charles pulled out the copy of the altered formula Humphrey and Jeremy had prepared and made to look suitably aged. He unfolded it, held it up where the foreigner could see it but not quite read it. "Why don't I just hold it here, then as soon as Martinbury has checked over his vowels, you can have it."

The foreigner was clearly unhappy, but had little choice; Charles was intimidating enough in civilized garb—in his present guise, he exuded aggression.

Duke took the vowels, quickly checked, then looked at Charles and nodded. "Yes." His voice was weak. "They're all here."

"Right then." With a nasty grin, Charles handed the formula to the foreigner.

He seized it, pored over it. "This is the right formula?"

"That's what you wanted—that's what you've got. Now," Charles continued, "if you're done, my friend and I have other business to see to."

He saluted the foreigner, a parody of a gesture; taking Duke's arm, he turned. They marched straight out of the gate. Charles hailed a hackney, bundled a now trembling Duke in, and climbed in after him.

Tristan watched the carriage rumble off. The foreigner looked up, watched it go, then carefully, almost reverently, folded the formula and slipped it into his inner coat pocket. That done, he adjusted his grip on his cane, straightened his back, pivoted on his heel, and walked stiffly back toward the lake.

"Come on." His arm around Leonora, Tristan straightened away from the tree and started off in the man's wake.

They passed Humphrey; he didn't look up but Tristan saw that he'd produced a sketch pad and pencil and was rapidly drawing, a somewhat incongruous sight.

The foreigner didn't look back; he seemed to have swallowed their little charade. They'd hoped he would head straight back to his office rather than into any of the less salubrious areas not far from the park. The direction he was taking looked promising. Most of the foreign embassies were located in the area north of St. James's Park, in the vicinity of St. James's Palace.

Tristan released Leonora, then took her hand, glanced down at her. "We're out for a night of entertainment—we've decided to look in at one of the halls around Piccadilly."

She opened her eyes wide. "I've never been to one—I take it I should treat the prospect with enthusiam?"

"Precisely." He couldn't help but grin at her delight—nothing to do with any music hall but the result of pure excitement.

They passed Deverell, who'd got to his feet and was brushing himself down preparatory to joining them in following their quarry.

Tristan was an expert at trailing people through cities and crowds;

so, too, was Deverell. They'd both worked primarily in the larger French cities; the best methods of the chase were second nature.

Jeremy would collect Humphrey and they'd return to Montrose Place to await developments; Charles would be there ahead of them with Duke. It was Charles's job to hold the fort until they returned with the last, vital piece of information.

Their quarry crossed the bridge over the lake and continued on toward the environs of St. James's Palace.

"Follow my lead in all things," Tristan murmured, his eyes on the man's back.

Just as he'd expected, the man paused just before the gate leading out of the park and bent down as if to ease a stone from his shoe.

Sliding his arm around Leonora, Tristan tickled her; she giggled, squirmed. Laughing, he settled her familiarly against him, and continued straight past the man without so much as a look.

Breathless, Leonora leaned close as they continued on. "Was he checking?"

"Yes. We'll stop a little way along and argue about which way to go so he can pass us again."

They did; Leonora thought they put on a creditable performance of a pair of lower-class lovers debating the merits of music halls.

When the man was once more ahead of them, striding along, Tristan grasped her hand, and they followed, now rather more briskly as if they'd made up their minds.

The area surrounding St. James's Palace was riddled with tiny lanes and interconnecting alleyways and yards. The man turned into the labyrinth, striding along confidently.

"This won't work. Let's leave him to Deverell and go on to Pall Mall. We'll pick him up there."

Leonora felt a certain wrench as they left the man's trail, continuing straight on where he had turned left. A few houses along, she glanced back, and saw Deverell turn off in the man's wake.

They reached Pall Mall and turned left, ambling very slowly, scanning the openings of the lanes ahead. They didn't have long to wait before their quarry emerged, striding along even more quickly.

"He's in a hurry."

"He's excited," she said, and felt certain it was true.

"Perhaps."

Tristan led her on; they switched with Deverell again in the streets south of Piccadilly, then joined the crowds enjoying an evening stroll along that major thoroughfare.

"This is where we might lose him. Keep your eyes peeled."

She did, scanning the throng bustling along in the fine evening.

"There's Deverell." Tristan stopped, nudged her so she looked in the right direction. Deverell had just stepped into Pall Mall; he was looking about him. "Damn!" Tristan straightened. "We've lost him." He started openly searching the crowds before them. "Where the devil did he go?"

Leonora stepped closer to the buildings, looked along the narrow gap the crowds left. She caught a flash of grey, then it was gone.

"There!" She grabbed Tristan's arm, pointed ahead. "Two streets up."

They pushed through, tacked, ran—reached the corner and rounded it, then slowed.

Their quarry—she hadn't been wrong—was almost at the end of the short street.

They hurried along, then the man turned right and disappeared from view. Tristan signaled to Deverell, who started running along the street after the man. "Down the alley." Tristan pushed her toward the mouth of a narrow lane.

It cut straight across to the next street running parallel to the one they'd been on. They hurried along it, Tristan gripping her hand, steadying her when she slipped.

They reached the other street and turned up it, strolling once more, catching their breaths. The opening where the street the man had turned down joined the one they were now on lay ahead to their left; they watched it as they walked, waiting for him to reappear.

He didn't.

They reached the corner and looked down the short street. Deverell stood leaning against a railing at the other end.

Of the man they'd been following there was absolutely no sign.

Deverell pushed away from the railing and walked toward them; it only took a few minutes for him to reach them.

He looked grim. "He'd disappeared by the time I got here."

Leonora sagged. "So it's a dead end—we've lost him."

"No," Tristan said. "Not quite. Wait here."

He left her with Deverell and crossed the road to where a streetsweeper stood leaning on his broom midway down the short street. Reaching under his scruffy coat, Tristan located a sovereign; he held it between his fingers where the sweeper could see it as he lounged on the rails beside him.

"The gent in grey who went into the house across the way. Know his name?"

The sweep eyed him suspiciously, but the glimmer of gold spoke loudly. "Don't rightly know his name. Stiff-rumped sort he is. 'Ave 'eard the doorman call him Count something-unpronounceable-beginning-wif-an-eff."

Tristan nodded. "That'll do." He dropped the coin into the sweep's palm.

Strolling back to Leonora and Deverell, he made no effort to keep his self-satisfied smile from his lips.

"Well?" Predictably, it was the light of his life who prompted him.

He grinned. "The man in grey is known to the doorman of the house in the middle of the row as 'Count something-unpronounceable-beginning-wif-an-eff.' "

Leonora frowned at him, then looked past him at the house in question. Then she narrowed her eyes at him. *"And?"*

His smile broadened; it felt amazingly good. "The house is Hapsburg House."

At seven o'clock that evening, Tristan ushered Leonora into the anteroom of Dalziel's office, secreted in the depths of Whitehall.

"Let's see how long he keeps us waiting."

Leonora settled her skirts on the wooden bench Tristan had handed her to. "I would have assumed he'd be punctual."

Sitting beside her, Tristan smiled wryly. "Nothing to do with punctuality."

She studied his face. "Ah. One of those strange games men play."

He said nothing, simply smiled and leaned back.

They only had to wait five minutes.

The door opened; a darkly elegant man appeared. He saw them. A momentary hiatus ensued, then, with a graceful gesture, he invited them in.

Tristan rose, drawing her to her feet beside him, setting her hand on his sleeve. He led her in, halting before the desk and the chairs set before it.

After closing the door, Dalziel joined them. "Miss Carling, I presume."

"Indeed." She gave him her hand, met his gaze—as penetrating as Tristan's—coolly. "I'm pleased to make your acquaintance."

Dalziel's gaze flicked to Tristan's face; his thin lips were not quite straight when he inclined his head and waved them to the chairs.

Rounding the desk, he sat. "So—who was behind the incidents in Montrose Place?"

"A Count something-unpronounceable-beginning-wif-an-eff."

Unimpressed, Dalziel raised his brows.

Tristan smiled his chilly smile. "The Count is known at Hapsburg House."

"Ah."

"And—" From his pocket, Tristan withdrew the sketch Humphrey had, to everyone's surprise, made of the Count. "This should help in identifying him—it's a remarkable likeness."

Dalziel took it, studied it, then nodded. "Excellent. And he accepted the false formula?"

"As far as we could tell. He handed over Martinbury's vowels in exchange."

"Good. And Martinbury is on his way north?"

"Not yet, but he will be. He appears genuinely appalled by his cousin's injuries and will escort him back to York once he— Jonathon—is fit enough to travel. Until then, they'll remain at our club."

"And St. Austell and Deverell?"

"Both have been neglecting their own affairs. Pressing matters necessitated their return to their own hearths."

"Indeed?" One laconic brow rose, then Dalziel turned his dark gaze on Leonora. "I've made inquiries among government ranks, and there's considerable interest in your late cousin's formula, Miss Carling. I've been asked to inform your uncle that certain gentlemen would like to call on him at his earliest convenience. It would, of course, be helpful if their visit could take place before the Martinburys leave London."

She inclined her head. "I'll convey that message to my uncle. Perhaps your gentlemen could send a messenger tomorrow to set a time?"

Dalziel inclined his head in turn. "I'll advise them to do so."

His gaze, fathomless, lingered on her for a moment, then switched to Tristan. "I take it"—the words were even, yet gentler—"that this is farewell, then?"

Tristan held his gaze, then his lips quirked. He rose, and extended his hand. "Indeed. As close to farewell as those in our business ever get."

An answering smile fleetingly softened Dalziel's face as rising, too, he gripped Tristan's hand. Then he released it, and bowed to Leonora. "Your servant, Miss Carling. I won't pretend I would much rather you did not exist, but fate has clearly overruled me." His lazy smile robbed the words of any offense. "I sincerely wish you both well."

"Thank you." Feeling far more in charity with him than she had expected, Leonora politely nodded.

Then she turned. Tristan took her hand, opened the door, and they left the small office in the bowels of Whitehall.

"Why did you take me to meet him?"

"Dalziel?"

"Yes, Dalziel. He obviously wasn't expecting me—he clearly saw my presence as some message. What?"

Tristan looked into her face as the carriage slowed for a corner, then righted and rolled on. "I took you because seeing you, meeting you, was the one message he could neither ignore nor misconstrue. He is my past; you—" He lifted her hand, placed a kiss in her palm, then closed his hand about hers. "You," he said, his voice deep and low, "are my future."

She considered what little she could read in his shadowed face. "So all that"—with her other hand, she gestured back toward Whitehall—"is at an end—behind you?"

He nodded. Lifted her trapped fingers to his lips. "The end of one life—the beginning of another."

She looked into his face, into his dark eyes, then slowly smiled. Leaving her hand in his, she leaned closer. "Good."

His new life—he was impatient to get on with it.

He was a master of strategy and tactics, of exploiting situations for his own ends; by the next morning, he had his latest plan in place.

At ten, he called to take Leonora for a drive, and kidnapped her. He whisked her down to Mallingham Manor, currently devoid of old dears—they were all still in London, busily devoting themselves to his cause.

The same cause to which, after an intimate luncheon, he devoted himself with exemplary zeal.

When the clock on the mantelpiece of the earl's bedchamber chimed three o'clock, he stretched, luxuriating in the slide of the silk sheets over his skin, and even more in the warmth of Leonora slumped boneless against him.

He glanced down. The tumbled mahogany silk of her hair screened her face. Beneath the sheet, he curved a hand about her hip, possessively caressed.

"Hmm-mm." The sated sound was that of a woman well loved. After a moment, she mumbled, "You planned this, didn't you?"

He grinned; a touch of the wolf still remained. "I've been plotting for some time to get you into this bed." His bed, the earl's bed. Where she belonged.

"As distinct from all those nooks you were so successful in finding in all the hostesses's houses?" Lifting her head, she pushed back her hair, then rearranged herself against him, propping her arms on his chest so she could look into his face.

"Indeed—they were merely necessary evils, dictated by the vagaries of the battle."

She looked into his eyes. "I'm not a battle—I told you before."

"But you are something I had to win." He let a heartbeat pass, then added, "And I've triumphed."

Lips curving, Leonora searched his eyes and didn't bother to deny it. "And have you found victory to be sweet?"

He closed his hands over her hips, held her to him. "Sweeter than I'd expected."

"Indeed?" Ignoring the rush of warmth over her skin, she raised a brow. "Well, now you've plotted and planned and got me into your bed, what next?"

"As I aim to keep you here, I suspect we'd better get married." Lifting one hand, he caught and played with strands of her hair. "I wanted to ask—did you want a big wedding?"

She hadn't really thought. He was rushing her—calling the shots—yet . . . she didn't want to waste any more of their lives either.

Here—lying naked with him in his bed—the physical sensations underscored the real attraction, all that had tempted her into his arms. It wasn't just the pleasure that wrapped them about, but the comfort, the security, the promise of all their lives combined could be.

She refocused on his eyes. "No. A small ceremony with our families would suit very well."

"Good." His lashes flickered down.

She sensed the spurt of relief he tried to hide. "What is it?" She was learning; rarely did he not have some plan afoot.

His eyes flicked up to hers. He shrugged lightly. "I was hoping you'd agree to a small wedding. Much easier and faster to organize."

"Well, we can discuss the details with your great-aunts and my aunts when we return to town." She frowned, recollecting. "It's the De Veres' ball tonight—we have to attend."

"No. We don't."

His tone was firm—decided; she glanced at him, puzzled. "We don't?"

"I've had enough of the ton's entertainments to last me for a year. And when they hear our news, I'm sure the hostesses will excuse us— after all, they love that sort of gossip and should be grateful to those of us who supply it."

She stared at him. "What news? *What* gossip?"

"Why that we're so head over heels in love that we refused to countenance any delay and have organized to be married in the chapel here tomorrow, in the presence of our combined families and a few selected friends."

Silence reigned; she could barely take it in . . . then she did. "Tell me the details." With one finger, she prodded his bare chest. "All of them. How is this supposed to work?"

He caught her finger, dutifully recited, "Jeremy and Humphrey will arrive this evening, then . . ."

She listened, and had to approve. Between them, he, his old dears, and her aunts had covered everything, even a gown for her to wear. He had a special license; the reverend of the village church who acted as chaplain for the estate would be delighted to marry them . . .

Head over heels in love.

She suddenly realized he'd not only said it, but was living it. Openly, in a manner guaranteed to demonstrate that fact to all the ton.

She refocused on his face, on the hard angles and planes that hadn't changed, hadn't softened in the least, that were now, here with her, totally devoid of his charming social mask. He was still talking, telling her of the arrangements for the wedding breakfast. Her eyes misted; freeing her finger, she laid it across his lips.

He stopped talking, met her gaze.

She smiled down at him; her heart overflowed. "I love you. So yes, I'll marry you tomorrow."

He searched her eyes, then his arms closed around her. "Thank God for that."

She chuckled, sank down, laying her head on his shoulder. Felt his arms settle, holding her tight. "This is really all a plot to avoid having to attend any more balls and soirées, isn't it?"

"And musicales. Don't forget those." Tristan bent his head and brushed a kiss to her forehead. Caught her gaze, softly said, "I'd much rather spend my evenings here, with you. Attending to my future."

Her eyes, the periwinkle blue intense and brilliant, held his for a long moment, then she smiled, shifted, and drew his lips to hers.

He took what she offered, gave all he had in return.

Lust and a virtuous woman.

Fate had chosen his lady for him, and done a bloody good job.

A Gentleman's Honor

One

ॐ౷౷ॐ

The Bastion Club
Montrose Place, London
March 15, 1816

"We've a month before the Season begins, and already the harpies are hunting in packs." Charles St. Austell sank into one of the eight straight-backed chairs around the mahogany table in the Bastion Club's meeting room.

"As we predicted." Anthony Blake, sixth Viscount Torrington, took the chair opposite. "The action in the marriage mart seems close to frenetic."

"Have you seen much of it, then?" Deverell sat beside Charles. "I have to admit I'm biding my time, lying low until the Season begins."

Tony grimaced. "My mother might be resident in Devon, but she has a worthy lieutenant in my godmother, Lady Amery. If I don't appear at her entertainments at least, I can be assured of receiving a sharp note the next morning, inquiring why."

There were laughs—resigned, cynical, and commiserating—from the others as they took their seats. Christian Allardyce, Gervase Tregarth, and Jack Warnefleet all sat, then, in concert, all eyes went to the empty chair beside Charles.

"Trentham sends his regrets." At the head of the table, Christian didn't bother keeping a straight face. "He didn't sound all that sincere. He wrote that he had more pressing engagements, but wished us joy in our endeavors. He expects to be back in town in a week, however, and looks forward to supporting the six of us through our upcoming travails."

"Kind of him," Gervase quipped, but they were all grinning.

Trentham—Tristan Wemyss—had been the first of their number to successfully achieve his goal, the same goal they all were intent on attaining. They all needed to marry; that common aim had spawned this, their club, their last bastion against the matchmakers of the ton.

Of the six of them as yet unwed, gathered this evening to share the latest news, Tony felt sure he was the most desperate, although why he felt so restless, so frustrated, as if poised for action yet with no enemy in sight, he couldn't fathom. He hadn't felt so moody in years. Then again, he hadn't been a civilian, an ordinary gentleman, for years, either.

"I vote we meet every fortnight," Jack Warnefleet said. "We need to keep abreast of events, so to speak."

"I agree." Gervase nodded across the table. "And if any of us has anything urgent to report, we call a meeting as needed. Given the pace at which matters move in the ton, two weeks is the limit—by then, the ground has shifted."

"I've heard the patronesses of Almack's are thinking of opening their season early, such is the interest."

"Is it true one still has to wear knee breeches?"

"On pain of being turned away." Christian raised his brows. "Although I've yet to ascertain just why that would be painful."

The others laughed. They continued trading information—on events, the latest fashions and tonnish distractions—eventually moving on to comment and caution on individual matrons, matchmaking mamas, dragons, gorgons, and the like—all those who lay in wait for unsuspecting eligible gentlemen with a view to matrimonially ensnaring them.

"Lady Entwhistle's one to avoid—once she sinks her talons into you, it's the devil of a job to break free."

It was their way of coping with the challenge before them.

They'd all spent the last decade or more in the service of His Majesty's government as agents acting in an unofficial capacity scattered throughout France and neighboring states, collecting information on enemy troops, ships, provisions, and strategies. They'd all reported to Dalziel, a spymaster who lurked, a spider in the center of his web, buried in the depths of Whitehall; he oversaw all English military agents on foreign soil.

They'd been exceedingly good at their jobs, witness the fact they were all still alive. But now the war was over, and civilian life had caught up with them. Each had inherited wealth, title, and properties; all were wellborn, yet their natural social circle, the haut ton—the gilded circle to which their births gave entrée and in which their titles, properties, and the attendant responsibilities made participation obligatory—was an arena of operations largely unknown to them.

Yet in gathering information, evaluating it, exploiting it—in that they were experts, so they'd established the Bastion Club to facilitate mutual support for their individual campaigns. As Charles had described it with typical dramatic flair, the club was their secured base from which each would infiltrate the ton, identify the lady he wanted as his wife, and then storm the enemy's position and capture her.

Sipping his brandy, Tony recalled that he'd been first to point out the need for a safe refuge. With a French mother and French godmother intent on encouraging any and all comers to bat their lashes at him—both ladies were aware such a tactic was guaranteed to make him take the matter of finding a wife into his own hands without delay—it had been he who had sounded the warning. The ton was not safe for such as they.

Set on in the gentlemen's clubs, hounded by fond papas as well as gimlet-eyed matrons, all but buried beneath the avalanche of invitations that daily arrived at their doors, life in the ton as an unmarried, wealthy, titled, *eminently* eligible gentleman was these days fraught with danger.

Too many had fallen on the battlefields of the Peninsula, and more recently at Waterloo.

They, the survivors, were marked men.

They were outnumbered, but they'd be damned if they'd be outgunned.

They were experts in battle, in tactics, and strategy; they weren't about to be taken. If they had any say in it, *they* would do the taking.

That was, at the heart of it, the *raison d'être* of the Bastion Club.

"Anything more?" Christian glanced around the table.

All shook their heads; they drained their glasses.

"I have to make an appearance at Lady Holland's soirée." Charles pulled a face. "I gather she feels she lent Trentham a helping hand, and now wants to try her luck with me."

Gervase raised his brows. "And you're giving her the chance?"

On his feet, Charles met his gaze. "My mother, sisters, and sisters-in-law are in town."

"Oh, ho! I see. Thinking of taking up residence here for the nonce?"

"Not at present, but I won't deny the thought has crossed my mind."

"I'll come with you." Christian strolled around the table. "I want to have a word with Leigh Hunt about that book he's writing. He's sure to be at Holland House."

Tony stood.

Christian glanced his way. "Are you still glorying in solitary state?"

"Yes, thank heaven—the mater's fixed in Devon." Tony resettled his coat with a graceful shrug. "I have, however, been summoned by my godmother to a soirée at Amery House. I'll have to put in an appearance." He looked around the table. "Anyone going that way?"

Gervase, Jack, and Deverell shook their heads; they'd decided to retire to the club's library and spend the rest of the evening in companionable silence.

Tony bade them farewell; grinning, they wished him luck. Together with Christian and Charles, he went downstairs and into the street. They parted on the pavement; Christian and Charles made for Kensington and Holland House, while Tony headed for Mayfair

Reluctance dragged at him; he ignored it. Any experienced commander knew there were some forces it was wise never to waste energy opposing. Such as godmothers. French godmothers especially.

"Good evening, Mrs. Carrington. A pleasure to meet you again."

Alicia Carrington smiled easily and gave Lord Marshalsea her hand. "My lord. I daresay you recall my sister, Miss Pevensey?"

As his lordship's gaze was riveted on Adriana, standing a few steps away, Alicia's question was largely rhetorical. His lordship, however, had clearly decided that gaining Alicia's support was crucial to securing Adriana's hand; while acknowledging Adriana, he remained by Alicia's side and made conversation in a distant, distracted fashion.

That last, something Alicia viewed with amusement, was due to his lordship's absorption with Adriana, talking animatedly with a coterie of admirers all vying for her favor. Adriana was an English rose gowned in pink silk a shade darker than that generally worn by young ladies, the better to exploit her luxuriant dark curls. Those sheened in the chandeliers' glow, creating the perfect frame for her bewitching features, her large brown eyes set under finely arched black brows, her peaches-and-cream complexion and lush, rosebud lips.

As for Adriana's figure, deliberately understated in the demure gown that hinted at rather than defined, it enticed. Even gowned in sackcloth, Alicia's sister was a package guaranteed to capture gentlemen's eyes, which was the reason they were here in London, in the very heart of the ton.

Masquerading.

At least, Alicia was; Adriana was who she purported to be.

While making the appropriate responses to Lord Marshalsea, Alicia monitored all those who paid court to her younger sister. Everything to date had gone exactly as they, sitting in the tiny parlor of their small house in Little Compton, in rural Warwickshire, which along with the surrounding few acres were all they—she, Adriana, and their three brothers—jointly owned, had planned, yet not even in their admittedly unfettered imaginations had they envisioned that events, people, and opportunities would fall out so well.

Their plan, desperate and reckless though it was, might just succeed. Succeed in securing a future for their three brothers—David, Harry, and Matthew—and for Adriana. For herself, Alicia hadn't thought that far; time enough to turn her mind to her own life once she'd seen her siblings safe.

Lord Marshalsea grew increasingly restless; taking pity on him, Alicia eased him into Adriana's circle, then stepped back, effacing herself as a good chaperone should. She eavesdropped, listening as Adriana handled the gentlemen surrounding her with her customary confidence. Although neither she nor Adriana had had any previous experience of the ton, of the ways of society's elite, since their appearance in town and their introduction to those exalted circles some weeks ago, they'd managed without the slightest hiccup.

Eighteen months of intensive research and their own sound common sense had stood them in good stead. Having three much younger brothers whom they'd largely reared had eradicated any tendency to panic; both jointly and individually, they'd risen to every challenge and triumphed.

Alicia was proud of them both, and increasingly hopeful of an excellent outcome to their scheme.

"Mrs. Carrington—your servant, ma'am."

The drawled words jolted her from the rosy future. Concealing her dismay, calmly turning, lips curving, she gave her hand to the gentleman bowing before her. "Mr. Ruskin. How pleasant to meet you here."

"The pleasure, I assure you, dear lady, is all mine."

Straightening, Ruskin delivered the comment with an intent look and a smile that sent a warning slithering down her spine. He was a largish man, half a head taller than she and heavily built; he dressed well and had the manners of a gentleman, yet there was something about him that, even hampered by inexperience, she recognized as less than savory.

For some ungodly reason, Ruskin had from their first meeting fixed his eye on her. If she could understand why, she'd do something to deflect it; her ever-fertile imagination painted him a snake, with her as his mesmerized prey. She'd pretended ignorance of the tenor of his attentions, had tried to be discouraging. When he'd shocked her by obliquely suggesting a *carte blanche*, she'd pretended not to understand; when he'd later alluded to marriage, she'd feigned deafness and spoken of something else. To no avail; he still sought her out, increasingly pointedly.

Thus far she'd avoided any declaration, thereby avoiding having outright to refuse it. Given her masquerade, she didn't want to risk an overt dismissal, didn't want to draw any attention her way; the most she dared do was behave coolly.

Ruskin's pale gaze had been traveling her face; it rose to trap hers. "If you would grant me the favor of a few minutes in private, my dear, I would be grateful."

He still held her fingers; keeping her expression noncommittal, she eased her hand free and used it to gesture to Adriana. "I'm afraid, sir, that with my sister in my care, I really cannot—"

"Ah." Ruskin sent a glance Adriana's way, a comprehensive survey taking in the besotted lordlings and gentlemen gathered around her, and Miss Tiverton, whom Adriana had taken under her wing, thereby earning Lady Hertford's undying gratitude. "What I have to say will, I daresay, have some impact on your sister."

Looking back at Alicia, Ruskin met her eyes; his smile remained easy, a gentleman confident of his ground. "However, your concern is . . . understandable."

His gaze lifted; he scanned the room, filled with the fashionable. Lady Amery's soirée had attracted the cream of the ton; they were present in force, talking, exchanging the latest *on-dits*, exclaiming over the latest juicy scandal.

"Perhaps we could repair to the side of the room?" Ruskin brought his gaze back to her face. "With this noise, no one will hear us; we'll be able to talk, and you'll be able to keep your ravishingly lovely young sister safe . . . and in view."

Steel rang beneath his words; Alicia dismissed any thought of refusing him. Inclining her head, feigning serene indifference, she laid her fingers on his sleeve and allowed him to steer her through the crowd.

What unwelcome challenge was she about to face?

Behind her calm facade, her heart beat faster; her lungs felt tight. Had she imagined the threat in his tone?

An alcove behind a chaise filled with dowagers provided a small oasis of relative privacy. As Ruskin had said, she could still see Adriana and her court clearly. If they kept their voices low, not even the dowagers, heads close swapping scandal, would overhear.

Ruskin stood beside her, calmly looking out over the crowd. "I would suggest, my dear, that you hear me out—hear *all* I have to say—before making any reply."

She glanced briefly at him, then stiffly inclined her head. Lifting her fingers from his sleeve, she gripped her fan.

"I think . . ." Ruskin paused, then continued, "I should mention that my home lies not far from Bledington—ah, yes! I see you understand."

Alicia struggled to mask her shock. Bledington lay southwest of the market town of Chipping Norton; Little Compton, their village, lay to the northwest—as the crow flew there could be no more than eight miles between Little Compton and Bledington.

But Ruskin and she had never met in the country. Her family had lived a circumscribed existence, until recently never venturing beyond Chipping Norton. In embarking on her masquerade, she'd been certain no one in London would know her.

Ruskin guessed her thoughts. "We never met in the country, but I saw you and your sister when I was home last Christmas. The pair of you were crossing the market square."

She glanced up.

He caught her eye, and smiled wolfishly. "I determined, then, to have you."

Involuntarily, her eyes widened.

His smile turned self-deprecatory. "Indeed—quite romantic." He looked back at the crowd. "I asked and was told your name—Miss Alicia Pevensey."

He paused, then shrugged. "If you hadn't appeared in London, no doubt nothing would have come of it. But you did appear, a few months later—as a widow of more than a year's standing. I wasn't fooled for a moment, but I comprehended your need of the ruse, and appreciated your courage in implementing it. It was a bold move, but one with every chance of success. I saw no reason to do other than wish you well. As my admiration for your astuteness grew, my interest in you on a personal level firmed.

"However"—his voice hardened—"when I offered you my protection, you refused. On reflection, I decided to do the honorable thing and offer for your hand. Again, however, you turned up your nose—quite why I have no notion. You seem uninterested in attaching a husband, solely concerned with watching over your sister as she makes her choice. Presumably, given you transparently have no need of funds, you've determined to make your own decision in your own time."

His gaze returned to her face. "I would suggest, my dear *Mrs. Carrington*, that your time has run out."

Alicia fought down the faintness, the giddiness that threatened; the room seemed to be whirling. She drew a slow breath, then asked, her tone commendably even, "What, precisely, do you mean?"

His expression remained intent. "I mean that your performance as a hoity widow in dismissing my suit was so convincing I checked my information. Today, I received a letter from old Dr. Lange. He assures me that the Pevensey sisters—*both* Pevensey sisters—remain unwed."

The room gyrated, heaved, then abruptly stopped.

Disaster stared her in the face.

"Indeed." Ruskin's predatory smile dawned, yet his self-deprecation remained. "But fear not—having concluded that marrying you would be an excellent notion, nothing I've learned has changed my mind."

His gaze hardened. "So let us be clear, my dear. *Mrs. Carrington* cannot continue in the ton, but if you consent to become Mrs. William Ruskin, I see no reason the ton should ever learn that Mrs. Carrington did not exist. I'm renewing my offer for your hand. Should you accept, there's no reason your plan to establish the lovely Adriana will suffer so much as a hiccup." His smile faded; he held her gaze. "I trust I make myself plain?"

Triumph had turned to ashes; her mouth was dry. Moistening her lips, she fought to keep her tone even. "I believe I understand you perfectly, sir. However . . . I would ask for a little time to consider my reply."

His brows rose; his untrustworthy smile returned. "Of course. You may have twenty-four hours—there isn't much to consider, after all."

She sucked in a breath, frantically gathered her wits to protest.

His gaze, hard, trapped hers. "Tomorrow evening you can formally accept me—tomorrow night, I'll expect to share your bed."

Shock held her immobile, staring at his face; she searched his eyes but found no hint of any emotion worth appealing to.

When she made no reply, he bowed punctiliously. "I'll call on you tomorrow evening at nine."

Turning, he left her, strolling into the crowd.

Alicia stood frozen, her wits careening, her skin icy, her stomach hollow.

A burst of raucous laughter from the dowagers, ineffectually smothered, jerked her back to earth. She glanced across the room at Adriana. Her sister was holding her own, but had noticed her distraction; their gazes met, but when Adriana arched a brow, Alicia shook her head.

She had to regain control—of their plan, of her life. Marry Ruskin, or . . . she could barely take it in.

Faintness still gripped her; she felt hot one minute, cold the next. Seeing a footman passing, she requested a glass of water. He brought it promptly, eyeing her warily as if she might swoon; she forced a weak smile and thanked him.

A chair stood against the wall two yards away. She walked to it and sat, sipping her water. After a few minutes, she flicked open her fan and waved it before her face.

She had to think. Adriana was safe for the moment . . .

Blocking out all thought of the threat Ruskin had made, she focused on him, on what he'd said—on what he knew and what he didn't. Why he was acting as he was, what insights that gave her, how she might press him to change his mind.

They—she, Adriana and the three boys—desperately needed Adriana to make a good match. Not with just any gentleman, but one with reasonable wealth and a sufficiently good heart not only to forgive them the deception they were practicing but to provide for the boys' schooling.

They were as near to penniless as made no difference. They were wellborn, but had no close connections; there were just the five of them—or more correctly Alicia and Adriana to look after them all. David was only twelve years old, Harry ten, and Matthew eight. Without an education, there would be no future for them.

Adriana had to be given the chance to make the match they felt certain she could. She was stunningly beautiful; the ton had already labeled her a "diamond of the first water" among other admiring epithets. She would be a hit, a wild success; once the Season proper commenced, she could take her pick from the wealthy eligibles, and she was wise enough, despite her years, to make the right choice, with Alicia's help.

One gentleman would be the right one for her, for them all, and then the family—Adriana and the three boys—would be safe.

Alicia had no other goal before her; she hadn't had for the past eighteen months, since their mother died. Their father had died years before, leaving the family with little money and few possessions.

They'd scrimped, saved, and survived. And now they'd risked all on this one throw that fate, in creating Adriana's undoubted beauty, had given them. In order to do so, Alicia had behaved in ways she wouldn't otherwise countenance; she'd taken risks she otherwise never would have—and thus far won.

She'd become Mrs. Carrington, a wealthy and fashionable widow, the perfect chaperone to introduce Adriana to the ton. Hiring a professional chaperone had been out of the question—not only did they not have the funds, but to the ton, especially the upper echelons, a wealthy widow presenting her ravishing younger sister was a significantly different prospect to two provincial spinsters with a hired chaperone, one whose relative standing would have illuminated theirs.

With her masquerade in place, they'd cleared every hurdle and succeeded in insinuating themselves into the ton. The ultimate success beckoned; all was going so well . . .

There *had* to be a way around Ruskin and his threat.

She could marry him, but the recoil the thought evoked made her cast that as a last resort; she'd return to it if and only if there was no other way.

One thing Ruskin had said clanged in her mind. He thought they had money. He'd discovered she'd never married, but he hadn't learned she was first cousin to a pauper.

What if she told him?

Would that make him turn aside from his plan, or simply place another weapon in his hands? If he learned she came with no money but only costs and responsibilities, would he decide not to marry her after all, but instead force her to become his mistress?

The thought made her nauseous. She gulped the last of her water, then rose to set the glass down on a nearby sideboard. The movement had her facing down the side of the room just as Ruskin stepped out through a pair of glass doors.

Moving into the crowd, she looked more closely. The doors, left ajar, led outside, presumably to a terrace.

The very fact she'd seen him go out into a place that would afford greater privacy hardened her resolve; she would go and speak with him. Despite what seemed an unhealthy wish to "have her," there might be some other reward he would accept in return for his silence.

It was worth a try. She did have acquaintances with money she could—or at least thought she might be able to—call on. At the very least, she might be able to talk him into giving her more time.

Tacking through the crowd, she came up beside Adriana.

With a smile at her cavaliers, her sister turned to her. "What's wrong?"

Alicia wondered again at her sister's facility for seeing straight through her. "Nothing I can't manage—I'll tell you about it later. I'm just going out onto the terrace to talk to Mr. Ruskin. I'll be back shortly.

The look in Adriana's eyes said she had many more questions but accepted she couldn't ask them now. "All right, but be careful. He's a toad, if not worse."

"I say, Mrs. Carrington, will you and Miss Pevensey be attending the opening night at the Theatre Royal?"

Young Lord Middleton was as eager as a spaniel; Alicia returned a vague answer, exchanged a few more comments, then slid out of the group and headed for the glass doors.

As she'd surmised, they gave onto a terrace overlooking the gardens. The doors had been left ajar to let air into the crowded and overheated drawing room; slipping through, she drew them almost closed behind her, then, shrugging her shawl over her shoulders, looked about.

It was mid-March and chilly; she was glad of the shawl. Not surprisingly, there were no others strolling in the still and frosty night. She glanced around, expecting to see Ruskin, perhaps indulging in a cigarillo, but the terrace, overhung with shadows, was empty. Walking to the balustrade, she surveyed the gardens. No Ruskin. Had he chosen to leave the soirée by this route?

She glanced down along the path that, from its direction, she assumed led to a gate giving onto the street.

A flash of movement caught her eye.

She peered, and glimpsed a man-sized shadow in the gloom beneath a huge tree beside the path. The tree was massive, the shadows beneath it dense, but she thought the man had just sat down. Perhaps there was a seat there, and Ruskin had gone to sit and smoke, or to think.

Of tomorrow night.

The idea had her stiffening her spine. Pulling her shawl tight, she descended the steps and set off along the path.

With every step Tony took along Park Street, his resistance to attending his godmother's soirée and smiling and chatting and doing the pretty with a gaggle of young ladies with whom he had nothing in common—and who, if they knew the man he truly was, would probably faint—waxed stronger. Indeed, his reluctance over the whole damn business was veering toward the despondent.

Not by the wildest, most exaggerated flight of fancy could he imagine being married to any of the young beauties thus far paraded before him. They were . . . too young. Too innocent, too untouched by life. He felt no connection with them whatsoever.

The fact that they—each and every one—would happily accept his suit if he chose to favor them, and think themselves blessed, raised definite questions as to their intelligence. He was not, had never been, an easy man; one look should tell any sane woman that. He would not be an easy husband. The position of his wife was one that would demand a great deal of its holder, an aspect of which the sweet young things seemed to have no inkling.

His wife . . .

Not so many years ago, the thought of searching for her would have had him laughing. He hadn't imagined finding a wife was something that would unduly exercise him—when he needed to marry, the right lady would be there, miraculously waiting.

He hadn't, then, appreciated just how important, how vital her role *vis à vis* himself would be.

Now he was faced with that anticipated need to marry—and an even greater need to find the right wife—but the right lady had thus far shown no inclination even to make an appearance. He had no idea what she might look like, or be like, what aspects of her character or personality would be the vital clue—the crucial elements in her that he needed.

He wanted a wife. The restlessness that seemed to enmesh his very soul left him in no doubt of that, but exactly *what* he wanted, let alone why . . . that was the point on which he'd run aground.

Identify the target. The first rule in planning any successful sortie.

Until he succeeded in satisfying that requirement, he couldn't even start his campaign; the frustration irked, fueling his habitual impatience. Hunting a wife was ten times worse than hunting spies had ever been.

His footsteps echoed. Another, distant footfall sounded; his agent's senses, still very much a part of him, flaring to full attention, he looked up.

Through the mist wreathing the street, he saw a man, well muffled in coat and hat and carrying a cane, step away from the garden gate of . . . Amery House. The man was too far away to recognize and walked quickly away in the opposite direction.

Tony's godmother's house stood at the corner of Park and Green Streets, facing Green Street. The garden gate opened to a path leading up to the drawing-room terrace.

By now the soirée would be in full swing. The thought of the feminine chatter, the high-pitched laughter, the giggles, the measuring glances of the matrons, the calculation in so many eyes, welled and pressed down on him.

On his left, the garden gate drew nearer. The temptation to take that route, to slip inside without any announcement, to mingle and quickly look over the field, then perhaps to retreat before even his god-mother knew he was there, surfaced . . . and grew.

Closing his hand on the wrought-iron latch, he lifted it. The gate swung soundlessly open; passing through, he closed it quietly behind him. Through the silent garden, heavily shadowed by large and ancient trees, the sound of conversation and laughter drifted down to him.

Mentally girding his loins, he drew in a deep breath, then quickly climbed the steep flight of steps that led up to the level of the garden.

Through ingrained habit, he moved silently.

The woman crouching by the side of the man lying sprawled on his back, shoulders propped against the trunk of the largest tree in the garden, didn't hear him.

The tableau exploded into Tony's vision as he gained the top of the steps. Senses instantly alert, fully deployed, he paused.

Slim, svelte, gowned for the evening in silk, her dark hair piled high, with a silvery shawl wrapped about her shoulders and clutched tight with one hand, the lady slowly, very slowly, rose. In her other hand, she held a long, scalloped stilletto; streaks of blood beaded on the wicked blade.

She held the dagger by the hilt, loosely grasped between her fingers, pointing downward. She stared at the blade as if it were a snake.

A drop of dark liquid fell from the dagger's point.

The lady shuddered.

Tony stepped forward, driven by an urge to take her in his arms; catching himself, he halted. Sensing his presence, she looked up.

A delicate, heart-shaped face, complexion as pale as snow, dark eyes wide with shock, looked blankly at him.

Then, with a visible effort, she gathered herself. "I think he's dead."

Her tone was flat; her voice shook. She was battling hysterics; he was thankful she was winning.

Tamping down that impulsive urge to soothe her, shield her, a ridiculously primitive feeling but unexpectedly powerful, he walked closer. Forcing his gaze from her, he scanned the body, then reached for the dagger. She surrendered it with a shudder, not just of shock but of revulsion.

"Where was it?" He kept his tone impersonal, businesslike. He crouched down, waited.

After an instant, she responded, "In his left side. It had fallen almost out . . . I didn't realize . . ." Her voice started to rise, became thready, and died.

Stay calm. He willed the order at her; a cursory examination confirmed she was right on both counts. The man was dead; he'd been knifed very neatly, a single deadly thrust between the ribs from the back. "Who is he—do you know?"

"A Mr. Ruskin—William Ruskin."

He glanced at her sharply. "You knew him."

He hadn't thought it possible, but her eyes widened even more. "No!"

Alicia caught her breath, closed her eyes, fought to summon her wits. "That is"—she opened her eyes again—"only to speak to. Socially. At the soirée . . ."

Waving back at the house, she dragged in a breath and rushed on, "I came out for some air. A headache . . . there was no one out here. I thought to wander . . ." Her gaze slid to Ruskin's body. She gulped. "Then I found him."

Ruskin had threatened her, her plan, her family's future. He'd been blackmailing her—and now he was dead. His blood oozed in a black pool by his side, stained the dagger now in the stranger's hand. It was a struggle to take everything in, to know even what she felt, let alone how best to react.

The unknown gentleman rose. "Did you see anyone leaving?"

She stared at him. "No." She glanced around, suddenly aware of the deep silence of the gardens. Abruptly, she swung her gaze back to him.

Tony sensed her sudden thought, her rising panic. Was irritated by it. "No—*I* didn't kill him."

His tone reassured her; her sudden tenseness faded.

He glanced again at the corpse, then at her; he waved back up the path. "Come. We must go in and tell them."

She blinked, but didn't move.

He reached for her elbow. She permitted him to take it, let him turn her unresisting, and steer her back toward the terrace. She moved slowly, clearly still in shock. He glanced at her pale face, but the shadows revealed little. "Did Ruskin have a wife, do you know?"

She started; he felt the jerk through his hold on her arm. From beneath her lashes, she cast him a shocked glance. "No." Her voice was tight, strained; she looked ahead. "No wife."

If anything, she'd paled even more. He prayed she wouldn't swoon, at least not before he got her inside. Appearing at his godmother's soirée via the terrace doors with a lady senseless in his arms would create a stir even more intense than murder.

She started shaking as they went up the steps, but she clung to her composure with a grim determination he was experienced enough to admire.

The terrace doors were ajar; they walked into the drawing room without attracting any particular attention. Finally in good light, he looked down at her, studied her features, the straight, finely chiseled nose, lips a trifle too wide, yet full, lush and tempting. She was above average in height, her dark hair piled high in gleaming coils exposing the delicate curve of her nape and the fine bones of her shoulders.

Instinct quivered; deep within him, primitive emotion stirred. Sexual attraction was only part of it; again, the urge to draw her close, to keep her close, welled.

She looked up, met his gaze. Her eyes were more green than hazel, large and well set under arched brows; they were presently wide, their expression dazed, almost haunted.

Fortunately, she seemed in no danger of succumbing to the vapors. Spying a chair along the wall, he guided her to it; she sank down with relief. "I must speak with Lady Amery's butler. If you'll remain here, I'll send a footman with a glass of water."

Alicia lifted her eyes to his face. To his velvet black eyes, to the concern and the focus she sensed behind his expression, behind the masklike, chiseled, haughtily angular planes. His was the most strikingly attractive masculine face she'd ever seen; he was the most startlingly attractive man she'd ever met, elegant, graceful, and strong. It was his strength she was most aware of; when he'd taken her arm and walked beside her, her senses had drunk it in.

Looking up at him, into his eyes, she drew on that strength again, and felt the horror they'd left outside recede even further. The reality around them came into sharper focus; a glass of water, a moment to compose herself, and she'd manage. "If you would . . . thank you."

That "thank-you" was for far more than the glass of water.

He bowed, then turned and headed across the room.

Suppressing an inner wrench, not just reluctance but real resistance to leaving her, Tony found a footman and dispatched him to revive her, then, ignoring the many who tried to catch his eye, he found Clusters, the Amerys' butler, and pulled him into the library to explain the situation and give the necessary orders.

He'd been visiting Amery House since he'd been six months old; the staff knew him well. They acted on his orders, summoning his lordship from the cardroom and her ladyship from the drawing room, and sending a footman running for the Watch.

He wasn't entirely surprised by the ensuing circus; his godmother was French, after all, and in this instance she was ably supported by the Watch captain, a supercilious sort who saw difficulties where none existed. Having taken the man's measure with one glance, Tony omitted mentioning the lady's presence. There was, in his view, no reason to expose her to further and unnecessary trauma; given the dead man's size and the way she'd held the dagger, it was difficult if not impossible to convincingly cast her as the killer.

The man he'd seen leaving the grounds via the garden gate was much more likely to have done the deed.

Besides, he didn't know the lady's name.

That thought was uppermost in his mind when, finally free of the responsibility of finding a murdered man, he returned to the drawing room and discovered her gone. She wasn't where he'd left her; he scouted the rooms, but she was no longer among the guests.

The crowd had thinned appreciably. No doubt she'd been with others, perhaps a husband, and they'd had to leave. . . .

The possibility put a rein on his thoughts, dampened his enthusiasm. Extricating himself from the coils of a particularly tenacious matron with two daughters to marry off, he stepped into the hall and headed for the front door.

On the front steps, he paused and drew in a deep breath. The night was crisp; a sharp frost hung in the air.

His mind remained full of the lady.

He was conscious of a certain disappointment. He hadn't expected her gratitude, yet he wouldn't have minded a chance to look into those wide green eyes again, to have them focus on him when they weren't glazed with shock.

To look deep and see if she, too, had felt that stirring, that quickening in the blood, the first flicker of heat.

In the distance a bell tolled the hour. Drawing in another breath, he went down the steps and headed home.

Home was a quiet, silent place, a huge old house with only him in it. Along with his staff, who were usually zealous in preserving him from all undue aggravation.

It was therefore a rude shock to be shaken awake by his father's valet, whom he'd inherited along with the title, and informed that there was a gentleman downstairs wishful of speaking with him even though it was only nine o'clock.

When asked to state his business, the gentleman had replied that his name was Dalziel, and their master would assuredly see him.

Accepting that no one in his right mind would claim to be Dalziel if they weren't, Tony grumbled mightily but consented to rise and get dressed.

Curiosity propelled him downstairs; in the past, he and his peers had always been summoned to wait on Dalziel in his office in Whitehall. Of course, he was no longer one of Dalziel's minions, yet he couldn't help feeling that alone would not account for Dalziel's courtesy in calling on him.

Even if it was just past nine o'clock.

Entering the library where Hungerford, his butler, had left Dalziel to kick his heels, the first thing he became aware of was the aroma of fresh coffee; Hungerford had served Dalziel a cup.

Nodding to Dalziel, elegantly disposed in an armchair, he went straight to the bellpull and tugged. Then he turned and, propping an arm along the mantelpiece, faced Dalziel, who had set down his cup and was waiting.

"I apologize for the early hour, but I understand from Whitley that you discovered a dead body last night."

Tony looked into Dalziel's dark brown eyes, half-hidden by heavy lids, and wondered if such occurrences ever slipped past his attention. "I did. Pure chance. What's your—or Whitley's—interest?"

Lord Whitley was Dalziel's opposite number in the Home Office; Tony had been one, possibly the only, member of Dalziel's group ever to have liaised with agents run by Whitley. Their mutual targets had been the spy networks operating out of London, attempting to undermine Wellington's campaigns.

"The victim, William Ruskin, was a senior administrative clerk in the Customs and Revenue Office." Dalziel's expression remained uninformative; his dark gaze never wavered. "I came to inquire whether there was any story I should know?"

A senior administrative clerk in the Customs and Revenue Office; recalling the stiletto, an assassin's blade, Tony was no longer truly sure. He refocused on Dalziel's face. "I don't believe so."

He knew that Dalziel would have noted his hesitation; equally, he knew that his erstwhile commander would accept his assessment.

Dalziel did, with an inclination of his head. He rose. Met Tony's eyes. "If there's any change in the situation, do let me know."

With a polite nod, he headed for the door.

Tony saw him into the hall and handed him into the care of a footman; retreating to the library, he wondered, as he often had, just who

Dalziel really was. Like recognized like; he was certainly of the aristocracy, with his finely hewn Norman features, pale skin and sable hair, yet Tony had checked enough to know Dalziel wasn't his last name. Dalziel was slightly shorter and leaner than the men he had commanded, all ex-Guardsmen, yet he projected an aura of lethal purpose that, in a roomful of larger men, would instantly mark him as the most dangerous.

The one man a wise man would never take his eye from.

The door to the street shut; a second later, Hungerford appeared with a tray bearing a steaming cup of coffee. Tony took it with a grateful murmur; like all excellent butlers, Hungerford always seemed to know what he required without having to be told.

"Shall I ask Cook to send up your breakfast, my lord?"

He nodded. "Yes—I'll be going out shortly."

Hungerford asked no more, but silently left him.

Tony savored the coffee, along with the premonition Dalziel's appearance and his few words had sent tingling along his nerves.

He was too wise to ignore or dismiss the warning, yet, in this case, he wasn't personally involved.

But she might be.

Dalziel's query gave him the perfect excuse to learn more of her. Indeed, given Whitehall's interest, it seemed incumbent upon him to do so. To assure himself that there wasn't anything more nefarious than murder behind Ruskin's death.

He needed to find the lady. *Cherchez la femme.*

He regretted not asking her name, but introductions over a dead body simply hadn't occurred to him, so all he had was her physical description. The notion of asking his godmother occurred, only to be dismissed; alerting *Tante* Felicité to any interest on his part—especially when he wasn't sure of his ground—didn't appeal, and the lady might have arrived with others. Felicité might not know her personally.

Over breakfast, he applied his mind to the question of how to track the lady down. The idea that occurred seemed a stroke of genius. Ham and sausages disposed of, he strode into his hall, shrugged on the coat Hungerford held, and headed for Bruton Street.

The lady's gown had been a creation of considerable elegance; although he hadn't consciously noted it at the time, it had registered in his mind. The vision leapt clearly to his inner eye. Pale green silk superbly cut to compliment a lithe rather than buxom figure; the fall of the silk, the drape of the neckline, all screamed of an expert modiste's touch.

According to Hungerford, Bruton Street was still home to the ton's most fashionable modistes. Tony started at the nearer end, calmly walking into Madame Francesca's salon and demanding to see Madame.

Madame was delighted to receive him, but regretfully—and it truly was regretfully—could not help him.

That refrain was repeated all the way down the street. By the time he reached Madame Franchot's establishment at the other end, Tony had run out of patience. After enduring fifteen minutes of Madame's earnest inquiries regarding his mother's health, he escaped, no wiser.

Going slowly down the stairs, he wondered where the devil else one of his lady's ilk might obtain her gowns. Reaching the street door, he opened it.

And saw, large as life, walking along the opposite side of the street, the lady herself. So she did come to Bruton Street.

She was walking briskly, absorbed in conversation with a veritable stunner—a younger lady of what even to Tony's jaded eye registered as quite fabulous charms.

He waited inside the doorway until they walked farther on, then went out, closed the door, crossed the street, and fell in in their wake, some twenty yards behind. Not so close that the lady might sense his presence, or see him immediately behind her should she glance around, yet not so far that he risked losing them should they enter any of the shops lining the street.

Somewhat to his surprise, they didn't. They walked on, engrossed in their discussion; reaching Berkeley Square, they continued around it.

He followed.

"There was nothing you could have done—he was already dead and you saw nothing to the point." Adriana stated the facts decisively. "Nothing would have been gained and no point served by you becoming further involved."

"Indeed," Alicia agreed. She just wished she could rid herself of the niggling concern that she *should* have waited in Lady Amery's drawing room, at least for the gentleman to return. He'd been uncommonly sensible and supportive; she should have thanked him properly. There was also the worry that he might have become embroiled in difficulties over finding a dead body—she had no idea of the correct procedures, or even if there *were* correct procedures—yet he'd seemed so competent, doubtless she was worrying over nothing.

She was still jumpy, nervy, hardly surprising but she couldn't allow even a murder to distract her from their plan. Too much depended on it.

"I do hope Pennecuik can get that lilac silk for us—it's a perfect shade to stand out among the other pastels." Adriana glanced at her. "I rather think that design with the frogged jacket would suit—do you remember it?"

Alicia admitted she did. Adriana was trying to distract her, to deflect her thoughts into more practical and productive avenues. They'd just come from visiting Mr. Pennecuik's warehouse, located behind the modistes' salons at the far end of Bruton Street. Mr. Pennecuik supplied the trade with the very best materials; he now also supplied Mrs. Carrington of Waverton Street with the stuffs for the elegant gowns in which she and her beautiful sister, Miss Pevensey, graced the ton's entertainments.

A most amicable arrangement had been reached. Mr. Pennecuik supplied her with the most exclusive fabrics at a considerable discount in return for her telling all those who asked—as hordes of matrons did and would when they clapped eyes on Adriana—that insisting on the best fabric was the key to gaining the most from one's modiste, and the fabrics from Mr. Pennecuik's were unquestionably the best.

As she patronized no modiste, the presumption was that she employed a private seamstress. The truth was she and Adriana, aided by their old nurse, Fitchett, sewed all their gowns. No one, however, needed to know that, and so everyone was pleased with the arrangement.

"Dark purple frogging." Alicia narrowed her eyes, creating the gown in her mind. "With ribbons of an in-between shade to edge the hems."

"Oh, yes! I saw that on a gown last night—it looked quite stunning."

Adriana prattled on. Alicia nodded and hmmed at the right points; inwardly, she returned to the nagging possibility that continued to disturb her.

The gentleman had stated he wasn't the murderer. She'd believed him—still did—but didn't know why. It would have been so easy . . . he might have heard her on the path, propped Ruskin against the tree, hid in the shadows and waited for her to "discover" Ruskin, then walked up and "discovered" her. If anyone asked, she would be honor-bound to state he'd come up after she'd found Ruskin already dead.

Already stabbed.

The memory of the dagger sliding out . . . she shivered.

Adriana glanced at her, then tightened their linked arms, pressing closer. "Stop thinking about it!"

"I can't." It wasn't Ruskin she was thinking most about, but the man who had emerged from the shadows; despite all, it was he who lingered most strongly in her mind.

Determinedly she redirected her thoughts to the crux of her worries. "After all our luck to date, I can't help but worry that some whisper of my involvement with so scandalous a thing as murder will out, and will affect your chances." She met Adriana's gaze. "We all have so much riding on this."

Adriana's smile was truly charming; she was no giddy miss, but a sensible female not easily influenced by man or fate. "Just show me the field and leave the rest to me. I assure you I'm up to it, and while I'm swishing my skirts, you can retreat into the shadows if you wish. But truly, I think it unlikely any news of this murder, much less your part in it, will surface, beyond, of course, the customary 'How unfortunate.' "

Alicia grimaced.

"Now," Adriana continued, "I gather from Miss Tiverton that there'll be quite a different crowd at Lady Mott's tonight. Apparently, her ladyship has a wide acquaintance in the counties, and what with everyone coming up to town early, there's sure to be many at her ball tonight. I think the cerise-and-white stripes will be best for me tonight, and perhaps the dark plum for you."

Alicia let Adriana fill her ears with sartorial plans. Turning into Waverton Street, they headed for their door.

From the corner of the street, Tony watched them climb the steps and enter, waited until the door shut, then ambled past. No one watching him would have noticed his interest.

At the end of Waverton Street he paused, smiled to himself, then headed home.

Lady Mott's ball had been talked of as a small affair.

The ballroom was certainly small. The ball, however, was such a crush Alicia was grateful that the size of Adriana's court gave them some protection.

As was her habit, after delivering Adriana to her admirers, she stepped back to the wall. There were chairs for chaperones a little way along, but she'd quickly realized that, not truly being chaperone material, it behooved her to avoid those who were; they were too inquisitive.

Besides, standing just feet away, she was near if Adriana needed help in dealing with any difficult suitor or avoiding the more wolfish elements who had started to appear at the periphery of her court.

Such gentlemen Alicia showed no hesitation in putting to rout.

The strains of the violins heralded a waltz, one Adriana had granted to Lord Heathcote. Alicia was watching, relaxed yet eagle-eyed as her sister prettily took his lordship's arm, when hard fingers closed about her hand.

She jumped, swallowed a gasp. The fingers felt like iron.

Outraged, she swung around, and looked up—into the dark, hard-featured face of the gentleman from the shadows.

Her lips parted in shock.

One black brow arched. "That's a waltz starting—come and dance."

Her wits scattered. By the time she'd regathered them, she was whirling down the room, and it was suddenly seriously difficult to breathe.

His arms felt like steel, his hand hard and sure on her back. He moved gracefully, effortlessly, all harnessed power, hard muscle and bone. He was tall, lean, yet broad-shouldered; the notion that he'd captured her, seized her and swept her away, and now had her in his keeping, flooded her mind.

She shook it aside, yet the sensation of being swept up by a force beyond her control, engulfed by a strength entirely beyond her power to counter, shocked her, momentarily dazed her.

Tangled her tongue.

Left her mentally scrambling to catch up—and filch the reins of her will back from his grasp.

The look on his face—one of all-seeing, patronizing, not superiority but control—helped enormously.

She dragged in a breath, conscious of her bodice tightening alarmingly. "We haven't been introduced!" The first point that needed to be made.

"Anthony Blake, Viscount Torrington. And you are?"

Flabbergasted. Breathless again. The timbre of his voice, deep, low, vibrated through her. His eyes, deepest black under heavy lids, held hers. She had to moisten her lips. "Alicia . . . Carrington."

Where *were* her wits?

"*Mrs.* Carrington." She dragged in another breath, and felt the reel her wits had been whizzing through start to slow.

His eyes hadn't left hers. Then he slipped his shoulder from under her hand, and that hand, her left, was trapped in his. His fingers shifted, finding the gold band on her ring finger.

His lips twisted fleetingly; he replaced her hand on his shoulder and continued to whirl her smoothly down the room.

She stared at him, beyond astonished. Inwardly thanking the saints for Aunt Maude's ring.

Then she blinked, cleared her throat, and looked over his shoulder into safe oblivion. "I must thank you for your help last evening—I hope the matter was concluded without any undue difficulties. I do ask you to excuse my early retreat." She risked a glance at his face. "I fear I was quite overcome."

In her experience most men accepted that excuse without question.

He looked as if he didn't believe it for a moment.

"*Quite* overcome," she reiterated.

The cynical scepticism—she was sure it was that—in his narrowing eyes only deepened.

Theatrically, she sighed. "I was attending with my *unmarried* younger sister. She's in my care. I had to take her home—my responsibility to her came first, above all else, as I'm sure you'll understand."

For a full minute, not a muscle moved in his classically sculpted face, then his brows rose. "I take it Mr. Carrington was not present?"

A whisper of caution tickled her spine; she kept her eyes on his. "I'm a widow."

"Ah."

There seemed a wealth of meanings in the single syllable; she wasn't sure she approved of any of them. Her tone sharp, she inquired, "And what do you mean by that?"

He opened his eyes wider, the heavy lids lifting; his lips, thin, mobile, the lower somewhat fuller, seemed to ease. His black gaze held hers trapped; he made no move to answer her question.

Not with words.

She suddenly felt quite warm.

Flustered—she was actually flustered.

The music reached its conclusion; the dance ended. She'd never been so thankful of any event in her life. She stepped out of his arms, only to feel his hand close once more about hers.

His gaze on her face, he set her hand on his sleeve. "Allow me to escort you back to your sister."

She had little choice but to accept; she did so with a haughty inclination of her head, and permitted him to steer her up the room, tacking through the crowd to where Adriana had returned to the safety of her court.

Taking up her position a few steps away, close by the wall, she lifted her hand from Torrington's sleeve and turned to dismiss him.

His gaze had gone to Adriana; he glanced back at her. "Your sister is very lovely. I take it you're hoping to establish her creditably?"

She hesitated, then nodded. "There seems no reason she shouldn't make an excellent match." Especially now Ruskin was gone. The recollection had her meeting Torrington's black gaze; it seemed fathomless, but far from cold.

Oddly intriguing. His gaze seemed to hold her, yet she didn't, in fact, feel trapped. Just held. . . .

"Tell me." His expression eased a fraction more. "Have you seen the latest offering at the Opera House? Have you been in town long enough to do so?"

He glanced away; she blinked. "No. The opera is one experience we've yet to enjoy." Studying him, she couldn't see him enthralled by opera or a play. Couldn't resist asking, "Have you succumbed to its lure recently?"

His lips twitched. "Opera isn't my weakness."

Weakness—did he have one? Given all she could sense, it seemed unlikely. She realized she was gazing at him, trying hard not to stare, not to show any consciousness of him, of the potent masculine aura of which, as the confines of the crowded ballroom necessitated them standing mere inches apart, she was very much aware.

She'd been going to dismiss him. She drew in a breath.

"I thought you'd want to know that the proper authorities were informed of Mr. Ruskin's sad end." Those fascinating black eyes returned to hers; he'd lowered his voice so only she could hear. "In the circumstances, I saw no need to implicate you. You knew nothing of the situation leading to Ruskin's death—or so I understood."

She nodded. "That's correct." As if in support of his judgment, she added, "I have no idea why he was stabbed, or by whom. I had no connection with him beyond a few social exchanges."

Torrington's black gaze remained steady on her face, then he inclined his head and looked away. "So from which part of the country do you and your sister hail?"

Given he'd just informed her he'd been instrumental in protecting her from precisely the sort of imbroglio she'd been frantic to avoid, she felt compelled to answer. "Warwickshire. Not far from Banbury." She and Adriana had decided it would be wise henceforth to avoid all mention of Chipping Norton.

"Your and Miss Pevensey's parents?"

"Are no longer alive."

That earned her a glance, black and sharp. "She has no guardian other than yourself?"

"No." She lifted her chin. "Be that as it may, I believe we'll muddle through."

He registered her acerbic tone; he glanced again at Adriana. "So you're solely responsible for . . ." He looked back at her. "Do you have any idea what you've taken on?"

She raised her brows, no longer amused. "As I said, I believe we'll manage nicely. We have until now, and quite well, I would say."

His black gaze held hers with a disturbing intensity. "I would have thought your husband would have had some hand in that."

She blushed. "Yes, of course, but he's been dead for some years."

"Indeed?" Torrington's black eyes gleamed. "Might one inquire from what he died?"

"An inflamation of the lung," she snapped, not at all sure to what in his question she was reacting. She looked away at the surrounding crowd, tried to realign her thoughts with the requirements of her charade. "It's unkind of you to remind me, sir."

After a moment came the dry comment, "My apologies, my dear, but you don't appear to be a grieving widow."

She made the mistake of glancing at him.

He caught her gaze, held it.

After a moment, she narrowed her eyes, then, deliberately, looked away.

Fought to ignore the soft, very masculine chuckle that fell, a distractingly warm caress over her senses.

"Tell me." He'd lowered his voice and shifted closer; the deep rumble teased her ear. "Why aren't you joining your sister in hunting for a husband?"

"I have other matters in hand, other responsibilities. I don't need to add a husband to the list."

She refused to look at him, but sensed she'd said something to make him pause.

Not for long. "Most ladies in your position would look to a husband to shoulder their responsibilities for them."

"Indeed?" Still surveying the crowd, she raised her brows as if considering, then shrugged. "Perhaps, but I have no ambitions for myself in that direction. If I can see my sister comfortably established, married to a gentleman worthy of her, then I'll retire from this Season well pleased."

Glancing at Adriana's court, she noted one particular gentleman who was making every attempt to monopolize her sister's attention. The surprising thing was he appeared to be succeeding.

"Well pleased from a guardian's point of view perhaps, but as a lady of some experience, a widow's lonely existence can hardly be fulfilling."

Distracted, she heard the deep, drawled words, but wasted no wit on divining their meaning. Frowning, she turned to him. "Instead of twitting me, you might attempt to be useful—who is the gentleman with my sister?"

Tony blinked. Thrown entirely off his stride, he looked. "Ah . . . there's at present seven gentlemen surrounding your sister."

She made a frustrated sound—the sort that intimated he was being willfully obtuse. "The one with wavy brown hair speaking with her now. Do you know him?"

He looked, and blinked again. It was several seconds before he replied, "Yes. That's Geoffrey Manningham, Lord Manningham."

An instant later, his prey prodded his arm. "Well? What can you tell me about him?"

He glanced at her. Far from observing the stiff formal distance she'd been working to preserve between them, she'd shifted closer; he could smell the perfume wafting from her throat. If he shifted his head just an inch, he'd be able to touch his cheek to her hair.

She'd been staring, frowning, at Geoffrey; now she glanced up at him, pointedly opened her green eyes wide.

"His estate is in Devon. It shares a partial boundary with mine. If I know anything of Geoffrey, and I've known him since childhood, then his estate, houses, and finances will all be in excellent condition."

Her green eyes narrowed. "You . . ." She glanced at Geoffrey.

"No." It was comforting to be with a woman he could read so easily; she made very little effort to hide her thoughts. "Geoffrey didn't send me to distract you so he could waltz your sister off from beneath your careful nose."

She looked up at him, still suspicious. "And why should I believe that?"

He held her gaze, then caught her hand, lifted it to his lips. Kissed. "Because I told you so." Her eyes flashed; he smiled, and added, "And because Geoffrey and I haven't met in over ten years."

Perfectly aware that with the simple caress he'd fractured her concentration, he gestured to the circle a few feet away. "Shall we join them?"

She gathered herself and managed a regal nod. Delighted, entranced, he tucked her hand in his arm and steered her to Geoffrey's side.

"Manningham?"

Geoffrey looked up from his pursuit of the lovely Adriana. The rivalry that in their youth had never been far beneath their surfaces instantly leapt to his eyes.

Tony smiled. "Allow me to present Mrs. Carrington—Miss Pevensey's sister and guardian."

Geoffrey's gaze deflected, then he threw Tony a speaking glance and made haste to bow and shake Alicia's hand. Others made hay of his distraction and reclaimed Adriana's attention. Tony noted that while she showed no partiality to those anxious to gain her approbation, she did sneak swift glances at Geoffrey, engaged by her sister in the customary social niceties.

Content to observe, he made no attempt to extricate Geoffrey. Instead, he listened to Alicia Carrington craftily confirm all he'd told her, and elicit a few details more. Her protectiveness toward her younger sister, her determination to ensure she was in no way taken advantage of, rang true and clear. Not one of the men gathered about Adriana could doubt it; her sister would always stand as her protector.

With her single-minded focus, she reminded him of a lioness watching over her cubs; woe betide any who dared threaten them. She was calm, determined, sensible, and strong-willed, mature yet not old; she was as chalk to cheese to the young misses he'd been exposed to over the past weeks—the contrast was a blessed relief.

Via the groom he'd sent to chat in the mews near Waverton Street, he'd learned that Mrs. Carrington hired her carriage from the nearby stables, and also that, as was her habit, she'd sent her evening's instructions to the coachman at midday. Armed with the information, he'd arrived early, much to Lady Mott's delight; he'd been in the ballroom waiting when Alicia Carrington had walked in.

He'd watched her for an hour before he'd approached; in that time, he'd seen her dismiss without a blink three perfectly eligible gentlemen who, as he did, found her quieter beauty, with its suggestion of maturity and a more subtle allure, more attractive than her sister's undeniable charms.

As with all else she'd revealed in response to his probing, her dismissal of marriage rang true. She was truly disinterested, at least at present. She was focused on her task . . . the temptation to distract her, to see if he could . . .

He refocused on her; she was still interrogating Geoffrey who, to Tony's educated eye, was finding the going increasingly grim.

He'd done his duty. He'd convinced himself that his first impression of Mrs. Carrington had been accurate; she hadn't slid a stiletto between Ruskin's ribs, and he could see no reason to doubt her assertion that she had known Ruskin only socially. There was nothing there to interest Dalziel.

Mission accomplished, there was no reason he couldn't retire and leave Geoffrey to his fate. No reason at all to remain by Alicia Carrington's side.

The distant scrape of bow on string heralded the return of the musicians and an impending waltz. Geoffrey straightened, stiffened, then threw him an unmistakable look of entreaty. Man-to-man. Ex-boyhood-rival-to-rival.

Tony reached for Alicia's hand. "If you would do me the honor, Mrs. Carrington?" He bowed.

Alicia blinked, startled by the sudden clasp of Torrington's hard fingers on hers. As he straightened, she glanced at Lord Manningham only to discover his lordship had grasped her single moment of distraction to turn to Adriana, who, from her smile, had been waiting, having already granted him this dance.

She opened her lips—on what words she didn't know—only to find herself whisked about. "Wait!"

"The dance floor's this way."

"I know, but I wasn't going to accept your offer."

He threw her a black glance, not irritated but curious. "Why?"

"Because I don't want to waltz."

"Why not? You're passably good at it."

"It's got nothing to do with . . . I'm a chaperone. Chaperones don't waltz. We're supposed to keep an eye on our charges even while they're waltzing."

He glanced over her head. "Your sister's with Manningham. Unless he's changed beyond belief in the last ten years, he's no cad— she's as safe as she can be, and you don't need to watch."

They'd reached the floor; the musicians had launched into their theme. He swung her into his arms, then they were whirling down the room.

As before, she found breathing difficult, but was determined not to let it show. "Are you always this dictatorial?"

He met her gaze, then smiled, an easy, warming, simple gesture. "I don't know. I've never been questioned on the subject before."

She threw him a look she hoped conveyed total disbelief.

"But educate me—I've been away from the ton for more than ten years—should your sister be waltzing at all? Wasn't there some rule or other about permission from the hostesses?"

"She had to get permission from one of the patronesses of Almack's. I spoke to Lady Cowper, and she was kind enough to give her approval." Alicia frowned. "But why have you been away from the ton for ten years—and more? Where were you?"

He looked at her for a moment, as if the answer should be obvious, tattooed on his forehead or some such, then his smile deepened. "I was in the army—the Guards."

"Waterloo?"

The concern in her face was quite genuine. It warmed him. "And the Peninsula."

"Oh."

Tony watched her digest that. Despite the fact he waltzed well— always had—the waltz wasn't his favorite dance; with a woman in his arms, he'd much rather be involved in a romp that heated up the sheets on some bed, rather than a sedate revolution about some tonnish ballroom.

And in this case, the woman in his arms teased and challenged on a level he'd forgotten what it was like to be challenged on. For too many years, women, ladies and all, had come to him easily; generally speaking, he'd only had to crook his finger, and there'd always been more than one willing to slake his lust. He was an accomplished lover, too experienced to be anything other than easy and generous in his ways.

Too experienced not to recognize when his senses were engaged.

Taller than average, supple and svelte, she was less buxom than those ladies who normally caught his eye, yet she hadn't just caught his attention, she'd fixed it—quite why he couldn't say. There seemed a multitude of small attractions that made up the whole—the sheen of the candlelight on her perfect skin, a soft cream tinged with rose, a very English complexion, her eyes and their green gaze—direct, without guile, amazingly open—the lush, heavy locks of her dark mahogany hair, the way her lips set, then eased and lifted.

He wanted to taste them, to taste her. To tempt her to want him. And more. With her in his arms, his appetite, along with his imagination, was definitely inclined toward a bed.

Alicia was conscious of an escalating warmth, one that seemed to rise from within her. It was pleasant, even addictive—her senses responded with a wish to wallow and luxuriate. It was something to do with him, with the way he held her, whirled her so easily down the room, with the reined strength she sensed in him but which triggered her innate defenses not at all—that strength was no threat to her.

His effect on her, however, might be; she wasn't experienced enough to know. Yet it was just a dance—one waltz—and she'd never waltzed like this before, never felt quite like this. Surely it couldn't hurt. And he was a military veteran, an ex-Guardsman, and a viscount.

Quite what that said of him she wasn't sure, but it couldn't all be bad.

He swung her through the turns at the end of the room; her heart leapt as his thigh parted hers. Letting her lids fall, she concentrated on breathing—and on the warmth her senses seemingly craved.

The music slowed, stopped, and they halted. And she realized just how pleasant—how pleasurable—the dance had been. She glanced at him, met his black gaze, and thought she saw a fraction too much understanding in his dark eyes. How black could seem warm she had no idea, but his eyes were never cold . . .

She looked to where Adriana's court waited, and saw Adriana on the arm of Lord Manningham ahead of them, moving that way. Torrington took her arm and steered her in their wake.

As seemed normal for him, he didn't offer his sleeve or ask her permission . . .

And, as was starting to be normal for her, she'd let him.

She frowned. Not once during the waltz had she thought to check on Adriana and Manningham—her distraction had been that complete.

The man on whose arm she was strolling was dangerous.

Seriously dangerous; he'd managed to make her forget her plan for a full five minutes, in the middle of a ton ballroom, no less.

Tony saw the frown form on her face. "What's the matter?"

She glanced up. He looked into her green eyes, watched as she debated, then decided not to tell him the truth—that he was disturbing her, ruffling her senses, undermining her equanimity—as if he didn't know.

Frown deepening, she looked down. "I was just wondering whether my demon brothers had behaved themselves tonight."

He felt his brows rise. "*Demon* brothers?"

She nodded. "Three of them. I'm afraid they're quite a handful. David is a terror—he pretends to be a pirate and falls out of windows. I don't know how many times we've had the doctor to the house. And then Harry, well, he has a tendency to lie—one never knows if the house really is on fire or not. And as for Matthew, he is only eight, you understand, if we could just stop him from locking the doors after people, and slipping around the house at night—we've lost three parlor maids and two housekeepers, and we've only been in town for five weeks."

Tony looked into her face, into her green eyes so determinedly guileless, and struggled not to laugh. She was a terrible liar.

He managed to keep a straight face. "Have you tried beating them?"

"Oh, no! Well, only once. They ran away. We spent the most awful twenty-four hours before they came home again."

"Ah—I see. And do I take it these demons are your responsibility?"

Head rising, she nodded. "My *sole* responsibility."

At that, he grinned.

She saw. Frowned. "What?"

He lifted her hand from his sleeve, raised it to his lips. "If you want to scare gentlemen off, you shouldn't sound so proud of your three imps."

Her frown would have turned to a scowl, but her sister came up on

Geoffrey's arm and effectively distracted her. Adriana's court trailed behind; within minutes they were once more part of a fashionable circle, within whose safety Alicia remained, shooting the occasional suspicious glance his way until, deeming his duty on all counts done, he bowed and took his leave.

Three

He repaired to the Bastion Club.

With a sigh, he sank into a well-stuffed leather armchair in the library. "This place is a godsend."

He exchanged a glance with Jack Warnefleet, ensconced in another chair reading an issue of *The Sporting Life*, savored a sip of his brandy, then settled his head against the padded leather and let his thoughts roam.

To his life—what it used to be, what it now was, most importantly what he wanted it to be. The past was behind him, finished, brought to a close at Waterloo. The present was a bridge, a transition between past and future, nothing more. As for the future. . . .

What did he truly want?

His mind flashed on snippets of memory, a sense of warmth in company, of rare moments of closeness punctuating long years of being alone. Of camaraderie, a sense of shared purpose, a passion for life as well as justice.

Dalziel and his mention of Whitley had brought Jack Hendon to mind. The last he'd seen of Jack he'd been firmly caught in his lovely wife's coils, trooping, gesticulating and protesting, at her dainty heels. A vision of Kit with their elder son in her arms, Jack hovering protectively over them both, swam through his mind. And stuck.

Jack and Kit were coming down to London this Season; they'd be here within a few days. It would be good to see them again, not only to renew old friendships but to refresh his memory, to sense again how a successful marriage worked.

The restlessness that for a few hours had been in abeyance

returned. Draining his glass, he set it aside and rose. With a nod to Jack, who returned a salute, he left the library and the club.

At that hour London's streets were quiet, the last stragglers from the balls already at home while the more hardened cases were ensconced in their clubs, hells, and private salons for what was left of the night. Tony walked steadily, his strides long, his cane swinging. Despite his self-absorption, his senses remained alert, yet none of those hanging back in the shadows made any move to accost him.

Reaching his house in Upper Brook Street, he climbed the steps, fishing for his latch key. To his surprise, the door swung open.

Hungerford stood waiting to relieve him of his coat and cane. The hall lights were blazing. A footman stood to the side, still on duty.

"The gentleman who called this morning has returned, my lord. He insisted on waiting for your return. I've put him the library."

"Dalziel?"

"Indeed, my lord."

From Hungerford's tone, it was clear that he, no more than Tony, was certain just who, or more correctly what, Dalziel was, other than someone it was unwise to disobey, let alone cross.

Tony headed for the library.

"The tantalus is well supplied. Do you require anything further, my lord?"

"No." Tony paused and glanced back. "You and the staff can retire. I'll see"—he'd been about to say his lordship; Dalziel was at the very least that—"the gentleman out."

"Very good, my lord."

Tony continued across the green-and-white tiles toward the library door. The hall was paneled in oak, an airy, high-ceilinged space . . . it was a night for memories. He could recall running here as a child, with a fire roaring in the hearth at the end, the dancing flames reflecting off the oak, a sense of warmth enveloping him.

Now the hall seemed . . . not cold, but it no longer held that encompassing warmth. It was empty, waiting for that time to come again, for that phase of life to return.

Hungerford and the footman had disappeared through the green baize door. Alone, Tony paused; with his hand on the knob of the library door, he looked around. Let his senses stretch farther than his eyes could see.

He was alone, and his house was empty. Like it, he was waiting. Waiting for the next phase of life to rush in and fill him, engage him.

Warm him.

For a moment he stood silent and still, then he shook off the mood and opened the door.

Dalziel was in an armchair facing the door, an almost empty brandy balloon in one long-fingered hand. His brows rose faintly; his lips curved, cynical and amused, in welcome.

Tony eyed the entire vision with a misgiving he made no attempt to hide; Dalziel's smile only deepened.

"Well?" Crossing to the tantalus, Tony poured a small measure of brandy, more to have something to do than anything else. He raised the decanter to Dalziel, who shook his head. Replacing the decanter, picking up the glass, he crossed to the other armchair. "To what do I owe this . . . unexpected visit?"

They both knew it wouldn't have anything to do with pleasure.

"We've worked together for a long time."

Tony sat. "Thirteen years. But I work for the government no longer, so what has that to say to anything?"

Dalziel's dark eyes held his. "Simply that there are matters I cannot use less experienced men for, and in this case your peculiar background makes you too ideal a candidate to overlook."

"Bonaparte's on St. Helena. The French are finished."

Dalziel smiled. "Not that peculiar background. I have other half-French agents. I meant that you have experience of Whitley's side of things, and you have a better-than-average grasp of the possibilities involved."

"Involved in what?"

"Ruskin's death." Dalziel studied the amber lights in the glass he turned between his fingers. "Some disturbing items came to light when they started clearing the man's desk. Jottings of shipping information derived from both Revenue and Admiralty documents. They appear to be scribbled notes for more formal communications."

"Nothing in any way associated with his work?"

"No. He organized Customs clearances for merchantmen, hence his access to the internal Revenue and Admiralty notices. His job involved the dates of expected entry to our ports. The information jotted down relates to movement of ships in the Channel, especially its outermost reaches. There is no possible reason his job required such details."

Dalziel paused, then added, "The most disturbing aspect is that these jottings span the years from 1812 to 1815."

"Ah." As Dalziel had prophesied, Tony grasped the implication.

"Indeed. You now perceive why I'm here. Both I and Whitley are now extremely interested in learning who killed Ruskin, and most importantly why."

Tony pondered, then looked at Dalziel, directly met his eyes. "Why me?" He could guess, but he wanted it confirmed.

"Because there is, as you've realized, the possibility that someone in Customs and Revenue, or the Home Office, or any of a multitude of government agencies is involved, in one capacity or another. It's unlikely Ruskin could use the information himself, but someone knew he had access to it, and either made use of him themselves, or put someone else on to him. In either case, this nebulous someone might be in a position to know Whitley's operatives. He won't, however, know you."

Dalziel paused, considering Tony. "The only connection you've had with Whitley's crew was that operation you ran with Jonathon Hendon and George Smeaton. Both are now retired; both are sound. Despite Hendon's background in shipping, he's had no contact with Ruskin—and yes, I've checked. For the past several years, both Hendon and Smeaton have remained buried in Norfolk, and their only links in town are either purely social or purely commercial. Neither is a threat to you—and as I recall, no one else of Whitley's crew ever knew who Antoine Balzac really was."

Tony nodded. Antoine Balzac had been a large part of his past.

"On top of that, you found the body." Dalziel met his gaze. "You are the epitome of an obvious choice."

Tony grimaced and looked down, into his glass. It seemed as if the past was reaching out, trying to draw him back; he didn't want to go. Yet all Dalziel said was true; he *was* the obvious choice . . . and Alicia Carrington was, at least peripherally, involved.

She wasn't part of his past.

"All right." He looked up. "I'll nose around and see what connections I can turn up."

Dalziel nodded and set his glass aside. "Ruskin worked at the main office of Customs and Revenue in Whitehall." He gave details of the building, floor, and room. "I suggested that his papers, indeed, all his office be left as was. I gather that's been done. Naturally, I've asked for no clearances. Let me know if you require any."

Tony's lips curved; he inclined his head. Both he and Dalziel knew he wouldn't ask for clearances. He'd been an "unofficial agent" for too long.

"Ruskin lived in lodgings in Bury Street—Number 23. His home, Crawton Hall, is near Bledington in Gloucestershire, just over the border of north Oxfordshire, southwest of Chipping Norton, the nearest market town."

Tony frowned, but his knowledge of England was nowhere near as detailed as his knowledge of France.

"Ruskin has a mother living, and an older spinster sister. They reside at Crawton Hall, and haven't left it in decades. Ruskin spent but little time there in recent years. That's what we know of him to date."

"Odd habits?"

"None known—we'll leave that to you. Obviously, we can't afford any overt activity."

"What about manner of death—any word from the surgeon?"

"I called Pringle in. According to him, Ruskin was knifed with the stiletto you found. Very professionally slipped between the ribs. Angle and point of entry suggest a right-handed assailant standing beside and a little behind his left side."

They both could see how it was done.

"So." Tony sipped. "A friend."

"Certainly someone he in no way suspected of murderous intent."

Such as a lady in a pale green silk gown.

Tony looked up. "Did Pringle give any guesses as to the murderer—size, strength, that sort of thing?"

Dalziel's eyes, scanning his face, narrowed. "He did. A man almost certainly as tall as Ruskin and, of course, of reasonable strength."

"How tall was Ruskin?"

"A trifle shorter than me. Half a head shorter than you."

Tony hid his relief behind a grimace. "Not much help there. Any other clues?"

"No." Dalziel stood, fluidly graceful.

Tony did the same, with even more innate flair.

Dalziel hid a grin and led the way to the door. "Let me know what you find. If I hear anything useful, I'll send word."

He paused as they reached the door and met Tony's gaze. "If I do have anything to send, where should I send it?"

Tony considered, then said, "Here. Back door. My butler's reliable, and the staff have been with me for years."

Dalziel nodded. They stepped into the hall.

Tony saw Dalziel out and locked the front door, then returned to the library.

He went straight to one of the bookcases and crouched, scanning the spines, then he pulled out a large tome. Rising, he crossed to where the lamp on the desk threw a circle of stronger light. Opening the book—a collection of maps of England's counties—he flicked through until he came to the pages showing Oxfordshire. He located Chipping Norton, and Banbury in the far north of the county.

It took a few minutes of flicking back and forth, comparing maps of Gloucestershire, Oxfordshire, and Warwickshire, before he had the geography straight. The only bit of Warwickshire "not far from Banbury" was also not far from Chipping Norton, and therefore, in turn, not far from Bledington.

Alicia Carrington's home lay within ten miles of Ruskin's.

Shutting the book, Tony stared across the room.

How likely was it, given the social round of county England that, living in such proximity, Alicia Carrington née Pevensey and Ruskin had never met?

The question suggested the answer. Ruskin hadn't spent much time in Bledington recently, and despite telling him she and her sister hailed from the area, Alicia Carrington could well have meant their home was there now. The home she'd made with her husband; most likely she was referring to his house, not necessarily the area in which she and her family, the Pevenseys, had lived most of their lives. Of course.

He returned the book to the shelf, then headed for the door.

Of course, he'd check.

That, however, would have to come later. The first thing he needed to do, and that as soon as humanly possible, before any whisper of an internal investigation into Ruskin's affairs could find its way to anyone, was search Ruskin's office.

The Customs and Revenue Office in Whitehall was well guarded and externally secure, but for someone who knew how to approach it from within, down the long, intersecting corridors, it was much less impenetrable. Even better, Ruskin's office was on the first floor at the back, and its small window faced a blank wall.

At four o'clock in the morning, the building was cold and silent. The porter was snoring in his office downstairs; lighting a lamp was safe enough.

Tony searched the desk, then the whole office methodically. He collected everything pertinent in the middle of the desk; when there was no more to discover, he transferred all he'd found to the deep pockets of his greatcoat.

Then he turned out the lamp, slipped out of the building, and went home, leaving not a trace of his presence, or anything to alert anyone that Ruskin's office had been searched.

Despite his late night, he was out again at noon, heading for Bury Street. It was a fashionable area for single gentlemen, close to clubs, Mayfair, and the seat of government; Number 23 was a well-kept, narrow, three-story house. He knocked on the door and explained to the landlady that he worked alongside Mr. Ruskin and had been sent to check his rooms to make sure no Customs Office papers had been left there.

She led him up to a set of rooms on the first floor. He thanked her as she unlocked the door. "I'll return the key when I leave."

With a measuring glance that read the quality of his coat and boots in much the same way as a military pass, she nodded. "I'll leave you to it, then."

He waited until she was heading downstairs, then entered Ruskin's parlor and shut the door.

Again, his search was thorough, but in contrast to Ruskin's office, this time he found evidence someone had been before him. He found a pile of old IOUs lying in a concealed drawer in the escritoire atop more recent correspondence.

Dalziel and Whitley would never have permitted any other from either the official or unofficial sides of government to meddle in an affair they'd handed to him; whoever had been through Ruskin's papers was from the "other side." Indeed, the fact the rooms had been searched—he found further telltale signs in the bedroom—meant there was, most definitely, an "other side."

Whatever dealings Ruskin had been involved in, someone had believed there might be evidence they needed to remove from his rooms.

Presumably they'd removed it.

Tony wasn't unduly concerned. There were always threads left lying around in the aftermath of any scheme; he was an expert at finding and following such flimsy but real connections.

Such as those IOUs. He didn't stop to analyze them in detail, but a cursory glance revealed that they'd been paid off regularly. More, the sums involved made it clear Ruskin had enjoyed an income considerably beyond his earnings as a government clerk.

Stowing the notes in his pockets, Tony concluded that discovering the source of that extra income was logically his next step.

After taking an impression of the key, he let himself out, returned the key to the landlady with typical civil service boredom, admitting to removing "a few papers but nothing major" when she asked.

Back on the street, he headed for Torrington House. He needed a few hours to study and collate all he'd found. However, the day was winging, and there was other information he needed to pursue that would, he suspected, be best pursued in daylight.

He'd been wondering how to approach Alicia Carrington and learn unequivocally all he needed to know. He'd left a corner of his brain wrestling with the problem; an hour ago, it had presented him with the perfect solution.

First, he needed to empty his pockets and let Hungerford feed him. Two o'clock would be the perfect time to essay forth to rattle Mrs. Carrington's defenses.

He found her precisely where his devious mind had predicted—in Green Park with her three brothers and an older man who appeared to be their tutor.

The two older boys were wrestling with a kite; the tutor was assisting. The younger boy had a bat and ball; Alicia was doing her best to entertain him.

He spent a few minutes observing, assessing, before making his move. Recalling Alicia's description of her demons, he grinned. The boys were sturdy, healthy-looking specimens with apples in their cheeks and shining brown hair. They were typical boys, rowdy and physical, yet they were quick to mind their elder sister's strictures.

Obedient demons.

Amused, he walked toward her. The bat in her hands, she had her back to him. The youngest—Matthew?—tossed the ball to her; she swung wildly and missed. The ball bounced past her, giving him the perfect opening.

He stopped the ball with his boot, with a quick flick, tossed it up, and caught it. Strolling forward, he hefted the ball; as he reached Alicia's side, he lobbed it to the boy.

And reached for the bat. "Here, let me."

He twitched the bat from her nerveless fingers.

Alicia stared at him. "What are you doing here?"

Torrington glanced at her. "Playing ball." He waved to the side. "You should stand over there so you can catch me out."

Matthew, blinking at the changes, shook his head. "She's not much good at catching."

Her tormentor smiled at him. "We'll have to give her a bit of practice, then. Ready?"

Alicia found herself stepping back in the direction Torrington had indicated. She was not sure about any of this, but . . .

Matthew pitched the ball to him, and he tapped it back between her and Matthew. Matthew squealed delightedly and pounced on it. A huge grin wreathing his face, he hustled to square up again.

After a few more shrewdly placed shots—one which came straight at her and surprised a shriek out of her—David and Harry left Jenkins with the kite and came hurrying to join in.

Normally, the older boys would have immediately taken over the game; she girded her loins to defend Matthew, but Torrington, bat still in his hand, elected himself director of play. He welcomed the older boys and waved them to fielding positions, leaving Matthew as bowler.

What followed was an education in how boys played, or could play if led by a competent hand. When Jenkins came up, the discarded kite in his hands, she waved him to take over her position. He might be more than twice her age, but he was better at catching.

The kite in her arms, she retreated to lean against a tree. Given the focus of the game, she naturally found herself gazing at Torrington.

Not a calming sight.

He literally made her pulse skitter and race. She was far enough away to appreciate his perfect male proportions, the wide shoulders and tapering chest, slim hips and long, lean legs. She'd yet to see him make an ungraceful move; she wasn't sure he'd know how. His reflexes were excellent.

She saw the laughing humor in his face as he skied a ball to Harry, who with a rowdy whoop caught it. Torrington's black locks, thick and lightly wavy, hugged his head; one fell forward across his broad brow as he good-naturedly surrendered the bat to Harry. He took the ball and bowled for a while, then tossed it to David.

And came strolling over the lawn to take up a fielding position near her. He grinned at her. "Coward."

She tipped up her nose. "As you've been informed, I'm hopeless at catching."

The look he gave her was enigmatic, but a ball hit his way recalled him to his duty.

She tried to watch the play and call encouragement as a good sister should, but having Torrington so close, watching him move and stretch and stand, hands on hips, then wave, directing her brothers, was distracting.

His occasional glances did nothing to slow her pulse.

What really worried her was why he was there.

As soon as David and Matthew had had a turn at batting, she called a halt. "Come along—we have to get back for tea."

Her brothers, flushed and glowing with happiness, ran up.

"I say." David tugged her hand. "Can Tony come home with us for tea?"

Alicia looked down into David's bright eyes. Tony—Torrington was *Tony* to them. That seemed dangerous. But David, even more than the other two, was lonely here in London, and what, after all, could Torrington do? She smiled. "If he wishes."

"Will you come? Will you come?" The chorus was instantaneous.

Joining them, Tony—Torrington—glanced at her. "If your sister doesn't mind."

She wasn't at all sure it was a good idea, and he knew it; she met his gaze, but kept her expression easy. "If you have no objection to sitting down to a nursery tea, then by all means do join us."

He smiled, not just with his lips but with those coal black eyes; if she'd had a fan, she would have deployed it. He bowed. "Thank you. I'd be delighted."

Thrilled, thoroughly pleased with their new acquaintance, the boys took his hands; surrounding him, they danced by his side all the way back to Waverton Street, peppering him with questions.

At first, following behind with Jenkins, she merely listened, learning that Tony was an only child and had grown up mostly in Devon, but also in part in London. He knew all the childhood haunts. But when Harry, military mad, asked if he'd served overseas, and he replied he had, her protective instincts flared.

Quickly lengthening her stride, she came up beside Matthew, tripping along, Tony's hand in his, gazing adoringly up at his new friend.

"So which were you in—the navy or the army?"

"The army—the Guards."

"And you were at Waterloo?"

"Yes."

"Did you lead a charge?"

She jumped in. "Boys, I really don't think we need to hear about charges and fighting over tea."

Torrington glanced at her briefly, a swift, penetrating look, then he turned back to her brothers. "Your sister's right—war is not fun. It's horrible, and frightening, and dreadful to be involved in."

David's eyes grew round. Harry's face fell.

Alicia only just managed to keep her own jaw from falling.

"But . . ." Harry blinked at Torrington. "I want to be a major in the Guards when I grow up. Or the cavalry."

"I was a major in both, and I'd suggest you rethink. Aside from all else, there are no more enemies to fight. Being in the cavalry in peacetime might not be the exciting life you imagine."

They'd reached the front steps of the house. Torrington waved the boys ahead of him, then waited for Alicia to precede him. She went quickly up the steps and opened the door, then stood back, and the three boys filed in.

Gracefully, Torrington waved her on, then followed.

"Upstairs and wash your hands, please." She shooed her brothers to the stairs. "Then you may join us in the parlor."

They flashed swift smiles at Torrington, then clattered up the stairs. Jenkins shut the door. She turned to him. "If you could order tea, Jenkins?"

"Indeed, ma'am." Jenkins bowed and left them.

She turned to Torrington. "Thank you." She met his black eyes. "That was just the right thing to say."

He studied her for a moment, then one black brow arched. "It's no more than the truth."

But one few ex-majors in the Guards would admit. Inclining her head, she led him to the parlor. Located at the back of the house, it was the room she and Adriana used most, when they were alone or with the boys, *en famille.* A comfortable room in which the boys could relax without worrying overmuch about the furniture, it was a trifle shabby, but she didn't care as she led Torrington in; she'd warned him it was to be a nursery tea.

Adriana was there, poring over the latest fashion plates. She glanced up, saw Torrington, and rose, smiling.

After Adriana and Torrington exchanged greetings, they all sat. Even though the room was decently sized, Alicia was aware of his physical presence, his strength. Adriana asked how he had come to join them; he related the story of the game in the park. Every now and then, his gaze would touch Alicia's, and a teasing smile would flirt about his lips. She was relieved when the boys rejoined them, bursting upon them in a noisy, albeit well-behaved wave, and the talk became more general.

Jenkins appeared with the tray; if Torrington noticed the oddity in that, he gave no sign.

She poured; on their best behavior, the boys offered Torrington the plate of crumpets first. He went up in their estimation—and hers—when he accepted one and smeared it with globs of jam, just as the boys did with theirs. All were soon munching happily.

Crumpet dealt with in three bites, Torrington wiped his fingers on his napkin, then reached for his teacup. He looked at her brothers. "Your sister told me you live in Warwickshire—is there much sport up that way? Shooting? Hunting?"

David wrinkled his nose. "Some fishing, some shooting, not much hunting just where we are. That's south Warwickshire."

Harry waved his remaining crumpet. "There's hunting around Banbury, but not down near us."

"Well," David temporized. "There's a small, really *tiny* pack runs out of Chipping Norton, but it's not what you'd call a real hunt."

From the corner of his eye, Tony saw Alicia and Adriana exchange a swift glance; the instant the boys had started mentioning towns, Alicia had tensed. He pressed harder. "Chipping Norton? Is that your nearest town? I've a friend who lives up that way."

Alicia leaned forward. "Harry! Be careful. You're about to drip jam."

Adriana grabbed his napkin and wiped Harry's fingers. Neither Tony nor Harry could see any physical reason for his sisters' sudden action.

"There." Adriana sat back. "Now why don't you tell Lord Torrington about that huge trout you caught last year?"

Instead, the boys fixed Tony with round eyes.

"Are you really a lord?" Matthew asked.

Tony grinned. "Yes."

"What sort of lord?" David asked.

"A viscount." Tony could see from their faces they were trying to recall the order of precedence. "It's a small lordship. The second smallest."

They weren't deterred. "Does that mean you get to wear a coronet at a coronation?"

"What sort of cloak do you get to wear?"

"Do you have a castle?"

He laughed, and answered as best he could, noting the relieved look Alicia threw Adriana; his presence in her parlor was making her skittish, and on more than one front.

Interrogating her brothers was not a gentlemanly act, yet he'd learned long ago that when it came to matters of treason, and that was what he and Dalziel and Whitley were dealing with in one guise or another, one couldn't adhere to gentlemanly scruples. In that particular theater, adhering to such scruples was a fast way to die, failing one's country in the process.

He felt no remorse for having used the three boys; they'd come to no harm, and he'd learned what he needed. Now he had to interrogate their elder sister. Again.

"Time for your afternoon lessons, boys. Come along, now." Alicia stood, waving her brothers to their feet.

They rose, casting glances at Tony; knowing on which side his bread was buttered, he gave them no encouragement to defy their sister, but rose, too, and gravely shook hands.

With resigned polite farewells, the boys trooped out; Alicia followed them into the hall, consigning them into Jenkins's care.

Seizing the moment, Tony turned to Adriana.

She'd risen, too, and now smiled. "I believe you're acquainted with Lord Manningham, my lord."

"Yes. He's an old friend."

Amusement flashed through her brown eyes, suggesting Geoffrey had painted their association with greater color.

He didn't have much time. "I wanted to speak with you. Your sister will have mentioned the matter of Mr. Ruskin." Adriana's face immediately clouded; like Alicia, she possessed little by way of a social mask. "I gather you hadn't met him in the country."

"No." Adriana met his gaze; her eyes were clear, but troubled. "He appeared a week or so after we arrived in town. We only met him a handful of times in the ballrooms, never anywhere else."

She hesitated, then added, "He was not a man either of us could like. He was . . . oh, what is the word . . . 'importuning'. That's it. He hovered about Alicia even though she discouraged him."

From her expression, it was clear that while Alicia was mother lion, Adriana would be fierce in her sister's defense. He inclined his head. "It's perhaps as well, then, that he's gone."

Adriana muttered a guiltily fervent assent.

Alicia reentered; he turned to her and smiled. "Thank you for an entertaining afternoon."

Her look said she wasn't sure how to interpret that. He took his leave of Adriana, then, as he'd hoped, Alicia accompanied him to the door.

Following him into the hall, she shut the parlor door. He glanced about; fate had smiled—they were alone.

He gave her no time to regroup, but struck immediately. "Ruskin lived at Bledington, close to Chipping Norton. Are you *sure* you never met him in the country?"

She blinked at him. "Yes—I told you. We only met recently, socially in London." Her eyes, searching his, suddenly widened. "Oh, was he a friend of your friend? The one you mentioned?"

He held her gaze; he could detect not the slightest hint of prevarication in the clear green, only puzzlement, and a hint of concern. "No," he eventually said. "Ruskin's friends are no friends of mine."

The reply, especially his tone, further confused her.

"I understand he'd been bothering you—in what way?"

She frowned, clearly wishing he hadn't known to ask; when he simply waited, she lifted her head and stiffly stated, "He was . . . attracted."

He kept his eyes on hers. "And you?"

Irritation flashed in her eyes. "I was not."

He felt his lips ease. "I see."

They remained, gazes locked, for two heartbeats, then he reached out and took her hand. Still holding her gaze, he raised her fingers to his lips. Kissed, and felt the tremor that raced through her. Watched her eyes widen, darken.

She drew in a quick breath, tensed to step back.

He reacted. Tightening his grip on her fingers, he drew her nearer. Bent his head and touched his lips to hers in the lightest, most fleeting kiss.

Just a brushing of lips, more promise than caress.

He intended it to be that, not a real kiss but a tantalizing temptation.

Raising his head, he watched her lids rise, saw surprise, shock, and curiosity fill her eyes. Then she realized, stiffened, drew back.

Releasing her, he caught her gaze. "I meant what I said. I truly enjoyed the afternoon."

He wondered if she understood what he was saying.

Before she could question him—before he could be tempted to say or do anything more—he bowed and turned to the door.

She saw him out and shut the door.

Gaining the pavement, he paused, letting the last moments fade from his mind, turning instead to running through all he'd learned thus far.

His instincts were pricking. Something was afoot, but just what he'd yet to divine. Turning on his heel, he headed for home and his library. There was a great deal he had to digest.

He spent the rest of that day and the entire evening analyzing all he'd retrieved from Ruskin's office and lodgings. Ruskin's scribbled notes and the receipts of his debts appeared to be the only clues, the only items warranting further investigation.

After assembling a schedule of the dates on which the debts, in groups, had been paid, along with the sums involved, Tony called it a night. At least working for Dalziel gave him an excuse not to attend the ton's balls.

The next day, just after noon, he girded his loins and dutifully presented himself at Amery House for one of his godmother's at-homes, to which he'd been summoned. He knew better than to ignore the dictate. Strolling into her drawing room, he bowed over her hand, resignedly noting he was one of only four gentlemen present.

Felicité beamed up at him. "*Bon!* You will please me *and* your *maman* by talking and paying attention to the *demoiselles* here, will you not?"

Despite the words, there was an ingenuous appeal in her eyes. He felt his lips quirk. Hand over heart, he declared, "I live to serve."

She only just managed to suppress a snort. She rapped his knuckles with her fan, then used it to gesture to the knots of young ladies gathered by the windows. "*Viens!*" She shooed. "Go—go!"

He went.

It was a cynical exercise; none of the young things to whom the matrons prayed he'd fall victim had any chance of fixing his interest. Why they thought he might be susceptible escaped him, but he behaved as required, pausing by first one group, then another, chatting easily before moving on. He did not remain by any lady's side for long; no one could accuse him of being the least encouraging.

He'd scanned the room on entering; Alicia Carrington had not been present. As he moved from group to group, he resurveyed the guests, but she didn't appear.

While moving to the fifth knot of conversationalists, he caught Felicité's eye, noted her puzzled expression. Realized he was giving the impression he was searching for someone, waiting for someone.

Mentally shrugging, he strolled on.

He was with the sixth group, inwardly debating whether he'd dallied long enough, when he heard two matrons standing a little apart exchanging the latest gossip—the items they considered too titillating for their charges' delicate ears.

His instincts flickered; he'd noticed there was some flutter—some piece of avid interest—doing the rounds among the older ladies.

The two biddies a yard behind him put their heads together and lowered their voices, but his hearing was acute.

"I had it this morning from Celia Chiswick. We met at Lady Montacute's morning tea. You've heard about that fellow Ruskin being murdered—stabbed—just along the path there?"

From the corner of his eye, Tony saw the lady point into the garden.

"*Well!* It seems he was blackmailing some lady—a widow."

"No! Who?"

"Well, of course no one knows, do they?"

"But someone must have some idea, surely."

"One hardly likes to speculate, but . . . you do know who he was speaking with just before he left this room and walked to his death, don't you?"

"No." The second woman's voice dropped to a strained whisper. "Who was it?"

Tony shifted and saw the first lady lean close to her companion and whisper the answer in her ear.

The second lady's eyes widened; her jaw dropped. Then she looked at the first. "*No!* Truly?"

Lips thinning, the first lady nodded.

The second flicked open her fan and waved it. "Great heavens! And she with that ravishing sister of hers in tow. *Well!*"

Tony fought to keep his expression from hardening, from revealing anything of the maelstrom of emotions that rose up and buffeted his mind—and him. Inwardly grim, he spent a few more minutes with the sweet young things, then excused himself and headed for the door.

Only to have Felicité step into his path. "You're not leaving so soon?" She put a hand on his arm; immediately concern flared in her eyes. She lowered her voice. "What is it?"

He hesitated, then said, "I'm engaged on some business. I have to go."

Her concern only deepened. "I thought you'd finished with such things."

His short laugh was harsh. "So did I. But not yet." He eased her hand from his sleeve and bowed over it. "I must go—there's someone I have to see."

Her gaze had flicked to where he'd been, then to the garden. He could see the connections forming in her mind. He stepped away.

She looked back at him. "If you must go, you must, but take care. And you must tell me later."

With a curt nod, he left. For once, he didn't stop to consider his plan.

Alicia strolled the clipped lawns of the park in the wake of Adriana and her swains. A morning promenade was becoming a regular event in their schedule. The gentlemen preferred the less-structured, less-cramped encounters such a stroll allowed; it gave them more time to worship at her sister's feet unfettered by any need to pay attention to any other young lady.

She'd countered that by inviting Miss Tiverton to walk with them. Adriana now strolled beside that young lady while five perfectly eligible gentlemen vied for their attention.

The most prominent, and most assiduous, was Lord Manningham. Alicia studied the undeniably attractive figure he cut in his morning coat, pale, tightly fitting breeches, and black Hessians. His address was polished without being oversmooth, his features were handsome rather than beautiful.

He was turning Adriana's head, and her sister knew it.

It was time, perhaps, to learn more of Geoffrey Manningham.

Especially as he was apparently a friend of Lord Torrington's. He who had almost-kissed her, who without provocation let alone permission had deliberately teased her in her own front hall.

The moment flared in her mind; her nerves tensed . . .

Ruthlessly, she bundled the memory aside—he probably did such things all the time. She refocused on Adriana and her court. Adjusting her parasol, she strolled on.

She had no warning, no premonition of danger, until she heard herself hailed in a voice that cut like a whip.

She whirled, but Torrington was already upon her. Hard fingers closing manacle-like about her elbow, he swung her around and marched her down the lawn, away from the carriageway.

"What—?" She tried to free her arm, but couldn't. She glared at him. "Unhand me, sir!"

He ignored her. He strode on, forcing her with him; she either had to keep up, or stumble and fall. His face was set like stone, his expression unforgivingly grim. Thunderclouds would have looked more comforting.

She glanced back at the others, strolling on unaware. "Stop! I have to watch over my sister."

He glanced briefly at her—too briefly for her to read his eyes—then lifted his gaze and looked back at the others. "She's with Manningham. She's safe." Looking forward, he growled, "You aren't."

He'd lost his senses. She tugged against his hold, then dragged in a breath. "If you don't stop this instant and let me go—"

Abruptly, he did both. She'd been strolling along the periphery of the fashionable throng; they were now in an area where no others were walking. They were out of earshot of everyone, too far from the carriageway for any to discern even the tenor of their exchange.

On top of that, he stood squarely between her and the rest of the ton. Cutting her off from the world. Stunned, she raised her eyes to his face.

His black gaze impaled her. "What was Ruskin blackmailing you about?"

She blinked; her eyes grew wide. The world lurched and fell away. "Wh—what?"

He gritted his teeth. "Ruskin was blackmailing you. About *what*?" His eyes narrowed to obsidian shards. "What was the hold he had over you?"

When she didn't answer, couldn't get her wits to stop whirling quickly enough—dear God, how had he found out?—his jaw set even harder. From the corner of her eye, she saw his hands clench; locking eyes, she sensed he wanted to seize her, shake her, but was exercising quite amazing restraint.

"Was. He. Blackmailing you?"

The words were uttered with such force they dragged the answer from her. "Yes—*no*! That is . . ." She stopped.

"Which?" He took a half step nearer, towering over her, menacing, intimidating. Aggression poured from him.

And ignited her temper. She straightened to her full height, tipped back her head, met his piercing black gaze. "Whichever, it is *no* concern of yours."

"Think again."

The low growl skittered over her nerves; she dug her heels in even deeper. "I beg your pardon?" Outraged, she held his gaze, absolutely determined not to quail. "You, my lord, are skating on thin ice. Don't *think* to browbeat me!"

For an instant, they stood, all but toe to toe, certainly will against will, then, to her surprise and immense relief, he eased back. Reined in the sheer male power that beat against her senses.

Yet he didn't shift back; his eyes didn't leave hers. When he spoke, his tone was dark, definite, but harnessed, fractionally more civilized.

"I've been asked to investigate Ruskin's death. I want to know what your connection with him was."

She stared. "Why? *Who*—?"

"Just answer the question. What was your connection with Ruskin?"

She felt the blood drain from her face. "We didn't have any—I told you!"

"Yet he was blackmailing you."

"No—at least, not in the way you mean."

He opened his eyes wide. "What other way is there?"

She had to reply; there was clearly no option. "It wasn't about money. He wanted me to marry him."

He blinked. His tone lost a little of it sureness. "He was blackmailing you to marry him?"

Lips tight, she nodded. "He . . . offered me a *carte blanche*. I refused, and he offered marriage. When I refused that . . . he thought to pressure me into agreeing."

"With what?"

She searched his eyes; his demand was precise, implacable. Who was he?—she didn't really know. "He'd learned something about us— about me—that if it became common knowledge, would make establishing Adriana . . . very difficult. It's nothing nefarious or terrible, but you know what the gossipmongers are like."

"Indeed." The word was clipped, imbued with meaning. "You spoke with him immediately before he left Lady Amery's drawing room. I want to know what was said, and exactly what happened to result in you going into the garden and finding his body."

Whoever he was, he knew far too much. The thought chilled her. He also knew how to interrogate; even restrained, there was a threat in his manner—avoiding his questions wasn't going to be possible. She had absolutely no doubt his claim of being asked to investigate was true.

"I . . ." Her mind slid back to that moment in the drawing room, when Ruskin had threatened to pull the rug from under their future. "As I said, I'd declined his offer of marriage. That evening, he came up and requested a private interview. I refused—I was watching Adriana. He insisted, so we retreated to the side of the room. He told me he lived near Bledington, and had seen us last Christmas, in the square at Chipping Norton."

She refocused on the black eyes fixed so intently on her face. "He'd seen us—we hadn't seen or met him. Not then. Only after we came to London."

"What was it he knew of you?"

Feeling compelled to keep her eyes on his, she considered, eventually moistened her lips. "It's not anything to do with his death. It can't be. It doesn't concern anyone but me."

Tony held her gaze for a full minute; she didn't waver, didn't offer anything more. She was no longer so defiant, but on that one point intractable; she wasn't going to tell him. He forced himself to look away, over her head, forced himself to take a deep breath and think. Eventually, he looked down at her. "Does anyone else in London know of this *thing* that Ruskin knew?"

She blinked, thought. "No." Her voice strengthened. "No one."

He digested that, accepted it. "So he propositioned you—threatened you with exposure." He forced himself to say the words, ignoring the violence the thought evoked. "What then?"

"I asked for time, and he agreed to twenty-four hours. He said he'd call on me the next evening." Remembered horror flitted through her eyes; he wondered what she wasn't telling him. "Then he walked away."

When she said nothing more, he prompted, "What then?"

"I was upset." She seemed not to notice the hand she raised to her throat. "I asked for a glass of water, sat, then I started to think again, and realized he . . . that it might be possible to buy him off. I stood and saw him slip out of the terrace doors. I decided to follow and speak with him—at least convince him to give me more time."

Remembered fear tinged her voice. Swallowing an oath, he suppressed the urge to haul her into his arms; she'd probably struggle. "So you followed him out?"

She nodded. "But first I crossed the room to Adriana. I told her where I was going."

"Then you went onto the terrace?"

"Yes, but he wasn't there. It was chilly—I looked around and saw movement beneath that huge tree. I assumed it was he, so I went down. Then I found him . . ." She paused. "You know the rest."

"Did you see anyone else go out on the terrace before you did—or before Ruskin did?"

"No. But I wasn't watching the doors."

Regardless, it was unlikely a gentleman wearing a coat and hat would leave Amery House via the drawing room and the terrace doors. Fitting her information with his, it seemed clear what had happened.

She'd taken advantage of his silence to regroup.

He met her gaze. "I take it Ruskin made no mention of going to meet anyone."

"No. Why? Oh . . . I suppose he must have met someone."

"He did. As I came up Park Street, I saw a gentleman in a coat and hat leave by the garden gate. He was too far away for me to identify, but he definitely came out of that gate. Allowing time for you to walk to the tree, and for me to walk to the gate, it must have been he—that man—you saw moving beneath the tree."

She paled. Looked at him, stared at him. After a long moment, she asked, "Who are you?"

He let two heartbeats pass, then replied, "You know my name."

"I know I have only your word that there was another man, that it wasn't you who stabbed Ruskin."

The accusation pricked; holding her gaze, he softly said, "You might want to consider that I'm all that stands between you and a charge of murder."

The instant he uttered the words, he wished them unsaid.

Her head snapped up. She stepped back. "I do not understand what right you have to question me—interrogate me—*or my family*." Her eyes blazed; her tone was scathing. "In future, please leave us alone."

She turned.

He caught her hand. "Alicia—"

She swung on him; fury lit her eyes. "*Don't* presume to call me that! I have *not* given you leave—and I won't." She looked down at his fingers circling her wrist. "Please release me immediately."

He had to force his fingers to do it, to slide from her skin; she snatched her hand away, backed two steps, watching him—as if she suddenly saw him for what he truly was.

Her eyes had widened; for an instant, he glimpsed a vulnerability he couldn't place.

Alicia fought to subdue the emotions roiling inside her. Her stomach was knotted, her lungs tight. He'd played with her brothers, interrogated them and Adriana, flirted quite deliberately with her. All because . . . and she'd thought he was honest, that he was trustworthy, genuine . . . how foolish she'd been.

When he said nothing, she dragged in a breath. "I've told you all I know. Please"—for the first time, her voice quavered—"don't come near me again."

With that, she whirled and walked quickly away.

Tony watched her go. Then he swore comprehensively in French and strode off in the opposite direction.

He hailed a hackney and headed into the city. Resting his head against the squabs, he closed his eyes and concentrated on getting his temper under control and his thoughts straight; it had been years since they'd been so tangled.

He'd stalked into the park furious with her for concealing from him such a potentially dangerous connection. Not because that concealment interfered with his investigation, but purely because the damned woman hadn't availed herself of his abilities—his protection.

Because she deliberately hadn't trusted him.

Stalking out of the park, he'd been furious with himself. She'd questioned who he was, his integrity, and he'd reacted by taking a high hand, which any fool could have predicted would fail miserably—in his case, spectacularly.

He hadn't meant it to sound as it had, hadn't in the least meant to threaten her.

Eyes still closed, he sighed. In thirteen years of operations, he'd never let his personal life interfere with his duty. Now the two were inextricably entwined. She hadn't killed Ruskin, but courtesy of whoever had started the rumors, she was now involved. Worse, he had a nasty suspicion that the person who had started the rumors would prove to be Ruskin's killer. If threatened, he might kill again.

He spent the rest of the day in the city, using his erstwhile talents to gain access to Ruskin's banking records. A combination of suggestion and implied threat, together with his title and the supercilious arrogance he'd learned long ago worked so well with those whose status depended on patronage, got him what he wanted.

His first stop was Daviot & Sons, the bank Ruskin had favored, exclusively as far as the notes in his rooms went. Ten minutes, and he'd gained access to all documents relating to Ruskin's dealings. The records revealed no major sums credited to Ruskin's account, only a trickle of income the bank verified came from Gloucestershire, believed to be derived from Ruskin's estate. There were no large deposits, nor any large withdrawals. Wherever the wealth Ruskin had used to pay off his considerable debts hailed from, it had not passed through the hands of the Messrs Daviot.

He proceeded to check all the likely banks; they were located in close proximity, scattered about the Bank of England and the Corn Exchange. Using his success at Daviots to pave the way, he encountered no resistance; by afternoon's end, he'd established that the city's legitimate financiers had not facilitated the flow of pounds to Ruskin's gaming acquaintances.

Hailing a hackney, he headed back to Mayfair. On the evidence of Ruskin's IOUs, the man had been not only a poor gambler but an addicted one. He'd lost steadily for years, yet there was no indication of any panic in his dealings. He'd paid off every debt *regularly* . . .

Muttering a curse, Tony tapped on the roof; when the jarvey inquired his pleasure, he replied, "Bury Street—Number 23."

There had to be—*had to be*—some record somewhere. Ruskin was a clerk by nature; the contents of his desks, both in his office and his rooms, testified to his compulsive neatness. He'd even kept those old IOUs in chronological order.

The hackney halted in Bury Street; Tony swung down to the pavement, tossed a coin to the jarvey, and strode quickly up the steps of Number 23. This time, an old man let him in.

"I'm from Customs and Revenue—I have to check Mr. Ruskin's rooms for something I might have missed when I checked yesterday."

"Oh, aye." The old man stood back. "You'll know the way, then."

"Indeed. I have his key. I'll be a few minutes—I can see myself out."

The old man merely nodded and shuffled back into the downstairs front room. Tony climbed the stairs.

Once in Ruskin's rooms with the door shut and relocked, he stood in the center of the rug and looked around. He imagined himself in Ruskin's shoes; assuming he'd kept a record of his illicit dealings and had wanted to keep that record secret, where would he have hidden it?

The room was clean, neat, dusted; the furniture was polished and well cared for. Someone came in to clean. Whatever secret hole Ruskin had, it would be somewhere not likely to be found by a busy char woman.

Behind the solid skirting boards was unlikely; the cleared floor space, even under the rugs, would be too risky. Working as silently as he could, Tony shifted the heavy furniture and checked beneath and behind, but found only solid walls and solid floorboards, and dust.

Undeterred, he checked inside the small closet, shifting the items he'd searched before. He pressed, prodded, gently tapped, but there was no hint of any secret place. Next, he examined the door and window frames, searching for any crevice opening into a useful gap within the walls. There wasn't one.

Which left the fireplaces and their chimneys.

There were two—one in the parlor and a smaller one in the bedroom. The mantelpieces and hearths were easily examined; no luck there. With a resigned sigh, Tony stripped off his coat and rolled up his shirtsleeves before tackling the chimneys.

He saw the place as soon as he crouched down, ducked his head, and looked into the parlor chimney. Enough light seeped past his shoulders for him to discern the single brick, up on the side well above the flames' reach, that was considerably less grimed than its fellows. Its edges were free of soot and the detritus of years. Reaching in, he pressed one corner; the brick edged out of place. It was easy to grip it and drag it free.

Setting the brick down, he dusted his fingers, then reached into the gaping hole. His fingertips encountered the smooth surface of leather. He felt around, then drew out a small, black leather-bound book.

Grinning, he laid the book on the floor and replaced the brick. That done, he cleaned his hands on his handkerchief, then rolled down his sleeves and shrugged on his coat. Picking up the book, he hefted it—then gave in to temptation and quickly leafed through it.

It was exactly what he'd hoped to find—a miniledger that many gamesters kept, noting their wins and losses. The book was almost full; the entries stretched back to 1810. Each entry comprised a date, the initials of the opponent, and sometimes the name of the game—whist, piquet, hazard—and the sum involved; the latter was placed in one of two columns ruled at the right of the page—either a loss or a win.

In Ruskin's little black book, the losses greatly outnumbered the wins. However, the tally of wins and losses, scrupulously noted at the end of each page, was readjusted every few months, being brought back into balance by an entry, repeated again and again, of a substantial sum, noted as a win.

Tony checked back through the book. The regular "wins" started in early 1812. Although always substantial, the sums varied; the initials noted for each payment did not.

A. C.

Tony felt his face harden. He looked up. His mind in a whirl, he closed the book and slid it into his pocket. A moment later, he stirred, and headed for the door.

He was on his way down the stairs when the old man stuck his head out of the downstairs room. He squinted at Tony, then recognized him, nodded, and moved to retreat.

Tony reacted. "One moment, sir, if you would."

The old man turned back.

Tony assumed a faintly harrassed expression. "Have there been any other visitors to Mr. Ruskin's rooms since he died?"

The old man blinked, thought, then opined, "Well, not since you folk came by, but there was a gentl'man called here the night Mr. Ruskin met his end. It was late, so mayhap that was after he died."

"This gentleman, was he one of Mr. Ruskin's friends? A regular acquaintance?"

"Not that I ever saw. Never seen him before."

"What happened on that night?"

The old man leaned on his cane; he peered up at Tony with eyes that retained a deal of shrewdness. "It was late, as I said. The man rapped politely, and as it wasn't after midnight, I let him in. I was sure Ruskin was out, but the gentleman insisted he'd go up and check . . . didn't seem any harm in that, so I let him. He went up the stairs, and a minute later I heard the door open, so I thought, then, that Ruskin must have slipped in, and I hadn't noticed. I left them to it and went back to my fire."

Tony stirred. "Ruskin hadn't come home. He spent most of the evening at a soirée in Green Street. It was there, in the garden, that he was killed."

"Aye. So we heard the next day. Howsoever, that night, the gentleman that called and went into Ruskin's rooms stayed for more than an hour. I could hear him moving around; he wasn't thumping about, but it's quiet around here at night. One hears things."

"Did you see him when he left?"

"No—I'd put the door on the latch and gone to bed. They can still let themselves out, but the door locks as it closes."

"Can you describe this gentleman?"

Running his eye up Tony, the old man grimaced. "I can't recall much—no reason to, then. But he was decently tall, not so tall as you though, but more heavily built. Well built. He was nicely kitted out, that I do remember—his coat had one of those fancy fur collars, like rippling curls."

Astrakhan. A vision flashed into Tony's mind—the glimpse he'd caught at a distance as the unknown man leaving the Amery House gardens had passed beneath a streetlamp. His thought had been "well rugged up"—prompted by the astrakhan collar of the man's coat.

"And," the old man continued, "he was a toff like you. Spoke well, and had that way about him, the way he walked and carried his cane."

Tony nodded. "How old? What color hair? Was there anything notable about him—a squint, a big nose?"

"He'd be older than you—forties at least, but well kept. His hair was brownish, but as for his face, there was nothing you'd notice. Regular features"—the old man squinted again at Tony—"though not as regular as yours." He shrugged. "He was a well-dressed gentl'man such as you'd find on any street about here."

Tony thanked the man.

Once on the pavement, he paused, then set off for Upper Brook Street; the walk would do him good, perhaps clear his mind. An A. C. had paid Ruskin large sums for the last four years. Be that as it may, he was perfectly certain things were not as they seemed.

A few hours closeted in his library clarified matters, at least as far as identifying his immediate next steps.

Through Ruskin's blackmail and fateful coincidence, Alicia Carrington was being drawn further and further into his investigation. Given his personal interest, he needed to regain lost ground rapidly—needed to regain her trust. Doing so would require an apology, and worse, explanations. All of which necessitated a certain amount of planning, which in turn required a certain amount of reconnoitering. His groom returned from the mews near Waverton Street with the necessary details, by which time he'd formulated his plan.

He began its implementation with a note to his godmother, then sent a different note around to Manningham House.

When the clocks struck nine, he and Geoffrey were propping the wall of Lady Herrington's ballroom, keeping a careful eye on the arrivals.

"I would never have thought of sending around a groom." Eyes on the throng, Geoffrey seemed to be relishing his role.

"Stick with me, and you'll learn all sorts of useful tricks." Tony kept his gaze on the ballroom stairs.

Geoffrey softly snorted.

The strands of old companionship had regrown quickly, somewhat to the surprise of them both. Tony was four years Geoffrey's senior; much of their childhood had been colored by Geoffrey's need to cast himself as Tony's rival. Despite that, there'd been many occasions when they'd combined forces in various devilry; the friendship beneath the rivalry had been strong.

"There they are." Tony straightened. At the top of the steps, he'd glimpsed a coronet of dark hair above a pale forehead.

Geoffrey craned his head. "Are you sure?"

"Positive." Which was of itself revealing. "Remember—the instant they reach the bottom of the steps. Ready?"

"Right behind you."

They swooped as planned, a perfectly executed attack that separated Alicia and Adriana the instant the sisters set foot on the ballroom floor. Geoffrey took Adriana's hand—offered with a delighted smile—and smoothly cut in, drawing Adriana forward while simultaneously insinuating himself between the sisters, cutting Alicia off from Adriana's immediate view.

Before Alicia could even gather her wits, she was captured, swept aside; Tony propelled her across the front of the ballroom steps and around into their lee, where a small and as yet uncrowded little foyer stood before a closed door.

They'd reached the foyer before she caught her breath.

Then she did. Her eyes swung to his face. They blazed.

He caught that scorching glance, held it. Her breasts swelled; her lips parted—on a scathing denunciation he had not a doubt. "*Don't* fight me." He spoke softly; there was steel in his voice. "Don't look daggers at me, and for God's sake don't rip up at me. I *have* to talk to you."

Her jaw set mulishly. She tugged her right arm, firmly gripped in his right hand; his left arm was around her waist, steering her on. She tried to stop, to dig in her heels, but she was wearing ballroom slippers. "If we must, we can talk here!"

He didn't pause, but looked down at her, leaned closer, drawing her into the shield of his body. "No, we can't. You wouldn't like it, and neither would I."

He released her arm to fling open the door, catching her in his left arm when she tried to step back. He swept her over the threshold and followed, shutting the door behind him, by sheer physical presence forcing her on along the corridor beyond.

She hissed in frustration, took two steps, then swung to face him and glared. "This is ridiculous! You can't simply—"

"Not here." He caught her arm again, propelled her on. "The door on the left at the end is our best bet."

He could sense her temper rising, seething like a volcano. "Our best bet for *what*?" she muttered beneath her breath.

He glanced at her, but held his tongue.

They reached the door in question; he sent it swinging wide. This time, she entered of her own volition, sweeping in like a galleon under full sail. He followed, shutting the door, taking note of her gown—a sleekly draped silk confection in bronzy, autumnal shades that became her extremely well.

She turned on him, faced him; the silk tightened over her breasts as she dragged in a deep breath—

He heard a click as the door at the head of the corridor opened. The noise of the ball washed in, abruptly cut off again as the door was shut. A woman giggled, the sound quickly smothered.

Reaching behind him, he snibbed the lock on the door.

Too far from the corridor to realize the danger, eyes blazing, Alicia opened her mouth to deliver the broadside he undoubtedly deserved.

He stepped forward, jerked her into his arms, and silenced her—saved them—in the only possible way.

Five

He kissed her.

Her mouth had been open, her lips parted; he slid between, caressed, claimed—and felt her attention splinter. Her hands had gripped his upper arms; they tensed, but she didn't push him away. She clung, held on.

As a whirlpool of want rose up and engulfed them.

He hadn't intended it, had had no idea how much he wanted, how much hunger he possessed, or how readily it would rise to her lure. Hands framing her face, he angled his head and flagrantly feasted. Asking for no permission, giving no quarter, he plunged them both into the fire. She was a widow, not a skittish virgin; he didn't need to explain things to her.

Such as the nature of his want. His tongue tangling with hers, aggressively plundering, he released her face and gathered her to him. Into his arms, against his hard frame. Glorying in the supple softness that promised to ease his ache, he molded her to him, blatantly shifted his hips against hers. He felt her spine soften as she sank into him.

As her bones melted and her knees gave way.

Alicia struggled to cling to her wits, but time and again he ripped them away. Her breath was long gone; with their mouths melded she could only breathe through him—she'd given up the fight to do otherwise.

Her head spun—pleasurably. Warmth, burgeoning heat, spread through her veins. Intoxicating. Shocking. She tried to cling to her anger, rekindle her fury, but could not.

She'd had only a second's warning, but she'd expected a kiss—a touching of lips, not this ravenous, flagrantly intimate exchange. Mild kisses she could cope with, but this? It was new territory, unknown and dangerous, yet she couldn't—*could not*—let her innocence, her inexperience show.

No matter how much her senses swam, how much her wits had seized in sheer shock.

She had nothing to guide her but him. In desperation, she mimicked the play of his tongue against hers, and sensed his immediate approval. In seconds, they were engaged in a duel, in a sensual game of thrust and parry.

Of lips and tongues, of heated softness and beguiling aggression, of shared breaths and, amazingly, shared hunger.

It caught her, dragged at her mind. Drew her in. Held her captive.

He urged her closer still, one hand sliding down her back to splay over her hips, her bottom, lifting her and pressing her to him.

Sensation streaked over her skin, prickling, heated; she clung tight, felt the world whirl.

And she was engulfed in his strength, enveloped by it, a potent masculine power that seemed to weaken every bone in her body, that promised heat and flames so dizzyingly pleasurable all she wanted was to wantonly wallow, to give herself up to them and be consumed.

On one level it was frightening, but she couldn't retreat—had wit enough left to know she couldn't panic, couldn't run.

She was supposed to be a widow. She had to stand there, accept all, and respond as if she understood.

Eventually his aggression eased, the tension riding him gradually, step by step, reined in. Gripping his arms, fingers sunk deep, she felt that drawing back; the kiss lightened, became a more gentle if still intimate caress, lips clinging, teasing, still wanting.

At last he raised his head, but not far.

Her lips felt swollen and hot; from beneath her lashes, she glanced at his eyes. His black gaze touched her eyes, held, then he sighed. Bent and touched his lips to the corner of hers.

"I didn't intend this. There were people in the corridor. A danger . . ."

Deep, gravelly, the words feathered her cheek; sensation, hot and immediate, flashed over her.

"I wanted to apologize . . ." He paused, raised his head. Again she met his eyes, again found them waiting to capture hers. Something predatory flashed in the rich blackness, then he continued, "Not for this. Not for anything I've done or even said, but for how what I said in the park sounded."

His tone was still low, slightly rough, teasing something—some response—from her.

Her gaze had drifted to his lips; his hands tightened on her back, and she looked up, eyes widening as she felt the heat between them flare again.

He caught her gaze, held it. "I'm not Ruskin. I will never hurt or harm you. I want to protect you, not threaten you." He hesitated, then went on, "Even this—I didn't plan it."

This. He was still holding her close, not as tight as before yet just as flagrantly. Only lovers, she was perfectly certain, should ever be this close. Yet she didn't dare pull back, fought instead to ignore the warm flush the embrace sent coursing through her. What had gone before no longer seemed terribly relevant.

"So—" She broke off, shocked by the sound of her voice, low, almost sultry. She moistened her lips, tried for a normal tone. Didn't quite manage it. "What had you planned?" She met his eyes, clung to her bold front.

He studied her face, then his lips twisted. "I spoke the truth—I do need to speak with you."

He made no move to release her. How would an experienced widow react? She forced herself to remain passive in his arms and raised a haughty brow. "About what? I wasn't aware we had anything to discuss."

One black brow arched—arrogantly; holding her gaze, he deliberately shifted her against him, settling her in his arms—sending her senses reeling again. "Obviously"—he gave the word blatant weight—"there's much we could, and later will, discuss. However . . ."

The room, a small parlor overlooking the gardens, was unlit, but her eyes had adjusted—she could see his face well enough. Although he didn't physically sigh, she sensed his mind lift from them and refocus on something beyond. A frown in his eyes, he looked down at her, studied her face.

"When did you marry Carrington?"

She stared at him. "Marry?"

His frown grew more definite. "Humor me. When was your wedding?"

"Ah." She struggled to remember when it must have been. "Eighteen months—no, more like two years ago, now."

She dragged in a breath, struggled to ignore the way her breasts pressed into his chest, how her nipples tightened, and dragooned her wits into order. He was investigating Ruskin's death; she couldn't afford to prod his suspicions. "It was a very short marriage. Poor Alfred—it was terribly sad."

His brow arched again. "So you've been Alicia Carrington for only two years?"

She checked her calculations. "Yes." She bit her tongue against adding anything more; better to keep her answers short.

He didn't seem to notice; he seemed, not exactly relieved, but pleased. "Good!"

When she looked her surprise, he smiled rather grimly. "So you can't be A. C."

"Who's A. C.?"

"The person who paid Ruskin for his treasonous services."

She stared at him. Her lips formed the word twice before she managed to utter it. *"What?"*

Tony grimaced. He looked around. "Here." Reluctantly releasing her, he steered her to a chaise. "Sit down, and I'll tell you."

It hadn't come easily, his acceptance that if he wanted her trust, he would have to tell her, if not all, then at least most of what was going on, how he was involved, how she was involved—how she was threatened. He needed her cooperation for reasons that struck much deeper than his mission; that mission—his investigation—was a whip he could use to command her, but only one thing would suffice to make her trust him. To lean on him as he wished her to.

Appeasement—a peace offering, some gift on his part—was the only way to nudge her onto the path he'd chosen. The most important element between them right now was the truth; as far as he was able, he would give her that.

He waited while, with a suspicious and wary glance, she sat and settled her skirts, then he sat beside her and took her hand in his. Looked down, played with her fingers as he assembled his words.

Then, keeping his voice low yet clear enough for her to easily hear, he told her simply, without embellishment, all he'd learned of Ruskin.

She listened, increasingly attentive, but made no comment.

But when he came to how and where he'd discovered the initials A. C., her fingers tensed, tightened on his. He glanced at her.

She studied his eyes, searched his face. Then she breathed in tightly. "You know I didn't kill him—that I'm innocent of all this?"

Not so much a question as a request for a clear statement.

"Yes." He raised her hand to his lips, held her gaze as he kissed. "I know you didn't kill him. I know you're not involved in any treasonous use of shipping information." He lowered their locked hands, then added, "However, you—we—have to face the fact that *someone* started the rumor I heard."

"I can't understand it—*how* could anyone know?"

"Are you sure, absolutely sure, that your secret, whatever it is, was known only by Ruskin?"

Frowning, she met his gaze, then looked away. Her hand remained resting in his. After a moment, she replied, "It might be possible that, in the same way Ruskin had learned what he had, then someone else might have, too. But what I can't understand is how that someone could know Ruskin was using the information as he was."

She looked at him.

"Indeed. Blackmail doesn't work if others know." He paused, then added, "From what I've learned of Ruskin, he wasn't the sort to give away valuable information. He'd have charged for it, and—"

Releasing her hand, he stood; he thought better on his feet. "The dates of payments noted in his black book not only match the dates he paid his debts, but also follow by about a week the dates he noted for certain ships." He paced, caught her eye. "However, there's no other payment—any unaccounted payment—entered. So I think we're on firm ground in assuming he hadn't sold any information other than the shipping directives."

Halting by the fireplace, he considered her. "So the question remains. Who would he have told about you, and why?"

Her brow creased as she looked at him; her gaze grew distant.

"What?"

She flicked him an impatient glance. "I was just wondering . . ."

When he moved toward her, she quickly continued, "When he left me, Ruskin was sure—absolutely confident—that I'd agree to his proposal. He"—she paused, blushed, but lifted her head and went on—"was so certain he expected to call the next evening and . . . receive my acceptance."

After a moment, she met his eyes. "I didn't know him well, but given his nature, he probably couldn't help gloating. About me—I mean, about gaining a wealthy widow as his wife."

Tony could visualize such a scenario readily, but he doubted it was her wealth Ruskin would have gloated about. Nevertheless . . .

"That would fit." He paced again. "If Ruskin, quite unsuspectingly, mentioned his coup—and yes, I agree, he was the type of man to gloat, then . . ." Bits and pieces of the jigsaw slid into place.

"What?"

He glanced at her, and found her glaring at him; he felt his lips ease. "Consider this. If Ruskin was murdered by whoever he'd been selling his information to—"

"By this A. C., you mean?"

He nodded. "Then if he mentioned he was about to marry, quite aside from any risk from the blackmail going wrong—it's always a risky business—the knowledge that Ruskin would soon have a wife would have increased the threat Ruskin posed to A. C."

"In case he told his wife?"

"Or she found out. Ruskin even mentioning knowing A. C., even years from now, might have been dangerous."

Alicia pieced together the picture he was painting. At one level, she could barely believe all that had happened since they'd entered the room. That searing kiss—it was as if it had cindered, felled, and consumed all barriers between them. He was talking to her, treating her, as if she was an accomplice, a partner in his investigation. More, a friend.

Almost a lover.

And she was reacting as if she were.

She was amazed at herself. She didn't—never had—trusted so readily. Yet if she was honest, it was why she'd been so furious with him in the park, when, despite her totally unwarranted trust—one he'd somehow earned in a few short days—it had seemed his interest in her and her family had all been fabricated. False.

That kiss hadn't been false.

It had been a statement, unplanned maybe, but once made, it couldn't be retracted—and he hadn't tried. It had happened, and he'd accepted it.

She had no choice but to do the same.

Especially as she, innocent or not, was being drawn deeper and deeper into the web of intrigue surrounding Ruskin's murder.

"Is this what you think happened?" She didn't look up, but sensed his attention fasten on her. "Presumably the man—let's assume he's A. C.—had arrived in the Amery House gardens via the garden gate. Ruskin went out to meet him—it had to have been an arranged meeting."

Torrington—Tony—drew nearer. "Yes."

"So then Ruskin babbled about his soon-to-be conquest—me—but . . ." Frowning, she glanced up. "Had Ruskin some information to sell, or had A. C. come there with murder on his mind?"

Tony mentally reviewed all Ruskin's notes on shipping. None had been recent. Even more telling . . . "I don't think there could be anything worthwhile for Ruskin to sell. With the war over, the information he had access to wouldn't be all that useful. . . ."

He was aware of her watching him, trying to read his face, follow his thoughts. He glanced at her. "I haven't yet defined how the information Ruskin passed on was used, but it's telling his association with A.C. began in early '12. That was when naval activity once again became critical. From '12 up until Waterloo, shipping was constantly under threat. Now, however, there is no significant danger on the seas."

He was going to have to pursue that angle hard, and soon.

She took up the tale before he could. "If Ruskin no longer had anything of real use to A.C., then . . ." She looked up at him.

He met her gaze. "A.C., assuming he has a position and reputation to protect, would have been threatened by Ruskin's continued existence."

"If Ruskin was not above blackmailing me . . ."

"Indeed. He may not have called it by that name, but given his debts, he would have needed an injection of capital quite soon, and almost certainly would have looked to A.C."

"Who decided to end their association." She nodded. "Very well. So while Ruskin is gloating, A.C. stabs him and leaves him dead. I come down the path—" She paled. "Do you think A.C. saw me?"

He considered, then shook his head. "The timing—when I saw him on the street—makes that unlikely."

"But then how did he know it was me Ruskin was blackmailing? Would Ruskin have told him my name?"

"Unlikely, but A.C.—and I agree, it most likely was he—didn't need your name to start the rumors."

She frowned at him. "These rumors—what exactly do they say?"

"That Ruskin was blackmailing some lady—a widow."

Her frown deepened. "But there are many widows in the ton."

"Indeed, but only one was seen talking to Ruskin immediately before he died."

Her gaze remained locked with his, then, abruptly, all color drained from her face. "Oh, good heavens!"

She sprang to her feet; her eyes flashed fire at him as if he was in some way culpable. "If they've decided I'm the widow in question, then what . . . ? *Good lord! Adriana!*"

Whirling, she raced for the door. He got there before her, closing his hand about the knob. "It's all right—calm down!" He caught her gaze as she paused, impatient before the door. "Manningham's with her."

Her eyes flashed again. "You and he planned this."

He tried to frown her down. "I had to talk to you."

"That's all very well, but what's been happening out there"—she jabbed a finger toward the ballroom—"while we've been talking?"

"Nothing. Most will be waiting, wondering where you are, hoping to catch a glimpse but not surprised given the crush that they haven't yet succeeded." He took in her wide eyes, the tension now gripping her. "There's no need to panic. They don't know it's you, and they only will know if you behave as if it is. As if you're frightened, or watchful. Ready to take flight."

Alicia met his steady gaze. To her surprise, she drew comfort from it. She drew in a breath. "So I have to carry it off with a high head and a high hand?"

"Absolutely. You can't afford to let those hyenas sense fear."

Despite all, her lips twitched. Hyenas? The hard line of his lips eased; she realized he'd deliberately tried to make her smile.

Then his gaze flicked up to her eyes.

He lowered his head—slowly; she sucked in a breath.

Held it as her lids fell and his lips touched hers—not in a tantalizing teasing caress, yet neither with their earlier ravenous hunger.

A definite promise; that's what the kiss was—as simple as that.

Slowly, he raised his head; their lips clung for an instant, then parted.

Lifting her lids, she met his black gaze.

He searched her eyes, then turned the knob and opened the door. "Come. Let's face down the ton."

She returned to the ballroom on his arm, calm, her usual poise to the fore. It was all a sham, but she was now an expert in the art of pulling wool over the ton's collective eyes.

One thing he'd said stuck in her mind: watchful. She had to stop herself from looking around, from searching for signs that people suspected her. She had to appear oblivious; it was the most difficult charade she'd ever performed.

He helped. On his arm, she strolled; he was attentive, charming, chatting inconsequentially as two such as they might. He was a wealthy peer; she was a wealthy, wellborn widow. They didn't need to hide a friendship.

They progressed down the room; she smiled, laughed lightly, and let her gaze rest on the dancers but no one else. He distracted her whenever the temptation to scrutinize those watching them burgeoned.

At one point, his lips curved rakishly; he bent his head to whisper, "They're totally confused."

She met his gaze as he straightened. "About what?"

"About which rumor they should spread."

When she looked her question, with a self-deprecatory quirk of his lips he explained, "The one about you and Ruskin, or the one about you and me."

She looked into his black eyes. Blinked. "Oh."

"Indeed. So all we need do is continue on our present tack, and their befuddlement will be complete."

Just which tack he meant she discovered a minute later.

She'd expected him to guide her to Adriana's side; her sister wasn't on the dance floor, which surprised and concerned her—she hadn't yet located her among the crowd. Instead, he led her to a chaise midway down the long ballroom. Lady Amery was seated on it, along with an older lady Alicia had previously met.

Nervousness struck; her fingers fluttered on Tony's sleeve. Instantly, his hand closed, warm and comforting, over hers. Steering her to the chaise, he bowed to the two dames. "*Tante* Felicité. Lady Osbaldestone."

Spine poker straight, Lady Osbaldestone nodded regally back.

"I believe you're both acquainted with Mrs. Carrington?"

Alicia curtsied.

"Indeed." Lady Amery reached for her hands; her eyes glowed with welcome. "My dear, I must apologize for this *dreadful* business. I am most distressed that it was your attendance at *my* soirée that has given rise to such unpleasantness. Why, there are any number of widows in the ton, and as we all know, many of those others are much more certain to have secrets to hide. So foolish of these *bourgeoisie*"—with a contemptuous flick of her hand she dismissed them—"to imagine you had any connection with Mr. Ruskin beyond the natural one of living nearby."

Her ladyship paused; bright eyes fixed on Alicia's face, she surreptitiously pressed her fingers. "Tony tells me you spoke with Mr. Ruskin, but it was purely an exchange about mutual acquaintances in the country."

In the corridor just before they'd reentered the ballroom, he'd primed her with that tale. Alicia longed to turn her head and glare at him; he hadn't mentioned this little encounter he'd arranged for her.

"Indeed." To her relief, the glamor she'd perfected over the last weeks didn't waver; she smiled with easy assurance tempered with just the right touch of innocent bewilderment. "We hail from the same area. Although we only met recently, here in town, we shared a number of mutual acquaintances. It was they we discussed in your drawing room that evening."

Lady Osbaldestone humphed, drawing Alicia's attention. The old black eyes assessing her were a great deal sharper and harder than Tony's ever were. "In that case, you'll have to excuse those with nothing better to do than wag their tongues and make mischief. For my money, they've hay for brains.

"I ask you," she continued, "even if Ruskin was blackmailing some widow, what has that to say to anything?" She gave a dismissive snort. "The idea of some lady in evening dress pulling a stiletto from her reticule and stabbing him to death is ludicrous. Aside from the fact he was no weakling, and would hardly have obligingly stood still while she poked him, where would she have carried the blade?" The black eyes flashed, at Tony as well as Alicia. "That's what I'd like to know. Have you ever seen one of those things? *Pshaw!* It's not possible."

Apparently entertained, Tony inclined his head. "As you say. I heard the authorities are looking for a man at least as tall as Ruskin."

"Indeed?" Lady Osbaldestone brightened at the news. "Not perhaps revealing, but interesting nevertheless." She rose; although she carried a cane, she rarely used it.

She was a tall woman, taller than Alicia; her face had never been pretty, but not even age could dim the strength of its aristocratic lines. Her piercing black eyes rested on Alicia, then her lips lifted, and she looked at Tony. "Send my regards to your mother when next you bestir yourself to write. Tell her Helena sends her fondest wishes, too." Lifting her cane, she jabbed it at him. "Don't forget!"

"Naturally not." Eyes on the cane, Tony bowed with a flourish. "I wouldn't dare."

With a glint in her eye, Lady Osbaldestone regally acknowledged Alicia's bobbed curtsy and Lady Amery's salute, then glided away.

"Well, there you are!" Lady Amery beamed at Tony and Alicia. "It is done, and Therese will do the rest, you may be sure." She lifted a hand, waved it at Tony; he took it and helped her to her feet.

"*Bien!* So now I am going to enjoy myself, too, and see what a stir I can cause." She glanced at Alicia, and patted her arm. "And you must go and dance, and pretend not to notice, and it will all blow over, my dear. You'll see."

Alicia looked into Lady Amery's button-bright eyes, then impulsively squeezed her hand. "Thank you."

Her ladyship's eyes glowed brighter. "No, no, *chérie*. That is not necessary—indeed, it is I who must thank you." Her gaze shifted to Tony. "I am an old woman, and I have been waiting an age to be asked to help. At last it has happened, and you are the cause. It is good." She patted Alicia's hand and released it. "Now go and dance, and I will go and make mischief."

The first strains of a waltz were percolating through the room; Tony offered his arm. "I suspect your sister will be located most easily on the dance floor."

Alicia narrowed her eyes at him, but consented to place her hand on his arm. He steered her to the floor; seconds later they were whirling.

She took a few minutes to adjust, to regain her breath, realign her wits and subdue her clamorous senses. The physical power with which he so effortlessly swept her along, the shift and sway of their bodies, the subtle repetitive temptation of their limbs brushing, touching, then moving away—the waltz was a seduction in itself, at least the way he danced it.

Surreptitiously clearing her throat, she looked up; she studied his expression, arrogant, latent charm lurking, yet difficult to read. "Why did you ask Lady Amery to help?"

He glanced down at her. "She's my godmother. You heard her— she's been waiting for the bugle call for years." He looked ahead, then added, "It seemed appropriate."

"It's *you* she wanted to help, not me."

His lips quirked. "Actually, no—it's *you* she's been waiting all my life to aid."

She frowned and would have pursued the odd point, but a flash of dark curls caught her eye. Turning, she saw Adriana whirling down the room in Geoffrey Manningham's arms. Her sister was . . . the only fitting word was scintillating. She drew eye after male eye, and a good many female ones, too. Her delight seemed to fill her and overflow.

Alicia looked at Tony, caught his eye. "Please tell me your friend is entirely trustworthy."

He grinned; after whirling her through the turns at the end of the room, he dutifully parroted, "Geoffrey is entirely trustworthy." He paused, then added, "At least where your sister's concerned."

"What does that mean?"

"It means he won't do anything you would disapprove of."

She blinked at him. "Why not?"

"Because if he makes you unhappy, then I'll be unhappy, and Geoffrey and I have been down that road before."

She studied his eyes. A vise slowly tightened about her lungs. Then she forced in a breath, lifted her head, fixed her gaze over his left shoulder, and stated, "If you imagine I'll be grateful . . ."

Her courage failed her; she couldn't go on. But he thought her a widow, and clearly had a certain interest, and just possibly imagined. . . .

He frowned at her; from the corner of her eye she watched . . . it took a moment for him to follow her reasoning, then his eyes flared. His lips set in a thin line. The fingers about her hand tightened; the hand at her back tensed . . . then, very slowly, eased.

Eyes narrow, Tony waited; when she didn't look at him, he looked away, unseeing. After a moment, he exhaled. "You are without doubt the most difficult female I've ever—" He bit the words off, abruptly stopped as his temper threatened to erupt. When he had his fury once more in hand, he drew breath and went on, his voice low, tight, very definitely just for her. "I'm not helping you in the expectation of gaining any specific . . ." He cast about in his mind, but could only come up with, *"Service."*

Her eyes flicked to his face, wide, curious, wanting to know.

He trapped her gaze. "I want you, but not as a result of any damned gratitude!"

Her eyes remained on his, then scanned his features. "Why, then"— her voice, too, was low, intensely private—"are you helping me?"

For an instant, he inwardly rocked, then he found the right words—words he could say. "Because you deserve it. Because you and your sister and your demon brothers *don't* deserve the censure of the ton, let alone being implicated in a murder."

For a long moment, she held his gaze, then her lips gently lifted. "Thank you." She looked away; he only just caught her last words. "You're a good man."

He wasn't quite so good as he would have her believe, but he definitely wasn't expecting her gratitude to stretch as far as an invitation to her bed. He *did* expect to be invited to her bed, but not because of his efforts on her behalf.

The next morning, he was still . . . not so much smarting as ruffled, a disordered sensation he appreciated not at all. A vague disgruntlement that she'd even *imagined* that he might *need* to resort to gratitude—

He cut off the thought and headed for the Bastion Club.

Sanity in a disconcerting world—a world with females in it.

He was looking for advice. In the club's drawing room, he found Christian Allardyce slouched in an armchair, his long legs stretched out, ankles crossed, a news sheet propped before his face. He lowered it as Tony entered.

"Ho! And here I've been wondering about these tales of you stumbling over a dead body."

Tony grimaced. "All true, I'm afraid, and there's a deadly twist. The game's fallen into Dalziel's lap, and guess who he's tapped on the shoulder?"

Christian's brows rose. "And you agreed?"

Elegantly sitting in another chair, Tony shrugged. "Aside from the fact that refusing Dalziel is marginally more difficult than taking an enemy battery single-handed, there were other aspects that attracted me."

"Quite apart from tripping over the body."

"Indeed. From what we have, the man was a traitor of sorts." Crisply, he outlined what he knew of Ruskin, omitting all mention of one lovely widow. After describing the payments made by A. C., he went on, "I wondered if perhaps, if A. C. was truly wise, he might have channeled the payments through a moneylender."

Christian opened his eyes wide. "Used a moneylender to draw the large sums, then paid them back with numerous smaller amounts much easier to explain from his own accounts?"

"Exactly. Do you think that's possible?"

Christian nodded. "I would say so." He met Tony's gaze. "Certainly worth asking."

"Next question: who do I ask? I've never had any dealings with such gentlemen."

"Ah! You've come to the right source."

It was Tony's turn to open his eyes wide. "I would never have imagined you deep in debt and reduced to dealing with moneylenders."

Christian grinned and laid aside the news sheet. "No, I never was. But I once bailed out a friend, and along the way I made the acquaintance of a good handful of the gentlemen. Enough, certainly, to start you on your way."

Folding his hands across his waistcoat, Christian leaned his head back; eyes on the ceiling, he started recounting all he knew.

Tony drank it in. At the end of fifteen minutes, he knew exactly who to approach, and even more importantly, how.

Thanking Christian, he left the club and headed into the city.

His interview with Mr. King, the most famous—or infamous depending on one's point of view—usurer in London was an unqualified success. Mr. King's office was a stone's throw from the Bank of England; as Christian had prophesied, Mr. King was perfectly happy to assist the authorities given their investigation in no way threatened him or his trade.

A traitor lost all claim to confidentiality; Mr. King had ascertained that no gentleman with the initials A. C. had borrowed large sums of cash from him. He'd confirmed that the practice of disguising major debts in such a way was not uncommon, and had undertaken to inquire on the government's behalf among the other moneylenders capable of advancing such sums.

Tony parted from Mr. King on genial terms. Hailing a hackney, he headed back to Mayfair. With the money angle in hand, he had two other avenues of inquiry to pursue; as the carriage rocked along, he considered how best to tackle them.

Nearing the fashionable quarter, he glanced out at the pavement. It was a glorious day, ladies walking, children laughing and dancing.

Temptation whispered.

Reaching up, he thumped on the roof, then directed the jarvey to Green Park.

He arrived to an exuberant welcome, and had just enough time to have a quick turn flying the kite before Alicia, feigning primness, gathered them all and herded them back to Waverton Street.

Although he quizzed her with his eyes, she remained spuriously aloof, walking smartly along, the boys skipping about them.

He matched his stride to hers, inwardly amused, not only with her but with himself. It had been a long time—thirteen years at least—since he'd felt so relaxed, experienced this kind of subtle content. He'd honestly enjoyed his time with her brothers; it was almost as if his military years, especially as he'd lived them, had been taken out of his life, excised, so the youth he'd been at nineteen had more in common with the man he had become.

Or perhaps all he'd seen, all he'd experienced in those thirteen years away, had left him with a deeper appreciation of life's little pleasures.

Reaching their house, she opened the door. The boys tumbled in.

"Blackberry jam today!" Matthew sang, and rushed for the stairs.

The older two raced after him, laughing and calling. Jenkins, the kite in his arms, smiled and trudged after them.

Alicia called after him, "Do make sure they're clean before they come down, Jenkins."

"Aye, ma'am." Jenkins looked back. "And I'll let Cook know about tea."

He nodded deferentially to the presence behind her; suddenly realizing, Alicia whirled. "Oh—yes." She met Tony's black eyes; uncertainty flared. "You . . . er, will stay for tea, won't you?"

They were suddenly alone in the hall. He smiled, slowly, into her eyes, then inclined his head. "Blackberry jam's my favorite."

His gaze dropped to her lips; the image that flashed into her mind was of him licking blackberry jam from them. Heat rising in her cheeks, she quickly turned away. "Adriana will be in the parlor."

She led the way, with some relief saw Adriana look up as they entered. Adriana and Tony exchanged easy greetings; as was her habit, Adriana was studying the latest fashion plates prior to designing their next round of gowns.

They all sat; a companionable, almost familial ease fell over them. From her corner of the chaise, Alicia watched as Adriana asked Tony's opinions on various styles depicted in the latest issue of *La Belle Assemblée*. He responded readily; it was quickly apparent he understood more about ladies' garments than one might suppose a gentleman would. . . .

She broke off the thought. His attention was on the plates Adriana had spread before him; she seized the opportunity to study him.

She wished she could see into his mind.

Since they'd parted the previous evening, she'd been plagued by one question: how did he think of her? How did he see her—what were his intentions, his expectations? What direction did he imagine they were headed in?

Given the circumstances, those were not only valid questions; learning the answers was vital to maintaining her charade and succeeding in their aim of having Adriana marry well.

Tony—*Viscount Torrington*—could easily scupper their plans. If he learned of them, and if he so chose. There was, at present, no reason he should stumble on their—her—crucial secret. That secret, however, was precisely the fact that most complicated her way forward.

Along with all the ton, he thought her a widow.

Last night had been a warning. If she was to maintain her charade long enough to establish Adriana, and then disappear, she was going to have to as far as possible restrict her interaction with Torrington.

And what she couldn't avoid, she was going to have to respond to as if she was indeed a widow; she couldn't risk all they'd done, all their success to date, by succumbing to any missish sentiment.

The thunder of feet on the stairs heralded her brothers' arrival. They burst in, full of chatter and exclamations. Jenkins followed with the tray. In seconds, the parlor was filled with rowdy, boisterous warmth and comfort; if anything was needed to remind her why she was playing the role she was, it was there before her in her brothers' smiling, laughing, happy faces.

Torrington—thinking of him by his title helped to keep a sensible distance between them, at least in her mind—gave his attention to the boys, answering questions, joining in their speculations and wonderings, occasionally teasing in a way the boys not only understood and accepted, but took great delight in.

As the guardian of three males, she'd long known they were incomprehensible beings; watching Tony—Torrington!—slouched on the floor, munching a muffin slathered with blackberry jam only compounded her wonder.

He caught her watching; their gazes touched, locked, then he smiled. A fleeting, wholly personal, even intimate gesture, then he looked again to David, who'd posed the question of when the animals in the zoo were most likely fed.

To the boys' disappointment, Tony admitted he didn't know; to their delight, he promised to find out.

It was time to step in. She leaned forward. "Enough, boys! Time for your lessons."

With artistic groans, they clambered to their feet; eyes alight, each shook hands with Tony. Armed with his promise to let them know what he learned with all speed, they left with remarkable alacrity for their books.

Inwardly frowning, Alicia watched them disappear. Jenkins entered and removed the tray.

As he was leaving, Adriana bounced to her feet. "I want to do some sketching. I'll be up in my room."

Before Alicia could think of a suitably worded protest, given he whose presence occasioned that protest was stretched at her feet looking thoroughly at home, Adriana had blithely taken her leave of him, then, without meeting her eyes, her sister whisked out of the room.

And closed the door behind her.

Alicia considered the closed door, then looked at Tony. *Torrington*! He remained on the floor, shoulders against the side of an armchair; his expression gently amused, he raised a brow at her.

She cleared her throat. "Have you learned anything more about Ruskin?" She needed to keep his mind away from her, from his interest in her; his investigation was assuredly her best bet.

His eyes opened a fraction wider. "Yes, and no. I haven't learned anything definite, but I have certain inquiries in train. Whether they bear fruit remains to be seen."

When she waited, pointedly, Tony grinned. "I spent a most illuminating morning learning about moneylenders."

"Moneylenders?" Alarm flared across her face; her hand instinctively rose to her breast.

"Not on my account." He frowned fleetingly at her. "It's not unknown for gentlemen like A. C. to move the large sums they use to pay their informants via moneylenders, thus concealing their part in the transaction. I visited Mr. King this morning, and asked if he knew of any gentleman with the initials A. C. who had borrowed large sums regularly over recent years."

She continued to stare at him; her stillness was strange. "Any gentleman . . ." She drew breath. "I see. And did he?"

"No." Tony studied her, trying to fathom the cause of her reaction. "He had no such borrower on his books. However, he agreed to check with the other moneylenders. Given he's something of an institution in the field, if A. C. has been using moneylenders to cover his tracks, I believe we can rely on Mr. King to unearth him."

She blinked; some of her tension had faded. "Oh." She searched his face, then abruptly rose; with a swish of skirts, she went to stand before the window. "Ruskin's information must have some bearing on this. Presumably A.C. used it to his benefit, or why seek and pay for it?"

"Indeed." His gaze on her, Tony got to his feet, resettled his coat, then approached. "There are other avenues I'm exploring."

His voice warned her; she glanced over her shoulder as he halted behind her, so close she was to all intents and purposes—certainly his intents and purposes—trapped between him and the wide windowsill.

Her eyes widened; she sucked in a quick breath. "What avenues?"

Standing this close, with the perfume of her hair and skin rising, wreathing his senses, his mind wasn't on his investigation. "The shipping is one." He slid one palm across her waist, then splayed his fingers and urged her back against him.

She hesitated, then permitted it, letting him settle her, warm and alive, against him. "How are you going to investigate that?"

The words were thready, starved of breath. He inwardly grinned, and sent his other hand to join the first, anchoring her before him, savoring the supple strength of her beneath his palms, her warmth and the softness of the feminine curves riding against him. "I have a friend, Jonathon Hendon. He and his wife will be in London in a few days."

Bending his head, he set his lips to cruise the fine skin above her temple. "Jonathon owns one of the major shipping lines. If anyone can indentify the likely use of Ruskin's information, Jonathon will."

There was a nervous tension in her he couldn't place, didn't understand.

"So you'll learn what A.C. used the information for from Jonathon?"

Beneath his hands, she stirred. Her pulse had accelerated; her breathing was shallow.

"Not quite." He bent lower, let his breath caress her ear. "Jonathon will be able to say what the information might have been used for, but proving that someone did use it, then following the trail back to that someone won't be quite so simple."

"But . . . it would work."

"Yes. Regardless of how we identify A.C., we'll still need to piece his scheme together. Eventually." He breathed the last word as he set his lips to her ear, then lightly traced with his tongue.

A telltale shudder racked her spine, then she surrendered and sank back against him. Feeling ludicrously victorious, he changed position so he could minister to her other ear.

Her hands closed over his at her waist, gripped. "What other route . . . you said avenues . . . plural . . ."

Her voice faded as he artfully teased; when he lifted his head, she sighed. He grinned openly—wolfishly—knowing she couldn't see. "There'll be some other connection between Ruskin and A.C. They'll have met somewhere, have known each other, even if only distantly. Their lives will have touched somewhere, at some time."

Sliding his hands from under hers, he ran his palms slowly upward. Heard the swift intake of her breath as his thumbs brushed the undersides of her breasts. She stiffened, stilled. He caressed knowingly, reassuringly; gradually, almost skittishly, she eased back.

"How—" She cleared her throat. "How do you plan to investigate . . . that?"

She was having trouble finding breath enough to speak; he decided to make it harder still. "I have a friend, not exactly up that way, but close enough." Boldly turning his hands, he cupped her breasts.

Alicia thought she might faint. Her lungs seized; her head whirled. Desperate, she clung to her wits. Dragged in a tight breath. "Ah . . . what . . . ?"

"I'll ask him to check in Bledington. See if the initials A.C. mean anything to people there."

She jerked as his hands shifted, frantically fought down all further reaction. She hadn't imagined he would . . .

His voice had grown deeper, darker, more gravelly. Would a widow protest? On what grounds?

Giddiness threatened. She hauled in a breath, briefly closed her eyes, battered by conflicting impulses. Panic that his friend might stumble on more than she would wish. The urge to stiffen—not just in response to that, but to his boldness, to the liberties he was taking . . . her head was spinning. The countering instinct to sink against him, to arch her spine, press her breasts, now aching so strangely, into his hard hands only added to her dizziness.

Then he closed his hands and kneaded.

She lost the last of her breath. Her senses fractured. Her wits fled.

Beyond her control, her spine softened, gave; she had to lean fully against him, her hands dropping helplessly to brace against his muscled thighs.

His fingers shifted, then closed again. Tightened.

Fire lanced through her. She gasped, arched; eyes shut, she let her head fall back as he repeated the torture, then he bent his head to her throat, now exposed. His lips cruised, then settled.

Hot, wet, his mouth covered the spot where her pulse raced. He kissed, licked, laved, all the while massaging her breasts, sending wave after wave of pure sensation rushing through her.

Heat built beneath her skin; the rasp of his tongue over her pulse point shocked and teased her senses. His hands were strong, his grip confident, knowing, his body a wall of hard muscle and bone, holding her there, a captive to delight.

To the pleasure even in her innocence she knew he was orchestrating.

She felt totally at his mercy. And witlessly content to be so.

Madness—but an oh-so-pleasurable insanity.

This had to be lovemaking, a part of it, of the type a nobleman indulged in with his mistress.

Illicit. Exciting. Enthralling . . .

The moment for protest was long past. Her role was set; eyes closed, head back, she gave herself up to it—she couldn't draw back now.

Tony was intrigued by her response, with the ardor he sensed beneath her restrained veneer. As he ministered to her senses, learned the curves of her breasts, their weight, their wonder, he cataloged, analyzed, noted for future reference. She was amazingly responsive; her breasts, now sensitive and swollen, filled his hands. She shifted under them, pressing back against him, sirenlike, openly sensuous.

Despite her reserve, an understandable defense for an attractive well-born widow, she couldn't hide her reactions; she understood what lay between them as well as he. The flames that leapt into being at just a touch were more than strong—they were scorching. They could both feel them licking, beckoning, hungry yet held back.

They couldn't take things much further yet, but their time would come. On the physical plane, the path ahead was straightforward, but there was much about her he'd yet to learn.

"Your parents." Releasing her breasts, he nuzzled her ear, gently blew. "When did they die?"

Eyes still closed, Alicia dragged in a breath—it felt like her first in ten minutes. Then she felt a tug at her neckline; opening her eyes, she looked down—to see his long fingers easing the top button of her bodice free. "Ah . . . Mama died almost two years ago."

Good Lord! She had to stop this—had to call a halt. If he touched her . . .

"And your father? From your brothers, I gather he's been gone a long time."

Her mouth was dry; she nodded. "Years and years." Gaze fixed on his busy fingers, she licked her lips.

"And you have no other family? No one close?"

"Ah . . . no." She dragged in a breath. "I really think—"

"You're not supposed to think."

She blinked, lifted her gaze. "Why not?"

"Because"—his fingers were inexorably descending, leaving her bodice gaping—"at the moment, you're supposed to be enjoying, simply feeling. You don't need to think to do that."

He sounded eminently reasonable, even faintly amused; the idea of a missish protest and consequent retreat seemed unwise.

"Have you always lived near Banbury?"

"Ah . . . yes." Once he'd opened her bodice, what did he plan to do?

He shifted behind her, easing back; the realization that she wasn't the only one affected by his play burst across her mind, stealing what few wits she'd managed to reassemble.

"I assume Carrington hailed from that area, too?"

The words sounded distant, vague, but whether that was due to the drumming in her ears, the titillating panic locking her lungs, or because he was no more interested in the subject than she was, she wasn't sure.

A cool wash of air slipped beneath her gaping bodice; she quelled a shiver. His hands drifted down, then fastened about her waist.

"Ah . . . y-yes. He came from there, too."

"How old are your brothers?"

She frowned. "Twelve, ten, and eight." His hands had settled; she gulped in a breath. "Why are you asking all this?"

His fingers gripped, then he stepped back, turned her and stepped forward once more, locking her against the windowsill, his hips to hers, his erection rigid against the softness of her stomach.

He trapped her gaze.

She couldn't think—not at all. Could only stare into his black eyes, and wonder if there really were embers glowing in them. The sheer maleness of him engulfed her; his gaze dropped to her lips—she felt them throb.

His lips quirked, wryly humorous. He released her waist; one hand rose to cup her jaw, angling her face upward as he bent his head. "Because I want to know *all* about you."

His lips closed on hers as his other hand slid boldly beneath her bodice, and closed about her breast.

She gasped, tensed; only a fine layer of silk lay between her sensitized skin and his burning palm. Her breasts instantly felt heavy, swelling, tightening, aching anew.

Then he entered her mouth, possessive and demanding, capturing her attention, insistent and commanding; she scrambled to meet him, to remember how, to play the experienced widow she was pretending to be. The hand on her breast shifted, knowingly cupping, then his fingers toyed with the silk, shifting it over the tightly ruched peak, heightening its excruciatingly sensitive state—then he closed his fingers around the pebbled tip, tugged gently, then tightened, tightened . . .

She tried to break from the kiss, but he wouldn't let her; his hand framing her face, he held her captive. Once again lavished delight and sheer sensual pleasure on her through the play of his lips and tongue, and the even more expert play of his fingers.

He captured her totally. Not just with the heat, with the sudden flare of hot desire, but with something simpler, more fundamental.

His hunger—and hers.

He didn't try to hide his want, his wish to have, to know, to take, to explore, to experience; it was there, laid before her, stated more clearly than in words. A hunger of her own rose in reply, not mere curiosity but something more definite—a need she hadn't known she had.

He angled his head, ravaged her mouth, and she consciously met him. Flagrantly urged him on. His fingers closed again and she shuddered, no longer trying to disguise her response. Her hands rose, of their own volition found his shoulders, then pushed on, around, back, then she speared her fingers into his black hair.

The silken touch of the heavy locks didn't distract, but only added to the tactile experience; her greedy senses, awakened and starved, welcomed and wallowed. His hand shifted on her breast, blatantly possessive; his fingers tightened again—hers clenched in response.

He moved closer, into her, deepening the kiss—and suddenly they were somewhere else, in some place they hadn't been before. Somewhere hotter, more fiery, where their needs escalated and their senses grew ravenous. Clamorous.

Urgent.

It was he who broke the kiss, lifted his head and hauled them free of the fire. Drew them back to earth, back to themselves, to their bodies locked close in the parlor.

To their breaths fast and shallow, to their pulses hammering in their veins. Lids lifting, their gazes locked; in his, the flames still smoldered. Her lips throbbed, appeased yet still hungry.

His gaze fell to them, then lower. To where his hand lay over her breast. He closed that hand, slowly, deliberately. Desire welled and washed down her spine; something inside her clenched tight.

His eyes lifted to hers. "Not here, not now." He bent his head and kissed her, slowly, deeply, intimately, then drew back. "But soon."

His hand left her aching flesh, yet he didn't step back. Instead, his gaze returning to her eyes, trapping her, holding her, he deftly rebuttoned her bodice.

Her head was whirling, but some part of her no longer cared. That part of her that seemed new, different—changed. Or perhaps revealed, called forth. That part of her that thrilled to that decisive "But soon."

She might have thought she was mad, but knew she wasn't. This was a facet of life she'd yet to experience, yet to explore.

As a widow, she couldn't pretend not to understand. The look in his eyes convinced her she'd never succeed in denying what she'd felt, in pretending her hunger didn't exist. He'd seen it, felt it, understood it—almost certainly better than she did.

There was nothing she could say—that she could think of that was safe to say—so she merely held his gaze and, her pulse still thundering, waited to follow his lead.

That seemed an acceptable response. When, stepping back, he quizzed her with his eyes, she merely arched a brow, and saw his lips quirk.

He took her hand, raised it to his lips. "I'll leave you. I'm afraid I won't be attending the Waverleys' ball tonight." He turned to the door; she walked beside him. "I need to consult with some others about the investigation."

He opened the door; she led him into the front hall.

"The rumors concerning you and Ruskin should be fading."

She glanced at him, saw a frown in his eyes. "I'm sure we'll manage."

Her even reply didn't reassure him. "Lady Amery will be attending, and Lady Osbaldestone, too, should you need any support."

Opening the front door, she held it, and looked at him. "I doubt that will be necessary, but I'll bear it in mind."

Pausing by her side, he looked into her eyes. She got the distinct impression he wanted to say something more, something other, but couldn't find the words.

Then he reached out, with the pad of his thumb caressed her lower lip.

It throbbed.

Swiftly, he bent his head, pressed a kiss, hard and definite, to the spot, then he straightened. "I'll call on you tomorrow."

With a nod, he went down the steps.

She stood at the door, watching him walk away, then shut it. She paused, waiting until her nerves steadied and untensed, then, lips firming, she headed for the stairs.

* * *

Alicia tapped on the door of Adriana's bedchamber, then entered.

Sprawled on her bed, her sketchbook before her, Adriana looked up, then smiled. Impishly. "Has he gone?"

"Yes." Alicia frowned as Adriana bounced into a sitting position. "But you shouldn't have left us alone."

"Why ever not?" Adriana grinned. "He was waiting to be alone with you, wasn't he?"

Sitting on the end of the bed, Alicia grimaced. "Probably. Nevertheless, it would be wiser if I didn't spend time alone with him."

"Nonsense! You're a widow—you're *allowed* to be alone with gentlemen." Adriana's eyes sparkled. "*Especially* gentlemen like him."

"But I'm *not* a widow—remember?" Alicia frowned. "And gentlemen like him are dangerous."

Adriana sobered. "Surely not—not him." She frowned. "Geoffrey told me Tony—Torrington—was totally trustworthy. An absolutely to-his-bones honorable gentleman."

Alicia raised her brows. "That may be so, but he thinks I'm a widow. His attitude to me is based on that."

"But . . ." Adriana's puzzlement grew; curling her legs, she shifted closer, studying Alicia's face. "Gentlemen do marry widows, you know."

"Perhaps." Alicia caught her eye. "But how many noblemen marry widows? I don't think that's at all common. And you know what the books said—unless of the nobility herself, a widow is often viewed by gentlemen of the haut ton as a perfect candidate for the position of mistress."

"Yes . . . but the books were warning of the general run of gentlemen, the bucks, the bloods, the—"

"Dangerous blades?" Alicia's lips twisted; reaching out, she squeezed Adriana's hand. "You're not, I hope, going to tell me Tony—Torrington—isn't dangerous."

Adriana pulled a face. "No. But—"

"No buts." Alicia spoke firmly, then stood. "In my estimation, it would be unwise for me to be alone with Torrington in future."

Adriana's eyes, fixed on her face, narrowed. "Did he kiss you?"

Her blush gave her away; she met Adriana's eyes fleetingly. "Yes."

"And?" When she said nothing, Adriana prompted, "How was it? How did it *feel*?"

The word brought back exactly how it had felt; warmth spread beneath her skin, her nipples tightened. One glance confirmed that

Adriana was not going to be deterred. "It was . . . pleasant. But," she quickly added, "indulging in such pleasantness is far too risky."

She could see more questions forming in Adriana's inquisitive mind. "Now that's enough about me." She reverted to her firmest tone. "I intend to avoid Torrington in future. But what about you? You're the reason we're here, after all."

Adriana gazed up at her. After a moment, she said, "I like Geoffrey. He's kind, and funny, and . . ." She drew breath and continued in a rush, "I think he might be the one."

That last was said with an almost stricken look. Alicia sat again. "If you only *think* he might be, perhaps we should cast around a trifle more until you're certain. There are three weeks yet before the Season begins, so you've plenty of time—there's no reason to feel you must reach a decision quickly."

"Indeed." Adriana frowned. "I wouldn't want to make a mistake."

The sisters sat side by side, both staring into space, then Alicia stirred. "Perhaps"—she glanced at Adriana—"to help in deciding, it might be time to ask Mr. King to dine."

Adriana looked at her, then nodded. "Yes." Her chin firmed. "Perhaps we should."

Alicia held her head high, her parasol deployed at precisely the correct angle as the natty barouche she'd hired from the livery stables rolled smoothly onto the gravel of the avenue through the park.

The morning was fine; a light breeze drifted through the branches of the trees, just coming into bud. She and Adriana sat in elegant comfort; on the box before them and clinging behind, the coachman and footman were attired in severe black with bright red ribbons circling the crowns of their hats. That last was Adriana's suggestion, a simple touch to add a hint of exclusivity.

Such things mattered when going about in the ton.

"I still can't get over Lady Jersey being so attentive." Adriana lifted her face to the breeze; her dark curls danced about her heart-shaped face. "She has *such* a reputation, but I thought she was quite nice."

"Indeed." Alicia had her own ideas over what had prompted Lady Jersey's kind words, and those of the other senior hostesses who had found a moment during the Waverleys' ball to stop beside her to admire Adriana and wish them both well. She strongly suspected Lady Amery and her dear friend Lady Osbaldestone had been busy. And she knew at whose behest.

"Oh! There's Lady Cowper." Adriana returned her ladyship's wave.

Alicia leaned forward and directed their coachman to pull up alongside her ladyship's carriage, halted on the verge.

Emily, Lady Cowper, was sweet-tempered and good-natured; she had from the first approved of Mrs. Carrington and Miss Pevensey. "I'm so glad to see you both out and about. The sun is so fickle these days one daren't let an opportunity pass."

"Indeed." Alicia touched fingers; Adriana smiled and bowed. "One can only attend a few balls each night, and there's so many one simply cannot find in the crowds."

Lady Cowper's eyes gleamed. "Especially when so many need to have their notions set straight. But that small *contretemps* seems to be sinking quite as quickly as any of us might wish."

Alicia shared a satisfied, understanding smile with her ladyship. They chatted about upcoming events for five minutes, then took their leave; the carriage rolled on.

To Lady Huntingdon, then Lady Marchmont, and finally Lady Elphingstone.

"That color so becomes you, my dear." Lady Elphingstone examined Alicia's maroon twill through her lorgnette, then turned that instrument on Adriana's gown of palest lemon. "I declare you both are forever at the very pinnacle of modishness—always just so, never a step too far. I only wish my niece would take note."

Alicia recognized the hint. "Is your niece in town?"

Lady Elphingstone nodded. "She'll be at Lady Cranbourne's rout tonight. I take it you both will be attending?"

"Indeed." Adriana smiled warmly; she knew her role well. "I would be pleased to make your niece's acquaintance, if that might be possible?"

Lady Elphingstone beamed. "I'll be sure to make her known to you."

Alicia returned her ladyship's smile. "We'll look forward to it." By such little strategems were valuable alliances formed.

They parted from Lady Elphingstone. Alicia glanced ahead, then instructed the coachman to return to Waverton Street. Adriana cast her a questioning glance. Settling back, she murmured, "I've had enough for today."

Adriana accepted the decree with easygoing cheerfulness; Alicia shut her lips on her real reason—she didn't need to burden Adriana with that.

She had had enough—enough of deceiving others. But she'd

accepted the role she had to play; any guilt associated with it was hers alone to bear.

As the carriage rolled under the trees, along the drive lined with the conveyances of the fashionable, she and Adriana continued to smile, wave, and exchange nods; the number of ladies with whom they were acquainted had grown dramatically over the past days. Or, more correctly, the number of ladies wishing to make their acquaintance had grown, courtesy of Tony—his lordship—and those he'd asked to look kindly upon them.

The gates of the park loomed; the carriage swept through, and they were free of the necessity of responding to those about them. Alicia couldn't help but wonder what their reception would be if the ton knew the truth.

The prospect increasingly impinged on her mind. Tony—Torrington—had allied himself with them; if her secret became known, he would be involved by implication. Guilt by association, something the ton was quick to indulge in.

That worry dragged at her; only when they turned into Waverton Street and her mind swung to her brothers and her small household did she realize her worry for Torrington was of the same type, that nagging insistent consideration that she felt for her dependents, all those in her care.

The carriage rocked to a halt. Inwardly frowning, she let the footman hand her down. She wasn't wrong in assessing how she felt, yet Tony wasn't a dependent, nor yet in her care. Why, then, was her feeling so strong—so definite? So *real*.

After handing Adriana down, the footman bowed, then left. The carriage rumbled off. Adriana started up the steps. Closing her parasol, Alicia followed more slowly.

Jenkins would be upstairs with the boys; Adriana opened the door and went in, then turned to take Alicia's parasol. "I'll put these in the parlor. I thought of a new design—a variation of that French jacket. I want to sketch it before I forget." With a swish of her skirts, she headed for the parlor.

Alicia paused in the hall, watching her sister . . . just for one instant pausing to give thanks, then she heard a footfall on the stairs.

She looked up—and her heart leapt.

There could be no doubt; as she watched Tony slowly, elegantly descend, his lips set in an easy line but his eyes watchful, intent, she understood what she was feeling, couldn't stop the welling tide of anticipation, the burgeoning of simple happiness.

She was in a very bad way.

With one hand, he indicated the upper floor. "I've been with your brothers." Reaching the bottom stair, he stepped down, walked closer.

With every step he took, she could feel her awareness come to life, feel her consciousness expand, reaching for him.

He stopped directly in front of her. His eyes met hers, their expression quizzical, faintly amused. Then, before she could stop him, he bent his head and kissed her.

Gently, warmly.

He raised his head, met her gaze. "I need to speak with you privately." He glanced around, then gestured. "Shall we use the drawing room?"

She looked at the closed door. Her lips still tingled; it was an effort to bludgeon her wits into working order. "Yes. If . . ." Had her brothers said something they shouldn't?

That thought and the incipient panic it evoked helped get her mind functioning. Turning, she crossed the hall by Torrington's side, her protective instincts abruptly on full alert. No matter what she felt for him, she shouldn't forget that if he learned the truth, he could pose as big a threat to her and her family as Ruskin had.

Indeed, the threat he could pose was even greater.

Tony opened the door, waited for her to enter, then followed her into the elegantly appointed room. His gaze went first to the windows—two long panes looking onto the street. Shutting the door, he glanced around, but there was nothing of her or her family there, on the mantelpiece or the occasional tables set between the two chaises and the well-padded armchairs.

She stopped in the middle of the richly colored Turkish rug; head up, spine straight, hands clasped before her, she faced him.

"You don't have enough menservants." He had no idea what she'd expected him to say, but it assuredly wasn't that. She blinked, then frowned as her mind shifted to the domestic arena. If he told her he'd discovered a certain delight in throwing her off-balance, in confusing her, she most certainly wouldn't approve, yet such moments revealed an underlying vulnerability, one she didn't normally show, but which he treasured seeing and knew he responded to. As he presently was.

"Menservants?" Her frown was definite. "We have Jenkins, of course."

"One man for a house of this size, with a family of this size?"

Her chin rose as he closed the distance between them. "We've never seen the need for a large staff. We're quite comfortable as we are."

Halting before her, he caught her gaze. "I'm concerned."

She searched his eyes. "About what?"

"About the direction my investigation is taking, and the fact someone started rumors about you. Specifically *you*—the widow Ruskin was blackmailing."

She hesitated, then said, "Adriana and I are always careful."

"Be that as it may, this house is large . . . and you have three young brothers."

He didn't need to say more; he watched alarm flare in her eyes, only to be replaced by consideration, then consternation. He picked his moment to murmur, "I have a very large house with a very large staff, most of whom have very little to do given I'm the only member of the family in residence." Her gaze lifted to his; he held it. "I would feel much happier, less concerned, if you would allow me to lend you a footman, at least until my investigation is successfully concluded."

She returned his regard steadily. A minute ticked by, then she said, "This footman . . . ?"

"I have one in mind who would suit admirably—Maggs. He's been with me for years. He's well trained, and I can assure you he'll know how to deal with your brothers and the rest of the household, Jenkins especially."

Her eyes narrowed; her look stated that she understood his tactics, that she recognized he'd left her little room to maneuver, no real excuse to refuse. "Just for the duration of your investigation?"

"You may have him for as long as you wish, but I'd urge you to allow him to stay at least until we have Ruskin's murderer by the heels."

She pressed her lips together, then nodded. "Very well. I'll warn Jenkins."

They were standing close; he sensed her impulse to step back, away. Instead, she fixed him with a direct look. "It may interest you to know that at the Waverleys' ball last night and in the park this morning, Adriana and I met with, not just a gratifying degree of acceptance, but a quite astonishing level of support."

He raised his brows. "Indeed?"

"Indeed." She held his gaze. "You arranged it, didn't you?"

His face remained impassive, unreadable; his eyes, he knew, gave nothing away while he debated his answer. Eventually, he said, "Although she no longer resides in the capital, my mother has a large circle of friends among the *grandes dames* of the haut ton. I used to find their existence a trial. Now . . . I'm prepared to admit they do have their uses."

She drew a slow, deep breath; although he kept his eyes locked with hers, he was highly conscious of the swelling of her breasts. "Thank you." She hesitated, then added, "I don't know why you're doing this—"

Alicia broke off when something flashed in his eyes—an expression so vibrant, so powerful, even as fleeting as it was, the glimpse distracted her.

In the same moment, he reached for her; hands sliding around her waist, he drew her to him. Against him. Into his arms as he bent his head.

"The reason I'm doing this . . ."

The words washed over her lips, suddenly hungry; for a second, their gazes touched, locked, then his lids fell. She felt his gaze on her lips.

"Ought to be obvious."

Deep, low, the words sank into her brain as his lips covered hers, and he sank into her mouth. Claimed her attention, then sent it spinning, fractured, dispersed. Called her senses, drew them to him, then trapped them, held them enthralled.

She kissed him back, found herself mentally floating as the slow, drugging kisses took their toll. Sinking her fingers into his shoulders, she tried to hang onto her wits, to some degree of control, but steadily, inexorably, implacable and irresistible, he drew it from her grasp.

Then he drew her hard against him, locked her body to his, and the flames and the magic flared.

It had to be magic, that surge of sensation, the giddy delight, the anticipation streaking down her nerves, tingling, tightening so that the need to sate it was suddenly more important than breathing, far more important than any consideration of social strictures.

His hands spread over her back, stroked possessively down the long planes, curving over her hips to close proprietorially over her bottom, provocatively kneading, then boldly caressing. Hot as a flame, heat spread beneath her skin; a deep-seated yearning flowered in its wake.

Then he angled his head and ravaged her mouth, took more, demanded more. Unhesitatingly she followed him deeper into the exchange, encouraging and enjoying the ever more intimate melding of their mouths.

The first inkling she had that he'd opened her bodice was the slithering caress of her silk chemise as, loosened, it slipped down, helped by his long fingers. And then those fingers were on her skin, and she lost touch with the world.

And plunged into another.

Into a realm where sensation and emotions were the only reality, where touches and caresses formed the language, with needs, wants, and desires the only goals. Every slow, possessive caress heightened her need, made her want with an ever greater certainty fueled by escalating, burgeoning desire. Yet that desire seemed entwined with his, with him, with his obvious reason. With what she sensed, in her bones knew, he wanted.

Their lips parted; from under heavy lids, their gazes met, held as his fingers moved on her, upon her, drawing whorls of flame on her skin, tightening her nerves to an excruciating degree. Unable to bear it, she closed her eyes, with a soft gasp let her head fall back. Felt him bend near, felt his lips on her throat, sliding down to fasten over her thudding pulse.

His hands shifted; her gown slid over her shoulders, then cool air caressed her heated skin. The bared skin he set his lips to tracing, with flicking licks and long trailing laves teasing, the hot, wet promise of his mouth withheld . . . as the fever built, as some need within her grew, and grew . . . until she moaned.

The sound, soft, nearly suppressed, surprised her, but through the hands at her waist holding her, supporting her, she sensed his satisfaction. A wholly male triumph that he crowned by closing his mouth— every bit as hot and wet as she'd imagined—over the taut, aching peak of one breast.

She tensed, her nerves clenched, not with rejection but delight. Her hands slid through his hair, tightened on his skull as he swirled his tongue about the ruched peak, then sucked gently. Sensation, pure and elemental, streaked through her, racing through her body to pool deep and low, a warming glow within her.

Cracking open her lids, she looked down. Watched as he feasted on her bounty—and wondered at her reaction. Some part of her was shocked, yet she couldn't, even now, summon any will to refuse him, deny him—to push him away. She couldn't tense her muscles, couldn't break the spell. She didn't want to, couldn't pretend. Could only watch, feel, learn, and experience.

Something new, something novel, something she'd never felt before.

Tony sensed her fascination and was content. For now. He knew her acquiescence was not, yet, freely given; he could draw her into such sensual exchanges, but she did not, yet, seek them of her own accord.

That was what he wanted. Needed. For her to want him as he wanted her.

Overwhelming her natural resistance, taking over, controlling her—
for one of his talents, that wasn't all that hard. For him, the challenge lay
deeper, in making her come to him, making her desire him enough to set
aside her reserve and actively seek to be intimate with him.

Only by that route would he gain the surrender he sought, the
complete and conscious giving that, for one of his nature, was the ultimate prize.

He raised his head; their gazes briefly touched, then he covered
her lips, and took her mouth again. In a slow, thorough, leisurely
engagement that left them both starved of breath.

Gradually, he drew back. Her breasts were swollen, tight beneath
his hands; her skin felt like hot satin beneath his fingertips. He kept his
lips on hers as he searched for and found the top edge of her chemise,
and drew it up, tugging the drawstring so it tightened and held.

She stirred in his arms. He ended the kiss and lifted his head. Their
eyes met for an instant, then she looked down; drawing her hands from
his shoulders, she resettled and retied the chemise, then, a blush tinting
her cheeks, she rapidly did up the buttons of her bodice.

He couldn't keep his lips straight when she glanced at him; his satisfaction was too deep to hide.

She saw it, read it; a frown in her eyes, she waved him to the door.

Smiling, he turned, glancing at her as she fell in beside him.
Before the door, he halted, caught her eye as she looked up. "I'll send
Maggs this afternoon."

She blinked at him. "Maggs?"

"The footman."

"Ah." She drew herself up, nodded. "Yes, of course. Thank you."

He grinned, ducked his head, and kissed her—stole one last kiss
from her luscious lips—then straightened and met her eyes, green and
slightly dazed. "I'll see myself out."

He managed to suppress a smirk; feeling positively virtuous, he
opened the door, gracefully saluted her, then closed it.

Alicia stared at the panels. Beyond them, she heard his footsteps
recede, then the front door opened, and shut.

He was gone.

Reason and logic returned in a flood; the last minutes—however
many minutes it had been—replayed in her mind.

Her increasingly horrified mind.

Her lips still throbbed, her skin still tingled, her breasts . . . she
could still feel the sensation of his mouth moving over them . . .

With a groan, she closed her eyes and slumped against the door.

What was she going to do?

Seven

"My dear Mrs. Carrington, may I present Sir Freddie Caudel?"

Lady Hertford beamed at Alicia, who divined that gaining Sir Freddie's notice was something of a coup. She extended her hand with a polite murmur.

Sir Freddie took her fingers and bowed gracefully. A gentleman in his middle years, he was handsome in a quiet, patrician way.

Alicia smiled. In a few short minutes, she established that Sir Freddie was a scion of an old and ancient house and consequently socially prominent, held a political post in the government, possessed a degree of polish and address to which younger men could only aspire, and was on the lookout for a wellborn, beautiful, and young bride.

Not surprisingly, Adriana had caught his eye.

Alicia hestitated, wondering if she should, in all compassion, nip Sir Freddie's aspirations in the bud; from all she could see, Adriana was fast losing her heart to Geoffrey Manningham.

Sir Freddie had followed her gaze to where Adriana stood by Lord Manningham's side. "I realize, of course, that youth and beauty go hand in hand, yet often you ladies have a remarkably discerning eye."

Alicia met Sir Freddie's blue eyes, guileless and amused. Geoffrey might be younger, yet Sir Freddie was undeniably distinguished, and his manners, while absolutely correct, had an ease about them, a comfortable confidence deriving from years of moving in the first circles.

Sir Freddie might give Geoffrey a run for his money.

More particularly for Adriana's heart, which her hand would follow.

Lips curving, Alicia inclined her head. "If you wish to join my sister's circle, I have no objection." She seriously doubted Sir Freddie would succeed, but there was no harm in him attempting to upset Manningham's applecart.

Sir Freddie offered his arm. "If you would introduce me?"

Placing her fingers on his sleeve, Alicia allowed him to lead her to Adriana's side.

Adriana was, as always, polite to anyone who sought her attention. Introduction completed, Alicia withdrew, rejoining Lady Hertford at the side of the room.

"He's very highly thought of," her ladyship whispered. "Marcus tells me he can be quite stiff-rumped on occasion, but always the true gentleman." Adriana drew Miss Tiverton into the conversation with Sir Freddie; Lady Hertford smiled delightedly. "Such a sweet girl, your sister. Who knows? If Sir Freddie doesn't fix her interest, perhaps he'll look at Helen. Of course, there's his age, but when men of his stamp look to take a wife, one can at least be sure they're in earnest. And his estates are quite respectable, I believe—they've been in the family for generations."

Alicia smiled easily; she let Lady Hertford's chatter wash over her, nodding here and there. Eventually, her ladyship departed, leaving Miss Tiverton along with Adriana under Alicia's watchful eye.

She did keep her gaze on her sister's circle, some yards away, but the instant Lady Hertford's distraction disappeared, Alicia's thoughts focused on her own distraction.

Anthony Blake, Viscount Torrington.

Her reaction to his practiced seduction surprised her; she'd assumed she'd be uninterested, disinterested, that repulsing any gentleman's advances, especially those of a predatory nobleman, would be instinctive, a natural response she wouldn't have to pause to consider, let alone battle to achieve.

It was a battle she was losing; she'd already lost significant ground. Quite why, she didn't understand.

When she was with him, in his arms or even simply alone with him, the world seemed to shift, the frame of reference by which she'd lived her life thus far to alter. It swung to focus on him, to accommodate him, to center, not just on him, not just on his wishes, but on hers—those wishes she hadn't known she had.

When with him, her attention shifted to a different landscape, one encompassing all that was growing between them. That change was unprecedented, unsettling, yet fascinating. Even addictive.

Something in him called to something in her; from the coalescing of those somethings grew the power she sensed, the power that was strong enough to suborn her wits, shackle her senses . . . and seduce her.

She shivered, and refocused on Adriana's circle, and saw Sir Freddie successfully solicit her sister's hand for a waltz. Noting Geoffrey Manningham's studiously impassive countenance, she smiled.

Hard fingers, a hard palm, closed about her hand.

She turned as Tony—Torrington!—raised it; eyes capturing hers, he pressed a kiss to her fingers. Faintly smiled.

"Come and dance."

Within seconds, she was whirling down the floor. She didn't bother trying to resist; instead, she turned her mind to her most urgent need—trying to understand what was going on.

He seemed content simply to dance, to hold her in his arms and revolve about the ballroom, his gaze resting on her face, on her eyes.

Drinking her in.

She lowered her lids, screening her eyes, shifted her gaze to look over his shoulder. Smoothly, he drew her closer as they went through the turns, and didn't ease his hold; abruptly she was aware of their bodies, the subtle brushing of their hips, of his thigh parting hers as they turned . . . as if he'd reached for her and enveloped her in a flagrantly intimate embrace. The memory leapt to her mind, instantly impinged on her wanton senses.

Instantly stirred her hunger.

She looked up, met his gaze. "This is madness."

The words were low, breathy. He smiled, but his eyes remained on hers, his gaze intent. "If it is, we're both infected."

Beyond recall. She drew breath, read his eyes; their expression was openly predatory—his intent could not have been clearer. Realization, as inescapable as the dawn, burst upon her.

Deep within her, something quivered.

Tony looked up, over her head, wishing for once that she possessed a more definite mask, a countenance less easy to read. One long look into her eyes, and he was aching. If Cranbourne House had boasted any suitable room, he'd have whisked her off to it, there to pursue, however impulsively, the connection growing between them. Unfortunately, Cranbourne House was small, pokey, a totally unsuitable venue. Added to that, her sister was present, which meant she'd be distracted. When he finally had her beneath him, he didn't want her thinking of anything else.

He noticed Geoffrey standing by the side of the room, not exactly scowling, yet clearly not happy. A quick glance about the floor located Adriana waltzing in the arms of a somewhat older man.

"The gentleman waltzing with your sister—who is he?"

Alicia had been studying his face; she answered evenly, "Sir Freddie Caudel." After a moment, she asked, "Do you know him?"

One distraction was as good as another. Resigning himself to yet another night of escalating frustration, he glanced down at her. "No, but I've heard of him. Very old family. Why? Is he interested in your sister?"

Alicia nodded. "How interested, I'm not sure, and I doubt his interest, at whatever level, will be reciprocated, nevertheless . . ."

His lips quirked; he glanced again at Geoffrey. "Another iron in the fire?"

Alicia narrowed her eyes. "Precisely." One with which she might prod things along.

"I take it the footman met with your approval?"

"Maggs?" Bearing a written introduction, the man had presented himself at the back door in Waverton Street. She met Torrington's gaze, let a moment pass; Maggs, as he had to be aware, was the most unprepossessing specimen. His features were irregular, his face appeared pushed in, yet he seemed possessed of an easy disposition and had already, in just a few hours, gained acceptance from Cook, Fitchett, and, most importantly, Jenkins. For which she was grateful. "I daresay he'll suit well enough. As I pointed out, we really have little use for a footman."

"Nevertheless." Torrington's black eyes quizzed her. "Just so that I can rest easy."

She suppressed a humph.

The waltz ended. Without instruction, Torrington led her back to her position not far from Adriana's court. He remained by her side, chatting inconsequentially on this and that, the customary exchanges of tonnish life. Others joined them, remained for a time, then moved on; she tried not to dwell on the fact that she preferred having him near, that his easy, in many ways undemanding presence made her evening distinctly more enjoyable.

More relaxing on one level, more unnerving on another.

It was the minor moments that tripped her up, that set her nerves jangling. That brought what was between them flooding back into her mind, blocking out all else, even Adriana.

Like the moment when having remained by her side, her cavalier through the rest of the evening, Torrington parted from them in the Cranbournes' front hall. They were among a small crowd of departing guests; to gain her attention, he touched her shoulder.

His fingertips brushed lightly. Despite being decently sheathed in ruby silk, her skin reacted. Goosebumps rose and spread in a wave; her nipples tightened.

Her eyes flew to his, wide, aware; he read them, his lips thinned, and she knew he knew, too.

Then he met her gaze fully. The expression in his eyes nearly slew her; the heat was so open, so intense, it was a wonder it didn't melt her bones.

His lashes swept down; he grasped her hand and very correctly took his leave of her.

She mumbled some response, then watched his back as he walked away through the crowd; only when he disappeared through the front door did she manage to breathe again. Manage to give her attention to the footman waiting to be told which carriage to summon. Thankfully, Adriana hadn't noticed; her sister seemed as distracted as she.

The journey back through the night-shrouded streets provided a welcome respite, a quiet moment all but alone when she could gather her wits, review what had happened, all she'd felt, how she'd reacted, without worrying about her betraying blush.

Finally to make some attempt at defining where she stood. And whither she was heading.

The first seemed all too clear; she stood teetering on the horns of a dilemma. As for the second, the possibilities were varied but uniformly unsettling.

Her dilemma was clear enough. She had to play the part of a tonnish widow, an experienced lady aware of, indeed personally acquainted with, all aspects of intimacy. The question now facing her was simple: how far should she go in preserving her charade?

To her perturbation, the answer was not at all simple.

Dedication to their cause argued the answer should be as far as she needed to go to see Adriana through her Season and secure their family's relief. But that immediately raised another highly pertinent question: how far *could* she go without Torrington realizing?

He was not just experienced; he was an expert. She'd been scrambling to keep up with him thus far; at some point she would falter, and he'd realize. . . .

The social strictures at least were clear. Regardless of her charade, she wasn't a widow, but a virtuous spinster—she shouldn't permit him even the liberties he'd already taken. Unfortunately, her inner voice was quick to argue, to speak in support of those wishes and needs she was only just realizing she possessed; where, that inner voice asked, was the harm?

She'd accepted over a year ago that she'd missed her chance at marriage; she was twenty-four—not unmarriageable by ton standards, yet in reality the likelihood had faded. Once Adriana was established, she, Alicia, would disappear from society; she'd imagined she'd retire to the country to watch over the boys, to keep home for them whether with Adriana and her husband or otherwise.

That plan still stood; nothing had happened to alter her path. Any liaison with Torrington would be, as such things generally were, temporary, fleeting. A liaison with him might, however, be her only chance to experience all she was presently pretending to know.

He was the only gentleman who had ever engaged her on that level; even now, she wasn't sure how he'd done it, how it had happened. Yet it had; the possibility now existed where it hadn't before. If she wanted to know more, wanted to experience all that could be between a man and a woman, all she had to do was let Torrington teach her.

The carriage rocked along, heading into Mayfair, pausing here and there as other carriages crowded the streets. She barely noticed the delays, indeed was grateful for the opportunity to let her mind range ahead, examining, imagining.

If she did indulge in a liaison with Torrington . . .

He would realize she was a virgin, would guess she'd never been married. However, she doubted he would expose her to the ton; there was no reason he should, not once she'd explained.

There was, however, another danger. One her instincts, uneducated though they were, had detected. Just how real that danger was she couldn't be certain, yet Tony—Torrington—was a nobleman to his toes. Arrogant, yes, with a definite streak of ruthlessness behind his charming facade, and . . . she searched for the word to describe what she sensed when he looked at her, held her, kissed her, caressed her.

Possessive.

If she gave herself to him, trusted him that far, would he agree to let her go?

She wasn't foolish enough to overlook the point; if she became his mistress, allowed him to become privy to her secret, he'd be in a position much as Ruskin had been, able to dictate her behavior. She recognized the possibility, viewed it clearly, yet she couldn't, despite all, see it happening. Adriana had mentioned Geoffrey's assessment of Torrington; it concurred with her own reading of the man. He was simply not the sort to hold a woman against her will. Regardless of all else, he was an honorable man.

If she did become his mistress, for whatever length of time, he would, in the end, let her go.

All of which left her precisely where she'd started, facing the question of what she should do and no nearer to finding an answer.

The only alternative to making a decision was to stave it off. Somehow to hold him off, to avoid the culmination he was clearly steering them toward. If she could hold to a line just short of surrender, then the instant Adriana was established, disappear . . .

With a creak, the carriage turned into Waverton Street. Adriana stirred, stretched. Alicia straightened, and gathered her shawl and reticule. The carriage halted; looking out, she saw the light burning above their door.

Thought of her brothers innocently asleep in their beds.

Resist Torrington. The problem with that strategy was that in order to implement it, she'd have to fight not only him, an experienced campaigner, but her own, largely unknown, desires.

She let the footman hand her down, then led the way up the steps. Their reckless but straightforward plan had developed serious complications.

The next morning, Tony headed for the Bastion Club. On foot. He needed the exercise.

Needed the physical activity to ease the building frustration of a type he'd rarely had to endure. Indeed, he couldn't remember ever wanting a woman so much, and not having her. Worse, in this instance, he recognized the need to go slowly, carefully; his relationship with Alicia was forever, not for a few weeks or a few months. It would be the most important relationship of his life; it demanded and deserved a degree of care, of respect, of attention.

He'd noticed her occasional hesitations, the sudden tensing, almost a skittishness that sometimes gripped her. He'd always succeeded in soothing it, in getting her to set it aside and relax, to trust him. To open her eyes, see and accept all that could be and would be between them.

Although he hadn't foreseen it, her reserve didn't surprise him; she might be a widow, but that wouldn't change the underlying truth of her nature—she was a virtuous lady, and as such would not easily be seduced. And in her case, there was yet more—a complicating factor. She was responsible for her family, and she took that responsibility seriously.

He hadn't imagined that in gaining his bride, he'd have to compete with her family for her attention. While the fact was a difficulty, and clearly would continue to raise hurdles, he didn't, as it happened, disapprove.

He enjoyed her family—enjoyed spending time with her brothers, even enjoyed watching Adriana make her choice, especially given Geoffrey was involved. But more, he found the circumstance of her family reassuring.

As an only child, he'd never experienced the relationships Alicia and her siblings took for granted. The warmth, the closeness that was simply there, the support it never occurred to them to question . . . all that was not only attractive, but spoke strongly of Alicia's ability to create for him, with him, the sort of home and family he wanted. And needed. How much he hadn't realized until he'd met her and her brood.

Regardless of his frustration, he wouldn't have her change, didn't wish she was otherwise. He valued her for what she was, as she was, and was fully prepared to accommodate that, to woo her as she needed to be wooed.

And pray he didn't do himself an injury in the meantime.

With a wrench, he hauled his mind away from that moment in the Cranbournes' front hall. Just thinking of that made him ache. Determinedly, he focused on the meeting he was heading for, with Gervase Tregarth and Jack Warnefleet.

They were waiting in the club's meeting room, comfortably slouched about the mahogany table. Christian Allardyce was also there; when he raised his brows, Tony waved him to stay. "You've already heard part of this affair—the more help the better."

Christian grinned. "And Dalziel is involved."

"Indeed." Tony sat and quickly, concisely, told them all he'd learned of Ruskin, his death, and his dealings with A. C. "This is a list of the ships mentioned in Ruskin's notes, and the associated dates, and these"—he handed over a second sheet—"are the dates on which Ruskin received large cash donations to his gambling fund."

Gervase studied the list of ships and dates, then compared them with the dates of the payments. Shifting to sit beside him, Jack perused the lists, too.

Christian, beside Tony, looked across the table at them. "I take it the payments in some way coincide with the shipping dates?"

Checking back and forth, Gervase nodded. "About a week in between, but not for every ship listed."

Tony sat back. "It appears Ruskin provided the information, it was used or in some way confirmed, and then he received payment."

"Whoever A. C. is, he ran a tight operation. No payment unless . . ." Jack stopped, looked up.

Grimly, Tony nodded. "Presumably no payment unless the information was useful."

"Which," Christian murmured, "suggests it was used for something."

"And if it was," Gervase was still studying the lists, "it wasn't for anything good."

"That," Tony agreed, "is the inescapable conclusion. What we need to determine is exactly how it was used."

Gervase nodded. "And trace it back to whoever that use benefited."

"Precisely." Tony paused, then asked, "Can you help?"

Gervase looked up, grinned. "I was intending to slip home for a few days. I can easily ask around in Plymouth, and along the coast there." He met Tony's gaze. "But you've more extensive contacts in the Isles and on the French side, and to the southeast on this side, I'd imagine."

"Yes, but my problem—our problem at present—is that that information"—Tony nodded at the lists in Gervase's hands—"is all we have. I compiled the list of ships from scattered jottings, more like reminders. Presumably the information Ruskin passed contained more detail."

"But what detail we don't know?" Jack asked.

"Exactly. Via the Revenue and Admiralty dispatches that passed through his hands, Ruskin had what amounted to each ship's sailing orders, at least for their approach to our shores." Tony looked at Gervase. "If you can find any hint of what was going on—how the information was used—I can put out feelers more widely. But given the nature of my contacts, if I ask general questions, rather than specific ones, I won't get any answers. Worse, I might alert whoever it is that's behind this."

They all understood how the informant system worked; he didn't need to explain further.

"Can I keep these?" Gervase held up the lists.

Tony nodded. "Those are copies."

Folding the lists, Gervase slipped them into his pocket. "I'll ask around and see if I can find any whisper of any action involving these ships on or about those dates. If I find anything, I'll bring it back immediately."

"Once we have a clue what we're dealing with, I'll follow up more widely."

Jack frowned. "Have you thought of inquiring via the shipping lines? If these ships are merchantmen . . ."

"I've a friend who'll be in town in a day or so—he has a similar background to ours. He's been out of the service for some years, but knows the game well. He also owns Hendon Shipping, one of the largest of the local lines. He has the contacts and will know how to make such inquiries without raising a dust."

Jack nodded. "So—what did you want me to pursue?"

"Ruskin himself, and how A. C. knew him. Ruskin lived at Bledington when he was in the country. Not often, admittedly, but it's an area we shouldn't overlook. Given you're the closest of us countywise, your inquisitive presence is least likely to attract attention. Our ultimate aim is to identify A. C. It's possible he's someone who lives out that way, and that's how he knew Ruskin, and most importantly where Ruskin worked."

"Right." Jack's gaze had grown distant. "I'll check into Ruskin's background and see if I can turn up anyone with the initials A. C. connected in however vague a fashion with our boy."

"While you're up there . . ." Tony hesitated, then went on, "You might check on a Mrs. Carrington and her family, the Pevenseys. Their connection with Ruskin appears to be via Chipping Norton. It seems Mrs. Carrington and the Pevenseys didn't know Ruskin, but he knew them."

"Carrington." Christian murmured. "That's a C."

"Indeed. More confusing, she's Alicia Carrington, so she is A. C., but she married Carrington about two years ago, so wasn't A. C. four years ago, when Ruskin first started receiving large sums from A. C. More to the point, her husband, deceased for two years, was Alfred Carrington. Although he can't be the A. C. involved either, given the way names run in families there may be a connection with Ruskin of which Mrs. Carrington is unaware."

"Oh, yes." Jack nodded; for one instant, the dangerous man behind his hail-fellow-well-met cheerily handsome facade showed through. "Second cousin, third cousin, whatever. I'll check."

They all exchanged glances, then, as one, pushed back their chairs. They stood, stretched, resettled their coats; as they turned to the door, Christian murmured, "That shipping business sounds decidedly nasty." He caught Tony's eye, then glanced at the others. They were all thinking the same thing—that someone had been using the war for their own ends.

"We definitely need to learn what the information was used for, and how," Gervase said.

"And, most importantly"—Tony followed Christian from the room—"by whom." That, indeed, was their primary interest.

* * *

Tony returned to Upper Brook Street and spent the next few hours attending to numerous matters of business. Under his father's hand, the Blake estates had grown considerably; he was determined that during his tenure, the family's fortunes would continue to expand.

The activity naturally brought to mind the family—the people— that fortune was intended to support. When the clock struck two, he set aside his papers and strolled around to Green Park.

David, Harry, and Matthew were delighted to see him. Alicia was rather more circumspect; she greeted him with a polite smile and sus- picious eyes. The wind was brisk, perfect for kites; together with the boys, he spent a thoroughly satisfactory hour making theirs soar higher than anyone else's.

"It'll get trapped in the trees," Alicia grimly prophesied.

"Nonsense." Halting before her, he looked into her eyes. Fought down the urge to see how she would respond if he kissed her there, in the middle of the park with all the nursemaids and Maggs looking on. He forced himself to turn and look at the boys. All three were hanging on to the kite strings, shrieking and whooping as the kite, courtesy of his maneuvering now high above the treetops, swooped and tugged in the wind. "I assure you I manage the reins better than that."

An instant's pause ensued, then she replied, "You might. They won't."

She was right, but before the kite could come to grief in the leaf- less branches, he stepped in and took control again, and gradually brought the flapping creation with its long tail safely back to earth.

The boys were ecstatic, their eyes shining, cheeks rosy, glowing with happiness. Walking to join the group, Alicia studied the man about whom her brothers danced; no matter her suspicions, she could not doubt that he, too, had enjoyed the play. His black eyes gleamed as he shared the moment with her brothers; his lips were curved, the nor- mally austere lines of his face relaxed.

As usual, he was dressed with consummate elegance in a perfectly cut dark blue coat over a white shirt, his long legs encased in tight buckskin breeches that disappeared into glossy black Hessians. The wind ruffled the black locks of his hair as he helped her brothers gather the long tail of the kite.

He was sophisticated, worldly, a gentleman of the ton, yet at moments like this she could almost believe she could see the boy he must have been, the boyishly open soul still lurking behind his adult glamor.

When she stopped beside the group, he looked up and grinned, still very much the boy. She smiled spontaneously in return. "Tea?"

The boys instantly raised a chorus of entreaty, but he didn't take his gaze from her; his grin eased into a smile of quite devastating charm. "Thank you. I'd like that."

With the boys about them and Maggs following with the kite in his arms, they headed back to Waverton Street.

Teatime was the usual relaxed and comfortable interlude. Maggs brought in the tray. The boys peppered Tony with questions on their latest interest—horses, curricles, and phaetons, and racing the same, while devouring their usual quota of crumpets and jam.

Alicia exchanged a smiling glance with Adriana and sat back, content to let Tony—Torrington!—manage as he would; although his knowledge of such male subjects was patently wide, she now trusted him to know what was appropriate to tell her brothers, and what was not.

It wasn't them he was intent on seducing; he was more than wise enough to know he'd have more chance with her—

She broke off that thought and looked at Adriana. Busy as usual with sketches of gowns, hats, and accessories, her sister seemed quieter than usual. She seemed to be thinking, mulling—over what Alicia could easily guess.

She leaned closer; under cover of a rowdy conversation about swan-necked phaetons and their propensity to overturn, she murmured, "Mr. King sent a reply. He'll gather his information and dine with us the day after tomorrow."

Adriana looked up, held her gaze for a moment, then, lips firming, nodded. "Good." After a moment, she added, "If there's any difficulty . . . I need to know now."

Alicia patted her hand, then drew back.

Although courtesy of her brothers' eager opinions Tony hadn't heard what was said, he noted the sisters' exchange and made a mental note to ascertain just how serious Geoffrey was. The last thing he wanted was for Alicia to become anxious over her sister's budding romance. He wanted her attention, as much of it as he could get, for himself.

Maggs reappeared to remove the tea tray, bending a glance on Tony that he read with ease: nothing to report. At Alicia's command, the boys stood and took their leave, resigned to returning to their lessons. As they trooped to the door, Tony looked at Adriana.

She met his gaze, then fleetingly, conspiratorially smiled. Gathering her papers and sketchbook, she stood; directing an airy, "I'll be in my room if you need me," to Alicia, she followed her brothers out of the door, shutting it behind her.

The instant the door closed, Tony rose and sank onto the chaise where Adriana had been. Alongside Alicia.

She directed a wide-eyed look his way. "Ah—have you learned anything more about Ruskin, about what he was up to?"

Habit prompted him to answer with a simple "No," and then distract her from the subject, but his decision not to conceal such matters from her weighed against such a tack. "Nothing specific—as I said, I've various inquiries under way."

Reaching into his coat pocket, he drew out the originals of the lists he'd made of ships' names, dates, and Ruskin's payments. "This"— stretching out his legs, crossing his ankles, he settled back. Straightening the lists, he held them up before him—"are all we have to work with at present."

She hesitated, but had to lean closer to look.

Her shoulder brushing his arm, Alicia read the entries; she was determined to keep their conversation focused on the safe and highly pertinent subject of his investigation. Relatively safe; clearly, he was not above using every opportunity that came his way to ruffle her senses, even this. His writing was neat, precise, but quite small; she had to press closer still to make out the dates—her senses flared with awareness, of him, of his strength, of the promise of sensual delight her wanton wits now associated with him.

She waved at the lists. "These dates. They seem to be related in some way—not exactly, but . . ."

He nodded. "We think—"

Without further prompting, he explained what the lists were, what he believed they meant. To her surprise, he even told her what his assumptions regarding the lists' significance were, what he hoped to learn from the shipping companies, the ports, and the mariners, and how that might indicate further avenues to explore . . . it was intriguing.

She found herself enthused with a zeal to in some way assist in working out the puzzle of what Ruskin's information was used for, and why. She'd intended to do something—pushing the investigation to a rapid conclusion would remove the most compelling excuse Torrington had to call on her, to be close to her.

About to ask how she could help, she stopped; why ask? Reaching for the lists, she drew them from his fingers. "May I make copies of these?"

His brows rose, but he nodded. "If you like."

Tony watched as she stood and crossed to the escritoire standing against the wall between the windows. She sat, drew out a sheet of paper, then settled to copy his lists. A slanting beam of sunlight struck coppery red glints from her dark hair. In the evenings, she wore it coiled high; during the day, the heavy loops were neatly constrained at her nape, the dark silk lustrous against her pale skin.

A fleeting notion of releasing that restrained abundance, of spreading it in a sheening mahogany veil over her bare shoulders, a distracting screen about her charms, filled him. Caught him. Momentarily held him.

She glanced at him, alerted, suspicious, but not knowing why.

He frowned, surreptitiously shifted. "What do you intend to do with those?"

Laying aside her pen, she blotted the lists, then rose and turned to him. "I don't know. If I have them, then when I think of something . . ." She shrugged. His originals in her hand, she walked back to the chaise.

His frown wasn't feigned. "If you do think of anything, or learn anything, promise me you'll tell me immediately."

Alicia halted before him, met his eyes. After a moment's consideration, she nodded. "I promise." What else was she to do with anything she learned?

She held out the lists. For one moment, his gaze didn't leave her face, then it slowly lowered, eventually fastening on the sheets in her hand.

He reached out—reached farther than the sheets and grasped her wrist. Long fingers locking, he tugged.

Before she could catch her breath, she was on his lap, in his arms. In a flurry of skirt and petticoats, she tried to right herself, tried to push back.

She heard a deep chuckle, felt it reverberate through her palms, braced on his chest. "We have a few moments . . ." His tone was pure temptation.

Resist, resist, resist.

She drew breath, looked up. And his lips came down on hers.

He captured them, captured her mouth, bewitched her senses. She was kissing him back, flagrantly participating in the exchange before her wits caught up with her actions. He shifted; she felt him pluck his lists from her nerveless fingers, fold them, and tuck them into his pocket.

Then his arms rose and closed about her, his head angled, and he parted her lips wider, his tongue evocatively thrusting deep, then settling to a typical, devastatingly intimate game. Of exploration, of enticement.

Soon her mind was whirling, senses locked with his as together they fed their mutual hunger, created and assuaged a mutual desire. Fingers tangled in his hair, she clung, savored, appeased, and demanded.

How long they indulged in the heated sensations she had no idea, but her wits returned with a jolt when she felt his hands between them, opening the buttons down the front of her walking dress.

It took a huge effort but she broke from the kiss; he was distracted, so let her go. On a gasp, she looked down, then glanced wildly around. "Ah . . ."

"Don't worry." From under his heavy lids, his black eyes caught hers. He searched, read, then his lips twisted wryly. "Your brothers are safe upstairs, so is your sister. Jenkins is with your brothers, and the rest are in the kitchens. No one is going to come through the door, not in the next half hour."

Half hour? What might he do in half an hour?

"That's—" She had to stop and moisten her lips, had to whip her wits into order. She was supposed to resist, or at least . . . she looked down, saw his fingers dark against the skin he was swiftly uncovering, couldn't quite suppress a tense, expectant shiver. "This is . . . really too . . . that is . . ."

Good Lord! Her words died along with her wits when he slipped a hand between the gaping halves of her bodice, with a flick of his fingers dispensed with her chemise, and boldly set his hand to her skin.

The touch was a sensual shock, not muted in the least by the fact she'd expected it, knew what his hand felt like there, cupping her breast, taking its weight, fingers gently kneading, then artfully teasing the already tightly ruched peak. Her lids drifted down, eyes closing as the sensations swept her—then she remembered and jerked her eyes open. Half-open. Enough to look into his face.

He was watching her. "Stop fighting it—just enjoy."

His hand moved on her, her wits started to slide . . .

"No! That is . . ." She drew a determined breath, only to discover she couldn't; her lungs had locked. Her nerves had tensed, not in rejection but in pleasured delight. The urge to press her breast into his warm hand was compelling, almost overwhelming. She held it at bay.

Fingers sinking into his shoulders, lids closing, she managed to shake her head. "I—you . . . this. We *can't*—"

She broke off with a sound very close to a moan.

His hand shifted, fingers closing more definitely about the aching peak he'd so effectively tortured, with expert ministrations soothed the pain, but that somehow only escalated the ache.

"I told you not to worry."

His words, deep and gravelly, reached through the fog of her whirling senses. "If you need to go slowly, we will. We have no need to rush."

On the words, his hand left her, fingers trailing upward, then she felt him ease her gown over the peak of her left shoulder. Baring her breast. His hand returned to its seductive play; she knew he was watching as he caressed her swollen flesh. As he knowingly tightened every nerve she possessed.

"We can take the long road." His voice had deepened, darkened, weaving a sorcerous spell. "And spend as much time as we wish enjoying every sight, every experience along the way."

Her breasts ached; her whole body seemed to throb.

He leaned nearer; his lips brushed hers. "Is that what you want?"

She nodded. "Yes." The word was a whisper between their lips.

"So be it," he whispered back. Then sealed the pact with a kiss.

A kiss that ripped her wits away and sent them spinning. That sent heat and flame pouring through her, down every nerve, down every vein. His hand left her and he gathered her closer; holding her in one arm, he sent his hand exploring again.

Caressing her through her clothes. Not just her breasts, but everywhere. His hand traced her shoulders, her back, her spine, delineated the muscles on either side, then spanned the back of her waist. His palm, hot and hard, passed over her hip, then boldly caressed her bottom. He traced the globes, over and around, all the while holding her to their kiss, to the slow, steady dizzying rhythm of thrust and retreat he'd established.

Her senses spun as he cupped the back of her thigh, then moved down, found her knee, then swept upward. Inward.

She gasped, would have stiffened in his arms, but he didn't allow it. His other hand shifted, gripping her bottom, holding her still. Then his questing hand splayed over her stomach; he pressed, kneaded, then held her tight, not just in his arms but sensually, too, as he reached lower, traced the tops of her thighs, then stroked, through the fine fabric of her walking dress gently probed the hollow between, caressed the soft curls beneath chemise and gown.

Teased her to life.

Until every nerve in her body was tingling, until heat pulsed just beneath her skin.

Eventually, gradually, he drew back. Eased her back.

Eventually he lifted his head, looked into her face, then brushed her lips once more with his. "If you want it slow, we'll go slowly. Very, *very* slowly."

From beneath her heavy lids, she caught the fire in his eyes.

The reassurance was what she'd wanted.

She wasn't sure she'd survive.

Eight

Afternoon tea in Waverton Street was a social engagement Tony felt he could easily grow fond of. In contrast, balls, routs, and soirées held far less appeal; there he had to share Alicia's attention with anyone else who thought to claim it.

However, she'd asked to go slowly, to rein in their progress, and if he was honest and viewed the whole dispassionately, there was much to be said in support of her request.

He was engaged in a serious and difficult investigation, one in which she was involved; it made sense to conclude the matter, to identify, locate, and nullify A. C. before addressing what lay between them. Before formally mentioning marriage and precipitating the associated hullabaloo.

She was right; they should take the long road. Entering Lady Cumberland's ballroom, he tried to tell himself he accepted the decree.

He found Alicia in her usual position by the wall near Adriana's circle. As more families returned to town, that circle grew; the quality of its members was also increasing. Adriana now had two earl's sons dancing attendance, along with six of lesser standing, including Sir Freddie Caudel and Geoffrey, who looked somewhat tense.

Recognizing in his childhood friend some of the impatience he himself was feeling, Tony inwardly raised his brows. Luckily in his case, Alicia seemed impervious to the frequent advances made by numerous gentlemen; she consistently dismissed them with an almost absentminded air. He was the only one she'd allowed to draw close, to impinge on her personal world. Unlike Geoffrey, he didn't need to worry that some rake would appear and turn her head.

Reaching Alicia, all thoughts of Adriana and her swains disappeared; taking Alicia's hand—the hand she now freely offered—he bowed, then placed her fingers on his sleeve, covering them with his.

She looked up at him, faintly arched a brow.

He simply smiled at her.

With a haughty look, she returned to her watching brief.

He studied her. Her gown of apricot silk, a warm and subtle shade, deepened the rich mahogany of her hair and made her creamy complexion glow. The gown hugged her curves, the silk flowing over her hips and down the long line of her legs. For the moment, he was content simply to stand and let his senses drink her in.

Two days had passed since he'd last had her to himself. He'd spent those days and the intervening evening pursuing a whisper Dalziel had heard of a possible link between Ruskin and someone in the War Office. Nothing, however, had come of it; while there might be someone in the War Office interested in things that were no business of theirs, there was no hint of a connection between Ruskin and anyone bar the mysterious A. C.

He'd caught up with Alicia at a ball yesterday evening; he'd had to content himself with a waltz before leaving to spend the rest of the night trawling through gentlemen's clubs and exclusive hells.

Jack Warnefleet was busy, Gervase likewise in Devon, and Jack Hendon would arrive in town late tomorrow. Jack had conveyed his willingness to place his time and contacts at Tony's disposal, an offer he intended to take up with all speed.

Tonight, however, the single question nagging him was: how slow was slow?

Cumberland House was a massive old mansion, one with numerous useful little rooms; he'd explored it years ago with some amorous young matron who had known more of its amenities than he. Such knowledge, however, was never wasted.

The musicians were resting; he wondered at his chances of convincing Alicia that Adriana would be perfectly safe for a time.

He glanced at her; she straightened, coming alert. He followed her gaze and saw Adriana looking questioningly Alicia's way.

Alicia responded; he moved with her as she glided to Adriana's side.

Adriana looked uncertain. "Sir Freddie was wondering . . ."

Smoothly urbane, Sir Freddie stepped in. "I was wondering, Mrs. Carrington, if you would permit me to take Miss Pevensey for a stroll in the conservatory. It's been opened for the evening, and many others are enjoying the cooler air. I thought perhaps you and"—Sir Freddie's gaze flicked, man-to-man, to Tony—"Lord Torrington might accompany us?"

Alicia smiled regally. "A stroll in the conservatory sounds an excellent idea—it's quite stuffy in here." She nodded encouragingly to Adriana, who smiled and accepted Sir Freddie's arm. "You go ahead, we'll follow." Alicia glanced at Tony as Adriana and Sir Freddie turned away. "If you're willing . . . ?"

He looked down at her, then slowly arched a brow. She blushed lightly and glanced away.

Ignoring Geoffrey and his suppressed displeasure—an emotion Tony had no difficulty interpreting—he tucked Alicia's hand more definitely in his arm and steered her in her sister's wake.

While crossing the crowded ballroom, they chatted of this and that, but once inside the long conservatory, with its glass doors latched open and a wide corridor down the center cleared for promenading, there was space enough to ask, "How lies the wind in that quarter?" With a nod, he indicated Adriana, conversing animatedly with Sir Freddie.

Alicia humphed. "Much as I feared. Your friend Manningham has stolen a march on all others. However, as the saying goes, true love never runs smoothly."

"Oh? How so?"

"Adriana believes she should be certain of her feelings before she bestows her hand on any gentleman. And how is she to be sure other than by testing the waters?"

"Ah. I take it Geoffrey isn't taking well to her testing program?"

"Indeed."

He glanced down; a distinctly satisfied expression was stamped on Alicia's fine features.

"It's only sensible that a lady should be sure of her choice before declaring it, and if a gentleman has problems with that, well . . ."

Her gaze was fixed on Adriana and Sir Freddie; Tony told himself she wasn't speaking of herself. Their conversation drifted to other things, yet as they returned to the ballroom, he couldn't quite rid himself of the suggestion.

If she needed assistance making up her mind, he was only too ready—and willing—to supply it. How slowly could slowly be, after all?

The musicians had resumed; Lord Montacute was waiting to claim Adriana's hand in a country dance. Sir Freddie nobly requested Alicia do him the honor; to Tony's irritation, she granted Sir Freddie's wish.

Deserted, he went searching for the refreshment room.

Geoffrey found him there. He eyed the glass in Tony's hand. "Don't tell me you've been given your congé, too?"

Tony humphed; through the arch, he was observing the dancers. "Just for this dance." He sipped, then said, "Incidentally, I was informed you're being tested."

It was Geoffrey's turn to humph. "So I'd supposed."

Shoulder to shoulder, they watched the couples swirl about the floor.

Geoffrey shifted, lifted his glass, and sipped. He glanced at Tony. "I don't suppose you'd consider staging a diversion?"

Tony's gaze was on Alicia, twirling down the set. "Divert the lioness while you whisk away her cub?"

Geoffrey swallowed a laugh, nodded. "Precisely."

Watching Alicia's body sway as, hand high, she turned beneath Sir Freddie's arm, Tony asked, "What's your interest there?"

Geoffrey's tone—insulted, a touch vulnerable—gave him his answer more than the words, "What do you think?"

Tony nodded. "Done." He set down his glass. "But I'll have to move first. If she gets any inkling of your intention, I'll never get her away."

"The field's yours." Setting down his glass, Geoffrey followed him into the ballroom. "Just make sure I get at least half an hour."

Tony glanced at him, then looked back at his prey. And smiled. "Half an hour won't be any problem."

Getting Alicia out of the ballroom and into the tiny withdrawing room at the end of the east corridor—a room Tony remembered from that long-ago exploration—was the principal difficulty. He managed it by the simple expedient of talking fast.

His topic was guaranteed to fix her interest—the contrast between sophisticated gentlemen such as Sir Freddie Caudel and backbone-of-the-country types epitomized by Geoffrey Manningham.

"I didn't know he'd been in the navy." Alicia looked thoughtful. "I don't think Adriana knows that."

"Understandably he doesn't speak much of it, but he served with distinction. And then, of course—"

He rattled on, borrowing from his knowledge of Geoffrey, inventing shamelessly with regard to Sir Freddie. Her eyes on his face, her mind on his words, Alicia barely registered entering the corridor running alongside the ballroom; when she went to look around, he mentioned Geoffrey's mother—her gaze immediately swung back to his face. His fingers firmly over hers, resting on his sleeve, he steered her on.

When he opened the door to the withdrawing room, she swept over the threshold of her own volition, held by the vision he'd painted of Geoffrey's manor house and the surrounding countryside, the rolling fields leading down to the river with the blue hills in the distance, the lowering plateau of Exmoor stretching to the horizon.

Gesturing, she turned to face him. "It sounds an almost idyllic place."

Much of what he'd described was his own land, his boyhood memories of home; his smile was genuine. "It is."

He closed the door; without taking his gaze from her face, he snibbed the lock. The sound broke the spell.

She blinked, glanced around. A three-armed candelabrum threw a warm glow through the small room. Aside from a chaise and a single armchair, the only furniture was a small table and a heavy sideboard. She looked at him. Directly. "Why are we here?"

He raised his brows, approached. "Guess."

Suspicion burgeoned in her eyes; as usual, she made no effort to hide it. He watched her cast about in her mind for some deflecting comment, yet as he neared . . . her eyes widened, darkened—he could almost see her senses awakening, stretching. Reaching for him. Could almost see her wits start to slow . . .

He reached for her, gently drew her to him.

She came without resistance, her hands rising to rest on his chest. Her gaze dropped to his lips. "I . . . ah . . . I thought we'd agreed to slow down."

"We did." He urged her closer, settled her against him, bent his head. "We are." He kissed her, made her lips cling. "Progressing step by small step."

He took her mouth again; she gave it freely, met him, parted her lips, welcomed him in. Her hands clenched, clutched as he captured her senses and drew her deeper into the exchange, into the sensual game they both so enjoyed.

Lips caressed, pressed, tongues tangled, stroked, probed, mouths melded. Both took, gave, delighted, then explored.

Sensation streaked through Alicia; warmth welled, pooled, and dragged her senses down to wallow, to luxuriate, to expand and experience a world of sensual delight, of wanton, illicit, addictive pleasure.

No matter how much a small part of her mind tried to warn her, tried to make her see how dangerous it could be, her body, her nerves, her skin and her senses, and the greater part of her whirling wits, were eager to go forward, to follow the path he opened before her, to seize the moment to learn and feel.

To learn of herself, of what could be, of all she could be. To feel the welling tide of compulsive emotions—the hunger, the need, the flagrant desire, and most especially the triumph.

A simple and pure triumph she hadn't known existed, the confidence, delight, and sheer pleasure of knowing he found her desirable, that he wanted her in the most blatantly sexual way, and the satisfaction that flowed from knowing not only that she could evoke his hunger, but also from the innate womanly knowledge that she could, indeed, sate it.

He'd drawn her close, fitting her body against his, but once they reached that plateau of more urgent, definite need—one she now recognized—his arms eased, then his hands, hard and demanding, slid over her silk-encased form. Over her back, over her sides, around over her already aching breasts.

Through the fog of desire flooding her mind, she inwardly smiled. She eased back from the kiss enough to murmur against his lips, "I'm afraid this gown has no buttons down the front." She'd worn her topaz silk for that very reason.

"I'd noticed," he murmured back.

His lips brushed hers, then settled, drawing her into a long, increasingly intimate exchange . . . as it ended her awareness slowly returned. And she realized the pressure about her breasts had eased.

Her bodice was loose.

She drew back from the kiss as he did. Looked down as he raised his hands to her shoulders. Slowly, very slowly, he pushed her now gaping gown off her shoulders, sliding the small puff sleeves down her arms.

He'd undone the laces.

Her mind seized; she stopped breathing. She hadn't thought . . .

The neckline caught across the peaks of her breasts. Leaving the sleeves at her elbows, he ran his fingers up, then slipped them beneath the neckline and eased it over and down.

She shuddered, told herself it was due to the cool caress of the air. Knew it wasn't. Desperate, she hauled in a breath. Ignored the sudden lifting of her breasts. "Wait—"

"Lift your arms." The words were half entreaty, half command. They were reinforced by his touch, fingertips running over her bared shoulders, down the sensitive skin of her arms to her elbows. He gripped lightly, urged.

She freed her arms from the clinging sleeves. "This—"

"Is the smallest step I could think of." His black gaze touched hers; the emberlike glow in the dark depths only heated her more.

She sucked in a tight breath. "But—"

"Going slowly isn't stopping." He held her gaze, his fingers lightly caressing—so lightly they barely touched the heavy, swelling curves of her breasts. "You don't want to stop."

Not a question, a statement, one verified by the shiver that streaked through her, a silvery sensation that brought every nerve alive.

His lips curved, openly predatory, entirely undisguised. He bent his head. His lips cruised over hers as his fingers drifted, as his hands followed, then firmed, taking possession as they had before. But before she hadn't been as aware, as blatantly near-naked. As heated.

Her breath caught.

One hand kneaded, the other slid away. His arm slipped about her waist; holding her, he backed her, step by slow, easy step until she felt the sideboard behind her.

Lifting his head, he fastened both hands about her waist and lifted her to the sideboard's top. He sat her there; hands clutching his shoulders, she glanced down. Her gown had slid to her hips. Before she could react, he bunched the skirts and raised them to her knees, allowing him to part them and step between.

Her mind was whirling, wits totally scattered.

He met her eyes; his lips curved, but it wasn't exactly in a smile. "For us . . . the only way to slow our inevitable progression is to indulge in more intensive play."

She searched his eyes, instinctively accepted that as truth. Yet . . .

He leaned closer, lips swooping, nearing as his hands rose, fingers reaching for the tiny ribbon bows securing her silk chemise. The last flimsy barrier screening her from his sight.

Dizzy desperation gripped her; she sank her fingers into his shoulders. "I—"

He hesitated, but when she couldn't find the words—any words that made sense—he closed the inch between their lips, kissed. Drew back enough to breathe, "You know where we're headed, don't you? You know what lies at the end of our road."

Her lips were dry, yearning, hungry. She forced herself to nod. "Yes."

"Then there's no reason I shouldn't see you, bare you, and look my fill. No reason I shouldn't take what pleasure I wish with you, in you—and you shouldn't take all you wish of me."

His lips closed on hers, warm and beguiling; he didn't rip her wits away, didn't send them spinning, but left her aware, attuned, every nerve tight and flickering.

So she knew when his fingers closed on the ribbon ties, so she felt the tugs as he unraveled the bows, then slowly, gently, inexorably eased the fine fabric down. Exposing her breasts.

And then his hands were on her, hot skin to hot skin. He caressed, fondled, kneaded, squeezed. Her senses filled, overflowed; sensation rushed through her, down her nerves, down her veins.

She couldn't think, no longer had space in her mind for that activity, swept away, consumed by the dizzying splendor, the bone-melting pleasure he pressed on her. His lips left hers; he nudged her head back, skated his lips down the taut tendon to settle over her pulse point, heating her blood still further. Her fingers, until then gripping his shoulders, eased; she sent her hands sliding over and back, found and caressed his nape.

His lips left her throat and slid lower. Splaying her fingers, she speared them through his thick locks, then clutched. Eyes closed, she held tight as his burning lips cruised the upper swells of her breasts. Then dipped lower still.

Her world stopped when his lips found one aching peak.

Splintered when he took it into his mouth.

Hot, wet, he caressed, laved, licked, than gently rasped.

Her breasts felt on fire, tight, taut; head tilting back, she gasped, spine tensing as he artfully teased, then openly feasted. Then he shifted, drew the aching, tormented peak deep, and suckled.

The jolt of sensation rocked her, shocked her, surprised a small cry from her. Her fingers spasmed on his skull. Eyes shut, she struggled to cope, to cling to sanity as with mouth, lips, and tongue, hard fingers and palms, he pressed sensation after sensation upon her.

Through her fingers, through the tension gripping her, Tony read her increasing desperation. Every sense he possessed was locked on her, watching, gauging . . . he eased back.

Heard in her tortured breathing a return from the brink of panic.

He didn't take his lips from her skin, but traced, kissed lightly, soothed with gentle caresses. When she'd calmed enough to be lucid, he cupped both breasts in his palms, straightened slightly, shifting between her spread thighs. Bent again to touch his lips to the hot satin skin of the now swollen mounds. "Didn't your husband caress you like this?"

Her lids cracked open. From behind the screen of her lashes, her eyes met his. A moment passed, then she licked her lips. Tried to speak, ended by shaking her head.

When he waited, she dragged in a breath. "No. He . . ."

Primitive joy streaked through him. He waited; when she remained silent, he prompted, "Wasn't inclined to see to your pleasure?" A common enough failing, after all.

She shuddered. Beneath his hand, he could feel her heart still pounding, but slower. Her skin was still heated; he kept it that way, idly kneading, caressing.

Again she drew breath, again met his eyes. "I . . . don't know all that much about . . . pleasure."

The word came out on a soft exhalation; she closed her eyes as he again bent and savored one tightly budded nipple. He released it, blew gently on it, then soothed it again.

Lifting his head to examine the effect, he murmured, "It'll be my pleasure to teach you." Shifting his hands, he set his thumbs to circle her nipples.

"I—that's why . . ." She broke off, drew in a hissed breath. "Why it must be slow . . ."

On his shoulders, her fingers tensed again, but not, this time, with any sense of desperation. He watched her face as he caressed. "Forget about your husband. Forget all you ever knew." Keeping one hand on her breast, he slid the other to the small of her back and eased her to the sideboard's edge. His hand still at her breast, he bent his head to take her mouth.

Before he did, he murmured, his voice low, gravelly, decided. "Start again. With me. I'll teach you all you should know, all you need to know."

Her fingers slid to his nape, cupped as he covered her lips, held tight as he plunged into her mouth and took possession. Plundered, ravished, devoured as he wished; she met him, went with him, followed him deeper. Until the exchange became a flagrant echo of that other intimacy, until hot and heated she clung to the rhythm, matching him, sating his hunger as it rose, learning of her own.

He'd pressed her thighs wide; her silk skirts lay in a spill covering her knees, but beneath . . . he knew precisely what he would find when he released her breast and slid his hand beneath the folds of silk.

The skin of her inner thighs was as fine as the silk, as delicate, but far warmer. She was too deep in the kiss to do more than vaguely register as he stroked, caressed. Deliberately, he let her surface, step by step until he sensed her sudden awareness, felt the gasp smothered between their lips as she realized.

She started to tense; he deepened the kiss, just enough to distract her, to fracture her attention long enough to let him explore further. To reach higher and find her, swollen and fever-damp, hot enough to scald.

Slow. Step by step.

He forced himself to do no more than touch her, to find the tiny nubbin within the folds and caress, but go no further.

Tiny shivers of sensation coursed through her as he stroked, gently pressed. He knew what he might do, knew the potential, but sensed she wasn't ready for that yet.

Alfred Carrington must have been an insensitive clod.

He continued to touch her gently, undemandingly exploring, letting her grow accustomed to him touching her there, to the intimacy, mild to his mind though it was.

Step by step.

He let her surface by degrees, let her awareness rise free from the drugging kisses, until at the last he could raise his head and watch her face. Watch her lips, parted and swollen as he circled, then pressed lightly. Catch her eyes as he stroked, and she shuddered.

Then softly sighed.

She dropped her forehead to his shoulder. After a moment, said, "This is all so—"

She broke off. He stroked again, felt her shiver. "More than you expected?"

Against his shoulder, she nodded. "Much, much more."

Satisfied with the way events were proceeding not just with Alicia but also with his investigation, Tony felt distinctly mellow, a prey to pleasurable anticipation as the next evening he went upstairs to change.

He'd reached the landing when a heavy knock fell on the front door.

He recognized the knock. Halting, he waited, one hand on the balustrade as Hungerford strode majestically to the door. He'd recognized the knock, too. He pulled open the door, revealing Maggs.

Hungerford looked down his nose. "I believe you know where the back entrance is?"

"'Course I do. Live here, don't I?" Maggs lumbered in, his hat in his hands. "But I'm supposed to be Mrs. Carrington's footman. If I came with a message, I wouldn't come to the back door, would I?"

Turning back down the stairs, Tony straightened his lips. "What is it, Maggs?"

Maggs looked up. "Oh, there you be." He hesitated, frown growing as Tony descended. As he gained the front hall, Maggs suggested, "You might want to hear this in private."

Brows rising, Tony looked at Hungerford. "Thank you, Hungerford. I'm sure Maggs can see himself out."

That last was said with a hint of understanding. Hungerford bowed stiffly. "Indeed, my lord. If you have need of anything, you have only to ring."

"Thank you." Tony turned to Maggs and waved to the study. Hungerford departed; Maggs opened the study door. Tony entered and went to sit behind his desk; closing the door, Maggs came to stand before it.

Maggs had been a stable lad at Torrington Chase when Tony had been a boy; he'd attached himself to the son of the house and followed him into the army. Whenever Tony had had need of a batman, Maggs had filled the position. He'd been a part of Tony's life for longer than he could remember, and continued as his most trusted servant. Despite Maggs's bruiser's countenance, the man was intelligent, capable, and effective.

"What is it?" Tony asked.

Maggs's frown hadn't eased. "I don't know as you'll believe this, but the ladies, Mrs. Carrington and Miss Pevensey, are sitting down to dinner—well, they'd be near to finished by now—with a gentleman goes by the name of Mr. King. Wouldn't've thought much of it 'cept I've seen him before, and I'd swear on my mother's grave he's Mr. King, the moneylender."

Tony blinked. After a long moment of staring at Maggs, he nodded. "You're right—I find that very hard to believe."

Maggs sighed heavily. "Well, there you are. But Collier's on watch at the corner, so you needn't think I've deserted my post and left the lady unguarded."

"Good." Tony was finding it hard to focus his thoughts. Mr. King? As a *dinner guest*? He refocused on Maggs. "What's the relationship between Mr. King and the ladies? How did they react to him?"

"Friendly." Maggs shrugged. "Nothing heavy-handed, if that's what you're thinking. They treated him like he was an old friend of the family."

Tony inwardly goggled. He stood. "Come on. I'll know Mr. King if I see him." He shook his head as he rounded the desk. "I can't believe this."

"Aye, well." Maggs lumbered after him. "I did warn you."

Half an hour later, from the shadows of his town carriage pulled up by the curb close to the end of Waverton Street, Tony watched a large, burly gentleman take his leave of Alicia and Adriana. The sisters remained just inside the front hall, but the hall and porch lights were lit; it was easy to make out the genuineness of their smiles as the three shook hands.

Then Mr. King turned and descended to the unmarked black carriage that awaited him.

Maggs had returned to his duties. Collier, the man Tony had set to watch the street, was in his accustomed place. Tony sat back and waited until Mr. King's carriage rumbled past. He didn't bother to glance again at the occupant; it was definitely London's most famous moneylender.

He remembered Alicia's odd reaction when he'd mentioned he'd visited the man.

The door of the Carrington abode shut. Slumped against the cushions, Tony waited, totally unable to formulate any possible scenario to account for what he'd seen. Five minutes later, he tapped on the roof and directed his coachman to return to Upper Brook Street.

Courtesy of Maggs, these days he always knew where Alicia would be. That evening, she was attending Lady Magnuson's ball; as usual, he found her by the side of the room, watching over Adriana.

Who, he inwardly admitted, now needed to be watched. The Season was nearly upon them; the wolves of the ton were back in force, actively hunting in their favorite ground. As he approached, he saw Alicia step forward and engage one of the younger brethren who, until then, had remained unwisely oblivious of her presence.

It was instantly apparent from the young buck's face that a few words had sufficed for her to draw blood; his face hardened, lips thinning. After one last look at Adriana, he sloped off to find easier—less well guarded—prey.

A flicker of unease tickled Tony's shoulder blades. Adriana and her beauty posed a danger. She was too young to fix the interest of the truly dangerous blades, yet she nevertheless drew their eyes, which then passed on—to her sister. Who was much more the sort to attract a connoisseur's attention.

Reaching Alicia, gowned in a pale bronze creation edged with tiny pearls, he took the hand she offered, almost absentmindedly raised it to his lips, then met her eyes as he kissed.

He watched a light blush rise to her cheeks.

She tugged; placing her hand on his sleeve, he covered it with his.

"I need to speak with you." He glanced at Adriana's court. "And before you tell me you need to remain here and protect your sister, regardless of your recent intervention, you don't."

She frowned. "That doesn't make sense."

"It does if you consider." Casting a last glance at Adriana's circle, he turned her, steering her down the long room. "If you hadn't stepped in, either Sir Freddie or Geoffrey would have. Or even Montacute. They've been dancing at your sister's feet for weeks—none of them will take kindly to any rakish interloper thinking to poach their prize."

She still frowned, more in puzzlement than irritation, but continued strolling beside him. "You make it sound like a competition. A sport."

"It's a game no matter which side you're on." He spotted an opening between two groups of potted palms; deftly, he whisked them into it. "Now, quite aside from that . . ."

He stopped, unsure how to proceed. How to ask what he had to. He glanced at her; she was studying him, not suspiciously but directly. "I was passing along Waverton Street earlier this evening and saw Mr. King leaving your house."

Her gaze didn't waver; she continued to regard him attentively.

"I mentioned meeting Mr. King in the course of my investigations. Is he . . . an acquaintance?"

Without hesitation, she nodded, then looked out at the room. "Yes—he's just that, an acquaintance."

Alicia let a moment elapse, then, her gaze still on the crowd, asked, "Do you want to know why he called?"

She heard a hiss, an exhalation through his teeth.

"Yes."

She'd assumed he would hear of King's visit; she'd rehearsed her explanation. "We made his acquaintance some months ago through matters arising from my late husband's estate. Mr. King knew of our wish to establish Adriana creditably." She glanced up, and found Tony watching her closely. "He offered to give us the benefit of his knowledge regarding the financial status of any gentleman Adriana was seriously considering."

The look in his eyes was priceless; he was astounded, could barely believe his ears . . . she sensed it the moment he did.

His gaze sharpened. "What did Mr. King say about Geoffrey?"

She grimaced, let her uncertainty show. "That he's perfectly sound. He's never had dealings with any moneylenders, but they would be happy to have him on their books. His credit is excellent, his estates are in exemplary order. Financially, he passed with flying colors."

"So why aren't you thrilled?" Two matrons took up position on the other side of one set of palms. Grasping Alicia's elbow, Tony guided her out of their nook. A waltz was just starting; the dance floor seemed the next safest place.

He drew her into his arms, looked down at her face as he started them revolving, noted the frown in her eyes. "It's obvious your sister favors Geoffrey, and he's intent on her. You've received reports from all and sundry that his character and situation are beyond reproach. Why, therefore, your hesitation?"

They revolved twice before she met his eyes. Her gaze was level and serious. "Money, title, and estate are all well and good, and character to date as well. But who can foresee the future?" She blew out a breath and looked away. "If I could be certain he's all Adriana *deserves*, I'd feel happier."

Tony steered her around the tight turn at the end of the room; she remained relaxed in his arms, warm, at ease, yet as so often was the case, focused on her family, in this case, Adriana. He studied her face as they precessed up the room; he could read her abstraction clearly.

What a lady deserved.

He'd never heard that advanced as a criterion for marriage, yet for the sort of marriage Alicia wished for her sister it was perhaps more pertinent, more relevant. And she was right; such a stipulation was much harder to guarantee—that a gentleman could and would provide what a lady deserved.

The waltz ended, but her concept remained, inhabiting his mind, directing his thoughts as they strolled through the glittering throng. Lady Magnuson was old but wealthy and well connected; all those of the haut ton already in town were certain to attend, to look in for at least an hour and show their faces. Many stopped them, most trying their hand at divining just what their relationship was; neither he nor Alicia gave them any joy. Which only fed the whispers.

He glanced at her. She was frowning, trying to catch a glimpse of her sister's court. Lifting his head, he looked over the crowd. "Adriana appears hale and whole." He glanced at Alicia. "She's managing perfectly well."

She frowned at him. "I should return to her—"

"No, you shouldn't." He anchored her hand more firmly on his sleeve. "She's too sensible to go out of the ballroom without your permission, and with both Geoffrey and Sir Freddie standing guard, no bounder will have any chance of whisking her off undetected."

"Yes, but—" She broke off as he whisked her into a dimly lit corridor. "Where are we going?"

"I don't know." That was the worst of having spent the last decade elsewhere. Taking her hand in his, he strolled on. "I don't know this house."

His hearing was acute; he passed door after door, hearing muffled giggles or grunts from the rooms within.

She tried to slow, but he kept her with him. She tugged at his hand. "We can't just—"

"Of course we can." He stopped outside a door, listened, then hearing nothing opened it silently. Caught a glimpse of a white rump plunging, and swiftly closed it. "Just not there."

He heard the growing frustration in his voice; from the odd glance she threw him, she heard it, too.

They turned a corner; it was instantly apparent they'd reached a wing that was no longer in use. No lights glowed; there was dust on the sidetable farther along. He stepped to the side and opened a door, cautiously. Looking in, he breathed again. "Perfect."

He drew her over the threshold and closed the door, with one finger snibbed the lock. Busy looking around, she didn't hear.

"What a lovely room."

He released her and she headed for the windows; uncurtained, they looked out over a stone-flagged courtyard with a long pond in its center, a fountain, still and silent, rising from the black water. Lily pads were unfurling, spreading across the obsidian surface. Moonlight, stark and ghostly white, poured softly over all, casting black shadows in the lee of the creeper-covered walls, edging each new ivy leaf in silver.

She glanced at him as he joined her. "I wonder why the room's unused."

"The Magnusons were a large family, but there's only Lady Magnuson left now. Her daughters are married and gone." He hesitated, then added, "Both her sons died at Waterloo."

She looked around the room, at the furniture swathed in holland covers. "It seems . . . sad."

After a moment, she glanced up at him.

What a lady deserves.

How unpredictable, how ephemeral, how precious life was.

Slowly, he bent his head and kissed her, despite all gave her the chance to deny him if she chose. She didn't. She lifted her face, met his lips with hers. They touched, caressed, firmed. She raised a hand and gently, tentatively, laid her fingers along his cheek.

He slid an arm around her, smoothly yet more slowly than usual; it seemed important to savor each moment, to draw each instant, each movement, each acceptance, each commitment out. To fully know and appreciate every subtle nuance as they came together, as without words, he steered her to the next step.

Heat blossomed, spread beneath their skins, pooled low, then coalesced. Tightened. Throbbed.

Alicia opened her senses, tried for the first time to deliberately explore the effect of each touch, each caress. Whenever she tried to cling to control, she was swept away, so instead she went forward of her own accord, eyes open, senses aware, ready to learn, to see, to know. To, perhaps, understand what this was, what fed the power he could so easily conjure between them.

And learn to manage it herself.

As he did.

The kiss lengthened, deepened, yet not once did his control even quiver. He knew what he was doing, scripted and directed their play . . . this time she participated without hestitation, eagerly, determinedly following his lead. Waiting to see where it led.

She was trapped in his arms, locked against him, flagrantly molded to him when he finally raised his head. He looked down at her face. She could feel their mutual need, a well-stoked furnace seething between them.

He eased his hold on her, held her until she was steady on her feet. His eyes were dark as they held hers, yet she could feel the heat in his gaze.

"Open your bodice for me."

The words were gravelly, deep, and dark. She held his gaze for an instant, then calmly looked down. Lifting her hands, she slipped the tiny pearl buttons free.

She felt him exhale. His arms fell from her. He looked around, then stepped back and lifted the holland cover from a large shape, revealing a big, well-padded armchair. It was set facing the windows so any occupant could enjoy the view.

Dropping the dust sheet to the floor, he looked at her. Met her gaze as she slipped the last button free.

He reached for her, still moving with that measured grace that only heightened her expectations, that gave time for anticipation to well before she felt the next touch as he drew her to stand before him.

She watched him watching her as his hands rose and closed on her shoulders. He pushed the gown down, inch by inch steadily slipped the sleeves down. Without waiting for any instruction, she lifted her arms from the narrow sleeves, then, emboldened, draped them about his shoulders and stepped closer.

Saw the dark flare in his eyes as she did. Felt his hands tense on the folds of silk at her waist, then, holding her gaze, he slowly slid his hands down, tracing the curve of her hips, sliding her gown over them until, with a soft swoosh, it fell to the floor.

She caught her breath, felt the air on her skin, felt panic rise—

He circled her waist, drew her against him, flush against his hard body, and kissed her. Not ravenously but forcefully, then he lifted his head. "Slowly. One step more." He lifted his lids, met her gaze. "Trust me. It'll be as you wish." His gaze dropped to her lips; he lowered his head. "And all you deserve."

The promise feathered over her lips. Then he kissed her.

She stood locked against him in a dark, deserted room clad only in her chemise and her even finer silk stockings. If she wished, she could retreat—she knew it—yet as he kissed her she could feel the strength of his control, could feel the tight rein he kept on his passions.

Therein lay safety.

Nothing ventured, nothing learned. And she had to learn more. At least his next step, so she could predict the one after.

Tightening her arms about his neck, she kissed him back.

Nine

ક(જ઼્જી) જ

Her chemise reached to midthigh; in the poor light, he wouldn't be able to see through it. Her stockings covered her legs, the garters hidden beneath the chemise's hem. She was clad, albeit thinly; wrapped in his arms, his lips on hers, his tongue tangling with hers, she certainly wasn't cold.

Committed to playing her part, she set aside all maidenly reserve and gave herself up to it—to his embrace, to the slow-burning embers that glowed between them. No flames yet; he kept them dampened, but she knew the potential was there. It was a measure of his control that he could so easily hold the conflagration at bay, at a safe distance so she could feel the warmth, experience the pleasure, but not be burned by it. Not be consumed.

He held to his slow, measured, almost languid pace. The intimacy deepened; the urgency did not.

His control—the trust she placed in him—was what allowed her to stand within his arms and with simple passion kiss him back. He took her invitation as offered, savored her mouth, her lips; she in turn savored his pleasure.

When he straightened, eased his hold on her, sat in the armchair and urged her onto his lap, her confidence, her need to know, and her trust in him held firm, allowing her to sit across his hard thighs, to let him lift her, arrange her as he would. Then he drew her to him, locking her again in the circle of his arms, and kissed her. She responded willingly, eagerly, waiting to learn.

They were taking the long road; there had to be more steps before they approached the ultimate intimacy. She'd done her homework as well as she could, yet although she'd found two texts purporting to describe the physical aspects of intimacy as indulged in by blue-blooded rakes, said texts were so riddled with euphemisms she'd ended more confused than instructed.

The manuals had, however, demonstrated that the spectrum of activity was wide, that if an experienced gentleman were so inclined, there were indeed a large number of steps between a first kiss and consummation.

From what she'd understood, his attentions to her breasts, even his stroking of her curls, were relatively early in the sequence. Tonight, he wished to take one step further; she wanted to know what that step was. With luck, it would allow her to gauge just how far along their long road they were and how fast they were progressing.

How much more time in his arms she had.

That knowledge—that her time with him was limited—dragged at her mind; he seemed to sense it. He lifted his head. Close, their breaths mingling in the darkness, from beneath his heavy lids, he caught her gaze. After a moment, he murmured, "You're not frightened, are you?"

She thought, then shook her head. "No." She hesitated, then boldly raised her hand, traced a fingertip down his lean cheek. "Just . . . unsure." As far as she could, she'd be honest with him.

His lips curved, but didn't soften. The lines of his face seemed harsher, harder. Swiftly turning his head, he trapped her fingertip between his teeth. Bit gently. Then he drew it into his mouth, sucked . . . she blinked, then shuddered lightly.

He released her finger. His grin was so fleeting she nearly missed it. His arms tightened; he drew her back down, bent over her, paused to whisper in his dark sorceror's voice, "Slow. As you wish. All you deserve."

Then he kissed her.

Tony pressed deep, let the kiss, not just a meeting of lips but a melding of mouths, sink into realms they'd not previously explored. Let the drugging, absorbing effect take full hold . . . until they were captive, both trapped, held but not tightly within the web of their mutual desire. A desire that glowed, warm, alive, real, not yet red hot but a thing of flame.

She was with him, as committed as he to their road; he read it in her lips, through the way she met each increasingly explicit exchange, in the way her body, lithe and supple, lay lightly tensed, poised and willing in his arms.

Regardless, he held back, held his own desires in a grip of iron and focused solely on hers. On awakening them, coaxing them, stirring them—step by step, as he'd promised—into full-blown life.

She hadn't been down this road before; to one of his experience that was clear. Her husband . . . was dead, of no importance now. He set himself to search out and eradicate any lingering difficulties, any unnecessary hesitations. Any instinctive drawing back. He was committed to teaching her what could be—what should be and would be between them. All the glory he was capable of summoning and laying at her feet.

Her chemise had no straps; a drawstring secured it above her breasts. He caressed, taunted, teased her breasts through the fine layer of silk, then tweaked the tie undone and slipped his hand beneath.

Closed it about one firm mound, and felt something in her, and in him, ease in sensual relief. He drew back from the kiss, lifted his head to look down as he played. As he filled his senses and hers with simple delight, with uncomplicated pleasure.

She—they—had been this far before; despite her harried breathing, despite her racing pulse, she didn't protest, didn't pull away. He could feel her gaze on his face, watching him savor her, watching him fall more deeply under her spell.

He glanced at her, caught the gleam of her eyes from under her weighted lids. His answering smile was tight, dangerous. Shifting his hold, he lifted her, raising her breasts, her spine bowing over his arm as he bent his head to do homage.

In that, he held nothing back. Deliberately sent fire racing through her veins, set desire chasing hard on its heels. Her fingers found his hair, tangled, clung, then clenched as he feasted. He took all he wished, all she wordlessly offered, gave her in return all the delight, all the tight, thrilling, illicitly intense pleasure his expertise could evoke.

Alicia gasped. Her body seemed no longer hers. He suckled more deeply. Taut in his arms, a soft moan escaped her, then the suction eased, and fire flared anew; hot and scalding, it raced through her to flow into the furnace building deep within her.

Her breasts were on fire, but it was the increasingly insistent, increasingly powerful demands of her body that gripped her, shook her. Unknown, as-yet-incomprehensible demands that threatened to overwhelm her, to sweep aside what wits she'd managed to cling to. She struggled against the tide; she wanted to know more, to learn what this and their next step would be. They'd gone no further than before— yet. He hadn't even touched her curls—yet.

This time, she knew, and waited—for that knowing touch, that oh-so-illicit caress. Her whole body was taut, quivering in anticipation. Of that, of what would follow the delight, the almost excruciating pleasure he, with clear intent, lavished upon her.

His mouth was scalding as he tasted her sensitized skin. Her nipples ached with a deep-seated pain that was intensely sweet. Then he placed his hand, large and heavy, over her waist; through the silk, she felt its heat and hardness, felt her muscles leap.

He raised his head. Looked down at her breasts. Even in the dimness, she could see the possessiveness limning his features.

His gaze rose. Black, hot, it searched her face, read her features, then his eyes returned to hers. He held her gaze, held her awareness.

His hand drifted lower.

The silk softly shushed, the last barrier between his hand and her flesh. Flesh that now pulsed hotly, nerves that slowly, slowly tightened with expectation.

Almost negligently, he caressed her stomach, then his hand drifted to the curve of her hip, then followed the line of one thigh.

Tony watched her, watched her senses follow his hand, his fingers. He did nothing to break the spell, held aside his own clamorous instincts and forced himself to keep to the same slow steady pace that had, from the moment they'd entered the room, contributed to the magic.

Orchestrated it, built it.

He needed that magic. He didn't just want to introduce her to passion, to take her and make her his. He wanted—needed—to expand her horizons, to bring her to know, to experience, and ultimately to want to explore the outer reaches of desire with him. To achieve that he needed to show her, to make her see and appreciate that there was a great deal more beyond the simple act.

So he held back his frustration, without compunction sacrificed it to their greater good, closed his mind against the drumming insistence of even deeper instincts, those that had reacted to the thought of other men—other rakes—coveting her as he did, those instincts that still, beneath all else, prowled, prodded to possessive life by the nebulous threat of her involvement with Ruskin.

He pushed them all aside, and concentrated on her. On the tale told by her rapid breathing, the way her nerves leapt as he stroked down her thigh. The armchair was commodious; her legs were a heated weight across his lap. Against one firm thigh, he was hard as rock, rigid and aching, but relief was not in the cards, not tonight. He'd survive, but he was determined in recompense to advance their one small step.

Still holding her gaze, he closed his fingers about one knee and lifted it, shifted it, parting her thighs. She permitted it, but tensed; her breathing tightened. Intent, he kept her with him and stroked his fingers, his palm, up the sensitive inner face of her thigh.

All the way to where her tight curls brushed his fingertips. He smoothed them aside, in the same movement boldly cupped her. Set his hand to her softness and covered it. Claimed it.

She caught her breath, stopped breathing entirely. His gaze locked with hers, he held still, then, adhering to that same slow steady beat, he eased his palm back, and with his thumb and one finger began to explore her.

Alicia quivered, and followed his every move. She couldn't do otherwise; he had her locked to him in some heightened state where she was shockingly aware of their flagrantly sexual play, where they were in some way connected so she both felt the sensations of his touch and simultaneously experienced something of his reaction.

Of what he felt as he learned her, caressed and boldly explored the soft, swollen folds between her thighs. She'd never known that part of her body to feel so hot, so wet, so achingly wanting. Pulsing, almost throbbing; her hips stirred, of their own volition lifted to his caress as if seeking more.

A glimmer of satisfaction flashed across his hard face. That he understood her body better than she did she didn't doubt; his caresses changed, became subtly more deliberate, more potent.

More satisfying to both of them.

He was showing her, teaching her. She remembered his words as his thumb swirled knowingly about the tight pearl of sensation he'd found, that exquisitively sensitive spot that seemed pleasurably connected to every nerve she possessed. He swirled again and her whole body reacted; she arched lightly, heard herself gasp, let her lids fall.

"Stay with me."

The deep words were an outright command. She forced her lids up, met his gaze. Tried to read it and failed. "Why?"

To her surprise, the single word was all sultry temptation. Not like her at all, or so she had thought, yet it was. Emboldened, she shifted her hands, until then slack on his shoulders, let her fingers stroke his nape.

In response, his fingers stroked, but more slowly, as if savoring the wetness they'd drawn forth.

"Because I want you to know this, and I want to know you—all of you. All that you feel, all that you enjoy."

On the words, as if to demonstrate, his wicked fingers shifted, parting her folds, this time gently probing.

The action captured her attention. Completely. She moistened her lips; her gaze once again locked with his, she felt him ease one blunt fingertip between the slick folds.

Her body reacted, flushed, heated. She dragged in a tight breath. "One step."

He held her gaze, his eyes black, intent. "Just one step."

Slowly, he slid his finger into her.

Into the heated softness of her body, into the scalding furnace of her desire. Mentally gritting his teeth, Tony held tight to his reins and watched her outward attention splinter. Watched her focus inward, on the steady penetration of his finger into her tight sheath.

Her breathing was labored; she struggled to do as he'd asked and cling to the contact, to keep her eyes open, locked albeit unseeing on his.

Still keeping to their slow, steady rhythm, he reached as far as he could, gently pressed, then equally slowly reversed, until his fingertip reached the tight constriction that guarded her entrance. Then he reversed direction, deliberately pressing in, stroking the soft tissues, teasing the nerves and muscles beneath.

She lay in his arms, not passive but accepting, following, letting him learn her body even more intimately. Aware, as her widening eyes testified, of the building beat in her own body, of the heat, the burgeoning need.

Relentlessly, he built the rhythm until, with a small cry, she lifted against his hand. He pressed deeper, faster, clung to their visual contact as she climbed the peak, as her nails sank into his shoulders, her body bowing as the tension tightened. Heightened.

Then broke.

She came apart in his arms. The shocked awareness on her face, the stunned expression that was washed away as rapture took her, was a revelation—she'd never known the pleasure before.

As her lids drifted down, fierce satisfaction broke over him. His innate possessiveness roared, pleased beyond measure that it had been he who had brought her her first taste of sexual bliss.

He kept his hand between her thighs, one finger buried deep within her, savoring her contractions, the telltale ripples as her muscles relaxed into satiation. All her tension melted; as it did, he slid another finger in alongside the first, gently worked both deep. Stroked as she floated; she was so tight . . . Alfred Carrington had clearly been inadequate in more ways than one. When their time finally came, she'd need help stretching to accommodate him. Perhaps it was as well their time was not yet. Would likely be some while yet.

Eventually withdrawing his fingers from her softness, smoothing her chemise down, he settled back in the chair. And tried to ignore the musky scent that teased his senses, compounded by the warm weight of well-pleasured woman in his arms. Not an easy task.

Only one topic held the power to distract him; he turned his mind to scripting their next step.

Alicia reached home in the small hours, her wits in disarray. Her body . . . felt glorious. The former was a direct consequence of the latter.

She now understood something she never had before—why ladies allowed themselves to be seduced. If that evening's sample of what a noble lover could produce was in any way indicative, it was a wonder any lady remained a virgin by choice.

A gloating whisper in her brain suggested only those ignorant of the possibilities did.

Leaving her cloak in Jenkins's arms, leaving him and Maggs to lock up the house, she headed for the stairs.

Adriana joined her, glanced at her face. "What's wrong?"

Alicia looked briefly her way. Wondered that her experience hadn't left some tangible evidence in her face. She felt different from her head to her toes, yet no one in the ballroom, whence they'd eventually returned, had seemed to notice. Apparently not even her perceptive sister could see the change in her. "Nothing."

Looking forward, she remembered the two texts on lovemaking she'd consulted. Remembered their shortcomings. "I wonder if there are *advanced* manuals?"

She'd mumbled—grumbled—the comment aloud. Adriana, passing on her way to her bedchamber, cast her a puzzled look. "What was that?"

She tightened her lips. "Never mind."

Opening the door to her bedchamber, the one nearest the stairhead, she nodded a good night to Adriana and went in.

Closing the door, she stood for a moment staring into space, then she moved into the room, dropping her reticule on the dressing table, quickly unpinning her hair. She undressed and donned her nightgown—then couldn't remember doing it. Finding herself ready for bed, standing beside the bed, she climbed in and lay down. Drew the sheet and coverlet over her.

Lay flat on her back and stared at the canopy.

Every nerve she possessed was still humming; warm pleasure still coursed her veins. Yet there was an expectation, an underlying anticipation that the evening's small step had done nothing to assuage.

Instead, that nebulous but definite anticipation had grown.

She didn't truly know what it was, could only guess for she'd never felt it before. But then she'd never indulged as she had that evening, never let any man touch her intimately at all, let alone as he had.

And now ... having learned what she'd wanted to know, she found herself facing an even bigger unknown. An even more frightening unknown.

Knowledge, it seemed, was a two-edged sword.

By the next morning, she'd talked herself around. Her analysis of her situation, her decision on her best way forward, had been right; there was nothing in the events of the past evening sufficient to deflect her from her path.

It would, however, clearly behoove her to make a serious effort to push Torrington's investigation along. The investigation provided his major excuse to spend time in her company, seducing her, being kind to her brothers, helping her with Adriana ...

Pushing aside such thoughts, she rose from the breakfast table and went in search of the lists she'd made.

Tony sat comfortably slumped in a leather armchair in the library of Hendon House. Idly swirling a glass of brandy, he recited the story of Ruskin's death, the subsequent revelations, and the ongoing investigation to Jack—otherwise Jonathon, Lord Hendon—who was similiarly comfortable in another chair, and his strikingly beautiful wife Kit, presently perched at Jack's elbow.

"So," he concluded, "Ruskin's been selling information on ships and dates to someone, who presumably used the information for their own gain—they certainly paid Ruskin well for it. However, we have no idea of the precise nature of the information Ruskin passed, so we don't know how it might have been used—"

"And therefore can't trace said user of same." Jack met his gaze, his expression hard.

"That"—Tony saluted him with his glass—"sums it up nicely."

Kit straightened. "Well, Jack will just have to help you learn what was important about those ships, but meanwhile, what about this widow? What was her name?"

Tony met Kit's violet gaze. The first time he'd met her, he'd thought she was a boy—understandable given he was half-dead courtesy of a brig full of smugglers, and she'd been traipsing about in breeches at the time. Now her glorious red hair was longer, elegantly cut to frame her piquant face. Her figure, previously slender and slim, had filled out a trifle, but that only made it all the more womanly. Two children had done little to curb her fire; she was one of the most disconcertingly active women Tony knew.

He was supremely thankful she was Jack's wife. "The widow isn't involved, other than by the unfortunate act of stumbling on Ruskin's body."

Kit frowned. "Why, then, are you being so careful not to use her name? You've mentioned her at least six times, but always as 'the widow.' "

Jack had turned to study his wife; now he turned, and studied Tony. "She's right. What going on with this widow?"

"Nothing." Tony sat forward, then froze. To Jack and Kit, who knew him well, both his tone and that movement had betrayed him. "Oh, all right." He slumped back. "The widow is Mrs. Alicia Carrington, and she is, as you've guessed, of more than passable charms, and . . ."

When he didn't go on, Jack pointedly prompted, "*And . . . ?*"

Kit was grinning.

Tony grimaced at them both. "And it's possible, perhaps, that . . ." He waved the question aside. "That's beside the point. The first thing"—he fixed Kit with a narrow-eyed look—"indeed, the *only* thing I need from you both is help with this shipping business. We need to make some headway on how the ships were involved."

Kit continued grinning. "And later?"

She wasn't going to give up. Tony closed his eyes. "And later you can dance at my wedding." Opening his eyes, he glared at her. "Good enough?"

She beamed. "Excellent." She looked at Jack. "Now what could be the crucial *thing* about those ships?"

Jack studied the list Tony had given him. "If I had information like this . . ." He looked up, met Tony's gaze. "These are all merchant ships. If the dates are convoy dates, the dates on which these ships were due to join convoys to come up the Channel, or alternatively the dates on which they left the protection of the convoy to turn aside to their respective home ports . . ."

"You think the information might have been used to take the ships?"

"As prizes?" Jack thought, then grimaced. "That's one possibility. Another is deliberate sinking to lay hands on the insurance—I won't tell you how frequent that is. Wrecking is another option."

Tony pointed at the list. "All those ships are still registered." That was the first thing he'd checked.

"That makes sinking or wrecking unlikely." Jack looked again at the list. "The next thing to determine is who owns these vessels and from where they were coming."

"Can you do that?"

"Easily." Jack looked at Tony. "It'll take a few days."

"Is there anything else we can pursue in the meantime?"

Jack pulled a face. "I can ask, quietly, as to whether there's anything noteworthy about one particular ship, and perhaps put out feelers about a few others, but until we know something more specific . . ." He grimaced. "We don't want to tip our quarry the wink."

"Indeed not. Anything I can do?"

Jack shook his head. "Lloyd's Coffee House is the obvious place to ask, but it's a closed group. I'm one of them, so I can ask nosy questions, but the instant you walk in . . ." He looked at Tony. "You'd have to make it official to get any word out of anyone there."

Tony grimaced, then drained his glass. "Very well, I'll leave it to you."

Kit rose in a rustle of skirts. "I'll tell Minchin you'll stay to luncheon."

"Ah—no." With a charming smile, Tony stood. "Much as I would love to grace any board presided over by your fair self, I've other engagements I must keep."

Taking Kit's hand, he bowed with consummate grace.

As he straightened, she arched a brow at him. "I must be sure to make Mrs. Carrington's acquaintance."

He grinned and tapped her nose. "I'll warn her to keep a weather eye out for you."

Coming up behind Kit, Jack wrapped his arms around her waist. "Well, you've one night's grace—we're staying in tonight."

Kit leaned back against her husband's broad chest. "It was a wrench to part from the boys. It's the first time we've left them."

Tony noted her misty-eyed expression as she thought of her two sons. Last time he'd seen them, they were robust and active—the sort to run their keepers ragged.

Jack snorted and glanced down at her face. "God knows, by the time we get home, they'll have exhausted everyone and be lording it over all and sundry."

Tony saw the pride in Jack's face, heard it in his voice. He smiled, kissed Kit's hand, saluted Jack, and left them.

Ten

"We found a clue! We found a clue!" Matthew rushed into the parlor and flung himself joyously into Alicia's arms.

"Well, we think it's a clue," David temporized, following Matthew in.

"We had a wonderful time!" Harry's eyes were shining as he plonked himself down on the chaise beside Alicia. "Are there any crumpets left?"

"Of course." Smiling, Alicia hugged Matthew, relieved as well as pleased. Five minutes of studying Tony's lists that morning had convinced her that she, personally, had no hope of making any sense of them. Adriana, too, had had no idea, but had suggested Alicia ask Jenkins and the boys, pointing out that their frequent excursions often took them to the docks.

She'd harbored reservations over the wisdom of such a course, but Jenkins had welcomed the challenge for himself and his charges. The boys, naturally, had been thrilled to assist Tony in any way. Soothing her sisterly concern by sending Maggs with them, she'd consented to an afternoon excursion.

Releasing Matthew, she signaled Adriana, who rose and tugged the bellpull. A moment later, Maggs and Jenkins both looked in. Alicia beckoned. "Come and tell us your news, but first we need to order tea to celebrate."

She wasn't sure how much credence to place in her brothers' "clue," but they undoubtedly deserved a reward for doing as she'd asked and looking.

Matthew and Harry told her which wharves they'd visited, glibly naming various seagoing vessels and their likely destinations. Then

Maggs opened the door, Jenkins carried in the tea tray, and everyone settled to hear the news. Both Matthew and Harry were busy with their crumpets, today dripping with honey; by unspoken consensus, everyone looked at David.

He asked for the list; Jenkins handed it over. David smoothed the sheet. "There are thirty-five ships listed, and for many, there's nothing odd or unusual to report." He glanced at Alicia. "We asked lots of stevedores, and we found at least one who could tell us about each of these ships. So we know that for nineteen of them nothing odd has happened, nothing anyone knows to tell or talk about. *But*." He paused, making the most of the dramatic moment, checking to see that both his sisters had recognized its import. "We learned that the other sixteen ships were all lost—on or around those dates!"

David's eyes gleamed as he glanced from Alicia's face to Adriana's; hardly surprising, they were both agog.

"Sunk?" Alicia asked. "All sixteen were sunk?"

"No!" Harry's tone indicated she'd missed the whole point. "Taken as prizes during the war!"

"Prizes?" Puzzled, she looked to Jenkins.

He nodded. "During all wars, merchantmen are targeted by opposing navies. It's a customary tactic to deny the country one is at war with vital supplies. Even a shortage of, for instance, cabbages, could cause internal civil unrest and pressure an enemy's government. It's a very old tactic indeed."

Alicia tried to put the information into perspective. "So you're saying that sixteen ships"—she reached for the list David held; little 'P's had been written in the margin beside nearly half the names—"these sixteen ships were taken as prizes of war by . . ." She looked up. "By whom?"

"That we didn't learn," Maggs replied. "But those we asked thought it was most likely foreign privateers, or the French or Spanish navies." He nodded to the boys. "Your brothers hit the nail on the head over who to ask—it was their idea to approach the navvies. They unload the cargoes, so they remember the ships they've been hired to unload that don't come in, because then they don't get paid."

Alicia sat and absorbed all they'd told her while they consumed their tea and crumpets. When, finished, the boys eyed her hopefully, she smiled. "Very well. You've done an excellent job, and doubtless learned a great deal this afternoon, so you're excused from lessons for the rest of the day."

"Yayyyy!"

"Can we go and play in the park?"

She glanced out; it was still light, but night would soon start falling.

"I'll take 'em if you like, ma'am." Maggs rose. "Just for half an hour or so—let 'em run the fidgets out."

She smiled at him. "Thank you, Maggs." Then she looked at her brothers. "If you promise to attend Maggs, you may go."

With a chorus of assurances, they jumped up, jostling as they raced from the room. With an understanding grin, Maggs followed.

Alicia watched him go. She owed Torrington a debt for sending him. Maggs was as careful of her brothers as she could wish.

Jenkins cleared the tea things and removed the tray; Adriana returned to her sketching. Alicia sat with the list in her hand, and wished Tony—Torrington—was there.

That evening, Alicia had elected to attend Lady Carmichael's ball. Thus advised by Maggs, Tony saw no reason to arrive early; better to let the first rush ebb before making his way up the Carmichaels' stairs.

He'd spent the best part of his afternoon with Mr. King, learning more about Alicia, specifically about her finances. As he'd suspected, she had had a contract with King, but to his surprise, the man hadn't jumped at his offer to buy out said contract.

A degree of verbal fencing had ensued, until both he and King had agreed to show their hands. Once he'd made the nature of his interest clear, King had been much more accommodating; he'd agreed to burn Alicia's contract in Tony's presence in return for a bank draft for the appropriate amount. As King's goal was to ensure that no one, not even he, could hold the contract over Alicia's head, and as *his* only aim was to lift the financial burden from her shoulders, he'd been happy to agree.

The amount he'd paid had been another revelation. He knew how much it cost to run his various houses and to meet his mother's milliners' and dressmakers' bills; how Alicia was managing on the frugal sum she'd borrowed was beyond his comprehension. Her gowns alone would cost more.

Yet King had assured him Alicia was not in debt to anyone else. Understanding what had occasioned his query, he'd added that he, too, had thought the amount far too small, but when recently he'd dined with them, he'd detected not the slightest frugality or lack.

Tony now understood that the face the Carrington household presented to the world was a facade—a superbly crafted one with no cracks. Behind the facade, however . . . he'd recalled the lack of servants and the simple but hearty fare Maggs had described.

Like crumpets and jam for tea.

Alicia's payment to King, capital plus interest, would fall due in July. Her life would have changed dramatically by then, but if she recalled the debt and inquired, as both he and King fully expected she would, King had agreed to simply say that an anonymous benefactor had paid the sum. She would guess it was he; he was looking forward to her attempts to make him admit it.

Lips curving as he entered Lady Carmichael's ballroom, Tony inwardly basked in a self-satisfied glow.

He made his bow to her ladyship, then joined the throng. The ball was in full swing, the ballroom a collage of silks and satins of every hue swirling about the black splashes of gentlemen's evening coats. He looked around, expecting to locate Adriana's court somewhere along the side of the room.

Instead, he saw Geoffrey Manningham, shoulders propped against the wall, his gaze, distinctly black, fixed on him.

Instincts pricking, he strolled the short distance to Geoffrey's side. Met his scowl with a questioning frown.

"Where are they?" Geoffrey growled. "Do you know?"

Tony blinked. Satisfaction fled. He turned to survey the room, but didn't see the crowd. "My information was that they'd be here."

"You can take it from me they aren't."

The tension in Geoffrey's voice, in his stance, had effectively communicated itself to him. Tony's mind raced; he tried to imagine what might have happened. Could Maggs have been wrong? He looked at Geoffrey. "How did you know they'd be here?"

Geoffrey looked at him as if that was a supremely silly question. "Adriana told me, of course."

That raised the stakes. The sisters had expected to be there, and were now seriously late.

A contained commotion by the door drew their attention. A footman was whispering urgently to the butler, proffering a note. The butler took it, straightened magisterially, then turned and surveyed the guests.

His gaze stopped on Tony.

The butler swept forward, not running, yet as fast as one such as he might go. He bowed before Tony. "My lord, this message was just delivered by one of your lordship's footmen. I understand the matter is urgent."

Tony lifted the folded note from the salver. "Thank you."

Flicking it open, he rapidly scanned the contents, then glanced at the butler. "Please summon my carriage immediately."

The butler bowed. "Of course, my lord." He withdrew.

Tony opened the note again, held it so Geoffrey, looking over his shoulder, could read it, too.

The writing was a feminine scrawl, the hand holding the pen clearly agitated. Adriana had been too overset even to bother with any salutation.

> *My lord, I don't know who else might help us and Maggs assures me this is the right thing to do. Just as we were about to set out for the Carmichaels', officers from the Watch arrived, along with a Bow Street Runner. They've taken Alicia away.*

The writing broke off; a blob of ink was smeared across the page. Then Adriana continued: *Please help! We don't know what to do.*

She'd signed it simply Adriana.

Geoffrey swore. "What the devil's going on?"

Tony stuffed the note into his pocket. "I've no idea." He glanced at Geoffrey. "Coming?"

Geoffrey sent him a grim look. "As if you need ask."

They went quickly down the stairs and reached the portico just as Tony's town carriage rattled up.

Tony reached for the door, opened it, and waved Geoffrey in. "Waverton Street! As fast as you can." With that, he followed Geoffrey, slamming the door behind him.

His coachman took him at his word. They rocketed along the streets, swinging about corners at a criminal pace. In five minutes, the coach was slowing; it lurched to a halt outside Alicia's front door.

Tony and Geoffrey were on the pavement before the carriage stopped rocking. Maggs opened the front door to Tony's peremptory knock.

"What's going on?" Tony shot at him.

"Buggered if I know," Maggs growled back. "Strangest bit of work I've ever seen. Nice thing it is when a lady getting ready to go to a ball is set on in her own front hall. What's the world coming to, I ask you?"

"Indeed. Where's Adriana—and do the boys know about this?"

"They're all in the parlor. Couldn't keep the boys from hearing—there was a right to-do. Mrs. Carrington gave the blighters what for, but they weren't about to go away, nor yet let her go out and wait until later. I'm thinking she went with them just to get them out of the house, what with the boys and Miss Adriana being so upset."

Tony's face hardened. He led the way to the parlor. The instant he opened the door, four pairs of eyes fixed on him.

A second later, Matthew flung himself at him, arms clutching limpetlike about his waist. "You'll get her back, won't you?"

The words, not entirely steady, were muffled by Tony's coat.

David and Harry were only steps behind. Harry caught Tony's arm and simply clung, the same question in his upturned face. David, older, tugged at Tony's sleeve. When Tony looked at him, he swallowed and met his gaze. "They've made some mistake. Alicia would never do anything wrong."

Tony smiled. "Of course not." Putting a hand on Matthew's head, he tousled his soft hair; laying an arm around Harry's shoulders, he hugged him, then urged the trio back into the room. "I'll go straight-away and bring her back. But first . . ."

One glance at Adriana's white face told him she was as upset as her brothers, but having to comfort the boys and contain their panic had forced her to master her own. Despite the shock, despite the way her fingers clutched and twisted, she was lucid, not hysterical.

Her eyes were wider than he'd ever seen them. "They said they were taking her to the local Watch House."

"South of Curzon Street, it is," Maggs put in.

Tony nodded. Urging the boys ahead of him, he made his way deeper into the room. Geoffrey followed on his heels. While Tony sat in the armchair, the boys scrambling to perch close on the padded arms, Geoffrey sat beside Adriana. He took her hand and squeezed it reassuringly. She smiled weakly, rather wanly, at him.

"Now," Tony commanded, "tell me exactly what happened."

Adriana and the boys all started talking at once; he held up his hand. "Adriana first—listen carefully so you can tell me anything she forgets."

The boys dutifully settled to listen; Adriana drew a deep breath, then, her voice only occasionally quavering, she described how, just as she and Alicia were about to leave for the ball, a heavy knock on the door had heralded the Watch, accompanied by a Bow Street Runner.

"There were two from the Watch, and the Runner. He was the one in charge. They insisted Alicia had—" She broke off, then dragged in a breath and continued, "That she had killed Ruskin. Stabbed him to death. It was ludicrous!"

"I presume she told them they were fools?"

"Not in those precise words, but of course she denied it."

"The men wouldn't believe her," Matthew said.

Tony smiled at him. "Fools, as I said."

Matthew nodded and settled back against Tony's shoulder.

Tony looked at Adriana. She continued, "We tried to reason with them—Alicia even used your name. She told them you were investigating the matter, but they wouldn't even wait while we sent for you. They were totally certain—absolutely—that Alicia was a . . . a *murderess*!"

Eyes huge, Adriana looked at him imploringly. "They were very rough men—they won't hurt her, will they?"

Tony bit back a curse, exchanged a swift glance with Geoffrey, and stood. "I'll go there now—I'll bring her back straightaway. Geoffrey will stay and keep you company. If I'm an hour or so, don't worry." Resettling his sleeves, he flashed the boys a reassuring smile. "I'll need to have a word with this Bow Street Runner, and make sure the gentlemen of the Watch don't make such a silly mistake again."

Five minutes later, he strode up the steps of the Watch House. Two stalwart members of the Watch were heading out on their rounds; they glanced at him—and rapidly got out of his way.

Tony's heels struck the tiles of the foyer; glancing swiftly around, he fixed his gaze on the supervisor behind the narrow desk, who was already eyeing him with increasing unease. This Watch House was situated on the edge of Mayfair; the hapless supervisor would know Trouble when he saw it. His expression as he hurriedly got to his feet suggested he recognized it bearing down on him now.

"Can I help you, sir—m'lord?"

I believe you have something of mine.

Tony bit back the words, reined in his temper, and quite softly said, "I believe there's been a mistake."

The sergeant paled. "A mistake, m'lord?"

"Indeed." Tony drew out his card case, withdrew a card and flipped it on the desk. "I'm Lord Torrington, and according to Whitehall I'm in charge of the investigation into the murder of William Ruskin, lately of the Office of Customs and Revenue. I understand two of your men in company with a Bow Street Runner visited a private residence in Waverton Street an hour ago and removed, *by force*, a lady—Mrs. Alicia Carrington. The taradiddle I've been told—no doubt you and your men can explain it—is that Mrs. Carrington is accused of having stabbed Ruskin to death."

At no point did he raise his voice; he'd long ago learned the knack of making subordinates quake with a quiet and steely tone.

With his gaze, he pinned the supervisor, who was now holding on to his desk as if he needed its support. "I should perhaps mention that it was *I* who discovered Ruskin's body. In the circumstances, I would like an explanation and I would like it now, but first, before all else, you will release Mrs. Carrington into my care." He smiled, and the supervisor visibly quailed. "I do hope you've taken exceptionally good care of her."

The man could barely draw breath. He bowed, bobbed. "Indeed, m'lord—she did mention . . . we've put the lady in the magistrate's office." He hurried around the desk, almost stumbling in his haste to conduct Tony thither. "I'll just show you, then I'll get ahold of Smiggins—he's the Runner, m'lord. We was acting under his orders."

"Very well." Tony followed the bobbing supervisor. "What's your name?"

"Elcott, sir—m'lord, begging your pardon." Elcott stopped outside a door, and gestured. "The lady's in here, m'lord"

"Thank you. Please send Smiggins here immediately. I wish to attend to this business and remove Mrs. Carrington as soon as possible. This is no place for a lady."

Elcott kept bobbing. "Indeed, m'lord. Immediately, m'lord."

With a curt nod, Tony dismissed him. Opening the door, he walked in.

Alicia was standing by the window, dressed in all her finery for the ball. She swung around as he entered; the pinched look in her face dissolved as she recognized him. "Thank God!"

She didn't exactly fly to him, but she crossed the room quickly, her hands rising; shutting the door, he grasped them, and pulled her into his arms.

He held her tight, his cheek against her hair. "I came as soon as I could. You needn't worry about Adriana and the boys—they know I'm here, and Geoffrey's with them."

A large part of her tension dissipated; she looked up, pushing back to look into his face. "Thank you. I didn't know what to do—and I've no idea what's going on. For some reason they think I stabbed Ruskin."

"I know." Tony heard footsteps approaching. Reluctantly releasing her, he urged her to the chair behind the desk. "Sit down—try not to say anything. Just listen and watch."

A hesitant tap sounded on the door.

Resuming his previous, grim expression, he took up a stance beside Alicia's chair. "Come."

The door opened; a heavily built man in the distinctive red coat of a Bow Street Runner looked around the edge. He saw Tony; his eyes widened. He cleared his throat. "Smiggins, m'lord. You sent for me?"

"Indeed, Smiggins. Come in."

Smiggins looked like he'd rather do anything else, however, opening the door wider, he entered, then ponderously shut the door. He turned to face them; meeting Tony's eyes, he stiffened to attention. "Sir?"

"I understand you saw fit to apprehend Mrs. Carrington this evening. Why?"

Smiggins swallowed. "I had orders to bring the lady in to answer questions seeing as she was said to have stabbed some gentleman called Ruskin. To death, m'lord."

"I see. I take it Elcott informed you that I have been placed in charge of the investigation into Ruskin's murder by Whitehall?"

Hesitantly, Smiggins nodded. "That were a surprise, m'lord. We hadn't been told that."

"Indeed. Who gave you your orders?"

"Supervisor at Bow Street, m'lord. Mr. Bagget."

Tony frowned. "I assume a warrant has been issued—who was the magistrate?"

Smiggins shifted; all color fled his cheeks. "Ah—I don't know about any warrant, m'lord."

Gaze fixed on the hapless Runner, Tony let the silence stretch, then quietly asked, "Are you telling me you seized a lady from her own house *without* a warrant?"

Smiggins looked green. Spine poker stiff, he stared straight ahead. "Information came in latish, about six, m'lord. Sir Phineas Colby—the magistrate on duty—he'd already left. It was thought . . . well, the information was that the lady was looking to leave the country, so . . ."

"So someone had the bright idea to send you, along with two ruffians, to take matters into your own hands and forcibly remove the lady from her home?"

Smiggins trembled and said nothing.

Again, Tony let silence work for him, then softly asked, "Who laid the information?"

It was abundantly clear that Smiggins wished himself anywhere but there. He hesitated, but knew he had to answer. "From what I heard, m'lord, the information came anonymous-like."

"Anonymous?" Tony let his incredulity show. "On the basis of anonymous information, you acted to remove a lady from her home?"

Smiggins shifted. "We didn't know—"

"You didn't think!"

The sudden roar made Alicia jump; she stared at Tony. He glanced briefly at her, but immediately turned back to the now quaking Runner. "What exactly did this anonymous information say?"

"That Mrs. Alicia Carrington presently residing in Waverton Street had stabbed Mr. Ruskin to death and was likely to do a flit any minute."

His gaze on the Runner, Tony shook his head. "We already know that whoever stabbed Ruskin was taller than he was and had to have possessed the strength of a man, not a woman. Ruskin was nearly as tall as me—taller than Mrs. Carrington. She could not have stabbed Ruskin."

The Runner glanced at Alicia, then quickly looked forward.

Tony continued unrelenting, his tone lethally quiet. "You, Smiggins, and your supervisor have acted completely outside the law—the law you are supposed to uphold."

"Yes, m'lord."

"In a moment, I will be taking Mrs. Carrington from here and returning her to her home. Henceforth as far as Bow Street are concerned, she is to be considered as being under my legal protection in this matter—is that clear?"

"Perfectly clear, m'lord."

"And in recompense to Mrs. Carrington for causing her distress, and to me for disrupting my evening, you will undertake, with your supervisor's full support, to track down the source of your 'anonymous information.' You will do nothing else, take part in no other duty, until you have accomplished that and made a full report to me. Do I make myself clear, Smiggins?"

"Yes, m'lord. Very clear."

"Good." Tony waited, then quietly said, "You may go. Report to me the instant you learn anything—Torrington House, Upper Brook Street."

Bowing, Smiggins backed to the door. "Yes, m'lord. At once."

The instant the door shut behind him, Tony reached for Alicia's hand. "Come. I'll take you home."

She rose with alacrity, more than ready to leave; as he led her to the door, she glanced at his face, at the hard, set planes, heard again his tone as he'd dealt with the Runner.

As she walked beside him out of the Watch House, her hand tucked possessively in his arm, she absorbed the other side of him she'd just seen.

It wasn't until the carriage moved off from the curb and she relaxed against the well-padded seat that the shock and panic hit her. Until then, she'd been thinking of her brothers, of Adriana, worrying about them; until then, she'd taken everything in, but hadn't spared any real thought for herself.

She shivered and twitched her cloak closer, huddled into its warmth. If he hadn't come . . . a chill washed through her veins.

He glanced at her, then his arm came around her; he hugged her to him, against his warmth.

"Are you truly all right?" He whispered the words against her temple.

Her teeth were threatening to chatter, so she nodded.

Even through their clothes, the solid warmth of him reached her; as the carriage rolled on, negotiating the swell of evening traffic along Piccadilly, her chill slowly faded. His strength, the decisive and effective way he'd dealt with the entire episode, the simple fact of his presence beside her, seeped into her mind, into her consciousness, and reassured.

Eventually, she drew breath, glanced at him. "Thank you. It was just . . ." She gestured.

"Shock." He looked out at the passing facades. "We'll be back in Waverton Street soon."

Silence descended. A minute passed, then she broke it. "I didn't stab Ruskin." She studied his face as he looked at her, but in the dimness couldn't read his expression. She drew a determined breath. "Do you believe me?"

"Yes."

Tony gave the word, simple, straightforward, uninflected, and unadorned, its moment, let it sink into her mind. Then he looked down; taking her hand, he played with her fingers. "You heard me tell the Runner, and *Tante* Felicité and Lady Osbaldestone before that. Physically, you couldn't have killed Ruskin. I—we—knew that from the day after his death."

Her fingers twined with his. He could almost hear her mind working, hear the questions forming, sense her searching for the words.

"I. We. You told me you'd been asked to investigate, but until this evening, in the Watch House, I didn't truly comprehend what that meant, that you were investigating at the behest of Whitehall."

He felt her gaze trace his features. Waited for the next question, wondered how she'd phrase it.

"Who are you?"

When he didn't immediately react, she drew breath, straightened within his arm. "You're not just a nobleman the authorities—even less the gentlemen in Whitehall—just happened to ask to look into a matter because you stumbled over a body." Turning her head, she studied him. "Are you?"

He let a moment pass, then met her gaze. "No. That isn't how Whitehall operates."

She didn't respond, but simply waited.

He looked away, rapidly sorted through his impulses. He shouldn't expect her to accept him as her husband without knowing who he was, all he truly was. Ingrained instincts urged continued and total secrecy, yet he recalled the trouble Jack Hendon had landed himself in when he'd failed to tell Kit the whole truth. He'd thought he was protecting her; instead, he'd hurt her, nearly driven her away . . .

He glanced at Alicia, then reached up and rapped on the roof. His coachman opened the trap. "Drive around the park." The gates would be locked, but the streets around the perimeter wouldn't be crowded at this time of night.

The trap fell shut; the carriage rolled on. The flare from a passing streetlamp briefly lit the carriage's interior. He glanced at Alicia; she met his eyes, and raised a brow. The light faded; the shadows closed in.

Fittingly, perhaps.

He leaned back, resettling his arm so she could rest more comfortably, curving his palm about her shoulder both to steady her and keep her close. He tightened his other hand about hers, locking their fingers; in the dimness he needed the contact to help gauge her reactions.

Telling her all was a risk, but a risk he had to take.

"I told your brothers I was a major in the Guards, in a cavalry regiment." Her fingers shifted; he squeezed them gently. "I was, but after the first few months, I didn't serve in either the Guards or the cavalry."

She'd turned her head and was watching his face, but he couldn't make out her expression. He drew breath and went on, "There was this gentleman named Dalziel who has an office in Whitehall—" He continued, telling her what he'd never told anyone, not Felcité, not even his mother; quietly, steadily, he told her the truth of the past thirteen years of his life.

His voice remained cool, steady, his tone dispassionate, almost as if his dark and murky past was at a great distance. The carriage rolled on; she didn't interrupt, didn't exclaim or ask questions. Didn't pass judgment, but he couldn't tell if that was because she was shocked speechless or hadn't yet taken in enough to believe and react.

He didn't know how she would react. A surprising number of those whose lives and privileges he and his colleagues had risked their lives repeatedly to protect held that such services as those he'd performed, predicated first to last on deceit, fell outside the bounds of all decency and branded him forever less than a gentleman.

The knowledge that some who welcomed him into their homes would respond to the truth of his life, if they ever learned of it, in such a way had never bothered him. But how she reacted . . .

It was tempting, oh-so-tempting, to gloss over the dark facts, to paint the details of his life in brighter colors, to lighten them. To hide and disguise their true nature. He forced himself to resist, to speak nothing more than the unvarnished truth.

To his surprise, his chest felt tight, his throat not as clear as he liked. At one point, when recounting in bleak black-and-white terms the cold facts of his existence among the seedier elements in the northern French ports, he realized he'd tensed, that he was gripping her hand too tightly; he paused and forced himself to ease his hold.

She tightened hers. Shifted on the seat, then her other hand touched the back of his, and settled, warmly clasping. "It must have been dreadful."

Quiet acceptance, quiet empathy.

Both flowed around him like liquid gold.

His fingers curled, gripping hers again; warmth blossomed in his chest. After a moment, he went on, "But that's all in the past. Along with most others, I got out last year." He glanced at her, sensed the contact when she met his gaze. "However . . ."

She tilted her head. "When Ruskin was stabbed, and *you* reported the body . . . ?"

"Indeed. Dalziel reappeared in my life." He grimaced. "If I'd been in his place, I'd have done the same. Whatever the business Ruskin was involved in, it's almost certainly treasonous."

They'd circled the park; ahead, the flickering streetlamps played over the stately mansions of Mayfair. He reached up, and instructed the coachman to head for Waverton Street. Once they were within the fashionable, well-lighted streets, he looked at her and found her watching him, not judgmentally, not even curiously, but as if she could finally see him clearly—and what she saw was something of a relief.

Her gaze shifted past him, then her lips eased and she sat back. "So that's why Whitehall—this Dalziel person—chose you for the investigation. Because you've proved beyond question to be true to the country's cause."

No one had ever described him like that, but . . . he inclined his head. "It's important that whoever is pursuing the investigation is beyond question true, because with Ruskin being within the bureaucracy, it's likely whoever he was dealing with is in some way connected either with a relevant department, or the government."

Waverton Street was approaching; Alicia spoke quickly. Her mind was racing, thoughts tumbling. "So is your investigation supposed to be secret?"

His reply was wry. "It was."

She glanced at him. "But now you've had to step in and rescue me—I *am* sorry. I shouldn't have—"

"Yes, you should have." His hand tightened about hers. "Indeed, if you hadn't, I'd have been . . . displeased."

She frowned at him. "Are you sure?"

"Perfectly. Neither the Watch nor Bow Street will be falling over themselves to say anything about what occurred tonight. Unless whoever was behind this evening's events was actually watching the Watch House, they won't be any the wiser."

"Whoever was behind . . ." She stared at him. "You mean the person who laid the information . . . that was deliberate? I assumed it was just a mistake. . . ." Hearing the words brought home the unlikelihood of such a supposition. She faced forward. "Oh."

"Indeed." His tone had hardened.

She glanced at him as the carriage rocked to a stop; his face had hardened, too.

He shifted forward; reaching for the door latch, he met her gaze. "We need to consider how to react—how best to meet this new development."

"She's back!" Harry reached Alicia first, wrapping his arms around her waist and hugging her tightly.

"I'm all right." She hugged him back, then opened her arms to Matthew, who clutched and wriggled until, with an effort, she lifted him into her arms. David hung back, feeling his age, yet clearly wanting reassurance; she smiled, freed a hand, and drew him to her for a quick kiss. "Truly," she whispered, then let him go.

His somber expression eased; turning, he led the way to the chaise.

Having followed Alicia into the parlor, Tony pressed a hand to her back, worried about Matthew's weight. She flashed him a smile, then glanced down at Harry's head.

Transferring his hand to Harry's shoulder, he gripped lightly. "Come on—let's get her to sit down."

Harry glanced at him, then released Alicia; tucking his hand in Tony's, he went with him to the armchair and perched on the arm. Still carrying Matthew, Alicia walked more slowly to the chaise. Matthew slid down and she sat, then he crawled into her lap.

Beside her, Adriana laid a hand on her arm. "It must have been awful—you must have been so afraid."

Alicia smiled reassuringly. "I wasn't there long enough to get into a state." She glanced at Tony, then looked down at Matthew, snuggling close. She ruffled his hair. "Sweetheart, it's long past your bedtime."

He looked up at her, for a minute said nothing, then, smothering a yawn, mumbled, "Have you told Tony about the ships?"

She looked at Tony. Everyone looked at him.

He stared back. "What about the ships?"

Three pairs of eyes focused in brotherly admonition on Alicia. She waved in exculpation. "There's been so much happening"—she exchanged a glance with Tony, the memory of their drive around the park and all it had revealed high in her mind—"I haven't had a chance. But now you can tell him yourselves."

They did, in a chorus of statements and explanations that left him dazed. "Prizes? Sixteen of them? You're sure?"

Tony studied the list Alicia had fetched from her escritoire. The boys had gathered about him, David leaning over his shoulder, Matthew and Harry balancing one on each chair arm. Scanning the list and the inscribed "P"s, he listened as they explained how they'd gleaned their information.

All the ships were still registered, therefore presumably still afloat, as they would be if they'd been taken as prizes and subsequently ransomed by their owners.

Alicia sank back on the chaise. "Jenkins can tell you more if need be. And Maggs—he went, too."

He glanced at her, then looked around at the boys, meeting their eyes. "This is excellent." He didn't have to fabricate his enthusiasm, the sincerity of his thanks. "You've shown us which direction to pursue. Thank you." Solemnly, he shook each boy's hand.

They grinned, and continued pelting him with information about the ships. One part of his mind listened, cataloging useful details; most of his mind was racing, assessing, formulating.

When the boys' observations slowed, then stopped, Alicia rose, clearly intending to gather them and send them upstairs. He stayed her with an upraised hand. "One moment."

One glance at Geoffrey's face, and Adriana's, assured him neither would let him leave without a comprehensive explanation of what was going on; they were merely biding their time. His professional habits urged secrecy—information shared only with those who needed to know—yet this time other instincts, deeper instincts, were increasingly suggesting that sharing knowledge was a wiser, infinitely safer way to proceed.

His gaze came to rest on Alicia's brothers, on the three tousled, silky brown heads, currently bent close as they again examined the list of ships.

If he were on the "other side" in this affair . . .

They'd already targeted Alicia, not once, but twice. They knew where she lived. Anyone watching the house and her would quickly realize what her strongest instinct was—and therein lay her greatest weakness. It would be remarkably easy to engineer, and her reaction would be one hundred percent predictable . . .

Raising his gaze to her face, he waved her to sit. Puzzled, she sank down on the edge of the chaise. He glanced at Geoffrey and Adriana, then looked back at her. "This household—Adriana and Geoffrey, and the boys, too, and Jenkins, Maggs, and any other servants you have—all need to know the basic elements of what's going on."

Concern filled her eyes. She frowned. Before she could voice any protest, he glanced at her brothers; all three had come alert at his words and were now looking expectantly at him.

He smiled slightly, then raised his gaze and met Alicia's eyes. "It's the best way to protect everyone. They all need to know."

Geoffrey and Adriana were quick to voice their agreement.

Alicia glanced at them, then looked again at the boys. A moment passed, then she lifted her gaze to meet his, and nodded. "Yes. You're right. The basic facts so they understand why they need to take care."

He inclined his head. "If you'll summon the others?"

She rose. He watched her, inwardly acknowledging his ulterior—ultimately his primary—motive: keeping her safe. Keeping her brothers safe was part of that, but it was she who stood in the line of fire. Conscripting her household in her defense was clearly in everyone's best interests; each of them needed her in their own way.

Within a few minutes, the entire household had assembled. He hadn't previously met the cook and their old nursemaid, Fitchett; both women bobbed deferentially, then retreated to sit on the straight-backed chairs Maggs and Jenkins fetched for them. Maggs had warned him of the small number of staff, so that came as no surprise; given what he now knew of the family's finances, the fact even made sense.

When everyone had settled, the boys seated in a semicircle before his chair, despite the hour alert and eager to hear of his investigation, he told them, simply and concisely, all they needed to know.

He started by telling them of finding Ruskin's body, omitting to mention that Alicia had been there. Her gaze touched his face; he met it, held it, continued explaining who Ruskin had been, and what they now believed he'd been engaged in—selling information on ship movements that had led to at least sixteen ships being taken as prizes by the enemy.

The boys exchanged significant—excited—glances. Tony noted it; he bore their reaction in mind as he admitted to being an agent for the government, stressing that he was in charge of the investigation regardless of the Watch's and Bow Street's imaginings. The boys were, predictably, even more impressed, their approbation edging into awe.

From there, it was a small step to explaining that the investigation, while no longer strictly secret, would progress more surely if pursued with discretion to avoid alerting the mysterious A.C. He asked that they all continue as usual, but if anyone noticed anything out of place, no matter how small or mundane, they should tell Maggs or, if that wasn't possible, send word immediately to him or, failing that, to Geoffrey.

Able to read behind his careful words, Geoffrey, his expression impassive, nodded, accepting the unstated commission.

Finally, he came to his peroration, specifically intended to impress on his audience, especially the three boys, that the matter was serious—deadly serious. It required tact to walk the line between frightening the boys and fixing it in everyone's heads that in no circumstance were they to court any risk whatever. He alluded to Alicia's recent trauma—a trauma her siblings and the household had shared—as an example of how A. C. might play his game, but he also cautioned that whoever he was, A. C. would not balk at more violent deeds—it was assuredly he who had murdered Ruskin.

From the looks on the boys' faces, worry, concern, but also determination all present in their expressions, he succeeded in his aim.

He glanced at Alicia, faintly raised a brow; she met his gaze, read his question, nodded almost imperceptibly.

Glancing around, surveying the faces, he said, "So now you all know what the problem is, and that there's a need to keep alert at all times."

"Aye." Maggs pushed away from the wall. He looked to the other servants, getting to their feet. "We'll keep our eyes peeled, you can count on that."

"Thank you." With a nod, Tony dismissed them.

Alicia flashed them a grateful smile as they filed out of the room, then turned to her brothers. "Bed for you three, now. It's been a very long evening, and you have lessons tomorrow."

They looked at her, then, somewhat to her surprise, quickly rose. They came to hug her; she kissed their cheeks, then they hugged Adriana and, without any argument, headed for the door. Alicia turned. Maggs and Jenkins had dallied in the doorway; they took the boys under their wings and herded them upstairs.

She sat back on the chaise, hugely relieved, amazed, given the events of the evening, to feel so. Then Geoffrey was bowing before her. She gave him her hand, smiled in gratitude. "I can't thank you enough for coming to stay with Adriana and the boys."

He looked faintly irritated; he frowned at her, reminding her of Tony. "Nonsense. Any gentleman would have done the same." He glanced at Adriana, who'd risen, too.

She beamed at him. "But you did." She squeezed his arm. "Come— I'll see you out."

With a tired but genuine smile for Alicia, Adriana led Geoffrey to the door; he closed it behind them.

Alicia turned to Tony. He'd been watching the door close; now he looked at her.

His gaze rested on her face for a long moment, then he said, "My apologies. I should have asked before I spoke—do you expect any trouble with your staff?"

She blinked. "You mean because of . . ." She let her words trail away, uncomfortable with their direction.

He refused to mince words. "Because despite the fact I avoided using the term, a threat clearly exists toward this household, and, consequently, there has to be a certain if unspecified danger. Household staff aren't partial to getting caught in any cross fire."

She smiled at the military allusion. "In this case, you needn't worry. Cook, Fitchett, and Jenkins have been with us for longer than even I can remember—they won't give notice. They're part of the family."

He looked at her—studied her—then inclined his head and rose.

Quickly, she rose, too. In the distance, she heard the front door shut; she paused, waiting, then the sound of Adriana's light footsteps on the stairs came clearly to her ears.

And Tony's. One glance at him—at the black eyes that were watching her—was enough to assure her of that. But he made no move, simply watched her.

There was a great deal she wanted, indeed felt compelled to say. Quite aside from her rescue, aside from his revelations, his taking the lead in dealing with the matter, here, within her household, had given her time to calm, to reassess and catch her mental breath. She felt infinitely more confident, more assured, than she had two hours earlier. Her latent panic had disappeared; she could face the immediate future sure in her ability to cope.

He didn't move, just watched, waited.

She drew breath, lifted her chin, and closed the distance between them. She stopped directly before him—or would have, but he reached out and smoothly drew her on, into his arms. Her heart leapt; her senses stirred, came alive. His arms settled about her, a loose cradle; her hands coming to rest on his chest, she looked into his face.

A face that gave little away; she couldn't guess what he was thinking.

"I wanted to thank you." Without his intervention, she couldn't imagine what might have happened, how matters might have developed.

He said nothing; instead, he slowly raised a brow. His black gaze touched hers, then swept down to her lips.

She knew exactly what he was thinking. She didn't stop to consider, to assess the wisdom of her response. Drawing in a quick breath, she gripped his arms, stretched up against him, and touched her lips to his.

It was an invitation rather than a kiss; when he didn't immediately respond, she eased back.

His arms tightened, locking her more definitely to him. Her lashes fluttered up; his dark gaze met hers for an instant, then he bent his head.

His lips touched her cheek, a light, insubstantial caress. He paused, then closed again; this time, his lips found the corner of hers, and slowly teased.

As he drew back, just an inch, she turned her head, fleetingly met his eyes. Then she raised one hand, laid her palm along his cheek, and guided his lips to hers.

He closed them over hers and took what she offered. Her mouth, herself. He drew her deeper into his arms, parted her lips, and sank deeper into the kiss. Into the explicit exchange she now knew well.

She responded, more than willing. It seemed very right that she should thank him this way, that she should give and appease the hunger she sensed in him, that elusive desire she exulted in evoking, equally exulted in sating.

As far as she dared.

The warning sounded in her mind—there could not be that many milestones left in the long road they'd agreed to travel. All but instantly, that small voice of caution was drowned out by the memory of his assurance that instead they would dally longer, more intensely, more intimately at every stage.

His mouth feasted on hers; his hands roamed, pleasuring her while feasting on her curves. He molded her to him, explicitly rocked the hard ridge of his erection against her.

Heat erupted inside her, spread through her veins, suffused beneath her skin. Raising her hands, she framed his face, then ran her fingers back, spearing them through his hair. She opened her mouth wider beneath his, with her tongue boldly taunted, deliberately incited him to take, and take more. Never had she felt so alive, so blatantly desirable.

So wanted.

They were standing locked together in her family's parlor; she was sure he wouldn't forget. Felt sure she could leave the decision on what was appropriate to him.

She knew, in her heart, in her soul, that he wouldn't let her down.

Tony had no intention of doing so, yet the demands of the moment were many. A wild and primitive emotion was burgeoning within him; he didn't recognize it, but he knew what it demanded.

Her. Not just her giving but his taking. A claiming, yet . . . this, he accepted, was neither the time nor place.

Not yet, not here. Soon, yes, but tonight . . .

He didn't question the instincts that told him what to do; he'd been their captive for too many years. Experience analyzed, instructed, informed; he fell in with its directives.

Breaking from the kiss, he murmured, unsurprised his tone was low, almost harsh, "Jenkins?"

Courtesy of their kisses, she was close to breathless. "Upstairs. He locks up the front of the house early, all except the front door."

Thank God. He kissed her again, ravenously, arms locking her against him, lifting her as he backed her toward the chaise. Stopping before it, he lifted his head and let her slide down until her feet touched the floor. "So we're alone?"

"Um-hmm." Her hand pressed under his collar and curled around his nape; she lifted her lips to his.

"Good." He took them, kissed her hungrily, in no way disguising his need. She met him, flagrantly urged him on—didn't so much as catch her breath when he eased her gown over her shoulders, then pushed it down to pool about her feet.

Still he held her to the kiss. Shifting to trap her between the chaise and him, he closed his hands about her breasts. Through the fine silk of her chemise, he teased the sensitive mounds, stroked and kneaded until they were full, until her breathing was tight, threatening to fracture.

Swiftly, he undid the ribbon ties and eased the fine fabric down; it fell in folds about her waist. Deciding his control didn't need further strain, he left the flimsy garment there. It was so fine, it was barely a sop to modesty, but having her completely naked on the chaise beneath him might be that one step too far.

At the first touch of his hands on her bare breasts, she murmured incoherently, the words trapped between their lips, and pressed closer.

He held her, for long moments simply savored the sensations—of her mouth freely offered, all his, of her tongue slowly tangling, caressing his, of the way she softened as he explored, claiming at will, then artfully stoking her fires. A deep pleasure coursed through him, part victory, part desire, at the tactile confirmation his hands reported; he had her in his arms all but naked, her breasts bare, pressed to his chest, her hips, the cradle in which he ached to lie, screened by nothing more than a thin barrier of silk.

Now she was his, it was time to feast.

His hands shifted over her body, then he lifted her, knelt on the chaise and laid her on the damask, following her down so their lips didn't part, settling beside her, his longer, harder frame trapping hers on the cushions. One hand rising to cradle her face, he plunged once more into her mouth.

Plunged them both back into the building flames.

Alicia went willingly, eager to know, to experience whatever and wherever he led. She knew it was dangerous, yet when he finally lifted his head and released her lips, and she struggled to breathe, to fill her starved lungs, there was no thought in her mind of drawing back.

Not when he looked at her with desire, hot and glowing, behind his black eyes. His gaze had dropped to her breasts; they were swollen and aching. Nerves tightening, she waited for his touch, waited for the burning delight of his mouth, for the sharp, addictive pleasure.

His gaze flicked up to meet hers, briefly locked, then his lips curved, knowing and sure. He looked down, bent his head, and gave her all she'd wanted, all her tight nerves craved, the intoxicating play of lips and tongue, the hot, wet suction of his mouth.

He orchestrated the whole until her gasps filled the room, until her fingers were clenched on his skull, her body bowing under the hand he'd splayed across her midriff.

A deep rumble of satisfaction reached her; he shifted lower, leaning over her. One hand still massaged her breasts, stroking, tweaking, caressing as his lips trailed down between, down over the centerline of her body. With one finger he drew the silk folds of her chemise aside, so he could continue his line of openmouthed kisses to her navel.

Raising his head slightly, he circled the indentation with one fingertip, then lowered his head and boldly probed with his tongue, an echo of their kisses, of the plunder, the claiming.

Dazed, her limp fingers retensing on his skull, she watched him minister to her body as if it was a thing worthy of his worship.

Finally lifting his head, his eyes met hers; they were dark and fathomless, hot yet unreadable. Watching her, he shifted, parted her legs and settled between, ran his hand up her thigh, sliding it under the layer of silk to lay it over her stomach, hard possessive palm to her hot, soft skin.

She couldn't take her eyes from his, from the intent, burning look burnished in the black, didn't dare shift her gaze even when she felt his hand move, felt his fingertips brush her curls, then slide further to caress her as he had before.

Her breath strangled, her lungs slowly seizing as he artfully, deliberately explored, then stroked, caressed, finally probed. One large finger slid a little way in, just enough to tantalize, to freeze her mind, and send her frenzied senses searching. Reaching.

He caressed and her body came to life, muscles tensing, flickering, her hips lifting in anticipation. Slowly, he slid one long finger into her, pressed steadily deeper, deeper.

Her lungs locked; her hips lifted, but he held her down, moving lower, his shoulders sliding from her weakened grasp.

He looked down, watched as he worked his hand between her spread thighs, as he worked his finger within her, then he glanced up at her face, with his thumb circled that critical spot he'd discovered before, simultaneously reaching deeper still.

On a moan, she closed her eyes, let her head fall back. This had to be wicked; it was too glorious to be right.

A wave of sheer sensual delight swept through her, caught her wits, trapped her mind in sensations. Wild, wanton, indescribable pleasure flooded her; this time, he seemed content to let the wave lap at her, lap at her, rather than build.

The deliberate, flagrantly intimate repetitive penetration encouraged her to wallow in the warmth, to let her body simply enjoy every moment.

She was hardly relaxed, yet with every minute the landscape grew more familiar, less threatening. The urgency hadn't infected her yet, but she knew it would. Before it did . . .

She managed to catch her breath and look down at him. Reach for him, with her fingers brush his shoulders. He looked up; his eyes were so black she could read nothing of his thoughts, but his face was a graven mask etched with a desire she comprehended instinctively.

"You . . ." She moistened her dry lips. "I'm the one who's grateful. I want to give to you, not . . ."

Her gesture encompassed her body, thrumming with warmth and pleasure, and him, now propped between her knees, one shoulder cushioned against one of her thighs.

His hot black gaze didn't flicker. He glanced briefly down to where his hand steadily pandered to her senses, then he looked up and met her eyes.

"Then lie back, close your eyes, and let me take this, at least." His thumb swirled about the tight nub nestled within the now slick and swollen folds.

She tensed, but he held her with his eyes.

His words reached her, gravelly, low, primitively dark. "If you can't be mine yet, give me this instead. Let me claim this much."

Caught in his eyes, captured by the sheer need she could feel pouring from him, she tried to think, couldn't—didn't care. "Take—whatever you wish." Caution reared. "But . . ."

His gaze seemed almost blank. "Just one more step." He shifted further back. "Do as I asked—lie back and close your eyes."

He waited; she could feel her pulse hammering in the soft flesh his fingers were tracing. She had no real idea . . . couldn't imagine . . .

She closed her eyes, let her head fall back.

"Just like that—try not to move."

She didn't get a chance to reply. At the first touch of his lips, she lost all capacity even to think. Sensations buffeted her, rose and crashed through her. The intimacy all but slew her.

She heard her gasp, followed by a long moan as his fingers slipped from her sheath and blatantly, holding her thighs wide, he settled to feast.

His mouth worked, and she thought she might die. Of their own accord her hips lifted, twisted, but his hands had closed about them and he held her down, held her in position so he could, as he'd wished, claim her in this way.

A brutally explicit, intensely intimate claiming.

As she squirmed helplessly, struggled to breathe, the fact he knew of no reason to hold back, to withhold from her any degree of his transparently well-educated expertise, was forcefully borne in on her. He knew just what he was doing, to her, to her nerves, to her senses, to her mind.

To, in some way she didn't comprehend, her heart.

She might be giving, he might be taking, yet he gave selflessly, too. If she'd harbored any doubts that lovemaking was in essence a sharing, the long, heated moments she spent under his hands, under his mouth, with his tongue stroking, probing, lapping at her softness, burned every shred of doubt away.

The flames built, expertly stoked, until the conflagration simply became too much. Too much for her to resist, to hold back from the beckoning delight. She would have warned him if she'd been able, but he didn't look up, didn't pause in his increasingly potent ministrations even when she tugged his hair.

And then she was there, at the heart of the firestorm, and for one blinding moment nothing else mattered but the intense, golden glory. It held her tight, a vise of his making, then she fractured, and the glory shattered, sharp shards streaking down her veins to melt deep within her, beneath her fingertips, under her skin.

Exulting, Tony savored the powerful contractions, savored her release, then licked, lapped. Eventually, he eased back and lifted his head.

Ignoring the fiery pressure in his loins, he looked at her, spent, dazed, gloriously sated. Gloriously exposed. He let his gaze travel slowly down her body, seeing and claiming anew, then he bent and placed a kiss on her damp curls, pushed up her chemise, and dropped a gentle, lingering kiss on her belly.

Next time. He promised himself that.

Lifting away, he shifted higher and lay down once more beside her. Propping on one elbow, he laid a hand on her breast, and settled to watch her return to earth and welcome her back.

An hour later, lying in her bed with the house silent about her, Alicia tried to take in, to understand, all that had happened. Not physically; shocking though that had been, stunning beyond her wildest imaginings—or, apparently, those of the authors of both sexual texts she'd consulted—she knew, to her bones, exactly what had happened, what part of him had touched what part of her, and how.

That was a problem in its own right, but what consumed her, what mystified her, was the connection she sensed, the link that steadily, day by day, interlude by interlude, seemed to be growing, forged in the fires between them.

That was something else. Something beyond the facts she'd considered when she'd decided to adhere to her widow's role, to pretend to be as experienced as she was not.

He'd agreed to go slowly; by his standards, he probably had. Even though it was now patently clear that they'd all but arrived at their final destination, it wasn't panic over that that filled her mind.

From the first, she'd responded to his practiced caresses instinctively, had been forced to rely on instinct to guide her. It seemed instinct had, but in a way she hadn't foreseen, in a direction she hadn't intended to take.

She hadn't foreseen the danger. Not at all.

Rolling over on her side, she clutched a pillow to her and tried not to think about him, tried not to feel . . . tried not to be aware of the compulsion that had grown to give him more than she at any stage had contemplated.

Yet the more she fought it, the more she tried to turn her mind from the prospect, tried to deny it, the more it grew.

Fascination had turned into something more.

Something a great deal more powerful.

At an unusually early hour the next evening, Tony entered Lady Arbuthnot's ballroom. Without glancing at anyone else, he made his way to Alicia's side.

Truth be told, he didn't truly register anyone else's presence; his mind, all of his awareness, was centered on her.

Not by choice. He felt driven, whipped along at the mercy of emotions he'd never before had to conquer. Mild possessiveness was one thing, but this?

There was so much in her life he wanted to spare her—more, that some part of him felt driven to fix, almost as if his very self—his honor, his name, his self-respect—depended on it. Taking care of her, protecting her, keeping her safe, ensuring her happiness, had become that important.

How, he wasn't sure, but to his mind reasons were by the by. He knew how he felt; he knew what he wanted. He knew how he needed to act.

Reaching her side, he took the hand she smilingly offered, raised it, and placed a kiss on her fingers, then without pause, pressed another to her palm.

Startled, she searched his eyes. "Are you all right?"

He hesitated, then nodded. "Perfectly."

A lie, but he didn't want her asking questions he couldn't answer.

Tucking her hand into his elbow, he pretended to survey the other guests. The dancing had not yet commenced. "Has anyone behaved oddly toward you or Adriana today—here, or in the park?"

She glanced at him. "No." After a moment, she went on, her voice lowered, "Are you expecting rumors about me being taken up by the Watch?"

"Possibly. I want to know if any surface."

He could feel her gaze on his face, studying; he glanced at her, arched a brow.

She held his gaze. "What have you done? Tell me."

He debated whether to inform her he wasn't one of her brothers, but couldn't see it stopping her interrogation. "I've asked *Tante* Felicité and her bosom-bows to keep their ears open. I told her the bare bones of what happened yesterday—she and the few other *grandes dames* who were present were shocked and suitably outraged." He squeezed her fingers before she could protest. "This is the sort of thing that in different circumstances might happen to them. They have a vested interest in ensuring the customs of the ton aren't manipulated for subversive purposes."

Alicia frowned, then nodded, conceding the point. "I'll tell you if Adriana or I encounter any difficulties." She continued to study his face; he seemed more tense, more on edge than he usually was. "What else did you do today?"

He paused, to her now-informed eye deciding where to start rather than deciding whether to speak.

"I passed the information about the ships on to Jack Hendon."

"The friend who owns a shipping line?"

"Yes. Now he knows what to look for, we'll get along faster. I also sent word to another friend who's checking along the southwest coast. With luck, we'll have a clearer idea of what's been happening soon, then we can start following the trail back to the perpetrator."

"A. C." Remembering the fright of the day before, she shivered. Feeling Tony's gaze on her face, she met it. "He must be someone quite knowledgeable, mustn't he? He knew how to start those first rumors, knew how to trick Bow Street into seizing me."

Lips set, he nodded. "He's intelligent, and cold-blooded."

He hesitated, then went on, his fingers absentmindedly stroking the back of her hand. "I heard back from Smiggins. It seems his 'anonymous information' came via a flower seller who'd been paid by a well-to-do gentleman, one expensively dressed, to take the information to the Watch. She can't describe the man beyond that."

The vision of a gentleman wrapped in an expensive coat with an astrakhan collar, viewed through the mists of a chilly night, slid through Tony's mind. For him, A. C. was no phantom, but a dangerous adversary, one he'd yet to put a name to.

Which, of course, only made it harder to protect Alicia from the danger. He let his gaze drift to Adriana's circle; through her connection with Alicia, she, too, was in danger. There were six gentlemen gathered about her; Sir Freddie Caudel was, as usual, one of the crew. He was engaged in describing some play to Adriana; prettily, she hung on his words, her attention politely all his, at least for the moment. Tony was not at all surprised to see Geoffrey hovering even more determinedly, more definitely possessive.

From beside him came a small humph. "I daresay, if Lord Manningham is all you and Mr. King tell me he is, then I'll shortly be entertaining an offer from him."

He glanced at Alicia, caught her eye. "I should think that's a foregone conclusion." He paused, then asked, "Will she, and you, accept Geoffrey's suit?"

She looked at Geoffrey and Adriana, hesitated, then nodded. "If she's happy, and if he wishes to hold to his offer once he's fully informed of the family's circumstances."

He arched a brow. "Circumstances?" He knew precisely what she meant—the fact she and her brood were as poor as church mice. She, however, didn't know he knew; he wondered when she'd tell him.

She met his gaze, her expression open. "There's the boys, of course, and myself—not every gentleman wants to marry into such a close family."

More fool them. He raised his brows noncommittally, and let the matter slide. Time enough to see how she reacted to his proposal once he'd made it. With her and her family in A. C.'s sights, eliminating A. C. had to be his top priority; there would be time aplenty to speak of marriage once they were safe.

More guests were arriving; her ladyship's rooms were fast filling. He remained by Alicia's side; with only two weeks to go before the start of the Season, tonnish entertainments once more resembled the melee he recalled, one through which wolves of various hues prowled.

Félicité waved from across the room, then Lady Holland stopped by to compliment Alicia on her and Adriana's gowns. The comment drew his notice; as usual, the sisters were superbly turned out . . . again he wondered how they managed it. Then he recalled Adriana's preoccupation with fashion; she was forever sketching the latest designs, or similar designs artfully modified.

He looked again at their stylish attire. Understanding dawned; he saw Adriana in a new light.

"Good evening, Torrington—I trust you will introduce me to your lovely companion. I do not believe I have yet had the pleasure of making her acquaintance."

The perfectly modulated tones, still distinctly accented, jolted him from his thoughts. Lowering his gaze, he smiled easily and bowed. "Your Grace." His gaze passed on to the lady—yet another *grande dame* if appearances spoke true—by Her Grace of St. Ives's side. The lady smiled with charm, and a hint of determination.

"Allow me to present my sister-in-law, Lady Horatia Cynster." The Duchess of St. Ives smiled at him, pale eyes alight. She waited while he bowed over Lady Horatia's hand, then continued, "*Bon*! And now you may introduce us both to this lady, if you please."

He nearly laughed; one of his mother's oldest and dearest friends, Helena, Duchess of St. Ives, was both incorrigible and unstoppable. She was a petite force of nature, and woe betide any who thought to say her nay. He turned to Alicia. She met his eyes; he smiled encouragingly. "Ladies—Mrs. Alicia Carrington, allow me to present Helena, Duchess of St. Ives, and Lady Horatia Cynster."

Alicia dipped into a curtsy of precisely the right degree.

Impulsively, Helena took her hand and waved her up. "Your sister is *ravissante*, as all the ton now knows, but you, too, will do very well I believe."

Alicia smiled, but demurred. "I seek only to establish my sister."

Helena bent on her a look of patent incomprehension, then glanced at her sister-in-law.

Whose lips were not straight. "My dear, a word of advice—*you* may not seek, but the gentlemen assuredly will. Indeed"—her gaze slid teasingly to Tony—"I'm quite sure they already are."

The only way to deal with such females was to meet their jibes with polite impassivity; Tony did so. They stayed by Alicia's side, chatting about this and that, for nearly ten minutes, then moved on.

Before Alicia had time to draw breath, two other haughty matrons stopped to speak kindly. He stood by her side, suavely urbane, and thought cynical thoughts along the lines of: where Cynsters led, others followed.

He was grateful for Helena's support; he knew her well enough to know the gesture had been intentional. To be seen to be accepted by the elite of the haut ton provided a social cachet which was of itself a protection. Rumors were simply much less likely to be credited. Socially, Alicia and Adriana were gaining a status it would require a major public indiscretion to shake.

As more of the ladies on whose opinion the ton turned made a point of acknowledging Alicia, either by stopping for a few words or by exchanging nods across the room, he felt increasingly reassured on the social front.

Other fronts, however, were not so secure.

"Good evening, Mrs. Carrington."

The deep timbre of the voice sent Tony's hackles rising. He turned to see a dashingly handsome gentleman with unruly blond curls bowing over Alicia's hand; from the look on her face, she hadn't meant to surrender it. The gentleman had approached from the rear, escaping Tony's watchful eye, which endeared him to Tony even less.

The gentleman straightened and smiled at Tony. "Your servant, Torrington." Exchanging a brief nod, he looked back at Alicia. "My mama chatted with you earlier—she told me your name. I'm Harry Cynster."

His smile thawed Alicia; she returned it, relaxing. "It's a pleasure to make your acquaintance, sir."

It took Tony a few seconds to make the connections. Harry Cynster, he of the guileless blue eyes and a distinctly predatory streak. Horses—he was a renowned whip, a legendary rider, in more than one sense, appropriately nicknamed Demon.

He was chatting with Alicia, his voice a deep, fashionable drawl, deploying the charm for which the Cynsters were notorious. "My mama dragged me along. Now we're all of us back from the wars, it seems our mothers and aunts are determined to marry us all off."

"Indeed?" Alicia returned his innocent look with one of polite scepticism. "And what of you? Doesn't marriage figure among your ambitions?"

His eyes met hers, their expression rather less innocent. "Not just yet."

The undercurrent beneath the words registered as a warning.

Harry raised a brow. "I believe that's a waltz starting up."

To her surprise, Tony reached across; his fingers closed about her hand. "Ah, yes. Thank you for reminding me, Cynster." He smiled urbanely, and drew her to him. "Mrs. Carrington has promised me this dance."

Over her head, blue eyes met black. There was something—some form of masculine challenge—behind Tony's polite mask. She glanced from one to the other, then Harry Cynster raised both brows, faint surprise in his face. "Well, well. I see." Then he grinned and saluted her. "A pity, but I wish you good riding, my dear."

Before she could reply to the strange comment, Tony whisked her away.

"Mrs. Carrington doesn't often dance at all," she informed him as he drew her into his arms.

He met her eyes. "Except with me."

With that, he whirled her into the revolving circle of dancers. The floor was crowded; he had to hold her close. So close his strength and that fascinating power he wielded, a potent blend of physical confidence and sexual prowess, wrapped about her, a seductive spell she wasn't even sure he knew he was weaving.

Then he guided her through the turns; his thigh parted hers, and all she could think of was . . .

She looked away, cleared her throat. Desperate to cool her thoughts, she struggled to find some distraction . . . "What did he mean?" Glancing up, she caught Tony's black gaze. "Harry Cynster— why wish me 'good riding'? He doesn't even know if I ride."

For an instant, Tony stared down at her; she couldn't interpret his expression. "He assumed," he eventually said. His tone seemed flat. "He's an exceptional rider himself . . ." He shrugged lightly. "Probably all he thinks of."

His lips tightened, as if he didn't want to say anything more. He looked up, steering her on; she wasn't sufficiently interested to pursue the point—whatever it was.

But that left her mind free, and her senses susceptible. Left her nerves leaping when they were jostled and he drew her protectively close, into the safe harbor of his arms. For a moment, their hips and thighs touched, brushed; when they moved on, she felt heated. She glanced up at him, praying the heat hadn't reached her cheeks, afraid it had, afraid that her eyes, too, would give her away, would hold some impression of her thoughts, reveal her sudden, unexpectedly flaring need.

His eyes met hers; darkly burning, they reflected thoughts that mirrored hers.

Abruptly, it seemed they were the only couple on the floor, the sole focus of their senses. They moved in a social vacuum charged with sensual heat, wracked with restrained passion. It flowed about them, caressed their skins. Teased, taunted, and left them yearning.

The music ended. It was a wrench to stop, to part, to step back even though both recognized they must. It was harder yet to pull back onto that other plane, to deny any expression to what was beating inside them, burgeoning between them, especially when each knew the other felt it, too. That the other wanted just as passionately, just as hungrily.

The need was there in his eyes; the answering tug was very real within her. But they had to play their parts, had to stroll easily, apparently nonchalantly back up the room, returning to take up her usual position near Adriana's circle, with him by her side.

Tony settled her hand on his sleeve, but didn't dare leave his hand over hers. He wanted her close, closer than she was; such unsatisfying skin-to-skin contact was almost painful.

Dragging in a breath, he glanced around, unseeing. How he would survive . . . one thing was certain—no more waltzes. Not until they'd danced to a different tune in a much more private setting.

Not until he'd felt her skin against his, naked body to naked body.

After . . . he assumed—fervently prayed—that the pressures that seemed to be building inside him, seething volcano-like from somewhere deep within, those emotions he accepted but didn't wish to examine, would ease. That he wouldn't feel like snarling when men like Harry Cynster hove near, that he'd be able to waltz with her without remembering . . . and imagining . . .

Without wanting to behave like some primitive caveman and toss her over his shoulder, seize her, and cart her away. And . . .

He had to stop thinking about it, or he'd go mad.

At the end of the ball, he and Geoffrey accompanied the sisters into the front hall. Adriana gave Geoffrey her hand; he bowed over it, whispered something Tony didn't catch, then took his leave of Alicia, who, distracted, had missed that little interaction entirely. With a nod to him, Geoffrey left.

Alicia turned to him, held out her hand. "Thank you for your company."

He looked at her, took her hand, and tucked it in his arm. "I'll escort you home."

She blinked, but allowed him to draw her close. "You don't need to do that."

He looked down at her, then softly stated, "I do." After a moment, his chest swelled; he looked ahead. "Aside from all else, you're in my custody."

She frowned. "I thought you just said that for the benefit of the Watch."

A footman came to tell them their carriage was waiting. Tony steered her onto the steps, then leaned close, and murmured, "I said it for my benefit, not theirs."

After that comment . . . Alicia spent the entire journey home in a fever of speculation. The waltz had left her nerves, her senses, primed and flickering; rocking over the cobbles in the dark with Tony beside her, his hard thigh riding alongside hers, did nothing to calm them.

Last night—or had it been this morning? Whichever, there was no doubt in her mind that there were no further halts along their road. Yet she hadn't until now seriously considered, hadn't asked herself the fateful question.

If it came to that, would she?

If the moment arose and she had the chance, would she take it? Or try to the last to avoid it?

A small voice whispered . . . how did one avoid the inevitable?

By the time they reached Waverton Street, and he handed her down, she felt as tense as a bowstring. Adriana followed her up the steps. Tony brought up the rear. Maggs opened the door and held it wide; Alicia stepped back and let Adriana precede her. Tony, she noticed, cast comprehensive glances up and down the street as he climbed to the door.

She entered; he followed.

Adriana, no doubt thinking thoughts of Geoffrey Manningham, drifted upstairs without so much as a good night. Uncertain if she should be grateful or irritated, Alicia nodded to Maggs. "Thank you. You may retire. I'll see his lordship out."

Maggs bowed and lumbered away.

She watched the green baize door swing shut behind him.

Leaving her alone with the man who would be her lover.

Slowly, she turned . . . and found herself alone.

Tony had gone. The drawing-room door stood open.

Frowning, she went to the threshold; a dark shadow in the unlighted room, he was standing before the long windows. Puzzled, she went in. "What are you doing?"

"Checking these locks."

The windows gave onto the narrow area separating the house from the street. "Jenkins checks the locks every night, and I suspect Maggs does, too."

"Very likely."

Halting in the middle of the floor, she folded her arms beneath her breasts. "Do you approve?"

"No." Tony turned from the windows, through the dimness studied her. "But they'll do." For now.

Until he could think of some way to improve the defenses he felt compelled to erect about her. He needed to know she was safe. He wanted her his. In the circumstances, satisfaction would—indeed needed to—come in that order.

The reality had come crashing down on him as he'd sat beside her in the carriage and sensed the flickering and skittering of her nerves, her growing agitation. After all she'd been through in the last two days, what woman wouldn't be on edge?

This was not the time to press his suit, regardless of the strength of their passions. Aside from all else, he hadn't forgotten her earlier mistake over him expecting her to be grateful. Hadn't forgotten Ruskin's diabolical scheme—"gratitude" demanded as payment for protection.

Now *he* was her protector, in more ways, more arenas, more effectively established than Ruskin had ever stood to be.

No. He wanted her safe, wanted her to know she was safe, and had no need to thank him further. No need to come to him out of gratitude.

He didn't want her in that way, didn't want her to come to him with any complicating emotions between them. He wanted much more from her.

When she came to him, it had to be because she wanted to, because she wanted him as he wanted her.

That simple—that powerful.

To gain all he wanted, to achieve all his goals, that point was critical. He didn't question why that was so, but knew absolutely that it was.

She was watching him, puzzled, increasingly tense.

He crossed the room to her. She watched him approach, but didn't move. Either toward him, or away.

Halting in front of her, through the shadows he looked down on her upturned face. Slowly raising both hands, he feathered his fingers along her delicate jaw, then cupped her face, framed it as he tipped it up, bent his head, and set his lips to hers.

She opened to him readily; she kissed him back, not urging him on, yet not denying their mutual hunger. Her hands rose, her soft palms lightly clasping the backs of his, a subtle, accepting, very feminine caress.

For long moments, they stood in the cool dark, their bodies inches apart and, mouths melding, giving and taking, drank each other in.

The distant chiming of a clock broke the silence, reminding him of time passing. Reluctantly, he drew back; equally reluctantly, or so it seemed, she let him.

Lifting his head, he looked into her face, into the soft pools of her eyes. He couldn't read their expression, but he didn't need visual cues to know that she was as aware as he, as achingly, tormentingly conscious of the sensual whirlpool that was swirling about them, of the sheer strength of the attraction that had grown into so much more between them.

He lowered his hands, had to clear his throat to find his voice. "I'll leave you then." Despite his determination, there was the tiniest hint of a question in the words.

She drew a deep breath, breasts rising, and nodded. "Yes. And . . . thank you for all you've done."

No words could have better convinced him he should go. He turned to the door. She followed. He stood back to let her step over the threshold; as she did, a heavy knock fell on the front door.

They both froze, then he reached forward and moved her to the side. "Let me see who it is."

She made no demur but stood quietly where he'd set her while he crossed the hall and opened the door.

One of his footmen looked up at him. The man smiled in relief. "My lord." He bowed and offered a letter. "This came from the Bastion Club with instructions it be delivered to your hand as soon as possible."

Tony took the missive. "Thank you, Cox." A quick glance at the seal informed him it was from Jack Warnefleet. "Good work. I'll take care of this. You may go."

Cox bowed and retreated. His footsteps faded along the street as Tony shut the door.

"What is it? News?" Alicia came to his side.

"Very likely." Breaking the seal, Tony spread the single sheet. Took in the single sentence with a glance.

"What? Who is it from?"

"Jack Warnefleet. He's been digging into Ruskin's county connections." Folding the note, Tony slipped it into his pocket. "He's returned with some news he thinks I should hear immediately."

Jack had written that he'd uncovered something significant and suggested Tony meet him at the Bastion Club "pdq." Pretty damn quick. Between such as they, that meant with all speed—urgent.

The possibility that they'd finally got some handle on A.C. sent anticipation, a keen sense of the hunt, rising through him. "He's at the club—I'll go there now."

He glanced at Alicia. His welling excitement had communicated itself to her; eyes wide, she reached for the doorknob. "You will tell me if you learn anything major, won't you? Like who A.C. is?"

Already speculating on what avenues the new information might open up, he nodded as she opened the door. "Yes, of course."

The words were vague, the nod absentminded; Alicia stifled an oath. She caught his arm and tugged until he looked at her, actually focused on her. "Promise me you'll come and tell me the instant you learn anything significant."

She held his gaze, prepared to be belligerent if he turned evasive.

Instead, he looked into her eyes, then smiled. "I promise."

He ducked his head, kissed her swiftly, then slipped out of the door she was holding half-open. "Lock it—shoot the bolts. Now."

Grimacing at him, she shut the door, dutifully reached up, and shot the bolt above her head, then bent and slid home the other near the floor. Straightening, she listened. An instant later, she heard his footsteps descending the steps, then he strode away down the street.

Half an hour later, in the shrouded darkness of her bed, she sat up, pummeled her pillow, then flung herself down on it again.

She hadn't wanted to take the final step.

She reminded herself of that fact in inwardly strident tones—to no avail. They didn't impinge on her restless moodiness in the slightest, didn't alleviate the deflated feeling dragging at her—as if she'd been on the brink of receiving some wonderful gift, but it had been delayed at the last moment.

The feeling was nonsensical. Illogical. But very real.

She'd spent the entire evening on tenterhooks, increasingly sharp ones, worrying over what would unfold between them next, worrying that she knew all too well, that Tony would press ahead, engineer the moment, and . . .

That she felt so ungrateful for his forebearance was damning indeed.

He'd clearly decided to hold back; she should grasp the time he'd

granted her to concentrate on those things that were most important—
Adriana and their plan and the boys. Closing her eyes, settling her
head on the down-filled pillow, she willed herself to keep her mind on
such matters, on the things that had always dominated her life.

Determinedly, she relaxed.

Within seconds her mind had roamed, to a pair of hot black eyes,
to the feel of his lips, firm and pliant on hers, to the sensations of his
hands stroking, caressing, to the intimate probing of his tongue . . .

Sleep crept into her mind and swept her into her dreams.

She woke sometime later to a preemptory knock on her bedchamber
door. She couldn't imagine . . . she stared through the shadows at the
door.

It opened. Tony walked—stalked—in. He scanned the room and
located her in the bed; even through the dark his gaze pinned her. Then
he turned and quietly closed the door.

She struggled up onto her elbows, struggled to shake off the cobwebs of sleep and make her mind work. What? Why? Had something
serious occurred?

Tony's calmly deliberate movements made that last seem unlikely.
He'd crossed the room. Without meeting her eyes, he turned and sat on
the end of her bed. It bowed beneath his weight.

She stared at his back, then wriggled and sat up, hugging the coverlet to her breasts. She'd caught only a glimpse of his face, but her
eyes were adjusted to the darkness; it had seemed somewhat harder
than usual, the harsh features sharply delineated, the angular planes set
like granite.

He didn't turn around, but bent forward.

She frowned. "What's going on?"

Her whisper floated out through the room.

He didn't immediately answer; instead, she heard a thud.

Realized with a sudden clenching of nerves that he'd pulled off
one shoe.

He shifted and reached for the other. "You made me promise to
come and tell you the instant I learned anything significant."

Those had been her exact words. She shifted, wondering . . .
"Yes? So what—" A sudden thought took precedence over everything
else. She stared at the back of his head. "How did you get in?"

His second shoe hit the floor. "I slipped the lock on the drawing-
room window. But you needn't worry." He stood and faced the bed. "I
locked it again."

That wasn't what was worrying her.

Eyes widening, mouth drying, she watched as he shrugged out of his coat, glanced around, then flung it over her dressing table stool. Then his fingers rose to his cravat, smoothly tugging the ends free.

"Ah . . ." Good heavens! She had to . . . had to . . . she swallowed. "Did you learn something from your friend?"

She had to distract him.

"From Jack?" His tone was flat, his accents clipped. "Yes. As it happened, I learned quite a lot."

He had the cravat undone; dragging it free, he flung it on his coat, then his fingers went to the buttons of his shirt.

It was getting harder and harder to think, to swallow, even to breathe. Had the moment really come? Just like that, without warning?

Panic inched higher and higher.

She clutched the edge of the coverlet. "So . . . what did you learn?" She tried to recall what had passed between them earlier—had she inadvertently issued some sexual invitation?

"Jack investigated Ruskin's background. In Bledington." Tony followed the line of buttons down, then glanced at her, yanked the tails from his waistband and stripped off the shirt. His eyes had adjusted; he could see how wide hers were. Wondered, cynically, intently, just how far she'd go before she broke.

He tossed the shirt aside, set his hands to his waistband, his fingers on the buttons of the flap. "Ruskin's estate amounts to little more than a few fields—he inherited his liking for gambling from his father. The income he enjoyed could not in any way derive from his ancestral acres." He slipped the buttons free. "If anything, the upkeep of the house in which his mother and sister live was a drain on his purse."

She didn't shift, made absolutely no sound as he removed his trousers and sent them to join the rest of his clothes. His determination hardened; it was an effort to keep his emotions—the mix of incredulity, anger, and hurt, and so much more he didn't want to examine—from his face.

Clothed only in shadows, he turned to the bed. Silent-footed, he prowled down its side; it was a large, canopied affair. He was aroused but, apparently stunned, she was following his face; she'd yet to look down.

She moistened her already parted lips. "Ah . . . so . . . what does that . . ." She made a valiant and quite visible attempt to focus her mind. "I mean, why is that important?"

"It's not." He heard the harshness in his tone. Watching her closely, primed to smother a shriek, he reached for the covers. "But there were other facts Jack discovered that were far more startling."

Her knuckles turned white as he grasped the covers, but when, jaw setting, he lifted them, her grip eased; the silky quilt slid through her fingers as he raised the sheets.

"Oh. I see . . ."

She was looking straight at him, but he would have sworn she wasn't seeing him. Her tone seemed distant, as if she was thinking of other things.

His temper, held in tight check until then, flared. He slid onto the bed, dropped the covers, and turned to her.

His plan—what plan he had—was to force her into admitting the truth, the truth Jack had uncovered. The truth she'd so artfully kept from him, her protector and would-be husband. He'd intended to shock her, to use that truth itself to chastise her, to embarrass her into admitting all; he'd imagined she'd succumb to virginal fluster long before now.

Still convinced she would, that at any second she'd panic, call a halt, and admit all, he reached for her. Closing his hands about her slender shoulders, feeling the fine silk of her nightgown slide over the soft skin beneath, he drew her to him.

Slowly, steadily, totally deliberately.

He looked into her face.

No hint of fear, of panic—of anything remotely resembling the frantic, embarrassed fluster he expected—showed in her features.

Quite the opposite. She was finally looking at him, studying his eyes, his face; her expression seemed almost serene, almost glowing.

Her eyes searched; her hands slid up to frame his face, then slid farther, her arms twining about his neck.

Abruptly losing patience, he pulled her to him.

Fully against him, body to body with only a fine layer of silk between.

He hadn't counted on the shock affecting him.

For one instant, the world about them rocked, quaked, then settled not quite as it had been before. His lungs seized; every muscle tensed; every nerve came alive.

Impulses—powerful, primitive, and sure—rose and rushed through him; his head spun.

He heard her breath catch. He looked into her eyes. Saw something like wonder in her expression.

Their gazes touched, held.

For three long heartbeats, time stood still.

Between them, heat welled. Flames ignited, greedily grew.

Her gaze dropped to his lips.

Beyond his control, his dropped to hers.

Who made the first move he didn't know. She lifted her head as he bent his. Their lips met.

And the fires leapt, then raged.

She pressed against him and he was lost. She opened her mouth to him, and he drowned in her bounty.

He sank against her, into her. In no way passive, she met him, her body firm and supple against his, her hands in his hair, her tongue dueling with his, inciting, inviting.

Wanting.

His control was gone before he even saw the threat. Vaporized by a need the like of which he'd never known. She was with him in want, in desire, in passion; her flagrant encouragement left no room for doubt.

Instinct claimed him, primal and unfettered. Unchained after being so long denied. He had to have her, all of her, had to have her beneath him, claimed and incontrovertibly his. It wasn't lust that drove him, but something deeper, more powerful, something that dwelled in his heart and his soul and paid scant attention to the dictates of his brain.

Within a minute, the kiss turned ravenous; his hands hardened, fingers kneading possessively.

Alicia sensed the change in him and exulted. Her own needs unleashed for the first time in her life, she wanted all he did, wanted to experience all he and she together could be.

She'd made her decision. Or had had it made for her; she wasn't sure, but either way she felt certain, confident beyond doubt, that this was meant to be.

The moment he'd turned to her, naked, aroused, yet somehow to her senses still unthreatening, she'd known. To her eyes, he was beautiful, incomparably male yet totally safe; never would she find another man she could trust as she trusted him—never with another would she feel the same certainty that she could go forward without fear, that she could surrender to him yet not lose herself.

That his victory would also be hers. That in his arms she would always be safe. Protected. Cared for.

Worshipped.

Despite the urgency that coursed through him, that hardened his body and shredded the veil of elegance that usually disguised his strength, that last was still apparent. His every touch was blatantly sexual, not rough but driven, forceful, demanding, even predatory, yet still each caress had only one aim, to awaken her senses and heighten their delight.

Pleasure was his currency, first and last.

She accepted it, and made it hers.

She sent her hands roaming, fingers flexing over his bare shoulders, glorying in the sculpted strength tensing beneath her fingertips, in the heavy resilence of his flesh, so unlike her own. He had her locked to him, lips devouring as his hands evocatively kneaded her bottom, his erection a hot heavy ridge impressed against her belly. She couldn't push back enough to press her hands between them; denied the chance of exploring his chest, she ran one hand down his back, reaching boldly for his waist, his hip, the subtle flare of his buttock. That was all she could reach, yet she sensed his pleasure in her touch; his lips clung to hers, distracted, then his attention returned to her in full measure, hotter, harder, more urgent.

Encouraged, determined, she pushed back, and he let her, shifting over her so his weight pinned her to the bed. His legs tangling with hers, he released her bottom; his hands rose to her breasts.

Their kiss continued unabated, mouths melding in a feast of mutual need, their hunger steadily growing, the heat between them swelling, escalating, this time out of control. Neither sought to rein it in; neither even considered it. By mutual accord, they let it rage, and rage it did.

He'd touched all of her before, had had her naked beneath his hands before, yet this was different. Her senses splintered, avidly trying to take in every new sensation. From the crisp, crinkly rasp of his hair-dusted legs against the fine skin of hers, to the unexpected weight of him above her, to the promise in the hard hot length now pressed to her hip, all was new, fascinating and enthralling.

As was the compulsion within her, building and swelling with every beat of her heart, with every knowing sweep of his hard hands. Without pause, he pushed her on and she went gladly, matching him, meeting him, even when she sensed him struggling to regain control, goading him.

Her hands had been resting on his shoulders; she swept them down, pressing her palms to his hot flesh, fingers searching, exploring, as wantonly sensual as he in learning him, in tracing the muscle bands, letting her fingers tangle in the mat of hair across them, finding a flat nipple beneath the pelt and tweaking it to a tight bud.

His hips shifted against her. Emboldened, she sent her hands lower, caressing the taut, ribbed muscles of his abdomen, then reaching lower yet.

Until she found him, hot, heavy, velvet over steel.

He'd taken his weight on his arms, allowing her her way. She took full advantage and traced, caressed, then took him between her palms almost reverently, amazed, enthralled by the feel of him, the weight, the length and thickness, the baby-fine skin so obviously shatteringly sensitive. She could feel his reaction to her every touch, feel the flickering of his locked muscles, the heat that flowed through their kiss, welling and swelling with every sweep of her fingertips, every gentle squeeze.

Abruptly he broke from the kiss, and rolled onto his back, taking her with him. The sudden change in position momentarily distracted her; while she was reassessing, her attention deflected by the feel of his body now beneath hers, he reached down.

He caught her nightgown, gathered the skirts until he held them bunched at her thighs.

What he intended burst into her mind. She looked down, met his black eyes.

And suddenly they were themselves again, sane, rational—yet no longer who they had been. They'd moved on, traveled the very last stage of their road, and arrived at their destination.

It was different from what she'd imagined.

He said nothing, simply waited, his need in his eyes, in his body taut and tense beneath her.

Within her, she felt her own need swell, recognized it as similar yet subtly different from his. Knew in her soul that their needs were complementary—they would be assuaged by the one act, sated and fulfilled in the same moment.

Their gazes remained locked, their lips mere inches apart, their breaths, panting and ragged, softly filling the silence between them.

She found it was impossible to smile. Instead, she shifted; fingers tangling in the silk, she twitched it. Upward.

He didn't wait for more, but drew the gown up, past her hips, past her waist, tugging it up over her breasts, waiting while she disentangled her arms before dragging it free and flinging it away.

And she was naked in his arms.

He reached for her; giving her no time to think, to dwell on the intimacy, the vulnerability, he drew her lips down, took them, took her mouth, and dragged her back into the flames, into the furnace of their mutual need.

His hands were everywhere, claiming anew, drowning her in glorious sensation.

The flames roared; heat engulfed them.

She was suddenly sure her skin was on fire; as for him, he burned. His hands felt like brands, spreading liquid flame as he caressed, boldly possessed. Then he rolled again and pinned her beneath him.

He spread her thighs and settled between; braced on one arm, he hovered above her, his lips feeding from hers, his hips holding her down as with his other hand he reached between them, and found her.

She was swollen, wet and wanting, all but aching with the need to feel him within her. She knew it, didn't try to deny it, hide from it.

His fingers briefly played, then penetrated her. Once, twice, delved deep, then withdrew.

He shifted, his hips pressing between hers, then she felt the broad head of his erection part her swollen flesh, sliding easily between the folds to press in.

He stopped. Bracing both arms he lifted above her, simultaneously breaking their kiss.

With an effort, she managed to lift her lids; panting, barely sentient, she raised her eyes to his.

He trapped her gaze. Held it.

Desire wrapped them in a cocoon of flames; her body felt molten, yet achingly empty. The need to have him fill that emptiness thrummed, a steady, compulsive beat in her blood. Eyes locked with his, her every sense was focused on where they would join, on the soft swollen flesh between her thighs, on the hard heavy rod of his erection.

He pressed in. He kept his eyes on hers, holding her with him as slowly, steadily, he thrust in, and filled her. Not in a rush, but inch by slow inch. She felt her body give, stretch, felt every inch of his thickness as he pressed deeper, as her body struggled to adjust to the invasion.

The difficult moment came, as she'd known it would. She tried to cling to calm, tried to find some ease by breathing yet more rapidly, but the pressure and the pain steadily built, built . . . she would have shut her eyes, turned her head away, but his black gaze held her trapped.

Held her through it all, steady as a rock, a primitive promise beckoning as fraction by fraction he pressed her farther . . .

Her body tensed, arching under his, and still he held her with his eyes. And sank deeper.

The pressure gave.

In one sharp flash of pain it was gone, leaving her gasping, breasts rising and falling, yet still locked in his black gaze.

She sensed rather than saw his satisfaction. He halted, held still for some moments as she struggled to recover, to assimilate the change; he watched her, waiting. He seemed to know the exact moment the burning sensation faded, and the vise about her lungs eased and fear left her; he resumed his invasion, still slow, yet more assured.

Tony watched her, held her eyes, drank in every nuance of her response as he claimed her, filled her, and made her his. He'd surrendered to instinct long ago, in that first heated moment when his need had broadsided him. Subsequently, no thought had been required. He knew what he wanted, what he needed. Ruthlessly he took it—and her.

And part of that taking was this, this slow, excruciatingly complete first invasion. A branding, a declaration, an acceptance.

A sharing.

He'd needed to know, to be with her, to appreciate what she felt, know how she reacted. He'd always noted the responses of the women he bedded, yet this time he was not simply cataloging, gauging a reaction in order to capitalize on it. This time, he was immersed in the moment, experiencing both her pain and that glorious rush of release, of sexual interlocking, with her.

Experiencing, through it all, a deeper sense of connection, a deeper meaning beneath the sensations, beneath the physical pleasure.

He continued to press in; her body continued to give, to enclose him, until finally he was fully seated within her. Still holding her gaze, he withdrew halfway, then pressed in again, watching for any sign of discomfort.

Seeing none, feeling her body ease beneath him, her scalding sheath clasping tightly about him, he bent his head.

She raised hers, offered her lips.

He took them, claimed them. Without further direction, let his body do as it wished, as it had to do, and claim her.

The tiny fragment of his mind that remained lucid fully expected a fast and furious engagement. Instead, he rode her slowly; even now, even freed from all restraint, his body remained attuned to hers, gauging without conscious direction, responding to each quickening clasp of her sheath, to each restless shifting of her thighs, ultimately to the tentative rocking of her hips as she learned to match him and meet him.

Their progression was slow, measured, deliberate—and all-consuming. As she took him in, and his body followed hers, it occurred to him to wonder who had claimed whom. Who was leading, who was in charge . . .

Not him, and it couldn't be her.

Never had he been so totally absorbed, so totally submerged in the moment, so totally aware. Not just of the woman beneath him, but of his own body, his own pleasure. Hers heightened his; like a series of mirrors, reflecting back over and again, each tiny gasp, each soft moan, every sudden tensing of her fingers on his skin, washed over him and welled, swelled the exquisite tightness in his groin, fueled the tension driving him.

She'd tugged him down so his body met hers; her breasts were trapped beneath the heavy muscles of his chest, the rough hair abrading their sensitive skin, her nipples tight crests, their arousing pressure shifting with every deep thrust. Their skins were aflame, sheened, slick; her hands roamed his back, sweeping over the long planes, increasingly urgent. Their stomachs met, his hips locked in the cradle of hers, her thighs widespread, knees clasping his flanks, calves tangling with his.

Their mouths had fused, lips still greedily clinging, a connection that completed some circuit, that kept them immersed, locked in the compulsion that drove them, wholly given over to it.

Surrender came with a sudden quickening, first of her body, then of his. He was so deeply buried inside her, she took him with her; release swept them both in a long, glorious golden wave. Locked together, they rode it, let it take them and fling them high into the heavens, into the realms of pleasured bliss.

He emptied himself into her, felt her womb contract powerfully, holding him, accepting, taking.

The wave receded.

They drifted slowly to earth, their bodies eased, all tension gone, boneless in the aftermath. Their lips parted; breaths mingling, they clung, eyes still closed, savoring the closeness.

He felt her arms steal around him, then rest, lax. With the last of his strength, he slumped to the side, trying not to crush her as oblivion, deeper than he'd ever known it, caught him and drew him down.

Remarkable.

It had been that and more; an hour later, Tony still couldn't rationalize how very different the interlude had been, that she, a rank novice, had been the one woman in all his years to shatter his control, capture him utterly, forcing him to rely wholly on instinct, thus taking him to . . . wherever they had been.

A plane on which the pleasure defied all description, in which the physical had been a golden echo of something else.

An unworldly, unearthly, otherworldly place.

In all his years, through all his experience, he'd never even imagined such an exchange could be, or that such a place existed.

On rousing, he'd disengaged and lifted from her. Lying on his back, he'd gathered her to him; unresisting, she'd let him settle her against him, within the circle of his arms, her head on his shoulder.

The covers lay warm about them. Night lay like a blanket over the house; the moonlight had strengthened. He glanced at her face; she still seemed sunk in pleasured oblivion. Lifting his hand, he tentatively touched her hair. When she didn't stir, he set his palm to the silky tresses, smoothing them, drinking in the feel of their warm softness.

Lying back, he looked up at the canopy; slowly stroking, he tried to think.

The gentle, rhythmic comforting caress gradually drew Alicia back into the world. Warmth held her; pleasure still lay heavy in her veins. A sense of safety she'd never before known, so deep, so solid its existence was beyond question, wrapped her about, supporting, reassuring.

She sighed, and her wits returned.

And she remembered. Everything. All of it.

Every moment that had passed since he'd drawn her into his arms, every touch, every blissful second.

His arms remained around her, steel bands cradling her, gently enough, yet still overtly possessive.

The stroking slowed; his hand stilled. He knew she was awake.

Opening her eyes, she shifted her head and looked up. Met his gaze. Excruciatingly aware that she lay naked in his arms, that he was naked, too. Aware that their limbs were tangled, that they lay slumped together in a warm cocoon of rumpled sheets.

His black eyes held hers; it was impossible to read anything from them or his face. "When did you intend to tell me?" His tone was even, uninflected.

She searched his face, remembered . . . refocused on his eyes. "You knew."

He'd known she was—had been—a virgin; he'd watched for every second as he'd taken her virginity, as she'd willingly yielded it to him.

He looked down, at her hand spread on his bare chest. He took it in his; his long fingers toyed with hers. "There wasn't any trace of any Carrington anywhere near Chipping Norton. No entry in the parish records. No one of that name known at any of the stables or inns. Yet many knew the Misses Pevensey—*both* Misses Pevensey."

He glanced up; his eyes were sharp as they found hers. "I would have stopped if you'd wanted me to."

A statement, but there was a question buried in it. She held his gaze steadily. "I know."

She let the two words stand alone, a simple acknowledgment of the decision she'd made. She'd gone to him willingly; she wasn't about to pretend otherwise.

What was done was done; she was his mistress now.

She frowned. "How did you learn . . . ?" The truth struck her, left her horrified. "Your friend?"

Incipient panic flared in her eyes; Tony closed his hand over hers. "There's no need to worry." He hesitated, then explained, "Jack Warnefleet—Lord Warnefleet—investigated Ruskin for me. He also asked after your supposed husband, Alfred Carrington. Another A. C."

Understanding lit her eyes; he added, "We can rely on Jack's absolute discretion."

She studied his face, his eyes; a long moment passed, then she asked, "That was the urgent information he sent you the note about last night?"

He felt his jaw set. "He knew I'd want to know."

She blinked, then her lashes veiled her eyes. "I couldn't tell you." A heartbeat passed, then she added, "I couldn't risk it."

There was no hint of excuse in her tone; she was stating a fact, at least as she'd seen it.

He drew in a breath, lifted his gaze to look, unseeing, across the room. Given all he now knew of her, of the plan she and, he assumed, Adriana had concocted, of her commitment to her sister and even more to her brothers, he couldn't fault her; any hint that she wasn't the widow the ton thought her would, even now, result in complete and unmitigated disaster. Any chance of Adriana making a good match would disappear. They'd be social pariahs, expelled from society, forced to retreat to their cottage in the country to scrape a precarious existence for themselves and their brothers.

Trusting him with the truth . . .

He suddenly realized she had. She just hadn't told him in words.

His silence had bothered her; she tried to edge away. Even before he'd thought, his arms were tightening, holding her to him. "No—I know." She stilled; he drew in another breath, glanced down at her bent head. "I understand."

When she didn't look up, he bent close, placed a kiss on her crown, hesitated, then gently nudged her head.

Alicia looked up, into black eyes that promised far more than understanding. Safety, protection from both the finite and the nebulous dangers of the world, but more precious, at least to her, was the strange and novel relief of having someone with whom she could share her thoughts, her concerns, her schemes. Someone who did indeed understand.

His eyes searched hers; as if to confirm her reading, he asked, "Tell me how this all came about—you, your sister, your plan."

It wasn't a command, but a request, one she saw no reason to refuse; better he know all than half the story. She settled against him, felt his arms close tighter. "It started when Papa died."

She told him everything, even explaining her connection with Mr. King. Although he said not a word, she could tell he didn't approve, yet still he accepted, and made no protest. She was surprised when he questioned her about their gowns, and gave mute thanks not everyone was so acute.

When she in turn questioned why he'd investigated her supposed husband, he explained his thoughts of some other Carrington being involved. The comment led them deeper into the possibilities surrounding Ruskin; they discussed, tossed thoughts back and forth, argued likelihoods—the sort of exchange she'd never indulged in with anyone else.

Gradually, the silences lengthened. Blissfully warm, totally comfortable, she lay in his arms and listened to his heart beat steadily beneath her cheek. The covers lay over them; she still lay half-atop him, stretched alongside, her legs tangled with his, her hand spread over his chest. One muscled arm was wrapped around her, his hand heavy over her waist.

She should, she felt sure, feel some degree of fluster, of maidenly, feminine embarrassment over their naked state, let alone all that had led to it. Instead, the intimacy was addictive, a strange sense of closeness, of inexpressible comfort, of a simple rightness she was loath to shake.

He glanced down at her, then she felt his lips brush her hair.

"Go to sleep."

The whisper floated down to her. Turning her head, she looked up, met his eyes. Then she lifted her head, and touched her lips to his. He met them, returned her kiss, but gently. Briefly. Softly sighing, she drew back. Settling more definitely on his chest, spreading her hand over his side, she relaxed, and closed her eyes.

He merged with her dreams in the darkness before dawn. For long moments as he caressed her, sending sensation after sensation spiraling through her, each exquisite touch driving her higher into the clouds, she wasn't certain where her dreams ended and reality began.

Then he moved over her, spread her thighs wide, and slowly filled her.

She woke as he thrust deep and embedded himself within her, to the sensation of him hard and strong and rigid within her, of her body clamping tightly, joyously, about him, her arms reaching out to embrace him—and knew her life would never return to what it had been.

That was her first and last lucid thought; the instant he started to move within her, her wits deserted her, submerged beneath her clamorous senses, greedy for him, for what was to come.

He stayed close this time, his body moving over hers, murmuring gruff encouragement as she shifted beneath him, tilting her hips, adjusting to the rhythm and the depth of his penetration.

Her body seemed to know what to do; she let herself flow with the tide, gave herself up to the powerful surging rhythm, let it sweep her away into a whirlpool of shattering sensation. He kept them there, held them there, each rocking thrust swirling the vortex higher, tighter. Their lips found each other's without conscious direction, and then they were there again, in the heart of the flames, the center of the furnace.

The heat cindered all barriers, locked them together, desire flowing molten through them, between them. For one glorious instant, she lost touch with the world, couldn't tell where she ended and he began, knew only that they were together, one in thought, in mind, in deed.

Their lips clung, their hands grasped, slipped, gripped; their bodies strove to reach the elusive peak, just beyond their reach.

Then they broke through the clouds and the sunburst took them. The glory fractured, shattered, and poured through them. Rained down on them. Drove them at the last, gasping and shuddering, onto some far-distant shore.

They lay tangled, entwined, struggling for breath, the last shards of ecstasy still shivering through them. Heated, swollen, their lips touched, brushed, then parted. In the instant before she surrendered to beckoning oblivion, one simple truth floated through her mind.

Each time he came to her, each time they joined, left her one step further from the woman she had been.

Tony woke as dawn began to streak the sky. Satiation lay heavy upon him; he didn't want to move.

Eyes closed, he lay still, savoring the sensation of Alicia's soft curves pressed to his side; he consciously considered leaping a few steps and simply staying where he was.

Reluctantly, he accepted that might be going too far, too fast. Although where they were headed was perfectly clear, taking women for granted was never wise.

Stifling a sigh, he disengaged, trying not to disturb her. She murmured sleepily and clutched at his chest, but then slid back into slumber. Gently lifting her hand from him, he slid out of the bed. She snuggled down in the warm depression where he'd lain. The sight of her burrowed there made him smile.

Quickly, he dressed, dropped a light, fleeting kiss on her forehead, then slipped out of her room, and out of the house.

"Are you all right, Miss Alicia?"

Alicia woke with a start, realized it was Fitchett who had spoken. "Ah . . . yes." A lie, but she could hardly explain. "I, ah, overslept."

Struggling to sit up, her gaze fell on the rumpled disaster of her bed. Thank heavens Fitchett was outside the door.

"Aye, well, we was wondering, seeing as you hadn't rung. I'll bring up your water if you're ready for it."

Alicia glanced at the window. A shaft of bright sunlight lanced into the room. Dear God, what was the time? "Yes, thank you. I'm getting up now."

Fitchett lumbered off. Dragooning her wits and her still too-lax muscles into action, Alicia flung back the covers and got out of bed.

By the time Fitchett arrived with her water, she'd stripped the bed; there'd been no possibility of putting things right enough to pass muster. When Fitchett stared at the pile of bedclothes, she airily waved. "I decided to change the sheets. It's only a day or so early."

To her relief, Fitchett merely humphed.

She washed and dressed quickly, then hurried downstairs to discover bedlam reigning at the breakfast table. Adriana had done her best, but she lacked Alicia's authority; called to order, the boys assumed their most angelic expressions and innocently resumed a more civilized rapport.

"I slept in," she replied to Adriana's questioning look. It wasn't a good excuse—she never slept in—but it was all she could think of. Reaching for the teapot, she poured herself a cup. She sipped, relaxed, then realized how hungry she was. Ravenous, in fact.

Jenkins came in, and they discussed the boys' lessons for the coming week while she polished off a mound of kedgeree.

When Jenkins departed, the boys in tow, Adriana frowned at her. "Well, you're obviously not ailing—there's nothing wrong with your appetite."

She waved the piece of toast she'd started nibbling and reached for her cup. "I just slept longer than usual."

Adriana pushed back her chair and rose. "You must have been dreaming."

Recollection flashed across Alicia's mind; she nearly choked on her tea.

"Are we still going to Mr. Pennecuik's warehouse today?"

She nodded. "Yes—we must if we're to make those new gowns." Setting down her cup, she picked up her toast. "In twenty minutes—I have to check with Cook before we go."

The rest of the day passed in the usual busy fashion; she hadn't before noticed how little personal time she had, private time alone in which to think. If she and Adriana weren't out, attending some function or event, then some member of the household would want to speak with her, or her brothers needed supervising, or . . .

She needed to think—she knew she did, knew she ought to stop and consider, and get her mind in order for when next she met Tony. She'd taken a major step, turned a hugely significant corner—one she definitely shouldn't have turned, perhaps, but she'd willingly taken that road; it was clearly imperative she stop and take stock.

All that seemed obvious, yet when she finally found herself alone in her room, bathing, then dressing for the evening, she discovered her mind had a will of its own.

When it came to all that had passed in the night, and in the small hours of the morning, while she could recall and relive every moment, every detail, her mind flatly refused to go any further. It was as if some dominant part of her brain had decided those events were in some way sacrosant, that they stood as they were and needed no further examination. No dissection, no analysis, no clarification. They simply were.

It was, indeed, as if she'd stood at a crossroads, and now she'd gone around the corner, she couldn't see where she'd been. Which left her facing forward along a road she'd never imagined traveling.

Putting the last touches to her coiffure, she paused and studied herself in the mirror. She still looked the same, yet . . . was it something in her eyes, or maybe in her posture, the way she stood, that assured her, at least, that she was no longer the same woman?

She had changed, and she didn't regret it. There was little in this world for which she'd trade so much as a minute of the time she'd spent in Tony's arms.

Indeed, there was no point looking back. She was his mistress now.

And if she didn't know what that new status would bring, or how to cope, she'd just have to learn.

She looked into her eyes for a moment longer, then let her gaze run down the sleek lines of the deep purple silk gown Adriana had designed and she and Fitchett had created. The heart-shaped neckline showcased her breasts without being obvious; the cut below the high waist made the most of her slim hips and long legs, while the small off-the-shoulder sleeves left the graceful curves of her shoulders quite bare.

Turning, she picked up her shawl and reticule, then headed for the door. Luckily, she learned quickly.

The cacophonous sound of the ton in full flight rose to greet Tony as he paused at the top of the steps leading down into Lady Hamilton's ballroom. Her ladyship's rout was one of the events traditionally held in the week before the Season began; society's elite were almost to a man foregathered in town—everyone who was anyone would be present.

Looking down on the sea of bright gowns, of sheening curls, of jewels winking in the light thrown by the chandeliers, he scanned the throng, relieved when he located Alicia standing by the side of the room, Adriana's court, some steps in front of her, partially screening her. Relief died, however, when closer inspection revealed that three of the gentlemen between Alicia and Adriana were not conversing with Adriana.

Jaw setting, he strolled with feigned nonchalance down the steps; cutting through the crowd, he made his way directly to Alicia's side.

She welcomed him with a smile that went some way toward easing his temper. "Good evening, my lord."

He took the hand she offered, raised it brazenly to his lips, simultaneously stepping close. "Good evening, my dear."

Her green-gold eyes widened a fraction. His easy, languid smile took on an edge as, setting her hand in the crook of his arm, he took up a stance—a clearly possessive stance—by her side.

With every evidence of well-bred boredom, he glanced at the gentlemen who had been speaking with her. "Morecombe. Everton." He exchanged the usual nods. The last man he didn't know.

"Allow me to present Lord Charteris."

The tall, fair-haired dandy bowed. "Torrington."

Tony returned the bow with an elegant nod.

Straightening, Charteris puffed out his narrow chest. "I was just describing to Mrs. Carrington the latest offering at the Theatre Royal."

Tony allowed Charteris, who appeared to fancy himself a peacock of sorts, to entertain them with his anecdote; he judged the man safe enough. Morecombe was another matter; although married, he was a gazetted womanizer, a rake and profligate gambler. As for Everton, he was the sort no gentleman would trust with his sister. Not even with his maiden aunt.

Both clearly had their eyes on Alicia.

Behind his polite mask, he took note of the undercurrents in the small group; focused on the men, it was some minutes before he noticed the swift glances Alicia surreptitiously cast him. Only then realized she was, if not precisely skittish, then at least uncertain.

It took a minute more before he realized her uncertainty was occasioned not by any of the three gentlemen before her, but by him.

He waited only until the notes of a waltz filled the room. Glancing at her, he covered her hand on his sleeve. "My dance, I believe?"

His tone made it clear there was no doubt about the fact; as he hadn't previously spoken, it should be patently clear that her hand being his to claim was an arrangement of some standing.

Fleetingly meeting his eyes, she acquiesced with a gracious inclination of her head.

The glances he noticed Morecombe and Everton exchange as, with a polite nod, he led her away gave him some satisfaction. With any luck, they would move on to likelier prey before the waltz ended.

Reaching the dance floor, he drew Alicia into his arms, started them revolving, then turned his full attention on her. He studied her eyes, then raised a brow. "What is it?"

Alicia looked into his eyes; she felt her lips firm, but managed not to glare. *I haven't been a nobleman's mistress before* hardly seemed worth stating. And now she was in his arms, sensing again the familiar reactions—the physical leap of her senses soothed by the feeling of comfort and safety—her earlier worries over how she should react—how he would behave and how he would expect her to respond to him—no longer seemed relevant. "Have you made any progress with your investigations?"

That, at least, was something she could ask.

"Yes." For a moment, he looked down at her as if waiting for her to say something else, then he looked up for the turn, and went on, "I heard from Jack Hendon this morning—he's confirmed all that your brothers learned." Glancing down, he met her gaze. "Incidentally, he was impressed—you might tell them."

"They don't need any encouragement."

His lips twitched. "Perhaps not." He looked up again, drawing her fractionally closer as they came out of the turn and headed up the long room. "Jack's pursuing the matter, trying to find a pattern to the ships that were taken versus those that were not. With luck, that might shine some light on who benefited from the losses."

He met her gaze. "I haven't yet heard back from the friend scouting down in Devon—he has contacts with smugglers and wreckers along that coast. As for myself, now I've got something specific to ask, I'll start putting out feelers among my own contacts."

He'd kept his voice low; she did the same. "Does that mean you'll be leaving London?"

The prospect filled her with a curious disquiet. An odd, novel, uncomfortable feeling; she'd never relied on others before—she'd always been self-sufficient. Yet the thought of coping with the unfolding events stemming from Ruskin's death by herself . . .

His arm around her tightened, drawing her attention and her gaze back to him.

"No—my contacts are primarily along the southeastern coast, from Southampton to Ramsgate, all within half a day from town. I can cover them in single-day journeys. Aside from all else, I need to be here to assess what the others discover, Jack Hendon from Lloyd's and the shipping lines, and Gervase Tregarth in Devon."

She nodded, aware of relief, but they were now *too* close, her bodice brushing his coat, her silk-sheathed thighs shushing against his . . . yet with the press of other couples about them, it was unlikely any would notice. And to the ton, she was still a widow after all.

Tony hesitated, debating, then murmured, "Incidentally, I've arranged for some men to keep a watch on your house. They'll be in the street—you won't know they're there, but . . . just in case you have need, there'll always be someone watching your front door."

She stared up at him; he could see her thoughts whirling behind the green-gold of her eyes. First Maggs, now . . . "Why?"

He had his argument ready. "First the rumor, then the Watch. I want to make sure whoever A. C. is, he gets no chance to do anything more to implicate you. Or your family."

He felt confident those last words would see her accept his arrangements without further question.

She frowned at him, but proved him right. "If you really think there's a need . . ."

Whether there was or not, he would feel much happier knowing that when he journeyed out of the capital, more of his trusted minions had her and her brood under their eye. The three men he'd set to keep a constant watch on the Waverton Street house were one hundred percent reliable; nothing suspicious would escape them.

The music slowed, then ended; they whirled to a halt. Reluctantly releasing her, he tucked her hand in his arm and turned her away from Adriana's court. "I'll go down to Southampton tomorrow."

Looking at him, she nodded, then cast a glance back up the room. "We should—"

"Behave as if we're lovers."

Her gaze snapped back to his face. "What?"

He resisted the urge to narrow his eyes at her; he opened them wide instead. "No one will find anything odd in that—it's what they're expecting." Given he'd laid the appropriate groundwork over the past several weeks.

She frowned. "Yes, but—" Again she glanced back toward Adriana.

"Stop worrying about Adriana. Geoffrey's beside her, and even if he's distracted, there's always Sir Freddie." He paused. "Has he made an offer yet?"

"Sir Freddie? No, thank heavens." She turned and settled to stroll by his side.

"Why so relieved? I thought you wanted Adriana to be able to choose among many?"

She narrowed her eyes at him. "I did. But as you very well know, she's already made her choice, so Sir Freddie making an offer will simply be an unnecessary complication."

He grinned, making a mental note to prod Geoffrey when next he had a chance. "Actually, I'm surprised you haven't been inundated with offers."

"I daresay I would have been if Adriana hadn't hinted many of them away." She shot him a severe glance. "Strange to tell, she seems to feel that avoiding trying Geoffrey's temper unnecessarily is a sound idea."

He looked down at her—and hoped she read the message in his eyes; he concurred with her sister's judgment and sincerely hoped she herself would exercise similar restraint.

The way she looked away, the hoity angle to which she elevated her nose, suggested she understood him well enough. Hiding an inward grimace at his own susceptibility, he steered her to where his godmother waited, surrounded by a number of her extremely interested friends.

Despite their interest and that shown by any number of the ton's matrons in the relationship between them, the rest of the evening passed well enough. Through a combination of exemplary scouting and good management, he kept Alicia to himself throughout, avoiding the other gentlemen who, prowling through the crowd and attracted by the faintly exotic, definitely sensual picture she presented in her deep purple gown—something he fully intended to enjoy removing later—continually hove on her horizon.

They indulged in another waltz, after which she insisted on returning to check on Adriana and her court. Instead of permitting her to hang back as she usually did, he led her to join the circle of gentlemen and two other enterprising young ladies gathered about Adriana.

Alicia shot him a suspicious glance, which he met with a bland, wholly deceptive smile, but she consented to do as he wished. Thus protected from further incursions—the gentlemen who looked her way were not the sort to dance attendance among the younger crew—they saw out the end of the evening.

As soon as guests started to leave, Alicia turned to him; he got the impression she was tired, then recalled . . . hiding a smug smile, he gathered Adriana and Geoffrey; together with Sir Freddie, they joined the exodus. In the foyer downstairs, they parted. Sir Freddie bowed easily over Adriana's hand, bowed courteously to Alicia, nodded to Tony, and lastly Geoffrey, then left. Geoffrey scowled after him, then turned to farewell Adriana and Alicia.

Tony exchanged a nod and a glance. Geoffrey returned both, an acknowledgment that Tony would see both ladies safe home.

When he accompanied them to their carriage, Alicia shot him a wary frown. He ignored it, handed first Adriana, then her up, and followed.

Adriana accepted his presence without the slightest question. Alicia glanced at him, then gave her attention to the facades they rolled past. He leaned back, content to feel her soft warmth beside him, perfectly aware of what was going through her mind.

When the carriage rocked to a halt in Waverton Street, he stepped down, and handed both sisters down. He shut the carriage door; the carriage lurched, then rumbled off. He turned to find Alicia standing on the pavement, eyeing him uncertainly. Suppressing a smile, he took her arm and guided her up the steps. Adriana had already knocked; Maggs opened the door, and she swept in. He steered Alicia in her wake.

"Good night." Adriana headed for the stairs with barely a backward glance.

Maggs shot the bolts on the front door, then bowed to them both and took himself off.

Alicia watched him go and wished she knew what would happen next. She shouldn't encourage any illicit interlude; she steeled herself to bid Tony good night. Determinedly ignoring the twitching of her senses, the skittering anticipation afflicting her nerves, she tensed to swing about—

His long fingers slid around her wrist. "Come into the drawing room."

She turned, tried to read his face, but he was already moving, drawing her with him. He opened the door; leaving it ajar, he led her into the dimness beyond the shaft of light shed by the candle left burning in the hall.

Halting, he faced her, smoothly drew her into his arms—and kissed her.

Stormed her senses.

She was kissing him back, fully participating in an increasingly heated exchange before she caught her mental breath. Even when she did, it was impossible to draw back, to pull away from the engagement and the spiraling escalation of hunger and need it fueled.

Whose hunger, whose need, she couldn't have said; they were both greedy, ravenous, both wanting.

Her hands were sunk in his hair, holding him to her as their tongues dueled, as their lips feasted. One of his hands had closed about her breast, kneading, leaving it swollen and aching; the other was wrapped about one globe of her bottom, crushing the silk as he held her to him.

He rocked against her, deliberately evocative; heat pulsed within her—she heard a soft moan.

Holding her tight, her body molded to his, he broke from the kiss, raised his head, but not far. With an effort she lifted her heavy lids, and found his black gaze on her eyes.

"There's no reason to step back."

She knew he didn't mean from their kiss.

His gaze fell to her lips, then returned to her eyes. "And don't think to deny this."

She couldn't; given what was so manifestly flaring between them . . . he was right—there was no point.

He bent his head again. She was lifting her lips to meet his when she heard his soft murmur, "Or me."

She set her hand to his cheek as he took her mouth again; he was all heat and fire, tempting and familiar. This, she accepted, was the way it would be; if he wanted her, she was willing.

A minute later, he broke from the kiss to murmur, his voice dark and gravelly, "Upstairs."

He turned her. His hand remained on her bottom as he guided her into the hall, then up the stairs to her bedchamber; her skin didn't cool in the least.

Then they were in her room, and he closed the door. She'd halted in the middle of the floor, the candle in her hand. The flame wavered, but was enough to shed a golden pool of light into the general gloom.

He glanced at her, then at her dressing table; he waved. "Put it down there."

She moved to do so. Leaning over the stool, she set the candlestick down on the polished top, straightened—and saw in the mirror that he'd followed her.

His hands slid around her waist. He shifted her slightly so that she stood directly in front of the three-paneled mirror with its wide central panel flanked by two narrower wings. The rectangular stool stood before her knees. She glanced down at it, then looked up as his hands slid farther and gripped, anchoring her as he stepped closer, trapping her before him.

She caught her breath as, in the shadowy mirror, she watched his dark head bend beside hers; releasing her waist, one hand rose, gliding upward over the purple silk, now deep as the midnight sky, to close possessively over one breast. His other hand splayed down, covering her stomach, pressing in, gently kneading, pressing her hips back against his hard thighs.

Turning her head, she glanced over her shoulder at his face; inches away, she saw his teeth gleam in a fleeting smile.

"Bear with me," he murmured, then his lips touched the corner of hers, then cruised back along her jaw to trace her ear. "I want to see you naked."

He whispered the words, dark and erotic, into her ear.

It took a moment before she realized what he meant—he wanted to see her naked in the mirror.

Her nerves seized; before she could think of any protest—even decide if she wished to protest—he nudged her head back. She complied without thought; his lips traced downward along the column of her throat, then fastened over the spot where her pulse leapt.

His lips moved on her skin; his hands moved over her silk-clad body, roaming, caressing, then his fingers found her laces.

She closed her eyes, leaned back against him as he loosened her gown, then his hands rose to her shoulders and pressed the soft fabric down.

"Lift your arms."

Opening her eyes just enough to see beneath her lashes, she watched her reflection in the mirror as she obeyed, sliding her arms free of the tiny sleeves. His palms swept down, over her breasts; the gown slithered down to her waist. His hands followed, pressed the folds past her hips; with a soft swoosh, the dress pooled at her feet.

For an instant, he paused, surveying what he'd uncovered. She caught the gleam of his eyes from beneath his heavy lids, felt his gaze briefly roam. In the flickering candlelight her chemise was opaque, the shadowy valleys and contours it hid mysterious.

He looked down. His hands rose and gripped her waist. "Kneel on the stool." He lifted her, and she did; with his knees he nudged her ankles wide and stepped between, so his chest was again a warm wall at her back, his erection a promise against the swell of her bottom.

The candlelight reached her, but didn't light him well; he was a dark presence behind her, his tanned hands contrasting starkly against the whiteness of her skin, the ivory of her chemise. He was a phantom lover, come to claim her, to lavish pleasure on her and take his own.

Her breath caught. He looked up, in the mirror trapped her gaze—as his hands slipped beneath the front hem of her chemise. She steeled herself, anticipating his touch, the fiery delight of his hands on her flesh, skin to bare skin. Instead, he turned his hands, caught the fine fabric and lifted it. Without touching her at all, he raised the diaphanous garment; lungs seizing, she lifted her arms and he drew it off over her head.

She put out a hand to steady herself as the cool air caressed her skin—the only firm purchase she could reach was his thigh behind her. Sinking her fingers into the hard muscle, giddy, she stared at the vision in the mirror—that of a slim, slender woman, her dark hair elegantly high, totally naked but for her silk stockings and the ruched satin garters that held them in place, circling her thighs.

Lifting her gaze to his face, she sensed rather than saw his satisfaction; it was a tangible thing, filling the air, surrounding her. She realized she still had on her ballroom slippers; even as the thought occurred, she saw him glance down, then his fingers caressed each ankle, and he slipped the shoes from her feet and let them fall.

He moved close again, and reached around to her garters. But instead of easing them down, as she'd expected, he ran his fingertips around the upper edge of each. And smiled. "They can stay. For now."

The timbre of his voice sent a shiver down her spine. It took effort to remain upright, yet pride dictated she keep her spine erect; she could feel the fabric of his coat and trousers gently abrading her bare skin.

His gaze had returned, slowly, to her face. He studied it, then shifted back a fraction, just enough to shrug off his coat. Seconds later, his waistcoat joined it on the floor.

He had to step back to deal with his cravat and shirt; she had to let go of him. She watched as he flung the shirt aside, then looked down, his hands going to his waist. His trousers hit the floor, and he stepped out of them, returning to her, his hands sliding over her hips, over her waist, drawing her back against him, against the heat of his skin, the rock-hard wall of his chest and abdomen, the hard columns of his thighs.

"Lean back. Let me love you."

The words were an erotic whisper in the darkness.

"Let me see you. Watch you."

She did as he asked, leaning back against him, eyes almost closed, committed to following his lead, only later, as his hands made free with her body, with her senses, fully understanding what he meant.

At first, his hands simply roved her body, a basic pleasure, heating her skin, teasing her senses to even greater awareness, evoking a deeper, persistent hunger. Flaring need grew as he weighed and caressed her breasts, taunting the tight, aching peaks, then tracing the lines of her body, sculpting the curves with his palms before gliding his fingertips down her thighs, then nudging her knees farther apart.

She watched, immersed in the sensations as he stroked the quivering inner faces of her thighs, then laid his hand over her stomach, the other sliding across her waist, holding her, surrounding her with his strength, giving her a moment to assimilate the heated, raspy reality of his skin, his muscled body pressed to her, locked about her.

In the mirror, she could see his shoulders above hers; his chest was wider than her back, his arms a cage in which she willingly waited.

He murmured something in French—she didn't catch the words but let her head rest back against his shoulder, watching, watching as he shifted, then the hand at her stomach slid lower, long fingers gliding over, then through the dark curls at the apex of her thighs. He reached farther; the breath strangled in her throat, her lungs seized. The vise about her chest locked tight as he stroked, caressed, then deliberately probed.

Farther, then yet farther, until his hand was pressed between her thighs, until her body was awash with flame. Her hands fastened on the arm locked about her waist, fingers sinking into the hard muscle as she watched him watching her—watched his hand, so much darker than her skin, rhythmically lavish fiery delight upon her senses.

She gasped, felt her body tighten, arching, reaching for the beckoning peak. He didn't stop but steadily pushed her on, on, on—until she fractured.

Her soft cry hung in the air; he wrapped her in his arms, in his strength, held her safe as she slowly drifted back from the crest.

She turned her head, glanced at him. He met her gaze, but briefly. His lips curving in what wasn't quite a smile, he glanced down at her body, soft, pliant, still locked against the hard aroused length of his. Then he bent his head and pressed a kiss to the point where her neck met her shoulder.

"First course."

His tone made it clear he intended to feast.

Reaching out, he moved the single candle, still burning bright, across and back on the dressing table, positioning it near the central pane of the mirror, at the very center. Reaching farther, he tugged first one side panel, then the other forward, angling them so they reflected the candlelight back at them. At her—it was her smooth, white skin the light illuminated; in contrast, his darker, tanned, and haired limbs seemed to disperse the light. Yet she could now see him clearly. The new position of the side panels let her see beyond her shoulders.

His hands returned to her body; they circled her breasts, gently kneaded, then slid down, tracing her sides, then he gripped her hips. Bent his head and murmured, his breath a heated promise, "Lean forward—hold on to the edge of the dressing table."

She did, and felt his hand caress the globes of her bottom. He traced the backs of her thighs, then reached between. Touched, stroked.

On a shuddering sigh, she closed her eyes; she had only an instant's warning—an inkling of what he would do—before he shifted, pressed close, and entered her.

Instinctively she locked her thighs, braced her arms, held still as he sank in, gasped when, with a last thrust, he filled her completely. His hands gripped her hips, anchored her as he withdrew, returned, then settled to a slow, steady plundering.

Her senses shook; her wits had long gone. Her breathing sounded ragged in her ears. Beneath her skin, her pulse throbbed, her body aflame as she rode the increasingly powerful thrusts.

The tempo escalated, degree by degree, until she was barely clinging to sanity, wrapped in heat, driven by desire.

"Watch."

The command reached through the flames fogging her mind. She dragged in a breath, forced her lids up. Looked.

And saw.

Him, behind her, his face etched with passion, set, his whole being focused completely on her, on the pleasure he found in her heated body. A body aglow with desire, softly sheened, his hands curved over her hips, his fingers locked on her skin.

She moved with him, not by thought but in instinctive concert, taking, giving, wanting more. Glancing to the side, into the side mirror, she watched their hips move, locked together in their sensual dance.

Her lungs seized; she glanced back at his face, saw the gleam of his eyes beneath his lashes as he watched her.

Then he shifted, thrust deeper, harder, higher. She gasped, let her lids fall; he was impossibly high inside her.

Faster, faster—and the flames roared. Took them, consumed them in an orgy of feeling, of sensations too sharp, too bright, too excruciatingly powerful to survive. And they were whirling, trapped in a whirlpool of delight, passion still driving, ecstasy beckoning . . . until it broke over them, drenched them, washed through them.

Leaving them shuddering, locked tight together, his arms wrapped around her, hers wrapped over them.

The tide faded, and left them.

The bed was close. He lifted her, staggered the few steps, then they collapsed amid the covers. It was a long time before either could summon the will or the strength to move.

Fourteen

෯෯෯

The following days were among the strangest Alicia had known. And quite the fullest.

With the Season about to commence, the social pace approached the frenetic; not only were there three or more major balls every night, but the days, too, were crammed with activities—driving in the park, at-homes, teas, luncheons, picnics, and all manner of diversions. So established were they now among the ton that their absence at such events would have been remarked; people expected to see them—they needed to be there.

She'd schemed, hoped, worked for, plotted so that at the start of the Season she and Adriana would be accepted members, indeed fixtures on the social scene. Fate had granted her wish, and they were dancing every night.

Those who had only recently come to town cast covetous eyes at their now-combined circle, with Tony, Geoffrey, Sir Freddie, and a bevy of others regularly forming part of that select company. But most, certainly the major hostesses and the matrons on whose opinion tonnish acceptance hung, had grown used to them; they merely smiled, nodded graciously, and moved on through the crush.

Of course, given Adriana's clear preference for Geoffrey's company, and his for hers, such social prominence was no longer necessary, yet Alicia would have managed society's demands easily enough—if it hadn't been for the distraction of all else in her suddenly and unexpectedly full life.

Tony left her bed every morning before dawn; through the day, he traveled—to the coast, to various towns and hamlets, over the Downs, to Southampton and Dover—speaking with his mysterious "contacts," constantly seeking information that might shed light on A.C.'s nefarious activities.

In the evening, he'd return, not to Waverton Street but his own house; later still, he'd join her at whichever ball or soirée, musicale or rout they had chosen to attend.

Each evening, she'd wait, chatting with those about her but with her thoughts elsewhere, wondering, circling . . . until he arrived. Every time he appeared to bow over her hand, then set it on his sleeve and take his place by her side, her heart leapt. Quelling it, she'd wait still further, impatient yet resigned, for the ballrooms were now too crowded to risk talking of his findings.

Only later when he'd escorted them home, then followed her to her bedchamber would they talk. He'd tell her all he'd done that day, all he'd learned. Snippets of information verified their suspicions that A.C. had somehow profiteered by ensuring certain ships had been taken by the enemy, yet nothing they'd discovered so far had shed enough light to show them how.

Later yet . . . they'd come together in her bed, and the day would fall away, and nothing else—nothing beyond the cocoon of the coverlets and the circle of each other's arms—seemed real, of any consequence.

Later still, she'd lie wrapped in his arms, surrounded by his strength, listening to his steady heartbeat, and wonder . . . at herself, at where she was, where she was heading . . . but those moments were fleeting, too brief to reach any conclusion.

And then the sun would rise, and there'd be another day of frantic activity, of ensuring her brothers' lives and their lessons stayed on track, that Adriana and Geoffrey's romance continued to prosper, and that all else—the facade of her making—continued as it needed to.

Beneath the social bustle, she was conscious of an undercurrent of action. Things *were* happening; Tony and his friends were steadily, quietly, chipping away at A.C.'s walls—at some point they'd break through. Twice, she glimpsed a watchful face in the street; the sight reminded her of the potential danger, kept her on her mental toes.

She tried, once, to find time alone to think, but Adriana burst in in a panic over a new gown that wouldn't drape straight, and she put aside her nebulous concerns. Time enough when the Season had run at least a few weeks, enough to take the edge from society's appetite, and A.C. had been exposed and her family was safe again, and Geoffrey had proposed . . . time enough, then, to think of herself.

That evening, she nearly suggested they stay home—perhaps send a note to Torrington House, and another to Geoffrey Manningham, inviting them to a quiet dinner . . . then she sighed and climbed into the fabulous apple green silk gown Adriana had fashioned. It was the Duchess of Richmond's ball tonight.

The traditional, recognized, start of the Season.

Even before they reached the duchess's door, it was clear the crowd would be horrendous; their carriage took forty minutes just to travel up the drive and deposit them beneath the awning erected to protect the ladies' delicate toilettes from the light showers sweeping past. Once inside, the noise of a thousand chattering tongues engulfed them; friends called greetings through the throng—it was impossible not to be infected with the gaiety.

Geoffrey was the first to find them. "Let me." He took Adriana's arm, offered Alicia the other, then steered them to where a trio of potted palms gave some respite from the packed and shifting bodies.

They stopped, caught their breaths. Alicia snapped open her fan and waved it. "Now I see why they refer to such events as 'crushes.'"

Geoffrey threw her a commiserating look. "Luckily, it doesn't get much worse than this."

"Thank heaven for that," Adriana murmured.

Gradually, the others with whom they'd become most friendly found them; it was a comfortable circle that formed by the side of the room, Miss Carmichael and Miss Pontefract, both sensible and well-bred young ladies, helping to balance the genders. They exchanged the latest stories they'd heard during the day; the gentlemen, most of whom kept to their clubs during the daytime, often had not heard what the ladies had, and vice versa.

Occasionally, a matron would stop by and engage Alicia; some brought their daughters to be introduced. Lady Horatia Cynster smiled and nodded; later, the Duchess of St. Ives stopped by Alicia's side and complimented her on her gown.

"You have become as *ravissante* as your sister." The duchess's pale green eyes quizzed her. "I confess I am surprised Torrington is not here. Do you expect him?"

She wasn't sure how to answer, in the end admitted, "I believe he'll arrive shortly."

"Indeed, and no doubt he will see you home." The duchess's smile deepened. She laid a hand on Alicia's wrist. "*Bien.* It is good. I am most pleased that he has had the sense to act, rather than prevaricate— it is pleasing to see that he takes such excellent care of you." Her pale gaze fell on Geoffrey. "And this one, if my eyes do not lie, will take good care of your sister, *hein*?"

Alicia raised her brows. "It appears he wishes to, certainly, although she has yet to tell him he may do so."

The duchess laughed. "*Bon!* It is wise to keep such as he wondering, at least for a little time."

With a nod to Adriana, and to Sir Freddie Caudel, who had noticed her and bowed low, the duchess patted Alicia's hand, then moved on into the crowd.

The dance floor was in the next salon, separated by an archway. Alicia refused all offers to lead her thence, remaining by the palms chatting with whichever gentlemen were not engaged with the ladies on the floor.

Such was the crowd, she was almost surprised that Tony managed to find them. It was late when he did.

His fingers slid around her wrist; she looked up, smiling in welcome, aware as usual of faint but definite relief. A relief that turned to concern when she met his eyes and saw her weariness mirrored there.

He raised her hand to his lips, using the gesture to mask his grimace. "I'd forgotten how bad these affairs could be."

She smiled, and let him draw her close. "The dance floor is unnavigable, I've heard."

He raised a brow at her. "There's always the terrace."

"Is there a terrace?"

He nodded. "Through the drawing room."

She considered the question in his eyes, then faintly smiled. "I'd rather go home."

His black eyes held hers. After a moment, he murmured, "Are you sure?"

"Yes."

He held her gaze for an instant, then nodded. With a look and a quiet word, he gathered Adriana; not surprisingly, Geoffrey came, too. Sir Freddie bade them a suavely courteous good night, remaining to chat with Miss Pontefract and Sir Reginald Blaze. Leaving the group, they made their way through the still dense crowd to the foyer.

Tony sent a footman for their carriage. Richmond was a long way from Mayfair; in response to a pointed look from Adriana, Alicia invited Geoffrey to share their carriage. He accepted; minutes later, the carriage arrived, and they set off on the long rocking ride back to town.

Once they were free of the gate and bowling along the main road, Geoffrey looked at Tony. "Have you learned anything yet?"

Tony felt Alicia's glance, shook his head. "Nothing definite. Corroboration, yes, but nothing that defines the game A. C. was playing."

"Was playing? You're sure of that? That it's all in the past?"

He wasn't surprised to find Geoffrey interrogating him; if he'd been in his shoes, enamored of the lovely Adriana, he, too, would want to know. "That much seems certain. Indeed, that's why Ruskin was no longer valuable—why he became an expendable liability."

Geoffrey thought, then nodded.

Conversation lapsed, then Adriana asked Geoffrey something; he looked down at her, and replied. They continued talking, their voices low.

Tony wasn't in the mood to chat; he was in truth tired—he'd traveled down to Rye and spent much of the day chasing men who rarely ventured forth in sunshine. Nevertheless, he'd found them, and learned all he'd needed to know.

He looked at Alicia; shifting his hand, he found hers and wrapped his fingers about it. She glanced at him; in the weak light he saw her smile gently, then she looked forward, leaned her head against his shoulder, her other hand finding and covering their clasped hands. He sensed she was as tired as he; he was tempted to put his arm around her and gather her against him, but in light of the pair on the opposite seat, refrained.

It took nearly an hour to reach Waverton Street.

Geoffrey jumped down; Tony followed. They handed their ladies down, then Geoffrey took his leave of Adriana and Alicia, and walked off.

Tony followed Alicia up the steps of the house, glancing as always to left and right. He'd caught a glimpse of his man on the corner, recalled the report that had been on his desk when he'd returned home that evening.

In the front hall, he waited with Alicia while Adriana went upstairs, and Maggs retreated to the nether regions; he was perfectly sure their charade wasn't fooling Maggs, but he suspected it was important to Alicia, at least at that point, to preserve her facade as a virtuous widow.

Once Maggs's footsteps had faded and Adriana had disappeared down the corridor to her room, he turned back to the front door and slid both bolts home. Alicia had picked up the candle from the hall table; on the lowest tread of the stair, she glanced back at him. He joined her; together they climbed the stairs to her room.

Her bedchamber was the largest, closest to the stairs. Adriana's room lay along the corridor, two dressing rooms and a linen press separating the rooms. He had no idea whether Adriana knew he spent the nights in her elder sister's bed; given the distance between their rooms, there was no reason she would have guessed.

The boys' rooms were on the next floor, the servants' rooms in the attics above. Following Alicia into her bedchamber and shutting the door, he reflected that thus far, her reputation remained safe.

If there was any reason to imagine it threatened, he would make his intentions public, but as things stood, with the ton believing her a widow and thus according her the associated license, there was no compelling urgency to declare his hand.

Indeed, he prayed the necessity wouldn't arise, that once A. C. was unmasked and they were free of his threat, he would have time to woo her, to ask for her hand with all due ceremony. That was, to his mind, the least she deserved, regardless of their established intimacy.

He hadn't intended that, but having once spent the night in her bed, the notion of not continuing to do so hadn't even entered his head. The fact he'd simply assumed her agreement occurred to him. He glanced at her. She'd crossed the room to set the candlestick on the dressing table; seated on the stool, she was calmly letting down her long hair.

The simple, domestic sight never failed to soothe him—to soothe that part of him that was not, even at the best of times, all that civilized.

She had not at any time drawn back, either from him or from their relationship; her quiet, calm acceptance was both balm to his possessive soul and a wordless reassurance that they understood each other perfectly.

Indeed, words had never featured much between them. Aside from all else, he'd always believed actions spoke louder.

Sitting on the bed, he removed his shoes, then shrugged out of his coat. He stripped off his waistcoat, untied his cravat, all the while watching her brush the long, mahogany tresses that spilled down her back, a silken river reaching nearly to her waist.

When she laid down the brush and stood, he crossed to her. Bending his head, murmuring an endearment, he set his fingers to her laces, and his lips to the sensitive spot where her white shoulder and throat met. When her gown was loose, he forced himself to move away, allowing her to remove the gown, shake it out, and hang it up.

Unbuttoning his shirt, he inwardly frowned, returning to a thought that frequently nagged; it would be nice to give her more servants, a maid at least to take care of her clothes and see to her jewels . . . frowning, he pulled his shirt from his waistband. As far as he'd seen, she didn't have any jewelry.

"Oh." At her armoire, she turned, through the shadows looked at him. "I meant to tell you—something rather strange happened today."

Clad in her chemise, she headed for the bed. He started unbuttoning his cuffs. "What?"

Picking up a silk robe, she slipped it over her shoulders. "A solicitor's clerk called this morning." Sinking onto the bed, she met his eyes. "Adriana and I were in the park. The man—"

"A weasely-looking fellow in black?" The description had been in Collier's report; he'd read it before setting out for Richmond.

She blinked, then nodded. "Yes—that sounds like him. He insisted on waiting to see me even though Jenkins told him I'd be a while. Maggs and Jenkins discussed it, then left him in the parlor, but when I arrived home with Adriana and Geoffrey, the man wasn't there." She shrugged. "He must have got tried of waiting and left by the front door, but it seems strange that he left no message."

He'd slowed, stopped undressing, giving her his undivided attention. He considered, then said, "The parlor?"

She nodded.

Biting back a curse, he swung on his heel and headed for the door. "Tony?"

He heard her whisper, but didn't answer. Glancing back as he went down the stairs, he saw her following, belting the silk robe as she came, her bare feet almost as silent as his.

Reaching the parlor, he opened the door. The fire was still glowing; picking up a three-armed candelabrum, he lit each candle from the embers, then, rising, set the candelabrum on the table beside the chaise.

Alicia silently closed the door. Her eyes felt huge. "What is it?"

Slowly swiveling, he studied the room, the window seat beneath the bow window, the bookselves flanking the fireplace and one corner of the room, the escritoire against one wall, and a high table with two drawers. "How long was he here—do you have any idea?"

Drawing the robe close, she considered. "It could have been half an hour. Probably not more."

He waved to the armchair by the fire. "Sit down. This might take a while."

Sinking into the chair, she drew her legs up, covering her cold toes with the hem of her robe, and watched him search the room. He was thorough—very thorough. He looked in places she'd never have thought of—like the undersides of the drawers of the table against the wall. He found nothing there, and moved on to the escritoire.

"Does this have a secret drawer?"

"No."

He checked every possible nook and cranny, then shifted to the bookshelves. She quelled a shiver. Barefoot on the cold boards, he hunkered down; his shirt flapped loose about his chest, but he didn't seem to feel the chill. He ran his hand along the spines, then started pulling out individual books, reaching into the gaps to check behind.

Tony had no idea what he was looking for, but instinct told him there would be something to find. He pulled out a slim volume; the title caught his eye. *"A Young Lady's Guide to Etiquette in the Ton."* Briefly, he raised his brows. Setting it aside, he pulled out a few more. They, too, dealt with similar subjects; clearly Alicia and Adriana had done considerable research before embarking on their scheme.

Making sure he missed no section of the shelves, he worked his way along.

He found what he was searching for behind a set of books on the lowest shelf, close by the room's corner. A sheaf of papers had been jammed behind the books; drawing them out, he turned to Alicia. One look at her face, her eyes, assured him they weren't hers.

"What are they?"

Rising, he moved closer to the candelabrum, and flicked through the sheaf. "Old letters." He straightened them out, laying each on the table. "Five of them." Sinking down on the chaise, he picked one up.

In a rustle of silk, Alicia left the armchair and came to join him. Sitting close beside him, she reached for one of the letters—he forestalled her, passing her the one he'd already scanned; she took it and he lifted the next.

When he laid down the fifth missive, she was still picking her way through the second. The letters were in French.

For a long moment, he sat, elbows on his thighs, and stared across the room, then he leaned back, reached for her, and drew her, letters and all, into his arms.

She shivered, and looked up at him. "I've only read one. Are they all similar?"

He nodded. "All to A. C. from French captains acknowledging ships taken on information supplied." Three of the letters were from French naval captains; he could personally verify two of the names. He could also identify from his own knowledge the other two correspondents, both captains of French privateers.

The letters were extremely incriminating. For A. C.

Alicia had never been A. C., and indeed, the letters all dated from before her fictitious marriage had supposedly taken place. The name wasn't what was worrying him.

She frowned at the letter she held, then shuffled the sheaf. "These are all addressed to A. C. at the Sign of the Barking Dog."

Her tone alerted him; he glanced at her. "Do you know it?"

She nodded. "It's not far from Chipping Norton."

He sat forward. "An inn?" Getting to his feet, he drew her with him.

She shook her head. "No, a hedge tavern. Barely even that. It caters to a very rough crowd—most of the locals avoid it."

He hid a grimace. The Barking Dog sounded like the perfect address for a villain. He doubted he would get any help from the innkeeper as to who had picked up the letters, but he'd send someone to inquire tomorrow.

Meanwhile . . . "Let's go upstairs. You're freezing."

He drew her out of the room; she went unresisting, frowning, refolding the letters. Closing the parlor door, he saw her tiptoeing awkwardly to the stairs. Shutting his lips on a query regarding the whereabouts of her slippers, he strode after her, bent, and hefted her into his arms.

She looked into his face, then settled back and let him carry her upstairs. She'd left the door to her bedchamber open; he entered and nudged it closed. The lock clicked shut. She shifted, expecting to be put down.

He strode to the bed and dropped her on it. Filched the letters from her grasp when she bounced. "I'll need those."

She struggled up, watched as he crossed to his coat and slipped the sheaf into a pocket. "That clerk put them there, didn't he? Why?"

"To confuse things."

She swung her legs off the bed, stood, shrugged out of her robe and laid it aside. "How?" Turning back to the bed, she frowned at him. "What do you think will happen?"

"I think"—he stripped off his shirt and dropped it on his coat— "that you can expect a visit from someone in authority within the next few days. They'll be looking for the letters, but"—he smiled evilly— "they won't find them."

Still clad in her chemise, she slipped under the covers. He looked down as he stripped off his trousers, hiding his smile, pretending not to notice as, once safely covered, she wriggled out of the fine chemise and tossed it to the floor. Once he joined her in the bed, it wouldn't stay on her; better she remove it than risk him tearing it, or so he had given her to understand.

She was still frowning. "What should we do?"

Naked, he crossed to the dressing table and doused the candle. "We'll talk about it in the morning. There's nothing to be done tonight."

He returned to the bed and slid under the covers beside her.

She was shivering, still frowning, but accepting his edict, turned into his arms as she always did, as ardent and as needy as he. Her openness was a blessing for which he would remain forever grateful;

the instant their limbs met, and their lips found each other's, there was only one thought between them, only one goal, one aim, one desire.

Her chill, her concern over the letters—and his—faded as that simple reality took control, claimed them, heart, minds, and souls fused them. Slumped, exhausted, and thoroughly heated, in each other's arms, they surrendered, and slept. And left tomorrow's problems for tomorrow.

Again, Alicia slept in. Lecturing herself that she couldn't let the practice become habit, she climbed into a new morning gown of forest green, quickly coiled her hair, then hurried downstairs, expecting mayhem.

She came to a teetering halt on the threshold of the dining room. Alerted by the deep rumble of Tony's voice, she looked in—stared.

He was seated at the foot of the table, keeping order, clearly in charge. Her brothers, of course, were on their best behavior; expressions angelic, they hung on his every word. Adriana . . . one glance at her sister as she slowly entered was enough to inform her that Adriana was intrigued.

The boys noticed her, and smiled.

Picking up her pace, as nonchalantly as she could she went to her accustomed place at the head of the table. "Good morning." Sitting, she met Tony's gaze. Inclined her head briefly. "My lord. To what do we owe this pleasure?"

A smile flashed behind his eyes; she prayed Adriana didn't catch it, or if she had, wouldn't be able to interpret it.

"I came to enjoy your company"—he smiled briefly at the boys; he was clearly their hero—"and also to discuss the most recent developments and remind you all to take care." His gaze returned to her face. "It seems matters are progressing, just not as I'd thought, or hoped. You"—his gaze swept the table—"all of you, need to stay alert."

"Why?" Eyes wide, David waited.

Alicia felt Adriana's glance, then her sister leaned forward and looked down the table at Tony. "That odd man who called yesterday but didn't wait—is it something to do with him?"

Looking straight down the table, Alicia met Tony's eyes and read the question therein. Briefly, she nodded.

"Yes." Assembling their collective interest with a glance, he went on to explain about the letters.

She listened, on one level monitoring his words and her brothers' reactions, on another, thinking rather more personally.

At least he'd changed out of his evening clothes; he was wearing a morning coat of rich, dark brown over ivory inexpressibles reaching into gleaming black Hessians. His waistcoat was striped in ivory and browns, his cravat starched white, severely simple. On the little finger of his right hand the gold-and-onyx signet ring he always wore gleamed; his gold watch chain and the gold pin in his cravat completed the picture, one of simple yet formidable elegance.

He'd left her bed at dawn, as usual; he must have gone home, then returned. She hoped he'd rung the doorbell, and hadn't simply waltzed in . . . then again, would anyone have deemed it odd if he had?

Was this a taste of things to come—a guide to how their relationship would develop? That gradually he would become more than just a frequent visitor, over time gaining the status of accepted member of the household, moreover a member whose edicts carried weight.

As they clearly already did with her brothers. Yet he was impressing on them the need to take care, more, to avoid taking any risks; she wasn't about to complain. They paid his warnings far greater heed than they would any from her.

Deep down, she was conscious of a small, very small, degree of irritation that he'd been able so easily to assume a role that for a decade had been hers, that her family—even Adriana—accepted his usurpation without question . . . yet as, with a glance, he extended his edicts to Adriana, too, who just as avidly as the boys had been drawn in by his glib, truthful but not unnecessarily revealing, or worrying, account of the planted letters and what he thought they would mean, she couldn't find it in her actively to oppose him.

Nevertheless, some part of her, the most private side of her, felt almost exposed. Most definitely uncertain, both of the rightness of the present and what next might come. Until this morning, what had grown between them had remained between them alone, yet now . . . perhaps this was how things were done in his world?

She honestly didn't know; she'd traveled far beyond the limits of the books in the parlor. Not one gave any description of the normal pattern of behavior, the day-to-day arrangements that might exist between a member of the nobility and his mistress.

Presumably he knew how things should be; she would have to, as she'd had to so often thus far, follow his lead.

"I don't know exactly what will happen, or when." Tony met the boys' eyes, then glanced briefly at Adriana. "It's possible nothing at all might occur—we might catch whoever it is before he takes the next step."

He didn't believe that for a moment; Alicia's slight frown suggested she didn't either.

Returning his attention to the boys, he reiterated, "But you can't be too careful—I want you all to be on guard, and not panic if there is some development. I, and others, won't be far away."

The boys, eyes wide, nodded solemnly.

Jenkins came in at that moment; Alicia forced a smile and spoke with him regarding the boys' lessons, then looked at her brothers. "Up you go."

Tony reinforced her command with a look. The boys finished their milk; he inclined his head as they bobbed bows before taking themselves off.

Letting his gaze drift past Adriana, he looked at Alicia. "If I could speak with you for a moment?"

She blinked, glanced at Adriana, and rose. "Yes, of course. If you'll come into the drawing room?"

Rising, he took his leave of Adriana, who seemed totally at ease over his unorthodox presence, then followed her across the front hall. She paused by the drawing room door; he waved her in and followed, closing the door behind them.

She stopped and faced him; halting before her, he met her gaze. "Regardless of what I just said, I fully expect something to happen." He grimaced, let her see his unease. "I just don't know what, or exactly when."

She studied his face, then said, "Thank you for speaking with them. We'll be on guard now."

"My men outside gave me a decent description of this clerk, but there must be thousands like him in London—I don't expect to be able to trace him, let alone his employer." He paused, wondered if she'd see his next maneuver for the revelation it was—decided he didn't care. "With your leave, I'll send another footman—he'll arrive within the hour. Maggs tells me there's room in the attics—I want him—Maggs—free to follow any other strange visitors who come to call."

She blinked. A frown grew in her eyes. "We have Jenkins. I'm sure he can cope—"

"Your brothers." Ruthlessly he fell back on the one argument he knew would overcome her resistance. "I'd rather Jenkins concentrated on keeping watch over them, and I don't want you and Adriana left without some degree of male support."

She held his gaze, evaluating, realizing he'd left her no option. Her lips tightened, but only fractionally. "Very well. If you truly think it necessary."

"I do." Absolutely, definitely necessary; if he thought he could get her to agree, he'd have half a dozen men about her. "I'll be staying in

London—Gervase should be back from Devon, and with luck Jack Hendon might have something to report."

"If you learn anything, you will send word, won't you?"

He smiled, a flash of teeth and resolution. "I'll bring any news myself." He studied her eyes. "If anything happens, Scully, the new footman, or Maggs, will get word to those watching—they'll find me. I'll come as soon as I can."

For an instant, her expression remained serious, sober, the reality of the threat, the potential but unknown difficulty she and her family might have to face—that he and she both felt sure they would face—dulling the gold and green, then a smile softened her eyes. "Thank you." Putting a reassuring hand on his arm, she held his gaze. "We'll manage."

Her "we" included him; that was clear in her eyes, in her inclusive smile.

His expression eased. He hesitated, then bent his head. Cradling her face in one palm, he kissed her, briefly yet . . . the link between them was now so strong, even that brief caress communicated volumes.

Raising his head, he stepped back. Saluted her. *"Au revoir."*

Tony returned to Upper Brook Street to discover messages from Jack Hendon and Gervase Tregarth awaiting him. Both expected to have firm information by noon; Gervase suggested they meet at the Bastion Club. Tony sat at his desk and dashed off a note to Jack, giving him directions and a brief explanation—enough to whet his appetite.

After that he sat and mentally reviewed all he knew thus far. Action was clearly imminent; why plant incriminating evidence if not to expose it? How, by whom, and precisely when he didn't know, but he could and did clear everything on his desk, all matters that might need his attention over the next few days.

Summoning Hungerford, he gave orders that would ensure, not only that his houses and estate would continue on an even keel were he to be otherwise engaged for a week or so, but also that the various members of his extended staff, some of whom did not fit any common description, were apprised of his intentions, and thus would hold themselves ready to act on whatever orders he flung their way.

At a quarter to twelve, he headed for the Bastion Club.

Climbing the stairs to the first floor, he heard Jack, already in the meeting room, questioning, clearly intrigued by the club and its genesis. He pricked up his ears as other voices answered—Christian, Charles, and Tristan were there, regaling Jack with the benefits of the club, especially as applied to unmarried gentlemen of their ilk.

"I'm already leg-shackled," Jack confessed, as Tony appeared in the doorway.

"To a spitfire, what's more." Tony entered, smiling.

Jack raised his wineglass. "I'll tell her you said that."

"Do." Unperturbed, Tony took a seat opposite and grinned at Jack. "She'll forgive me."

Jack mock-scowled. "I'm not so silly as to encourage her."

Quick footsteps on the stairs heralded Gervase. He strode in quickly, brown curls windblown, the light of the hunt in his eyes. Every man about the table recognized the signs.

Christian, Charles, and Tristan exchanged glances. Christian made as if to rise. "We'll leave you . . ."

Tony waved him back. "If you have the time, I'd value any insight you might have on these matters. For our sins, we're all sufficiently connected with Dalziel, and Jack worked for Whitley."

Gervase drew out a chair and sat. "Right, then." He looked at Tony. "Who do you want to hear from first?"

"Jack's been checking the specific ships." Tony looked across the table. "Let's start there."

Jack nodded. "I concentrated on the sixteen vessels listed in Ruskin's notes that we know were taken. Thus far, I've only been able to get a general picture of their cargoes—asking too many specific questions would attract too much interest."

"Were they carrying anything in common?" Christian asked.

"Yes, and no. I've got word on six of the sixteen, and each was carrying general cargo—furniture, foodstuffs, raw products. No evidence of any peculiar item common to all ships."

"Six," Tony mused. "If there's nothing in common between six, then chances are that's not the distinguishing factor."

Jack hesitated, then went on, "All the ships are still registered—there's no hint of any insurance fraud. On top of that, all the ships I've got information on were owned by various lines, their cargoes by a variety of merchants. There's no common link."

Tony frowned. "But if you think of what's lost when a ship is taken as a prize, rather than sunk . . ." He met Jack's eyes. "The lines buy back their ships—it's the cargo that's lost irretrievably."

"To this side of the Channel." Charles looked at Jack. "But aren't cargoes insured?"

His gaze locked with Tony's, Jack shook his head. "Not in such circumstances. Cargoes are insured against loss through the vessel being lost, but they aren't covered if the goods are seized during wartime."

"So it's considered a loss through an act of war?" Tristan asked.

Jack nodded. "The cargoes would be lost, but there'd be no claim to worry the denizens of Lloyd's Coffee House, no fuss perturbing any of the major guilds like the shipowners."

"And if the merchants were unconnected individuals, and the losses varied and apparently random . . ." Tony paused, frowning. "Who would that benefit?"

None of them could offer an answer.

"We need more information." Tony looked at Gervase.

Who smiled grimly. "It took a bit of persuasion, but I heard three separate tales from three unconnected individuals of 'special commissions' being offered in the Channel Isles. The contacts were all English, and all were miffed that these 'commissions' were being offered solely to, not specifically French, but only to non-English captains."

Gervase exchanged a glance with Tony. "You know what the sailors in and about the Isles are like—they consider themselves a law unto themselves, and largely that's true. It never was clear where they stood in recent times."

Tony humphed. "My reading is that they're for themselves, regardless."

"Indeed," Charles put in. "But I assume the links between our shores and the Isles, and the Isles and Brittany and Normandy continued to operate throughout the war?"

"Oh, yes." Both Tony and Gervase nodded; Jack, too.

"Located as they are . . ." Jack shrugged. "It would be wonderful were they not the haunt of 'independent captains.' "

Tony turned to Gervase. "Did you get any confirmation on those particular ships?"

Gervase shook his head. "None of my contacts had information on specific ships—they'd never been in the running for those 'special commissions' and it seems whoever was making the offer played his cards very close to his chest."

Tony grimaced. "I could go over and scout about, but . . ."

Jack shook his head. "Aside from all else, there'd be more than a few who might remember one Antoine Balzac, and that not fondly."

Tony raised his brows fleetingly. "There is that." He reached into his pocket. "Which brings us to my discovery, which makes me even less inclined to go fossicking on foreign shores."

He tossed the bundle of letters on the table; the others' eyes locked on them. "Yesterday, a greasy-looking clerk in dusty black called at Mrs. Alicia Carrington's house in Waverton Street while she and her sister were in the park, as might have been predicted, the hour being what it was. Said clerk insisted on waiting, and was shown into the parlor, but when Mrs. Carrington returned home, no sign of this clerk could be found.

"Later, when I searched the parlor, I found these, wedged behind books in a corner bookshelf."

The others all glanced at him, then reached for the letters. Their faces grew more and more impassive as they read each, passing them around the table. Finally, when all five letters had been tossed back on the table, Christian leaned forward and looked at Tony. "Tell me why Mrs. Alicia Carrington cannot be A. C."

Tony didn't bridle; Christian was playing devil's advocate. "She's been married just less than two years—before that, she was Alicia Pevensey, and that's been checked." He gestured at the letters. "All five of these were written while she would still have been A. P."

Christian nodded. "Her husband—what was his name?"

"Alfred." Tony didn't like pretending Alfred Carrington had ever existed, but life would be easier if he stuck to Alicia's fabrication. "But he died nearly two years ago, so he wasn't the A. C. who was continuing to seek and buy information from Ruskin. Further, the Carrington family have no connections through which they might have used such information, nor wealth enough to have played A. C.'s game. The payments, the system, are consistent throughout—we're looking for one man, A. C., who's very much alive."

"And up to no good, what's more." Charles flicked one of the letters. "I don't like this."

Tony let a moment elapse, then softly said, "No more do I."

After a moment, he went on, "However, the letters confirm that the track we're pursuing is correct. They show A. C. did engage French naval captains and French privateers to capture ships, presumably using information Ruskin supplied." He added his knowledge of the Frenchmen involved.

"Stop a minute." Tristan said. "What have we got so far? How could a scheme based on what we've surmised work?"

They tossed around scenarios, pooling their experience to approve some suggestions as possible, discounting others.

"All right," Tony eventually said. "This seems the most likely then: Ruskin supplied information on convoys, especially when and where certain ships would leave a convoy to turn aside to their home ports."

Charles nodded. "That, and also when frigates were called off convoy duty to serve with the fleets—in other words when merchantmen would be sailing essentially unprotected."

"The merchantmen would have made a good show"—Jack looked increasingly grim—"but against an enemy frigate, they'd stand little chance."

"So, armed with said knowledge, A. C. arranges for a foreign captain to pick off a specific merchantman. Once the deed was done, and Ruskin's information proved good, A. C. paid him, and both he and A. C. went home happy." Tony grimaced. "We need to work out why A. C. was so keen on removing specific merchantmen, thus preventing their cargoes from reaching London."

He looked at Jack, who nodded. "We need the specifics of the cargoes, not just the general description. The only way to access those details after all this time is via Lloyd's—they always keep records."

"Can you learn what we need without alerting anyone?" Tony held Jack's gaze. "We have no idea who A. C. might be, nor yet what contacts he might have."

Jack shrugged. "I wasn't planning on asking anyone—I know where the records are kept. No reason I can't drop by late one night and take a look."

Charles grinned. "A man after our collective heart—are you sure you don't want to join the club?"

Jack answered with a brief grin. "I have my hands full just at present."

"How long will it take you to gather what we need?" Tony asked.

Jack considered. "Two days. I'll need to scout things out before I go in. Wouldn't do to get caught."

"No, indeed." Christian looked at Tony. "This business of those letters planted in Mrs. Carrington's parlor more than worries me. Whoever A. C. is, he's blackguard enough to happily deflect blame onto an innocent lady, without regard for the damage to her—"

Heavy thuds fell on the front door, reverberating up to the meeting room.

They all froze, waited . . .

The door downstairs opened; voices were heard, then footsteps, not precisely running but hurrying, came up the stairs.

Gasthorpe, the club's majordomo, appeared in the doorway. "Your pardon, my lords." He looked at Tony. "My lord, a footman has arrived with an urgent summons."

Tony was already rising. "Waverton Street?"

"Indeed, my lord. The authorities have descended."

Fifteen

They'd anticipated something of the sort, but Tony was nonetheless surprised and made uneasy by how swiftly the expected had arrived.

Jack demanded the number of Alicia's house, then parted from him on the pavement outside the club, saying he'd meet him there. Together with Christian and Charles, Tony piled into a hackney; Tristan intended to join them, but just at that moment Leonora, his wife, emerged from the garden next door—her uncle's house where she'd been visiting. She saw them, and instantly wanted to know what was going on.

Tristan stopped to talk to her; behind his back, he waved to them to go on without him. They did.

In Waverton Street, Tony jumped down from the hackney. Collier, masquerading as a street sweeper, was lounging on the railings close by the Carrington residence.

The heavily built man tipped his cap as Tony paused beside him. "Five redbreasts, m'lord. Never seen the like in all my born days— they pushed in like it was a thieves' den. Pompous little sort leading from the rear."

Tony murmured his thanks. "Keep watching."

"Aye." Collier eased upright. "I will that."

Christian had paid off the hackney; he and Charles followed as, jaw set, Tony strode up the steps. He didn't knock, but flung the front door wide and stalked in.

A young Runner standing before the drawing room door started, instinctively snapping to attention, then pausing, confusion in his face.

From the direction of the parlor, a stocky sergeant barreled forward, belligerence in every line. "Here, then! Who'd you think you are? You can't just barge in 'ere."

Tony reached into his coat pocket, and withdrew a card. "Viscount Torrington." Face impassive, he handed the card to the sergeant, gestured to Christian and Charles. "The Marquess of Dearne and the Earl of Lostwithiel. Where are Mrs. Carrington and her family?"

The sergeant fingered the expensive card, tracing the embossed printing. "Ah . . ." His belligerence fled. He glanced at his junior barring the drawing-room door. "The inspector placed the lady and her household under guard, m'lord. Took 'em all into custody, like."

"Your inspector seems to have overlooked the point that Mrs. Carrington is already in *my* custody, a fact of which the local office of the Watch is well aware." Tony let his fury ripple beneath his words, subtly scathing.

Yielding to instinct, the sergeant came to attention, eyes fixed forward. "We're not local, m'lord. We came directly from headquarters—Bow Street."

"That's no excuse. Who's in charge here? What's your inspector's name?"

"Sprigs, m'lord."

"Fetch him." Tony caught the hapless sergeant's eye. "I'm going to check on Mrs. Carrington, to make sure neither she nor any member of her household has suffered any ill effects from your inspector's reckless action. Your inspector better pray they haven't. When I return here, I expect to find him waiting, along with every member of your force currently within this house. Is that clear?"

The sergeant swallowed. Nodded. "Yessir."

Tony turned on his heel and made for the drawing-room door. The young Runner gave way, hurriedly stepping back. Tony opened the door; pausing, he scanned the room, then released the knob and walked in.

Relief flooded Alicia; she jumped up from the chaise and went quickly to meet Tony. Two other gentlemen followed him in; from their appearance and actions, they were friends. The one with black curling hair moved to intercept their guard, struggling out of the armchair he'd commandeered with a weak "Hey!"

Tony turned his head and looked at the man.

Suddenly the object of two unnerving gazes, he stopped, apparently paralyzed by caution.

She reached Tony; his gaze returned to her, searched her face. He took her hands, squeezed lightly. "Are you all right?"

His gaze had gone past her to the boys, Adriana, and all their staff gathered about the chaise.

"Yes." She glanced back to see them all on their feet. "Just a trifle shocked." In truth, she was furious, still seething; the inspector's insinuations had made her blood boil. Looking back at Tony, she lowered her voice. "Is this about the letters?"

He squeezed her fingers again; instead of answering—an answer in itself—he kept his attention on the others. "This is all a mistake— we're here to sort it out. I want all of you to stay here quietly. There's nothing to fear."

Adriana nodded; forcing her lips to curve, she sat down again. The boys glanced at her, uncertain, then looked again at Tony.

He nodded. "Stay here with Adriana. Alicia and I will be back in a few minutes." She was close enough to sense the tension that held him, yet he smiled with beguiling charm at her brothers. "I promise I'll explain all later."

The smile and that promise reassured them; with fleeting if brittle smiles, they went to cluster around Adriana.

Alicia noted the look Tony exchanged with Maggs, and more briefly with the new footman, Scully, both of whom had refused to be shifted from her and her family's sides, then he took her arm and turned her to the door.

The other two gentlemen flanked them. Beside her, the larger smiled, as charming in his way as Tony, and half bowed. "Dearne. A pleasure to meet you, Mrs. Carrington, even in such trying circumstances. Rest assured we'll have this settled in short order."

She bobbed a brief curtsy.

"Indeed," the second gentleman said. He saluted her. "Lostwithiel, for my sins." His grin was unrepentant. "We can deal with the introductions later."

Tony shot him a glance as he opened the door.

They emerged into the front hall just as the inspector, a short, red-haired man of uncertain temper with an aggressive attitude and an abrasive tongue, came charging up from the direction of the parlor. "What the *devil's* going on here?" The demand fell just short of a raging bellow.

Fixing on their company, his eyes momentarily widened, then he recovered. "Scrugs! Dammit, man—don't you know better than to allow visitors in?"

He rounded on the sergeant, who held his ground. Scrugs nodded at Tony. "This here's his lordship, what I told you about, sir. And the marquess and the earl." There was enough emphasis in Scrugs's tone to convey the fact that if his superior didn't know when to back off, Scrugs certainly did.

"Inspector . . . Sprigs, is it?" The words were mild, Tony's tone was not. It cut.

Sprigs swung to face him, glaring belligerently. "Aye. And I'll have you know—"

"I assume you checked with the local Watch supervisor before barging onto his patch? Elcott, that would be."

Sprigs blinked; faint wariness crept into his piggy eyes. "Aye, but—"

"I'm surprised Elcott didn't inform you that Mrs. Carrington is already in my custody."

Sprigs cleared his throat. "He did mention it—"

"Indeed?" Tony raised his brows. "And did he also happen to mention that my orders in this matter come from Whitehall?"

Sprigs drew himself up. "Be that as it may, my lord, the information we've received—'deed, the people we received it from—well, we couldn't hardly ignore such, Whitehall or no."

"What information?"

Sprigs pressed his lips together, glanced at Alicia, then ventured, "That Mrs. Carrington here had hired some villains to do away with this man Ruskin, on account of she was in league with the French. Word had it that if we searched this house thoroughly, we'd find evidence enough to prove it."

"From whom did this information come?"

Again Sprigs hesitated; again the stretching silence forced him to answer. "Brought to us indirect, it was." He saw Tony's welling contempt and rushed on, "From the gentlemen's clubs. Seems a number of the high-and-mighty heard the story—wanted to know what we were doing about it. Questions were asked. They even had the commissioner himself in to explain."

Sprigs glanced at Charles and Christian, then looked at Tony. "It's treason we're talking about here. Don't suppose toffs like you care all that much, but if you'd served in the recent wars—"

"I wouldn't suppose quite so readily, Inspector."

The voice, languid, even soft, chilled. Everyone looked toward the front door. They'd left it partially open. A gentleman stood just inside; he walked forward as they stared.

His dark eyes remained fixed on Sprigs. Alicia had grown used to Tony's elegance—this man was equally impressive, moving with innate grace, slim, dark-haired, dressed in dark clothes that exuded that same austere style, a reflection of bone-deep confidence, of their assurance in who they were.

There was one difference. While Tony's tones could cut, whiplike, this man's voice projected a patently lethal threat, quietly efficient, like a scimitar slicing, unhindered, into flesh.

Suppressing a shiver, she glanced at Tony, then at his friends, and realized the newcomer was both known to them and accepted by them. An ally, definitely, yet she sensed he was someone around whom even they trod carefully.

Sprigs swallowed. He glanced at Tony. Behind him, the sergeant and his other two men were rigidly at attention.

"Dalziel." The newcomer answered Sprigs's unvoiced question. "From Whitehall." He halted at Tony's side and looked the unfortunate Sprigs in the eye. "I've already spoken with your superiors. You are to report back to Bow Street immediately, taking all your men, leaving this house in precisely the same state as it was when you, so unwisely, entered. You will not remove so much as a pin."

He paused, then continued, "Your superiors have been somewhat forcefully reminded that, together with Lord Whitley, I am handling this matter, and that contrary to their suppositions, Bow Street's mandate does not extend to countermanding or interfering with Whitehall's actions."

Sprigs, now all but at attention himself, nodded. "Yes, sir." He sounded strangled.

Dalziel let a moment pass, then murmured, "You may go."

They went with alacrity. At a nod from Sprigs, the junior stuck his head into the drawing room and summoned his companion; in short order, the five men from Bow Street were clattering down the steps, routed by a superior force.

All four gentlemen—Tony, Dalziel, Dearne, and Lostwithiel—stood in and about the front door and saw them off, watched them go. Trapped behind, screened from the sight by their broad shoulders, Alicia waited, somewhat impatiently. She knew the instant they all let down their guards.

Tony and Dearne visibly relaxed.

"Importunate devils," Lostwithiel quipped.

"Indeed," Dalziel replied.

They all started to turn inside—

Then paused.

Along with the others, Tony watched two carriages come clattering up, one from each end of the street. Both carriages pulled up before the house. The carriage doors swung open. Tristan sprang down from one carriage; from the other, Jack Hendon stepped down to the pavement. Both turned back to their respective carriages; each handed a lady down.

Kit, Jack's wife, and Leonora, Tristan's wife.

Barely pausing to shake out their skirts, both ladies swept toward the house—and saw each other. At the bottom of the steps, they met, exchanged names, shook hands, then, as one, turned and, beautiful faces decidedly set, swept up the steps.

On the pavement, Jack and Tristan exchanged long-suffering glances, and followed in their wakes.

All four men at the door gave way.

With barely a glance at them the ladies swept in. They saw Alicia, and pounced.

"Kit Hendon, my dear." Taking Alicia's hand, Kit waved toward Jack. "Jack's wife. How terribly distressing for you."

"Leonora Wemyss—I'm Trentham's wife." Leonora waved vaguely at her husband, too, and pressed Alicia's hand. "Are your family quite all right?"

Alicia found a smile. "Yes—I believe so." She gestured to the drawing room.

"It's quite insupportable," Kit declared. "We've come to help."

"Indeed." Leonora turned to the drawing room. "This is going to need action to set right."

Together, the three entered the drawing room. The door shut behind them.

All six men in the front hall stared at the door, then glanced, briefly, at each other.

Dalziel sighed, pityingly or so they all took it, and turned to Tony. "I take it you have whatever Bow Street's minions were sent to find?"

"Yes." Succinctly, Tony described the letters, and how they fitted the scenario they now thought most likely, confirming that A. C. had used Ruskin's information to arrange for merchantmen to be captured by the enemy.

At the end of his explanation, Dalziel, still and silent, stared out, unseeing, through the open door. Then, quietly, he said, "I want him."

He glanced at Tony, then at the others. "I don't care what you have to do—I want to know who A. C. is. As soon as possible. You have my full authority, and as for Whitley, suffice to say he's ropeable. If you have need of his name, you have permission to use that, too."

Briefly, he glanced at them again, then nodded. "I'll leave you to it."

He walked to the door. On the threshold he paused, and looked back. At Tony. "Incidentally, the information against Mrs. Carrington—there's no way to trace it. I've tried. Whoever this man is, he's extremely well connected—he knew exactly in whose ears to plant his seeds. When asked, every concerned soul said they heard it from someone else. I'll continue to keep my ears open, but don't expect any breakthrough on that front."

Tony inclined his head.

Dalziel left, going lightly down the steps, then striding away along the street.

The five men in the front hall remained where they were until his footsteps had faded, then all dragged in a breath and glanced at each other.

"I'm suddenly very grateful I only had to deal with Whitley," Jack said.

"Indeed, you should be." Tony stepped forward and shut the door.

Charles met Tony's gaze as he rejoined them, then glanced at Christian and Tristan. "How did he know?"

Christian raised his brows, openly resigned. "I suspect he knows one of our staff at the club rather well, don't you?"

"Our club?" Charles looked pained. After a moment, he shook his head. "I don't even want to think about that."

Tristan clapped him on the shoulder.

They turned to the drawing room. The door opened; Maggs, Scully, Jenkins, Cook, and Fitchett all slipped out, bobbing before disappearing through the green baize door.

With a glance, Tony halted Maggs. "Check the parlor—I doubt the good inspector's men had time to put their mess right."

Maggs nodded and headed down the corridor.

Tristan opened the drawing-room door and led the gentlemen in.

Kit and Leonora were seated in armchairs facing Alicia and Adriana on the chaise. All four heads were together; they glanced up as the men entered, but the comments that clearly hovered on their tongues had to wait—the three boys had been crowding around the front window; seeing Tony, they flung themselves at him.

"Are they gone?"

"What did they want?"

"Who was that man? The one who just left."

Tony looked down into three pairs of hazel eyes, all very like Alicia's. When he didn't immediately reply, Matthew tugged at his sleeve.

"You promised to tell us."

He smiled and hunkered down to be more on their level. "Yes, they've gone, and they won't be coming back. They'd been given false information, and thought there were documents hidden here—those letters I found. That's what they were searching for. And that man who just left was from the government—he came to tell them they'd made a big mistake, and that they weren't to bother you or your sisters anymore."

Three pairs of eyes searched his, then all three boys smiled.

"Good!" Harry said. "It might be exciting, but they weren't nice."

"And they worry Alicia and Adriana," David whispered.

Both his younger brothers nodded solemnly.

Smiling, Tony rose, ruffling Matthew's hair. "You'll do." He exchanged a fleeting glance with Alicia; with her eyes, she indicated upstairs. He looked back at the boys. "Now you'd better go and see if they searched your rooms." He lowered his voice. "You could help Jenkins and Maggs make sure there's nothing around to upset your sisters."

The boys exchanged glances. Solemnly nodded again.

They looked at Alicia. "We're going upstairs," David said.

She smiled encouragingly. "You can come down for tea."

Everyone waited while the three boys filed out and closed the door behind them.

"Thank heavens," Kit said. She looked at the men, still standing in a loose gathering in the center of the room. "Now! We need to move quickly on this. The damage has to be contained—better yet, turned around."

Jack and Tristan strolled forward.

Tristan shrugged. "I don't know that it's all that serious." He glanced at the other men. "I can't see that A. C. is likely to gain much from this—"

"*Not* your investigation!" Leonora glared at him. "That isn't what we're concerned about."

Tristan blinked at her. "What, then?"

"Why the potential social disaster, of course!"

They were right—that was the most urgent threat arising from Sprigs's visit; this time, Bow Street had come calling in daylight, and there'd been considerable activity visible from the street. Luckily, their counterstrategy was easy to devise and quickly set in train. Aside from Alicia and Adriana, there were seven of them in the room; each had multiple contacts among the *grandes dames*, contacts they normally avoided, yet contacts who, in this instance, once they were apprised of the situation, were very ready to come to their collective aid.

By the time that evening's entertainments commenced, all was in place, the cannons primed.

Tony, accompanied by Geoffrey, made privy to the latest developments, escorted the ravishing Mrs. Carrington and her even more ravishing sister to a formal dinner, followed by three major balls.

They'd barely entered the first ballroom, Lady Selwyn's, when he overheard his godmother spreading the word.

"It is *quite* beyond the pale!" Lady Amery's tones were hushed yet outraged. "This secretive gentleman seeks to manipulate us, those of the haut ton, with rumors and sly tricks, to make us turn on Mrs. Carrington and drive her from town so that her fleeing our wrath will appear an admission of guilt, and so confuse the authorities and hide his infamous deeds."

Lady Amery twitched her shawl straight, both the action and her expression indicating absolute disgust. "It is beyond anything that a gentleman should seek to use us thus."

Wide-eyed, the Countess of Hereford had been drinking in her eloquence. "So none of the rumors is true?"

"*Pshaw!*" Lady Amery flicked her fingers. "Nothing more than artful lies. The reason he has focused on Mrs. Carrington is purely because she had the ill fortune to be the last person poor Ruskin spoke with before going to his death—at this very man's hands, no less! She was attending a soirée—I ask you, what is one supposed to do at a soirée if not talk to other guests? But now the devil seeks to deceive and deflect the authorities, and to use us to accomplish his evil ends."

"How diabolical!" The countess looked shocked.

"Indeed." Lady Amery nodded significantly. "You can see why we—those of us who know the truth—must be vigilant in ensuring these lies are quashed."

"Unquestionably." Transparently horrified, Lady Hereford laid a hand on Lady Amery's arm. "Why, if the ton could be used so easily as an instrument of harm . . ."

Her thoughts were easy to follow: no one would be safe.

Lifting her head, the countess patted Lady Amery's arm. "You may rest assured, Felicité, that I'll correct any idle talk I hear." She gathered her skirts. "Poor Mrs. Carrington—she must be quite prostrate."

Lady Amery waved. "As to that, she is one of us and knows how to behave—she will be here this evening, I make no doubt, and with her head high."

"I sincerely wish her well." Lady Hereford stood. "And will do all I can to aid her and bring this dastardly plot to nought."

With a regal nod, which Lady Amery graciously returned, Lady Hereford stepped into the crowd.

From where he'd halted, two paces behind the chaise where his godmother sat, Tony moved quickly forward, drawing Alicia, another fascinated observer, with him. Courtesy of the dense crowd, neither recent occupant of the chaise had noticed them. Now he rounded the chaise and bowed to his godmother, then bent and kissed her cheek.

"You were superb," he murmured as he straightened.

Lady Amery humphed. "It's hardly difficult to act outraged when I am." She held out her hands to Alicia, and when she took them drew her down to the chaise. "But you, *chérie*—I vow it is unconscionable." She looked at Tony. "You will find him soon, yes? And then this nonsense will be over."

"There's a crew of us pursuing him—we'll unmask him, never fear."

"Bon!" Lady Amery turned to Alicia. "And now you must tell me how that lovely sister of yours is faring. Has Geoffrey Manningham truly turned her head?"

Standing beside the chaise, Tony scanned the company. A number of senior hostesses had nodded pointedly their way, their acknowledgment marked and openly so. Others less prominent had stopped by to assure Alicia of their support. The tide was already turning.

He saw Leonora and Tristan arrive, and promptly start circulating. Deeming Lady Selwyn's event well covered, he summoned Geoffrey and Adriana with a glance, and they moved on through the crowded streets to the next major event.

The Countess of Gosford's ball was in full swing by the time they arrived. There, they met more hostesses, more *grandes dames*, all supportive. Lady Osbaldestone summoned them with an imperious wave of her cane; she gave them to understand that she hadn't had so much fun in years, and fully intended to make "the blackguard's" attempt to use the ton against Alicia a *cause célèbre*.

"A judgment of sorts on our malicious ways—we'd be fools not to see it." Her black eyes locked on the golden green of Alicia's, she nodded curtly. "So you needn't think to thank us—any of us. Do us the world of good to realize we've created a system so amenable to such dastardly manipulation. Help keep us honest." She grimaced. "Well, more honest."

Switching to Tony, she fixed him with a basilisk gaze. "And how long do you expect to take to lay this villain by the heels?"

"We're doing all we can—some things take time."

She narrowed her eyes at him. "Just as long as you don't at the last seek to sweep this blackguard's name under any rug." Her expression was a warning. "Rest assured we—none of us—will stand for that."

Tony smiled urbanely. "Rest assured," he returned, "no matter who else might think otherwise, I won't be a party to protecting him."

His answer gave Lady Osbaldestone pause; she searched his face, then humphed, apparently appeased. "Very good. You may now take yourselves off. Indeed, I suggest a waltz—that ought to be one starting up now. Last thing you want to appear is too concerned to enjoy yourselves."

Tony bowed; Alicia curtsied, and he led her away. To the dance floor.

She went into his arms readily. After three revolutions, his hand tightened on her back. She dutifully shifted her attention to his face.

"What is it?" There was a frown behind his eyes.

She smiled—more easily than she'd ever imagined she would be able to in such circumstances. "I just . . . find it all a trifle unreal. I've been transported Cinderella-like to an unimagined place. I never expected so many would so readily give me their support." She blushed lightly. "For all that it's you, and Kit and Leonora and the others asking the favor, it's me they have to agree to back."

His smile was slow, genuine and warming. "You take too little credit to yourself." He looked up as they swept into the turn. "Consider this." He drew her closer, bent his head so his words fell by her ear. "You've made few, if any, enemies—you and Adriana have been openly friendly, you've made many real friends over the last weeks. You've been pleasant companions; you've not sought to cut others out, nor to blacken anyone else's name. You've not lent your standing to any less-than-admirable social thrust; you've avoided all scandal."

He caught her eye as they whirled out of the tight turn. Lips curving, he raised a brow. "Indeed, you're the epitome of a lady of whom society is pleased to approve—one of those the *grandes dames* delight in holding up as an example to others less adept, living proof of the type of lady they are happy to acknowledge."

Except she wasn't. She returned his smile lightly and looked over his shoulder as if accepting his description. Inside, the small kernel of disquiet that had been with her for weeks—ever since he'd first singled her out in some long-ago ballroom—grew, but she didn't have time to dwell on it, not then.

After the waltz, she and Tony strolled the ballroom, eventually rejoining Geoffrey and Adriana; together, they left for their last port of call.

The Marchioness of Huntly was one of the ton's foremost hostesses. When they arrived, Huntly House was ablaze with lights. A theme of white and gilt was repeated throughout the imposing reception rooms; the ballroom was festooned with white silk sprinkled with gilt stars and looped back with gold cords. The light from three brilliant chandeliers winked and glinted in the jewels circling ladies' throats and encrusting the combs in their coiffures.

Born a Cynster, Lady Huntly had been watching for them; she swept forward to greet them, and strolled down the ballroom chatting amiably, then handed them into her sister-in-law's care.

The Duchess of St. Ives positively glowed with social zeal. She smiled brilliantly at Alicia. "He is defeated, you see." Irrepressibly French, she gestured about them. "Oh, it may take a day or so more to complete what we have begun, but there will be no repercussions. He will not succeed in using us in so cowardly a way to attack you, and thus hide his own infamy."

Here, the company were the *crème de la crème*; only those accepted into the most rarefied of tonnish circles were present. The duchess remained with them for some time, introducing them to numerous others. Her generosity and determination added to the weight bearing down on Alicia's conscience.

Then a waltz started up, and Tony swept her onto the floor and into an interlude of pleasant distraction. She knew better than to think of the nebulous worry dogging her, not while in his arms; he was guaranteed to notice, and question, then interrogate further, and that she was not ready for.

So she laughed and smiled at his witticisms, eventually insisting he return her to Adriana's side. They joined her sister's circle. Although in this venue the attractions of those who had gravitated into Adriana's orbit was exceptional, it was clear, at least to Alicia, that her sister's decision to lean on Geoffrey Manningham's arm was not affected in the remotest degree.

Inwardly sighing, she made a mental note to arrange to speak with Geoffrey soon, to explain their financial state. Oddly, the prospect did not fill her with the dread she'd once thought it would.

Brows faintly rising, she realized she now knew Geoffrey too well to imagine mere money, or even their scheme, would weigh overmuch with him. His devotion to Adriana had remained unwaveringly constant throughout the weeks; indeed, it had only strengthened and grown. Adriana, at least, would achieve the goal they'd aimed for.

Her thoughts turned to herself; feeling a stir beside her, she abruptly pushed them aside, away, and turned.

"My dear Mrs. Carrington." Sir Freddie Caudel bowed and shook the hand she offered. He glanced around, then met her gaze. He lowered his voice. "I can't tell you how distressed I am to have learned of the problem besetting you."

Alicia blinked; the phrasing sounded rather strange, but Sir Freddie was one of the old school, somewhat formal in his ways.

"However, it seems the ladies of the ton have rallied to your cause—you must be grateful to have gained the support of such champions."

She'd learned that many gentlemen disapproved of the social power the *grandes dames* wielded; the edge to Sir Freddie's words suggested he was one. "Indeed," she replied, calmly serene. "I can't tell you what a relief it's been. The ladies have been so kind."

He inclined his head, looking away over the crowd. "It's to be hoped this man will be identified soon. Is there any information as to who the blackguard is?"

She hesitated, then murmured, "There are a number of avenues of investigation in hand, I believe. Lord Torrington could tell you more."

Sir Freddie glanced at Tony, on her other side, presently engaged with Miss Pontefract. Sir Freddie's lips curved lightly. "I don't believe I'll disturb him—it was purely an idle question."

Alicia smiled and turned the conversation to the latest play, which she hoped to see during the next week. Sir Freddie remained for several minutes, urbanely chatting, then he excused himself and moved to Adriana's side.

Turning back to Tony, Alicia saw he'd been tracking Sir Freddie. She raised her brows quizzically.

"Has he spoken—or even hinted—yet?"

"No—and don't speak of it. I'm hoping not to tempt fate." On a spurt of decision, she made a silent vow to speak with Geoffrey as soon as possible. There was no need to put Sir Freddie to the trouble of asking for Adriana's hand—no need for her to have to face the ordeal of politely refusing him.

To her relief, the evening rolled on in pleasant vein. Nothing of any great note occurred, no difficult situation arose to challenge her, or them. The small hours of the morning saw them heading back to Waverton Street, tired but content with the way their plans had gone. Geoffrey parted from them at their door. Tony accompanied them in, ultimately accompanying her up the stairs to her bedchamber, and her bed.

Tony shrugged off his coat, dropped it on the chair, felt very much as if he was shedding some physical restraint along with his social facade.

I don't like this. No more do I.

Charles's words, his answer. A statement that grew more accurate with each passing day. Despite his erstwhile occupation, its shadowy nature and often nebulous threats, he and his colleagues had always, ultimately, dealt with foes face-to-face. Once the engagement had commenced, they'd always known the enemy.

Never had he had to cope with a situation like this. The action had commenced with Ruskin's murder; subsequent acts, strikes at their side, had been mounted and executed with impunity, causing damage and difficulty in their camp. A. C. had forced them to respond, to deploy to meet his threats and the actions he'd unleashed, yet even though they'd managed thus far to weather all he'd thrown at them, they'd yet to sight his face.

An unknown enemy, with unassessed capabilities, made the battle that much harder to win.

Yet it was a battle he could not lose.

Glancing across the darkened room, he watched Alicia, sitting at her dressing table, brush out her long hair.

He couldn't even contemplate conceding a minor skirmish; there was too much here that was now too precious to him.

Yanking his shirt from his waistband, he looked down, started sliding buttons free. Beneath the loosening linen, he shifted his shoulders, aware of muscles subtly easing in one way, tensing in another. A primitive want welling as the civilized screen fell.

I want him.

Dalziel's tone had been lethal, yet no more than an echo of his own resolve. Whatever it took, he would find A. C. and ensure he was brought to justice. The villain had focused on Alicia, struck at her not once but multiple times; for him, there could be no rest until A. C. was caught.

Yet they did not, after weeks of searching, even know his name.

He shrugged off his shirt and felt the last shreds of social restraint fall from him. For a long moment, he stood, his shirt bunched in his hands, staring unseeing at the floor, inwardly watching the volcano of his emotions surge and swell.

The scraping of wood on wood snapped him out of his state. Alicia stood, pushing back her dressing stool.

He dropped his shirt on the chair; unbidden, he padded barefoot across the room to help with her laces.

She glanced at his face, then gave him her back. He could feel his need building; rapidly, with far less than his customary languid sophistication, he unpicked the knots, hooked the laces free.

He glanced up, met her gaze in the mirror.

Saw that she'd sensed the change in him.

She searched his face, then looked down.

Normally, he would have stepped back, given her space to remove her gown . . . he didn't move.

Nor did she. Instead, she looked up, again met his eyes.

Her gaze was direct, questioning, waiting.

He dragged in a slow, deep breath, and reached for her.

Stripped the gown from her, let it and her chemise pool about her feet. Murmured darkly as he stepped close and wrapped his arms about her, locking her silken back to his bare chest, spreading his hands and claiming her glorious bounty. He shifted evocatively against her. Bending his head, he whispered, half in French, half in English, asking her to put her foot on the stool and remove her ruched garters and silk stockings.

Her breath shuddered as she breathed in, and complied.

While she did . . . he let his hands roam. Let them take and claim as his need willed, set his senses free to wallow and seize all she surrendered to him, would surrender to him, in that moment, and the moments to come.

One arm crossing her body, his palm covering one breast, fingers evocatively kneading, with his other hand, he lightly gripped her nape; as she bent forward to roll the first garter and stocking down, he traced her supple spine, possessively stroking down, over the back of her waist, through the indentation below it, smoothly stroking over the swell of her bottom, down and around to caress the soft, slickly swollen flesh between her thighs.

With one foot on the stool, she was open to him. He parted the soft folds and found her, flagrantly caressed, then worked two fingers deep.

By the time she'd paused, gathered herself, changed legs, when she finally dropped the second stocking to the floor, Alicia was hot, wet and quivering with need.

Her foot still on the stool, her body riding the repetitive probing of his fingers, she looked into the mirror, from under heavy lids met his gaze.

Breasts swollen and full, peaks tight and aching, her skin heated, her breathing already ragged, she waited.

Withdrawing his hand, he grasped her waist; the instant she straightened and her foot touched the floor, he turned her.

She'd expected something else. Instead, he stepped back, drawing her with him, with one hand unbuttoning the flap of his trousers, the only clothing he still wore.

The backs of his thighs hit the bed. He paused only to free his fully engorged staff from the folds of his trousers, then he lifted her. Ignoring her smothered gasp, he sat and brought her slowly down, setting her on her knees astride his hips.

With the broad head of his staff nudging into her body.

She could feel him there, throbbing, sense the promise of all that was to come. The hot, aching emptiness within her swelled.

She looked into his face, into his black, fathomless eyes. Raising her hands, she framed his face as his hands closed hard about her hips. Under mutual direction, their lips met. Clung, held.

Beneath his control she sensed all he held back, sensed the power, the desperate need.

She shifted fractionally on him. He caught his breath, broke from the kiss. Screened by their lashes, their eyes met.

He whispered against her lips, his breath a hot flame. "Take me. Give yourself to me." His gaze dropped to her lips. "Be mine."

Gravelly, rough, another seduction, a dark temptation to a deeper level of giving.

She didn't hesitate. Drawing in a breath, tightening her hands about his face to anchor her, she angled her head, set her lips to his, and slowly eased down.

Inch by slow inch, she took him inside her, gloried in the feel of him filling her, stretching her. She'd never before been so aware of how her body closed about him, enclasped him. Took him in.

His hands were hard as iron about her hips as he ruthlessly guided her down; he let her set the pace only until he was fully seated within her, then he took the reins, took control, and the giving began.

Hard, hot, and complete.

Without restrictions, limits, or reservations.

Their bodies merged deeply, compulsively riding a wave of sensual desire higher than any before, a tide of need more desperately urgent, more powerful. More addictive.

Their tongues tangled, their mouths feeding in frenzy. He took her as he would, seizing and claiming every sense she possessed, demanding more even as she gave him all.

In the end, on a gasp, she surrendered completely, opened her body, her soul, her heart, and let him plunder.

Let him capture, take, and make her his.

Beyond all thought. Beyond all denial.

Beyond this world.

She was his. Forever. He would never allow anyone to take her from him.

When he slumped back on the bed, drained, replete, to the very depths of his soul sated, the darker side of his nature for the moment wholly satisfied, as he tumbled her down with him, then kicked off his trousers and wrapped them in the covers, those were the only thoughts to cross Tony's mind.

They were the only thoughts that mattered.

Sixteen

୧୦\~ଡ଼ଋ

In the darkness before dawn, Alicia stirred.

Awareness slunk into her brain. Her body still thrummed; her hair was a wild tangle, a fine net ensaring them, wrapped about the muscled arm lying protectively about her. Eyes closed, she lay still, safe, secure, warm. Freed by the night, by the silence, her thoughts crept from the corners of her mind, dwelling on the strange twist her life had taken—the deception she'd never intended to practice, not on so many, not to this degree.

The role of her own making now haunted her.

Not in her wildest dreams had she expected to rise to such social prominence, never imagined calling so many of the powerful friend. Yet in her and her family's time of need, they'd come to her aid—how could she now draw back from them, from the protection they'd so generously offered?

Thanks to A. C. and his latest attempt to cast all suspicion on her, she couldn't even slip away, fade from the scene. She had to remain, head high, and face down his rumors, at least for the next weeks.

Had to continue to pretend she was the widow she was not, while parading through the haut ton, the subject of the latest *on-dit*, the central character in the most amazing, attention-getting story.

The idea that someone from her little part of the country might, like Ruskin, pop up and recognize her had assumed the status of a nightmare. No amount of reasoning, of reiterating that there truly were few families of standing near Little Compton, and none who had known her, did anything to lessen its effect; like a dark, louring cloud it hovered, threatening, not breaking but always there, swelling in the back of her mind.

What if the cloud burst and the truth came raining down?

Her heart contracted; she dragged in a breath, conscious of the vise closing about her chest.

Tony had so publicly nailed his flag to her mast, had so openly committed himself to her cause, and brought with him so many of his aristocratic connections . . . if the ton ever learned the truth of her widowhood, how would that reflect on him?

Badly. Very badly. She'd now gone about in society enough to know. Such a revelation would make her an outcast, but it would make him a laughingstock. Or worse, it would cast him as one who had knowingly deceived the entire ton.

They would never forgive him.

And no matter any protestations to the contrary, deep down, in his heart, he would never—could never—forgive her. By making him a party to her deception, she would have ripped from him and put forever beyond his reach the position to which he'd been born, the position she suspected he never even questioned, it was so much a part of him.

She wanted to twist and turn, but with him breathing softly, deeply, beside her, she forced herself to lie still beneath the heavy arm he'd slung across her waist. Dawn was sliding over the rooftops when she finally accepted that she could do nothing to change things—all she could do was move heaven and earth to ensure that no one ever learned her true state.

She glanced at his face on the pillow beside hers. His dark lashes lay, black crescents over his cheekbones; in sleep, his face retained the harsh lines, the austere angularity of nose and jaw. In her mind, she heard his voice dispassionately reciting, describing what the last ten years of his life had been, how they'd been spent, and where; he'd avoided stating in what danger, but she was not so innocent she couldn't read between his lines. When his mask was off, as now, the evidence of that decade still remained, etched in the lines of his face.

Last night—early this morning—he'd needed her. Wanted her. Taken all she'd given, and yet needed more, a more she'd found it possible to give.

His satisfaction was hers, deep, powerful, and complete. She had never imagined such a connection, that a man such as he would have a need like that, and that she would be able so completely to fulfill it.

Her joy in that discovery was profound.

Lifting a hand, she gently brushed back the heavy lock of black hair that lay rakishly across his brow. He didn't wake, but stirred. His hand flexed, lightly gripping her side before easing as, reassured, he sank once more into slumber.

For long moments, she looked, silently wondered.

Faced incontrovertible fact.

He now meant more to her, at a deeper, more intensely emotional level, than all else in her life.

Tony left Waverton Street before the sunshine hit the cobbles. The tide of satisfaction that had swept him last night had receded, revealing, to him all too forcefully, the vulnerability beneath.

He couldn't—wouldn't—lose her; he couldn't even readily stomach the fact she was at risk. Therefore . . .

Over breakfast that morning, as always efficiently served by Hungerford who, despite knowing full well Tony hadn't slept in his own bed for the past week and more, remained remarkably cheerful, he made his plans. Those included Hungerford, but his first act was to repair to his study and pen two summonses. The first, to Geoffrey Manningham, took no more than a few minutes; he dispatched it via a footman, then settled to write the second, a communication requiring far more thought.

He was still engaged in searching for the right approach, the right phrases, when Geoffrey arrived. Waving him to the pair of armchairs before the hearth, he joined him.

"News?" Geoffrey asked as he sat.

"No." Sinking into the other chair, Tony smiled, all teeth. "Plans."

Geoffrey grinned, equally ferally, back. "You perceive me all ears."

Tony outlined the basics of what he intended.

Geoffrey concurred. "If you can get everything into place, including your beloved, that would unquestionably be the wisest course." He met Tony's gaze. "So what do you want me to do? I presume there's something."

"I want you to remove Adriana for the afternoon—or the day, if you prefer."

Geoffrey widened his eyes. "That all?"

Tony nodded. "Do that, and I'll manage the rest."

Just how he would do that last . . . they sat for ten minutes debating various options, then Geoffrey took himself off to accomplish his assigned task.

Tony remained before the fire for a few minutes more, then, struck by inspiration, returned to his desk and completed his second summons, disguised as a letter to his cousin Miranda, inviting her and her two daughters, Margaret and Constance, to visit him in London, to act as chaperone while the lady he intended to make his viscountess spent a week or so under his roof.

If he knew anything of Miranda, that last would ensure her appearance as soon as he could wish—namely, tomorrow.

The letter dispatched in the care of a groom, he rang for Hungerford.

Dealing with his butler was bliss; Hungerford never questioned, never made difficulties, but could be counted on to ensure that, even if difficulties did arise and his orders no longer fitted the situation, that his intent would be accomplished.

Telling Hungerford that he proposed protecting his intended bride from social and even possibly physical attack by installing her under this roof, within the purlieu of Hungerford's overall care, was all it took to get everything in Upper Brook Street ready.

He had little notion of what arrangements would be required to prepare the house to receive not only the widowed Miranda and her daughters, ten and twelve years old, but his prospective bride, her family, and her household, but he was sure his staff under Hungerford's direction would meet the challenge.

Beaming, clearly delighted with his orders, Hungerford retreated. Tony considered the clock; it was not yet noon.

He debated the wisdom of his next act at some length; eventually, he rose, and headed for Hendon House.

At two o'clock, he paused beside Collier, leaning on his street sweeper's broom at the corner of Waverton Street.

The big man nodded in greeting. "Just missed her, you have. She returned from some luncheon, then immediately headed off with the three lads and their tutor to the park. Kites today, if you've a mind to join them."

"And Miss Pevensey?"

"Lord Manningham called 'bout eleven and took her up in his curricle. They haven't returned."

Tony nodded. "I'm going to talk to the staff, then perhaps I'll fly a kite." He paused, then added, "I plan to move Mrs. Carrington and her household to Upper Brook Street, but I'll want you and the others to keep up your watch here. I'll leave Scully and one other in residence, to keep all possibilities covered."

Collier nodded. "When will this move happen?"

Today if Tony had his way. Realistically . . . "At the earliest tomorrow, late in the day."

Leaving Collier, Tony strode on; reaching Alicia's house, he went quickly up the steps. Maggs answered the door.

Tony frowned; Maggs forestalled him. "Scully's with 'em. No need to fret."

His frown darkening at the thought that he was *that* transparent, he crossed the threshold. "I want to speak with the staff—all of you who are here. It might be best if I came down to the kitchens."

From beneath the wide branches of one of the trees in Green Park, Alicia watched, a smile on her lips, as Scully and Jenkins wrestled with the second of the two kites they'd brought out.

The first kite, under Harry's narrow-eyed guidance, was soaring over the treetops. David was watching Scully and Jenkins, a pitying look in his face; Matthew's eyes were glued to the blue-and-white kite swooping and swirling above the trees.

"There you are."

She turned at the words, knowing before she met Tony's eyes that it was he. "As always."

Smiling, she gave him her hand; his eyes locking on hers, he raised it to his lips and pressed kisses first to her fingers, then to her palm. Retaining possession, he lowered his hand, fingers sliding about hers, and looked out at the scene in the clearing before them.

"I wonder . . ." He glanced at her, raised a brow. "Should I rescue Jenkins and Scully from sinking without trace in your brothers' estimation?"

She grinned; leaning back against the tree trunk, she gestured. "By all means. I'll watch and judge your prowess."

Over numerous afternoons, he'd taught the boys the tricks of keeping their kites aloft. He'd transparently enjoyed the moments; something inside her had rejoiced to see him caught again in what must have been a boyhood pleasure.

"Hmm." Studying the kite flyers, he hesitated; she got the impression he was steeling himself to resist the lure of the kites and do something else, something he was reluctant to do.

A moment passed, then he looked at her. "Actually, I wanted to speak with you."

She widened her eyes, inviting him to continue.

Still he hesitated; his eyes searched hers—abruptly she realized he was metaphorically girding his loins.

"I want you to move house."

She frowned at him. "Move? But why? Waverton Street suits us—"

"For safety reasons. Precautions." He trapped her gaze. "I don't want you or your household subjected to any repeat of yesterday."

She had no wish to argue that; no one had enjoyed the experience. But . . . she let her frown grow. "How will a different house avoid . . ." The intentness in his black eyes registered. Her lips parted; she stared, then baldly asked, "To which house do you wish us to move?"

His lips thinned. "Mine."

"No."

"*Before* you say that, just consider—living under my roof you'll have the protection not just of my title, my status, but also of all those allied with me and my family." His eyes pinned her. "So will your sister and brothers."

Folding her arms, she narrowed her eyes back. "For the moment, let's leave Adriana and the boys out of this discussion—it hasn't escaped my notice that you're always quick to drag them into the fray."

He scowled at her. "They're part of it—they're part of you."

"Perhaps. Be that as it may, you can't seriously think—"

He cut her off with a raised hand. "Hear me out. If it's the proprieties that are exercising you, my cousin and her two young daughters—they're ten and twelve—will be arriving tomorrow. With Miranda in residence, there's no reason—social, logical, or otherwise—that you and your household cannot stay at Torrington House. It's a mansion—there's more than enough room."

"But . . ." She stared at him. The words: *I'm your mistress, for heaven's sake*! burned her tongue. Compressing her lips, she fixed him with a strait look, and primly asked, "What will your staff think?"

What she meant was: what will the entire ton think. To be his mistress was one thing; the ton turned a blind eye to affairs between gentlemen such as he and fashionable widows. However, to be his mistress and live openly under his roof was, she was fairly certain, going that one step too far.

His expression had turned bewildered. "My staff?"

"Your servants. Those who would have to adjust to and cope with the invasion."

"As it happens, they're delighted at the prospect." His frown returned. "I can't imagine why you'd think otherwise. My butler's going around with a smile threatening to crack his face, and the staff are buzzing about, getting rooms ready."

She blinked, suddenly uncertain. If his butler thought her living in the Upper Brook Street mansion was acceptable . . . she'd always understood tonnish butlers to be second only to the *grandes dames* in upholding the mores of the ton.

Tony sighed. "I know we haven't properly discussed it, but there isn't time. Just because we've trumped A. C.'s last three tricks doesn't mean he won't try again." His expression resolute, he met her eyes. "That he's tried three times to implicate you suggests he's fixated on the idea of using you to cover his tracks. I'm sure he'll try again."

An inkling of why he was so set on moving her into his house, having her, at least for the present, under his roof, reached her. She hesitated.

He sensed it. Shifting closer, he pressed his point. "There's a huge schoolroom with bedrooms attached, and rooms for Jenkins and Fitchett nearby. There's a back garden the boys can play in when they're not having their lessons—and the staff truly are looking forward to having boys running up and down the stairs again."

Despite all, that last made her smile.

He squeezed her hand, raised it to his chest. "You and the boys and Adriana will be comfortable and safe at Torrington House. You'll be happy there."

And he'd be happy if she was there, too—that didn't need saying, it was there in his eyes.

"Please." The word was soft. "Come and live with me."

Her heart turned over; her resolution wavered.

"There's no reason at all you can't—no hurdle we can't overcome."

Lost in his eyes, she pressed her lips tight.

Felt a tug on her gown. She looked down.

Matthew stood beside them; neither of them had noticed his approach. Face alight, he stared first at one, then the other, then breathlessly asked, "Are we really going to live at Tony's house?"

By the time they got back to Waverton Street, Alicia had a headache. A frown had taken up permanent residence on her face; she couldn't seem to lose it.

She was seriously annoyed, not specifically but generally—she couldn't blame Tony for involving her brothers, but involved they now were, and determined to convince her of the huge benefits of removing with all speed to Torrington House.

If Tony was ruthless, they were relentless. She went up the steps, shooing them before her, feeling almost battered.

Despite their arguments, she felt very sure she needed to think long and hard about this latest proposition. She needed to investigate, and make sure that her presence in his house wouldn't harm his standing.

Nor make her own any more perilous.

"Off to wash your hands. No tea until you do."

It was blackberry jam day again, so they rushed off without argument.

With a short sigh, she swung to face Tony.

He was watching her closely. "Come and sit down."

She let him steer her to the parlor. Scully and Jenkins disappeared. Sinking onto the chaise, she fixed Tony with a darkling glance. "I haven't agreed."

He inclined his head and, wisely, made no reply.

Tea should have soothed her temper. Unfortunately, her brothers were not so perspicacious as Tony; although clever enough not to directly argue their case, their artful comments, tossed entirely among themselves, on the possibilities they imagined might accrue should they go to live in Upper Brook Street—possibilities like having suitable banisters to slide down, possibilities they innocently requested advice on from Tony—filled the minutes.

She kept her lips shut and refused to be drawn.

Then she heard the front door open, and Adriana's and Geoffrey's voices. She turned as they came in.

Adriana's face glowed. "We had a lovely drive around Kew. The gardens were well worth the visit."

Alicia sat forward and reached for the spare teacups, wondering how to broach the subject of Tony's proposed move, preferably in a way that would ensure her sister's cooperation in holding back what had started to feel like an inexorable tide.

Adriana tossed her bonnet onto the window seat, took the cup of tea Alicia had poured to Geoffrey, sitting in the second armchair, then sat beside Alicia on the chaise. Taking the cup she handed her, Adriana's gaze went to Geoffrey; he was being served crumpets and jam by Harry and Matthew.

Following her gaze, Alicia watched, noted. Despite their love of crumpets, the boys had readily shared; they'd accepted Geoffrey, not perhaps in the same unquestioning way they'd accepted Tony, yet they clearly counted him one of their small circle and trusted him.

Smiling, Adriana turned to her. "Geoffrey told me about Tony's suggestion that we move to Upper Brook Street." She sipped, then met Alicia's eyes. "It sounds an excellent idea . . ." Her voice trailed away; seeing Alicia's reaction, she blinked. "Isn't it?"

Alicia looked at Tony. He returned her regard steadily, giving not an inch. She glanced at Geoffrey, but he was—quite deliberately she was sure—chatting with her brothers about the merits of blackberry jam.

Slowly, she drew breath, then met Adriana's gaze. "I don't know." The unvarnished truth.

"Well—"

Adriana tried to persuade her all over again; her arguments echoed Tony's, yet were sufficiently different to assure Alicia he hadn't been so foolish as to plot with her sister against her.

He knew the thought crossed her mind; when, recognizing her suspicion was misplaced, she glanced at him, he searched her eyes, then faintly raised a brow. Raising his cup, he calmly sipped. And left her fighting a rearguard action against everyone else in the room.

Her brothers didn't press her directly; instead, they supported and elaborated on Adriana's themes. And then Geoffrey, more quietly but also more seriously and with considerably more weight, threw his support behind Adriana and Tony.

Looking into Geoffrey's steady brown gaze, Alicia felt her resistance waver. She could see why Geoffrey wanted Adriana and the rest of them under Tony's roof. Glancing at Tony, she knew the same reason was a significant part of his motivation, too. Was she being irrational in refusing to agree?

She needed reassurance, but not the sort anyone present could give—

The doorbell pealed. She glanced at the clock; time had flown. Hearing feminine voices in the hall, she rose. She tugged the bellpull to summon Jenkins, and instructed her brothers they could finish the crumpets before returning to their lessons.

Turning, she headed for the door, Adriana behind her. Tony and Geoffrey followed.

"Ah—there you are, Alicia!" In the hall, Kit Hendon beamed at her.

Beside her, Leonora Wemyss smiled. "I hope we haven't called at an inopportune moment, but there's a gathering at Lady Mott's that it would be wise to attend, and we wanted to coordinate which events we'll go to tonight."

Alicia smiled, touched hands, waited while they greeted the others, then ushered both ladies into the drawing room. As they all sat, disposing themselves on the chaise and the chairs, she realized that neither Kit nor Leonora had evinced the slightest surprise at discovering Tony and Geoffrey present.

The middle of the afternoon was not a common time for gentlemen to call.

Leonora plunged immediately into a discussion of the most promising events planned for that evening. "I think Lady Humphries' rout, then the Canthorpes' ball and the Hemmingses', too. What do you think?"

They tossed around the possiblities, eventually replacing the Hemmingses' ball with the Athelstans'. "Much better connected," Tony said, his eyes capturing Alicia's, "and that helps at the end of a long night."

"Yes." Leonora nodded, gaze distant as if reviewing a mental list. "That should do it." She glanced at Alicia. "A very good night's work."

"Now," Kit said, sitting forward, "the reason we think visiting Lady Mott's in the next hour would be wise is that her gatherings invariably attract all the busiest bodies in town. They're of the older, more crotchety crew, and while our story will doubtless have reached some of them, there are others who are highly active but only during the day."

"If we concentrate our activities solely on the evening events, we'll miss them," Leonora put in. "Not only would that leave an avenue open for A. C. to exploit, but those old ladies themselves won't thank us—they hate to be behindhand with gossip."

The observation made them all grin.

Alicia glanced down at her lilac gown; she'd worn it to luncheon at Lady Candlewick's, but courtesy of her sojourn in the park, grass stains now adorned the hem. "I'll have to change my gown."

"So will I." Adriana waved at her carriage dress, quite unsuitable attire for an afternoon call on Lady Mott and company.

"No matter." Sitting back, Kit waved. "Leonora and I will wait."

Alicia looked at Tony and Geoffrey. The opportunity to talk privately to Kit and Leonora, to sound them out over Tony's suggestion, was a godsend—but she didn't want to leave Tony alone with them in case he wooed them to his cause before she'd a chance to assess their true reactions.

As if bowing to her wishes, he uncrossed his long legs and stood. With a glance, he roused Geoffrey, then turned to her. "We'll leave you. I'll call for you at eight, if that's suitable?"

She rose to see them out. "Yes, of course."

He and Geoffrey farewelled Kit and Leonora. Adriana also rose and accompanied them into the hall. Maggs stood ready to open the door.

Alicia gave Tony her hand. He held it, looked into her eyes; reading them, his lips tightened. "You will consider my suggestion, won't you?"

"Yes." She held his gaze. "But I don't know that I'll agree."

The urge to argue welled strong; she could see it in his eyes, feel it in the clasp of his fingers about hers. But he quelled it. Suavely inclined his head.

Releasing her hand, he nodded to Adriana. With Geoffrey following, he went out of the door and down the steps into the street.

Alicia let out the breath she'd been holding and turned.

Saw Adriana's lips open and held up a hand. "Not now. We need to get changed—we can't keep Kit and Leonora waiting."

Adriana, every bit as stubborn as she, pressed her lips tight, but acquiesced. They went quickly up the stairs side by side. Alicia turned into her room—and then hurried like a fiend, selecting a pale green gown of the finest twill and struggling into it, then expertly tweaking and resetting her coiled hair.

She was ready long before Adriana; quickly, shoes pattering, she hurried back down to the drawing room.

Regardless of the fact she'd only made their acquaintance yesterday, with Kit and Leonora she'd felt an instant rapport. Indeed, *they* had only met on her front step, yet the directness, the ready understanding on which friendship and trust were based, were already there between them. She could ask them about Tony's suggestion; they were two of the very few people whose opinion on such an issue she would trust.

Kit was describing one of her eldest son's antics; she smiled as Alicia rejoined them, and quickly brought the story to a close.

Sinking onto the chaise, Alicia clasped her hands in her lap. Both Kit and Leonora looked at her; she drew breath and stated, "In light of the difficulties A. C. seems intent on causing, Torrington has asked me to consider moving this household to Upper Brook Street. To his house."

Leonora opened her eyes wide.

Kit frowned, tapped her fingers on the chair arm. "Who else is resident there?"

"A widowed cousin and her two young daughters—ten and twelve—are expected tomorrow."

Leonora's face cleared; she glanced at Kit. "It would certainly be—" She looked at Alicia and grimaced. "I was going to say an improvement, but by that I mean that while this address is perfectly respectable, Upper Brook Street would place you in the heart of the ton. It would be a statement in itself."

"Indeed," Kit agreed. "And given we suspect A. C. knows the ropes quite well, it's a statement he'll understand." She shifted, her bluey violet eyes studying Alicia. "I know Torrington House—Jack and Tony are old friends. It's a *huge* mansion, and currently only Tony lives there—you can imagine him rattling around like a pea in a cauldron. And it's fully staffed—he's never been able to bring himself to let anyone go, even though there's really no call for three parlormaids when there's only a bachelor to cater for. From what I've seen of his butler, Hungerford, he'll be in alt at the prospect of having a houseful of people to organize for again."

"It sounds like an excellent suggestion." Leonora looked at Alicia. "And it certainly sounds as if your household—boys and all—will fit."

Alicia studied their faces. There was not the slightest hint that either saw anything in any way remotely socially unacceptable in the notion of her living at Torrington House. In the end, she put her question directly. "You don't think it will be seen as scandalous—my living there?"

Leonora opened her eyes wide, clearly surprised by the question. "With his cousin in residence, I really can't see why anyone would disapprove."

She glanced at Kit, who nodded in agreement.

They both looked at Alicia. She summoned a smile. "I see. Thank you."

Adriana came in, a stunning breath of fresh air in a frilled gown of white muslin sprigged with blue. "Ready?"

The three ladies seated smiled and rose. Linking arms, they headed for Lady Mott's.

How he managed to keep his tongue between his teeth Tony didn't know, but he held his peace on the subject of the move for the entire evening.

Kit helped. She swanned up to him in Lady Humphries' ballroom and claimed his arm for a waltz. Alicia laughed and waved them away, remaining chatting with a group of others, all sufficiently harmless. Reluctantly, he let Kit lead him to the floor.

"Mission accomplished," she informed him the instant they were safely revolving. "And I was superbly subtle, I'll have you know. I didn't even have to mention it—she asked, and Leonora and I reassured her. We told her it was an excellent idea."

She smiled at him. "So next time Jack's being difficult about something, remember—you owe me."

He humphed and whirled her about, and forbore to mention that if Jack was being difficult about something, he'd almost certainly agree with him. "How did she take it?" he asked when they were once more precessing sedately up the room.

Kit frowned. "I'm not sure, but the impression I got was that her resistance stemmed primarily from a concern that in accepting your invitation she'd be committing some sort of social solecism." She looked up at him. "She's more or less on her own, with no older lady to guide her. For what it's worth, I don't think her resistance is all that entrenched."

"Good."

They spoke no more of it; at the end of the dance, he returned Kit to Jack's side.

Jack sent a significant glance his way. "I'll be dropping by that other venue later. I'll catch up with you tomorrow if I learn anything to the point."

He'd lowered his voice, directed his words specifically to Tony, yet Kit caught not only the words, but their subtext. "What point? What other venue?"

Jack looked into her narrowing eyes. "Just a little business matter."

"Oh? Whose business?" Kit sweetly inquired. "A. C.'s?"

"Sssh!" Jack glanced around, but there was no one close enough to hear.

Kit saw her advantage and pressed it, drilling one finger into Jack's chest. "If you imagine you're going out skulking tonight *alone*, then you'll need to promise to inform not just Tony but *all* of us of anything you discover."

Curling his hand around hers, Jack scowled at her. "You'll learn soon enough."

Kit opened her eyes wide. "When you deign to tell us? Thank you, but no—I much prefer to set a time and place for your revelations."

Tony nearly choked; he was privy to the story of what had happened in the early days of their marriage, when Jack had refused to tell Kit what he was involved in. Clearly, Kit had not forgotten. From the look on Jack's face, one of chagrin and uneasy uncertainty, he hadn't either.

When Jack glanced at him, Kit cut in, "And you needn't look to Tony for support." She fixed her violet eyes on him. "He already owes Leonora and me a favor. A very telltale favor."

In her eyes, he read a threat of doom should he fail to capitulate. He sighed and glanced at Jack. "I was going to suggest the club, but let's make it my library. What time?"

Jack humphed. "I'll send word first thing in the morning, once I know what I've managed to find."

Kit beamed at them both. "See? It doesn't hurt."

Jack snorted. Tony fought down a grin. He chatted for a while, then headed back up the ballroom to Alicia, still safe within Adriana's circle.

Which circle was growing less and less intent as more of those aspiring to Adriana's attention *vis à vis* claiming her hand took note of the glances she shared with Geoffrey, and sloped off to pay court to someone else. One gentleman who remained apparently oblivious of the clear firming of Adriana's intention was Sir Freddie Caudel.

As he drew near, Tony wondered if Sir Freddie was biding his time, perhaps thinking to give Adriana more experience of the ton before making his offer, or if he was instead merely using her as a convenient and unthreatening excuse to avoid all other possible candidates. If the man hadn't spoken yet . . . but then, he himself and Geoffrey were of a more direct generation.

Sir Freddie had been conversing with Alicia. He saw Tony approaching, smiled benignly, and excused himself as Tony joined her.

She turned to him, raised a brow. Wariness showed behind the green of her eyes; with an easy smile, he claimed her hand, set it on his sleeve, and inquired if she'd like to stroll.

She agreed, and they did. Because of the many eyes fixed on them courtesy of the story on so many lips, it was impossible to slip away. Resigned, he reminded himself of the true purpose behind their evening's endeavors and conducted her to chat with the next fashionable lady waiting to have her say.

They caught up with his godmother in the Athelstans' ballroom. Dispatched to fetch refreshments, he left Alicia seated on the chaise beside Lady Amery and shouldered his way into the crowd.

Alicia watched him go, then drew breath and turned to Lady Amery. "I hope you won't think me presumptuous, ma'am, but I need advice, and as the person most nearly concerned is Torrington . . ."

She and Lady Amery were alone on the small chaise; there was no one else close enough to hear—and she might never have another such opportunity to ask the one person in London who held Tony's welfare closest to her heart.

Lady Amery had turned to her; now she smiled radiantly. Reaching for Alicia's hands, she clasped them in hers. "My dear, I'd be delighted to help in any way I can."

Alicia steeled herself to see that sentiment change in the next minutes. Lifting her head, she confessed, "Torrington has asked that I and my household move into his house in Upper Brook Street—his widowed cousin and her daughters will be staying there, too."

Lady Amery's gaze grew distant as she considered, then she refocused on Alicia's face. "*Bon.* Yes, I can see that that would be much more comfortable, especially for him, what with this latest brouhaha." Her eyes twinkled, then, reading Alicia's troubled expression, she grew serious. "But you do not wish this? Would it be difficult to move to Upper Brook Street?"

Alicia stared into her ladyship's transparently sincere eyes. Blinked. "No . . . that is . . ." She dragged in a breath. "I just don't want to do anything to give the gossips food for slander—I don't want inadvertently to do anything to damage his name or his standing."

Lady Amery's concerned expression dissolved into smiles. She patted Alicia's hand. "It is very right that you think of such things— such sentiments do you credit—but I assure you in this case, there is nothing to concern you. The ton understands such matters—*oui, vraiment*." She nodded encouragingly. "There will be no adverse repercussions to your moving to Upper Brook Street in such circumstances."

The assurance with which she made the statement put the matter beyond argument.

Her expression easing, the weight on her shoulders lightening, Alicia smiled and let herself accept it. Despite her worries, her reservations, everyone—absolutely everyone—insisted Tony's suggestion was not only sound, but an outcome to be desired.

Despite that . . . she said nothing when he returned bearing glasses of champagne. Lady Amery claimed his attention and chatted animatedly about shared acquaintances, to Alicia's relief making no allusion to their discussion or her advice.

Finally, the long evening drew to a close, and they headed home. Geoffrey held to his new habit and accompanied them to their door; Tony, as usual, stayed with them beyond it.

In her bedchamber, they undressed—in silence. She felt herself tensing, waiting for him to ask her again, to press his case . . . instead, he said nothing. She climbed into the big bed; he pinched out the candle, and joined her beneath the covers.

He reached for her, drew her to him, then hesitated. In the dimness, he looked at her face. "You're still considering?"

There was no hint of a frown, of irritation or impatience in his voice; he simply wanted to know.

"Yes." She held his gaze. "But I haven't yet made up my mind."

She felt him sigh, then he tightened his hold on her, lowered his head. "We can discuss it in the morning."

When she awoke the next morning, however, he'd already left her bed. She lay staring at the canopy as minutes, then half an hour ticked by, then she sighed and rose.

Washed, gowned, her hair severely coiled, she headed downstairs.

Pausing in the doorway of the dining parlor, she studied the back of Tony's broad shoulders; she wasn't surprised to find him there, in the chair at the end of the table.

Her brothers saw her and turned; Tony glanced around and rose as she entered. Going past him, she waved him back to his seat, exchanged greetings with her brothers and Adriana—then, to Adriana's amusement, remembered to bid their guest a good morning, too.

He returned it with aplomb, recommending the kedgeree. She poured herself a cup of tea, then rose and crossed to the sideboard. She made her selections, all the while conscious of her brothers' whispers, of the anticipation welling, notch by notch, around the table.

Calmly, she returned to her chair, set down her plate, then sat, thanking Maggs, who held the chair for her.

That done, she picked up her fork—and looked around the table.

At four pairs of expectant eyes. And one black gaze she couldn't read.

She drew in a deep breath, exhaled. "All right. We'll move to Torrington House."

Her brothers cheered; Adriana beamed.

She looked down at her plate, poked at the pile of kedgeree on it. "*But* only when Lord Torrington's cousin is ready to receive us."

The cheering didn't abate, instead it broke up into excited speculation, mixed with whispered plans. She glanced at her brothers, then looked at Tony.

Raised a brow.

Tony knew better than to allow his satisfaction, let alone its depth, to show; looking down the table, holding Alicia's gaze, he inclined his head. "I'll send word when Miranda is recovered from her journey and ready to meet you."

Knowing Miranda, he predicted that would be about ten minutes after she arrived.

As he'd prophesied, so it proved. Miranda arrived agog to meet the lady who had finally, as she put it, snared him.

An openhearted lady of considerable charm, her husband's early death had left her sincerely bereft.

"Although I doubt that will last forever." Blond curls framing her heart-shaped face, she looked up at Tony as he stood before the fire in his drawing room. "Meanwhile, I'm on pins, positive pins, waiting to meet this widow of yours. Dare I guess she's ravishingly beautiful?"

Tony fixed her with a not entirely mock-severe glance. "You will behave. Furthermore, you will not regale Alicia with tales of my youth, nor yet of my childhood."

Miranda's grin deepened. "Spoilsport."

He snorted, and turned to the door. The clock on the mantelpiece chimed—twelve *tings*. "I'll go and inform her of your great willingness to make her acquaintance."

At the door, he paused, glanced back. "Just remember—she and I haven't yet formally discussed our marriage." By which he meant she hadn't yet, in so many words, agreed.

Miranda looked both intrigued and delighted. "Don't worry—I won't scuttle your punt."

Feigning disbelief, he left.

The atmosphere reigning in Waverton Street was as close to pandemonium as anything he'd experienced. He stood in the front hall transfixed by the activity. Crates lay open on the tiles; the green baize door stood propped wide, and a hum of noise pervaded the house. The boys were rushing up and down the stairs, calling to each other, ferrying books and toys, clothes and shoes, stuffing them joyously into the crates before, pausing only to flash him wide grins, racing up the stairs once more.

Through the open dining-room door, he saw Cook and Fitchett carefully wrapping glassware. A sound drew his attention to the gallery; he watched as Maggs, a heavy case on one shoulder, slowly descended the stairs.

"Madhouse, it is." Depositing the case beside two closed crates, Maggs grinned at him. "Almost as bad as one of your mama's journeys."

"Heaven forfend," Tony muttered. "Where's Mrs. Carrington?"

"In her room packing." Maggs stepped aside as the boys came whooping down once more. "Think she's nearly done, but she did say as she'd be out to organize these three devils betimes."

The boys looked up from where they were carefully squeezing slippers and dressing robes in around their toys. They grinned.

Tony fixed them with a direct look. "Do you three devils still need your eldest sister to organize you?"

"'Course not." David shrugged. "But she does anyway."

The other two nodded.

Tony raised his brows. "So if I take her away, you'll be able to manage on your own? My cousin is waiting to meet her, and I thought it might be easier if Alicia came first, on her own."

David and Harry exchanged glances, then nodded encouragingly.

"Good idea," Harry opined. "Then she won't be here to fuss over us."

Matthew looked less certain; Maggs lumbered forward and held out a hand. "Here then, I'll help. We can get you all packed, and meanwhile your sister can go and make Mrs. Althorpe's acquaintance, and make sure she's ready to meet you three, heh?"

Nodding, Matthew took Maggs's hand, but he kept his gaze on Tony's face. "So we'll come to your house later?"

Tony hunkered down, lightly squeezed Matthew's other hand. "I'll send my coach around for you as soon as I get home. It's large enough to take all of you at once, and the luggage can follow. That way, you'll be in Upper Brook Street, in my house, all the sooner."

"Hooray!" David and Harry turned and raced up the stairs. Grinning, reassured, Matthew dashed after them. Maggs brought up the rear.

Tony watched until they disappeared along the corridor, then he went up the stairs and along to Alicia's room.

She was bending over a box at the foot of her bed; straightening with a sigh, she shut the lid.

Smiling, he strolled in. "Finished?"

Alicia looked at him, returned his smile, then glanced distractedly around the room. "Yes—I think that's it for in here."

"Good." Halting before her, he reached for her.

Before she realized what he intended, he'd caught her, bent his head, and was kissing her . . . thoroughly. Her head spun pleasurably . . . then she remembered and struggled.

He ended the kiss; raising his head, he looked down at her. "What?"

She wriggled from his hands, firm about her waist. "The boys!" She peeked around him at the door, but there was no sign of them.

Tony met her warning look with a quizzical one, then he glanced around. "I came to take you to meet Miranda." His gaze returned to her. "She's waiting, so she assured me, on pins."

"Already? Oh." She scanned the room, but she had indeed packed everything. "But the boys aren't yet ready and—"

"The boys assured me they had their packing under control. Maggs has elected to watch over them, and you know Jenkins will as well, and Fitchett and Adriana." He fixed her with a direct look. "So there's no reason you can't come with me now. I'll send my carriage once we reach Upper Brook Street, so they'll all be only an hour or so behind."

She frowned. "But—"

"And don't forget the engagements we have tonight. You'll need to settle in, and then we have a meeting at two o'clock in the library— Jack sent word he's got what we wanted—I'm assuming you still wish to attend?" Innocently, he looked inquiringly at her.

She narrowed her eyes at him. "Of course."

He inclined his head. "And then we've dinner at Lady Martindale's followed by two balls, so we'll be out again within a few hours. I think you should look over the rooms before the others arrive, just in case there's any difficulty, anything you'd like changed."

Lips setting, she looked into his black eyes; she'd seen that expression of immovable purpose before—knew he wouldn't change tack, not easily . . . and perhaps he was right.

She grimaced. "Your cousin—she only has two daughters?"

Tony nodded; taking her elbow, he turned her to the door. "If you're worried she'll have the vapors over the boys' antics, you can rest easy—Miranda was a tomboy to the depths of her soul. We spent much of our childhood together—we were both only children. If anything, she'll be in her element with your brothers—and, incidentally, so will her daughters. If I'm any judge, they'll give your three a run for their money."

That distracted her, enough for him to steer her to the stairs. But—

"I must speak with Fitchett, and Cook, too, before I can leave."

At least she was going down the stairs. He went with her, resigned yet on guard. Stoically, he stuck to her side, determinedly herding her back to the front hall. Finally there, he picked up the pelisse she'd left lying on a chair and helped her into it.

Taking her hand, he drew her out of the front door, pulled it shut, then led her down the steps to where his curricle stood waiting. One of his grooms was holding his matched bays. He helped her in, waited while she'd settled her skirts, then climbed up beside her. Nodding to the groom, he set the horses pacing. Glancing at her, he saw her watching his hands on the reins, watching the horses, still skittish, coquettish.

He realized she was nervous; he kept the horses to a slow trot. "Don't worry—they won't bolt."

She glanced at him. "Oh—I just . . . have rarely had occasion to be behind such beasts. They're very powerful, aren't they?"

"Yes, but I have the reins."

The comment took a moment to sink in, then she relaxed. She looked at him. "You haven't driven me anywhere before."

He shrugged. "There hasn't until now been a need."

But today was different; he wanted her to himself, free of her family. When she first crossed the threshold of his house, he wanted to be with her, just her and him alone, without any distractions. He wanted to have that minute to himself; he refused to waste any time wondering why.

Luckily, she accepted his comment without question; relaxing a trifle more, she looked around as he took her deeper into the heart of Mayfair.

The moment, when it came, was as simple and as private as he'd wished; only Hungerford was there, holding the door as, his hand at her elbow, Tony guided her into his front hall.

She glanced at Hungerford, nodded, and smiled, then looked up, ahead, and around, and paused, stopped.

Hungerford closed the door, but hung back in the shadows. There was no footman hovering in the hall, no one else to intrude.

Pivoting, she looked around; Tony wondered how she would see it, how she would react to his home.

After a moment, she met his gaze. She sensed his waiting, and smiled. "It's much less intimidating than I'd imagined." Her smile deepened, softened; she glanced around again. "More comfortable. I can see people here—children . . . it's a welcoming house."

Her relief was transparent. It warmed him, eased a small knot of trepidation he hadn't until then acknowledged he carried. Joining her, he took her hand. "This is Hungerford. He's the ultimate authority here."

Hungerford approached and bowed low. "At your service, ma'am. Should you need anything—anything at all—we are at your disposal."

"Thank you."

Hungerford stepped back.

Tony gestured to the drawing-room door. "I'll introduce you to Mrs. Swithins, the housekeeper, later—she can show you the rooms they've prepared. But first, come and meet Miranda."

Buoyed by her impression of the hall, Alicia went forward eagerly. Entering the drawing room, she glanced around—and was again struck by the house's warmth. Without consciously considering it, she'd been expecting a house like him, coolly, austerely elegant, but that wasn't the pervading atmosphere here. The furniture was not new, far from it; every piece looked antique, lovingly polished, the tapestry and brocade upholstery and hangings carrying the rich, jeweled tones of a bygone age.

An age that had valued comfort and convenience as well as luxury, that had expected pleasure and enjoyment to be part of daily life. Hedonistic, but rich, warm, and very much alive.

Like the bright-eyed lady rising from a chair by the hearth. She came forward, smiling widely, hands extended.

"My dear Mrs. Carrington—Alicia—I may call you Alicia, may I not? I'm Miranda, as Tony's doubtless told you. Welcome to Torrington House—may your stay be long and happy."

Miranda's smile was winning; effervescent laughter lurked in her blue eyes. Alicia gave her her hands, smiled back. "Thank you. I hope you won't be too inconvenienced by our descent."

"Oh, *I* certainly won't be, and I doubt anyone could inconvenience Hungerford—he's terrifyingly efficient—all the staff are." Miranda looked at Tony. "You may take yourself off—we want to talk, and we'll do so much more readily without you. I'll take Alicia to meet Mrs. Swithins, so you're relieved on that score, too."

Alicia barely smothered a laugh. She glanced at Tony, saw chagrin briefly flare in his eyes as he sent Miranda a sharp glance, then he turned to her. "I'll send the carriage around for your family."

She smiled. "Thank you."

He hesitated, then, reluctant to the last, nodded and left them.

"Now!" Miranda turned to her, curiosity and delight in her face. "You must tell me all about your family—you have three brothers and a sister, that's all Tony's told me." Waving her to a chair, Miranda resumed her seat.

Alicia sank into the velvet comfort of an armchair, felt a solid sense of safety and security reach for her and wrap her about. Meeting Miranda's expectant gaze, she smiled and assembled her thoughts.

By the time Hungerford brought in the tea tray and she and Miranda had shared a pot, they'd progressed from acquaintances to friends, to newly found bosom-bows. The fictitious nature of her widowhood notwithstanding, they shared many interests—family, country pursuits, household management, and social necessity.

Miranda sent for her daughters; the girls arrived and made their curtsies, then asked polite but curious questions about her brothers. Alicia answered, inwardly heaving a sigh of relief; the girls were well-brought-up, well-bred young ladies, but not in the least sweet, retiring, or weak. They would, indeed, give her brothers pause.

Then it was time to meet Mrs. Swithins and look around the rooms before the others arrived. After performing the introductions, Miranda hung back, letting the housekeeper, a woman of considerable age but imposing presence, softened by a twinkle in her eye, guide Alicia through the house.

"We thought your young brothers would be most comfortable up here, ma'am." Mrs. Swithins led the way into the schoolroom; she waved to rooms opening off the central room. "There's three beds in the long room, and two in the next, so they can sleep together or separate if they wish." She smiled at Alicia. "We weren't sure, so both rooms are prepared."

Alicia frowned. "They're used to being together, but David is twelve."

Mrs. Swithins nodded. "We can leave it to them to decide what's most comfortable."

With a grateful inclination of her head, Alicia allowed herself to be led on to view the bedrooms for Fitchett and Jenkins.

"So they'll be close enough should the boys have need." With an airy wave, Mrs. Swithins sailed on.

The rooms on the first floor that had been prepared for her and Adriana filled Alicia, not with surprise, for she'd expected something of the sort, but with a sense of having stepped into a fairy tale, or, more specifically, into her own dreams.

Her room lay in the central wing of the mansion, above the long ballroom and overlooking the rear gardens. A wide, spacious chamber, it possessed a sitting area with two chairs before the fireplace, a delicate escritoire against one wall, a bank of large windows with a padded window seat beneath, a gigantic armoire, and a huge four-poster bed hung with pale green silks and covered with an ivory silk coverlet embroidered in green.

"The master mentioned your maid was not with you, so I've assigned Bertha." Mrs. Swithins beckoned to a young girl, who came forward and shyly curtsied. "She knows her way around a lady's wardrobe and is quick with her hands."

Alicia returned Bertha's smile, a trifle shy herself. She'd never had a maid, just Fitchett, not quite the same thing.

"I've hung your gowns in the armoire, ma'am." Bertha's voice was soft, carrying a country burr. Greatly daring, she glanced up and met Alicia's eye. "Absolutely stunning, they be."

"Thank you, Bertha." Alicia hesitated, then added, "I'll need you this evening to help me dress—we've a dinner and two balls to attend."

"Oh?" Miranda pricked up her ears; she came forward to link her arm in Alicia's. "What's this? Tony gadding about in society? Whatever next? You must tell."

Alicia laughed. She thanked Mrs. Swithins, then let Miranda sweep her back downstairs.

The others arrived just in time for luncheon. Emerging from a room Alicia took to be the library, Tony joined the melee in the front hall, then shepherded her family into the dining room, where Miranda waited with her daughters.

Introductions between children could sometimes be awkward; in this case, the arrival of the luncheon dishes cut short any difficult moment. Quickly wriggling onto the chairs to which Tony and Miranda directed them, both her brothers and Miranda's girls were at first on their best behavior, their responses stilted. That lasted only until the platter of sausages was uncovered. Thereafter, needing to ask each other to pass this or that, they quickly lost their shyness in the quest for sustenance.

Margaret and Constance were sturdy young ladies with long blond plaits; both ate heartily, showing no overt sign of consciousness of the boys. That piqued David's and Harry's interest enough for them to extend an invitation to go kite flying in the park.

The girls exchanged looks, then agreed.

When three faces turned up the table to Alicia, and two to Miranda, at the table's other end, the ladies exchanged pleased glances and nodded permission; with just one whoop—from Harry, valiantly smothered—they all pushed back from the table, bobbed curtsies or bowed, then, dismissed with nods, they headed in a bumbling crowd for the door, and Maggs, Jenkins, the park, and the sky.

"Well," Miranda said, turning back from watching them go, "they seem to have fallen on their feet."

Tony shrugged. "Why not?" His gaze went to Alicia, sitting beside him, lingered, then he looked down the table at Adriana, seated beside Miranda. "The others should be arriving any minute." To Miranda, he explained, "We're holding a council of war, so to speak, in the library this afternoon, to discuss the latest developments in our search for A. C."

Miranda's eyes opened wide; she glanced at Alicia. "Is this a private meeting, or can I listen in?"

Tony grimaced. "All in all, it might be as well if you did."

A knock sounded on the front door, and he rose. He didn't trust A. C., not on any level; given Miranda was here with her girls, sharing his roof with Alicia and her family, it was only fair she knew the whole score.

He ushered the three ladies, all determined to attend the gathering, into the front hall as Hungerford opened the door. Members of the Bastion Club streamed in. Tony nodded in greeting; beside him, Miranda murmured, "Well, well—you didn't mention them. And they are?"

The introductions took a few minutes, by which time Tristan and Leonora, Geoffrey, and, most importantly, Jack Hendon and Kit, had arrived. Once everyone was comfortably seated in the library, the large room looked unusually full.

A knock fell on the front door; it opened. A deep voice, not Hungerford's, was heard. An instant later, the library door opened, and Charles walked in. Seeing all eyes on him, he raised his brows. "Am I late?"

Tony waved him to a chair. "I thought you were away."

"No such luck." Charles drew up a chair and sat. "Merely a visit to Surrey with my sisters, sisters-in-law, and dear mama. I got back"—he glanced at the clock—"two hours ago, but matters are so fraught in Bedford Square, I dared not remain. I took refuge at the club, and Gasthorpe told me of the meeting."

His dark gaze, along with a piratical smile, swept the room. "So, what do we have?"

Alicia followed that sweeping glance around the faces, saw in each an impatience, an eagerness, a determination to get on with the business of unmasking A. C. They were quite a crowd, five ladies and eight gentlemen, an intelligent and talented company focused on their common goal.

"So what did you find?" Tony's gaze rested on Jack Hendon.

Jack had settled on a straight-backed chair. "I got the information from Lloyd's, unfortunately not as much as I'd have liked. There's a watchman who goes around every half hour. I could only chance three passes—I had to put out the light every time he came by. Without it, I couldn't see to make copies of the bills of lading." He drew a sheaf of papers from his inside coat pocket. "I got the full details of six ships before I called it a night. However—"

He distributed the papers, handing three to the men on his right, three to his left; the ladies, on the two chaises perpendicular to the hearth, had to contain their curiosity until the men had scanned the pages and passed them their way.

"As you can see," Jack resumed, as the men finished with the papers and looked up, "there's nothing obvious, no particular goods or commodities that were carried on all six ships." He paused, then added. "I'm not sure where that gets us. I was assuming there would be something in common."

The men frowned; they looked at the six sheets, now in the ladies' hands.

"How did you choose which ships to examine?" Christian asked.

"More or less randomly over the years '12 to '15." Jack grimaced. "I thought that would be most useful, but now I wonder whether whatever's the crucial element changes over time. One thing for so many months, another later."

Gervase Tregarth leaned forward, peering at the lists Kit and Alicia had spread on a low table before the chaise. "Is there definitely no item in common?"

Kit, Alicia, and Leonora shook their heads.

One of the men muttered something about the seasons.

Alicia tapped an item on one list. "Three hundred ell of finest muslin. Remember how expensive muslin was? The price is much better now, but when this was brought in, it would have been worth a small fortune."

"Hmm." Leonora studied the entry. "I never thought of it before— one simply grumbles and pays the price—but it must have been due to the war."

"Supply and demand," Kit said. They were speaking quietly, their lighter voices a counterpoint against the men's rumblings. "Jack says it's the merchants who best supply the demand who get on in business."

"True," Miranda put in, "and during the war, the demand was always there, never satisfied. Anything imported was by definition expensive. Just think how the prices of silks—"

"Let alone tea and coffee." Alicia tapped another entry on one list.

Miranda nodded; so did the others. "All those things became hideously dear. . . ." Her words faded.

Their gazes met. They all exchanged one long wondering glance, then looked at the lists.

"You don't think . . . ?" Adriana leaned nearer.

All five ladies bent over the lists again.

The gentlemen continued to reassess and revisit their reasoning, trying to see a way forward.

Alicia straightened. "That's it." She pointed triumphantly to items listed on each of the six bills of lading. "Tea and coffee!"

"Yes—*of course*!" Kit snatched up one of the lists and checked the entry, then reached for another.

"Ah—I see!" Leonora, face lighting, picked up another list.

Tony, Tristan, and Jack exchanged glances. "What do you see?" Tristan asked.

"The item in common." Alicia picked up another list and pointed to a line. "Tea—one thousands pounds of finest leaves from Assam."

Handing that list to Tony, she picked up another. "On this one, it's coffee—three hundred pounds of best beans from Colombia."

Kit sat back. "So sometimes it's coffee, and sometimes it's tea—one from the West Indies, the other on ships from the East."

"But they're often both handled by the same merchant," Leonora informed the men as the lists made their way around the circle again. "Not necessarily sold through the same shops, but it's usually the same supplier."

"Which supplier?" Christian asked.

The ladies exchanged glances. "There are many, I imagine," Miranda replied. "It's a profitable area, and fashionable in its way."

"But it's the price that's so important." Alicia looked around the male company. "It's always difficult to get good-quality coffee and tea—there never is enough brought into the country, even now. As Kit said, it's supply and demand, so the price always remains high."

"For good quality," Adriana stressed.

"Indeed." Kit nodded. "And that, perhaps, is where A. C. might have made his money. During the war, certainly over the years '12 to '15, the price of tea and coffee—the better-quality stuff—fluctuated wildly. It was always high, but sometimes it reached astronomical heights."

"Because," Leonora took up the tale, "you men always insist on your coffee at the breakfast table, and we ladies, of course, must have our tea for our tea parties, and the ton wouldn't go around if those things weren't there."

There was an instant's silence as the men all stared at them.

"Are you saying"—Charles leaned forward and fixed them with an intent look—"that during the war, the price of tea and coffee was often driven high—very high—because of sudden shortages?"

All five ladies nodded decisively.

Miranda added, "Only the best-quality merchandise, mind you."

"Indeed. But tea and coffee—the finest quality—appears on each of those lists? One or the other at least?"

Again, the ladies nodded.

"That," Alicia concluded, "seems the only link—the only thing in common, so to speak."

"Held to ransom over our breakfasts." Gervase gathered the lists and shuffled through them. "Doesn't bear thinking of, but it certainly looks—and sounds—right."

Tristan was looking over his shoulder. "Two ships from the West Indies with coffee, the other four, all East Indiamen, carried tea."

"These prices." Jack fixed his wife with a questioning glance. "How much of an increase are we looking at—prices twice as high, three times?"

"For the best coffee?" Kit glanced at Leonora and Alicia. "Anything from ten, to even fifty times the usual price, I would say."

"For tea," Miranda said, "it could easily be from ten to thirty times the price before the war—and even that price was always high."

"How high?" Tristan asked.

The ladies pursed their lips, then tossed around figures that made the men blanch. "Good God!" Charles stopped, calculating. "Why that's . . ."

"One hell of a lot of money!" Jack growled.

"One hell of a lot of profit," Gervase said.

"One very good reason to ensure that the supply failed at critical times." Tony fixed the ladies with an inquisitorial look. "From what you're saying, the person who would stand to gain—"

"Is the merchant who had brought in a cargo of tea and coffee safely just before any shortage occurred."

It was Jack who had spoken. Tony looked at him. "Before?"

Jack nodded. "The warehouses and docks know when a ship and its cargo doesn't arrive, and the merchants mark up the prices of the goods they have in stock accordingly—that I know for fact."

"So . . ." They all sat and thought it over, then Tony called them to order. "Assuming the answer is tea and coffee, how do we go on from here?"

"We first check the waybills of the other ten ships we know were lost courtesy of Ruskin's information." Jack glanced at Tony. "Two of us, now we know what we're looking for, could probably check all the waybills at once."

Tony nodded. "We'll do it tonight."

"Meanwhile," Christian said, "the rest of us can start investigating the merchants who specialize in tea and coffee. The connection to A. C. must be through them." He frowned, then glanced around. "What could the connection between A. C. and a merchant be, given we know, or at least can surmise, that A. C. is one of the ton?"

Charles grimaced. "Can we surmise that, do you think? That he is one of us?"

"I think that's beyond question," Tony answered. "Who else would have known how to manipulate the ton against Alicia? And Dalziel confirmed that the third round of information against her had been laid through the most exclusive gentlemen's clubs. There seems little doubt A. C. is a member not just of the ton, but the haut ton—our circle." A memory floated through his mind; he grimaced. "Indeed, I suspect I've seen him."

"You have?"

"When?"

He briefly explained, describing the man he'd seen through the mists in Park Street all those nights ago.

"Astrakhan—you know, that's not all that common," Jack Warnefleet said. "A point to remember, especially if he didn't know you'd seen him."

"That leaves us still facing the final question," Christan said. "What link could there be between a tea and coffee merchant and a member of the haut ton?"

The room fell silent; only the ticking of the mantelpiece clock could be heard, then Charles looked at Tony. "It couldn't be *that*, could it—the reason behind Ruskin's murder?"

"It's certainly feasible." Tristan leaned back in his chair. "There's many in the ton would move heaven and earth to hide any contact with trade."

"Add to that the illegality involved, let alone its treasonous nature . . ." Gervase glanced around. "That's a powerful motive for removing Ruskin."

"And then going to *any* lengths to cover his tracks." Tony's gaze was fixed on Alicia.

There were slow nods all around. Charles leaned forward, hands clasped. "That's it—we might not yet be able to see the player, but that assuredly is the game. A. C. is directly involved in trade via some tea and coffee merchant."

Suddenly needing to move, Tony rose. Crossing to the fireplace, closer to Alicia, he braced an arm on the mantelpiece and looked around the circle. "Let's recapitulate. A. C. is at the very least a sleeping partner with a merchant who imports the finest tea and coffee. In order to increase profits by driving up prices, he sets out to manipulate the supply of tea and coffee through having ships carrying competitors' supplies taken by the French."

He looked at Jack Hendon. "How did he know which ships to target?"

Jack shrugged. "Easy enough if you're inside the trade. The merchants know each other, and each merchant usually has contracts with only one or at most two shipping lines, and the ships run by each line are listed in a number of registers, none hard to access. It wouldn't have been difficult."

Tony nodded. "So he knows which ships to target to make his plan work. With the information from Ruskin, he knows when each returning ship will not be under frigate escort, and thus an easy and vulnerable target for a foreign captain."

His voiced hardened. "So A. C. arranges for the target ships to be taken, then sits back in London and counts the inflated return from the cargo he's already landed."

A long silence followed, then Christian straightened. "That's how it worked. We need to identify all possible merchants, then investigate which one had safe cargoes to exploit."

"And from there," Jack Warnefleet murmured, "we dig until we uncover A. C.—there'll be some track leading back to him, one way or another."

The soft menace in his tone was balm to them all.

Christian looked at Tony. "I'll act as coordinator in the search for the merchant, if you like." He glanced at the other members of the club. "We can take that on. I'll let you know the instant we identify the most likely firm."

Tony nodded. "I'll go with Jack tonight and confirm that the link holds good—if there's any ship taken that wasn't carrying tea or coffee, it might give us a link to another aspect of A. C.'s trade interests."

"True." Christian stood. "The more links we can get to A. C.'s trading activities, the easier it'll be to identify him conclusively."

The men rose. The ladies did, too, exchanging plans for meeting that evening at the balls they'd attend.

As the group emerged into the front hall, Charles paused beside Tony, his gaze uncharacteristically bleak. "You know, I might have understood if A. C.'s motive was in some way . . . well, patriotic even if grossly misguided. If he was the sort of traitor who sincerely believed England should lose the war and follow some revolutionary course. But be damned if I can understand how any Englishman could so cold-bloodedly have sent so many English sailors to almost certain death at the hands of the French"—he met Tony's gaze—"all for money."

Tony nodded. "That's one point that sticks in my craw."

Along with the fact A. C. had cast Alicia as his scapegoat.

Expressions grimly determined, they made their farewells and parted, all convinced of one thing. Whoever A. C. was, the man had no soul.

"Take care!"

In the crush of Lady Carmody's ballroom, Alicia watched Kit lecture her handsome husband, then she turned on Tony, standing beside Alicia.

"And you, too. I suppose I feel responsible after pulling you out of the water all those years ago, but regardless, I would prefer not to have to come to some dockside Watch House and explain to the interested who you both are."

Tony raised his brows. "If we're caught, it'll be your husband's fault—I haven't been retired as long as he."

From the look on Kit's face, she didn't know whether to take umbrage on Jack's behalf or be more worried still. When no eruption ensued, Jack, behind her, glanced around at her face. Sliding his arm around her, he hugged her. "Stop worrying. I'll—we'll—be perfectly safe."

Alicia turned to Tony. She fixed him with her most severe look, the one guaranteed instantly to wring the truth from her brothers. "Is he speaking the truth? *Will* you be all right?"

Tony smiled; lifting her hand, he pressed a warm kiss into her palm. "There's no danger to speak of. Lloyd's is just a coffeehouse—easy pickings."

She wasn't entirely convinced and let it show; his smile deepened.

Glancing around at the jostling throng, at the many gentlemen moving through its ranks, looking over the available ladies, he murmured, "I'm more concerned about you. Geoffrey will stay close, and Tristan and Leonora will meet you at the Hammonds', then Geoffrey will see you home." He met her gaze. "You face more danger than I." He added, pointedly, "Take care."

It was her turn to smile. "If worse comes to worst, I can always claim Sir Freddie's arm." And perhaps divert him from Adriana's side; the baronet remained assiduously attentive despite Adriana's hints.

Tony grimaced. Jack tapped him on the shoulder; he looked around.

"We'd better go." With a nod, Jack took his leave of her.

Tony's eyes returned to hers, lingered, then he released her hand and turned. With Jack, he moved into the crowd. They were taller than most, yet in seconds, neither Kit nor she could see them.

"Humph!" Kit pulled a face, and linked her arm in Alicia's. "We've been deserted." Surveying Adriana's circle, she set her chin. "This is far too tame—come on." She set off into the crowd, drawing Alicia with her. "Let's find some useful distraction. I don't know about you, but without it, I'll go mad."

Alicia laughed, and let herself be towed into the melée.

Gaining access to the records they sought wasn't quite as easy as Tony had painted it, yet soon enough he and Jack were flicking through files in the offices above the coffee house, searching for, then poring over the bills of lading lodged for the other ten ships Ruskin had identified and which were subsequently taken.

While he worked, Tony's mind revisited their logic, their strategies. "The connection had better not be through Lloyd's itself."

"Unlikely," Jack answered from across the room. "As far as I know, they've never handled tea."

Half an hour later, Tony wondered aloud, "In all of this"—he waved at the cabinets ringing the room—"do you think there's any chance of identifying ships that docked with cargoes of tea or coffee say in the week before one that was taken?"

Jack looked up, then shook his head. "Needle in a haystack. Virtually every ship that passes through the Port of London will have a waybill in here. That's often hundreds a day. We'd never be able to check enough to identify the ship we want."

He resumed his searching. "Mind you, we *will* be able to confirm the link once we know the merchant and his shipping line."

Tony nodded, and continued flipping through files.

It took them two hours to locate and examine the ten waybills. Then they quietly put the room to rights, eradicating any sign of their visit, and silently retreated from the room and the building.

* * *

By the time Tony reached Upper Brook Street, Mayfair was silent, the streets dark with shadows. Miranda, Adriana, and Alicia would have returned home long ago. They should all be asleep in their beds.

Closing the front door, he shot the well-oiled bolts, then crossed the hall. There was no lamp or candle left burning; Hungerford knew him better than that. Quite aside from his excellent night vision, he knew this house like the back of his hand, knew every creak in the stairs, every board that might groan.

At the top of the stairs, he turned away from the gallery leading to the east wing where Miranda, her daughters, and Adriana had their rooms, and headed for the room Alicia had been given, three doors from the master suite. Hand on the doorknob, he paused, struck by a sudden thought.

How had Mrs. Swithins known . . . ?

The answer was obvious. He really was *that* transparent.

Grimacing, he turned the knob.

Alicia was in bed, but not asleep. Cocooned beneath the luxurious embroidered silk coverlet, silk sheets sliding seductively over her skin, she'd been waiting for the past hour, waiting to at least hear Tony's footsteps, passing her door . . . or not, as the case might be.

Unable to sleep, made edgy by her own expectation—that he would come to her, that she wanted him to, even needed him to—an expectation she found somewhat damning—she was after all in his house, an old aristocratic mansion, yet while that fact might inhibit her, she doubted it would influence him—she had forcibly turned her mind to reviewing the day. A long day in which much had happened, and much had changed.

So easily.

That more than anything else, the ease with which the changes had been wrought, the ease with which she'd simply *flowed* into the position he'd created for her, niggled. In some odd way seemed to mock her. Everything had fallen into place so smoothly, she was still struggling to come to grips with the ramifications. As if he'd once more swept her off her feet, and her head had yet to stop whirling.

Not, for her, an uncommon feeling where he was concerned.

It wasn't that she wished things were otherwise; she couldn't convincingly argue against the move, not even to herself. But the uncertainty, the lack of clarity regarding her position here—the lack of sureness made it impossible to feel confident, at ease . . .

She never heard his footsteps; only a faint draft alerted her to the opening door. He was no more than a dark shadow slipping through; she recognized him instantly.

Her eyes had adjusted to the dimness; watching him cross the wide room toward her, she searched his face, all she could see of him, but could detect not even a limp. Kit's worry had infected her, yet here he was unscathed, moving with his usual fluid grace toward the bed.

He stopped by a chair and sat, reaching down to pull off his boots. She sat up, wriggling in the sheets onto her side; he heard the shushing and glanced across, smiled a touch wearily.

"Did you find the lists? From the other ships?"

He nodded. Setting his boots aside, he stood, stretched. "We found all ten—your theory was right. It's tea and coffee that's the link."

He lowered his arms, weary tension falling from him.

She watched him undress—coat, cravat, waistcoat, and shirt hit the chair. Realizing her mouth was dry, she swallowed, forced her gaze to his face. "So now we have to look for the merchant."

He nodded, looking down, bending down as he stripped off his trousers. "With all of us involved, that won't take long." Straightening, he grimaced. "Maybe a week." He flung the trousers at the chair, then turned to the bed.

Her pulse leapt. "So we're one step away from identifying A. C?"

"One step." Lifting the covers, he slid in beside her. Dropping them, he turned to her. Framed her face with his hands and kissed her.

Deeply, thoroughly, druggingly . . . until she was swept away, her mind whirling on a sensual tide.

Leaving one hand cupping her jaw, with the other Tony reached down and tugged the sheet from between them, then settled his body against hers. Letting the sheets fall, he plundered her soft mouth while with his palm he traced the long, smooth curve from her shoulder, over the supple planes of her back to the swell of her bottom, molding her to him, easing her beneath him, spurred by the realization that her skin was already warm, by the immediate leap of her pulse to the caress, the dewed flush that spread over the silken skin of her bottom, the evidence of her arousal he discovered when he pressed his hand down between them, slid his fingers between her thighs, and found her.

Ready, waiting, urgent for him.

He pressed her back into the bed, parted her thighs with his and filled her, surged slowly into her, taking his time, glorying in the ease with which he could forge in, in the way she tilted her hips and took him deep, to the fluid harmony with which they then moved, sliding into the dance their bodies now knew so well.

A different dance to any he'd enjoyed with any other woman.

Mouths melded, tongues tangling, hot yet languid, their bodies moved, merged, flexed to a rhythm that held a deeper tune, a more powerful cadence.

A heady, dizzying delight, a pleasure that soared higher and reached deeper, that slid past their slick skins, through muscle and bone, past straining sinews and tightening nerves to their cores. To touch, sink into, and hold something there.

Something precious, fragile, yet strong enough to fuse their hearts.

He sensed it before they'd even started to scale the peak. Their bodies held, thrummed with, a driving urgency, yet they had the strength to dally—neither was in any rush, delighting instead in every small touch, each delicate caress.

Slowly, powerfully, he rode her, feeling her body surrender and take him in, feeling the heat of her draw him deeper, tempting him further into her fire. He went, but kept the reins firmly in his hands, as always orchestrating the moment; after all these years, pleasuring women was all but second nature.

Gradually, the tempo built. Beneath him, her body rose, meeting his, matching his, urging him on. Her fingers, on his back, tensed, nails lightly scoring. Without easing the steadily escalating rhythm, he drew back from the kiss, through the dimness studied her face; her eyes were closed, her lips swollen and parted, telltale concentration etched in every line.

He thrust deeper, harder, and she gasped, her body arching greedily under his.

Lifting his shoulders a fraction farther, enough to appreciate the way her body, all sumptuous curves and hot flushed skin, undulated with each thrust, absorbed each forceful penetration as he rode her, filled her, he watched as he pushed her step by slow step closer to sensual fulfillment.

He felt the tension inside her coil, felt her tighten beneath him, her thighs gripping his flanks as release flickered and beckoned. Her ragged breathing filled his ears, a softer sound overlaying his own raspy breaths.

She reached for him, tried to pull him down to her.

Without breaking their rhythm, he shifted his hips, pressing more intimately between hers, then thrust deeper still, harder still.

She gasped, tugged, but the sight of her held him. Eventually lifting his gaze to her face, he saw the glimmer of her eyes beneath her lashes.

Alicia studied his face, licked her lips, felt her world teeter. She was so close to that joyous edge, yet, as always since that first engagement, no matter how desperate the moment, he held to his control, waiting, watching, certain to follow her, yet still . . .

"Come with me." She struggled to find breath enough to add, "Now."

His black eyes, until then hooded, opened wide—enough for her to realize she'd asked something no other ever had.

Her nerves shivered, started to unravel. Dragging in a breath, she lifted a hand to his face, traced his cheek. "*Be* with me. Please."

She wasn't sure how, but she knew what she wanted. Needed.

He knew, too. He gave a shuddering sigh; the tension rippling through him increased, hardening his body as it rode against hers, thrust into hers.

Their gazes remained locked. He shifted his weight, freed a hand, held it open close by her head. "Give me your hand."

She did, shifting her hand from his face, watching as he interdigitated his fingers with hers, then closed them, locking their palms. Then he pressed their linked hands into the pillow.

"Wrap your legs about my waist."

She could barely make out the gravelly command. The silk sheets caressed her skin as she complied, then gasped as he shifted fully over her and drove deep. Her spine bowed, but his weight pinned her, held her down as his hips flexed in a faster, more urgent, more compulsive rhythm.

For an instant, gasping and breathless, she rode it, then she felt his eyes on her face, met his black gaze, once again screened. Felt the flames inside rise, coalesce, fuse to an inferno.

He lowered his head, drove into her harder, faster, more powerfully.

"Now." He breathed the word against her lips, then took them, took her mouth as the conflagration roared—and caught them. Overwhelmed them. Consumed them.

As one. Together, as she'd asked.

Tony felt the reins he'd released whip away, sensed them cinder, all control sundered and gone. For only the second time in his life, he plunged into the heart of that familiar fire *with* a woman, by her side. Her hand was his anchor; he clung to it as her body tightened beneath his, closed powerfully around his, hot, scalding, driving him on, taking him with her into the world beyond the flames, into the pleasure of sexual satiation.

If she wished, so he would; they whirled, joined more intimately than he'd ever been with any other, not just their bodies but their awarenesses fused, experiencing together, simultaneously soaring. Higher, then yet higher.

Until they were both gasping, bodies locked and straining. Until they were there, twined together at the peak.

Until they fell, hearts thundering, senses merged, glory pouring through them. Souls as one.

She was his. Totally, completely, beyond recall.

The words drifted of their own volition across Alicia's brain.

Her body, trapped beneath his, thighs vulnerably wide with him buried so deep inside her, was no longer hers.

Her lips curved in sleepy satisfaction. No matter her thoughts, her will, her determination, logic had no place here. Despite all uncertainty, despite the nebulous unease that even now she could sense, a fog hovering just beyond the bed, even now, despite all, her heart rejoiced.

Lifting the hand he hadn't claimed, she laid it on his hair, then gently stroked. Let her fingers play among the silky strands.

Let her emotions have their way.

Let them well, and fill her mind, fill her throat and her chest, fill her heart, and overflow. Let them slide through her veins and sink into her flesh, a part of her, forever.

He lay heavy upon her; she delighted in his weight. Within her, the warmth of his seed radiated a glow of deep and abiding pleasure. She'd given him all she was; tonight, he'd taken, claimed, but when she'd wanted and needed, he had surrendered and given, too.

No matter what else the days might bring, tonight, he'd been with her.

As totally hers as she'd been his.

The gentle tangling of Alicia's fingers in his hair drew Tony back to earth. To a world that was almost as wonderful as the one they'd visited; her body was a sensual cushion beneath him, her breasts beneath his chest, her hips and thighs cradling his, their bodies still intimately joined.

He was more comfortable than he'd ever thought to be, not just in body but on all other levels. Physically, mentally, emotionally, he was at peace, at home in her arms. Where he was meant to be.

His satisfaction was so profound it was frightening. It lay like a golden sea about him, deep, timeless, ageless, weighing on his limbs, soothing his mind, infinitely precious.

Eyes closed, he savored it, held it, let its waves lap about him— and tried not to think of ever losing it.

Eventually, he felt forced to stir, to draw back from that contented sea. Lifting from Alicia, he ignored her sleepy protest; she seemed as addicted to the moment as he. Settling beside her, he drew her to him, against him, brushing aside her long hair so he could see her face. He looked into her eyes, shadowed pools, mysterious in the night.

Marry me tomorrow.

The words burned his tongue; all the reasons he shouldn't say them—not yet—doused them. Instead, bending his head, he touched his lips to hers, and spoke from his heart.

"Je t'aime." He breathed the words across her lips; closing his eyes, he tasted them. *"Je t'adore."*

He wasn't even conscious of speaking in French; it had always been the language of love to him.

She touched his cheek, returned his kiss, soft, clinging.

Their lips parted; he drew breath, softly asked, "Is everything here as you wish? If there's anything you need—"

She stopped him, laying her fingers across his lips. "There's nothing—everything's perfect." She hesitated, then added, "I like your house."

They were speaking in whispers, as if not to disturb the blanket of shared pleasure that still surrounded them. It was the deepest part of the night, the small hours of the morning, yet neither was sleepy. Sated, content, they lay in each other's arms, limbs tangled, hands occasionally touching, brushing, stroking.

Time drifted, and with it the tide of their loving. It slowly turned. Returned. Alicia didn't think, but simply flowed with it, knew he did the same.

Effortless. Their communication in that moment needed no words, no careful phrases. It was carried by their hands, their lips, mouths, tongues, every square inch of their bodies.

They moved over and around, worshipping, first one, then the other. Pleasure bloomed, ecstasy blossomed.

He opened her eyes to pleasures she hadn't imagined, sensual delights beyond her ken. In turn, she set aside her inhibitions and let instinct and his guttural murmurs of appreciation guide her.

When at last they joined and again crested the final peak, and found the now-familiar splendor waiting, they were again together, senses open yet wholly merged, deliberately and completely one.

Later, when they lay spent, exhausted, in each other's arms, Alicia heard his words echo in her mind. *I love you. I adore you.*

She wondered if he'd understood her reply.

* * *

Tony sank toward sleep, sated to his toes, his mind unfocused. Thoughts drifted, melted into the fogs as they closed in.

He'd told her he loved her, had said the words aloud. He'd surprised himself; he'd always imagined they would be so hard to say.

They'd slipped out, almost without conscious direction, a statement of fact with which he had no argument.

So easy. Now all that remained was to organize their wedding.

They were one step away from identifying A. C. One step away from being free to face their future, to give it their full and undivided attention.

If he had his way—and he was determined he would—the next time they indulged as they just had, they would be in his big bed at Torrington Chase, and Alicia would be his wife.

The following days passed in a frenzy of activity—social commitments on the one hand, covert investigation on the other.

To Alicia's relief, the staff at Torrington House truly were, as Tony had told her, delighted to have three boys rampaging through the house. Once she realized how safe, secure, and cared for the boys now were, with so many benevolently watchful eyes on them, she relaxed her vigilance—one item she didn't need to worry over.

She had plenty of others on her plate.

One was a lovers' spat between Adriana and Geoffrey. It blew over in twenty-four hours, but left Alicia, the recipient of both principals' outpourings, feeling battered. The event precipitated the long-desired meeting between Geoffrey, Adriana, and herself. She and Adriana made their financial situation crystal clear; Geoffrey looked at them as if they were mad, and then asked why they'd thought he would care. Without waiting for an answer, he formally offered for Adriana's hand. Adriana, somewhat stunned by his unwavering singlemindedness, accepted him.

Alicia retired, pleased, relieved, but wrung out. They all agreed that any announcement should wait until Geoffrey had written to his mother in Devon and taken Adriana to meet her. On all other counts, Alicia felt justified in leaving them to plan their own future.

When, later that night, she regaled Tony with a description of the meeting, he laughed, amused. Later still, when she was lying sated and warm in his arms, he murmured, "Did you tell him you weren't a widow?"

"No." He sounded serious; she glanced up. "Should I have?"

He was fiddling with a lock of her hair; he met her gaze, after a moment, replied, "There's no need to tell anyone, not anymore. It doesn't concern anyone but you and me."

She considered, then resettled her cheek on his chest. She listened to his heart beating strongly, steadily, and told herself all was well.

Only it wasn't.

It took her until her fourth day in Torrington House to realize what was wrong, what was increasingly troubling her, converting nebulous unease into a more tangible fear.

In addition to Hungerford's delight at her presence, the open acceptance by the *grandes dames* and hostesses of her sojourn in Upper Brook Street had allayed her concerns on one score. Contrary to her beliefs, it clearly was acceptable for a nobleman's mistress to reside openly under his roof, in certain circumstances. She assumed the ameliorating circumstances included that she was a fashionable widow of whom society approved, that Miranda was present, and that A. C. had attempted to use her as his scapegoat.

Regardless, her initial fears on that point had proved groundless; society took her relocation in its stride. So did everyone else—except her.

Only she was having difficulties, and that in a way she hadn't foreseen. At first, when Miranda had consulted her over this and that, deferring to her suggestions on the menus, the maids, the day-to-day decisions of managing the large household, she'd assumed Miranda was merely trying to ensure she felt at home.

But on the third morning, Miranda threw up her hands. "Oh, stuff and nonsense—this is all so silly. You're hardly an innocent miss with no experience. Here"—she thrust the menus at her—"it's only right and proper *you* should be handling this, and you don't need my help."

With a brilliant smile, Miranda rose, swung her skirts about, and left her to deal with Mrs. Swithins alone. Which, after swallowing her amazement, she did; it was transparent Mrs. Swithins fully expected her to.

From that point, the servants openly deferred to her. From that minute she became, in all reality bar the legal fact, the lady of Torrington House.

Tony's wife.

It was a position she'd never thought to fill; now, she found herself living it. Bad enough. The associated development that transformed the situation into a deeply disturbing, unsettling experience was something she not only hadn't foreseen, but hadn't even dreamed of.

On the fourth morning, the truth hit her like a slap.

Since she'd moved into his house, Tony left her bed only minutes before the maids started their rounds. That morning, she rose from her disarranged couch, only to feel the dragging effects of real tiredness.

The first weeks of the Season were packed with entertainments, morning, noon, and night; she, Adriana, and Miranda had attended six events the day before.

When Bertha appeared, she retreated to the bed, and let the little maid tidy away her evening gown. "We've a luncheon at two o'clock—I'll dress for that, but now I'm going to rest. Please tell Mrs. Althorpe and my sister that I'm still sleeping." If they had any sense, they'd be doing the same.

Bertha murmured sympathetically, efficiently tidied, then with a last whispered inquiry if she wished for anything else, which Alicia denied, the maid whisked out.

Left in blissful peace, Alicia snuggled down, closed her eyes. She expected to fall asleep, there was after all no urgent matter awaiting her attention, nothing she need worry about . . .

Her mind emptied, cleared—and the truth was suddenly there, abruptly revealed, rock-solid and absolute. Inescapable and undeniable.

Being the lady of Torrington House was the future her heart truly craved.

The revelation rocked her.

Lying back in the bed, she stared up at the silk canopy and tried to understand. Herself. How, why . . . when had she changed?

The answers trickled into her mind. She hadn't changed, but never before had she allowed herself to think of what she wanted for her own life; she'd spent her life organizing the lives of others, and had deliberately spared no thought for her own. Intentional self-blindness; she knew why she'd done it—it had been easier that way. The wrench of sacrificing dreams . . . one never had to face that deadening choice if one never allowed oneself to dream at all.

Looking back at her younger self, to when she'd made that decision . . . she'd done it to protect her heart against the harsh reality she, even in her relative naïveté, had foreseen. But she was no longer that naive young girl trembling, trepidatious and alone, on the threshold of womanhood, weighed down by responsibilites and cares.

She hadn't changed so much as grown. She was now experienced, assured. Her own actions in formulating and successfully carrying out her plan, and all that had flowed through her association with Tony, had opened her eyes, not just to what might be, but even more powerfully to who she was and what lay within her. Her own strengths, her own will, her abilities.

Beneath all ran a belief, a conviction, in her right to her own life—and a determination, quiet, until now unrecognized and unstated but definitely there, to seize what she wanted.

With the position of Tony's wife hers in all but name . . . the role fitted her like a glove, soothed her by its rightness, fulfilled some deep-seated yearning, an unrealized but essential, fundamental part of her.

That was what she wanted.

Her breath caught; a vise tightened about her heart. Her determination didn't waver.

Yet she was his mistress, not his wife.

He'd said he loved her. Her French was not good—she'd never had time to do more than learn the rudiments; he often murmured phrases during their lovemaking that she couldn't make out, yet she felt confident she hadn't misheard or mistaken those particular words.

She even believed them, or at least believed that he believed them.

What he *meant* by them was another matter.

Marriage had never been part of their arrangement. Just because she now yearned for it, wanted it—and not just because he got along so well with her brothers and had the wherewithal and character to guide and support them precisely as she'd always wished—just because she now realized that marrying him would satisfy every dream she'd never allowed herself to have, she couldn't now turn back the clock.

Couldn't now expect him to think in those terms just because her eyes had been opened. Shouldn't be so naive as to read too much into a simple declaration of love. Pretending to herself would be the ultimate folly, the ultimate way to break her heart.

When Bertha returned at one o'clock, she rose, washed, and dressed. Calmly serene, she went downstairs and threw herself into the social round.

A note arrived from Christian Allardyce just as Tony was about to embark on another round of balls and parties at Alicia's side. Also gathered in his front hall waiting for the coach to be brought around were Adriana, Geoffrey, and Miranda. Lady Castlereagh's was to be their first port of call.

Tony scanned the note. Christian wrote to suggest they should meet at the Bastion Club to review progress. Tony surmised that the others—Christian, Charles, Tristan, Gervase, Jack Warnefleet, and even Jack Hendon—were keen to use the investigation as an excuse to avoid their social obligations.

Even with Alicia's presence as reward, he, too, felt the temptation. For men of their ilk, balls were boring, pointless, and severely drained their never very deep reserves of civility. They'd spent the last decade avoiding fools—why change their ways now?

Noting Alicia, beside him, watching him, he handed her the note.

While she read it, he glanced at Geoffrey. If it hadn't been for the little chat they'd had that afternoon, he'd be irritated by Geoffrey's and Adriana's total absorption in the how and where of their nuptials; luckily, Geoffrey had had no argument with his assertion that he and Alicia should marry first, even if by no more than a week.

Given the way Geoffrey was watching over Adriana, as if determined now he'd won her no other would get close, it was clear he, at least, would resist the lure of the investigation.

Tony turned to Alicia as she looked up from the note.

"Are you going?"

He looked into her green eyes, hesitated. "If you would prefer I escort you to the balls tonight, I can put off the meeting until tomorrow."

She looked at him steadily; he couldn't tell what she was thinking. Then she glanced down at the note. "But that would mean actions that could be instigated tomorrow if you met tonight would be delayed, wouldn't it?"

She looked up again. He nodded. Put like that, it was almost incumbent upon him to leave her to Geoffrey's care and devote his attention to unmasking A. C. Still he hesitated, not liking the fact he couldn't follow her thoughts, or see her feelings in her eyes. He usually could. "Are you sure? Geoffrey will stay with you—"

She smiled, confident, and assured. "Yes, of course. Indeed, I'm sure we're starting to be the butt of comments about being forever in each other's pockets." Turning to Miranda, she caught her eye. "Tony's been called away—I'm assuring him we'll be perfectly happy with just Geoffrey as escort."

"Oh, indeed!" Miranda flicked her hand at him. "Go, go!" She grinned, a devilish light in her eye. "I assure you Alicia and I will be *excellently* well entertained."

She meant it in purely teasing vein, yet the barb slipped under Tony's guard and pricked. He glanced at Alicia; turning to him, she gave him her hand.

"I'll bid you a good night, then. I daresay we'll be home long before you get back." She raised her gaze to his face, but not as far as his eyes.

A sudden chill touched him.

Having heard his name and ascertained from Miranda what was going on, Geoffrey turned to him. "Don't worry, I'll bring them all safely back at the end of Lady Selkirk's affair." Meeting Tony's gaze, he quietly added, "Send word tomorrow morning if there's anything I can help with."

Tony nodded. He released Alicia's hand to shake Geoffrey's.

When he looked back, he found she'd turned away and was embroiled in a discussion with Adriana.

There seemed no reason to dally. "I'll leave you, then." He made the comment general; with a single nod for everyone, he headed for the door.

What he learned at the club drove all other thoughts temporarily from his mind.

"We've narrowed the field to three possibilities." As he'd suggested, Christian had acted as a central contact, compiling and disseminating information as the others brought it in. They'd all been involved, but in order to keep things moving, they'd simply reported, then got on with the next task, and left Christian to make sense of the whole. This was the first time they'd all gathered since the meeting in Tony's library—the first time they'd heard the results to date.

"Between them, Jack"—Christian nodded at Jack Warnefleet— "and Tristan came up with a list of tea and coffee merchants they've since verified as exhaustive."

"Can one ask how?" Charles asked.

Jack Warnefleet grinned. "Not if you want details. But I'm sure those merchants would be amazed at how much their wives, especially their competitors' wives, know."

"Ah!" Charles turned a limpid glance on Tristan.

Who smiled. "I left that endeavor to Jack. My contribution was verifying the information via the appropriate guilds. By a sleight of argument, I convinced the guild secretaries that I needed to examine their registers for cases of accidental cross-listings, where coffee merchants had been listed as tea merchants, and vice versa."

"Which naturally left you with a list of those who were both. Very nice." Charles looked back up the table.

"The list comprised twenty-three companies," Christian continued. "We eliminated those we know lost cargoes, assuming no merchant is going to send a precious cargo to France just to cover his tracks. That took twelve names out—some of the sixteen ships carried cargoes for the same merchant."

"Poor beggars," Jack Hendon said. "Knowing how close some of them sail to the wind, I'd be surprised if none have gone bankrupt."

"Some have," Gervase answered. "Yet more damage to add to A. C.'s account."

Tony stirred. "So that left us with eleven companies."

Christian nodded. "Courtesy of you all and your chameleon like talents, passing yourselves off as potential coffee-shop proprietors and the like, not to mention your ability to tell barefaced lies, by focusing on who had stock after the last A. C.-induced shortage, we've ended with three names—three merchants. All had stock to sell when the price last soared, and even though that incident was nearly a year ago, we have enough corroboration to conclude that *only* those three had stock to sell at that time."

A general hubbub ensued, centering on whether there was any easy way to narrow the list further.

Tony didn't contribute; reaching out, he took the sheet lying in front of Christian and read the names. "So," his voice fell into the lull as the prospect of a simple next step faded, "A. C. is associated with one of these three."

"Yes, *but*," Christian stressed, "two of the three are not involved. Given what we'll need to do to ferret out a hidden partner, we need to be absolutely certain which of the three it is before we move in."

Tony nodded. "If we get it wrong, we'll alert A. C., and given his record in covering his tracks, all we'll find is another corpse."

Jack Warnefleet sat forward. "So how do we pinpoint the right merchant?"

"The right merchant landed cargoes before each prize was taken." Tony looked across the table at Jack Hendon. "You said once we had a merchant's shipping line, we could verify the safe landing of A. C.'s cargo via the records at Lloyd's. We have three merchants—if we learn which shipping lines they use, could we check all three lines for safe landings in the relevant weeks preceding each prize-taking, and check the cargoes landed?"

Jack held his gaze for a long moment, then asked, "How much time do we have?"

"By my calculation, not a lot. A. C.'s been quiet for nearly a week, but he must know we haven't given up. He'll try something else to deflect the investigation—he won't succeed, but the faster we can conclude it, the better." Tony paused, then added, "Who knows what he might do next?"

It was a point on which he tried not to speculate, yet it hovered in his mind, a constant threat. To Alicia, to him, to their future.

Jack was thinking, calculating—glancing around the table, he nodded. "Given our number, it's possible. And it might be the best way. The first thing we need to learn is which shipping lines those three companies use, but to do that without alerting the companies, you'll need to ask the shipping lines."

"Can you do that?" Christian asked.

"Not me. As the owner of Hendon Shipping, the instant I start asking questions like that, there'll be hell to pay."

"No matter." Charles shrugged. "You tell us what answers we need, and what questions will best elicit them, and leave it to us."

"Right."

"Easy enough."

The others nodded. It was Tony who asked, "How many shipping lines are there?"

Jack met his gaze. "Seventy-three."

When the others stopped groaning, Jack continued, "I'll put a list together tonight—we can meet here first thing tomorrow. If we push, we should get the information by evening, and then"—he met Tony's gaze again—"we'll first need to get access to the shipping registers and get the ships' names, then we'll revisit Lloyd's. We'll be able to find the answer—which company A. C. is behind—there."

Tony returned Jack's gaze, then nodded. "Let's do it."

Nineteen

The next day was chaotic.

Six members of the Bastion Club attired as no gentleman would normally be met with Jack Hendon in the club's meeting room at eight o'clock. Over breakfast, they divided his list on the basis of the location of the shipping lines' offices, then each took a section and set out. They were masquerading as merchants, all appearing older and a great deal more conservative than they were.

Whoever discovered a link between any of the three merchants and a shipping line would send a messenger back to Jack at the club. They'd decided against calling a halt until all seventy-three shipping lines had been assessed; there was always the possibility that a merchant used more than one, especially if that merchant had something to hide.

Tony had taken a group of fourteen offices congregated around Wapping High Street. Charles, who had drawn the area next to that, shared a hackney down to the docks. They parted, and Tony began his search for a reliable shipping line to bring tea from his uncle's plantations in Ceylon. Once he had a shipping manager keen to secure his fictitious uncle's fictitious cargo, it was easy to ask for references in the form of other tea merchants the line had run cargoes for in the last few years.

By eleven o'clock, he'd visited six offices, and scored one hit. One line which, so the manager believed, had an exclusive contract with one of their three merchants.

Tony stopped in a tavern to refresh himself with a pint. Sitting at a table by a window, he sipped and looked out. He appeared to be watching the handcarts and drays and the bustling human traffic thronging the street; in reality, he saw none of it, his mind turned inward to more personal vistas.

Things had started to move; the pace always escalated toward the end of a chase. They'd soon have A. C., or at least his name. Dalziel would have his man; Tony would take great delight in delivering him personally.

He needed to keep his eye on the game, yet the very fact it was nearing its apogee had him thinking of what came next. Of Alicia and him, and their future life.

The closer the prospect drew, the more it commanded his attention, the more sensitive to threats to it he became. Last night in the hall, he'd been touched by premonition, by an unfocused, unspecific belief that something was wrong, or at least not right. Something in the way Alicia had reacted had pricked his instincts.

Yet when he'd returned home just after midnight, it was to find the others already back, and Alicia waiting for him in her bed. Explaining that they'd all wished for an early night, she'd encouraged him to tell her all he'd learned; she'd listened, patently interested, to their plans.

Then he'd joined her under the covers and she'd turned to him, welcomed him into her arms, into her body with her usual open and generous ardor. No hesitation, no holding back. No retreat.

When he'd left this morning, she'd still been asleep. He'd brushed a kiss to her lips and left her dreaming.

Perhaps that was all it was—that the social round, now frenetic, combined with the stress of watching over Adriana, was simply wearying her. God knew, it would weary him. When he'd returned to her last night, there'd been no sign of whatever he'd detected earlier, that slight disjunction that had seemed to exist between them.

He spent another five minutes slowly sipping his ale, then downed the rest in two swallows. He had eight more shipping lines to investigate. The sooner they could bring A. C.'s game to a conclusion, the better for them all.

Tony got back to the Bastion Club just after three o'clock. He was one of the last to return; the others were lounging around the table in the meeting room with Jack Hendon waiting impatiently for his report.

"Please say you've found a line working for Martinsons," Jack demanded before Tony could even pull out a chair.

He sat and tossed his list on the table. "Croxtons in Wapping have, so the manager assures me, an exclusive contract."

"Thank God for that." Jack wrote the name down. "I was beginning to think our plan would go awry. We've identified two shipping lines for Drummond, one from the east, one from the west, reasonable in the circumstances, and four—two in each direction—for Ellicot. Croxton runs ships both east and west, so Martinsons can indeed use them exclusively. Now"—he looked down his list—"all we need is for Gervase to confirm none of the three—Martinsons, Ellicot, or Drummond—use any other line."

But when Gervase came striding in fifteen minutes later, it was with different news. "Tatleys and Hencken both carry goods for Ellicot."

They all looked at him; Gervase slowly raised his brows. "What?"

"You're sure?" Jack asked. When Gervase nodded, he opened his eyes wide. "That's six shippers who carry Ellicot's goods, and two of those lines run ships to both the East and West Indies."

Tony caught Jack's eye. "Is it wise to place any great emphasis on that?"

Jack grimaced. "No, but it's tempting. If you wanted to disguise any pattern in shipping around the dates the prizes were taken, then the use of multiple lines and therefore different ships for each safe cargo brought in would totally obscure any link."

"The most likely people to check any connection would be the Admiralty," Gervase said, "yet their records show only the ships and shipping lines. There's no way to detect a link that exists at the level of cargo."

Tony frowned. "Customs and Revenue have records of the cargoes, but even there, the records are sorted by ports, and different lines use different home ports."

"So," Charles said, "this was an extremely well-set-up scheme. It's only because we used Lloyd's that we've been able to put things together."

"Which leads one to conclude," Christian said, "that the scheme's perpetrator knows the administrative ropes well. He knows how the civil services work and which avenues to block."

"We'll still get him." Jack had been reexamining his list. "We have nine shipping lines—more than I'd like, but seven are small. We now need a list of all the vessels each has registered."

"Can we get that before tonight?" Tony asked.

Jack glanced at the clock on the sideboard, then pushed back his chair. "We can but try."

"I'll help." Gervase rose, too. "I know the business well enough to deal with the intricacies of the registers."

"You two concentrate on getting a list of the ships' names," Tony said. "We'll take care of the rest."

Jack and Gervase left, conferring as they went. The others turned to Tony.

"Once we have the list of ships," he said, "we're going to have to search Lloyd's records. We need to identify which merchant consistently brought in a cargo in, say, the week before a prize was taken. Searching in the weeks before three separate incidents should give us one name and one only. If not, we can look at a fourth incident, but chances are three incidents will give us only one merchant who fits our bill."

The others nodded.

"Once we know the particular merchant involved, we should confirm that in each case they did indeed bring in tea or coffee."

"Can we do all that via Lloyd's?" Charles asked.

"Yes. If Jack and Gervase get the ships' names by this evening, I'll revisit Lloyd's tonight."

"I'll come, too" Charles said. "There's this horrendous ball my sisters want to drag me to—I'd much rather hone my filing skills."

"You can count me in," Jack Warnefleet said. "I've never had to track anyone through such a maze before."

They made arrangements to meet later that night.

Only Tristan demurred. "I'll keep a watch on things in the ballrooms. Having had the good sense to get married I, at least, am safe from the harpies."

Charles grimaced. "Half your luck. I don't know how you managed it so quickly—and now look at Tony. You're both safe. What I want to know is how long *I'm* going to remain dead center in the matchmakers' sights. It's deuced harrowing, I'll have you know."

Both Tony and Tristan made sympathetic noises. The mood of teasing camaraderie disguising their implacable resolve, the meeting broke up and they each headed home.

Tony found Alicia in the garden.

Admitted to the house by Hungerford, he'd slipped upstairs and changed into more normal attire before setting out to search for her.

She was walking alone; Hungerford had told him the boys were in the park—it was a perfect day for kites. It seemed odd to find Alicia by herself; pensive, head down, deep in thought, she slowly, apparently aimlessly, wandered the lawn.

He watched from the terrace—Torrington House was centuries old, the gardens stretching behind it extensive—then went down the steps and set out to join her. She didn't hear him; not wanting to frighten her by suddenly appearing beside her, he called her name.

Halting, she swung around and smiled. She straightened as he neared. "Did you learn anything?"

He would have taken her in his arms and kissed her, but she held out a hand; the swift glance she cast at the house was a warning.

Reluctantly bowing to her wishes, he took her hand and raised it to his lips. Kissed it, then, noting that her smile had faded, an expression he couldn't read taking its place, he tucked her hand in his arm, anchored it with his. He let a frown show in his eyes. "What's wrong?"

She blinked her eyes wide. "Wrong? Why . . . nothing." She frowned lightly back. "Why did you think there was?"

Because . . .

He felt confused, not a normal feeling, not for him. The expression in her eyes assured him she honestly didn't think anything was wrong, yet . . .

She shook his arm and started to stroll again. "*Did* you learn anything? What has Jack been up to—I met Kit at Lady Hartington's luncheon, and she said he was out, too, looking for A. C.'s connections."

He nodded. "We've all been out for most of the day."

He explained. Alicia listened, put a question here and there, and continued to reiterate to herself: *You are his mistress, his lover, not his wife.*

That, she'd decided, was the only sane way forward, to keep their relationship on a fixed and even keel. If she let herself get seduced— emotionally seduced by her emerging dreams—she'd end hurt beyond measure. She'd accepted the position; if she adhered strictly to that role, she and he could continue as they were. That would have to be enough.

If she was forced to make the choice between being his mistress or not being with him at all, she knew which she'd choose. She never wanted to lose him, to forgo those golden moments when they were so close, when each breath, each thought, each desire was shared. If to hold on to that closeness she had to remain his mistress, so be it. It was, she'd decided, worth the price.

The news he had was exciting; they were clearly closing in on A. C. As they discussed their findings, she was conscious of Tony's gaze on her face, black as ever but not so much intent as keen, sharp. Observant.

Finally, she felt forced to meet his eyes and raise her brows in mute question.

He searched her eyes, then looked forward, steering her along a path leading to a fountain. "Given I need to visit Lloyd's tonight, I won't be able to escort you to whatever entertainments you're sched-uled to attend."

She forced herself to smile easily; she patted his arm. "Don't worry—I'm perfectly capable of attending by myself." Even though, in his absence, there was nothing at such events to hold her interest. She didn't even need to watch over Adriana anymore.

She'd learned there were indeed couples, noblemen and their well-born mistresses, of whose relationship the ton was patently aware, but to which it turned a blind eye. Her and Tony's situation wasn't unusual. However, one relevant and undoubtedly important aspect was that those involved in such accepted affairs never drew attention to their relationship in public.

Such couples did not spend time together in ballrooms or drawing rooms; she should undoubtedly grasp this opportunity to ease their interaction into a more socially acceptable vein.

"You find the balls a bore." She looked ahead at the circular foun-tain set in the lawn. "There's no reason you need dance attendance on me there. Not anymore."

She glanced at him. There was a frown gathering in his eyes. She needed to discourage him from acting so overtly possessively. She smiled, trying to soften the hint. "And tonight, you need to be else-where searching for A.C.—there's no need to feel it's necessary to escort me, or that your absence will bother me—that I'll be in any way discomposed."

Her words were gentle, clear, her expression as always open and honest; Tony heard what she said, but wasn't sure he understood. She was explaining something to him, but what?

His brain couldn't seem to function as incisively as usual. The odd feeling in his chest, a deadening, dulling sensation, didn't help. Halting, he drew in a breath, glanced, unseeing, at the fountain. "If you're sure?"

He looked at her face, into her eyes—and saw something very close to relief in the green.

Her smile was genuine, reassuring. "Yes. I'll be perfectly content."

The assurance he'd asked for, yet not what he'd wanted to hear.

A babel of youthful voices spilled down from the terrace; they both looked and saw the three boys and two girls come tumbling down to the lawns.

Turning, they headed toward the children. As they reached the main lawn, Tony felt Alicia's gaze, glanced down, and met her eyes.

Again, she smiled reassuringly, then patted his arm as she looked ahead. "I'll be here, waiting, when you get home."

* * *

He'd accepted the arrangement because he'd had little choice. Yet the suspicion—now hardening to conviction—that something was going awry between them grew, fueled by that part of him that had heard her words as something approaching a dismissal.

A dismissal he'd had neither justification nor opportunity to challenge.

The incident had jolted him in a way he wasn't accustomed to; faced with a raft of unexpected uncertainties, he'd concluded he needed to think before doing anything, before reacting. Yet by one o'clock the next morning, when he silently let himself into his house, his uncertainty had only grown, until he, his usual forceful personality, felt paralyzed.

One thing he'd realized: he didn't have any real idea of what she was thinking, of how she saw their relationship.

He'd told her he loved her; she hadn't reciprocated.

He'd never before said those words to any woman, but in the past he'd been the recipient of such declarations too often for his comfort.

Alicia hadn't said the words. Frowning, he climbed the stairs. Until now, he hadn't thought he needed to hear them; until now, her physical acceptance, all that had passed between them, had been assurrance enough, guarantee enough.

But no more. Now he was uncertain. Of her.

Even though she'd assured him she'd be waiting, he wasn't at all sure what he'd find when he entered her room. But she was indeed there, yet not quite as he'd expected. She wasn't in bed, but standing by the side of the bow window, wrapped in her robe, arms folded beneath her breasts. Shoulder and head resting against the window frame, she looked out on the moonlit gardens.

As usual, she hadn't heard him enter. He made no sound as he closed the door, then stood in the shadows and studied her.

She was deep in thought, her body completely still, her mind elsewhere.

He hesitated, then stepped forward more definitely; she heard him and turned. Through the shadows he saw her gentle smile. She settled back against the window frame. "Did you manage to identify A. C.'s company?"

He halted by the bed. "It's Ellicot."

"The one that used many different shipping lines?"

He nodded; the subject was not the one uppermost in his mind. He eased off his coat. "Tomorrow, we'll start closing in, but we'll need to be careful not to alert A. C. We want him still in England when we learn his name."

He tossed the coat onto a chair, then looked at her. She'd remained at the window, leaning back against the frame, the silk robe draped about her, her arms folded. He sensed she was comfortable, at ease, yet distant.

The bed was behind him; stepping back, he sat on its side. Through the shadows, continued to study her.

He'd manipulated the situation and gained his objective—her, here, under his roof. In his house where he could share her bed easily, where she was protected constantly by his servants. He'd achieved all he'd wanted, all he'd thought they needed, yet . . . something was askew. The situation had developed undercurrents, ones he couldn't read well enough to counter.

She seemed to be drawing back. Not turning away, but sliding from his grasp. Inch by inch, step by tiny step . . .

He needed to hear words, yet he couldn't—didn't know how to—ask for them. Dragging in a short breath, he looked down at his hands, loosely clasped between his thighs. "Perhaps"—keeping his tone ruthlessly even, he looked up—"we should discuss the wedding."

She shook her head—instantly, without the smallest hesitation. "No, not yet. There's no sense making any plans until Geoffrey tells his mother, and they set a date."

He opened his lips to correct her; there was no reason he and she had to wait on Geoffrey and Adriana's arrangements . . .

The realization she'd thought he'd meant Geoffrey and Adriana's wedding, not theirs, burst on him before he uttered a word. It was superseded almost instantly by a blinding insight—the idea of their wedding—that he might be alluding to that—hadn't even occurred to her.

She shifted to stare out of the window once more. "It'll be upon us soon enough, but you needn't worry about the details. I'm sure they'll want to marry in Devon, and that would be wisest . . ." She paused, then softly added, "Considering my deception. A small, private affair would be best . . ."

Alicia let her words trail away. She'd been thinking of the wedding, of Geoffrey and Adriana's growing happiness, and struggling to contain a reaction perilously close to jealousy.

She drew in a slow breath, felt a welling need to rail, not against Geoffrey and Adriana—heaven forbid, she'd worked so hard to bring about her sister's happiness—but against a fate that was so twisted as to make her live through, have to smile through Adriana and Geoffrey's joy while knowing she would never achieve the same. Worse, while knowing she'd willingly and intentionally sacrificed her own chance at such happiness to ensure her sister made the marriage she deserved.

When she'd made the decision to leave behind any thought of marriage and masquerade as a widow, the critical decision from which all else had flowed, she hadn't known what she'd been so ready to turn her back on. Hadn't appreciated her until recently suppressed dreams, hadn't felt their tug.

Now she knew, now she had. Fate was indeed cruel.

Yet among her regrets there was one she didn't have. She didn't regret, couldn't regret, her relationship with Tony. If she couldn't marry him, then she wouldn't marry anyone else, so there was, she'd finally, bitterly, ironically and rather sternly concluded, no point in dwelling on her dreams.

Aside from all else, given his possessiveness, given all she sensed in him, honor notwithstanding, she wasn't at all sure he'd let her go.

Her senses suddenly leapt; she looked up, eyes widening as she found him—as she'd suspected—by her side. Straightening, she faced him.

He met her gaze briefly, searched her face, then his eyes returned to lock on hers. "I'll never let you go."

The words were quiet, steely—infinitely dangerous.

Almost as if he'd been reading her thoughts.

She held his gaze steadily, returned his regard. As always, his black eyes held a measure of heat, yet tonight, she could almost feel the flames. Not simply caressing, languidly artful, but greedily reaching, engulfing, hungry and urgent. Passion fueled them, but tonight there was something else, too, something she couldn't identify— something hotter, more potent, more powerful.

Something that touched her, reached deep, and thrilled her, as nothing had before.

"I know." There was no point in denying the strength of what bound her to him. She held his gaze. "I haven't asked you to."

"Good." The word was guttural in its harshness. His hands closed hard about her waist; she was instantly and shockingly aware of his strength. He pulled her to him, the movement lacking his usual grace. "Don't bother."

That something she couldn't name flared in his eyes.

"You're mine." He bent his head. *"Forever."*

The word was uttered as a vow, with the full force of all he was. Then his lips closed on hers.

He took them, claimed them, then parted them. She offered her mouth, appeasing his demand, ruthless, intent and dominant. His tongue thrust deep, knowing, commanding, then settled to plunder.

Not, as usual, with heated but languid caresses that spun a seductive web, but with unveiled passion, with a driving, ravenous, ruthless desire that stormed her mind and sent her wits careening.

His need hit her, an elemental force that literally shook her to her toes. Before she could react, she felt his hands shift, felt the tug—almost violent—as he jerked the tie of her robe undone. Then his hands, hard and forceful, were at her shoulders, pushing the robe over and down, stripping it away.

He gave her no chance to catch her mental breath. In seconds, the ribbon ties of her chemise were loose, then he pushed the garment down, his hands rough on her skin as he thrust the folds past her hips until they slithered down her legs to the floor.

His hands spread over her naked back and he pulled her fully to him, locked her against him. Angled his head over hers and ravaged her mouth, seizing, taking, ravishing, presaging what was to come.

Hands on his shoulders, fingers sinking into the embroidered silk of his waistcoat, she clung desperately to sanity, held tight as about her the world whirled.

She was naked in his arms, locked against his hard and unquestionably aroused body, her bare skin pressed to his clothes, the steely muscles trapping her screened by fabric. Even in her close-to-witless state, she recognized his clothed state as a deliberate ploy, a sexual taunt expertly aimed. He never cared about his nakedness; him naked she could deal with. Being naked, exposed, disturbed her still, at least beyond the confines of a bed.

He knew it. The way his hands moved over her body, not just possessive but tauntingly so, made that clear. Every touch escalated the tension gripping her, made her even more aware, deepened her feeling of vulnerabilty.

Heightened every sense she possessed until all, every last shred of her awareness, was focused completely on her own body, on what he was doing, on what he made her feel.

His lips held hers trapped as his hard hands moved over her breasts, closing, weighing, kneading, then retreating to play with her tightly budded nipples, causing havoc with nerves already excruciatingly taut. When her breasts were swollen and aching, he moved on, his touch openly hard, demanding, commanding. Not rough, but ruthless, relentless in pushing her on, in demanding and taking from her a surrender beyond all she'd previously given.

She didn't hesitate, didn't draw back. She met his lips, met his ravaging tongue, and let him have his way.

Let him trace her curves as he wished, explore her body as he wanted.

Let him sit on the window seat and lift her over him, let him settle her on her knees straddling his thighs, her own spread wide.

Let him hold her there as he broke from the kiss and trailed hot, burning kisses down her throat. Clinging to his shoulders, she arched her head back, caught her breath as he laved the pulse point at the base of her throat, then moved lower. To the ripe swells of her swollen breasts. To the tight, painful peaks.

He feasted, laving, licking, nibbling, sucking. She slid her fingers into his hair and held tight. Just breathing was a battle, one that only grew worse.

Along with the hot, empty ache deep within her. It welled, swelled, until it seemed to fill her.

Usually, with his hot body pressed to hers, she wasn't so shockingly aware of it. Tonight, held as she was, naked, but with him clothed, her thighs widespread, her body open but unfilled, she felt her own need keenly, clearly, more physically hers, not clouded by his.

Her breasts felt tight, skin hot and burning. He licked one nipple, then rasped it with his tongue; she heard a soft cry, and realized it was hers.

His hands, until then locked about her waist, holding her steady before him, eased; his palms slid down, curved over and around her bottom, then closed, kneading powerfully, evocatively. He continued to tease and taunt her nipples, then releasing her bottom, he ran his cupped hands down the backs of her spread thighs.

Her muscles quivered, then locked; above her knees, his hands swung around and he pushed both hands, lightly gripping, thumbs cruising the sensitive inner faces, up her thighs.

Slowly. Deliberately.

She stopped breathing when, reaching the tops of her thighs, he paused. Then his hands left her.

She sucked in a breath—lost it when he opened his mouth and drew one tortured nipple deep, and suckled. Her shattered cry echoed through the room.

Then she felt his left hand close about her hip, holding her steady once more. His other hand returned to her mons, with a strong, firm stroke brushed over her curls, then reached beyond.

He opened her, explored her, tracing the entrance to her body while he continued to suckle her breasts, first one, then the other, constantly racking the tension that held her tighter. The emptiness inside her expanded, waiting for him to slake it. Nerves flickering, she waited, breath bated, expecting the slow penetration of his fingers, needing his touch, wanting it.

It didn't come.

She was ready to beg when his hand left her. Desperate, she caught her breath on a sob, felt the fingers wrapped about her hip dig in, anchoring her. Releasing her breast, he lifted his head, found her lips—took them. Ravaged them.

Her world teetered, rocked, then she realized on a rush of quivering relief that his other hand was at his waist, flicking the buttons free. He laid the flap of his trousers open. She immediately went to press closer, to sink down and take him in.

His hands gripped her hips, held her still for an instant, poised as he adjusted himself to her. She felt the broad head of his erection touch her, press fractionally in.

Eyes tight shut, her whole body a mass of urgent, heated need, she tried to gasp through the kiss.

He pulled her down onto him. Impaled her.

Her senses shattered.

He was fully aroused, engorged, more rigid unforgiving iron than velvet.

A low moan escaped her; he lifted her and ruthlessly drew her down again. Further, this time, so she took more of him. He thrust deeper, shifted beneath her, then his hands were at her hips, sculpting her legs, lifting them, rearranging them. As he wished. As he wanted.

He didn't ask, didn't order. He lifted her knees and wound her legs about his waist, leaving her helpless with no purchase to move.

Totally in his control, totally at his mercy.

He showed none; for her part, she asked no quarter.

All she wanted was him deep inside her, and he gave her that, as much as she wished, as much as she wanted.

Arms twined about his neck, she clung as he moved her. He set a steady rhythm, hard and deep, the head of his staff nudging her womb. She felt so full of him, as if he was pressing against her heart—and he only drove deeper, sure and true.

He held her to their kiss, tongues tangling, mouths merged.

Held her on his lap, naked and exposed, more vulnerable in the moonlight than she'd ever been.

More his.

All his.

When he finally released her lips and returned his attentions to her breasts, she let her head fall back, eyes closed.

Tensing as he again teased her nipples until they ached, then suckled anew, hard enough to make her fight to swallow a scream.

The next time, she lost the fight.

He was lifting her, working her on him, around him; simultaneously he was feasting at her breasts. She couldn't take much more stimulation, more of the sensations he was ruthlessly pressing on her, heightened, made infinitely more powerful by their position.

She licked her lips, managed to gasp, "Take me to the bed."

He didn't miss a beat. "No. Here. Like this."

His voice, all she could hear in it, very nearly made her weep.

With joy, with a pleasure that was far beyond the physical.

Need—simple, abiding, far deeper than she'd expected.

Never before had he been like this, never before had he dropped all pretense, every last vestige of sophistication, and allowed her to see so far, so clearly, to see that naked need. To know by her own experience so no lingering doubt could remain what truly drove him.

I love you.

She wanted to say the words. They welled in her chest, pushed up through her throat, but she swallowed them. If she told him that . . .

She had no wits left with which to think; instinct was her only guide. So she left the words unsaid, sobbed instead as her body started to convulse.

And he slowed.

Thrust harder, deeper, but slower.

So she felt every tiny slither as her senses unraveled, felt every last fraction of her helplessness as she climaxed more powerfully than she ever had before.

Tony raised his head and watched her, her ivory limbs silvered by the moonlight as she came apart in his arms. He drank in the sight, one he'd needed, one the prowling beast inside him had simply had to have.

Sunk to the hilt in her body, bathed in its scalding heat, he set his jaw and relentlessly drove her through the longest, most extended climax he'd ever forced on any woman. The soft strangled cries that fell from her lips were balm to his raging soul; the ripples of her release, the contractions that beckoned, her body helplessly gripping and releasing his erection, soothed that most primitive side of him.

It would be an easy matter to finish with her there, but that wasn't what he wanted. Tonight he needed more.

He waited until her muscles relaxed, until she was limp, wholly pliant in his arms. Then he lifted her from him, simultaneously stood, and carried her to the bed. He laid her on the coverlet, then stepped back and stripped off his clothes.

Then he joined her.

Propped beside her, he ran a hand down over her back, over the smooth globes of her bottom. Slowly, surely, he roused her again, then positioned her curled over her knees before him. He entered her slowly, eyes closed, savoring every fraction of an inch as her soft, swollen sheath closed about him.

Then he rode her.

Slowly at first, then without restraint.

Until she was sobbing, hair threshing as she struggled for breath, incoherent in her need, totally wild, completely wanton.

She was usually neither; that last rein of restraint she'd not before released had snapped, broken.

He savored every second of her abandonment, of her complete and absolute surrender, listened to her cries as she fell from the peak—then found his own surrender beckoning.

This time he went willingly. He knew, in some dark corner of his mind, just what he'd been doing. Knew it wouldn't work.

Didn't care.

He'd had to do it—to show her all there was, to tempt that side of her he didn't think she realized she possessed. She was a deeply sensual woman, but exploring her sensuality, opening her eyes to its true nature, had only more clearly demonstrated his own weakness, his own vulnerability.

This was one battlefield on which he was helpless. This was one fight in which there was no enemy.

Only surrender.

On a groan, he did, gave her all he was, all he could ever be.

Spent, he collapsed, then gathered her to him. He'd given her far more than his body. He'd lost his soul. And his heart. And perhaps even more.

He left Alicia's side just after dawn, earlier than recent habit but after last night, he wanted nothing more than to have done with A. C.

After last night . . . he had even less idea what was wrong between them. Something, yes, but he'd be damned if he had a clue. If he pushed, twelve hours might result in them unmasking A. C., then he would be free to devote himself to the most important endeavor of his life—wooing Alicia, even winning her anew, if that's what was required.

Frowning, he left his apartments. After last night, he could hardly have missed the fact that she was as he'd hoped, openly, generously, totally his. If that was so, then what else was there? From where did their problem, whatever it was, spring?

Confusion reigned. Reaching Alicia's door, he determinedly put it from him, turned the knob, and entered.

She was still asleep. He sat on the bed and looked down at her, then gently shook her shoulder.

"Hmm?" She opened her eyes; he notched up her lack of surprise when she focused on him as a minor victory.

"I'm off to hunt down A. C. We're breakfasting at the club to work out our best approach. We need to learn who owns Ellicot, then proceed from there, but whatever we do—"

"You have to make sure you don't alert A. C." She was wide-awake now, studying his face, her gaze earnest but watchful.

He hesitated; he wanted to say something about last night, about them, but didn't know what, and couldn't find the words.

"Stay on guard." Squeezing her hand, he rose. "If we stumble and alert him, I'd expect him to run, but . . . he's kept his head until now."

"We'll be careful." She struggled up on her elbows.

"Good." Backing, he raised a hand in farewell. She was naked beneath the covers, now sliding slowly down; he didn't trust himself to kiss her, and stop at just a kiss. Last night had left them both with enough to think about. "I'll be back this evening, if not before."

She nodded. "Take care."

At the door, he glanced back and saw her watching him. He inclined his head, and left.

Closing the door, he turned. David, Harry, and Matthew stood shoulder to shoulder across the corridor staring unblinkingly up at him.

"I was just telling Alicia where I'd be today."

"Oh." David considered his reply to their unspoken question, then nodded and turned to the stairs. "Are you going down to breakfast?"

Harry and Matthew swung around and followed.

Drawing a relieved breath, Tony fell in in their wake. "No—I have to go out straightaway."

Reaching the stairs, David and Harry clattered down.

Matthew stopped and turned to him. "Are you going to marry Alicia?"

Tony looked down into the big eyes fixed innocently on his face. "Yes. Of course."

The other boys had stopped halfway down to listen; now they whooped joyously, and thundered on down.

Matthew simply smiled. "Good." He took Tony's hand and, with simple gravity, accompanied him down the stairs.

Two hours later, Alicia strolled the lawns in the park, alone but for Maggs, tactfully keeping watch from a distance.

All about her was quiet and serene. It was too early for the fashionable throng; a few latecomers were still exercising their horses on Rotten Row, but most riders had already clattered home while the matrons and their daughters had yet to arrive.

The solitude and fresh air were precisely what she craved.

After the door had closed behind Tony, she'd lain in bed for ten minutes before the insistent refrain playing in her brain had prodded her into action. Ringing for Bertha, she'd washed, dressed, and joined Miranda and Adriana in the breakfast parlor.

Miranda and Adriana had been busy organizing their morning's engagements; she'd excused herself on the grounds of a slight headache and her need for a quiet walk to refresh herself. Accepting her excuse, the other two had left to get ready to visit Lady Carlisle; she'd climbed to the schoolroom and checked on her brothers, then quit the house, Maggs at her heels as per his "master's orders."

She'd accepted his escort with equanimity; she'd grown quite fond of the unprepossessing man. Interpreting his orders to watch over her literally, he'd retreated to stand beneath a large tree, now some distance away, leaving her to her thoughts.

Which were what she'd come to the park to confront.

It—her present tack—wasn't going to work. She'd thought her best way forward was to adhere strictly to her position as Tony's mistress and not wish for more, to rein in her dreams and accept what she'd been given, what he'd freely offered. But that view was fatally flawed—last night had proved it, had illustrated the truth beyond doubt.

The connection between them, so much more, so much stronger than any mere physical link, was not compatible with, would not remain constrained within, the bounds of the relationship of a nobleman and his mistress. Their connection was a vital thing, a living force in and of itself; it was growing, burgeoning, already demanding more.

Last night, she'd nearly told him she loved him, had had to fight to swallow the words. Some night soon she'd lose that fight. One way or another, the truth would out—*in toto*, there was more to it, more depths, more aspects than even that powerful fact.

She might already be carrying his child; it was too early to know, yet the possibility existed. In the beginning, she'd assumed he'd know what to do, would take precautions, yet he hadn't, nor had he expected her to. If she'd been shocked by her wanton behavior last night, her reaction to the idea of bearing Tony's child had only confirmed how little attention she'd paid her to her latent hopes, aspirations, and dreams. Until now.

In her heart, and now very clearly in her mind, she knew what she wanted. The question facing her was how to get it; leaving matters as they were was, she now accepted, no longer an option.

Drawing in a breath, she lifted her head and looked unseeing at some distant trees. She'd taken serious risks to secure Adriana's and her brothers' futures, boldly gambled and won. It was time to act in pursuit of her own future—to realize the dreams she'd never allowed herself to dream but which Tony had brought alive.

She would speak with him. She felt her chin set. Just as soon as A.C. was in custody, she would talk to Tony, explain how she felt about them, about their future. How he would react was the risk, the unknown, yet . . . she had his declaration of love to lean on, and, indeed, more. Their connection itself; through it she sensed how he felt, his need, even if he didn't consciously acknowledge it. In time, he would recognize the truth as she had, and reassess as she had, and adjust.

Grimacing, she looked down. She would be gambling that their love truly was as she saw it—a huge risk, yet one she felt compelled to take.

The thud of footsteps approaching over the grass reached her. Looking up, she saw a footman in plain black livery striding purposefully her way.

Glancing to the left, she saw Maggs, leaning against the tree trunk, come alert, but as the footman halted and bowed, Maggs relaxed and resumed his unobtrusive watch.

"For you, ma'am."

The footman proffered a note. She took it, opened it, read it, and inwardly cursed. Chickens were coming home to roost thick and fast. Sir Freddie Caudel most formally and politely requested an interview.

She looked across the lawn to the black carriage drawn up on the gravel drive. With a sigh, she tucked the note into her reticule. "Very well."

The footman bowed and escorted her to the carriage. Maggs, closer to the carriage than she, remained where he was, half-obscured by the tree.

Reaching the carriage, the footman opened the door and stood back, clearly expecting her to enter. Puzzled, she looked in, and saw Sir Freddie, dapper and urbanely elegant as usual, sitting inside.

Smiling easily, he half rose and bowed. "My dear, I hope you'll forgive this unusual approach, but for reasons that will become clear as we talk, I wished to speak with you in the strictest privacy. If you will do me the honor of sharing my carriage, I thought we might roll around the Avenue—it's quite peaceful at the moment—and conduct our discussion in relative comfort, out of sight of prying eyes." He smiled, his pale gaze somewhat rueful, gently humorous, and held out his hand. "If you would, my dear?"

Inwardly sighing, she gave him her hand; gathering her skirts, she climbed into the carriage. Sir Freddie released her and she sat opposite him, facing forward. Sir Freddie nodded to his footman. The man shut the door; an instant later, the carriage started slowly rolling.

"Now." Sir Freddie fixed her with a calmly superior smile. "You must let me apologize for this little charade. I'm sure you understand that, given the nature of my interest and thus the reason behind my request for an interview, there would be nothing more unappealing to me than in any way whatever giving the gossipmongers reason to wag their tongues."

Alicia inclined her head; from her experience, now extensive, of Sir Freddie's circumlocutory periods, she knew it was pointless to try to rush him. He would get to his peroration in his own good time. Nevertheless . . . "Now we are here, you perceive me all ears, sir."

"Indeed." Sir Freddie returned her nod. "I should also explain that I did not think it appropriate, in the circumstances, to call at Torrington House." He held up a hand as if to stem a protest she hadn't made. "I'm quite sure I would be treated with all due consideration, indeed graciousness, however, I am aware that Manningham is an old and valued friend of Torrington's." Sir Freddie paused, as if weighing that fact anew. Eventually, he said, "Suffice to say I deemed it impolitic to call on you there."

Again, she inclined her head and wondered how long he would take to come to the point. Given that point—his offer for Adriana's hand—she turned her mind to finding the words with which to refuse him.

Sir Freddie rambled on and on; his voice, polished, light, his accents refined, was easy on the ear. Smoothly, he described his current position, his reasons for looking for a wife, then moved on to Adriana's manifold charms.

The carriage suddenly rocked, the wheel dipping in a pothole; mildly surprised that such a thing existed on the fashionable carriageway, Alicia refocused on Sir Freddie's eloquence, and discovered he was still describing, in phrases both flowery and convoluted, just what it was about her sister that had attracted his notice.

Counseling patience, she folded her hands in her lap, and waited. Her mind slid away . . . she imagined Maggs, under his tree, watching the carriage go around and around the park . . .

Instinct flickered. The carriage blinds had been drawn from the first, she'd assumed to prevent the interested seeing Sir Freddie speaking with her. The carriage rocked again; the blinds swayed—and she caught a glimpse of what lay outside.

It wasn't the park.

She looked at Sir Freddie as the sounds outside registered. They were traveling down some major road, not one lined with trees, not even with shops, but with houses—a road that led not into the city, but out of it.

Her shock, her realization, showed in her face.

Something changed in Sir Freddie's expression, as if a thin, obscuring veil was drawn aside; abruptly she realized that he was watching her closely, a coldly calculating look in his eyes.

He smiled. Before the gesture had been urbanely charming; now it chilled.

"Ah—I did wonder how long it would take." His voice, too, had subtly changed, all pleasantness leaching from it. "However, before you think of making any heroic attempt to escape, I suggest you listen to what I have to say."

His eyes held hers, and they were colder than a snake's. Alicia sat transfixed, her thoughts tumbling, churning. "Escape" implied . . .

"The most important thing you need to bear in mind is that there's another carriage ahead of us on this road. It contains two rather rough men—I wouldn't distinguish them with the title of gentleman—in company with your youngest brother. Matthew, as I'm sure you know, has a habit of slipping outside when he grows bored with his lessons. He did so, with a little encouragement I admit, this morning, just after you'd left the house. He's an enterprising young chap, quite capable of evading all supervision when he chooses." Sir Freddie smiled. "But I'm sure you know that."

Alicia's heart lurched; the blood drained from her face. She did know of Matthew's occasional excursions—just to the area between the house and the street to watch the world rumble by—but since they'd moved to Torrington House, she'd thought they'd stopped. "What do you want with Matthew?"

Sir Freddie's brows rose. "Why nothing, my dear—nothing at all. He's merely a pawn to ensure *you* behave as I wish." His gaze hardened. "If you do as I say, no harm will come to him. Those two men I spoke of have strict orders, ones it's to their advantage to obey. They'll take your brother to a safe place, and wait with him there for word from me. Depending on how matters transpire, I will instruct them either to return him to Upper Brook Street unharmed"—his lips curved lightly, tauntingly, "or to kill him."

He held her gaze. "The instruction I send will depend on you."

Alicia fought to met his gaze levelly, to keep her expression impassive, to keep her fear, her panic, at bay. Icy chills ran up and down her spine. *Matthew* . . . a vise squeezed her heart even as, instinctive and immediate, she searched for the means to free him. Maggs—he would fetch Tony . . . she couldn't work out the how and when, not with Sir Freddie's cold and sharply observant eyes on her.

She licked her lips, forced her lungs to work. "What do you want me to do?" She frowned. "What *is* this all about?" Why kidnap her and Matthew if it was Adriana Sir Freddie wanted?

She allowed her confusion and total incomprehension to show in her face.

Sir Freddie laughed.

The sound chilled her to the marrow.

Then he smiled, and she wanted nothing more than to flee. "This, my dear, is about me covering my tracks, an unfortunate necessity brought on by Ruskin. He couldn't seem to understand that the war was over and the easy pickings with it."

She stared at him. "*You're* A. C?"

"A. C?" Sir Freddie blinked, then his face cleared. "Ah, yes, I'd almost forgotten."

He shifted. With a graceful sweep of his arm, he bowed, the gesture full of his customary elegant charm. Face, lips lightly curved, and manner were all one, but as he straightened, his cold, pale eyes met hers. "Sir Alfred Caudel, my dear, at your service."

Tony returned to Torrington House midmorning. After reviewing their information, the group had agreed that Jack Warnefleet and Christian, neither of whom had been visible thus far in the affair, should visit Ellicot's offices and extract by whatever means they could some idea of who was behind the company.

There was a limit to how unsubtle they could be; there was no guarantee of a quick and favorable outcome. Restless, impatient, sensing matters were nearing a head but with nothing he could reasonably do, Tony had returned home.

He'd only just settled behind his desk when the study door burst open and panic—carried by David, Harry, Matthew, and Jenkins— rushed in.

"*Alicia!*" Matthew shrieked. "You've got to go and save her."

Tony caught him as he charged around the desk and flung himself at him. "Yes, of course," he replied, his gaze locking on the others.

David and Harry had rushed to the desk, gripping the front edge, their expressions as horrified as Matthew's. Jenkins, close on their heels, was not much better, and out of breath as well.

"My lord," Jenkins puffed, "Maggs sent us to tell you—Mrs. Carrington was inveigled into a carriage which then took off to the west."

Tony swore, started to rise. "Where's Maggs?"

Jenkins struggled for breath. "He's following the carriage. He said he'd send word as he can."

Tony nodded curtly. "Sit down." Lifting Matthew into his arms, he turned his attention to the older boys. "Now, David—tell me what you know, from the beginning."

David dragged in a huge breath, held it for a second, then complied. The story came out in reasonable order: Alicia visiting the schoolroom, mentioning she was going for a walk—Tony had imagined her out with Miranda and Adriana—the boys then prevailing on

Jenkins to take their nature lesson in the park; they'd arrived to find Maggs running toward them, swearing and cursing, watching a black carriage that had passed the boys turn out of the park and roll away to the west. Maggs had pounced on them, given them the message, hailed a hackney, and set off after the carriage.

"All right." Tony felt none of their panic; he'd spent the last decade dealing with similarly fraught situations. He welcomed, even relished what he recognized as the call to arms; he couldn't yet see how it related, but he knew a bugle when he heard it. "Did Maggs say who was in the carriage?"

The boys shook their heads. So did Jenkins. "I don't think he saw who it was, my lord."

"It was Sir Freddie someone's carriage." The mumbled words, spoken around a thumb, came from Matthew.

Tony glanced at him, then sat him on the desk so he could see his face. He pulled up his chair and sat, too, so he wasn't towering over the boy. "How do you know that?"

Matthew took his thumb out of his mouth. "Horses. This time, he had four, but the front two were the ones that always pull his carriage. I know them from when he came to call at the other house."

Tony wondered how much reliance to place on a small boy's observations. He felt a tug on his sleeve and looked into Harry's face.

"Matthew notices things—and he really does know horses."

Tony looked at David, who nodded, then at Jenkins, recovering in a chair. Jenkins nodded, too. "He's very good about details, my lord. Excellent memory."

Tony paused, then swallowed the curse that rose to his lips. Rising, he turned to the bookshelves behind the desk, scanned, then pulled out his copy of *Debrett's*.

A tap fell on the door, then it opened. Geoffrey Manningham strolled in. Across the room, Tony met his gaze.

Instantly, Geoffrey came alert. "What? What's happened?"

"Caudel has kidnapped Alicia." Tony opened the book, swiftly flicking pages. He found the entry for Caudel. He read it, and swore beneath his breath. "Sir *Alfred* Caudel."

He slammed the book shut. "A.C. Currently with the Home Office. From an old if not ancient family, his principal estate is in north Oxfordshire, near Chipping Norton, not far from the tavern where those letters from the French captains were sent."

Geoffrey's mouth had fallen open; he snapped it shut. "*Caudel?* Good God—no wonder he's so desperate to scotch the investigation."

"Indeed, and no wonder he knew so much about the investigation itself." Standing behind the desk, fingers lightly drumming, Tony rapidly assembled a plan, checking and re-checking, mentally listing all the necessary orders. He glanced at the three boys, spared them a reassuring smile. "I'll go after them."

Geoffrey frowned. "You know where they've gone?"

"Maggs has them in his sights—he'll send word as soon as he passes a hostelery." Tony spoke to the boys. "Maggs knows what to do—he won't stop following Alicia. I'll head out as soon as I know which road—Maggs and I have a system we've used before. It'll work, so don't worry that we'll lose the trail." He looked at Geoffrey. "I need you to get word to the others, and then wait here with Adriana, Miranda, and the rest—no need for vapors, I'll bring Alicia back."

Geoffrey nodded. "Right. Who do you want me to get hold of?"

Tony gave him a list. Dalziel first; Tony wrote a short note summarizing the evidence that Sir Freddie was A.C. He handed it to Geoffrey. "Give that to Dalziel—into his hand, don't show it to anyone else. Use my name, that'll get you through his pickets. Then go to Hendon House and tell Jack, then to the club, and tell the majordomo, Gasthorpe. Tell him the others—Deverell's out of town but the other five—all need to know."

While he'd talked, he'd risen and tugged the bellpull. Hungerford appeared; Tony ordered his curricle brought around with the bays put to. Without comment, Hungerford left.

Almost immediately he returned. "A message from Maggs, my lord, brought by an ostler from Hounslow. Maggs says it's the Basingstoke road."

Having assimilated the fact that Sir Freddie was A.C., which he verified beyond doubt by telling her the details of how his scheme had operated, and of how he'd worked since Ruskin's death to turn all blame on her, Alicia still didn't know the answer to her question. She fixed Sir Freddie with a steady gaze. "What do you plan to do now? What do you want me to do?"

"At the moment, nothing." Reaching out, he lifted a window flap, glanced out, then let the flap fall and looked back at her. "We'll be journeying through the night. When we stop to change horses, you'll remain in the carriage, calm and composed. At no time will you do anything to attract attention. You won't forget that your brother's future lies in your hands, so you will do exactly as I say at all times."

She debated telling him that Tony and his friends knew about Ellicot, but decided to hold her fire, at least until she knew more. "Where are we going?" Through the night suggested deep into the country.

Sir Freddie studied her, then shrugged. "I don't suppose it will hurt to tell you." His tone was cold, unemotional. "Given how forthcoming I've been, I'm sure you've realized by now that this last and, I fancy, winning throw of the dice involves your demise."

She had, but refused to let it panic her. She raised a brow, faintly haughty. "You're going to kill me?"

He smiled his chilling smile. "Most regretfully, I assure you. But before you waste breath trying to tell me such an act won't get me anywhere, let me explain how things will appear once you're no longer about to state your case.

"First, I'm aware of the activities of Torrington and his friends. They really are quite tediously tenacious. Ellicot was an obvious liability—he, naturally, is no longer with us. His family, however, are most likely aware that he had a sleeping partner, so I took care to remove all evidence of my association with him . . . and replaced it with evidence of *your* association with him.

"When Torrington and his friends look, they'll find a circle of evidence that leads them back to you—where their attention should have stayed all along. I'm sure they won't be happy about it, but they won't have any choice in laying the blame at your door. I've become quite adept at bending society and the upper echelons to my bidding; there'll be such irritation that you've escaped, your guilt will be established by default.

"Naturally, you won't be there to answer the charges, which will only reinforce them. Your disappearance will be seen as an admission of guilt, one your supporters will be at a loss to counter. When your body is eventually found, as I'll ensure it is, everyone will conclude that, weighed down with remorse, with the investigation closing in—something you would know with Torrington as your lover—with social disaster of ever-greater proportions looming over you and your precious family . . . well, you took the only honorable way out for a lady."

She let contempt infuse her voice. "You said you know of Torrington and his friends and how tenacious they are. My death won't convince them—it won't stop their investigation, it'll intensify it." She was perfectly certain of that.

Sir Freddie, however, smiled, coldly condescending. "The key is Torrington, and how he'll react to finding your dead body."

She couldn't stop her lashes from flickering.

Sir Freddie saw; his smile deepened. "He's in love with you, not just a passing fancy, I fear, but well and truly caught. What do you think it will do to him to be the one to discover you dead?"

She refused to react, to give him any indication of what she thought; the arrogant fool had just said the one thing above all others guaranteed to make her fight to the last.

"With you gone and nothing left to save, Torrington will retire to deepest Devon. The others won't be able to sustain the investigation without him." He paused, then added, "And that, my dear, will finally be the end of the story."

She drew breath, but didn't challenge him; there had to be some way to scuttle his plans. She kept her mind focused on that, refusing even to think of defeat. Defeat meant death, and she definitely wasn't ready to die.

Leaning her head against the squabs, she went over his plan. He was right in predicting she would do nothing to put Matthew at risk, but the risk came from Sir Freddie. He'd said his men would hold Matthew *until* they heard from him; if they didn't . . . there'd be time to find them and free Matthew unharmed.

She needed to escape and simultaneously take Sir Freddie captive, ensuring he could send no message. Once they'd turned the tables, Sir Freddie would tell them where Matthew was held . . . she needed Tony for that, but . . .

In her heart, she was sure he'd come for her. Maggs had been watching; he'd probably realized she'd been kidnapped before she had. Maggs would get word to Tony, and Tony would come. However, she couldn't rely on Tony catching up with her before Sir Freddie tried to kill her.

She looked across the carriage. Sir Freddie's eyes were closed, but she didn't think he was asleep. He was some years older than Tony, a few inches shorter, but of heavier build. Indeed, he'd be described as a fine figure of a man, still in his prime; he'd never looked out of place in Adriana's court.

Physically, she couldn't hope to win any tussle, yet if Sir Freddie had any weakness, it was his overweening conceit. He believed he'd get away with everything. If she played to that belief, there might be one moment, almost at the end of the game, when he might be vulnerable. . . .

It would likely be her only chance.

She saw a glint from beneath his lashes; he'd been watching her studying him. "You didn't say where we're going."

He was silent, clearly weighing the risk, then he said, "Exmoor. There's a tiny village I was once stranded in. The evidence will suggest you stopped there, then wandered out onto the moor, threw yourself down a disused mine shaft, and drowned."

Exmoor. Closing her eyes, leaning her head back again, she focused on that. An isolated moor. They'd have to walk to any mine . . . the coachman would have to stay with the horses . . .

As the day rolled into evening, she behaved precisely as Sir Freddie wished. She considered pretending to fall apart, weeping and despairing, but she wasn't that good an actress, and if Sir Freddie suspected she wasn't resigned to her fate . . . instead, she behaved as she imagined a French duchess would have on her way to the guillotine. Head high, haughtily superior, yet with no hint of any struggle against an overwhelming fate.

He had to believe she'd accepted it, that she'd go haughtily but quietly to her death. Given his background, that was very likely the behavior he'd expect of her, a lady of his class.

The farther they traveled, stopping at inn after inn to change horses, the more evidence she detected of his natural conceit overcoming his caution. He even allowed her to use the convenience at an inn, although she had no chance to speak to anyone, and he remained within sight of the door at all times.

Night fell; four horses pulled the coach steadily on. Closing her eyes, feigning sleep, she felt her nerves tensing and tried to relax. Exmoor, he'd said, and Exeter was still some way ahead; it would be hours yet before she got her chance. Her one chance at the life she now knew beyond doubt she wanted. The life she was prepared to fight for, the life she was determined to have.

Not as Tony's mistress, but as his wife. As his viscountess, the mother of his heir, and other children, too. She had far too much to live for to die.

And she knew he loved her; not only had he said so, but he'd shown her. If she'd had any doubt over what his feelings truly were, the picture Sir Freddie had painted, the question he'd asked: how would Tony react to finding her dead? had blown all such doubts away.

Devastated was too small a word—she knew precisely how he would feel because it was the same way she'd feel in the converse circumstance.

They loved each other, equally completely, equally deeply; she no longer questioned that. Once they were past this, free of Sir Freddie and his deadly scheme, she would speak with Tony. He might not yet see things as she did, but she was perfectly marriageable, after all. He'd established her as his equal in the eyes of the ton; if his mother was anything like Lady Amery and the Duchess of St. Ives, she doubted she'd have any difficulties there.

She wanted to marry him, and if that meant she had to broach the subject herself, then she would. Brazenly. After last night, she could be brazen about anything, at least with him.

The prospect—her future as she would have it with Tony by her side—filled her mind. Joy welled; fear hovered that it would not come to be, but she shunned it, clung to the joy instead.

Held to the vision of a happy future. Let it strengthen her. Her determination to make it happen—that it would be—soared.

Unexpectedly, she slept.

The noisy rattle of the wheels hitting cobblestones jerked Alicia from her doze. It was deepest night, past midnight; she'd heard the sound of a bell tolling twelve as they'd passed through Exeter, now some way behind.

Sir Freddie had fastened back one of the window flaps. Through the window, she glimpsed a hedgerow; beyond it, the ground rose, desolate and empty. The coach slowed, then halted.

"Well, my dear, we're here." Through the gloom, Sir Freddie watched her. Holding to her resolve, she didn't react.

He hesitated, then leaned past her, opened the door, and climbed down. He turned and gave her his hand; she allowed him to assist her to the cobbles, leaving her cloak on the seat. When the time came to run, she didn't want its folds flapping about her legs. Her skirts would be bad enough.

She'd slipped the cloak off sometime before; Sir Freddie didn't seem to notice—there was no reason he should care. He'd stepped forward to speak to the coachman; she strained her ears and caught the words she'd hoped to hear.

"Wait here until I return."

When she'd first emerged from the coach at an inn, there'd been no footman; she assumed he'd been set down in London. The coachman had avoided her eye; she knew better than to expect help from that quarter. All she needed was for the man to wait until his master returned. If things went her way, his master wouldn't return, not before she did and raised help from the cottages she could see just ahead, lining the road.

Sir Freddie turned to her. Again, he studied her; as she had all along, she met his gaze stonily.

He inclined his head. "Your composure does you credit, my dear. I really do regret putting an end to your life."

She didn't deign to answer. Sir Freddie's lips quirked; with a wave, he indicated a path leading from the narrow road. Within yards of the hedge, the path plunged into a dark wood; beyond, the moors rose, alternately illuminated, then shrouded in gloomy shadow as clouds passed over the moon.

"We have to walk through the wood to reach the moors and the mine."

Sir Freddie reached for her arm, but she forestalled him and turned, and calmly walked to the opening of the path.

Tony swore; hauling on the reins, he swung the latest pair he'd had harnessed in Exeter onto the road to Hatherleigh.

Why here, for heaven's sake? Was it the isolation?

He'd had hours to consider what Sir Freddie was about while following his path across the country. It had been decades since he'd driven at breakneck speed—he'd been pleased to discover he hadn't forgotten how—but even the exigencies of managing unfamiliar cattle hadn't stopped him from thinking first and foremost of Alicia, of the danger facing her.

Up behind him, Maggs was hanging on grimly, every now and then muttering imprecations under his breath. Tony ignored him. He'd caught up with Maggs at Yeovil; before then, whenever Maggs had stopped to change horses he'd sent a rider wearing a red kerchief back along the road. Tony had stopped each flagged rider, and thus known which road to follow.

As it happened, it was a road he knew well—the same road he'd traveled countless times between Torrington Chase and London. The familiarity had helped; he'd have missed their turning to Hatherleigh if he hadn't known to ask at Okehampton.

Sir Freddie taking Alicia so far from London had been a boon initially, giving him time to catch up. Even though Sir Freddie had been rocketing along, always using four fresh horses, Tony knew he was close on their heels.

While they were traveling, he had no fears for Alicia. Once they stopped . . .

His experience lay in pursuing someone he needed to catch, not save. Every time he thought of Alicia, his heart lurched, his mind stilled, paralyzed; shutting off such thoughts, he concentrated on Sir Freddie instead.

Why this route? Was Sir Freddie intending to drive through to the Bristol Channel and rendezvous with some lugger? Was Alicia a hostage? Or was she intended as the scapegoat Sir Freddie had from the first sought to make her?

That was Tony's blackest fear. The landscape, the desolate sweep of the moors rising up on either side of the road fed it. If Sir Freddie intended to stage Alicia's murder and make it appear a suicide, and thus quash the investigation . . .

Tony set his jaw. Once he got hold of her, he was taking her to Torrington Chase and keeping her there. Forever.

Sending the whip swinging to flick the leader's ear, he drove the horses on.

Twenty-one

❧❦❧

Alicia emerged onto the moor with a sense of relief; the wood had been dark, the trees very old, the path uneven and knotted with their roots. Here, at least, she could breathe—dragging in a breath, she looked up, tracing the path they were following to where it skirted a pile of rocks and earth, the workings of the disused mine in which Sir Freddie planned to drown her.

Every nerve taut and alert, she kept walking, head high, her pace neither too fast nor yet slow enough to prompt Sir Freddie to hurry her. Scanning the area, she searched—for a rock, a branch, anything she could use to overpower him. Closer to the mine would be preferable, yet the closer they got . . .

She was supremely conscious of him walking steadily at her heels. He seemed relaxed, just a murderer out to arrange another death. Quelling a shudder, she looked again at the mine. The path rose steadily, steeper as it led up the shoulder of the workings before leveling off as it skirted the lip of the shaft itself.

The clouds were constantly shifting, drifting; there was always enough light to see their way, but when the moon shone clear, details leapt out.

Like the discarded spar she glimpsed, just fleetingly, to the right of the steepest section of the path.

Her heart leapt; her muscles tensed, ready . . .

Quickly, she thought through what would need to happen. She had to distract Sir Freddie at just the right spot. She'd already decided how, but she needed to set the stage.

Reaching the spot where the steep upward slope commenced, she halted abruptly. Swinging to face Sir Freddie, she found the slope was sufficient for her to meet his gaze levelly. "Do I have your word as a gentleman that my brother won't be harmed? That he'll be released as soon as possible in Upper Brook Street?"

Sir Freddie met her eyes; his lips twisted as, nodding, he looked down. "Of course." After a fractional pause, he added, "You have my word."

She had lived with three males long enough to instantly detect pre-varication. Lips thinning, she narrowed her eyes, then tersely asked, "You haven't really got him, have you? There is no second carriage."

She'd wondered, but hadn't dared call his bluff or even question him while trapped in the carriage.

He looked up, raised his brows. Faintly shrugged. "I saw no reason to bother with your brother. I knew the threat alone would be enough to get you to behave."

The relief that surged through her nearly brought her to her knees. The weight on her shoulders evaporated. She was *free*—free to deal with Sir Freddie as she wished, with only her own life at stake. A life she was willing to risk to secure her future—what choice did she have? She fought to keep any hint of her upwelling resolve from her face. She glared at Sir Freddie, then swung on her heel and walked on.

Trusting to his overweening confidence to keep him from wonder-ing at her continued acquiescence for just a few steps more . . .

From behind, she heard a faint chuckle, then his footsteps as he followed. Up ahead to her right lay the wooden spar. Just a *little* far-ther; she needed the greater steepness, the change in their relative heights . . .

Again she stopped dead, swung to face him.

At the last second let her contempt show. "You *bastard*!"

She slapped him. With the full force of her arm as she delivered the blow, with him lower than she, his face at the right height to take the full brunt of her momentum.

He had no chance to duck; the blow landed perfectly. Her palm stung; he staggered.

She didn't pause but turned and raced, scrambling up the few steps to the spar. She heard him swear foully, heard his boots scrabble on the path. Bending, she locked both hands on the spar, hefted it, and swung around. Driven by resolution laced with very real fear, she put every ounce of strength she possessed behind her swing.

He didn't see it coming.

She wielded the spar like a rounders bat. He was still lower on the path than she; the spar hit him across the side of the head.

The spar cracked, broke, fell from her hands.

He slumped to his knees, groggy, dazed, but not unconscious. He weaved. Desperate, she glanced around.

There were no other spars.

She grabbed up her skirts, stepped around him, and ran. Fled like a fury down the path, leaping down from the workings and streaking across the moor to plunge into the dark wood.

Chest heaving, she forced herself to slow. The roots were treacherous; she couldn't afford to fall. If she could get to the cottages and raise the alarm, she'd be safe. She didn't even have to worry about Matthew anymore.

From behind her came a roar; the thud of heavy footsteps reached her, rapidly gaining.

Fighting down panic, she kept her eyes down, locked on the path, feet dancing over the tree roots—

She ran into a black wall.

She shrieked, then stilled as the familiar scent, the familiar feel of Tony's body against hers, of his arms wrapping about her sank into her senses. She nearly fainted with relief.

He was looking beyond her, over her head. "Where is he?"

His words were a lethal whisper.

"On the path leading up to a disused mine."

He nodded. "I know it. Stay here."

With that he was gone. He moved so swiftly, so silently, surefooted in the darkness, that by the time, dazed, she turned, she'd nearly lost him.

She followed, but carefully, as quiet as he. She'd expected him to wait in the shadows and let Sir Freddie blunder into him as she had, but instead, he paused, waited until Sir Freddie was nearly to the trees, then calmly, determinedly, walked out of the wood.

Sir Freddie saw him. Pure horror crossed his face. He skidded to a halt, turned, and fled.

Back up the path.

Tony was at his heels almost immediately. Following as fast as her skirts would allow, she could see that he could have overhauled Sir Freddie anywhere along the upward slope. Instead, he waited until Sir Freddie gained the level stretch beside the gaping mine shaft before he reached out, spun Sir Freddie around, and plowed his fist into his face.

She heard the sickening thud all the way down the path where she was laboring upward. The first thud was followed by more; she couldn't see either man but felt sure Sir Freddie was on the receiving end. She hoped every blow hurt as badly as they sounded. Gaining the level stretch, she looked, just in time to see Tony slam his fist into Sir Freddie's jaw.

Something cracked. Sir Freddie fell back, onto a pile of rubble. He slumped, winded, but quick as a flash he grabbed a rock and flung it at Tony's head.

She screamed, but Tony hadn't taken his eye from Sir Freddie. He ducked the missile, then, lips curling in a snarl, bent, grabbed Sir Freddie, hauled him to his feet, punched him once in the face, grabbed him again, shook him—and flung him backward into the mine shaft.

There was a huge splash; water sprayed out.

Tony stood where he was, chest heaving until he'd regained his breath, then he stepped forward and looked down just as Alicia joined him.

She cast one brief look at Sir Freddie, spluttering, desperately searching for handholds on the slippery shaft wall, then looked at him. Reached out with both hands and touched him. "Are you all right?"

He looked into her eyes, searched her face—saw she was far more concerned for his well-being than hers—and felt something inside him give. "Yes." He briefly closed his eyes. If she was all right, he was, too.

Opening his eyes, he reached for her, drew her to him. Wrapped her in his arms and gloried in the reality of her warmth against him. Cheek against the silk of her hair, he sent a heartfelt thank-you to fate and the gods, then, easing his hold on her, looked down at Sir Freddie, fighting to hold his head above the dank water. "What do you want to do with him?"

She looked down. Her eyes narrowed. "He told me he'd killed Ellicot, and he was going to kill me. I say we let him drown—poetic justice."

"No!" The protest dissolved into a gurgle as Sir Freddie's terror made his fingers slip. "No," came again as he scrabbled back to the surface. "Torrington," he gasped, "you can't leave me here. What will you tell your masters?"

Tony looked down at him. "That you'd sunk before I reached you?"

Folding her arms, Alicia scowled. "I say we leave him—a hemlocklike taste of his own medicine."

"Hmm." Tony glanced at her. "How about a trial for treason and murder?"

"Trials and executions cost money. Much better just to leave him to drown. We know he's guilty, and just think—*who* forced him to come here from London? Did *I* make him spin me a tale about kidnapping Matthew?"

Tony stiffened. "He told you that?"

Lips tight, she nodded. "And just think of all the brave sailors he's sent to watery graves! He's a disgusting and debauched worm." She tugged Tony's arm. "Come on—let's go."

She didn't mean it, but she was more than furious with Sir Freddie, and saw no reason not to torture him.

"Wait! Please . . ." Sir Freddie coughed water. "I know someone else."

Tony stilled, then, releasing her, he stepped closer to the edge and crouched down to peer at Sir Freddie. "What did you say?"

"Someone else." Sir Freddie was breathing shallowly; the water in the shaft would be freezing. "Another traitor."

"Who?"

"Get me out of here, and we can talk."

Tony rose; stepping back, he drew Alicia to him, pressed a kiss to her temple, whispered, "Play along." More loudly, he said, "You're right, let's just leave him." His arm around her, he turned them away.

"No!" Spluttering curses floated out of the shaft. "Damm it—I'm not making this up. There *is* someone else."

"Don't listen," Alicia advised. "He's always making things up—just think of his tale about Matthew."

"That was for a reason!"

She glanced over the edge. "And saving your life isn't a reason? Huh!" She stepped back. "Come on, I'm getting cold."

They started walking, taking tiny steps so Sir Freddie could hear.

"*Wait!* All right, damm it—it's someone in the Foreign Office. I don't know who—I tried to find out, but he's wilier than I. He's very careful, and he's someone very senior."

Tony sighed; he moved back to crouch at the edge. "Keep talking. I'm listening, but she's not convinced."

In gasps and pants, Sir Freddie talked, answering Tony's questions, revealing how he'd stumbled on the other traitor's trail. Eventually, Tony rose. He nodded at Alicia. "Stand back—I'm going to haul him out."

Tony had to lie full length on the ground to do it, but eventually Sir Freddie lay like a beached whale, shivering, coughing, and convulsing. Neither Alicia nor Tony felt the least bit sympathetic. Yanking Sir Freddie's cravat free, Tony used it to bind his hands before hauling him to his feet and, with a push, starting him back along the path.

Alicia's hand in his, Tony followed his quarry back through the wood and out onto the road. Maggs was waiting beside Sir Freddie's coach.

Alicia looked up at the box. "He had a coachman—he told him to wait."

"Oh, aye. He's waiting right enough, inside the coach." Maggs held out Alicia's cloak and reticule. "Found these when I shoved him in."

"Thank you."

Maggs nodded at Tony. "I was thinking we'd best leave 'em in the cellars at the George. I've had a word to Jim—he's opening up the hatch."

"Excellent idea." Tony prodded Sir Freddie along the road toward the nearby inn. "Bring the coachman."

Maggs had to lug him, for the coachman was unconscious. After a brief discussion with the landlord of the George, they left their prisoners in the cellars under lock and key.

Jim came out and led Sir Freddie's carriage away. Alicia was on the seat of Tony's curricle and he was about to join her when they heard the unmistakable rumble of a carriage heading their way.

Tony exchanged a glance with Maggs, then reached for Alicia. "Just in case, get back down here."

He had her on the ground behind him when the carriage rocked around the corner. The driver saw them and slowed.

"Thank God!" Geoffrey pulled the horses to a halt beside them.

Tony caught the leader's head, quieted the team. "What the devil—?"

In answer the doors of the carriage burst open and Adriana, David, Harry, and Matthew came tumbling out.

They rushed to Alicia, hugged her wildly, a cacophony of questions raining down. They waited for no answers, but danced and jigged, cavorted around Tony, too, but then returned to hug and hang on to their elder sister.

Geoffrey climbed down from the box; he stretched, then came to stand beside Tony. "Don't say I should have stopped them—it was impossible. It's my belief once they take an idea into their heads, Pevenseys are unstoppable." He smiled. "At least Alicia's a Carrington—she's been tamed."

"Hmm," was all Tony said.

Both he and Geoffrey were only children. The performance enacted before them left them both bemused and a trifle envious. They exchanged a glance, for once had no doubt what each other was thinking . . . planning.

"Come on," Tony said. "We'd better get them moving, or we'll be here for the rest of the night."

They rounded up their charges. With joy in their faces, still asking questions, the triumphant Pevenseys eventually climbed back into the carriage. Climbing up to the box, Geoffrey looked at Tony. "The Chase?"

Tony turned from handing Alicia into his curricle. "Where else?" Taking the reins, he climbed up. "It's the only thing Sir Freddie got right."

The comment puzzled Alicia. She waited until they were rolling along, heading farther up the road not back toward town with the heavy carriage rumbling behind. "Where are we going?"

"Home," Tony replied, and whipped up his horses.

She was determined to speak with him, to address the subject of marriage, but no opportunity came her way that night. They traveled for nearly an hour, steadily northward along the country road, then Tony checked the horses and turned in through a pair of tall gateposts with huge wrought-iron gates propped wide.

He'd refused to tell her more about where he was taking her, but she guessed when she saw the house. A large Palladian mansion in pale brown and grey stone with both double-and single-story wings, it sat peacefully in the moonlight, perfectly proportioned, comfortable, and settled within its park.

Tony drew the horses to a halt in the wide gravel forecourt. He leapt down, scanned the house with fond satisfaction, then turned and held out his hand. "Welcome to Torrington Chase."

The next hour went in pleasurable chaos. Servants tumbled from their beds and came rushing, their eagerness a comment on how they viewed their master. Tony flung orders this way and that; in the midst of the flurry, a calm, feminine voice was heard inquiring what her son was up to now.

In the drawing room, Tony exchanged a glance with Geoffrey, then looked at Alicia. Briefly, he lifted her hand to his lips. "Don't panic."

Releasing her, he went out; a moment later, he reappeared with his mother on his arm.

There could never be any doubt of the relationship; the viscountess's dark, dramatic, rather bold beauty was the feminine version of Tony's. Before Alicia could do more than assimilate that, she was enveloped in a warm embrace, then the viscountess—"You will call me Marie, if you please"—was asking questions, meeting the boys, exclaiming over Adriana, all with an understanding that made it clear she was excellently well served by correspondents in London.

Hot milk arrived for the three flagging boys, then they were bundled upstairs to bed. Maggs said he'd stay with them; he lumbered off. The housekeeper—Alicia felt sure the woman must be Mrs. Swithins's sister—came to say that chambers had been prepared for Alicia, Adriana, and Mr. Geoffrey, and that, as usual, the master's apartments lay ready and waiting.

With a recommendation that they all get some sleep, saying she would speak with them all in the morning, the viscountess graciously retired.

Tony asked Mrs. Larkins, the housekeeper, to show Adriana and Geoffrey their rooms. Taking Alicia's hand, he led her up the stairs in their wake, but then turned down another corridor off the main gallery.

He opened a door at the end of the wing and drew her into a large room. It was a private sitting room overlooking the gardens; she got barely a glimpse as he led her through a doorway into a large bedchamber.

She glanced around, taking in the heavy dark blue hangings, the richly carved mahogany furniture, none of it delicate. Her gaze stopped on the huge four-poster bed.

Tony drew her into his arms; she met his gaze. "This is your room."

His eyes held hers for an instant, then he murmured, "I know." He bent his head. "Tonight, very definitely, this is where you belong."

The first brush of his lips, the first touch of his hands as they spread and held her, then moved over her back and pulled her against him, verified the statement, told her how true it was—how very much he needed her.

The raw hunger in his kiss, the undisguised passion, the raging desire that fueled it, spoke eloquently of all he—and she, too—had feared, all they'd known they'd had at risk. Now the threat was behind them, conquered, vanquished, and in the aftermath, in the clear light of their victory, nothing was more apparent than the wonder and rightness of their dreams.

Their strength, their vulnerability—both sprang from the same source. The same overwhelming emotion that laid waste to all barriers and left them burning with one urgent and compulsive need.

Neither questioned it.

They shed clothes in the moonlight, let their inhibitions fall with them to the floor. He lifted her and they came together in a frenzy of need, of lust, of greedy passion, of molten, exultant desire. His need was hers; hers was his. They fed and gave succor, took, yielded, and let the raging tide swell.

Wrapped together, incandescent with glory, they gave themselves

up to it, surrendered anew. She gave him all and he returned the pleasure, again and again, over and over until ecstasy built, rose and
engulfed them. Caught them, trapped them in its golden fire.

They burned, clung, gasping as they reached the peak and soared,
and the flames fell away.

Leaving them somewhere beyond the stars, far beyond the physical world.

Locked together, merged, as one they breathed, and felt, and knew.
The moment stretched; full and deep, awareness touched them. Their
gazes locked. A moment of heartbreaking stillness held them.

Passion, desire, and love. The smallest word held the greatest
power.

This—all of this—was theirs. If they wanted. If they wished.

They both breathed in. The shimmering net released and fell
away; the physical world returned and claimed them. With soft murmurs, soothing kisses, and caresses, they sank onto his bed.

Tomorrow, Alicia promised herself as, wrapped in his arms, she
drifted into sleep.

He woke her the next morning, fully dressed, to explain that he'd sent
a messenger to London last night, and now had to take Sir Freddie
back to the capital.

Watching her as she blinked, valiantly trying to reassemble her
wits, he grimaced. "I'll return as soon as I can. Stay here with the
boys. I suspect Geoffrey will want to take Adriana to meet his
mother."

He leaned close and kissed her, then rose and strode out.

Alicia stared at the doorway, then heard the door beyond close.
No—wait! was her instinctive reaction. Instead, she sighed and rolled
onto her back.

Foiled again, yet there was no point in ranting. Aside from all else,
when she spoke to him of marriage, she wanted Sir Freddie and all his
works finished with, no longer in any way hanging over them.

Which left her facing her current situation—in his room, in his
bed—and how best to deal with it.

In the end, brazen and resolute, she decided to behave within his
house precisely as she meant to go on; she had had enough of decep-
tions. She rang for water, washed while a round-eyed maid shook and
brushed her gown, then, determined to be completely open and honest
with Tony's mother, she found her way back to the hall and was deferentially conducted to the breakfast parlor.

There, she found her four siblings in high spirits. Geoffrey rose as she entered; she smiled and waved him back, then bobbed a curtsy to the viscountess, seated at the end of the table.

Marie smiled warmly. "Come and sit here beside me, my dear. We have, I think, much to talk about."

The light in her eyes was delighted, frank, and encouraging; Alicia took her words to heart, piled her plate high at the sideboard, then returned to sit at her side.

She'd barely taken the first bite when Geoffrey asked if he could take Adriana to visit at his home. "I'd like her to see the house and meet Mama."

The viscountess, busy pouring Alicia a cup of tea, murmured, "Manningham Hall is but two miles away, and Geoffrey's mama, Anne, is waiting to welcome your sister."

Alicia glanced at Adriana, read the eager plea in her eyes. "Yes, of course." With a flicker of her own resolve, she added, "It's only sensible to seize the moment."

Geoffrey and Adriana glowed with happiness; with various assurances, they excused themselves and left.

They passed Maggs in the doorway. He lumbered in, saluting both ladies. "If you're agreeable, ma'am," he addressed Alicia, "I'll be taking these scamps down to the stream. I mentioned it this morning—seems they've been an age without holding a rod, and I'm happy to watch over them."

As Alicia glanced at her brothers, Marie again murmured, "Maggs is entirely trustworthy." She smiled at the large, homely man. "He's been watching over Tony since he was no older than your David."

Alicia regarded her brothers' shining eyes and eager expressions. "If you promise to behave and do exactly as Maggs says . . ." She glanced at Maggs and smiled, too. "You may go."

"H'ray!" Setting down napkins, pushing back their chairs, they rushed to Maggs, pausing only to make their bows to Alicia and the viscountess before happily heading off.

Alicia watched Matthew, his hand in Maggs's, walk confidently out, and felt a rush of emotion. Not just for Matthew, but for the children she would bear; here, like this, with this sort of continuity was how children should be raised.

"Now!' Marie settled back in her chair. At her signal, the young butler departed, leaving them alone. "You can eat, and I will talk, and we will learn all about each other, and you can tell me when your wedding is to be. With his customary flair for avoiding details, Tony hasn't told me."

Lifting her gaze from her plate, Alicia looked into Marie's bright black eyes. "Yes, well . . ." She dragged in a breath; she hadn't expected such a direct approach. "Indeed, that's a subject I wished to discuss with you."

She glanced around, confirming that they were indeed alone. She drew another breath, held it for a moment, then met Marie's gaze. "I'm Tony's mistress, *not* his intended bride."

Marie blinked. A succession of emotions played across her features, then her eyes flared; she pressed her lips tight and reached across to lay her hand on Alicia's arm. "My dear, I greatly fear I must, most contritely, apologize—not for my question, but for my oh-so-tardy son."

Marie shook her head; Alicia realized with some surprise that she was struggling to keep her lips straight. Then Marie met her eyes again. "It seems he hasn't told you either."

Over the next hour, she tried to correct Marie's assumption, but Tony's mother would have none of it.

"No, and no and *non, ma petite*. Believe me, you do not know him as I do. But now you have told me your background, I can well see how you, through his laggardliness, have come to think as you do. You have had no mentor, no guide to rely on—no one to . . . what is the word . . . 'interpret' his behavior for you. Rest assured, he would not have allowed anyone to know of you, much less established you as his consort in the eyes of the ton, or, indeed, brought you here, if he hadn't, from the first, seen you as his bride."

It was increasingly difficult to cling to her argument in the face of Marie's conviction, yet Alicia couldn't—simply could not—believe that all along . . . "From the first?"

"*Oui*—without doubt." Marie pushed back her chair. "Come—let me show you something, so you will see more clearly."

They left the breakfast parlor; while they walked through the large house, Marie quizzed her on her brothers' education. On the one hand, Alicia's heart soared; this—this house, this sense of family, of immediate and natural care—was the stuff of her dreams. Yet her wits were whirling—she couldn't accept it, couldn't take joy in it, stymied by her uncertainty over Tony's intentions.

Had he always seen her as his wife? Did he *truly* do so now?

Marie led her to a long gallery lined with paintings. "The *famille* Blake. Most we need not consider, but here—here are the ones that might make things clear."

She halted before the last three paintings. The first showed a gentleman in his twenties, dressed in the fashion of a generation before.

"Tony's father, the last viscount." The middle picture was of a couple—Marie herself and the previous gentleman, a few years older. "Here is James again, now my husband." She turned to the last painting. "And this is Tony at twenty. Now look, and tell me what you see."

One aspect was obvious. "He looks very much like you."

"*Oui*—he looks like me. Only his height, his body, did he get from James, and that one does not notice. He looks French, and that is what one sees, but one sees only the surface." Marie caught Alicia's eye. "What a man is, how he behaves—that is not dictated by appearance."

Alicia looked again at the portrait. "You're saying he's more like his father inside?"

"*Very* much so." Marie linked her arm in hers; turning, they strolled back along the gallery. "In the superficial things, he is clearly French. How he moves, his gestures—he speaks French as well if not better than I. *But* it is always James in the words he speaks, always—without fail—his Englishness that rules him. So, in deciding the question of did he always mean to marry you or no, the answer is clear."

With a gesture encompassing all the Blakes, Marie said, "You are English yourself. You know of honor. A gentleman's honor—*a true English gentleman's honor*—that is something inviolate. Something one may set one's course by, that one may stake one's life and indeed one's heart on with absolute certainty."

"And that's what rules Tony?"

"That is what is at his core, an inner code that is so much a part of him he does not even stop to think." Marie sighed. "*Ma petite*, you must see that it is not so much a deliberate slight, but an *oversight* that he has not thought to tell you, to ask you to be his bride. To him, his direction is obvious, so, like most men, he expects you to see it as clearly as he."

They'd reached the top of the stairs. Alicia halted. After a moment, she said, "He could have said something—we've been lovers for weeks."

"Oh, he *should* have said something—on that you will get no argument from me." Marie looked at her, frowned. "*Ma petite*, in telling you this, I would not wish you to think that I would counsel you to . . . how do the English say it—let him off easily?"

"Lightly," Alicia absentmindedly returned. She told herself she didn't have a temper, that not being informed she was to marry him—that he intended to marry her, indeed, from the first had so intended—that he'd taken her agreement so completely for granted he hadn't even thought to mention it was neither here nor there . . . she drew a deep breath, felt her jaw firm. "No. I *won't*—"

The boys came clattering into the hall below them. Seeing her and Marie, they came rushing up the stairs; if any shyness toward the viscountess had ever afflicted them, it had already dissipated. A rowdy report of their excellent fishing expedition tumbled from their lips.

Both Alicia and Marie smiled and nodded. Eventually, the boys ran out of exciting news, and paused.

David fixed his bright eyes on Alicia. "When are you and Tony getting married?"

"What he means," Harry put in, jostling his older brother, "is if it's soon, can we stay here?"

Matthew lined up, too. "There's ponies in the stable—Maggs said he'd teach me to ride."

Alicia waited until she was sure she had her voice and expression under control. "How did you know we were going to get married?"

"Tony told us." Harry grinned hugely.

"When?"

"Oh, days ago!" David said. "But can we stay here, please? It's so much fun."

Alicia couldn't think.

Marie stepped in and assured the boys their request would be considered. They grinned, briefly hugged Alicia, then ran off to wash and get ready for lunch.

As their footsteps faded, Marie drew in a long breath. Again, she linked her arm in Alicia's. "*Ma petite*, I think—I really do feel"—she glanced at Alicia—"*not* lightly."

"No." Jaw set, Alicia lifted her head as she and Marie descended the stairs. "And not easily, either."

The coach rocked and swayed. Beyond the flaps, the rain poured down; the wheels splashed through the spreading puddles. Evening had come early over Exmoor, dark clouds roiling up from the Bristol Channel to blanket the moors. Then the clouds had opened.

Alicia felt entirely at one with the weather, but she prayed they wouldn't get bogged. She'd hoped to get a lot farther before halting for the night; now her sights were set on the next town, South Molton, where Maggs had told her they could be sure of a decent inn.

Harry was curled up beside her, asleep with his head in her lap. He shifted, snuffled, then settled again. Absentmindedly, she stroked his curls.

Through the unnatural gloom, she looked across the coach at Maggs, burly and bearlike, with Matthew asleep in his arms and David slumped against his side. When he'd heard of her decision to quit Torrington Chase and go home to Little Compton, he'd volunteered to come with her and help with the boys. With no Jenkins or Fitchett, she'd accepted his help gladly.

Once the idea of going home had occurred to her, she'd seized on it and refused to be swayed. Not that Marie had tried; she'd considered, then nodded. "Yes, that will work. He'll have to speak then."

Indeed. Alicia's only question was what he would say, assuming, as both she and Marie had, that Tony would come after her.

Adriana, returning with Geoffrey and an invitation to visit for a few days with Lady Manningham, with whom Adriana had got on well, had been concerned, more about what was going on between Tony and Alicia than anything else. So Adriana was now at Manningham Hall; Marie had smiled and approved the arrangement.

The boys, of course, didn't understand. They'd argued vociferously when she'd informed them they were returning to Little Compton immediately, but Marie had broken in to state, in her most imperious tone, that if they wished to return to the Chase soon, they would go without complaint.

They'd considered Marie, exchanged glances, then consented to accompany Alicia without further grumbling.

Marie had lent her traveling coach and a knowledgeable coachman; she'd also insisted on a groom. "I have no intention of drawing Tony's fire by allowing you to set out insufficiently protected."

So the poor groom, as well as the coachman, was getting drenched up on the box. They would have to stop at South Molton.

She had no idea how long it would be before Tony returned from London. Three days? Four? She hoped to be home in two days.

Head back on the squabs, eyes closed, she tried yet again to calm her chaotic emotions, to bring order to her mind. The greater part was still seething, the rest confused, still innocently querying: he hadn't really intended to marry her, had he? But some part of her knew—he did, he had, from the first. She shouldn't have overlooked how dictatorial he was—how many times had he simply seized her hand and whirled her into a waltz, or into some room? She knew perfectly well how used he was to getting his own way.

In this instance, he still would—she wasn't so far gone in fury she'd deny herself her dreams—but not before, absolutely *not* before he got down on his knees and begged.

Jaw tight, she was imagining the scene when the rhythmic thunder of galloping hooves came out of the night behind them.

The coachman slowed his horses, easing to the side of the road to let the other carriage past. Disturbed by the change in rhythm, the boys stirred, stretched, and opened their eyes.

Listening to the oncoming hooves, Alicia wondered who else was out on such a night, chancing his horses at such a wicked pace.

That pace slowed as the carriage neared, then the sound of hooves lightened further, eventually disappearing beneath the steady drumming of the rain. She strained her ears but heard nothing more.

Then came a shout, indistinguishable from within the coach, but in response the coachman reined his plodding horses to a halt.

The coach rocked on its springs. The boys came alert, eyes wide.

Alicia looked at Maggs. Head on one side, he was listening intently.

No highwayman would use a carriage, surely, and it couldn't be—

The coach door was wrenched open. A tall dark figure was silhouetted in the opening.

Tony glanced once around the coach, then reached in and locked his fingers around Alicia's wrist. "Stay there!"

At his tone, one of rigid authority, the four males jerked upright. He didn't wait to check their expressions, but unceremoniously yanked Alicia—stunned speechless, he noted with uncompromising satisfaction—out of the coach.

He steadied her on her feet, then stalked down the road, towing her behind him. She gasped, but had no option but to go with him.

Courtesy of her totally witless flight, he was already soaked; she was, too, by the time he reached a point out of bellow range of the coach.

Releasing her, he swung around and faced her. He glared at her through the rain. *"What the devil do you think you're doing?"*

The question cracked like a whip. Over the miles, he'd lectured himself not to overreact, to find out why she'd run before reading her the riot act; just the sight of her in a coach leaving him had been enough to lay waste to all such wisdom.

"I'm going home!" Her hair clung to her cheeks, wisps dripping down her neck.

"Your home lies that way!" He jabbed a finger back down the road. "Where I left you—at the Chase."

She drew herself up, folded her arms, tipped up her chin. "I am not continuing as your mistress."

If Alicia had had any doubt that Marie had held to her promise to play the dumb innocent and not explain her complaint, it was put to rest by the expression on Tony's face. Expressions—they flowed in quick succession from totally dumfounded, to incredulous, to believing but unable to follow her reasoning . . . to not liking her reasoning at all . . . then back to absolutely incredulous dumbstruck fury.

"*You*—?" He choked. Black eyes blazing, he jabbed a finger at her. "You are not my bloody mistress!"

She nodded. "Precisely. Which is why I'm going home to Little Compton." Picking up her skirts, she went to swing haughtily about. Her skirts slapped wetly about her legs; catching her arm, he hauled her back to face him.

Held her there. He looked into her face; his, the austere planes wet, his hair plastered to his head, had never looked harsher. "I have no idea what"—he gestured wildly—"*idiot* notion you've taken into your head, but I have never considered you my mistress. I have always— since the first time I saw you—thought of you as my future *wife*!"

"Indeed?" She opened her eyes wide.

"*Yes*, indeed! I've shown you every courtesy, every consideration." He stepped close, actively intimidating; she quelled an instinctive urge to step back. "I've openly protected you, not just through the investigation, not only via your household and mine, but socially, too. As God is my witness I have never treated you other than as my future wife. I've never even *thought* of you as anything else!"

Male aggression radiated from him. Uncowed, she held his black gaze. "That's quite amazing news. A pity you didn't think to inform me earlier—"

"*Of course* I didn't say anything earlier!" The bellow was swallowed by the night. He locked his eyes on hers. "Just refresh my memory," he snarled. "What was the basis of Ruskin's attempt to blackmail you?"

She blinked, recalled, refocused on his face—read the truth blazoned there.

"I didn't want you agreeing to be my wife through any damned sense of gratitude." Tony growled the words; sensing her momentary weakness, he pounced. Lowering his head so they were eye to eye, he pointed a finger at her nose. "I waited—and waited—*forced* myself to wait to ask so you wouldn't feel pressured!"

Panic of a kind he'd never before known clawed at his gut; anger and a largely impotent rage swirled through him; an odd hurt lurked beneath all. He'd thought he'd done the right thing—*all* the right things—yet fate, untrustworthy jade, had still managed to trip him up. Yet the truth was slowly seeping into his brain—he wasn't going to lose her. He just had to find a way through the morass fickle fate had set at his feet.

He scowled at her. "Regardless of what I did or didn't say, or why, what the *devil* did you think the last weeks have been about?" He stepped closer, deliberately crowding her. "What sort of man do you think I am?"

"A nobleman." Alicia refused to budge an inch; elevating her chin, she met him eye to eye. "And men of your class often take mistresses, as all the world knows. Are you going to tell me you've never had one?"

A muscle leapt in his jaw. *"You are not my mistress!"*

The words resonated between them. Slowly, she raised her brows.

He dragged in a breath. Easing back, he released his tight grip on her arm, plowed his hand through his hair, pushing sodden strands from his eyes. "Damn it—the whole bloody ton knows how I see you—*as my wife!*"

"So I've been given to understand. The entire ton, all my acquaintances—even my brothers!—know you intend marrying me. The only person in the entire world who hasn't been informed is *me!*" She narrowed her eyes at him, then more quietly stated, "I haven't even been asked if I'm willing."

Precisely enunciated, the words gave him pause. He held her gaze for a long moment, then, also more quietly, said, "I told you I loved you." His eyes suddenly widened. "You do understand French?"

"Enough for that, but I didn't catch much else. You speak very rapidly."

"But I said the words, and you understood." His voice gained in strength. "It was *you* who never returned the sentiment."

She lost her temper. "Yes, I *did*! Just not in words." She could feel the heat in her cheeks, refused to let it distract her. "Don't tell me you didn't understand." She gave him a second to do so; when his face only hardened, she jabbed a finger into his chest. "And as for saying the words, *believing* as I did that I was your *mistress*, such a confession would have been entirely unwise."

She realized the implicit admission, sensed by the flare of heat in his gaze that he hadn't missed it.

Lifting her chin, she continued, determined to have all clear between them, "It's all very well to say you love me, but many men doubtless think they love their mistresses, and tell them so—how could I tell what you *meant* by the words?"

For a long moment, he held her gaze, then he gestured, as if brushing the point aside. In the same movement, he reached for her; grasping her elbows, holding her steady, face to face, he locked his eyes with hers. "I need to know—do you love me?"

The question, the look in his eyes, went straight to her heart.

She closed her eyes, then opened them and searched his. The rain was cascading down, the night was wild and black about them, yet he was totally focused on her, as she was on him. She drew breath, shakily said, "In *my* world, love between a man and a woman usually means marriage. In *yours*, that isn't necessarily so. You said one word, but not the other. You knew my background—knew I wasn't up to snuff. I couldn't tell what you meant, but . . . that didn't make any difference to how I felt about you."

He studied her for a long moment, then released her, stepped close, framed her face with his hands. He looked down into her eyes. *"Je t'aime."* The words resonated with a conviction impossible to doubt. "I love you." He held her gaze. "I want no other woman, not for a day, not for a night—only you. And I want you forever. I want to marry you. I want you in my house, in my bed—you already reside in my heart. You *are* my soul. Please . . ." He paused, still holding her gaze, then more softly continued, "Will you marry me?"

He didn't wait for her answer, but touched his lips to hers. "I never wanted you as my mistress. I only ever wanted you in one role—as my wife."

Another subtle kiss had her closing her eyes, swallowing to get her words out. "Do you think you could see me as the mother of your children?"

He drew back and met her eyes, his expression faintly quizzical. When she said nothing more, he replied, "That's understood."

"Good." She cleared her throat. "In that case . . ."

She paused, holding his black gaze; she still couldn't entirely take it in, that the future of her dreams was here, being offered to her, hers for the taking. He hadn't got down on his knees and begged, yet . . . smiling, she reached up and wrapped her arms about his neck. "*Yes*, I love you, and *yes*, I'll marry you."

"Thank God for that!" He pulled her to him, kissed her thoroughly—let her kiss him back in a wild moment of untrammeled joy with the rain drenching them and the moors a black void about them, then he sighed through the kiss, sank deeper into it, wrapped his arms about her and held her close. Until that moment, she hadn't appreciated just how tense—how keyed up, how uncertain—he'd been.

Through the kiss she sensed their emotions meet, touch, ease—the fraught worry of recent times, the uncertainties, the fears, all faded, submerged beneath a welling tide of unfettered happiness.

When he lifted his head, dragged in a huge breath, and eased his hold on her, all that fraught tension was gone, and he'd reverted to his usual dictatorial self.

"Come." He kissed her hand and turned her back to the coach. His curricle stood across the road, the pair with their heads hanging. "There's a good inn in Chittlehampton, just off the road a little way back. It's closest." Hard hand at her back, urging her along, he glanced at her—met her eyes. "We should get out of these wet clothes before we take a chill."

She seriously doubted, once they got out of their clothes, that they would be in any danger; she could feel the heat in his gaze even through the darkness.

He called orders to the coachman, then opened the coach door and looked in. "We're going back to the Chase."

A chorus of wild cheers and a "Good-oh" from Maggs greeted the pronouncement. She stuck her head past Tony to add, "But we have to stop at an inn for the night. I'm too wet to get back in. I'll follow with Tony."

Her brothers were thrilled, in alt at the prospect of returning to a house she suspected they saw as paradise, and not at all averse to spending the night at an inn along the way.

Tony helped the coachman turn his team, then he drew her protectively back while the coach lurched and started back down the road. In its wake, they walked to his curricle. Closing his hands about her waist, he lifted her to the seat. The rain was easing; she waited until they were rolling along before saying, "About my brothers."

He glanced at her. "What about them? They'll live with us, of course."

She hesitated, then asked, "You're sure?"

"Positive."

She tried to think of what else remained, what else needed to be settled between them . . .

"Good gracious!" She looked at him. "What happened with Sir Freddie?"

Later, kneeling before the fire roaring in the hearth of the best bed-chamber of the Sword and Pike in Chittlehampton, one towel wrapped around her while with another she dried her wet hair, she remembered how Tony had laughed.

How delighted he'd been that he—the question of becoming his wife—had exercised her mind to the total exclusion of Sir Freddie.

She had Dalziel to thank for Tony's rapid return. Tony had sent a rider hotfoot to London as soon as they'd reached the Chase the previous night; by return, Dalziel had sent word to bring Sir Freddie to London, but then had changed his mind. He'd met Tony on the road, and taken Sir Freddie into custody; apparently Dalziel wanted to visit Sir Freddie's home in his company.

It seemed clear Dalziel's interest had been sparked by Sir Freddie's claims of another, still unidentified ex-traitor. For her part, she'd learned enough about ex-traitors to last her a lifetime.

Yet Tony's reaction out on the road buzzed in her head. Almost as if he hadn't been sure that her connection with him wasn't in some way dependent on the threat of Sir Freddie. That that threat somehow ranked more prominently in her mind than it did.

The latch lifted; Tony entered. He'd taken it upon himself to see her brothers settled; Maggs would sleep in their room, just to make sure.

A smile curved his lips as he paused, studying her, then, smile deepening, he came toward her.

"Stop!" She held up a hand. "You're still dripping. Take off your clothes."

His brows quirked, but he obediently halted. "As you wish."

The purr in his voice was distinctly predatory, the speculation in his eyes equally so. She inwardly grinned, turned back to the fire, and continued to dry her hair.

But the instant he was naked, she rose, crossed the few steps to him. Holding his gaze, with the towel she'd been using on her hair in one hand, with her other hand she whisked the towel she'd wrapped about her free.

One towel in each hand, she started to caress him, to dry him.

She tried to make him keep his hands to himself, but failed. Miserably.

Within minutes, their skins were hotter than the flames, their mouths and hands more greedy. Then she felt his hands close about her waist, his arms tense to lift her. She pulled back from their kiss. "No. On the bed."

She'd never given orders, never taken the lead before, but he acquiesced, releasing her and drawing her to the curtained bed.

He held back the drapes, caught her eye as she climbed through. "How on the bed?"

She smiled, and showed him.

Had him lie flat on his back, and let her straddle him, let her take him in and ride him to oblivion.

She'd taken an hour to ransack his library; as she'd suspected, he had an excellent collection of useful guides. She had every intention of studying them extensively and putting the knowledge to good use.

As she did that night, lavishing pleasure upon him, taking her own from his helpless surrender. Hours later, when the fire had burned low and she lay exhausted, deeply sated in his arms, she murmured, "I love you. Not because you'll protect me and our family, not because you're wealthy, or have a wonderful house. I love you because you're you—because of the man you are."

He was silent for a long moment, then his chest swelled as he drew breath. "I don't know what love is, only that I feel it. All I know is I love you—and always will."

She lifted her head, found his lips and kissed him, then snuggled down in his arms, where she belonged.

He'd wanted a big wedding. At the Chase, with half the ton and all of the Bastion Club looking on. As he wished, so it was—the only person invited who sent his regrets was Dalziel.

Just over a week later, they all gathered to watch her walk down the aisle of the church in Great Torrington to take her place at Tony's side. Her gown was a confection of ivory silk and pearls that Adriana, her bridesmaid, assisted by Fitchett, Mr. Pennecuik, and numerous others in London, had slaved over to have ready in time. About her throat, three strands of pearls glowed; more pearls circled her wrists and depended from her lobes—a gift from Tony, along with his heart.

As, meeting his black eyes, she placed her hand in his, gave herself into his keeping, she had no doubt which gift was the most precious to her, and in that moment, what was most precious to him.

With him, side by side, she faced the minister, ready and very willing to claim their future.

The ceremony ran smoothly; the wedding breakfast was held on the lawns of the Chase. Everyone from the staff to the Duchess of St. Ives threw themselves into the celebration, resulting in a day filled to overflowing with happiness and simple, unadulterated joy. The boys were in fine fettle; along with Miranda's girls they dodged here and there among the guests, weaving laughter and exuberance through the throng, leaving benevolent smiles in their wake. The horrors of the wars still shadowed many minds; it was at moments like this that the future glowed most brightly.

Late in the afternoon, when the ladies had settled in chairs on the lawn to chat and take stock, their husbands, released from attendance, gathered under the trees overlooking the lake or wandered down to stroll the shores.

Together with Jack Hendon, who along with Geoffrey had stood as his groomsman, and the other members of the Bastion Club—Christian, Deverell, Tristan, Jack Warnefleet, Gervase, and Charles—Tony retreated to a spot in the pinetum from where they could keep the ladies in view but also talk freely.

The topic that interested them most was Dalziel's absence.

"I've never seen him anywhere in the ton," Christian said. He nodded toward the assembled ladies. "I'm starting to think if he appeared, someone would recognize him."

"What I want to know is how he manages it," Charles said. "He must be in similar straits as we, don't you think?"

"It seems likely," Tristan agreed. "He's definitely 'one of us' in all other respects."

"Speaking of which," Jack Hendon put in, "what happened to Caudel once he was in Dalziel's clutches?"

"Oh, he sang loud and long," Charles replied. "And then sat in his library and put a gun to his head—only way left for a man of his name. Far less messy than a trial and the attendant flap."

"Did he have any immediate family?" Gervase asked.

"Dalziel said a distant cousin will inherit."

Tony looked at Charles. "When did you see him?"

"He called me in." Charles grinned. "Seems this other sod who's been using the war for his own ends has been active for the most part in Cornwall, from Penzance to Plymouth. My neck of the woods. He's in the ministries, most likely the Foreign Office, and he's apparently someone in the higher levels, someone trusted, which is what is most deeply exercising Dalziel. If Caudel was bad, this other has the potential to be even worse."

"Has he been actively spying, or was it something more like Caudel's racket?" Tristan asked.

"Don't know," Charles replied. "That's one of the things I'm supposed to find out. I'm to go in and ask questions, creating the sort of ripples no self-respecting spy wants to know about, and then watch what happens."

Christian grimaced. "A high-risk strategy."

"But oh-so-welcome." Charles glanced at the others, his dark blue eyes alight. "So now I must leave you and be on my way. I'm driving on to Lostwithiel tonight."

He grinned, a touch devilishly. "Courtesy of our erstwhile commander, I have a gold-plated reason to escape London and the ton, and my sisters, sisters-in-law, and dear mama, who are all up for the Season and now fixed in town for the duration. Of course, they expected to spend much of their time organizing me and my future. Instead, I'm on my way home. Alone. There to sit in my library, surrounded by my dogs, put up my feet, and savor a good brandy." He sighed contentedly. "Bliss."

With a rakish smile, he saluted them. "So I must leave you to fight your own battles, gentlemen."

They laughed. Charles turned away.

"Let us know if you need any help," Jack Warnefleet called.

Charles raised a hand. "I will. And if you need to hide, you all know your way to Lostwithiel."

The group under the trees shifted, broke up. Tony, Jack Hendon, and Tristan remained, watching Charles as he glibly made his excuses to Alicia and Tony's mother, then deftly extricated himself from the clutches of the other matrons present.

As Charles headed toward the stables, Tony took note of his jaunty, cocksure stride. He glanced at Jack and Tristan, briefly met their eyes, then all three grinned and looked at their ladies—Alicia, Kit, and Leonora—heads together as they chatted in the sunshine on the lawn.

"I fear," Tony murmured, "that Charles's view of bliss is severely limited by his restricted experience of the state."

"He doesn't know what he's talking about," Tristan averred.

"True," Jack said.

Tony's grin widened into a smile. "He'll learn."

The three of them stirred and headed out onto the lawn.